Freedom of the Mask

For my daughter, Skye.

One

Awakenings

One

It was a worried man who came down the gangplank from the packet schooner *Ann Marie* and set foot upon the wharf of Charles Town.

Hudson Greathouse stood upon the sun-bleached boards with the expanse of the walled city before him, its stone buildings of white, pale green, lavender, sky blue and assorted Caribbean-inspired hues shimmering in the dusty air of August's final week. The salty smell of the sea—of which he had inhaled quite enough this last week of travel from New York—blew in from behind him, and before him wafted the oily perfume of the swamp from which the noble town had grown, and which also still held sway as a kingdom of moss and murk for many miles around.

He hoped that same swamp had not claimed the body of Matthew Corbett.

It was one river of thought he'd been beckoned along during the coastal voyage. The *Ann Marie*'s captain was an affable gent who kept a supply of brandywine aboard and was keen to share it with someone who could spin a good yarn. Hudson's yarn had been the rope of truth, an account of his nearly-fatal adventure last September at what he called the House At The Edge Of The World. The brandywine had been strong, but it was not strong enough to gull Hudson into doubting that some mishap—perhaps, God forbid, of the violently deadly variety—had befallen his young problem-solving friend. And thus he had arrived with questions that Charles Town would be called to answer.

Under the spell of the morning's sunshine, the harbor was busy with people who had gathered to greet the *Ann Marie*'s passengers and, the same as in New York, hawk their wares of trinkets and dance to a fiddler's tune with their palms turned outward. Fishing boats were gliding out to sea. A little navy of small sloops, square-rigged ketches and larger ocean-going brigs creaked upon the ropes that held them fast, and here and there cargo was being loaded or brought up from the holds. It was quite the industrious scene, but Hudson had not the time to dawdle; he swung the canvas bag of his belongings across a shoulder and strode forward with what might appear to be furious intent, for indeed those who saw him coming gave way to let him pass, and in so doing females of all ages looked upon him with curiosity and appreciation while the menfolk examined the grain of the docktimbers or smoked their pipes with more of a clench to their teeth. Thus it was ever so with the advance of Hudson Greathouse, whose broad-backed physical size combined with the intelligent, handsome features of a swordsman and adventurer compelled some and sent warnings to others. At the moment his face was set upon the west, with purpose to visit the three establishments the Charles Town-bred captain of the *Ann Marie* had told him took in paying guests.

One of them had to have some knowledge of Matthew, Hudson reasoned. Unless the boy had been cut off at the knees before he'd even reached Charles Town. And by now, if that damned Professor Fell had him, it would be Matthew's head that had been cut off.

"*Stop that!*" he snarled at himself, so vigorously that one of the fiddling ragmen immediately obeyed and cowered back as if the approaching man's shadow might itself leap at him like a panther. Then, once again more or less in control of the direction of his thoughts, the man Matthew Corbett referred to as "The Great One" strode by the poor trembling wretch and almost plunked a coin in his tin cup but he wasn't feeling particularly charitable this day. Or any day, really.

At forty-eight years of age, Hudson had passed his prime but damned if he'd let anyone know it but his own self. His days of tavern brawls, back-alley swordfights and battles against cloaked assassins and hell-tempered ex-wives had worn him down, but far from out. He was, after all, still on this earth. And still a credit to his gender, if praise by the beautiful and vivacious Widow Donovan—who now simply went by the name of Abby, a free spirit who wore her blonde hair down about her shoulders even on the Sabbath—was to be believed. Well, he chose to believe it.

He stood three inches over six feet, which made him tower above most men. He remembered his father calling him a bull and his mother calling him a prince. Rest their souls. He imagined himself a bit of both. His thick iron-gray hair was pulled back in a queue and tied with a black ribbon, and he wore a cream-colored shirt with the sleeves rolled up, dark blue breeches, stockings a near color to his shirt and a pair of unpolished, sensible ebony boots. His jaw was square, his eyes deep-set, brooding and as dark and dangerous as tar-pits. A jagged scar sliced through the charcoal-gray field of his left eyebrow. Two things he had recently given up: the beard he'd grown because Abby liked the one Matthew had when the boy returned from Pendulum Island back in April, and the cane that Hudson had been using to steady himself after being nearly stabbed to death by Tyranthus Slaughter last October. The beard had been a brief exercise in making Abby "tingly", as she put it, but himself itchy, and though in younger years tingly might have won out over itchy, this year it was more about the prince than it was about the bull.

The cane had gone because Hudson had realized he was depending on it too much, and such a thing could not be permitted. Yes, he was still sometimes unsteady and needed to grab onto something, but—dear God, man, wake up!—there was always Abby. The worst of that Slaughter episode had been the fact that for the first time in his life he'd been helpless; he'd felt the cold yet soothing hand of Death upon his throat, promising an end to pain and a path to rest. Except for Matthew's efforts, he might have given into it. For without the boy pulling him upward to the top of that well, Hudson knew he would have sunken down and been done with it.

Boy? Matthew at twenty-four years of age—having celebrated a birthday among friends at the Trot Then Gallop tavern in May—was certainly not a boy, but Hudson still considered him so.

Then why did you let him come to this town alone, you fool? Hudson asked himself as he stalked along the wharf, winding his way between dandies, damsels, hawkers, beggars and everything it seemed but Indian chiefs. At the end of the wharf, when he stepped upon the street of crushed oyster shells, he smelled the merchandise baking under the sun before he spied it: a wagonload of fresh alligator hides and selling them a raggedy man and woman with three teeth between them and three eyes as well. Three hands also; the man had reached for one alligator too many. This pair had joined the throng to welcome the purses of passengers and were erecting a tent over the wagon to shield their hides from what promised to be a brutal sun as the day wore on.

And on any other day the man from New York might have been tempted to hear tales of how these scaly monsters were captured and skinned, but today with his urgent purpose he continued toward the first establishment that had been described to him, an inn owned by a Mr. and Mrs. Carrington, which stood nearest to the waterfront.

"Something has happened to Matthew."

"What? What are you saying? Hudson, come back to bed."

"I'm saying," he had repeated to Abby very quietly on a very quiet morning one week ago, with light rain tapping at the dimpled window-glass and the sun yet shining on the other side of the world, "that something has happened to Matthew, and damned if I didn't goad him into going to Charles Town. After all else that's happened to him…I sent him off like a grinning fool. I said it would be *good* for him to get out of New York. That Pandora Prisskitt thing…it was a makepiece for him…a time-waster, really. We both knew it, and so did Madam Herrald."

"Hudson…come back to bed…calm yourself."

"*Calm* myself? I have awakened now for four nights in a row with this on my mind. I have sat right here in this chair and watched you sleeping and wondered if my friend wasn't lying dead somewhere.

Abby…he should've been back by now. Lord knows he wouldn't stay gone so long, without there being…something."

"And how long has it been? Really that long?"

"More than two months for a one-night task. Consider the travel time there and back, give him a few days to make the rounds of coffee houses and taverns—which he likely would not do—and… you see?"

"I do see, but there is always the possibility."

"Of what?"

"That—my darling Hudson, whose loss of beard must have shaved off some of your sensibilities—he has met a young lady and been smitten. Or perhaps knocked to his knees by that Pandora Priss person. Come to bed now, I need to curl myself around you."

Hudson had been determined not to let his wagon be pulled off the road. He'd said, "Matthew Corbett is smitten by only one person: Berry Grigsby. Oh, he doesn't fool me for a mad hare's second. He wouldn't be knocked to his knees by any woman, because he's already sitting on his ass on the love fence. He just can't make up his mind which way to jump. But…I've been thinking about this these last few nights and not wanting to pursue it. I've thought…give it another day. And then another and another, but no more. I'm going to see Berry tomorrow and find out if she's heard from him. If she hasn't, I'll ask at the Trot. And if no one there has heard anything I'm going to Charles Town on the next boat out, and when I find that boy I'll teach him the value of letter-writing with a boot to the rump. Why didn't I go with him, Abby? *Why?*"

"Because," she'd said in the way she had that was all cool lemonade on a sultry night, "Matthew may be your friend and associate but he is not your son, and if you thought nothing of him being in danger, recall that neither did Madam Herrald. Matthew prides himself on being a professional. You should also give him that honor. Now come back to bed, I insist upon your company at half-a-candle before dawn."

Her insistence had won him over but it had not settled the matter. At first light Hudson had been up and dressed and, leaving Abby to weather at breakfast the silent storm of the landlady Mary Belovaire's disapproval with her own sunny disposition and amazing disregard of public opinion, he was out the door of the boarding house and on his way to Queen Street and the home of Marmaduke Grigsby, the town's printmaster and Miss Berry's grandfather.

His hard-fisted knock at the door was loud enough to set dogs barking. On the river behind him a light mist held sway, and from it emerged small fishing vessels moving back and forth like old dowager ladies in white veils, searching for suitors.

Moon-faced and google-eyed, the printer of the town's news sheet—this month called the *Earwig*, but next month it might be something different at the whim of its master—answered the door in his blue-striped nightshirt, his face with its odd proportions and its prestigious slab of a forehead still wrinkled from sleep. The elderly gentleman was beginning to stoop over so much that it wouldn't require such an effort for Marmaduke to take a bite from one of Hudson's kneecaps, and the way his watery eyes appeared to bulge from their sockets under the heavy white eyebrows it seemed he was measuring the distance.

"Lord's mercy, Greathouse!" came the voice that along with his quill had launched a thousand fits. "What's all this hammering?" The single tuft of hair that adorned the front of his bald pate stood up like a white plume of smoke from a Mohawk's war fire.

"I need information. Have you or Berry heard lately from Matthew?"

"From Matthew? Greathouse...no...my Lord, have the roosters stopped their yawning yet?"

"It's not that early. Now shake the sleep out of your brain. Matthew's been gone for more than two months. I haven't heard a word from him, and I want to know if—"

"We have not," said the young woman who had emerged from the corridor to stand in the room behind her grandfather. "Should we have?" Her voice carried a touch of frost on such a steamy summer morn, and Hudson knew that whatever had transpired between Berry Grigsby and Matthew in the time since they'd both returned from their captivity on Pendulum Island, it wasn't for the good.

"I suppose not," Hudson replied after a short pause. "Matthew left here on a very minor errand. It shouldn't have taken him this long."

"Hm," she said, still seemingly distant of concern, yet she did come nearer to the door and the early gray light.

Hudson had no idea how this lovely creature could have sprung from the rather unsightly Grigsby line, if Marmaduke should be one example of the family's progress. She was tall and proud in her bearing, was fresh-faced and blue-eyed and had a beautiful abundance of curly coppery-red tresses that fell about her shoulders. A scattering of freckles decorated, in the most pleasant sense, her cheeks and the bridge of her nose. Hudson believed she had recently turned twenty years of age, and thus she was well into her marriageable years; from what he knew, the town's eccentric coroner—the king of bones up in that attic workshop of his atop City Hall—Ashton McCaggers was seen with her on many occasions. Any questions Hudson might have posed to Matthew regarding Beryl Grigsby went unanswered, and by Matthew's grim silence on her account Hudson took it that she had become in the past few months a forbidden subject. No matter that Matthew and Berry had together cheated death several times, it seemed to an observer that they were quits with each other. Which must be an uncomfortable situation, Hudson mused, since Matthew lived in a converted dairyhouse mere steps away from the front door of Grigsby's domain.

Used to live, Hudson thought. And then: *Stop that.*

"Is there anything else?" Berry asked, and she reached past her grandfather to put one hand on the door.

Hudson didn't know why, but whenever he was in the presence of this young woman he thought of the particular season that was beginning to be popularly known as "Indian summer", a combination of sunny warmth and bracing chill that came and went as the weather bode. Her affinity for eye-startling colors was well-known, as demonstrated by her green sleepgown adorned with red and purple ribbons, much like the first touchings of autumn to the Manhattan island trees. Her eyes reminded him of clear blue skies and—a little sadly—the great promise of youth that he now realized was a fleeting time that youth would ever waste. In her voice and manner now was the chill that did not brace the spirit as much as it promised to break it; she wanted nothing further to do with Matthew, and that was a declaration even a dunce like himself could quickly grasp.

"Nothing else," Hudson said.

"Good day, then," she told him. He reasoned that even the hint of concern for Matthew's welfare from her was beyond the pale.

He nodded and started to turn away, and she was in the process of closing the door when she paused and said, in the same frosty tone, "When you find Mr. Corbett, you may tell him that Ashton and I are discussing marriage."

"Fine," Hudson answered, turning again to give her the full view of an expression that looked as if he'd been chewing lemons. "I'm sure you'll be very happy, living up there amid all those—"

The door closed, firmly.

"—skeletons," Hudson finished.

Surely, he thought as he strode back toward the Trot Then Gallop to wait for its owner, Felix Sudbury, to show up for the morning sweep, that girl would not be happy married to the coroner. Why Matthew had let her get away, he had no clue. Of course, in Matthew's line of work…there was much danger, particularly with this business of Professor Fell. And there the blade of truth pierced his heart afresh, because he had pushed Matthew into this damned trip. It came to him that Sally Almond's would be opening sooner with its breakfast offerings, so that might be a place first to ask if anyone had heard from Matthew and also to feed his own appetite; a pity the kitchen couldn't get anymore of Mrs. Sutch's spicy sausages, but the only constant in this world was change.

Now, on this August morning in Charles Town, Hudson advanced along Front Street to where the crushed oyster-shells underfoot gave way to a more civilized pattern of white-and-gray stones, indicating a city that intended to improve its position among the colonies. Palm trees and palmetto bushes as well as trimmed hedges stood about, casting welcome shade. Carriages were on the roll, and as yet the horse-droppings on the street were not too bad. Hudson saw that some of the shops were already open, though it was yet early, and well-dressed figures of men and women under their parasols strolled along the sidewalk.

The Carringtons' inn was a two-storied house, very neatly kept and painted white with a dark green trim. Hudson entered through the front gate and went up three steps into the house, where he found both the man and his wife drinking tea in a parlor while they went over figures in a logbook.

To the question from the bewigged and nattily-dressed Mr. Carrington about how their new arrival could be helped, Hudson said, "I'm looking for a friend of mine. His name is Matthew Corbett. He might have stayed here—"

"Oh yes," said Mrs. Carrington, who turned a few pages back in the hide-bound book and showed Matthew's familiar signature to Hudson. "He did stay here, in late June. He attended the Sword Of Damocles Ball. You say…he was a friend of yours?"

"Yes." Hudson did not like the sound of that word *was.*

"A pity, then," said Mr. Carrington. "To perish at such a young age."

"*Perish*," Hudson repeated, and suddenly felt very cold on this nearly tropical day. "Trace back a ways," he said, his voice tight. "What happened to him?"

"He became involved in the murder of Mr. Kincannon's daughter Sarah," said the woman. "At the Green Sea plantation. Oh, that was a terrible thing. People so loved Sarah."

"Matthew is also held in high regard in New York. Please… about Matthew…go on."

"Oh, yes. Well…sorry to say, the young man lost his life in the swamp up the Solstice River. But justice was done, I can tell you that. Your young friend discovered Sarah's proper killer and pursued him—I should say, pursued the both of those villains—though he paid for that the ultimate price."

Somehow, Hudson found himself sitting in an overstuffed chair though he had no recollection of doing so. Through a window he could see the ships in the harbor, and in this unobstructed view he made out a group of hagglers at the dock trying to coax money from the well-to-do with a monkey that was turning flips.

"Would you like half of a griddle cake?" Mrs. Carrington offered. "I fear it's all we have left this morning. We've had a full house these last few days."

"No," said Hudson, who felt a weariness crash upon him as if he had been hit by the most vicious wave of the sea. "Thank you," he added. He thought he might sit here until the next call for breakfast, but the idea of spending a night in the inn that was Matthew's last residence on this earth...no. *Think!* he told himself. *I'm missing something! Think, for God's sake!* His brain, alas, was a pit of sludge. But then he got his mind and his mouth working together, somewhat, and he asked quietly, "Where is he buried?"

"A thousand pardons, as we're a Christian town, and also our deepest sympathies," said the man of the mansion. "Mr. Corbett was not buried, as his body unfortunately was never recovered."

"Never recovered?" Hudson sat up a little straighter in his chair. "Then how are you sure he's dead?"

"Well sir, he did not return from the Solstice River swamp. He did not bring his rented horse back to the stable, nor did he settle his bill with us. Those particulars were taken care of by Mr. Magnus Muldoon. It was from him we learned of the young man's regrettable passing."

Hudson stood up; he no longer had need for a chair when there was urgent travelling to be done. "This Muldoon fellow. Where can I find him?"

So it was that Hudson's large, scuffed boots took him nearly the length of Front Street, to a small shop with a front window adorned by the declaration *Items Of Interest, Magnus Muldoon, Glassblower.* In that window was a display of several cunningly-shaped, multicolored bottles, along with what appeared to be small glass figures—a horse and rider, an intricate sailing ship, a tree stylized to appear blown by a restless wind. Hudson wasn't particularly impressed by so-called artistic talent, believing such to be an outlet only for a weak mind. He saw no one in the shop through the window, and he imagined this Muldoon person to be a prancer. He was about to turn the knob of the shop's door when he heard whisperings behind him and he looked around to see two very lovely young creatures, one in pink and the other in violet, standing under their lacy parasols. Miss Pink was whispering behind her hand to Miss Violet, who was staring with excited eyes in Hudson's direction.

Even on so terrible a day as this a little of the bawdy cocksman awakened, and though Hudson had no time for these playthings it was a gratitude to know he was still—

But the two young women came nearer, and they peered through the window as if the Great One was himself made of glass yet inconsequential to their attentions, and Miss Violet said to Miss Pink, "Do you see him? Is he there?"

"No," said Miss Pink, "I don't see him. I can't bear to go in, I'd be all nervous shakes. Let's try later, Fran." And without giving the visitor from New York a second—or even a first—glance the chattering pair of Charles Town daisies moved on with a wiggle and a giggle and left Hudson thinking how shallow was this new generation of female, and thank God he was long past their like.

Hudson entered the shop, causing a bell to ring over the door. It wasn't a high-pitched little feminine ring, either; the bell that hung above his head was nearly the size of his head, and let out a coppery clang that he figured told the Carringtons at the other end of the street he'd arrived at his destination.

It wasn't ten seconds before a pair of curtains behind the counter parted to give way to a man who Hudson realized was certainly larger than himself, not in terms of bulk but in terms of height, shoulder-size, and—damn!—the prancer was a giant. He had a thick but neatly-combed mane of black hair, a sharp nose and a square chin that looked as sturdy as a warship's prow. Hudson figured him to be twenty-five or twenty-six years of age, surely this side of thirty. He was a handsome specimen, to be sure, and he was dressed simply in a plain white shirt and dark blue breeches.

"Help you?" The deep and rather rough-edged voice was polite but matter-of-fact.

"Muldoon?"

"Yep." The man's iron-gray eyes took on a glint of curiosity. "And who be you?"

"My name is Hudson Greathouse. I was...*am* a friend of Matthew Corbett." He saw Muldoon's expression darken, and it appeared the glassblower had flinched just a fraction when that name was mentioned. Hudson braced himself for trouble, already trying to determine where to hit the man to put him down, if need be. Not that chin, unless he craved a broken fist. "I've come from New York and I'm not leaving here until I hear every word about what happened...and you'd better make it good."

Muldoon didn't answer for a few seconds. He stared into Hudson's eyes, as if gauging the other man, and then looked at his own hands that gripped the counter's edge. "Ah," he said at last, in a quiet tone. "Figured it was a matter of time 'fore somebody came lookin' for him." He lifted his gaze to meet Hudson's. "Who sent you here? The stablemaster or the Carringtons?"

"The Carringtons."

"Yep, I settled Matthew's account with 'em. You in the same line of work as he was?"

"What work would that be?"

Muldoon's mouth crooked just a bit in a smile. "Stickin' your nose in where it don't belong. Oh, I ain't down on that, mister. I know Matthew came to that ball with Pandora Almighty Prisskitt on account of *me*. But then...he come to see me, to make me—can you bear this?—into a *gentleman*. Like he was, and indeed he was quite the gentleman. Well, I've got a ways to go but he started me off." Muldoon cast an appreciative eye around the shop with its colorful items of interest. "Makin' some good money now. My Pap would never have believed such a thing possible, not in this town."

"I have no idea what you're talking about," said Hudson, "but I figure you're going to sooner or later get to what happened to Matthew. I'm ready to hear that now."

The giant nodded. His smile was gone, and his eyes were sad. "All right, then. Pull up a chair." He motioned toward one on the other side of the counter. "It'll take me a spell to tell it. How Matthew died, I mean."

Hudson considered standing, but he realized that he would probably need to sit to hear this tragedy, lest he fall upon the telling of it. He drew the chair over and sat down, and with a heavy heart and an ache somewhere south of his conscience he waited for Muldoon to lay out the wretched tale. If the man was lying for any reason he would soon know it, and giant or not there would be some shattered glass and broken bones in this damned place today.

"It started with a duel at the ball," Muldoon began, "and it ended in a boat in the Solstice River swamp. 'Twixt those two things... that's the hell of it."

Hudson said nothing; he had decided to let the man take his own time in recalling this descent into the underworld...or perhaps, he wished to delay as long as possible the details—which he *had* to know—about the death of a young man who he would have been proud, in some other time and place, to have called his son.

Two

"I STILL can't believe," Hudson said as he brushed a swirl of mosquitoes away from his face, "that you didn't go into her house. How could you put faith in a demented girl?"

"Like I said five or six times now," Muldoon retorted, with a definite air of irritation, "she invited me in but I reckoned it best to let her grieve in private. I had no reason to think that Matthew was in there. Why should I? And if he *was* inside, why would he stay? If she invited me in, she wasn't tryin' to hide nothin'. That makes not a shillin' of sense."

Hudson grunted and concentrated on guiding his stable-rented horse, Helios, along this rough track that served as a road edging the Solstice River swamp. He would not add fuel to a slow-burning fire by pointing out that the difference between a glassblower and a professional problem-solver was just this: the glass-blower might make pretty bottles and have empty-headed little pipsqueaks peeking in his window, but the professional looked at a problem from all angles and considered that what made not a shilling of sense to some was the first sensible thing to have done. This insane girl,

Quinn Tate by name, who lived in the swamptown of Rotbottom was, according to Muldoon, the last person to see Matthew alive. She fancied in her madness that Matthew was the second-life of her dead husband Daniel, this according to the young giant as well. It didn't take the intellect of a giant to suspect that something might be amiss…to hell with the idea of Matthew falling into the river and being torn to pieces by alligators. To hell with it!

Then again…Muldoon had a point. If Matthew was indeed in Quinn Tate's house, then why had he *stayed* there?

Well…they'd soon find out.

The afternoon's heat had finally reached full sweltering blast. Before they'd started out from Charles Town on a trip that had necessitated crossing the Solstice by ferryboat to reach this backwoods road, Hudson had had the presence of mind to buy a broad-brimmed straw hat similar to the one Muldoon wore to save his brains from being boiled. He could smell the fetid, green and nostril-assaulting odor of the swamp, and how anyone could live out here nose-to-arse with this huge steaming pile of God's torment he had no earthly idea. Then again, he recalled those wretches—"opportunistic individuals", Matthew might have corrected him—selling their alligator hides at the harbor, and someone had to be out here catching the beasts to make a paltry profit. No alligator had yet lumbered across the track, but Hudson had seen a number of brown and black snakes hanging from tree branches or curled up on rocks to heat their blood, and he had decided that when he found the boy some punishment was in order for making him pass this way. Taking care of his laundry for a month might do it…yes, that would serve the purpose…clean laundry in exchange for this dirty job of extricating Matthew from whatever hole he'd gotten himself down.

Muldoon glanced back at Hudson, his own horse being a few strides ahead. "I did row out past Rotbottom a few times to try to find…" He paused, measuring his words. "Anythin' that might remain," he said. "I didn't want to believe he was dead. Just like you're not wantin' to believe it now."

"Show me the body," came the terse reply. "When I see that, I'll know for sure."

"The 'gators grow big up in here. They don't leave a lot to be—"

"Just guide," Hudson interrupted, and again he had to brush a maddening swarm of mosquitoes out of his face. God's mercy that he wouldn't be laid low with the fever after this. Maybe two months of laundry duty would be more equitable.

The two riders passed on under the burning sun, each taken with their own thoughts. Another hour and more swarms of countless mosquitoes later, the first rude hovels of Rotbottom came into view; that and the odor of alligator hides drying in the heat wafted forth, which made Hudson appreciate the horse-fig-dappled streets of New York as being akin to the perfumed gardens of paradise.

Magnus recalled which house belonged to Quinn Tate, and he aimed them in that direction. It was amid other small ramshackle wooden cabins of its like planted on the swampy earth, though he remembered that it did stand out for its relative cleanliness and order; the Tate girl might be addled, but it appeared she was proud of her home. As he and Hudson approached the house on their horses, they attracted the attention of a few raggedy residents who were repairing nets, chopping wood, cleaning fish and other chores of import. A wizened old white-haired woman who sat on her porch with a corncob pipe between her teeth and a little brown jug at hand hollered a greeting to them in a voice stolen from a bullfrog, and when Magnus nodded in response she lifted her jug and swilled from it as if she needed any further excuse to drink firewater on a day when the trees themselves might burst into flame.

Dogs came up barking like little pistols going off and rattled the horses until a thin man with a gray beard down to his bellyhole ran the canines away with foul-yelled oaths and the thrusts of a wooden pitchfork. Hudson had seen poor villages before, but this place was the poorest. He thought that even the meager bits of paint that clung to the wooden walls looked sad, and the garments hanging from their lines to dry were more patches than clothing. A few horses drooped around, trying to find grass on the trampled ground. Chickens roamed the yards, pigs lay in their stuporous slumbers, a couple of goats butted heads over some affront, and everywhere the smell of alligator carcasses freighted the air like heavy smoke. Hudson was beginning to grasp what Muldoon had been telling him; why in the world would Matthew stay in a place like this, if indeed he was still alive?

It was a mystery, but he couldn't allow himself to drift in that direction. If Quinn Tate was the last person to see Matthew alive, then she had questions to answer and Hudson by God was going to make sure no stone was left unturned, or in this case no rotten bottom left unexposed.

A woman was sweeping the porch of the house they were approaching. Her back was to them as she labored, and she wore around her head a sweat-stained blue wrapping-cloth. She was a small woman, finely-boned, but she worked with fierce intensity as if she had until sundown to live. It was all Hudson could do not to call to her, to blurt out his question of *Where is my friend Matthew.* But suddenly she must have heard the crunch of horse hooves on the earth or sensed herself being examined, for she turned toward the two new arrivals and was content for the moment to lean on her broom and watch them coming.

"That's her?" Hudson asked.

"No," said Magnus, "it ain't." He was puzzled at this, and caught a new puzzlement: the one time he'd been out here, all the windows of the house were shuttered tight. Now they were not.

A heavy-set man with a bald pate and a reddish-brown beard emerged from the house, either to speak to the woman or he'd seen the riders through a window. He planted his hands on his wide hips and said as the two men neared, "Afternoon! You lookin' to buy skins? Got some fine-grained ones bein' cured, make a few pairs of sturdy boots fit for gentlemen like y'selves."

"Not in the market for that," said Hudson as he reined his horse in just short of the porch steps. He aimed his stare at the woman, who had a hatchet-blade chin and eyes that made him think of an angry dog tensing itself to leap, snapping, at a man's throat. "I'm looking for Quinn Tate."

"Ain't here no more," said the woman, who hardly moved her mouth when she bit the words off.

"Where can I find her?"

"Go back to the road," the man spoke up. "Turn to the left and go on 'bout four or five rods. You'll see the cemetery plain enough, it's got a wall of stones around it to keep the 'gators out."

"The *cemetery*?" Hudson frowned, which itself was enough to put any man on guard for his life. "This is a poor joke, sir, and I am in no mood for such."

"Ain't no joke," said the woman. "Me and Clem been next on the list for a real house. Don't care how we got it, just so's there's a roof over our heads for the baby. Pity that woman got herself murdered, but she was warranted for it."

"Murdered?" Now it was Magnus' turn to be aghast. *"When?* And by *who*?"

"What're you men doin', disturbin' the dust for Quinn Tate?" The bullfrog voice issued from the old white-haired woman who had come from her porch, pipe in mouth and jug in hand, to follow the visitors on their route to this cabin. She removed the pipe to nearly bellow, "Leave that child to rest in her grave, and go on with you!"

"I have business with her," said Hudson, who felt dazed by the heat and skull-scorched in spite of his straw hat.

"*Nobody* has business with that child no more! Listen here, I been planted in this place for near on fifteen year, and I seen all that a human eye can hold. Saddest sight of all was seein' how that poor girl lost her mind after Daniel died. Her husband, killed by the Soul Cryer. Ahhh, you Charles Town fools don't know nothin' 'bout nothin'!" She waved a disgusted hand that had two fingers and a thumb.

"Enlighten us," Hudson insisted. He was aware that this woman's voice was summoning other Rotbottom residents to gather around. Men, women and children of all ages were seemingly emerging from the earth like dirtied ghosts, and some appeared so thin and frail they were near their departure from this world.

"I will so enlighten you, sir!" said the woman, with an exaggerated bow that ended in a stumble. To steady herself she took another swig of fortitude. "When Quinn come back with that fella she claimed was Daniel, nobody said nothin' and so we're all part of it! Yes we are!" She looked around ferociously at the gathering assembly of ragtags. "Oh, we talked about it 'mongst ourselves, but ain't one of us had the cock to tell that girl she was out of her head, that she needed to get that fella out of her house 'fore…well…somethin' bad was bound to happen! And it did! God's Eyes, it did!"

"Settle down, mother!" Hudson advised. "I'm here to make some sense of—"

"Ain't no damned sense to *be* made of it!" The old woman, a sinewy sack of wrinkles, looked like she could call up the furies if she needed them. "And I been mother to three sons and a daughter, all dead 'fore their time, and I been a wife to two men gone to the 'gators with no stone to mark 'em, and I done some right things and some wrong things but mister…the wrongest thing I ever done was not to speak up when that child brought a fella she said was Daniel here to share a house and bed with her! And *nonnnnnne* of us fine people said a damn word! Sure enough that man was moonstruck himself, or he would never have took Daniel's name! Then he ups and murders her, near cuts her head off with a blade to the throat!" She paused to wet her foghorn. Her eyes had become black holes with no bottom. "Buried her a week ago Tuesday, you can go look at the Cross *I* made for her grave. Me, of all people who don't think God's got a lick a'sense or a shadow of heart in this world no more. Well, she's in the ground and her killer's done gone, so that's the story. Go do your business with her, sonny! Go on, tell her Maw Katty sent you to bother her bones!"

All this had hit Hudson and Magnus like a storm of stones. Hudson feared his injuries from Tyranthus Slaughter yet weakened him, because he felt as if he might slither from his saddle into a puddle of flesh-colored mud.

"Her…killer's *gone*?" Magnus managed to say.

"Lit out right after it happened." Maw Katty took a puff and a pull. "He was seen leavin' in a wagon with that foreign gent. The mean one who took up with Annabelle Simms and beat her so bad. I asked her myself why she took up with him…said he was *royalty*, some kind of a Count. Guess that gave him special right to bust her nose and arm. Lord a' mercy, how these children delude themselves!"

"A *Count*," Hudson repeated, getting his brain and mouth connected again only with a supreme effort. "What was his name?"

"Hanged if I can remember it."

"I recall it," said a younger, sun-darkened man who stepped forth from the throng. "It was Dahlgren. Man owed me money from a game of Hazard. His English wasn't so good, but he said he'd give me lessons in swordplay instead of the shillings. I put a deaf ear to that."

"He was a swordsman, then."

"Thought himself so, but his left wrist was crooked. Said it made him unbalanced."

Hudson was remembering that last October, during Matthew's investigation of what he'd termed the 'Queen of Bedlam', a Prussian so-called count who was indeed a dangerous swordsman had nearly carved the boy to pieces in that mansion owned by the villain Simon Chapel, who was working in concert with Professor Fell. Hudson recalled Matthew telling him that the Count's left wrist had been broken in the fight. Also that—alas for the use of all that energy and defense of life—the man had somehow fled the mansion even as it was being attacked by a rescue party led by New York's then-High Constable Gardner Lillehorne, who at the end of May had left for London with his shrewish wife 'the Princess' to accept a position as Assistant to the High Constable there. An added plus to that departure was that Lillehorne had taken the little red-faced bully Dippen Nack with him to serve as *his* assistant.

Hudson was still stunned by what Maw Katty was telling him. And this about Count Dahlgren...could it be that Dahlgren had found refuge in this wretched town? Judging from Matthew's hair-raising tales, the Professor did not take failure of his plans and underlings lightly, so Dahlgren might very well have sought out a place where he could vanish from the earth, the reach of the law and—hopefully—the Professor's deadly grasp.

But now...what was to be made of the murder of Quinn Tate and Matthew leaving Rotbottom in a wagon with Count Dahlgren?

"Just so I know we're talking about the same person," Hudson said to the old woman, "can you describe for me the man who Quinn Tate called 'Daniel'? If it really was him, his given name is Matthew Corbett."

"*You* describe him. I'll tell you true if it fits."

When Hudson was finished, Maw Katty said, "He had a black beard and he looked most thin and haggard, but that was him. Had the scar 'cross his forehead plain as I'm seein' you. That was him, pulled out little more than a week ago with that foreign bastard."

Magnus could hold his tongue no longer. "I don't believe this for a minute! Matthew was—I mean to say, Matthew *is*—no killer!"

"Come take a look at my floorboards," said the new woman-of-the-house, with a bitter scowl. "Them bloodstains ain't never scrubbin' out. When that murderin' moonspinner left the body it must've been near white as the Queen's ass in winter."

"*Damn*," was all that Hudson could think to say, because even though he was relieved beyond words that Matthew was not dead—at least had not been dead when he'd left here—his heart was still heavy and many questions remained, the most important being: "Do you have any idea where they've gone?" When the old woman shook her head, Hudson posed the same question again to the larger group of people, but no one could answer.

"Sonny, you look like you might use a drink," said Maw Katty, and she stepped forward a couple of paces to offer Hudson the jug.

He took it. The corn liquor was not the strongest he'd ever put down, but it was strong enough to make him feel as if a maniac had him clutched by the throat, and to see dark spots whirling before his eyes. Still, it was what he needed to clear his head.

"You too, if you like," Maw Katty offered to Magnus, who did not hesitate in taking the jug from Hudson's hand and drinking a great draught of the liquid fire, for the realization of how he'd walked away from this house with Matthew shuttered away inside it was something he was going to have to deal with for many days ahead. Firewater would not cure the ill, but for the moment it would serve as an easement to his error in not entering that house at the girl's request. Then again…how would he have ever known Matthew was in there? She had likely asked him reasoning, even in her madness, that he would decline and thus Matthew's presence would go unknown to him. But surely—

Hudson voiced it before Magnus could think it: "Something had to be wrong with the boy. I don't know what…I can't figure it… but for Matthew to have stayed here, with the life he had in New York…*why*?"

Magnus returned the jug to Maw Katty, who squinted up at the scorched sky through the branches of overhanging oaks. "Might as well ask the sun why it burns and the wind why it blows. Ask the snakes why they curl up on rocks and the 'gators why they sleep in the mud. Some things you'll never know, and in the end they ain't important. Things just be what they be."

"*No*," said Hudson.

"What?" she asked.

"If my friend's still alive, I'm going to find him wherever he's been taken. I'm going to find out *exactly* what happened here, who killed that girl and why. So, many thanks for your time, the information and the drink. We'll be on our way now."

"You find Quinn's killer, you ought to turn him over to the law," said another woman in the crowd, this one several decades younger than Maw Katty but no less bedraggled. "Only right that he hangs for murder."

Hudson nodded at Magnus for them to start off again. Magnus wheeled his horse around and they retraced their path through the village back to the road. In another few minutes they were surrounded again by the steamy forest, the shrill calls of birds from the trees, the chitter and drone of an army of insects and the flying clouds of mosquitoes.

Magnus said, "I'm—"

"Don't speak for a little while," Hudson interrupted. "I've got to do some thinking." He glanced over at the other man, who had lowered his head as if he'd been struck, and reconsidered his harshness. "We're square," Hudson said quietly. "How were you to know Matthew was still alive if that girl said she saw him go in the river? I mean...*I* might have questioned it, but why should *you*? I'm a professional in these things, so that's my job. Anyway, I hardly ever believe anything I'm told until I see it with my own eyes. I still can hardly believe *this*, but...that part about the foreign Count...and Matthew leaving with him in a wagon...Christ, I don't like that!"

Magnus was silent for awhile longer, and then he asked, "What are you gonna do next?"

"I'm presuming Charles Town has a printmaster?"

"Yep."

"A dependable man who can work quickly?"

"Yep. I've used him to print some broadsheets."

"That's just what I need him to do for me. Print up broadsheets with Matthew's name and description on them. Also mention of a reward for any information. I'll post them around town and see if anybody bites."

"I'll help you post 'em," said Magnus. "Seems like the least I can do."

"Thank you." Then Hudson was quiet again, because this business of Count Dahlgren was weighing heavily on him. But why... *why*...would Matthew have gone anywhere with the man? And the murdered girl…well, it was beyond him at the moment to figure out. Time would have to tell.

Immediately on their return to Charles Town, Hudson left Magnus and secured a room at the Brevard House on Broad Street, after which he marched in haste upon the printmaster's shop and collared the man in the act of closing up for the evening. By strength of will and show of gold coin he was just able to get an order in for twenty broadsheets stating Matthew's name, description, a reward of a guinea for any reliable information—to be ascertained by circumstances—and two guineas to actually lead directly to the young man's whereabouts. He wished he'd brought more coin with him to sweeten the tea, but as he was far from being a rich man this was all he could afford, including the inn and the printmaster's work. Finally upon the broadsheet would be Hudson's name and locality at the Brevard House. When the printmaster vowed to have this work done within two days, all that was left for Hudson to do was to go find some dinner, have a drink or two, and perhaps enjoy the voice and music of a lass wandering with gittern in hand among the tavern tables. Anything to forget for a little while that, though he was overjoyed to find Matthew at least alive a couple of weeks ago, he was distraught to know the boy might be in the hands of the enemy.

In two days' time, Hudson and Magnus nailed up the twenty broadsheets across the width of the town. After that, all the man from New York could do was to hunker down, wait, and hope.

On the afternoon of the second day after the sheets had gone up, Mrs. Brevard knocked at Hudson's door to tell him he had a visitor, though she wrinkled her nose when she said it. In the parlor he entertained for a very few moments a garrulous drunkard who insisted that not only had he seen Sir Matthew Corbett that very morning, but Sir Matthew Corbett was his long-lost son who the Indians had taken along with his wife back in the summer of '89. Yes, indeed…the young man was seen among the beggars at Smith's Quay and did not know his own father, so tortured his mind had become. So…would the good gentleman consider giving over a guinea, or better still two of them, to help provide a way for a suffering father to give help to a Christian soul struck down by heathen evil?

"No," said Hudson, "but I'll give you some grudging admiration for pulling as many strings as you can. Now leave here and take your odor with you before I kick you out the door."

To which, the drunkard sat very still for a moment and then, as tears began to slowly roll from his yellowed eyes down the scabby cheeks, he rose to his feet and with the dignity of a silent statesman departed the Brevard House.

This, Hudson thought, was not going to be easy.

The following day thunder spoke and a light rain fell from morning until dusk. Steam rose from the streets and the roofs, and ensconced in the Brevard House's parlor Hudson entertained himself by playing games of draughts with a fellow traveller from Baltimore, a clothier who had come to Charles Town to buy the dyes—in particular the indigo—that were so famous among the colonies. No one came to offer any information. Hudson's coins were burning a hole in his pocket and he became more agitated and irritable by the hour, but there was nothing to be done for it.

In the evening he dined with the Brevards on whitefish, boiled potatoes, corn cakes, leek soup and very remarkable mincemeat pie. Not long after dinner, Hudson was again summoned by the lady of the house to the parlor, for another visitor had come calling.

This gentleman was tall and lean, had a brown goatee and mustache trimmed with gray, a mane of flowing brown hair that began at a widow's-peak, and wore stylish clothing and a wine-red cloak. He had a copy of the broadsheet in one hand and in the other carried a brown walking-stick with a large knotty grip. As Hudson entered the room the gentleman took his measure from head to toe and back again.

"Zounds!" he said, "you're a big one!"

"You have information for me?" Hudson pressed.

"Uh…well…I was—"

"Do you have information, or do you not?" He reached into a pocket and showed the gentleman a gleaming guinea coin. The man's eyes took on a fever. Hudson had noted that the man wore a ring on almost every finger, which he found a distasteful show of vanity.

The gentleman hesitated, but his gaze never left the gold. "I… suppose I do."

"Let's hear it."

The story was: the young man described upon the broadsheet was sitting this moment in the Full Fathom Five tavern not two streets from this parlor. The young Corbett was commonly seen there, was always in his cups, but he answered to the name of Timothy.

"Take me there," said Hudson.

"Well…I mean to say…and this may be indelicate…but I have been elected to come here from the regulars at the Full Fathom Five, and they would hold it grievously against me if I did not suggest they also might be paid."

"I'm not paying anything until I see the boy."

"Yes, of course, but I'm just suggesting you bring enough coin with you to reward myself and the six others."

"I have enough." Hudson touched another pocket where a small pouch of coins was secured. This would nearly clean him out, but if this really was Matthew it was a bargain and he would figure out how to pay the return packet boat fee later. He spent a moment to inform Mrs. Brevard where he was headed, if someone else came to ask for him, and then he said to the gentleman, "Let's go."

The streets were quiet, still wet with rain. Candlelight showed in many of the windows they passed. Somewhere a squeezebox was being played quite fervently and there came the sound of raucous male and female laughter, but the cloaked gentleman was leading Hudson away from the noise of festivities.

When the gentleman turned into the narrow mouth of an alley and said, "This way, sir, it's quicker," Hudson smelled the skunk and knew the game.

The two men who'd been hiding in the darkness of a shopfront rushed upon Hudson with their cudgels upraised. A third man, the fourth of the robbers' gang, seemed to think better of tangling with someone Hudson's size and he hung back, pretending to suddenly have a stone in his boot.

The cloaked gentleman lashed out with the knobby end of his stick, the action accompanied by the flash of a dirk drawn from its concealed sheath. Hudson parried the blow with his left arm, stepped into this rank amateur of a combatant before the dirk could be brought to bear, and hit him so hard his goatee and mustache nearly flew in separate directions from the body that collapsed bonelessly in a pudding of rainwater and horse figs. The second man got in a grazing blow to Hudson's shoulder with his cudgel, but in the next instant his front teeth were gone and his nose was of a new geometric. The fourth man had already fled for the safety of his skin, regardless of how many stones agonized his foot.

The third would-be-robber feinted with the cudgel, but Hudson simply stood his ground.

"You look to be all of sixteen years old," Hudson noted. "Is it necessary for me to severely hurt you?"

The answer was almost immediate. "No sir," said the youth, and he was gone like a shot.

Hudson undid his breeches and peed upon both the unconscious cloaked gentleman and the groaning new-nosed fellow. Then he stood in the damp night air rubbing the pain out of his not-too-damaged shoulder. He felt both sad and yet strangely full of energy, and thus decided not to waste his jaunt. He turned around and headed toward the noise of squeezebox and laughter, determined to get a tankard of ale and perhaps a wink from a comely girl out of this sorry misadventure.

Sure enough, it was the Full Fathom Five from which the carousing issued. Hudson's entry into the smoke-filled, noisy, dimly-candled, stained-walled and absolutely delightfully dirty establishment went entirely unnoticed by the clientele, who were too busy jabbering or laughing or quaffing from their cups or thumping their tables in time to the three-hundred-pound red-haired woman who played the Devil's own tune on that squeezebox. Hudson looked around at the happy flotsam and jetsam of Charles Town society and had to grin; this was more his liking, as it reminded him of New York.

He settled himself at a small table well amid the hurrahicano and ordered his ale from a serving-girl who looked as if she had winked at the patrons a few too many times, as her right eye was afflicted with a continual twitch. Still and all, she commanded a bright smile and clean blonde hair and in the low candlelight she was the Duchess of Desire, so well to the good and squeeze on, sister!

He had his tankard of ale, an apple-based concoction that might melt the hair off a man's chest, and a second one to wash down the first. The serving-girl brought him a little plate of half-burnt sausages when he asked for something to chew on. The female squeezebox player finished a last tune and waddled around collecting coins, then she went on her way. Some of the other patrons left and the place quietened down. Hudson was loathe to return to the Brevard House, because there in his room with a single candle throwing more shadows than light he would begin to believe that Matthew might never be found, and that would be a hard reality to stomach. He was contemplating this grievance against Fate and Circumstance and watering his rising anger with the second apple ale when someone at his left side said, "Mr. Hudson Greathouse?"

He looked up into a man's face that seemed more prune than flesh, so many were the wrinkles. The dusting of white face powder and cheek rouge the gent wore served only to make his appearance more garish, even frightful. The man was long and lean, was impossible to assign an age to because of the makeup but it was certain he was no young chicken. A leathered rooster he might be, Hudson mused…or, perhaps, a slippery snake. This unpretty picture of a nobleman wore a gray suit with a fancy and surely very expensive ruffled shirt, a pale blue waistcoat and a gray tricorn atop a powdered wig of a thousand curls, the wig being nearly high enough to tip the tricorn off its perch.

"You *are* Hudson Greathouse, aren't you?" The man had a voice that contained a hint of blustering storms, yet tonight he was doing his best to play Zeus and control his own bolts of lightning.

"I am," came the reply. "Who wants to know?"

"Oh dear, disagreeable so soon? Lady Brevard told me you were here and described you. She said that you seemed…how did she put it?…*edgy*."

"I was born edgy. I'm working past irritated to livid. Who the hell are you?"

"Earl Thomas Kattenberg, at your service." The man gave a slight nod that threatened to truly dislodge the tricorn. Hudson found himself tensed, ready to catch it. The prune- and powder-faced individual cast a gaze around the room through dark eyes buried in hoods of flesh, and then he focused his full attention upon Hudson again. He said, "Matthew knew me as Exodus Jerusalem, in the fledgling settlement of Fount Royal. God forgive their foolishness there." He shrugged and his mouth drew as tight as a miser's purse. "Another page is turned in the book of Life."

Hudson had been reaching for his tankard but his hand had stopped with the speaking of the name. "You...*know* Matthew?"

"I do. I saw a broadsheet this afternoon. I thought it best to seek you out."

"Well...my God, man! Sit down!"

"I shall, thank you." Thomas Kattenberg, the earl of a province that would never be found on any map, seated himself in a rickety chair as if lowering his hind upon a golden throne. His smile in the candlelight was ghastly. "Let us tend to the financials before we travel this road any further. How much money have you brought?"

"I have..." Hudson recovered his wits in a flash. He snapped, "Now hold that horse a minute! Are you telling me you have information to sell?"

"Not just any information. *The* information. You're wanting to know where Matthew is, correct? I can tell you that."

Hudson now did reach for the tankard and took a long drink. His anger at Matthew's disappearance and the indignity of being attacked by would-be Jonathan Dooms threatened to boil over and make quite a mess. He felt his face reddening. "Listen here!" he said, and he grasped hold of one of Earl Kattenberg's lacy cuffs, "I suggest you tell me what you know and tell me *now*, or you might not—"

The earl laughed. It was even more ghastly than the smile.

"Dear Mr. Greathouse," he said smoothly, with a little thunder behind it and the dark eyes catching a glint of crimson, "threats of violence and *acts* of violence do nothing but scramble the brain and impair the memory. You're from New York, you're supposed to be a *sophisticate* in such things. Alas," he said as he gently worked Hudson's fingers loose, "I rather think you're more hayseed than whipweed. Now: my question stands, sir. How much money have you brought?" He waved away his own query. "Never mind. However much it is, I want it all."

"Information first."

"Absolutely not. Money first."

"I have eight guineas."

"Oh, please do better than that."

"All right. Ten."

"Keep climbing, the peak is in sight."

"Were you Matthew's friend or enemy?" Hudson asked, his eyes narrowed into slits.

"We *understood* each other," said Earl Kattenberg, with a slight smile that moved across the wrinkled face like an oilslick of corruption. "As we do understand each other presently. Your next offer, please?"

Hudson had decided this man—rooster, snake, whatever he was—could read his mind. "Twelve guineas," he said, and from his pocket he produced the leather pouch. He dangled this between his fingers before the earl's so-called face. "That's it. Everything I've brought. I give this to you and I don't know how I'll pay for these ales and sausages."

"I'm sure," said Kattenberg, as he daintily took the offering, "an intelligent sophisticate like yourself will think of something." He opened the pouch to grin at the sight of gold. "I have to say, this is not as much as I'd hoped for, but—"

A hand closed on his chin, gripped hard, and then patted a rouged cheek with the most gentle of deadly threats.

"Where is Matthew Corbett?" Hudson asked, leaning forward like an approaching maelstrom.

"Where, indeed," said the man who had been Exodus Jerusalem and in fact carried within himself several identities as suited the purpose of the moment. His tongue worked saliva into his lips. "I shall tell you what I saw at the harbor little more than a week ago, and let us hope—dear Jesus, let us hope—that by now young Master Corbett's bones are not coral made, that he has not suffered a sea-change and that nymphs do not hourly ring his knell, as he lies sleeping in the deep, full fathom five."

Freedom of the Mask

Robert McCammon

Subterranean Press 2016

First Edition

Limited Edition ISBN
978-1-59606-774-5

Trade Edition ISBN
978-1-59606-775-2

Subterranean Press
PO Box 190106
Burton, MI 48519

subterraneanpress.com

Three

A STRENGTHENING breeze. An ominous curtain of clouds from horizon to horizon. A rolling of the sea, a chop of whitecaps, a fluttering of sails and clatter of block-and-tackle as the wind became not friend to the ship but its adversary. Then as the darkness of ink-black clouds came sweeping across the gray expanse, the thunder blasted its mighty bass voice and forks of lightning stabbed the water, the dolphins abandoned their positions at the prow of the two-masted brigantine *Wanderer*, bound from Charles Town to the port of Plymouth, and dove away from the calamities of the world of men.

The *Wanderer*, being an old ship and beaten by not only other storms but by the neglect of its owners and succession of captains, was hardly seaworthy, yet now came her most perilous hour. From the blackness of clouds shot through with streaks of angry violet, a banshee of winds took the sea within their power and whipped it to a frenzy. One instant the *Wanderer* was climbing a green mountain, the next it was sliding over a liquid cliff that seemed bound to break the vessel in two, yet a turbulent white fist of water came up

and in equal parts supported the ship and slammed the vengeance of Nature into the worm-eaten hull. As the prow descended at an angle that caused women to scream, children to wail and men to soil breeches already damp, the bowsprit knifed the sea and in its rage and indignation the sea exploded over the *Wanderer*, shuddering its timbers and making its masts shriek out like the high-pitched voices of humans who had unwittingly wandered into a fight for survival, and the realization that Hell was wet, salty, and unforgiving. Though the sails had been reefed, everything possible lashed down and the ship heaved-to before the awesome might of Neptune's wrath, the *Wanderer* was ill-prepared for such a blast, and in truth the newest and strongest of any fleet would have been tossed like a trinket.

Then the real storm began.

"Where is the captain? In the name of God, where is the captain?" shouted a gaunt man in a sopping-wet black suit stained with yellow mildew, his eyes near bursting from his head. He held a dirty oil lamp that in the ship's passageway illuminated one of the few crewmen who on the voyage so far seemed to give a damn about the welfare of the vessel and its fourteen passengers. Water sloshed calf-deep in miniature tidal waves, carrying with it debris that had broken loose from its moorings. "Mr. Roxley!" cried the lamp-bearer, as the ship rose up to what seemed a frightening height. The Right Reverend Enoch Fanning grabbed hold of a rope that had been tied along the passageway just for such purpose, and would have been dashed against the ceilingwork when the *Wanderer* came down again. As it was, his shoes slipped out from beneath him, he splashed down but was full-witted enough to save the lamp's flame, and Roxley—who himself seemed already brain-damaged by a previous collision with a bulkhead—was swept away by the fresh torrent of green water that poured through an open hatch the storm had unhinged.

"Captain Peppertree! Captain Peppertree!" Fanning yelled at the top of his lungs, though his sermon-shout was no match for the whirlwinds. "Jesus Christ, someone take command of this ship!" he wailed. Near sobbing, he struggled up and fought his way aft through the vicious little waves, as small silver fish jumped in panic around him.

The ship's manger had been broken open in this tumult, and as Fanning pushed on toward the captain's quarters one of the three goats brought aboard blocked the passage, its body crashing back and forth with the *Wanderer*'s violent dance. A dead chicken feathered the sloppy murk. Fanning shouted again, "Captain Peppertree!" but his voice only reached Bessie's ears. Then the ship rose…rose…rose…the timbers screaming, cracking, near bursting their joints…and very suddenly came down so hard Fanning's arm was almost torn from its shoulder as he gripped the safety-rope. The goat hit a bulkhead with such force surely its back was broken. Fanning barely dodged being crushed as it tumbled past him along the passage, its hooves scrabbling for purchase. Another Atlantic wave rolled through the ship, and water rained in from the deck overhead.

Fanning kept going. The door to the captain's quarters was open, the small nasty compartment aslosh with ocean, littered with wet papers and debris. No light shone there. The sea beat at the hull with both fists and a battering-ram the size of the tower of London. Fanning thrust his lamp into the dark. And there…there at his desk which certainly must be nailed to the floor as well as was the ragged leather chair he sat in…was Captain Gabriel Peppertree, who clenched a half-drained bottle of rum in one hand, his gray-bearded face fully drained of color, his reddened eyes lost, his expression blank, his shoulders hunched forward as if he were either sitting on the hole of his latrine or the edge of his grave.

"Captain!" the minister shouted, as he supported himself in the doorway. "This ship is breaking to pieces! Please take command and *do* something!"

Captain Peppertree stared at him, or at least in the minister's direction. His eyelids were at half-mast. His mouth gave a twitch, and nothing more.

"I beg of you!" Fanning pleaded. "You have crew and passengers in your care! Please rouse yourself to the task!"

Captain Peppertree, whose name suggested perhaps it had been better he remain rooted to the earth his entire existence, regarded the bottle of rum, took a long drink from it and then started to stand, battling the roll of his vessel and the crash of the sea on all sides and above.

He hesitated in mid-rise.

Then he vomited a terrible outpouring upon his desk, slumped down and passed out with his face in yesterday's porridge and today's sugarcane swill.

Fanning let out a moaning cry, for with Roxley out of his senses and the captain gone from this world there was literally no one left to take charge. The rest of the crew had burrowed even deeper into the ship to hide than had the passengers. There was nothing to be done. The minister turned away from this sorry sight of tragedy toward another sorry sight: a drowned pig being washed along the passageway, drowned as they all must surely be when this Godforsaken and masterless ship was dashed apart...which, by the sound of the Devil's waves and wind gnawing at the spars, was not to be long in coming. Fanning had no choice but to splash and careen his way forward again, and to the hold where his fellow passengers were huddled, soaked and trembling, awaiting word from the decrepit captain that there was hope yet to be found and a plan to keep this ship from capsizing.

The ocean-drenched space was nearly beneath the *Wanderer*'s figurehead, a carved female who might have once appeared serene as the moon, yet whose face had been wiped clean by the violence of past storms. The thirteen other passengers were gathered together and held onto ropes to keep from being tossed like bowling pins. Hezekiah Montgomery, a businessman from Liverpool, held an oil lamp and so did the blacksmith Curt Randolph, who had the misfortune of sharing his approaching death with his wife and two daughters, one hardly out of her swaddling. There was the farmer Noble Jahns, along with his wife, his young son, his mother and his one-legged father. There was the Charles Town lawyer Grantham Briarfield, a shrill-voiced dandy who was in a hurry to reach London for a business deal that meant he could not wait for a better ship to book passage upon, and...

...there was the Prussian Count Anton Mannerheim Dahlgren, and his black-haired, black-bearded, taciturn and decidedly strange young servant who he called Matthew.

"It's all up!" cried the minister to this assembly of despair. "Roxley is out of his head and the captain is useless!"

To which, as if in taunting reply, the ocean lifted the ship once more and plunged it down again. The sea burst through a thousand cracks and swamped the space before it ran off through a thousand more cracks into the hull below, and the shoals of human beings were nearly ripped from their ropes.

"Let us pray!" said Randolph's wife, a sturdy woman who cradled her infant child with her free arm while her husband's thick forearm gave a purchase for the elder daughter to hold onto. "Please, reverend! Lead us in prayer, that at least our souls and those of our children be saved!"

"Yes, yes!" Fanning agreed, though that last violent rise, plummet and cannonblast of sea against the prow had nearly unhinged his own senses. "God will have mercy on our souls if we pray!"

"*Ha! Vat a load of shit!*"

The half-choked, half-growled response had come from the Prussian, who stood at the far edge of the light with his servant behind him, both of them clinging to ropes, the servant with both arms and the Count with the one that did not have a severely crooked wrist. Dahlgren's dirty blonde hair was plastered to his skull, seaweed caught in his beard, his green eyes sunken and his gray teeth bared in the wolfish face. "Ve are dead! And your God is haffing a good laugh!" he said. "Listen to him roar!"

"*Please,*" the woman repeated to the minister. "For all of us who believe."

"Yes...of course. Let us bow our heads."

Everyone who could understand did, except the Count and his servant. And then, just before Fanning began, the servant also bowed his head. Water ran from his hair, over the crescent scar on his forehead, and dripped from the sharp tip of his nose.

"Dear God," the minister started. The sea and wind gave no mercy in the volume of their attack, thus Fanning had to speak as loudly as he could. "Dear God," he repeated, for quite suddenly and after fourscore and ten of sermons he did not know what to say, at this moment of moments. He floundered, searching, and then it came upon him as if it had been quilled upon his heart.

"We praise Thee," he said, "even in this hour of our trial. We praise our Heavenly Father, and lift our eyes and trust, for we know we live in the great house of the Lord, and though the seas may crash asunder and the wind tear apart what Man has created, the Word and Deed of the Lord Almighty goes on and on, and..."

The sea and wind did not like this and they let the *Wanderer* and her passengers know it, but the minister went on after the Atlantic had rolled over their backs again.

"...and we love the Word and Deed, for that is our bond for everlasting life, and in this...this great house that the Lord has created...we know there will be storms aplenty, and suffering too, and trials and tribulations to be conquered for that is the way of things, and we cannot ask why, we can only try our best to walk in God's light and do...what is right, for our loved ones and the community of Man."

"*Vashing of the hogs!*" Dahlgren sneered, but no one looked up from the prayer.

"So...we pray to Thee now...do what Thy will. We beg Thee to be merciful and to prepare a place in Paradise for all...especially these children...these young innocents...these lambs in dire need of a shepherd. If Thy will is so...take us all into Thy hands and deliver us to the realm of Heaven, where we might find peace...believers and unbelievers alike. It is this I sincerely ask, as Thy friend and child upon this earth...as Thy servant and exhalter. By Thy grace, Amen."

"*Amen*," said some of the others.

Dahlgren laughed harshly.

His servant spoke.

"Great house," he said.

He spoke the two words like a man who'd been struck, had been dazed and lost, himself wandering a dark wilderness, and who had just seen a glimmer of light through the tangled trees.

Matthew Corbett pressed his free hand against his forehead, for it seemed his brain was bruised. The ship went up, slammed down, the timbers shrieked, the water swept through, but suddenly the young man was an immovable object, and though at the end of his rope he held firm, and indeed something within himself began to climb back.

He had wondered so many things since starting this voyage with the monster who had murdered his wife, Quinn...or, who *said* she was his wife. And this man, this Prussian count who had slashed Quinn's throat right in front of him, said he was not Daniel Tate but was instead someone named *Corbett*, and that he did not belong in Rotbottom, but that a man Dahlgren called Professor Fell in England would receive him with open arms and explain everything to his satisfaction. But why did Quinn have to die, and if he wasn't her husband Daniel then how had he gotten to

Rotbottom? It was all mixed up, it was pain upon pain and a center of blankness. Why did he have such strange thoughts that streaked through his mind like comets, leaving blazing images that just as quickly faded away?

Who was the woman who appeared to be in a filthy gaol cell, and dropping her hooded cloak she stood naked to the world and defiantly said, *Here is the witch…*?

Who was a girl named Berry, for that name kept coming to him, and brief glimpses of her face as if seen only through frosted glass? And there was something about birds…hawks, maybe they were, and it was a fearful thing but he could make no sense of it.

Who was the man with him in the cold water at the bottom of a well, and the second man with a patchwork beard standing looking down, and his laugh like a slow funeral bell?

A girl that he somehow knew was of the Iroquois tribe sitting nude upon a rock at sea…two orange-haired brothers, devils both, but their names were gone…a massive explosion, and a burning wagon falling from the sky…a deadly swamp, and what appeared to be skeleton-men playing sport with human heads…

What did all that mean?

And one of the strangest things was that he knew a great deal about a sailing ship. He knew the difference between a cat's-head and a topgallant, a holystone and a gaff-rig; he knew the system of bells that kept time for the watch, though Peppertree failed to follow them with the same military precision as had Captain Falco. Of this he was somehow certain…but *who* was Captain Falco? A name that had come to him one day out of the mists, as had the girl's name Berry? He never recalled being at sea before, so…another mystery, among a multitude of them.

But the time for answering those questions was not of the moment; the problem to be solved, and quickly, was how to save this ship and all aboard.

The great house of the Lord, he thought.

The great house.

The greathouse.

Greathouse.

Why did those two words, put together, make him think that he was able to get out of this hold, face that storm and try to save himself and these people? Not only that...but he thought that even with the odds against him, he had a good chance of doing so.

Think! he told himself, as the ship pitched and fell, rolled and groaned and the water streamed over him and the others. Those two words...no, no...not just any two words...oh, his brain was hurting...not just two words...no...a *name*.

"If this ship is to be saved," he suddenly spoke up, already beating by three words the longest sentence he'd uttered to anyone on this voyage, "we're going to have to do it."

"*Us?*" said Noble Jahns' one-legged father. "I don't know a damn thing 'bout seacraft!"

"None of us do!" Briarfield's shrill voice was made even sharper and more shrill by his terror. "We're all landlubbers!"

"We've got to get up to the deck!" Matthew said. "Tie down every heavy rope we can find and throw them over! Let them trail in the water!"

"For what purpose?" the blacksmith asked.

"Slowing the ship down. The ropes will help that, and give us stability. If we can get the port and starboard anchors dropped, so much the—" He was interrupted by another slam and crash of prow against waves and *whoosh* of the sea rushing through the compartment. "Better," he finished when he could breathe again.

"No one's going up there!" said Briarfield, whose sharp-chinned face had taken on the color and sheen of spoiled cheese. "And *you*... you're nothing but a *servant*! You don't know anything about ships! Jesus Christ, what you're suggesting may well *sink* us!"

"I know this tub can't take much more! We can't just stay here and wait for it to break up!" When no one responded, Matthew said, "I'll do it myself, then!"

"Ohhhhhh, no!" It was the harsh voice of Count Dahlgren. "You are *not* going anyvhere! You are too waluable to me, to be lost in such a folly!"

Matthew despised the man. Not only was Dahlgren a murderer, he was filthy in his habits and expected his "servant" to wait upon him as if he had been elevated to the status of emperor. He had sworn to someday kill Dahlgren for Quinn's murder, but he had to stay his hand to find out who the enigmatic Professor Fell was, and what this person knew about his history.

In the meantime he had no intention of waiting here like a trapped bilge rat. The ship heeled violently and the women and children screamed but not as wildly as Grantham Briarfield. There was a sick instant when Matthew was certain the masts must be touching wavetops, and then with the noise of bursting timbers the *Wanderer* fought back. After the next wave smashed through, Matthew took the lamp from Hezekiah Montgomery. "I'm going," he said, but before he made two unsteady steps on this nautical nightmare Count Dahlgren was upon him.

"I said, *nein*!" Dahlgren hooked his good arm around his servant's throat. "You are svept off, and vhere does this leave *me*?"

"Let him go."

"*Vhat?*"

"Let him go," Randolph repeated. "If he's got guts enough to go out on this deck...by God, I do too. That trick with the ropes... it might steady us!"

"He is my property! I say vhat he does and does not do!"

"I'll go," said Montgomery. "If I'm going to drown, it won't be *inside* a ship!"

"I'll go," the one-legged old man said with a fierce intensity, but Noble Jahns shook his head. "I'm with ye," the farmer said to Randolph. "Pa, you're stickin' here to look out for the fam'ly. No arguments, now!"

"Yes," said Fanning, who gave his lamp to Jahns' father. "Take my light."

"Either let him go or come with us," Randolph said to Dahlgren. "We'll need all the hands we can get!" He didn't look at Briarfield, who had moved as far away from the light as he could.

"I say again...*nein*! I vill not haff—oh, *Jesu*!"

The next blood-curdling pitch and fall of the *Wanderer* had loosened Dahlgren's grip on Matthew, and the blast of water from the deck was strong enough to part master from servant.

"Let's get to it!" Randolph said to Matthew when he could speak again. He led the way out of the hold and into the flooded passageway with Matthew right behind him, followed by Jahns, Fanning and Montgomery.

Amid floating dead chickens and a pig swimming for its life, water-soaked boards that served as risers led up to a hatch set flush with the deck. The hatch had been hastily secured with a leather cord, but the sea was pouring in through every possible crack; it occurred to Matthew that neither Captain Peppertree nor his crew had ever heard of pitch or tar. A knife drawn from a sheath at Randolph's belt made quick work of the leather, and pushing the hatch upward and open the blacksmith was the first to step out into the whirlwinds. He was nearly blown out of his boots, and whether it was rain or seaspray that was crossing the deck in torrents made no matter; it was going to take strength, fortitude and just plain luck to even crawl on this pitching bitch without being thrown into the Atlantic.

When Matthew emerged he too was hit by the wind and water and he skidded several yards before he could grab hold of a rope. The deck was a tangle of lines, collapsed shrouds, and debris that had been torn loose. The lid of a toolbox had been battered open and its contents expelled. Several mallets, a couple of handsaws, some hatchets and a full-sized axe were underfoot for the taking, if such might be useful for the task. What caught Matthew's attention and held it, though, was the vista of mountainous black waves around them, under a dark violet sky through which it seemed a half-dozen whips of lightning flared at any given second. One instant the ship was rising with frightening speed toward the summits and the next it turned bowsprit down and slid into the canyons between them, with a thunder of water crashing over the prow, a shuddering and eerie groaning of distressed hull and masts, and a smash of water over the small figures that gripped onto any handhold to keep the deck beneath them.

Matthew's nerve faltered. He was on his knees, gripping desperately to a line. A wall of seafoam that felt as hard as church bricks struck him in the face and pounded his skull. The world was a black-and-purple tumult and a shriek of storm and vessel. *I can't do this!* he thought, as the terror flailed within him. *No...no...I can't!*

But then, in his mind, that name again: *Greathouse*. Yes, he was sure it was a name. Whoever it belonged to was strong, he thought. Whoever it belonged to...a man...yes...a man who would get up off his knees and do what he had to do, no matter if it cost him his life. And whoever it was, he would expect the same. It was not that Greathouse was without fear; it was that fear did not rule him, and however he went down he would go down fighting. Of this, Matthew was very sure.

He was not Greathouse, but whoever Matthew was—husband to Quinn, servant to Dahlgren, lost soul bound for either death at sea or an audience with Professor Fell in England—he had to stand up now, put on his big-boy boots and do what had to be done.

He was aware of the blurred figures of Randolph, Fanning and Jahns making their way aft, staggering hither and yon. Montgomery's head appeared in the hatch but his nerve must've collapsed because after only a few seconds he retreated, and he closed the hatch to seal his shame in with him.

Matthew got up. The wind pushed and pulled him at the same time. It caught him at the knees and hit him in the chest. He clung to whatever woodwork or lines he could find as he struggled aft, one moment climbing a mountain, the next trying to keep from sliding over a cliff. When he reached the others he found that Randolph had broken open one of the rope lockers and he and Jahns were pulling out the thicker mooring lines. Other ropes of various thicknesses lay about in tangles. Fanning was at work tying one of these to a cleat, his back braced against the storm. Matthew reached him between waves and helped him toss all sixty feet of the rope over the side, so the first line was in the water. Randolph and Jahns got one of the hawsers tied up, and there was an anxious moment when a wave swept in with tremendous force from starboard and nearly carried both men over the side but for the blacksmith's strength in holding them. The hawser went over the stern, and the two men started tying up a second heavy rope while Matthew and Fanning concentrated on securing and throwing over as many smaller ropes as they could gather.

"*You are coming vith me!*"

A hand with a crooked wrist grabbed the collar of Matthew's shirt. Water streamed from Dahlgren's hair over the vulpine angles of his face. "Come *now*!" he shouted, and pulled his servant away from the rope he'd been working on with Fanning.

"Leave me alone!" Matthew shouted back. "We've got to finish this!"

"You are *finished*!" said Dahlgren. He then lifted the club-like wooden belaying-pin he'd picked up from the deck and struck

Matthew a hard blow across the left side of his skull, very near the temple.

Matthew collapsed, his head full of fire. Darkness overwhelmed him.

"Are you *insane*?" Fanning yelled. "He's trying to save this—"

"Shut your mouth, you pious pigfucker!" Dahlgren hooked his bad arm around Matthew's chest and began dragging him toward the open hatch. Before he reached it, a sizzling bright bolt of lightning that forked into six spears before it plunged into the sea showed him the gargantuan wave that was bearing down on the unlucky *Wanderer*. It was a black monster, a leviathan of waves, topped with a white crest of boiling foam and shot through with streaks of iridescent green, deep blue and slate gray. Dahlgren realized he would not reach the hatch. He dropped Matthew and scrambled to find a handhold on something solid, at the same time as Fanning saw the wave and shouted for the others to brace themselves.

It lifted the ship on high, balanced it there for a heart-stopping few seconds...and then dashed the vessel down, down and down into a seething valley. The sea crashed over the prow with demonic force, splintering the bowsprit and tearing most of the figurehead away. The upper third of the mainmast snapped and fell overboard. The water picked up the body of the unconscious young man and tossed him like a boneless poppet, and being unconscious most likely saved his neck; in the next instant he was thrown back to the deck and pushed along by the rush of the sea until his left shoulder and the left side of his head struck the rough surface of the starboard bulwark, hitting very near to where the Count's belaying-pin had fallen.

Almost half-drowned, Dahlgren crawled over the debris toward Matthew, who lay like one dead. "Get up!" Dahlgren commanded, for he could see that at least his prize was still breathing. He staggered to his own feet and pulled at one of Matthew's arms. "Get up, damn you!" There was no reaction. Dahlgren looked over his shoulder, terrified lest another beast of a wave smash him down. He heard Matthew begin coughing; he saw the young man shudder and convulse and with an effort get up on hands and knees, and then Matthew began to retch out what seemed a bucket of seawater.

"Up!" Dahlgren said, and again there was no reaction but coughing and retching. He reached down to get his arm around Matthew, haul him up and drag him to the hatch. And then Matthew's head turned and the eyes opened, and blood had burst from the nostrils and the eyes too were reddened while his face had gone ghost-white and the lips gray.

"*You*," he said, more of a croak than speech. One hand came up to touch his left temple, and try to soothe the pulsing pain there. And quite suddenly, as if a veil had been torn away or a fog lifted, he remembered everything...not only what had happened since the murderer Griffin Royce had slammed him in the head with an oar... but everything of the past and present...Hudson Greathouse... Berry Grigsby...Captain Falco of the ship *Nightflyer* that had delivered himself and Berry from Professor Fell's Pendulum Island... Minx Cutter...Madam Herrald...the agency...everything. And though his head was killing him and his vision seemed to fade in and out, he knew exactly who this mongrel was beside him, exactly where he was and why. "You're not..." He tried it again, because his tongue was a heavy weight. "You're not...taking me to Professor Fell, you foul piece of shit."

FOUR

AT this center of the storm, another maelstrom threatened.

"I *remember*," Matthew gasped, still woozy from two blows to the head. The next thing he said he was able to shout over the roar of the wind. "I know who I am!" Perhaps the most important five words he'd ever shouted in his life. He hauled himself up by clinging onto a hanging mass of shrouds and looked defiantly into Dahlgren's face. "I said I'd kill you! So…when we get to England… the first thing I'm going to do is make sure you're arrested and hanged for the murder of Quinn Tate!"

Dahlgren also reached for support into the hanging lines, as the ship shuddered beneath their feet and rain thrashed their faces. "*Ist das so*?" The realization of Matthew's condition sank in. "A regretful situation," he said, and he glanced quickly aft where the others were still occupied throwing out the ropes. The *Wanderer* was yet bucking up and down at the whim of the sea, but it had steadied somewhat and was not heeling so dangerously to port or starboard. Dahlgren gave a thin, tight smile but his eyes were dead. "I no longer haff use for you, do I?"

"Smile all you please! I'll have you locked in the brig as soon as—"

An arm went around Matthew's throat with choking force. The Prussian braced himself to bodily throw the young problem-solver from New York over the side.

The *Wanderer* had been lifted up on a wave and now it sank rapidly into a green trough. The water that crashed over the damaged prow and flooded across the deck was not what saved Matthew's skin; it was the dozens of silver flying fish that exploded out of that wave, and struck at both the struggling men in a flurry of vibrating fins and tails.

In that miniature silver hurricane, Matthew fought free. He slipped on flopping fish and went down on the deck, and Dahlgren turned toward him with rage contorting his face and a flying fish caught for an instant in the tangle of his beard. Then Dahlgren saw something that suited his purpose, and he plucked up the axe that had been broken out of the toolbox.

"You *die*," said the Prussian, the wind whipping the words away so that Matthew only heard the passing intent of the growl behind them, but he could read Dahlgren's lips well enough to know that the axe was not going to be used to part only his hair.

Dahlgren's boots crushed fish as he advanced. He lifted the axe with a two-handed grip and brought it down with ferocious strength.

Matthew was already picking up a splintered spar that lay beside him in the debris as the axe rose. When it fell the spar was held horizontally before Matthew's face and so caught the blade yet very nearly was chopped in two. The spar served an additional purpose of trapping the axeblade, and as Dahlgren struggled to pull it free and Matthew fought to keep hold of the piece of wood, Matthew kicked the Prussian as hard as he could in the right knee. Dahlgren let out a cry of pain that shamed the storm's howl, but he held onto the axe and as he staggered back he tore the weapon loose from the wooden spar.

Matthew got up from the deck, slipped again on flopping fish and slanting deck but he kept his balance. Dahlgren came limping at him with the axe raised for another killing blow. Matthew stopped the blade with his spar. This time the length of wood cracked in two and he was left with a shorter length in each fist. Dahlgren's axe was rising again and so was the *Wanderer*, to a fearsome height. Lightning shot across the sky, a half-dozen white crackling whips snapping from black clouds to black sea. Matthew gritted his teeth and stepped toward Dahlgren while the axe was still going up, and he struck the Prussian on both sides of the jaw, right and left with his fists gripped around the pieces of wood. Dahlgren's head snapped back but still he kept control of the axe, and then the *Wanderer* crashed down and the sea burst over the wrecked prow. The wave hit both men with equal force and swept them off their feet and tumbling toward the stern.

Matthew collided with Enoch Fanning and nearly sent them both over the side. Randolph's strength was a blessing for himself and Noble Jahns, for as they'd been throwing out the hawsers he had twice saved them both from going over. As Matthew came up spitting water, he saw that Dahlgren was also rising from the foam, and damned if by the dint of at least one powerful grip he *still* had the axe.

Matthew had lost the two lengths of spar, and now here came the Prussian limping toward him as the remainder of the wave rushed away. Fanning was dumbstruck when Dahlgren swung the axe at Matthew, the young man dodged aside, and the axeblade sank into the transom. Matthew struck Dahlgren in the face again with a blow that, if it nearly broke his knuckles, certainly broke Dahlgren's nose for the blood spurted from both nostrils.

The Prussian pulled at the axe but this time Matthew was not going to let him free it. He hit him again, squarely on the crushed nose, and with a bellow of pain Count Dahlgren let go of the axe's handle and flung himself upon Matthew in a clawing fury.

"Stop that!" Fanning shouted. "Have you two gone *mad*?"

Matthew and Dahlgren fought toward the stern, as the blacksmith and the farmer ceased their work to watch in incredulous amazement at what was certainly a death-battle. Dahlgren clawed at Matthew's eyes and then got both hands around the young man's throat. Matthew pounded at the bloody face, but the Count was oblivious to everything except killing his enemy. They careened wildly across the deck. Randolph stepped in to pull them apart but suddenly the ship was rising again…climbing at a frightening speed to another terrible height. Dahlgren squeezed Matthew's throat with as much force as both hands could supply and the blood pounded in Matthew's head and dark spots swirled before his eyes.

The *Wanderer* fell toward another deep valley, walls of rolling ocean rising up on both sides. The hull's timbers let out a shudder and moan as the ship hit the bottom of the trough, and just as Randolph grabbed hold of Matthew's shirt and chopped Dahlgren's hands away from the young man's throat the next bow wave came at them all with a vengeance.

In that blast of sea Matthew thought he must've gone over the stern, for he seemed to be completely underwater and his shoes could not find the deck. Randolph must've fallen with him, for he could still feel the man's knotty hand holding cloth that at any second must rip away. Then his shoes touched timbers, his body hit what must've been the stern transom and knocked the fool out of him, the breath he'd been able to grab exploded from his lungs, he was about to draw in a draught of the sea, and then his face was out of the water and he pulled in air and collapsed against the transom like sack of soggy clothes.

"You all right?" The question was not directed from Randolph to himself, but to Jahns, who answered shakily that, God be praised, he was still aboard and still in one piece.

Fanning sputtered and retched, having been knocked to his knees and also thrown hard into the stern. Randolph held onto Matthew's shirt while the young man breathed like a bellows and came to his senses.

He realized in the next few seconds, as they all did, that the Prussian swordsman was no longer among them.

"The Count went over!" Jahns shouted. "I see him! He's grabbed hold of a rope!"

Over the roar of wind and the pounding of rain, Matthew thought he heard Dahlgren's ragged cry for help but that could have been a trick of the storm. He looked over the stern and saw in that madhouse of crashing waves and flying foam a blonde-haired head maybe forty yards out, and it was apparent Dahlgren had indeed seized one of the lines and was holding on for all his life was worth.

"Jahns! Fanning! Help me pull him in!" Randolph shouted, and having ascertained which rope the Prussian had grabbed he went to that line and began to haul the man home. Jahns gave his strength to the task, and so did the minister.

Matthew Corbett, however, did not join in the attempt at life-saving. He was recalling the moment when Dahlgren's blade slashed across the throat of a poor addled girl who already had been dealt a miserable hand in this lunatic game of living. He recalled her expression of shock as she fell, and his own helplessness to do anything but watch as her life streamed away across the floor. Oh, there had been so much blood...so much pain in that room...the cabin that Quinn had thought would be the loving home for herself and Daniel.

It was not right, Matthew thought. It was not fair.

He stood alone, and hardly moved when the next wave came in and washed around his legs and spray hit him across the back like buckshot.

The three men were doing an admirable job of hauling Count Dahlgren to safety. They would soon have him up on the deck. The rope was taut between the three Samaritans and the Son of Satan.

Well, Matthew thought.

In a daze he found himself putting a foot against the transom, pulling hard, and freeing the axe. He waited for the ship to rise and fall again, and the angry water to flow over his back. Then, aware of this cold-blooded instinct that had taken hold of him yet realizing also that once aboard this ship Dahlgren's main purpose would be to kill him before they reached England, Matthew strode through the swirl of sea on the deck toward the three men at the stern.

His face was a mask, showing no emotion. It was all locked within, and perhaps that was a freedom of the mask...the ability to show the world a false face, while holding all the torment deep inside, to show the world in essence a false person, a construct of circumstance.

Who among this ship's company would believe him when he demanded that Dahlgren be put in the brig and kept there until they reached port? The drunken captain? These well-meaning but unknowing men? Hell, was there even a brig aboard this crippled tub?

No, the decision must be made now.

He reached the stern. The rope was taut. Dahlgren was near being hauled up.

Matthew lifted the axe and with as much strength as his cold rage could produce he brought it down where the rope scrubbed over the stern transom.

The blow did not completely sever the rope, as it was a hawser as thick as the wrist of Magnus Muldoon. But it did serve to loosen the three men's grips upon it, as they all looked with astonishment at Matthew, and as Matthew raised the axe again Fanning fell back with an arm up as if he feared being struck by the mad young man and both Jahns and Randolph could only gape at him.

The second blow...and the rope was almost severed, but not quite.

"Please! Pull me up!" Dahlgren was right at the stern. His mouth sounded already full of water. A little more, and that accursed Prussian voice would be a gurgle.

"What are you *doing*?" the blacksmith shouted. Jahns had backed away from the task, and now only Randolph held the rope, which itself was held together by a fraying horse's-tail of strands.

"I am doing justice," the young man replied, very calmly, and with a very calm expression he slammed the axeblade down a third time, the blade sank into the wood and completely cut the line, and Randolph staggered back because what he was holding was tethered only to the air.

There was a high, sharp scream when someone's so-called master realized the falling rope meant he would not be putting his boots on the *Wanderer*'s deck after all. Matthew wondered if the man would have the presence of mind to swim for another rope, but it had been sheer luck he'd been able to grab one in the first place. Matthew let go of the axe, which remained embedded where it had struck. He stood at the stern as the ship rose away from Count Anton Mannerheim Dahlgren on the shoulders of the Atlantic as if a giant had awakened from the deep. There was a last glimpse of a blonde-haired head, or perhaps a mass of floating kelp torn from its muddy moorings fathoms below, and then the vessel slid downward, the hull and forecastle took a thunderous blow, the water surged around them but now with noticeably diminishing force, and the black waves tossed and foamed.

Matthew realized, dumbly, that his nose was bleeding. He could taste the blood that had gotten into his mouth. He put his hand to his nostrils and then looked at the blood as rain washed it out of his palm.

"We've done it!" someone shouted behind him.

All turned toward the voice, and there stood Hezekiah Montgomery in all the glory of a half-drowned rat. But behind him, at the tortured prow, were other figures only half-seen through the gloom though two of them had oil lamps…four figures, moving about as if they somewhat knew what they were doing.

"I went below!" Montgomery said breathlessly, for it appeared he'd taken a worse beating forward than had the men at the stern. "Told the crew what we were trying! Got four of them with balls enough to help!"

"What did they do?" Jahns asked.

"Dropped the anchors! Put a drag on this ship, they figured it would keep us from heeling over!"

"Exactly," said Matthew; it was a dazed mutter, and he wasn't sure anyone had heard. Did it matter? No.

"What's happened here?" Montgomery asked. He saw the cleaved end of the hawser Randolph was still holding and took it from the expressions, the postures and the fact that an axeblade was embedded in the transom top that something amiss had occurred. "The count! Where's Dahlgren?"

"Over the stern. Drowned by now, most likely," said the blacksmith. "His servant has murdered him."

"*What?*"

"I saw it all!" Fanning said. "They began fighting like two animals. Dahlgren had the axe…maybe he'd taken it from his servant, I don't know. It looked like he was trying his best to kill the boy, but…I don't know what happened to start it! Then…well…the man went over, and that one—" and here a finger pointed at Matthew Corbett "—cut his lifeline and committed cold-blooded murder! It can't be called self-defense in any court in England!"

"My God!" Montgomery said. "A servant killed his master? Lord, boy, why did you do such a crime?"

Matthew had no answer. At least none that these men could understand at the moment.

His head still hurt, his ears rang, and he was very weary. But they were waiting for a reply, so he said, "I thought this voyage needed a bit more excitement."

The blacksmith dropped the useless rope. "We'll see how excited you become when you spend the next two months in chains! You can't be trusted to be around the others! Here, let's get him below! Will you walk or shall you be carried?"

"I shall walk, thank you," Matthew said, and so he did.

On a bright September afternoon in New York, as birds sang in the trees, cattle grazed on the hillside pastures, boats sailed up and down the rivers, wagons trundled along the town's streets and all seemed right with the world, Berry Grigsby waited with dread to deliver a message.

She had arrived at Robert Deverick's Crown Street Coffee Shoppe at the appointed hour, taken a table and ordered a small light brew with cream. It was served to her not by Robert himself, who was making so much money off this endeavor that he could afford to hire help and was looking at another location in Philadelphia, but by one of the many ebullient and ambitious youths who, it seemed, were flooding into the town these days, with or without their elders. In this case it was a cheerful girl of about seventeen, with tresses of chestnut-brown hair and sparkling light blue eyes, and looking into that peach-fresh face Berry wanted to say, *Enjoy all life has to offer, but for the sake of peace guard your heart.*

But she did not, for such advice from an older personage as herself would be cast aside as surely as leaves were now beginning to be blown from the trees. It was not such a long way from seventeen to twenty but it could be a world of distance. So Berry smiled at the girl's smile, commented favorably on the bright yellow ribbons in the maiden's hair, and settled down to wait for Ashton McCaggers to arrive.

Dear, sweet Ashton. He was a little peculiar, of course...living up there in the attic of City Hall with his collection of skeletons and macabre geegaws, but...well, as coroner he took his responsibility very seriously, and Berry appreciated someone who dared to be different. He was a kind young man also, he was handsome in a studious fashion, was highly intelligent and could be funny when the mood struck him to be jocular, which was at every blue moon. Also, he seemed a bit lonely now that his dependable and silent assistant Zed was gone. But...here was where the soap should rinsed from the linen...

Were these attributes enough to accept his hand in marriage?

Berry sipped at her coffee. She listened to the noise of horse hooves on the cobbles and the sounds of city life that drifted into the shop. She came into this place a few occasions a week, after her duties teaching at the schoolhouse were done, and she knew that this time of day there were only a few other patrons here, if any. Today, Effrem Owles and his bride-to-be, Opal, had been here when she arrived; they had passed a few pleasantries but no one had mentioned the topic of the day. Then Effrem and Opal had left, arm in arm, and in her heart Berry wished them good fortune and long lives together.

What she would say to any young girl asking her advice in such matters of the heart was: never, ever fall in love with someone who cannot—or *will* not—love you in return. That road led not to the mountain of happiness, but to the valley of regret.

Today she wore a dove gray gown decorated with pale green ribbons, gloves of the same green hue, and a cocked gray hat with a small brown feather in its band. It was her idea of mourning apparel.

Ashton arrived, prompt as usual. He was a slim young man of twenty-seven, had light brown hair and darker brown eyes, wore spectacles of thin wire and his favorite brown suit, of which he had four exactly the same. Since he'd been seeing Berry throughout this past year and had come out more into the world from his aerie, this rather eccentric bird had improved his grooming habits, always meeting her with perfectly combed hair, spotless clothing and a fresh, clean shave. Berry reasoned he bathed before their appointments, for the odors of death did tend to cling to a coroner. Still, she sometimes caught beneath his fragrance of patchouli soap a whiff of graveyard matters. He was very proficient at his job and enjoyed being of service to the town in such a position, so how could one fault a hard-working young man who was on call all hours of the day and night to, as it were, tidy up. Berry had never had the misfortune to see this, but she recalled Matthew telling her that, for all his interest in skeletons, Ashton could not stand the sight or smell of blood and organs and thus had to keep a bucket nearby in which to release his objections. Matthew had said he'd witnessed Zed hold the bucket and minister to Ashton during this process, and Berry presumed one of the new young arrivals to town had found himself quite a job, though she and Ashton never spoke of this.

Matthew.

That name, the image of his face and the sound of his voice were always so close. It frightened her sometimes, how close they were. Close also, and still very painful, were the last words they'd spoken to each other, on the Broad Way back in April. *I thought we were friends,* she'd said. *I thought...we were something, I don't know what.*

His reply: *I don't know what either.*

I can't...I don't understand...why...

Oh, he'd said, *stop your prattling.*

I came to help you, if you needed me. That's all I ever wanted, Matthew! To help you! Can't you see that?

That's the point I'm trying to make, he had gone on, and then delivered a knife thrust to her heart that the world's worst killer could not have bettered. *I was wrong to have confided in you on the ship that night. It was weak, and I regret it. Because the fact is, I have never needed you, I didn't yesterday, I don't today and I will not tomorrow.*

Fine, Berry had replied. And the realization of what Matthew had just said fully hit her and nearly crushed her down, and to hang onto the wildly spinning world she had lifted her chin in defiance to fate and circumstance and repeated *Fine* as if that word had any true meaning. She had said *Good day to you, then.* And it was in turning away from him and trying to walk home along the Broad Way that she almost lost her balance and fell, and within six strides the helplessness and anger at Matthew's dumb stupidity and the way he was throwing away both their friendship and whatever else they might have had made the tears burst from her eyes. She had turned again, to face him one last time, and say *We are done.*

After that she had not spoken to him or seen him, and though she wished he would come ask—beg—her forgiveness and try to make everything right between them again, which she would have done after the proper length of time for him to lie in his dog kennel, he never did even try. Therefore she tightened her composure further, and went out of her way to avoid his comings and goings to the little converted dairyhouse behind the Grigsby home.

Good riddance to him, she had thought many times as she brushed her hair before the mirror in preparation to move on with her interests. Good riddance to him, by Mother Mary's grace.

But now…now that not only she but the whole of New York was rid of him…the grace of Mother Mary did not seem so kind.

Ashton came toward her smiling. He did have a nice smile, but he didn't wear it enough. Still, he wore it more with her than with anyone. And another way she had affected him: he did not share her affinity for colors that smote the eye, but by his own methods he was trying to appreciate life as she did. Today he wore a cravat that was a lighter brown than his suit, and was decorated with small black squares.

"My!" he said as he reached her. "You look lovely today!" This was a variation of what he said every time they met, and she replied as always in some variation, "Thank you, you're so sweet." Then he sat down at the table, and she found it very hard to look into his eyes because she knew she was going to have to kill him a little bit today, and this would be as sad for her as it was for him, and this was why she had dressed in mourning.

Ashton ordered a tea from the serving-girl. Coffee was not his taste of choice, though he did like the place and he wished Robert Deverick to do well in business since the young man had shown such ambition and drive after the unfortunate murder of his father last year, an affair in which both Berry and Matthew had gotten tangled up in and nearly lost their eyeballs to hawk talons.

They spoke for a few moments about her teaching, and the progress of the students at the school. She went on at some length concerning several of the most promising pupils, and one boy who vowed he would one day be governor of the colony. They stayed away from the topic of Ashton's work, unless there was something particular interesting that he wished to share, and also stayed away from that topic of the day that both had foremost in mind.

Ashton's tea came. He lifted the cup, the handle broke off in his hand and his lap was dowsed in oolong tea lightly flavored with lemon. Fortunately the tea was not so hot as to scald anything important, so after a little discreet mopping up and with fresh tea in a new cup in hand, Ashton shook his head and smiled wryly. "It seems to never fail!" he said. "Whenever I'm with you, I have the strangest of accidents! Breaking my shoe heel, or stepping into a puddle of mud that seemed only dust a moment before, and last week when that chair broke under me at Sally Almond's! I sincerely hope my bad luck doesn't rub off on you!"

"Ah," said Berry after a moment's silent reflection, "we should talk about luck, Ashton."

The way she'd spoken his name instantly made his smile fade, for she had heard it in her voice the same as he had: it announced a change coming, but as yet he didn't understand what it might be. He put his cup aside, and he waited with the patience of a coroner dissecting the dead.

"The bad luck," she said, with a soft smile of her own, "is unfortunately all mine to give to others. I have been—or thought myself—afflicted with bad luck all my life. You're being kind in ascribing it to your own ill fortune, but the truth is—and you must know it to be so by now—I am…how would you put this…a human black cat, crossing the paths of dozens of unsuspecting pedestrians every day."

"Oh, that's nonsense! Really! Who in the world has put this into your pretty head?"

"My own observations," she replied. "And…maybe…my father and mother did point it out to me on occasion."

"Well, that's ridiculous! They should be ashamed of such a thing!"

"Please," she went on, with a motion of her hand to still his agitation, "hear me out." She sipped at her coffee, putting together what she was going to say; she had rehearsed this, but still it was difficult because she did like Ashton, he was good company, and she knew he presumed, as she had said to Sir Corbett back in April, *I thought we were something.*

"I believe," Berry said, "that what I have always suspected was my bad luck was—is—in actuality a…well…a road map, of sorts. A set of directions. A course to be followed. And if I fail to follow that course…I will be calamity for whoever I marry."

"*What?* Berry, you're making no sense!"

"I have not gotten to the sensible part yet," she answered. "Now…this is difficult for me to express, Ashton, but you must believe it's true. I have had a few beaus…a few interested young men, back in England. Within days they were afflicted with various tribulations: a broken leg here, thrown from a horse there...and poor Munfrey did have such a bruised bottom he couldn't take a chair for a week, a chance meeting with poison ivy, a badger loose in the house—"

"Oh, you're making that up!" Ashton said.

"No, I am not." When it was clear to him from her intense response and her steady gaze that all these things—and many more—had actually happened, she continued: "You must know that I...have had an interest in Matthew."

"Ah yes. The topic of the day. Not your interest in him, of course, but the fact that he's been kidnapped and is on his way to England, according to Hudson Greathouse." And Ashton need not elaborate that this was the talk of the town, the tale having been carried far and wide by the regulars at the Trot Then Gallop after Greathouse's return from Charles Town three days ago.

"I tested Matthew," she said. "Because of my interest in him, and what I thought at the time was his interest in me. So...I tested him, to see if my bad luck would strike at him."

"You tested him? How?"

"I sat drawing in my sketchpad at the end of the worst pier I could find, because I didn't wish to be bothered by anyone. He came to speak to me. Instead of going to him, I made him walk the length of the pier out to where I sat. The boards were rotten and full of holes...any step could have sent Matthew through them and down into the mud. Oh, it wouldn't have been a long drop, he wouldn't have broken anything. I *suppose.* I kept drawing, but I was waiting to hear him shout when he fell." She lowered her eyes because she instantly had a pang of regret for saying that, for it sounded cruel but it had been the only way to know. "Suddenly," she said, "he was there beside me. He had made it, all that way. I was...well, I was *amazed.* Because...I have always believed that when I found the one who was right for me...call it Fate, or the will of God, or whatever you please...I would be *good* luck for him, instead of bad." She took the last sip of her coffee, pushed the cup aside and lifted her gaze to his again. "Do you see what I mean?"

It was a moment before Ashton could answer. He blinked several times behind his spectacles, as if stunned by this revelation. "You're saying...that because Matthew didn't fall through the rotten boards of an old pier, you believe him to be the one Fate has decreed to be your groom?"

There was no use in hesitation or denial. She said, "Yes. And besides that, in spite of his...*spite*...I am in love with him. I just cannot let that go."

"Hm," he said, and nothing more for awhile. Berry noted that the sounds of the town seemed far away now, as if she and Ashton were on a different plain. Ashton cleared his throat. "You mean to say," he ventured, "that you have been *good* luck for Matthew, regardless of all the scrapes he's been in, and now he's been kidnapped by a murderous ruffian and is on his way to England?"

"Yes," she said.

"How so?"

She gave him a slight smile. "He's still alive," she answered.

"You *hope*."

She nodded. "Yes, I hope. But more than that. When Mr. Greathouse leaves for England on the *Bonny Chance* in two days' time, I'm going with him."

"No! You can't mean it!" When she didn't respond, Ashton knew she absolutely did mean it, and knowing her as he did she certainly already had her ticket and was packed. He fumbled for words. "I...well...I don't quite...listen here, what does Greathouse say about this?"

"He has been resistant." That was an understatement, but she had her own money and she could do as she pleased. This morning she had contacted one of the new arrivals, who had applied for a position at the school, to take over her duties. "My grandfather is resistant as well, but both are beginning to see the light."

"Really? Please enlighten *me* exactly why you wish to go on this...very wild and, I'm sure, dangerous endeavor. Which may be entirely fruitless, I suppose you know."

"It may well be," she admitted. "Mr. Greathouse and I may never find him. But...I do love him, Ashton. Why? I know what he is and what he *can* be. I was bitterly hurt by him last April, and I think that trip to Pendulum Island affected him in a way he can't even understand. He played his part there too well. But knowing that he's in trouble...no matter what, I have to try to help him. If I do nothing but stay here...I couldn't sleep, I couldn't eat, I certainly wouldn't be any good for the students. I have to feel I'm doing *something*."

"Travelling across the Atlantic, in storm season? You and Greathouse are both risking your necks on a very slim possibility that Matthew is still alive…and certainly he may not be in the passage of time it's going to take to reach England." Ashton realized that, having gone this far in her plan, Berry was not going to change her mind and surely Greathouse wouldn't either. His next question was delivered in a quieter voice: "How will you ever find him?"

"Let's hope," she said, "his luck holds."

"His *luck*," Ashton said, in a quieter voice still. He removed his spectacles and, finding nothing with which to polish the lenses, took off his cravat and used that. He was flubbergasted and flabbercapped. This sunny day had turned as dark as a bad dream. He put his spectacles back on, the lenses newly polished, the better to see her more clearly. "Well," he sighed, "I trust that Greathouse will watch over you. The Lord and the Kingdom of Heaven also." He looked across the table into her face, was determined to burn every lovely feature and every freckle into his memory. He would never tell her that on this day he had planned to ask her to marry him, and in his pocket was a golden ring adorned with two hands clasping a heart between them. "My hope," said the eccentric coroner of New York, whose attic quarters and collection of bones would have to serve him as true companions a bit longer, "is that someday I meet a kind and beautiful woman who will cross an ocean to find me, if I ever become lost."

"Thank you," said Berry, and she put her hand upon his.

"Go find Matthew and bring him back," Ashton told her, and then there was nothing more to be said.

Five

THE breaking of dawn, a red slash across a cloudy sky, roosters crowing to greet the uncertain sun, dogs barking to quiet the roosters, and ships straining at their moorings at the Great Dock, where the *Bonny Chance* was readying to take aboard the last of its cargo, secure all passengers and provisions, and be ferried out by a number of longboats and strong oarsmen to catch the favorable tide and the rising wind.

The ship was captained by a tam-wearing, pipe-puffing Scotsman named McClendon, who kept company with a small brindle-colored terrier and who had perhaps the loudest holler Hudson Greathouse had ever heard. Greathouse stood on the deck, well out of the way of the stowing and hauling, as McClendon shouted orders to his crew and silenced roosters and dogs across the island and far to the yellow-flecked hills of New Jersey. Greathouse had come aboard an hour before when the starshine was just fading and the little irridescent stripers jumped away from the early morning fishermens' nets. He had lugged his trunk up the gangplank and into his quarters, which made Matthew's dairyhouse seem a mansion and was as expensive as a pair of new boots with golden heels, but he wished the privacy. Madam Herrald had paid for this uncommon luxury. She and Minx Cutter had gone to dinner last night at Sally Almond's with himself and Abby Donovan. Though Abby professed true and enduring love for Hudson and said she would be anxiously waiting his return, he doubted such a vivacious creature of lusty appetites would spend too much time watching the candle-clock burn down these many nights ahead. So be it, he'd decided. He was not one to have a rope tied around him, let him not be the one to tie ropes around anyone else.

Word had spread about this journey. It seemed their dinner table last night was a veritable monument to the impact Matthew had had upon the citizens of this town, so many came to wish Hudson well and express their hopes that young Corbett would be found and returned. Sally herself was the first to offer her promise to pray for success in this venture, and to prove her merit she treated the whole table to a free repast. Then came the sugar merchant Solomon Tully, the very well-to-do pottery merchants Hiram and Patience Stokely, Chief Prosecutor James Bynes, Dr. Artemis Vanderbrocken, the laundress and queen of local gossip Widow Sherwyn, Robert Deverick, Gilliam Vincent the rather prissy proprietor of the Dock House Inn and last but not least the buxom blonde force of nature Polly Blossom, whose eminence as the madam of New York's best dollyhouse did not diminish her financial standing and so commanded the respect of all who sought to better their positions by hard work and shrewdity.

Hudson had been getting along better with Minx Cutter lately, though he still had trouble fully trusting her motives. Still, she seemed to have completed to satisfaction that task of finding the stolen scorpion brooch in Boston back in June. At least she hadn't stolen it herself and fled back to Professor Fell. *Yet.* But...a funny thing...she seemed changed after that trip to Boston. Something about her...different...darker, perhaps. At any rate she hadn't gone into the particulars of this adventure with either himself or Katherine Herrald. To their inquiries the answer had been simply, *Job done.* And with the handsome fee paid by the Sutton family for the scorpion's return, no further questions need be asked.

In a way, Hudson was glad for the presence of Minx Cutter. He understood that Madam Herrald had plans to send her out on future assignments that needed the special touch of a woman who could slice a throat as easily as Hudson might carve a peach; the world was certainly rough, and getting rougher. Madam Herrald herself was interested in putting her own problem-solving talents to work, so woe to the villains, charlatans, flamboozlers, thieves, and killers in fact or in threat who roamed the colonies in Hudson's absence. He wished he could someday read of their exploits while he was away…and, of course, he ardently hoped both Lady Cutter and Katherine managed to keep their own throats unsliced and their hearts unstilled by the wicked blades they would surely have to outwit.

The time to sail was fast approaching.

As the dawn strengthened, here came the rest of the passengers—about twenty of them, it appeared, a couple of families and a few lone individuals, a number of black slaves and white servants carrying the trunks and various items of luggage. The pipers, jugglers, fiddlers, beggars and dancers had arrived on the wharf to cajole money from the throng of well-wishers, relatives and others who always enjoyed seeing the big ships off. Among the arrivals Hudson saw the bright yellow gown of Berry Grigsby and a yellow hat upon her red tresses. She was pulling a large trunk and Marmaduke was behind her, struggling at trying to hold up the trunk's other end. As much as Hudson did not want the girl along on this trip, he couldn't stop her; she paid her own way, and she was content to live for the duration of the voyage down in the hold where most of the others would be, their attempts at privacy maintained by sheets on clotheslines serving as flimsy boundaries that would very soon be sodden with mold. But he had to admire her pluck, and he thought Matthew was lucky to have someone who cared enough about him to endure the indignities of the hold.

He decided the gentlemanly thing to do was to go and help her. He pushed down the gangplank against the current of passengers and servants and was nearly to Berry's side when a strapping young man with a cherubic face and curly blonde hair stepped in and with stately grace lifted the entire trunk upon one muscled shoulder. Berry thanked Matthew's friend John Five, who as a blacksmith had no trouble with such items, for coming to her aid while Marmaduke wiped his own furrowed brow with a handkerchief and let out a whoosh of wind that might have set the *Bonny Chance* in motion.

Then Hudson realized that standing in this crowd he was amid everyone who likely had ever had any dealings with Matthew Corbett. There were Effrem Owles and his bride-to-be Opal Blackerby, Effrem's father Benjamin, Felix Sudbury, Madam Kenneday the baker, Israel Brandier the silversmith, the hulking Mother Munthunk and her two hapless sons Darwin and Davy, the constable Giles Wintergarten, Mary Belovaire the landlady of his own boarding house, Jacob Wingate the wig shop owner, Tobias Winekoop the stablemaster, Sally Almond up at an early hour, all the regulars from the Trot Then Gallop plus those from the Blue Bee and the Laughing Cat, Trinity church's reverend William Wade, his daughter Constance who was John Five's wife, a dolly from the Blossom house who Hudson knew went by the name of Missy Jones, and so many other faces and names he thought New York had coughed and thrown them out of their beds whether they'd liked it or not.

In this swirl of people and shatter of noise, someone tugged hard at Hudson's sleeve. He turned to look down into the life-weathered face of old Hooper Gillespie, whose wild white hair stood up from his head in bursts of cowlicks and thick cottony whorls that had rarely known a brush.

Old Hooper had lost a few more of his remaining teeth recently, which made his usually near undecipherable voice even more of a mystery. But today he said four words that he must've spent some time rehearsing to his satisfaction, for above a pair of determined eyes his pinched mouth spoke with the eloquence of an Oxford linguist.

"Bring the boy home," he said.

And then he was gone, swept away into the crowd.

Others surged forward to grasp Hudson's hand or clap his shoulder and convey the same message. Mother Munthunk's slap on his back nearly popped his eyeballs out. Berry, her grandfather, Constance and John Five shouldering the trunk passed him, going up the gangplank.

"Hurry up there, we've got a tide to catch!" bawled McClendon, pipe clenched between his teeth and brindle terrier in his arms. "Give 'em room there, you lot!"

"I wish you good fortune," Reverend Wade said to Hudson. "I'll pray and ask my congregation to pray for your success."

"Thank you, sir. I have a feeling all the help I can get will be most welcome."

Suddenly there seemed to be a different sort of disturbance in the crowd and they parted like the Red Sea.

They were making way for the approach of a tall, fleshy man in a pale blue suit with a ruffled shirt and ruffles at the cuffs. He wore a tricorn the same shade of blue and he carried a thin black cane. His face, daubed with white powder, might have made him popular among the horses at Winekoop's stable, as they would think him an equine miracle walking on two legs. He passed through the throng, looking neither left nor right, as if it were a given that he owned all assembled, their clothing, houses, possessions and every brick in the town.

This, then, was the Right Honorable Lord Cornbury, Edward Hyde, Governor of New York and New Jersey and cousin to Queen Anne. He was rarely seen without his usual feminine clothing and makeup, but today he was playing at being a man.

The lord who was most times a lady came right up to Hudson and stopped within the length of a nose hair.

"I understand," said Lord Cornbury, in the very same dour tones he used when he wore his gowns, "that Mr. Corbett is in some difficulty and you are bound to...shall we say...*rescue* him?"

"I'm planning on *finding* him, yes."

"Hm," said Cornbury, with a nod. He took no interest in the crowd, but remained focused solely on Hudson. "That young man *does* get into trouble, doesn't he?"

"I don't think they're usually of his own making."

"True enough, though Mr. Corbett seems to enjoy stirring up the muddy bottom of dark waters. High Constable Lillehorne told me many times that the young man's pride would lead him to disaster." Cornbury let that linger for a moment, expecting Hudson to respond but none was forthcoming.

"The ship's soon to get underway," Hudson said. "If you'll pardon me?"

"Yes, of course. Go about your business. And let me say that whatever Mr. Corbett is, he is one of *us*...therefore I do hope you find him and bring him back...but I have a feeling that before this is done, you'll be the one needing rescue."

"I'll bear that in mind, sir. And may I ask, just for the sake of curiosity, why you're not—"

"Dressed in my usual splendor? Ah…the question. I will tell you," and here he pitched his voice a little lower so it carried no further than Hudson's right ear, "that the letters I've sent a year ago to my cousin have not been answered, so why should I represent Her Majesty's presence on these streets?" His upper lip curled, an ugly sight on an already unfortunate face. "From here on, Mr. Greathouse—or at least until I hear favorably from that *person*—I am walking in my own two shoes."

Hudson looked down. What a sight he got, for he thought he'd smelled such but had considered it to be Lord Cornbury's breath at close quarters. "I fear you've already stepped in something," he said.

"Oh misery! Oh, damn it all, what a mess!" was Cornbury's reaction, and perhaps the question of why the crowd had parted to give him room was answered. With as much decorum as a man could muster wearing clodhoppers that had failed to hop the clods, he turned about and stalked away leaving his untidy footprints on the boards.

A bell was rung, and another sounded back. "All ashore who ain't bound for seventy-six days on the *Bonny Chance*!" boomed Captain McClendon from the quarterdeck. In a previous conversation between Hudson and McClendon, the captain had confided that his fastest crossing stood at seventy-eight days, but he was determined to beat that by forty-eight hours. With luck and the captain's resolve, Hudson hoped they wouldn't be too far behind the *Wanderer* in reaching Plymouth…and maybe, if they were really fortunate, they might make harbor within a few days of what he understood was an ignoble vessel captained by a drunken sloth.

But time would tell the tale.

It took awhile longer for everything to be put in order. Marmaduke Grigsby stopped to ask Hudson to please watch over a headstrong granddaughter who he sincerely hoped would live to see the age of twenty-one. Hudson vowed to do his best, and Marmy departed. A few of Matthew's friends and other relations of the passengers remained on the dock while the longboats began the task of rowing the *Bonny Chance* out of the harbor. Hudson stayed on deck, figuring he would have to get used to this as his cabin was so small; when the hammock was suspended from the overhead it was so tightly wedged between the walls that it wouldn't swing.

He watched the town diminish in size as the longboats rowed them out, and he had the strange feeling that New York was leaving him, rather than the other way around. He had the feeling it was getting smaller and smaller as if to make room for the larger—and more civilized yet many times more deadly and brutal—world beyond the Atlantic. There was a lot of world out there, and the people who had constructed it had had a long time to build their massive stone monstrosities of violence and brutality. He hoped finding Matthew was a real possibility and not a fool's errand, but he would be a fool if it meant he had any chance of success.

They passed the wild forest and rough rocks of Oyster Island on their passage toward the edge of the sea. The shops, taverns and houses on the rolling green hills of Manhattan seemed as toys to be played with by the hand of God. The sailing ships with their tall masts had become miniatures. All the people there…the hundreds of them…ants in the anthill that never slept.

Berry joined him at the port side. She had removed her hat, and the freshening breeze had begun to blow through her tresses. She did not speak, but instead visored her hand over her eyes to look back toward the town, as the sun had strengthened and shards of golden light reflected off water that remained as gray as the morning's mist.

"You can't see him from here," Hudson said.

"Pardon?" She dropped her hand and gave him a quizzical expression.

"I'm sure he came out to watch the ship leave. He may be standing there still, but you can't see him from here." Of course Hudson knew Ashton McCaggers had certainly emerged from his attic domain at City Hall to watch the vessel—and Berry—take leave of New York, just as he was sure Katherine Herrald and Minx Cutter had watched from their own balcony or window.

"Yes," she answered quietly, "he probably did. I just…thought I'd take a look."

"Listen here," he said, and summoned up the sternest gaze he could bludgeon her with, "I told Marmaduke I'd watch over you, so—"

"You certainly don't need to—"

"Yes, I *do*," he said forcefully. It was enough to cork her mouth. "If you've insisted on coming along against both my wishes and Marmy's as well, you're going to at least listen to me." He paused for a few seconds to let that sink in, and it seemed to because suddenly she was all eyes, if not all ears. "When we reach Plymouth," he went on, "you're not to leave my side. The first thing we'll do is check with the dockmaster to find out when the *Wanderer* arrived...and let's hope to Christ it does arrive." He declined to tell her that from what he'd heard at the Charles Town harbor, only the ship's barnacles were holding the hull together. "Until then..." He didn't know what else to say, because she was going to be down in the hold with those passengers who could afford only the least and most crude of accommodations, and though the crew seemed all business and very attentive to the captain's orders as they prepared to lower the sails, Hudson knew that after a few weeks at sea things would be different. He was an avowed landlover, but he'd had enough nautical voyages to know that a crew could get very...the word would be *rowdy*...if not managed by an iron hand, and even then the goats and cows in the manger had to be on guard.

"Yes?" Berry prompted.

Hudson watched the town shrink to the size of an engraving on a pocket watch. *"Hell,"* he muttered, for there was only one way to make good his vow of protection.

"A comment or a destination?" she inquired.

He let go a long sigh before he returned his gaze to hers. "I want you to take my quarters. They're tight, but at least the air's fresher and there's a latch on the door."

"Certainly not. I paid for what I'm getting."

"And you may pay a bit more, men being men and long at sea. I don't like your being so close to the crew's quarters, or to the manger for that matter. Pretty soon the aroma down there will not be—"

"I sailed perfectly fine from England to New York before," she said, but she conveniently left out the unfortunate incident of the dropped soap on the *Sarah Embry*.

Hudson pulled up all quarter ton of his darkest scowl and thrust his chin toward her like a declaration of war. When he spoke, his voice came from the deepest cavern of his guts. "This is not a *request*, miss. You're taking my quarters. You'll be safer there and I'll sleep easier down in the hold. Are we understood?"

No, she wanted to say, but how could one say no to an approaching thunderstorm? In fact, he scared the blazes out of her. A little bit of anger danced in her eyes but it very quickly danced away. "All right," she said. "Over my protest."

"Noted and discarded. I'll bring your trunk up for you."

The longboats had dropped their lines. The sails came down and the rigging hummed with the power of the wind. Before they went below, both Hudson and Berry gave one last look across the gray water at the town they were leaving, and each held the memory of someone there who was being left behind. Neither of them shared this with the other, but both had the feeling that a very different chapter in their lives was in the process of unfolding, and who could know how long it would be before they set foot in New York again, and what changes would be wrought before they did?

Up on the quarterdeck, McClendon hollered a course to the helmsman though the sailor at the wheel stood only a few feet away. The open sea stretched ahead, and dolphins rose from the depths to happily ride the skirts of the *Bonny Chance*.

Time passed, and it did tell the tale.

The tale it told for the *Wanderer* was one of continued wandering, under ill stars and a callous sun. Captain Peppertree had all but abandoned his command for the warmth and forgetfulness of the rum supply, which he had to protect from the angry crew at pistol point. Eventually someone broke into his cabin, the rum was seized and with that Captain Peppertree became an afternote in the story of nautical history. He might have been hanged from a yardarm had not Reverend Fanning promised the vengeance of God for such a crime. Thus Peppertree joined Matthew Corbett to be bound hand and foot with ropes in the soggy bowels of the ship's lowest hold, while the other bilge rats were free to nip and hiss in the dim light of a single hanging oil lamp that swung back and forth over a thousand times a day. Matthew knew, for one day he kept count though the days themselves could only be counted by the ration of bread and water brought by a crewman at first light. At least the ropes had been tied so that the hands of the prisoners were in front of them, and they could brush the rats away from the hunks of dark-veined bread.

Soon after being put into this makeshift brig, Matthew had heard the noise of much hammering and sawing above and figured the ship's carpenter and the crew had seized upon a way to, if not fully repair the broken mast, at least jury rig the sails to catch as much wind as possible. Whoever had taken on the role of captain would now be trying to figure out how much foodstuffs and clean water had survived the storm, to calculate the remaining length of the trip with what canvas they had, and how best to keep himself and everyone else alive. The *Wanderer* staggered on, and Matthew figured everyone up top was terrified to the roots of their hearts by any dark cloud on the horizon.

All in all, it was a sorry passage through Damnation that gnawed at the mind and sought to reduce a human being to an animalistic state. Determined not to fall again into that abyss from which he'd just crawled, Matthew kept himself mentally occupied by replaying games of chess he remembered playing at the Trot, and also turning over again and again the problem of how to get out of this situation and back to New York. Peppertree unfortunately was reduced to a babbling wreck after a few days, and after two weeks reduced to a silent heap that hardly moved except to throw himself upon his daily ration and fight the rats with all the fury of seven slavering madmen.

Came the morning when the hatch was unlocked, and Reverend Fanning and Curt Randolph descended the ladder carrying oil lamps and the rations of the day.

Though thin and weakened, Matthew had the presence of mind not to eat and drink everything he was given in a desperate few moments, but to make the bread last a few hours and the water a full day. He noted that Fanning and Randolph were filthy and wearing mold-greened clothes that hung on them like the rags of scarecrows. Their cheekbones had begun to show and their yellowed eyes seemed to be slowly pushing themselves out of their faces. He reasoned that everyone up there was on rations; by now the food and drinkable water must nearly be gone.

When Fanning reached the bottom of the ladder, he retched and had to turn away for a moment.

Matthew started to say *Pardon our condition*, but to his surprise no voice emerged. He had a brief horror that, just as his completeness of memory had returned, his ability to speak had departed. He tried again, and this time got out in a harsh croak, "*Pardon*." Then the rest seemed too much effort to say so he gave it up.

"Captain Spragg says we're four days out," said Randolph, and even he sounded labored with the rigors of speech.

Peppertree made a gobbling noise that Matthew deciphered as *BastardSpraggstolemyshipseehimhanged*, the last of it rising to what was a nearly a shriek of revenge.

"We are told the last of our food will see us through," Randolph continued. "I regret to say—on the captain's orders—you will get no more bread, but your water ration will remain as it is."

"Kind of him," said Matthew. He wanted to say *I'm sick of bread anyway*, but it suddenly seemed very important not to waste his remaining strength.

"You must know we've had a bad time. Jahns's wife passed away last month and Mr. Montgomery died less than a week ago. Most of us have been very ill."

Matthew nodded. He spoke into the lamp that Randolph held. "Things are bad all over," he said.

Fanning had regained his composure and kept in his possession the meager contents of his stomach. He staggered toward Matthew and reached out to brace himself against a support post, as the ship's rolling down here was truly vicious. "We have decided," he said, in a weakened voice that yet carried the firm conviction of his faith, "what we must do with you.

"We all agree that your master was a disagreeable man, and mayhaps there was bad blood between you, but to murder him…when he was so near to being saved…it's a monstrous thing you've done."

"I told you before, when we came below after the storm," said the bearded and half-starved problem-solver from New York, who could have stood before anyone he knew in that town and be called naught but an unclean beggar, a stranger in his own land. "Dahlgren wasn't my master. I told you…he was taking me to England by false measures."

"Yes, you told us," Randolph agreed, "but it makes no sense. False measures? He held no pistol to your head or blade to your back. Why would you be with him if not by your own free will?"

BastardSpraggstolemyship sobbed Peppertree, who had curled himself up as best he could into a little ball of misery.

"I'm very tired," Matthew said. "I can't explain everything to you. Just let me say…Dahlgren would've made certain I didn't live to see Plymouth."

"You cannot plead self-defense," said the minister, who clung to the post as the ship rolled in what seemed another storm, yet he knew that outside the sun was shining and the wind a gentle favor. "I—we all—fail to understand why your master was trying to harm you with that axe, and why you both fought so viciously, but… murder is murder. I saw that with my own eyes and by my oath to God and the common good I cannot let that pass."

"And neither can I," Randolph added. "We have decided therefore—and all of us are one in this decision, including Spragg—that you be turned over to the law as soon as we reach port. Even though the Count may have been of foreign birth and the murder committed on the high seas, some accounting must be made."

To this Matthew made no reply, for what was to be said? He would have the chance to explain his situation to the law in Plymouth, and that at least was a blessing. And a greater blessing: barring any horrendous mishap between here and the coast, he had survived this voyage while others had perished. Also…if he were in the position of Fanning and Randolph and he didn't know the whole picture, might he be of like mind in turning a murderer over to the law? Yes, he certainly would be. Therefore he said nothing, and after another moment the reverend made his unsteady way to the ladder, climbed up and went through the hatch.

"We will all be glad to set foot on solid earth, I'm sure," Randolph said. He lifted his lamp a little higher to have more of a view of Matthew's face. "Listen…I think I can get you—both of you—a little drink of rum, if you'd care for that."

Peppertree made a noise like a dog drooling for a beefbone.

"Thank you," Matthew answered. "Much appreciated."

Randolph nodded, and then he too climbed out of the fetid chamber.

Matthew was left with his thoughts and Peppertree's soft, tragic whining. Surely the law in Plymouth would have heard of Professor Fell, Matthew reasoned. As soon as he mentioned this name and gave the particulars, no one was going to hold him accountable for the death of a Prussian killer. So there was just the remaining problem of how to get back to New York, and perhaps contacting the members of the Herrald Agency in London would see him to success. The name of that agency, too, would be known to the law.

Things were looking up. He would drink that sip of rum in a mood of celebration, for once these ropes were removed and he was cleaned up and shaved—and perhaps rested for a few days, with a few good meals in his belly—he would be back to, as the Great One might say, "fighting fit".

Then…somehow back to New York…and after this experience he was going to crawl to the front door of Berry Grigsby's house and beg for her forgiveness, and explain to her that though he longed to be at her side he'd thought running her off was the only way to keep her safe from Professor Fell. The professor had a long memory and many arms of evil, as his symbol of the octopus represented; Matthew did not want one of those arms to find and crush that beautiful girl.

What was to be done? Where could they go, together, to find peace and safety?

First things first. He had awakened from one ordeal, and was better prepared now to handle what lay ahead. First things first.

Bring on the rum.

Two

A Merry Town Black as Sin

Six

The coach's doors slammed shut. Double bolt-locks were thrown. The team of four horses started up under the whip's crack, and Matthew looked through the barred window at the passing gray buildings of Plymouth as an equally gray drizzle swirled from a vault of leaden clouds.

His wrists and ankles were free of ropes but weighted with chains. An iron thunder-ball lay at his feet like a mean black dog. When asked, the arresting officer had told Matthew the journey would take seven days, give or take. The man, named Moncroff, was at this moment sitting up with the coach driver, both of them shrouded in black cloaks and hoods to shield against the dampness as best they could. Beside Moncroff was a cowhide valise containing the reports and signed statements of the two witnesses to the indefensible murder of Count Anton Mannerheim Dahlgren.

Matthew was on his way to stand before judgment in Londontown. As the Chief Constable of Plymouth had told him, "John Roper's window" yearned to snap his neck. Never had Matthew heard a hangman's noose described with such ferocious glee. Yet there was hope!

It seemed, as he sat on the hard plank and was bounced about by the rutted road like a dry pea in a gourd, that he would not be returning to New York anytime in the near future. In fact his plans had begun to go awry when he first stood before the magistrate's court in Plymouth, the third morning after being led down the *Wanderer*'s gangplank like the most common of criminals.

"As I say," Matthew went on, at the conclusion of his tale concerning his relationship with the deceased and his escape from being turned over to Professor Fell, "Dahlgren surely planned to kill me before we reached England. I was of no further use to him in what he thought would redeem him with Professor Fell, so—"

"A moment," said Magistrate Akers, who had a face like an iceberg and thin eyebrows that were painted on. He spoke his words slowly and precisely, with a slight pursing of the lips after each sentence. "I have read thoroughly the sworn statements of the witnesses." The parchment papers were before him, atop his desk. The pale light of a chill November morning through a pair of high windows further painted Akers, the room, the attendant guards and Matthew in shades of austere winter. "Nowhere is there indicated," Akers went on, "any proof that your Prussian master planned to kill you aboard the *Wanderer* after he was saved from the sea. True, it appears you and he had a...violent disagreement...but we are here concerned with *his* murder, not yours."

"He would have killed me! I'm telling you, I—"

"Murdered him first, in fear for your life? The statements here assert that your attack upon the Count's lifeline is indefensible, as you were under no clear and immediate threat."

"Dahlgren was already a killer!" The sound of rising panic in Matthew's voice further alarmed him; he realized it would do him no good to appear frantic, so he took control of his breathing and steadied himself. "You do understand what I'm telling you about Professor Fell, don't you?"

"I understand you mean such to help your case," said Akers, "but...unfortunately for you, young man, I have never heard of this person. He is a professor of what? And where does he instruct?"

Oh my God, Matthew thought. Again the flames of panic flared high. Matthew stood with his head lowered until he could find the sense to speak again; he was still weak from the voyage, had not been allowed to shave and wore baggy gray clothing after a brisk-broom scrubbing that had left his flesh raw. Two days and nights in the grim Plymouth gaolhouse, sharing a cell with a wizened madman who had raped and murdered a ten-year-old child, had not aided Matthew's attitude of relief at being off that damned ship, and neither had the wretched watery pea soup enriched with shreds of barely-cooked horse meat.

"Please," the prisoner said to the magistrate, "contact the Herrald Agency in London. Someone there will at least have heard of me."

"I know of this request from Chief Constable Scarborough. Again, neither of us...and no one within our jurisdiction of Plymouth...know anything about this Merrell Agency."

"Not *Merrell*," said Matthew. "*Herrald*. It's—"

"Yes, I've heard what you told Scarborough." A lily-white hand adorned with a trio of rings rose up to wave Matthew's voice away. "An agency that solves *problems* for people?" He gave a little crooked ghost of a smile at the burly bald-headed chief constable who sat at the back of the room. "Lord above, isn't that *our* responsibility? I would hate to think what might happen to English civilization should problem-solving be taken away from the courts and given to the dirty hands of the population. But as I say, there is no such record of a Merrell Agency." The magistrate's small eyes had taken on the blankness of disinterest, for there were many more defendants to be prosecuted. "To be sure, young man, your story reeks of the madhouse. In the opinion of this court it seems to have been scribed by the hand of Bedlam. Do you have anything further to say?"

Matthew's mind was working...sluggishly, deprived of solid food and easy rest...but working all the same.

He felt Roper's window tightening about his neck.

"Let me ask a question," he said, as a bright beam broke through the overcast in his brain. "I realize that my crime is made worse for a servant murdering his master. That's not something to let stand as an example for other servants, is it?" He kept going before Akers could shut him down. "My question is...where is the proof that I was servant to Count Dahlgren? Where are the papers of servitude? You have the word of Count Dahlgren through the word of other passengers that indeed I was a servant, but can that be proven? If I were not a servant, does that still make the murder of a Prussian-born individual upon the high seas, *not* in the realm of the English empire, a hanging offense? Should I not be removed from here to Prussia to stand trial? And indeed, what jurisdiction does an English court have over the murder of a Prussian count on the high seas? And can you even say it was a murder? Where is the corpse? Who to say that Count Dahlgren did not grab hold of a floating spar or piece of debris from the ship, and last until the sharks got him? Therefore should you not send a man-of-war out to gather up in nets all the sharks of the Atlantic and bring them to Plymouth to be hanged? Perhaps Count Dahlgren was stung to death by jellyfish or choked by seaweed. Well, then…there you have your murderers, and it only falls to this court to solve the problem of which jellyfish or piece of seaweed should be incarcerated in the Plymouth gaol-house. Of course he might have simply drowned…which leaves the entire ocean to appear in this court. To be exact, I did *not* murder the man, sir. To be exact, I only cut a rope."

"Ah, but the cutting of the rope *caused* him to be killed," said Akers, with a defiant lift of the pointed chin.

"Are you absolutely *certain* he's dead?" Matthew let that dangle for a few seconds on its own Roper's window. "Are the two witnesses certain? Did they actually see him perish? *I* did not. The man had more lives than Satan's cat. He might wash up here any day, and the first thing he'll do is murder someone for their clothes and money, so watch your beaches."

Akers put fingertips to mouth and patted his lips, his eyes firmly fixed upon the accused but now bearing a spark of renewed…might it be called *respect*?

"I have a solution," said Matthew. "I know the newly-arrived Assistant to the High Constable of London. His name is Gardner Lillehorne. Do you know that name?"

It was a moment before the magistrate answered. Then, "I do."

"Lillehorne's assistant is named Dippen Nack. Do you also know that name?"

Said cautiously: "I have heard it spoken."

"Rid yourself of me and throw me upon their briarpatch," Matthew went on. "You have done your duty in introducing me into the legal system. These questions of Prussian nationality, unproven servitude and unproven murder should be foisted upon the London courts, and good riddance for the halls of Plymouth and for yourself, whom I am sure has more pressing matters to attend."

Silence reigned o'er the court.

At last Magistrate Akers made a small noise, perhaps a clearing of the throat, and he quietly spoke the word, "Ha," without any note of humor.

Thus it was that within twenty-four hours Matthew was on his way to London in the prison coach. His spirits had risen for he'd had a good meal of beef stew last night—real beef, and one could taste the difference from meat of a diseased horse—and a mug of ale to wash it down, plus he had been removed from the presence of the muttering madman and afforded his own cell, which meant he'd had a full night's sleep. He still wore the gray outfit of a Plymouth gaolhouse prisoner and had been refused a shave as it was not the policy to let the inmates anywhere near a razor, but at least he was out of that grimy box and on his way to see someone he knew. And if he'd known a year ago that he would relish the sight of Gardner Lillehorne and Dippen Nack he might've crawled into the cell beside Tyranthus Slaughter and told the keeper to swallow the key for he was surely struck with incurable moon madness.

The horses went on at a quick walk, the wheels turned over English mud, the little villages drifted past one after another, and Matthew thought he had won a small victory in getting out of Plymouth with his neck unbroken. Now to play his cards right, explain this whole mess to Lillehorne and be granted a pardon... then, with—gad, the thought!—the help of that erstwhile gentleman get his tail back aboard a ship and—gad, that thought too!—be sailed again across the Atlantic to his dairyhouse paradise.

It was not an easy trip. The English roads were as rough as those around New York, and perhaps rougher for the amount of coach and wagon traffic they sustained. He, Moncroff and the coach driver stayed in a succession of inns along the route. Most times Matthew was obliged to sleep on the floor but Moncroff turned out to be an amiable companion and usually bought his charge a good kidney pie, boiled sausage or some such stomach-filler. Though yet thin and still recovering from his ordeal aboard the accursed *Wanderer*, Matthew was steadily gaining back his strength and resolve, and to Moncroff's credit the young New York problem-solver was never allowed to go hungry. He was beginning to take note of the quality of some of these English countrymen—and women—who seemed to delight in rattling his chains, pretending to poke at him with a blade or longstaff until Moncroff called them to account, or otherwise harass him with injurious actions or foul names. The children were just as bad as the adults, and in fact worse because they moved faster after they gave Matthew a kick to the ribs or shins. In every village they stopped for the length of the week, word quickly spread that a convicted murderer was on his way to London to be hanged by the neck until gray-faced and dead, and this brought mobs of people gawking at the inn's windows and the braver ones pounding at the door for a closer look-see. By the time they reached their last stop, Matthew learned through Moncroff who had heard from the inn's owner that this young wild-haired, black-bearded killer had decapitated three women and a number of children in Plymouth, had planted the heads atop fenceposts after painting them up with garish colors, had regularly bathed in blood in a room decorated with furniture made from human bones, and kept two nanny goats that he dressed in women's clothing. That night the mob almost tore the place down to get a look at him, so much so that Moncroff stationed himself on the front porch with a blunderbuss and remained there until another drizzly dawn.

Now, as the coach travelled on along a path that was more rut than road, a plank-weary Matthew Corbett looked out the barred window upon a dank morning of gray fog, with glimpses of gnarled trees, stone cottages with thatched roofs, and the occasional shadow of a green hill. The air was not bitterly cold, yet carried a bite. After awhile he noted that the number of thatched-roof cottages was increasing, and they stood closer together along the road. Also, the coach's speed fell when the driver put his concentration to more tightly controlling the horses, as an army of wagons, coaches and carriages of all description seemed to materialize out of the gloom. Matthew knew it before Moncroff pushed back the little viewslit between them and said, "London's just ahead."

Matthew pressed his face against the bars and craned his neck to get as much of a first look as possible.

There was only fog, pale gray, making ghostly figures of the wagons and other vehicles that shared the widening road. But ahead and to the right about fifteen degrees, the fog became a sulphurous yellow color shot through with streaks of darker brown. The area of discoloration was massive, and it was then that Matthew had a sense of the size of London though he could see none of its buildings. Ten times as large as New York? Oh, twenty times at least. Matthew knew from his reading that this was a city founded by the Romans, with a checkered history of triumphs and disasters; it had suffered extreme destruction in the Great Fire of 1666, and therefore—according to articles in issues of the London *Gazette*, which Matthew had read in New York—mostly done away with wooden buildings in favor of brick and stone. The wharves and warehouses along the Thames had already existed for generations, had collapsed and been rebuilt over and over again; indeed there were such a number of those, in Matthew's impression, that counted alone they would be many times the size of New York. This was the central point of the home country, from which all blessings flowed to the colonies and a major power in the world at large, so naturally it would be a huge and sprawling city, a nearly-living thing that took disaster in stride and grew larger from it.

For now, though, all Matthew could see was the ugly discoloration of fog that shrouded London's towers. Even so, and even in his remembrance while in the comfort of New York of wishing someday to see this great city, now that the day had arrived he was struck with a sense of dread; he had come here in chains, burdened with a thunderball and under threat of hanging unless he could silver-tongue his way out of this. In New York he was someone, known and for the most part liked...here he was no one, a thin and bearded prisoner whose only hope for survival was the mean-spirited individual whom he disliked and he knew felt equally toward himself. He began to feel smaller and smaller as the coach advanced through the fog, as it was locked in by other vehicles and its progress slowed to the walk of a one-legged man, as it had to sit still for over an hour with the horses nickering and nervous because a haywagon ahead had broken a wheel and crashed into a carriage, causing a traffic jam while the road was cleared, and again a long delay at a stone bridge over a dirty river lined with what must be slaughterhouses because

Matthew saw blood in the sluggish water and smelled the bitter scent of terrified beasts.

As the coach neared the city proper, there arose what seemed an endless assemblage of small villages—a few houses, a stable, a tavern, a number of shops and the like—separated by patches of woods, reedy ponds or stretches of marshland. Indeed, it seemed to Matthew that London must have been constructed atop a vast swamp, for the wet morass at places came up over the roadway and mud sucked at the wheels and hooves.

Then he was aware of two things at about the same time: an odor of damp rot, as one might catch at the oldest and most decrepit wharf in New York, commingled with the burnt smell of gunpowder, or the scent left in the air after the striking of a flint against stone, and the second thing...a noise.

It began as a humming, discernible over the sound of the coach's wheels and the other London-bound traffic. It was as much felt in the bones as heard by the ears. Within a few minutes, the hum had built to what Matthew likened to the low growl of an unseen animal in its lair. He realized it was the sound of the city, all the thousands of voices at different volumes and pitch, all the sound of cart wheels and horse hooves, all the noise of latches opening and closing, of the rusty hinges of iron gates, of the footfalls of boots on wood and stone, of the great river hissing around the multitude of pilings and hulls of ships, of hammering and sawing at more towers going up, of retchings and belches and farts, of shouts of delight and screams of rage, all there...all there.

And then the city suddenly opened up through the brown fog before them, and pulled them in as if into a seething whirlpool of humanity.

Seven

"I KNEW this day was coming," said Gardner Lillehorne, who was dressed in pale lavender and wearing a tricorn the same color, topped with a dark purple feather that matched the hue of his waistcoat. He reached out with his thin black-lacquered cane. Its silver lion's-head tapped Matthew none too gently on the shoulder. "Here you sit accused of murder," said the assistant to the High Constable of London, "and much too far from home, I do believe."

"Too far from home! Too far from home!" Dippen Nack chortled. His small shoulders were hunched forward and the teeth showing in a cherubic, fat-cheeked face reddened with the flow of excited blood. The brutal little billyclub-toting bully had come up in the world; he wore a dust-colored suit—though marred by food stains on the front—with silver buttons and upon his head a black tricorn. Beneath the tricorn was a white wig of many ostentatious curls. Nack's eyes, which always held red centers of anger, were accentuated with dark brown makeup, which made them appear as ugly pits of mud. But same as before, for he lifted that accursed ebony billyclub and placed its blunt end beneath Matthew's bearded chin. With it, he forced the young man's head up. "Looky looky!" grinned Nack. "Crumble yer cookie!"

"I have no idea what that means," said Matthew, pulling his head back from the billyclub's kiss.

"It means we gots the power now, Mr. High-And-Mighty!" came the heated response, with plenty of spittle flying from between the jagged teeth. "Ain't nobody steppin' in to save yer bacon!"

"You're making me hungry," said Matthew.

"*Please*, Nack. Restrain yourself." Lillehorne used his cane to push the billyclub away in what seemed for a few seconds might become a battle between the villainous instruments.

Nack allowed the cane to win, though he hissed, "Seems yer forgettin'...this ain't New York, Sir Lillehorne. The rules is changed here."

"I forget nothing, dear friend. But let's not break Mr. Corbett's jaw before he has a chance to speak."

Some chance he had! Matthew thought. These two would not make a full brain between them. Still...the old adage that beggars could not be choosers was never more *à propos*.

They were sitting at a table in a small, dank conference room. An oil lamp glowed atop the table and two half-melted candles burned in wall sconces. Beyond the single shuttered window Matthew could hear rain hitting the glass; he had not seen the sun in the four days since he'd arrived in London and been brought directly to this gaolhouse, where he shared a cell with three other unfortunate men, one who lay silently on the floor, curled up as if accepting Fate's decision that he should die a soul-shattered scarecrow. Moncroff had referred to the building as St. Peter's before handing over all the papers to an official and wishing Matthew well, but whether the place was really named that or it was a gaoler's grim jest he did not know.

Matthew's impression of London had been blocks of massive buildings, streets choked with all manner of conveyances and mobs of people, the smells of unwashed humanity and what seemed a sour scorched odor remaining from the Great Fire of thirty-seven years ago, as incredible as that might be, and that incessant sound of life in progress. Was there any place in London where one might find a silence? Certainly not in St. Peter's gaolhouse, where the screams and cries of desperate men became a kind of depraved music throughout all hours of the candle-clock. Other than those cursory impressions of the city, fog had masked the details and street placards and so Matthew had no idea where he was on a map of London, what was around him, where the Thames was, or much of anything else. His world had become the small cell, his dirty bunk and a blanket that smelled of death; at least in this perdition he had been relieved of the thunderball, though to have this audience with the assistant to the High Constable—who had taken his own sweet time in coming after Moncroff had made the official request and passed Matthew's name along through the proper channels—Matthew was required to again wear his shackles, wrists locked to chain locked to ankles. Therefore he was forced to shuffle along with his back bent over as if in reverence to the holy law of London.

"You," said the nearly-diminutive Lillehorne, "are in a predicament." Lillehorne had the hands of a child and looked as if a hard wind could break his bones. His black goatee and mustache were, however, as precisely-trimmed as they'd been in New York, his hair—pulled back into a queue with a lavender ribbon—had the same artificial hue of black dye with a pronounced blue sheen, his nose was still small and pointed, his lips still like those of a painted doll's, his arrogance and sense of importance to the world also the same. In this case, his importance to Matthew's world was paramount. Matthew figured Lord Cornbury had pulled some strings to get Lillehorne this position, but that probably meant that Cornbury had been found at some skullduggery by Lillehorne, and Nack's presence meant that Nack had found Lillehorne at some skullduggery, and it was a wonder the colonies of New York and New Jersey still had a guinea left in their treasuries. Mayhaps the money bags in the vaults were filled with wooden tokens or Indian beads. Something to look into when he got back home, he decided.

"A predicament," Lillehorne repeated. "I have read the statements of the witnesses and your own tale of this nasty business as recorded by the clerk at the court of Plymouth. I am to take it that this Count Dahlgren was the same individual who escaped justice by fleeing the Chapel estate when we raided the place? And... incidentally...saved your life, for which I believe there has yet to be proper recompense."

"The same man," Matthew answered. "Intent on delivering me to Professor Fell while I was in a state of distress. As I said, I had no memory of who I was or what had—"

"Yes, yes." The small fingers waved that away like so much smoke. "I've heard of such things happening but never witnessed it. Few have. It would be very difficult to prove at court."

"If I hadn't lost my memory, why would I be travelling with him? And being taken to the professor to be murdered? I believe Dahlgren wanted to trade me to get into Fell's good favor, perhaps be brought back into the fold. Listen...Gardner...surely they know Fell's name here! And they must know about the Herrald Agency! Why is that I'm sitting in that cell when all this could be explained in half-a-day's work?"

"Because," Lillehorne replied, and for once his voice was patient and nearly soothing, in his own way, "no one has half-a-day to spend on you. I am here *unofficially*, taking time from other pressing matters." He cocked his head to one side and his lips pressed tightly together before he spoke again. "You have yet to realize where you are. London is *not* New York. There we had a few robberies, a few altercations in taverns, a little strife between lovers or husband and wife, a murder now and again. *Here,* Matthew...you have a merry town black as sin. If a gentleman can walk two blocks at night and not be robbed and killed, he might consider his life charmed. I do understand that Professor Fell brought the gangs together into what might be considered a business organization, but time moves on. The gangs have been reborn with much younger and more vicious members. They control entire sections of the city. And murders...oh, Lord God! In this town knives are used more for cutting throats than for gutting fish. Every morning we take the wagons out to load up the corpses, and you never know what you might find: a headless little girl of eight or nine, a man torn open and his intestines carefully displayed on either side of the body like precious artifacts, a woman with her private parts cut away and missing...never to be found. Dozens of murder victims, nameless and often literally faceless, each and every day." Lillehorne paused, because there had been a tremor of emotion in his voice and it had surprised him as much as it surprised Matthew.

Rain was beating harder at the window. One of the candles in its sconce hissed and flared as its wick fired a particularly oily remnant of hog's fat.

It was a moment before Lillehorne steadied himself to go on.

"Some know the name of Professor Fell," he said quietly. "Most do not. It does not serve his purpose to be known by the population at large. But I will tell you, Matthew...that from what I have heard...from what I've seen, in just these few short months...there are *worse* than Professor Fell out there. As I say, time moves on. There are younger hands eager to take filthy money and many innocent lives, if need be. In New York there is a conscience, Matthew... there is a respect for other people. Here...well...New York had a population of around six thousand at the last census. London holds a population of six *hundred* thousand, all jammed together wanting what the other has, and fighting to stay alive any way possible. More are pouring in every day from all points of the compass. Do you get my drift?"

"Yes," Matthew said.

"And the law here is also fighting for survival," Lillehorne continued. "A bitter struggle, to be sure. There are parts of London no sane man will enter. They are fit only for animals. Here a whorehouse where the eldest girl is twelve and the youngest six, there a back alley den where impoverished men and women are induced to fight each other to the death for the benefit of the gamblers' pockets. Bring a new influx of cheap and mind-robbing gin to the equation, and you have the makings of Dante's Inferno upon English earth." Lillehorne stared into the flame of the oil lamp, and it was not just the low temperature of the mean little room that gave Matthew a chill but the expression of pain in the man's eyes. Obviously he hadn't been totally prepared for the job, nor for the realities of Londontown in the year 1703. "This city," Lillehorne said, "eats its young and weak. It cuts the heads off children and batters the faces of men and women into pulp for the taking of a few shillings. It corrupts the mind and destroys the soul. It has no bottom. So...no, there is no one to spend half-a-day on you, young man. Better for you than here," he said, "would have been to jump overboard and follow to a watery grave the unlamented Count Anton Mannerheim Dahlgren."

A silence fell but for the noise of the rain. Nack's mouth contorted as he was about to loose a further insult at Matthew. Lillehorne said in a dry and distant voice, "Don't speak," and his cohort in some unknowable crime remained mute.

It occurred to Matthew that Lord Cornbury might not have done either Lillehorne or Nack such a favor.

Matthew drew in a long breath and then let it go. He asked the question he'd never thought he would have to pose to Gardner Lillehorne: "Can you help me?"

Lillehorne regarded the flame for a few seconds more as if transfixed by it, or if its light was for a brief time a torch of sanity in a world of madness. Then he returned to his senses and the present moment, and he answered with no hint of the irony involved, "I will convey your situation to the general clerk at the Old Bailey and ask to see Judge Thomason Greenwood. Judge Greenwood is a fair and honest man…a young man, known to be lenient under compelling circumstances. The questions you brought up before Magistrate Akers are also in the papers I read and they will be of interest to the judge. I will stand up for you, and we shall devise some method of repayment for this service at a later date."

"Fine," said Matthew, with an almost overwhelming rush of relief. "May I ask how long this will take?"

"I'll contact the clerk in the morning. After that…I can't say with any certainty, but hopefully we can get you standing at the Old Bailey by the end of the month."

"The…end of the *month*? But it's barely November! You mean I have to stay here for nearly another whole month?"

"Appreciate where you *are*, young sir," said Lillehorne with a cutting edge to his voice. "You are fortunate because St. Peter's Place is the Dock House Inn of prison facilities here. You're a reader of the *Gazette*, you know you could do worse. Nack, fetch the guard."

Nack was up and knocking on the door at Lillehorne's command. The door was unbolted from the other side and a man who made Magnus Muldoon look puny came in, though most of his bulk was fat and he had a shaven head with a little chunk of it missing above the left eye.

"Mind your manners while you're in here," Lillehorne advised as the guard hauled Matthew up from his chair as if he were the weight of a potato sack. "Do what you're told and stay out of trouble...if that is *possible* for you, I mean."

"I will." The guard's hands on Matthew's shoulders were like bands of iron. No chains were needed with this goliath around. Too bad the man seemed to have the sense of a ten-year-old child. "And thank you, Gardner. I mean it sincerely."

"Of course you do." This was followed with a small smirk. "A prison cell has a way of producing sincerity as well as humility. Let's hope these life lessons *stick*."

The last word—four of them, to be exact—was delivered by Dippen Nack, with a scowl and a spit and a brandishment of the billyclub to which he evidently was married: "Too far from home!"

Then the guard took Matthew hobbling away, back to the cold cavern of cells, and the two gentlemen of London took their leave, out into the gray rain and the vast metropolis of gray buildings, gray sidewalks, and gray faces.

As soon as the *Bonny Chance* had fixed its lines to its berth in the Plymouth wharf and the gangplank lowered, Hudson Greathouse and Berry Grigsby were off to find the harbormaster. They were tired and grimy in their mold-streaked clothes and their first steps on an unmoving surface had them grabbing hold of each other as if one spinning top might secure the balance of another, but somehow they made it down the plank without splashing into the drink.

It was late afternoon, the *Bonny Chance* having been made by signal flag to sit at anchor in the harbor for four hours before the longboats could be sent out. The wharves at Plymouth had been exceptionally busy today and a mishap at unloading cargo had, in a series of increasing delays, caused in turn delays of the mooring of all new arrivals. Those four hours had seemed the longest in their lives to both Berry and Hudson, who could do nothing but wait. Now, though, it was time for action, and weariness, grime, mold and the torment of Hudson's itchy gray beard be damned...where was the harbormaster in this confusion of crates and trunks, ropes, horses and wagons, cursing sailors, shouting captains, caterwauling cargo chiefs and—the same as in New York—a more-than-motley crew of fiddlers, squeezeboxers, beggars, dancers and higglers hawking pastries and geegaws. All in all, a chaotic scene...and then quite suddenly from the leaden sky the rain began to beat down upon captain and fiddler alike.

Both drenched to the skin and resembling nothing more than beggars and ragmops themselves, Hudson and Berry after a time of searching found the harbormaster snug in his dockside cabin next to a roaring fire and with a cup of rum halfway to his mouth.

"The *Wanderer*," said Hudson when it was apparent business was meant and no man was going to dislodge him from this purpose. "Look through your records. Has it arrived? And if so—I *hope*—when?"

The answer was forthcoming on the arrival to the harbormaster's palm of twenty shillings, plus sped to speech by the sight of Hudson's fist cocked back to make a shredding of his lips. The ledger showed that the *Wanderer* had indeed arrived two weeks ago, that it was under legal seizure concerning a lawsuit Captain Sullivan Peppertree had filed against his crew, that the ship had unfortunately sunk at its berth three days after being tied up, and it was still there serving as a headache, an eyesore and a roost for a hundred seagulls. So what of it?

"You have a list of passengers?"

"I do not. God speed them on their way. I have only listings for cargo."

"We're looking for a young man named Matthew Corbett," Berry said, hoping to ease some of the tension in the room. "He was a passenger on the—"

"Oh, I remember that name!" came the reply. "There was quite a fuss on the wharf when the ship docked. It's not often that a constable is summoned to arrest a murderer as soon as he's brought down the plank. I know, because the preacher came first to me to arrange it."

"A *murderer*?" Hudson frowned. His heart had jumped. "Who was murdered?"

"A foreign count, I heard. I don't know all the details. But this Corbett fellow you're askin' for...he did the killin'."

Hudson and Berry looked at each other, both for the moment at a loss for words.

Berry recovered first, though her head was still swimming. "Where has he been taken?"

"The gaolhouse, I suppose. I know Constable Moncroff came here to make the arrest. Hey now!" His already-beady eyes narrowed. "What are all these questions about, anyway? You got a stake in this?"

"You might say that," Hudson replied. "Direct us to the gaol."

"Not a place most people *want* to visit, but I'll direct you. Got five more shillings on you?"

Within the hour Hudson and Berry had taken a carriage through the rainy streets of Plymouth to the Town Hall and gaol, a distance of about a half-mile from the harbor. In this dismal building they found that Constable Moncroff had gone for the day, the prisoner was no longer in the Plymouth gaol, the records of the matter were not for public display, and no—said the constable on duty, a rather strapping young fellow with a knife scar on his chin and hard eyes that dared an altercation—they could not have the home address of Constable Moncroff. They would have to come back tomorrow morning and that was that.

"At least tell us where he's been taken," Berry said, with a note of pleading in her voice. She felt near crying from frustration. "Won't you *please* do that?"

"Away from here. Moncroff signs in at seven o'clock sharp," said the young constable, and the set of his jaw told Berry there would be no more information.

Hudson would have smacked the fool out of this gent and been done with it but he cared not to spend a night behind bars. There was nothing more to do but return to the harbor, get their luggage taken off, and find an inn for the night. At this rate, Hudson thought, Matthew was going to owe him a year's worth of doing his laundry.

The rain was still falling. Darkness had begun to spread over the town. They got into the carriage that Hudson had wisely asked to wait for them, and they set off again toward the docks.

To Berry's silence, Hudson said, "We've come this far, one more night won't make a difference."

"It *might*," she said, and then lapsed again into quiescence. She was bedraggled, her hair was wet and dirty, there were dark circles under her eyes and never had she felt so weary. She'd forgotten the toll a sea voyage took on a person, even a voyage as calm and uneventful—mostly—as that on the *Bonny Chance.* At least she'd not been the reason for anyone falling overboard, breaking a leg on a stairway, or any other calamity she might imagine. True, one of the women passengers did give birth to twins on the trip and Berry had been the one to assist the ship's doctor in this event, but that had certainly been a positive and not a negative.

"We know three things," Hudson said as the horse clopped along, heedless of the driver's occasional whipstrikes. "Count Dahlgren is dead, Matthew has been held to account for it, *and* Matthew survives, wherever he might be. Look, we need to get our chins out of the mud. Matthew is *alive.* That's all I need to know to make me want to have a good dinner and a cup of the best wine a poor traveller can afford. How about you?"

"I could eat a horse with the skin still on it," she said, "and break open a bottle with my teeth to get at the wine. But...his not being here...there something about that I just don't like."

"Well, maybe that gaol is crowded and they put him somewhere else. We'll find out in the morning, but until then there's no use worrying ourselves to a pity. I'm already gray enough, thank you."

She looked at him, at the earnest and caring expression on his tired, hollow-eyed face, and gave him as much of a sunny smile as she could pry from behind her own dark clouds. He had been like this all through the voyage: always positive when she needed him to be, always a strong shoulder to lean on, always a gentleman and certainly always a loyal and unswerving friend to Matthew. Indeed, whatever Matthew had been through and whatever faced him now, he was lucky to have such a pillar of fortitude at his back. Her smile faded, though, as she pondered an imponderable. "I have two things to ask you," she said. "The first...do you think he actually did murder the man?"

Hudson scratched his bearded chin. If he didn't have a legion of lice in there, he would dance a jig and piss a pickle. "Murder," he repeated solemnly. "That can be one man's opinion. It appears Matthew may have aided Dahlgren's departure from this earth, but I'm not ready to call him a murderer." This was a quicksandy area, so Hudson pressed on. "Your second question?"

"One I've wished to ask you for some weeks now," she told him, and yet the question was—unlike the emergence of the twins—a difficult birth. At last she brought it to air. "Matthew was very unkind to me the last time we spoke. It was so *unlike* him. I thought...his experience on that damned island—excuse my tongue—caused him to lose his senses for awhile. But...nevertheless, he said to me some terrible and hurtful things. Is it that...he has feelings for Minx Cutter, and wishes me out of his sight?"

"Lord, no!" came the immediate response. "I don't know about you, but being in the same room with Minx Cutter makes me want to be wearing a suit of armor...or at least an armored codpiece. No, I don't think it's that at all."

"What, then? Can you say?"

"I can guess," said Hudson. He had to spend a few seconds in formulation of this guess, for he realized she was hanging on his words. "If I were Matthew," he ventured, "I'd be trying to run you off, too."

"Why?"

"Can't you understand it? Of course Matthew cares for you. He'd be a fool if he didn't and that boy is no fool. His reasons are plain. The closer he allows you to come to him, the more in danger you are from those who wish him harm. Speaking particularly now of Professor Fell." He paused for emphasis, and she got that because she nodded. "We know that even at a distance," he went on, "the professor can loose the devil's own Hell against his enemies. After Matthew was a part of blowing up that gunpowder supply and was responsible for destroying the whole—as you put it—damn island, Fell will be coming after him with every weapon he can bring to bear. Matthew doesn't want you to be one of them."

"Me? A *weapon*?"

"If Fell's people got hold of you, yes...a weapon with which to attack Matthew. And no telling what would be done to you before he could meet Fell's demands. Minx Cutter plays her part of being tough and unconcerned, but I believe she wishes for a second face on the back of her head to watch out for the professor's vengeance. It's coming. She knows it, I know it, and Matthew knows it. Therefore Matthew wants to keep you at a distance, though by now that's likely a futile plan."

"You're right," she said. "I won't give up on him."

"Of course you won't. That's why you're here. That's why you most probably turned down a marriage proposal from Ashton

McCaggers, and left New York on this journey with a crude, rude wild man you hardly know." Hudson offered the faintest spirit of a sly smile. "I won't ask you if I'm correct about McCaggers, but I know I'm correct about the other part."

"No, you're not. I find you anything but crude, rude and wild."

"My dear old Mam always taught me to be on my best behavior with a school teacher," he said. He glanced out the window into a torrent of driving rain. "Ah, here's the harbor! As wet above the sea as below. The dock's cleared out a bit." He reached up and rapped with his knuckles on the driver's viewslit. "If you wish an extra pence you can help us with our trunks," he told the man. "Then direct us to an inn, and not one where we have to share rooms with wharf rats, either."

"Yes sir, very good."

Berry didn't mind the rain or the discomfort of sopping-wet hair, clothes and skin. Her worried expression was due to her feeling—call it a woman's intuition—that wherever he was, even in the hands of the law, Matthew was still in terrible danger and there was nothing she nor Hudson could do about it. But tomorrow was tomorrow, and if Heaven must be moved to find him she would search out a lever big enough to reach from Earth to the Plain Of Paradise. Of this she made a solemn vow to herself.

"Ready?" Hudson asked before opening the door.

She nodded.

He said, "Chin—"

Eight

"—Up," spoke the prisoner with the mane of filth-matted white hair and one eye covered with a gray film. "Ya look like you're already climbin' the thirteen."

"Pardon?" It had been the first time this man had addressed him in the four days of being in the cell, and Matthew had a sluggish moment of not understanding. "The thirteen what?"

"Thirteen *what*, he asks!" White Hair elbowed the second prisoner, Broken Nose, in the ribs. "He don't know nothin', do he?"

"Thirteen steps to the gallows!" growled Broken Nose. "Where ya been all ya life?"

"As far away from the hangman as I could get," said Matthew.

"Ha! Ain't we all been!" White Hair grinned, showing a mouthful of green disaster. "Caught up with us now though, ain't it? But I say chin up, 'cause you could be like that poor feller!" He jerked a misshapen thumb in the direction of the aged gent who lay shivering in a heap on the floor, which was what the decrepit individual did except for eating lightly and defecating heavily. "He's gave the game to God!" said White Hair. "Won't be long 'fore they carries him out to the beetle yard!" He focused his working eye on Matthew. "What're you in for?"

"Someone's mistake."

Those two words might have been the most comical ever spoken in London, the way White Hair and Broken Nose howled with laughter while their nostrils shot goo and their three eyes leaked tears of hilarity.

"I presume that's what everyone says," Matthew amended, his own face as straight as a plowman's path.

"Honest now!" said White Hair when he could again speak. He wiped his nose on a sleeve that was black with such dried tidbits. "What'd ya do?"

"It is claimed," Matthew answered with great dignity, "that I committed murder."

Instantly the two men were nearly at his feet.

"Ya killed a constable?" asked Broken Nose.

"A preacher?" prodded White Hair. "I've always wanted to kill me one a'them!"

"Neither. It is claimed I killed a Prussian count."

Their faces sagged, if they could sag anymore than the usual. "Ahhhhh, that ain't nothin'!" White Hair made an expression of disgust, which on its own was a murderous sight. "Them foreign counts is a bob a bag, ain't worth wipin' the blade for."

"And him bein' Prussian!" Broken Nose added. "'Tain't nobody likes them pigsuckers! You'll be out of here 'fore the wrens fly on St. Stephen's Day!"

"I hope long before that."

"Well, them things has to go through what they call 'the proper channels'," said Broken Nose, with a philosophical air. "Hey, y'know we thought you was a pigeon, that's why we wasn't speakin' to ya."

"A pigeon?"

"Sure and it's the truth!" said White Hair. "A pigeon. Y'know. Somebody brought in from outside, dressed up to look like they belongs here. See, they ain't found the money I…um…helped myself to from the Widow Hamm's house after the poor old bitch fell down them steps and busted her head wide open. Lord, that was a sight! How was I to know she was gonna come a cropper 'gainst that boot brick? I ain't no fortune teller!"

"They ain't got my money neither!" said Broken Nose. "And damned if they'll find it. That old skinflint was robbin' me and everybody else worked in the shop, I'm just the one had guts enough to knock his brains out and take what was mine. 'Course, I took everybody else's money too, but they was all the yellowest of cowards!"

"So," White Hair continued, "they are known to send pigeons in here to find out where the money's stashed. Then they go and take it for themselves. But you been in here long enough, none of 'em stay more than two days. Who would if they didn't have to, even for the money? We figured we might be right when they took you out awhile ago, but then when they brung you back and that guard give you such a shove…naw, you ain't no pigeon. You're a regular fella."

"But I *still* ain't talkin' about where I stashed my loot," said Broken Nose adamantly. "I'm gettin' out of here, one way or 'nother. Knowin' that's waitin' for me…keeps me wakin' up to see the sunshine."

Matthew grunted. The only way sunshine could get into this place would be if someone could smuggle it here in a bottle. The clammy walls were mottled with brown, black, and green lichens, the floor laid with cold flagstones likely quarried by Roman slaves, the iron bars absolute in their rigidity, the only light—and blessed they were to have any at all—was the meager glow of a single candle stuck to a brown clay plate on a small ledge above Broken Nose's foul-smelling bunk. Matthew's own bunk smelled terribly foul as well; one fear he had was that when he got out of here he would find his sense of smell totally destroyed.

Down the corridor a man screamed as if his heart had been burst with a blade. Someone else laughed brokenly, a haunted hollow sound, and another voice further away began to speak curses at a slow, methodical pace as if reciting a schoolboy's lesson.

"You seem a smart lad," said Broken Nose, who paid no heed to this commotion and likely didn't even hear such anymore. "Know why it's thirteen steps to the gallows?"

"No, I don't."

"Let me lighten ya. Each step eight inches. Gives ya a height total of eight feet, six inches. What they call in their profession an 'acceptable drop'. Enough to break the neck clean…usual, that is. Don't pay to be tall if you're to be hanged. Height of eight feet, six inches also leaves 'nough room to handle the corpse, get a cart underneath it and cut it loose. That's why thirteen steps. Now you're smarter than ya was a minute ago."

"Thank you," said Matthew, a little uneasily. "I don't plan on ever needing that knowledge, but thank you."

"Hey now!" By the light of the candle White Hair looked as if he'd just had an epiphany. "Can you read, boy?"

"Yes."

"Gimme me the paper!" White Hair said to his companion. "The ass-wiper, right over there!" He took hold of the darkly-stained small yellow broadsheet, which appeared only to be stuck together with unmentionables, and held it out toward Matthew. "Here. Would you read this to me? Please?"

"Uh," Matthew said, "I'm not sure I really want to—"

"I'm *beggin'*. Please. My dear Betsy used to read it to me, twice a week. Oh, it's all dried, ain't nothin' to fear."

"It's not that I fear anything, it's just that...well...what *is* it?"

"*Lord Puffery's Pin*. Ain't you never heard of it?"

"No."

"That boy must be from the moon!" said Broken Nose. "*Everybody* knows the *Pin*!"

"Comes out twice a week," White Hair explained. "When the guards finish readin' 'em they bring 'em in sometimes for us to... y'know...clean ourselves with. But looky here, this one's hardly a week old!"

"It's a news sheet, I gather?"

"Oh, more than that! If it wasn't for the *Pin* you'd never know what was goin' on in London! It's like...like..."

"Balm for the soul," said Broken Nose.

"Yep, that!" The offensive sheet was held out closer to Matthew, who realized that despite the foulness of the paper it might not do to get on the wrong side of these two cellmates. "You bein' able to read," White Hair went on, with a desperate note in his voice, "that's kinda like a Godsend. I'm—the both of us—we're starvin' for the news. You see?"

"No, I can't see. Very well, at least." Matthew decided there were worse things in the world than handling a news sheet laden with a week's crust of manure. Or perhaps not, but the issue was diplomacy. It was a good way to make himself valuable to these two, as they both seemed to be as anxious as children awaiting the most delicious tray of sweetmeats. He reached out, grimaced only a little, and took the sheet in one hand. "Bring the candle closer, if you will," he said, and no quicker expressed than done.

"Start at the top," said White Hair, his single eye gleaming. "My Betsy always started at the top."

Matthew began to read the headline there. "*Lady Everlust Gives Birth To Two-Headed*—" He looked up in amazement. "What *is* this?"

"I knew Lady Everlust was gonna birth a freak!" White Hair said excitedly to his companion. "The way she was paradin' herself around, drinkin' gin by the barrel and spreadin' her legs for every man Jack! I knew it! Go on, was it a boy or a girl?"

Matthew read a little further into the so-called article. "Gave birth Thursday last," he reported, "to a two-headed child, one head that of a boy and one head that of a girl, with the sexual organs of—oh, *really*!" He couldn't bear to read on. "This is absurd!"

"It's God's judgment on Lady Everlust, is what it is," said Broken Nose. "You ain't been followin' the story, you don't know. That is one mean, wicked, hateful woman! So go on, what's the freak's sex?"

"Both," said Matthew, and the two men hollered with glee so loudly the sad sack on the floor shifted and put his hands to his ears.

"Next story!" White Hair urged. "Don't leave us hangin'!"

"*Great Ape Escapes From Zoo, Rampages Through House of Lords*... listen, do you really be—"

"Plucked their wigs off one by one, I'll bet! Can't you see it?" howled Broken Nose. "I'd 'a opened up that floorboard and given a pound of my money to see...I mean...that would've been worth payin' to see!"

"Next! Go on, go on!"

"*Famed Italian Opera Star Still Missing, Feared Kidnapped.*"

"Oh yeah." White Hair nodded. "Happened a couple of weeks ago. Lady was supposed to sing first for the Earl of Canterbury, then gonna do a singin' at the Castle Oak Theater. Pity, that. I heard she's a looker. Some knave's got her knocked up by now. Go on, the candle's burnin'."

"*Albion Attacks Again, Murder Done In Crescent Alley.*"

"*That* bastard!" seethed Broken Nose. "Does it say who he killed?"

Matthew had to read around a piece of what appeared to be oatmeal that had made its way from north to south. "Benjamin Greer, I think the name is."

"Not Benny Greer!" Broken Nose sat up as straight as if an iron rod had been introduced into his nether regions. "I know *a* Benny Greer, but it can't be the same one. Must be dozens of Benjamin Greers in London. Right?"

"What else does it say?" White Hair prompted, without answering the other.

"This is a little difficult to read, as it has done its job a bit too well, but..." Matthew angled the sheet toward the candlelight and tried his best to make out the murky printing. "Benjamin Greer, aged twenty-five or thereabouts...address unknown...recently released from St. Peter's—"

"God A'mighty! Benny!" gasped Broken Nose. "He was in here not a month ago! Does it say how Albion did it? Slashed throat, I'm guessin'. That's how he kills 'em all."

"Yes," Matthew saw in the article. "A cut throat, done after midnight in Crescent Alley. No one to claim the body, it seems." He looked up at the two prisoners, who had become very subdued. "Who is Albion?"

"Jesus save you, you must not be from around here." White Hair was staring at the floor, his interest in the *Pin* suddenly punctured. "Albion's the talk of London. Bastard's in the *Pin* all the time, killin' somebody or 'nother. Benny...damn, he was a good feller. Ran with them Black-Eyed Broodies over in Whitechapel, and maybe he did some things that weren't so upstandin', but...hell...he had a good heart."

"Let out of here hardly a month past," the other man added. "And dead by Albion's blade. Ain't right. Makes ya wonder what this world is comin' to."

Matthew was glad to put the sheet aside. In his opinion most of the articles seemed to be fashioned from the same substance that blighted the paper. "Albion," he repeated. "This person has killed many others?"

"Many," said Broken Nose. "There and then gone, he is. A phantomine if there ever was one."

"*Phantom*," White Hair corrected. "That's the proper word." He looked to Matthew for assurance. "Ain't it?"

Matthew hardly heard him. He watched the candleflame gutter at some breath of wind from a crack in the ancient walls. "Robbery is the motive, then?"

"Albion kills men who ain't got a shillin' to their names," Broken Nose said. He had curled himself up on his bunk so his back was firmly against stone. "Ain't robbery. It's killin' for the thrill of it, seems like. Oh, there's been a couple of people say they seen him, always after somebody's been laid low. Says he wears a black cloak and hood and a golden mask. Yessir. A golden mask. Carries a blade as long as your arm."

"That would be a sword?" Matthew inquired.

"Sword…long knife…whatever it is, it cuts deep. Heard tell Albion can walk through walls. Solid stone don't stop no phantomine…a *phantom*, if you please. Nossir. Heard he's in one place one minute, next he shows up halfway 'cross the city. Heard he jumped off a roof once…just disappeared right in midair. Albion flies with the wind, that's what he does. And anybody unlucky enough to see under that golden mask…they're gonna die for it, 'cause Albion is Death itself, and under there is a skull just a'grinnin'."

"May I ask who you heard these tales from?"

"It was read to me from the *Pin*, of course. That's how I get all my news."

"I see." Matthew realized Lord Puffery, whoever that entity might be, could just as well have made up the personage of golden-masked Albion as much as Lady Everlust and her two-headed lovechild had been invented. Of course Benjamin Greer was probably really dead, killed by a perfectly ordinary villain as had been the others, but ascribing these deaths to a phantom who travelled with the wind was much more compelling to the masses. "You say this *Pin* is published twice a week? How much is the cost?"

"Goes for five pence," said White Hair. "And worth every bit of it, to keep up with events. There's persons rather starve and go thirsty than do without their *Pin* twice a week."

"Cheap gin for the mind, I presume," Matthew said, but he was speaking mostly to himself. Gardner Lillehorne had been correct; this was not New York, as surely the citizens there would see through such blatant lies in Marmaduke Grigsby's *Earwig*. In fact, Marmy would be ashamed to show his face after printing such twaddle.

However, Matthew found himself again reaching for the sheet as if tranced, for that part about Lady Everlust's freak child was ridiculous but entertaining in its own way, and it made a small bit of gaol-time evaporate without effort. Scanning the articles, he surmised that Lord Puffery—if indeed there was in reality such a person—had quite an imagination and had been made by this thin one-sided five-pence meal of execrable porridge a very, very wealthy individual. At the bottom of the page was the boldface line *Buying Items Of Interest at Sm. Luther, Printer, 1229 Fleet Street.*

Samuel Luther? This person held the eyes, ears and voices of London's hundred thousands. Matthew played with the idea that when he got out of this he might find Lord Puffery, and give the *Pin* a real story concerning a certain Professor Fell, who made Albion's supposed wickedness a child's play. He was in Fell's territory, Berry and everyone else he cared for—loved—was at a safe distance. So if the professor wanted him so badly, let Fell first have a bellyful of *Pin*s.

It was a plan. But first for himself, to regain his freedom. Perhaps—hope upon hope—tomorrow.

Nine

Tomorrow dawned. In Plymouth, Hudson and Berry were accepted to be seen by Constable Moncroff at just after seven in the morning, were informed that the prisoner in question had been transferred to London, namely the holding facility at St. Peter's Place, and the case given over to the Honorable Gardner Lillehorne, Assistant to the High Constable. Moncroff did reveal that the victim of this murder, Count Anton Mannerheim Dahlgren, had been killed at sea during a storm and there might be some mitigating circumstances but other than that he could not say.

Hudson and Berry then went directly to the coach office to secure transfer to London, were told all the coaches were currently out but one to make the trip would be available on the morrow, if it arrived back in Plymouth on schedule tonight. The trip would take at least seven days and more if the infernal rain kept up, and word had it that parts of the road were being washed out. Therefore tickets could be sold to them, but there was no assurity they would reach London within a week's time.

The two travellers bought their tickets and then returned to the Hartford House in a dismal downpour.

In London as the day progressed, Matthew's expectations waned. The prisoners were taken out to file along in their chains and receive a wooden cup of ox-meat soup, light on the ox-meat, but no mention was made of his going before Judge Greenwood nor was there any further communication from Gardner Lillehorne. He and the others were returned to their cells, and Matthew realized he might indeed be made to stay here an intolerable month, a thought that dashed his spirits down to the very stones.

The following day, the rain still fell, no coach was available to Hudson and Berry, and Matthew went through the exact same routine as the day before. The only difference in this day was that when their candle burned out they were not given another, as it was explained to Matthew by his two coherent cellmates that they had used up their taper allowance for the week.

On the next morrow, with the rain ceased but the sky still low and threatening, success was had at the Plymouth coach office. A stop at the Hartford House to put aboard their trunks, and Hudson and Berry settled in for the journey along with a recently-arrived wig-crafter from Philadelphia and a Norwegian businessman in the timber trade.

Thus it was that Matthew had no sense of the time when the guard came to their cell with chains over his shoulder, unlocked the door and said to him, "*Out*."

Matthew stood up and obeyed. The guard first locked the cell door and then went about securing the chains to Matthew's ankles and wrists. His cellmates, who had been entertained by Matthew's tales of his youth growing up in the New York orphanage and of the Rachel Howarth incident in Fount Royal, pressed themselves against the bars. Broken Nose, whose name Matthew had learned was Thomas Leary, unsuccessful prize fighter and ex-carpenter, called out, "Steady, lad! Duck whatever they throw at ya!"

"Move on," said the guard, followed by a shove to Matthew's back.

Along the corridor they went, assailed by the rough voices, ragged curses and juicy spits aimed not at Matthew but splattering him just the same. The guard used his billyclub, quite similar to Dippen Nack's, to strike at the fingers that were curled around bars and might have managed to break a few according to the howls of pain that ensued. Matthew was made to wait while another door was unlocked, he was pushed through into a cleaner-smelling area with barred windows that allowed the meager light of what might have been early afternoon, and while one skinny guard held his own bludgeon under Matthew's chin the hulking one unlocked the prisoner's chains at wrists and ankles.

Then Matthew was guided through a long passageway adorned with the oil paintings of famous men with large heads and cautious eyes, and into a chamber where a bewigged official sat at a desk before a wall of shelves holding a multitude of ledger books. There Gardner Lillehorne stood waiting, dressed in dark brown with a red feather sticking up from his taupe tricorn. Beyond him was the pair of heavy oak doors that Matthew had been brought into this building through, and outside were seven stone steps to the street.

"Judge Greenwood," Lillehorne said, "will see you today."

"Luck to you," the offensive guard offered, and he put a hand on Matthew's shoulder like the most considerate of brothers.

Weak London light was yet strong enough to sting Matthew's eyes as he emerged from the gaolhouse alongside Lillehorne. The rain had stopped but the air was cold and clammy, the clouds dark, and in his tatty prison rags Matthew was chilled to the bone. A coach, again with barred windows, waited at the curb and there also waited another club-wielding guard who wore a black skullcap and a jacket made of wolfhide.

"Necessary," said Lillehorne in advance of Matthew's objection. "Get in and remain silent."

Matthew did as he was told, and gladly. The guard sat beside him in the enclosed cab while Lillehorne took the seat across. Lillehorne tapped on the roof with the silver lion's-head of his cane and the coach started off.

Though the sun was definitely hidden behind a ceiling of clouds, this afternoon there was neither rain nor fog. The light was low, tinged a shade blue, but Matthew had the chance to observe the city in greater detail as they moved along. Firstly, the buildings were close-packed together and huge; New York had never seen the like of such monuments to Mammon. There were businesses of all kinds and descriptions to go along with the incredible, head-spinning variety of edifices. Two stables within one block? The anvils and fires of two blacksmiths, the same? Here a corral of livestock, there a shop selling wedding gowns. The store of a tricorn-shaper stood next to a gunsmith, a nautical goods emporium next to a shop specializing in Japanese fans, jadework, and kimonos of every hue or so it seemed from the astounding variety in the front window. Three taverns stood within stagger distance of each other, two facing each other directly across the street. Matthew realized there must be several hundred taverns here for they were everywhere, with names like The Mad Parrot, Abraham's Pleasure, and The Restless Owl. He thought he might try the Owl when he got out of this; it sounded like it might be his kind of place.

But could he even find that particular tavern again? Even with instructions? These streets were a maze: one cutting across another, narrowing then widening and narrowing again, made black in the shadows of columns and towers, curving to cross another street, broken cobbles under the hooves and wheels, here a wagon stalled by a stubborn mule fighting against its driver and several other men, there a huge hole filled with muddy rainwater that had already bitten off two wheels for they were lying half-submerged in the morass. And everywhere more coaches and carriages, some sturdy and workmanlike and others painted up like brothel dollies. Then there were the wagons, and Matthew thought that if one third of the traffic on this very street was put upon the Broad Way that thoroughfare would collapse down to the tombs of the Mohawk Adam and Eve. Just within his limited sight they were hauling coal, barrels, lumber, haybales, the carcasses of dead horses, a cathedral's worth of bricks, windowframes, bolts of material, piles of burlap bags, a small mountain of gravel, and a massive bronze church bell.

And the people and their noise, and even without the shouting and wild laughter that seemed to soar up from the doorways and windows the sound of boots tramping on street stones was that of an army on constant march though no army had ever been so chaotic. Beggars here and beggars there, legs and arms missing from some real warfare or dread disease, gents and ladies in finery strolling yet here a stroll was a fight to move through the masses, two men at bloody fisticuffs over by the Gentleman Bear tavern and a crowd urging them on, a fiddler daring fate by playing his tune in the street, a young girl with long brown hair standing on a rooftop watching the river of life flow by below.

Before long Matthew was nearly exhausted from taking all this in, and finally in spite of his natural curiosity he had to pull his eyes away and concentrate on staring at the red feather in Lillehorne's tricorn.

"I felt much the same way, coming back here after such a time," said Lillehorne with a knowing half-smile. "I'd forgotten that New York is a rustic town compared to this." The coach suddenly came to a dead halt. "Oh mercy!" he said, his expression severe again, and he banged on the roof with his cane.

"Traffic jam up ahead, sir," said the driver through the viewslit. "Looks like an ale wagon's broke down. People are swarmin' all over, lootin' the barrels."

"Sweet breath of Christ!" In his dismay Lillehorne removed his tricorn to scratch in the glossy sheen of his hair. "Can you find another route?"

"We're jammed in. Stuck for awhile, looks like."

"I feared as much. Get moving when you're able."

The driver slid the viewslit shut and Lillehorne stared at Matthew with a baleful eye as if blaming him for this delay. "Unfortunately," he said, "one's time can be wasted here in many ways. I have a meeting with High Constable Lord Rivington within the hour. I don't want to be late for that."

"And neither do I want to be late to meet with Judge Greenwood."

"Yes, he's a lenient man but he does value time, as do all successful professionals." He heard something—a boy's voice, strongly calling out—at about the same time as Matthew did, and he looked to his left through the bars.

"Lord Shepsley deserts Lady Caroline for an African chambermaid!" the boy shouted, with lungs of leather. "Tipsy Viceroy tavern burned to the ground, the Mohocks claim they done it! Famed Eyetalian opera star kidnapped by her pirate lover! Fresh news from the *Pin* here, fresh news from the *Pin*!"

The bellowing salesboy, perhaps twelve years of age, stood at the curb with a bundle of the news sheets in his arms. He wore an apronlike garment with pockets in which to deposit coins. They were already bulging. "Boy!" Lillehorne called over the noise of London. "Come here!" He dug for a five-pence piece, paid the boy through the bars and took a copy as other customers swarmed around. The guard also coughed up a coin for his own sheet. With gleaming eyes and an air of excitement Lillehorne began to read the so-called news of the day. Matthew noted that both Lillehorne's and the guard's mouths moved as they read.

"Any further word of Lady Everlust's two-headed child?" Matthew asked.

Lillehorne glanced up for only an instant. "What? Oh, that's old news. I presume your cellmates were devotees? Almost everyone is."

"I see." Matthew watched the boy selling the sheets one after another until he moved out of sight, still hollering the headlines. "I'm wondering, though, how one separates fact from fiction in such a publication."

"It's all fact *based*," said Lillehorne, with a defensive edge to his voice. "Of course much of it is embellished for the entertainment of the common man, but it's done so *smoothly* one winds up not caring to make a distinction. Now quiet, please, and let me catch up."

"A slippery slope," Matthew said.

"Pardon?"

"A slippery slope, relinquishing the distinction between fact and fiction to a faceless Lord Puffery. Is there really such a person?"

"I have no idea. Does it matter?"

"I'd like to be sure what I'm reading is the word of a truthful writer. The story about the kidnapped opera star, for instance. Is that true?"

"It is. When Madam Alicia Candoleri arrived at Portsmouth she was met by what we presume she thought was a coach sent by the Earl of Canterbury. It turned out the real coach had been waylaid and the driver and the madam's escort murdered, their bodies found in a wood. Madam Candoleri disappeared and has not been seen since. That was two weeks ago."

"She had no protector travelling with her?"

"Two persons. Her manager and her makeup girl. Both also missing."

"What's the ransom?"

"No ransom has been requested, as far as I know."

"Hm," said Matthew. "No ransom demand after two weeks? The murder of the earl's driver and the escort makes it clear someone was very serious in their intent...but why would a famous opera star be abducted for anything but a queen's ransom? I'm guessing also that the part about the pirate lover is where fiction overtakes fact?"

"I haven't gotten there yet, please let me advance."

Matthew allowed him a few more seconds before asking the question that was of real interest. "Has Albion struck again?"

Lillehorne lowered his *Pin*. "What do you know of that?"

"Just what I read, which was a brief article in one of last week's issues." Matthew frowned at Lillehorne's obvious discomfort. "You mean...Albion is *real*? Not a fiction?"

"Not a fiction," was the reply. "Now, I'm sure the *Pin* does somewhat exaggerate Albion's exploits, but suffice it to say this personage is a true thorn in the side of the law."

"Black cape and hood? Golden mask? And he kills with a sword? That's all correct?"

"Yes."

"A dramatic individual definitely trying to make a statement," said Matthew. "But saying *what*?"

"Saying that he violently disagrees with the way the law is handled in this city. Albion has killed six men, all after midnight, all in areas where decent citizens would fear to tread. The connection between these victims is...oh, we're moving at last! Very good!" The coach had given a lurch as it started up. "The connection," Lillehorne went on brusquely, for it appeared he was highly irritated in not being able to read his *Pin* in peace, "is that all six were common criminals, had served time in the gaolhouse, but were released due to the machinations of lawyers, up to and including bribery."

"Are you speaking from your own personal experience?"

"Certainly not! It may be that I was rewarded for some of my decisions in New York, but here I am the straightest of arrows. Register that firmly in mind, Sutcliffe," Lillehorne said to the guard, who gave a nearly-imperceptible nod as he continued his mouthy reading. Lillehorne's attention returned to the prisoner. "There are unfortunately many in the halls of justice who are open to filling their pockets, but I vow to you I am not one of them. Princess and

I have been too long wanting to return here to risk losing my position for a few guineas."

"Ah," said Matthew. It helped Lillehorne's case that the father of his shrewish and socially voracious wife—Maude by name but referred to as "Princess" at her demand—was the well-to-do proprietor of a shellfish eating-house on East Cheap Street and was himself known as the "Duke of Clams". Matthew listened to the strident music of the city, which was both compelling and repellent. Thoughts floated through his mind like chess pieces in search of a board. "Interesting," he said.

"What?" Lillehorne again tore himself away from what seemed to Matthew nearly an addiction the entire city shared. "Interesting that I am above bribery?"

"Not that. I trust what you say. Interesting that six common criminals can afford lawyers schooled enough to manipulate the courts, and that six common criminals are for some reason worth the effort and cost of bribery. Is there nothing more to connect these men?"

"Matthew," said Lillehorne with a cool air of superiority, "you might have been a so-called 'problem-solver' in New York, but here you are simply a problem. If you will look deeply into your situation, you will see a prisoner fresh loosed from chains, riding in a prison coach *en route* to stand before a judge and hope—quite fervently hope—Judge Greenwood is not suffering from indigestion, gout or any itchy thing that might cause him discomfort, for this is far from being a sure thing. Now do you mind if I do *some* bit of reading before we reach our destination, which will be in about ten minutes if another ale wagon doesn't burst its barrels?"

"Oh, no, I don't mind," said Matthew. "Go right ahead."

Within ten minutes the coach turned into an alley and stopped alongside an oak door set in a wall of brown stones. The door appeared scorched and might well have been a survivor of the Great Fire. Matthew figured prisoners such as himself, particularly dressed as he was, were not allowed to sully the front steps of the palatial courthouse complex. "Get out and remain silent until you're asked to speak," said Lillehorne. "They brook no hint of disrespect here."

Matthew nodded, though it seemed to him that bringing a copy of the *Pin* into the Old Bailey was a form of disrespect to the law of common sense, yet neither Lillehorne nor the guard had qualms about this. He followed the guard through the door with Lillehorne behind him, and once inside he was made to stop in a chamber where chains and padlocks hung from hooks on the walls. A bewigged officer sat at a desk with an oil lamp, a ledger book, a quill and inkpot before him. Two other guards emerged from a hallway. Quick work was done to lock the chains once more to Matthew's wrists and ankles, making him again have to bend over in a back-aching position. He stared at the floor in disgust; to appear before a judge in this condition was a disgrace. He could feel lice crawling in his hair, he smelled his own terrible body odor, his gray shirt and trousers were filthy and he knew he must look a fright. But so be it. He had no choice but to trust Lillehorne and hope this entire ordeal would soon be ended.

"This way with you," said one of the newly-arrived guards. Matthew was guided toward a narrow staircase, the risers worn down by the shoes of many unfortunates before him.

They ascended three floors, went through a door and into a corridor with a black-and-white checkered floor. High windows admitted as much light as the London clouds would allow, which meant a murky atmosphere illuminated by oil lamps fixed to the walls. Massive paintings of stern men in black robes and huge white wigs glowered down upon the prisoner; they were the kind of paintings whose eyes stayed upon Matthew until he reached the domain of the next, and that eminent painted personage then took his turn applying the evil eye. The noise of the guards' and Lillehorne's boot heels clacking upon the checkered floor sounded like pistols going off, and Matthew's chains clattered in a place that most likely usually held the hush of a cemetery.

"Here," said Lillehorne, motioning toward another passageway. They turned down it, came to a door inset with panes of colored glass, and the guards stood back to surround Matthew as Lillehorne opened the door.

It was a regular office with a single oval window, the floor carpeted in dark green. A young man with straw-colored hair and square-lensed spectacles sat at a tidy desk before a row of wooden filing cabinets. He'd been scribing something as Lillehorne, Matthew and the guards entered. His eyes darted to Matthew and then quickly away again, and he put aside his quill. "Good afternoon, Mr. Lillehorne. You have an appointment with the judge, I see."

"Yes, Steven. Is he ready to speak to us?"

"Not quite yet. Judge Archer asks that you be patient. He just returned from the gymnasium a short while ago."

"Judge...*Archer*? Oh...well...I fear there's been a mistake. My appointment is with Judge Greenwood."

"There's been a change." Steven picked up a sheet of parchment from his desk and offered it to Lillehorne. "By formal decree, Judge Archer has taken responsibility in this matter."

"Let me see that! *Please*," he added, so as not to sound so disturbed. He took the parchment and read it silently, his mouth moving. He gave Matthew a stricken look that made the prisoner's heart start thumping harder and rise to the vicinity of his throat, for something had definitely gone wrong with this plan. Lillehorne returned the paper to the clerk's hand. "I don't understand. This morning all was agreed with Judge Greenwood. Why has Judge Archer taken an interest?"

"I'm sorry, sir," said the lad, "you'll have to ask him." He motioned toward a pendulum clock in the corner, the time being eight minutes after three. "Sir Archer has asked that you go ahead to his courtroom."

"His courtroom instead of his office?"

"I am told to inform you of where to meet him, sir. I trust I've done my duty."

"Yes. All right. Very well," said Lillehorne, who seemed to be struggling with inner difficulties involving his process of thought. He took a step toward the desk, reversed himself and took a backward step, and for a moment Matthew thought the man was going to bow before the clerk. Then Lillehorne said tersely, "Come with me," and Matthew had an extra added twinge of unease—of fear, really—because the assistant to the High Constable of London would no longer make eye contact with him.

They retraced their steps. Out in the corridor under the grim-faced paintings, Lillehorne said to the guards, "Step away and give us some privacy, please."

They obeyed. Matthew couldn't help but note that as soon as they distanced themselves the one with the *Pin* began reading the articles to the others and they all started grinning like pure fools.

"We are in serious trouble," said Lillehorne. "I mean to say, *you* are in serious trouble."

"What's happened?"

"What has happened…is that for some reason our lenient Judge Greenwood has excused himself from hearing your case, and Judge William Atherton Archer has stepped into the breach."

"Well…can't this Judge Archer be reasoned with?"

"Matthew, Matthew, Matthew," Lillehorne said, if speaking to an idiot child. "You don't grasp the situation. Judge Archer is known as the 'Hanging Judge'. It is said he cannot eat his breakfast until someone dangles from a noose at his order. And I can warrant you…he does not miss many breakfasts. This is who will hear your statements. Are you ready?"

"No," said Matthew.

"Gird yourself," said Lillehorne, who at this moment seemed Matthew's only friend in the world. "And for God's sake don't stand close enough him to let him get a whiff."

Ten

MATTHEW Corbett had never been afraid of a door before, but this one terrified him.

It was glossy ebony and had a shining brass handle that made him think of the grip and trigger of a pistol. The small brass nameplate across it read *W. A. Archer.* The door was situated next to the high bulwark of the judge's bench, which itself was a testament to the power of English law; sitting tall up there one might have a bird's-eye view of the entire kingdom, or at least the view of a hawk upon the tattered crows that came hopping in their chains upon the polished planks below.

Any second now Judge Archer would come through that door. Matthew could not stop his heart from pounding. His breathing was ragged; he wondered if he hadn't been poisoned by the moldy air at St. Peter's Place. All the air of London was moldy, it seemed to him. Today London smelled like bread that had been left to ferment in pickle juice, or perhaps that was just himself. In any case, he felt light-headed and near passing out as he stood before the bench, with Lillehorne positioned a few paces to his right. The guards had remained in the vestibule. Not another soul occupied this great columned courtroom with its vaulted ceiling, its upper balcony and its row upon row of spectator seats. Behind the bench there was a white wall sculpture of a heroic male figure at the reins of a six-horse chariot, the horses bounding forward and the muscles of the driver tensed as he held the steeds in check. Matthew noted that the driver wore a breastplate, his teeth were clenched and he'd been given a grin that said he was equal to the challenge of controlling this vehicle. Matthew had to wonder if the driver was modelled after the judge who sat beneath it.

There came the sound of the door's handle being turned. Matthew's heart stutter-stepped. Then…nothing. Perhaps the judge had forgotten something and gone back for it, or for some reason he'd paused in his entry. A few seconds passed, as Matthew watched the door that did not open.

Quite abruptly the handle turned, the door was nearly thrown open, and a slim man of medium height, his blonde hair bound in a queue with a black ribbon, came through. He was wearing a pearl-gray suit and waistcoat and he held a brown leather valise. He looked neither right nor left nor did he cast a glance at either of the two supplicants awaiting him, and he climbed up to his chair with the quick movements of a man who had energy to burn.

He situated himself, opened the valise and drew out some papers. He began to silently page through them. His mouth did not move as he read. Matthew had expected an older man but Judge Archer looked probably to be only in his early forties, or perhaps he was just well-maintained. He appeared a man who enjoyed a healthy breakfast. He had a high forehead, now furrowed as he digested the documents, and a long, narrow aristocratic nose. His eyes looked to be either dark blue or gray, it was difficult to tell at this distance. All in all, Judge Archer was a handsome man who certainly appeared to be cut from the upper crust, and Matthew figured he was from a long line of good breeding, exquisite manners, family money and mansions and of course the Oxford or Cambridge education. A doting wife, two delightful children with great prospects—if one was male certainly a future as a lawyer and judge himself—and all the English world spread out before him like a gigantic banquet on the best table money and old family connections could buy. Matthew felt very, very small—and very poor—indeed.

"*Damn*," said the judge without looking up. Though he had the appearance of an Oxford gentleman, he owned the voice of a dockside brawler. "When's the last time you had a *bath*?"

"Your Honor," said Lillehorne, "Mr. Corbett was imprisoned in Plymouth, directly he disembarked from the—"

"Was I asking you?" The lean face with its sharp cheekbones came up. The equally-sharp gray eyes under thick blonde brows pierced Gardner Lillehorne as an archer's arrow might pierce a soft, ripe apple. "Can this man speak, or is he as dumb as he looks?"

Matthew cleared his throat. God help him, he gave a little squeak in doing so. "I can speak, sir. My last bath was—"

"Forever ago, I'm sure. If I'd known your condition I would have met you in the alley and been done with this." He slapped the papers down with a force that made Matthew jump and caused Lillehorne to nearly lose his grip on his cane. The gray eyes shifted toward the sheet in Lillehorne's possession. "Is that what I think it is?"

"Your Honor, it's the latest—"

"Oh, *that's* what I'm smelling! The offensive odor of a beggar's rag, printed with ink strained from the bowels of diseased lepers! *Dare* you bring that into my court? Here, approach the bench and deposit it, I'll have my clerk come in and take it to be burned after we're done."

"Yes sir." Lillehorne flashed a helpless glance at Matthew that said *We are all up here, good luck and God's mercy on your neck.* He approached the bench, stood on tiptoes and reached up so high his back cracked, but he did deliver the *Pin* as instructed. Then he backpedalled, his head lowered and his eyes firmly fixed upon the floor.

"Mr. Matthew Corbett," said Judge Archer, and then he simply sat staring at the prisoner as if getting ready to test the reins of this particular chariot, as broken-down and filthy as it was.

The silence stretched.

"Your tale interests me," he went on. "An associate of the Herrald Agency? Well, I wouldn't brag on that, as they cause the legal system here more trouble than they're worth. Dealings with Professor Fell? A myth, as far as I'm concerned, and no one can make me believe he's a single man. If indeed there is a 'Professor Fell', he is a stewpot of various other criminals who have forged some kind of alliance with each other, the better to do their harm to England."

"Your Honor," said Matthew, "I can tell you that—"

"Don't interrupt me." The fierce expression would have caused a lion's balls to shrivel. "To continue: loss of *memory*? An abduction by a Prussian count who *you* say meant to kill you? And this business aboard the ship...what was its name?" He found the item in his papers. "*Wanderer.* Mr. Corbett, from what I have read you have committed murder. Now...your plea upon the magistrate at Plymouth that there is no proof of this man's death, for there is no body, carries some truth, but to allow you to walk away from this incident with no penalty whatsoever would be an affront to my colleagues here and to my entire career. *You* know you meant to commit murder. The witnesses know it, and *I* know it. Even Lillehorne there, who has very inably come to your defense, must know it. It's all here." Archer lifted the papers in a sinewy hand and then let them fall, one after the other, while maintaining his nearly mocking gaze upon the prisoner. "You try trickery upon this court, Mr. Corbett, and we shall not abide it."

Matthew saw his future tumbling away in the fall of those papers and this man's callous—even sadistic—attitude. The panic that leaped up within him was tinged with the first embers of anger. "Please listen to me," he said. "When I regained my memory and was going to tell the law about the murder of Quinn Tate, I was no longer of use to—"

"Ah, the murder of a poor madwoman in a wretched hovel! How is the court to know that is true, and not a lie or a delusion in keeping with this nonsense about Professor Fell?"

"You're not hearing me!" This was delivered more loudly than Matthew had intended, and he felt his cheeks reddening not with shame but with indignation. "I was in the presence of Professor Fell! I have *spoken* with him and I know part of his history! He's real, I can assure you! Didn't Lillehorne tell you about Pendulum Island and the gunpowder—"

"That is *Mister* Lillehorne to you, sir!" Archer snapped. "And refrain from raising your voice to me in my courtroom! No, he has told me nothing of that, and he knows what I think of that whole mythology! I sincerely doubt your tale, sir, and so should the

Honorable Mr. Lillehorne, for one central and inescapable reason... you are still alive, which should not be if indeed you did what you purport to have done! Now facts are facts, and the overwhelming fact is that you cut a lifeline in a storm at sea that doomed a man to certain death, and please don't go jabbering on and taunting this court with melodies of whether the man is actually dead or not! My father was—and remains—a sea captain and I was born at sea. I know what a raging ocean does to a man in peril, and in this case it aided the murderous use of an axe to—"

"*You need to see a physician immediately!*" Matthew shouted, and at once there was silence.

"Matthew!" Lillehorne grasped his arm. "Don't! Please remember your—"

"Hush," Matthew said, and pulled his arm away. He kept his own hot gaze fixed on Judge Archer's; where they met the air should have sizzled. He knew he ought to shut his mouth, he knew he ought to cower like a whipped dog...but he had to speak, and by God he was no whipped dog, even in these chains. "You need to see a physician immediately," Matthew repeated, in spite of all the gongs and chimes of alarm ringing in his head, "to have him clean the tonnage of wax from your ears that prevent you from hearing anything you don't wish to hear." He let that simmer for a few seconds. Lillehorne gave a soft groan, but Archer sat without speaking or moving. "Everything I have stated is the truth," Matthew vowed. "Count Dahlgren would have surely killed me before we reached port. I was never his servant, I was his unwitting captive. Should I have chopped that rope? No, I should not have. But at the moment... in that storm...after the fight and with my memory back...I lost my balance. And I'm telling you also that Professor Fell is no myth. If you think so, woe to you and woe to England because you're playing directly into his hands. If I were sitting on that bench I would at least have the sense to interview my constables, to verify—"

"*That*," said Judge Archer, in a very quiet voice, "will do."

"Oh no it won't! I'm not done!"

"Yes," still said quietly, "you *are* done. Constable, if the prisoner makes one more offensive and belligerent noise in my courtroom I wish you to strike him across the face." To Lillehorne's expression of dismay, Archer added, "Or you too will find punishment for disobedience."

"You can't stop me from speaking!" Matthew objected.

"I'm sorry," whispered Lillehorne under his breath, and he struck Matthew across the cheek with the flat of his hand.

"You call that a *strike*?" Archer asked. "That was a weak-willed tap."

Matthew stared daggers at the judge. "A court can't stop a man—"

He was hit again, harder.

"—from *speaking*!" Matthew shouted. "You refuse to even con—"

The next blow was much harder still, though delivered with a child-sized fist. "I'm sorry," Lillehorne repeated. "Please... don't—"

"—consider my circumstances!" Matthew continued, his voice ringing from the balcony, from the vaulted ceiling, from the sculpture of the heroic figure commanding the chariot, though now through a haze of pain Matthew thought the figure was not so heroic, it was not grinning so much as it was grinding its teeth trying to hold in check a team of runaways determined to run to freedom or die trying.

"You're a danger, sir!" Matthew exploded. "A small-minded man in a great man's—"

His eyes wide with fear for his own skin, Lillehorne hit Matthew with all the strength he could summon, a fist to the side of the bearded jaw.

Matthew staggered but did not fall. Damned if he would fall in this travesty of a court. His eyes watered a bit but he kept their focus on Archer, who was actually giving this scene a thin smile of approval. "*Position*," Matthew said, finishing his previous statement. He spat blood upon the polished planks. "There," he said. "Is that what you want?"

Lillehorne had cocked his arm back for another punch.

"That will do, Constable," said the judge, and immediately Lillehorne's arm dropped. He turned his back on the bench and walked away a few feet, where he leaned heavily on a railing. He was trembling, and he convulsed as if he were about to spew. "Restrain yourself," Archer told him, in a voice that demanded obedience. "I wish you to hear your instructions." He waited for Lillehorne to compose himself and turn around again. Matthew wiped blood from his lips and thought of a hundred other things he could—and should—hurl at this effigy of a judge, but the time had passed.

Archer folded his hands before him and looked down upon the prisoner. His smile had gone. His face was vacant of all emotion.

"You raise intriguing questions of life and death, of happenstance and responsibility," he said. "I commend you for assembling these observations. That is all I commend you for. The court cannot and will not let you walk away from your actions without penalty, Mr. Corbett, yet research must be done to determine if this crime truly falls under the jurisdiction of the Old Bailey. Does it merit hanging if you're found guilty? Well, that's to be determined at an official hearing, which this is not. In the meantime..."

He tapped his fingers together, and Matthew had the sense that the man was enjoying this way too much.

"In the meantime," Archer said, "the constable will with the necessary caution and the number of guards he deems appropriate... escort you to Newgate Prison, where—"

Lillehorne gave an audible gasp.

"Where," Archer went on, "you will be held in confinement until your case appears officially on the docket, which could be... oh...six months?"

"Your Honor," Lillehorne dared to venture, "may I ask that—"

"You may remain quiet," came the reply, "and do your duty as ordered by a justice of the realm, unofficially speaking or not. The proper documents will be drawn up by day's end. This is what I wish and it shall be done."

"Yes sir," was all that Lillehorne could say.

Matthew was stunned, to say the least. His brain reeled. *Newgate Prison.* The worst of the worst. Six months in that hole of Hell. Probably longer, if Archer could manage it and well he could; he had all the power now, and a bearded and bloody problem-solver from New York had none.

"You may prove yourself useful, Lillehorne," Archer said. "Instead of standing on muddy ground with common criminals, use your means to pressure your office in two worthy areas: finding Madam Candoleri and putting an end to this madman who calls himself Albion. Don't waste the court's time and yours otherwise. That is all."

Without a further word or glance at either of them the arrogant eminence got up from his chair, descended from the bench, and removed himself through the terrifying ebony door.

Even in the depths of his distress, Matthew could not help to note that Archer had taken the *Pin.*

Eleven

"Steady," Lillehorne said, but his weak voice was of no comfort to Matthew, who watched from the coach's barred window as the entrance arch of Newgate drew nearer.

The dark castle of Newgate Prison, made even more gloomy by the chill, rainy weather and the overhanging clouds, stood as the next building to the Old Bailey's Court Of Session House. It was connected to that structure by a flagstone walk between two stone walls. Matthew knew from his reading of the *Gazette* that many thousands had taken the journey along that path, which was referred to as the "dead man's walk" since a high percentage of those who undertook it were destined for the undertaker. It was also called "the Birdcage", for the walkway itself was covered over by a grating of iron bars. Lillehorne had arranged for the coach to drive Matthew and the two attendant guards the short distance into the prison, possibly making a statement that Matthew was not yet convicted and should be treated as such. Matthew thought Lillehorne was not all bad, just as certainly as William Atherton Archer was not all good.

Lillehorne leaned forward toward his charge. The two guards were sitting on either side of Matthew, pinning him in, but their show of strength was not necessary since under the burden of his chains the young man was virtually helpless.

"Listen to me *well*," Lillehorne said, both quietly and pointedly, as the *clip-clopping* of the horses' hooves drew the coach ever nearer to that grim monument to despair. "I am going to speak to the warden on your behalf. That may do some good with him, but you'll be on your own with the other inmates. Needless to say...within Newgate lies another world...and not one that will be kind to you."

"This one has been no Father Christmas."

"The time for witticisms is over and the time for wits beginning. If ever you used your good sense and careful tread, prepare to use them now." Lillehorne's eyes had become small black holes. "I cannot stress to you strongly enough the animal nature of—"

The coach slowed. The coachman hollered "More fuel for the furnace!" There came the sound of an iron portcullis being drawn upward in the medieval fashion, the wooden gears making the noise of a battery of bludgeons hammering flesh.

"The animal nature of this place," Lillehorne continued. "As I say...I'll do what I can for you...but...as I am a fairly new member of the legal establishment here...I hope you realize that my powers of influence are limited."

A whip snapped. The horses picked up their pace. The portcullis was cranked down behind them.

"I'm sorry," said Lillehorne, and he leaned back against the seat of cracked leather, for he had come to his finish.

Matthew nodded. His heart was beating hard, but he knew he had a long haul ahead of himself and it would not pay to lose his senses at this early point. How easy it would be to cry out for mercy, to rail against a seemingly-distant God, against the cold marble of the law and the distressing ignorance of mighty men. How easy... yet such would do him not a candle's wink of good, and it would simply open his soul up to further torment.

The coach began to slow again. They were near stopping, their destination reached.

What swirled in Matthew's mind was a memory. Back in Fount Royal in the Carolina colony in 1699, during the problem of Rachel

Howarth's supposed witchcraft, the true villain in that piece had spent time in Newgate Prison, and now Matthew recalled part of that man's hideous recitation of survival against the unholy predators within those walls.

The days were sufficiently horrible, he'd said, *but then came the nights! Oh, the joyous bliss of darkness! I can feel it even now! Listen! Hear them? Starting to stir? Starting to crawl from their mattresses and stalk the night fantastic? Hear them? The creak of a bedframe here—and one over there, as well! Oh, listen...someone weeps! Someone calls out for God...but it is always the Devil who answers.*

Even if it was so terrible a place, Matthew remembered saying to that near-demonic killer, *you still survived it.*

And his answer: Did I?

The coach's wheel creaked to a stop. One of the horses snorted. Someone else out there gave a muffled shout, a guttural sound.

More fuel for the furnace.

The coach's door on the right hand side was opened from without. Two men wearing dark coats and leather tricorns stood ready to receive the prisoner; both were carrying billyclubs, one of the implements glinting with a coating of pitch spiked with bits of broken glass. Without a word the two guards on either side of Matthew nearly lifted him off his seat and out of the coach onto bare earth that was pebbled with cinders. He stood in a courtyard with high walls of dark, soot-stained stone on all sides. Faces peered from barred windows up to the very top, which must have been four floors. Turrets with conical roofs stood at the corners of the walls. Up in the sky black banners of coalsmoke drifted from massive chimneys that were not part of the prison but were industries of London, yet as Matthew stood getting his bearings he was aware that burning bits of coal flared high above like dying comets, and by the hundreds the cinders of these little deaths rained down upon Newgate.

"In with ya," said the man with the glass-spined billyclub; his voice also was spiny and rough, and Matthew knew at once that a second's disobedience would here be a bloody mistake. He was pushed toward the yawning mouth of what appeared to be a tunnel entrance where a few torches burned against the walls. He obeyed without hesitation. Over the clanking of his chains he heard a harsh bestial rumbling, a sound that seemed to be issuing from both the bowels of the earth and the vaults of the clouds; it was, he realized as he entered the tunnel, the sound of the prison itself, or more specifically the noise of the prisoners as they crowded at barred windows, pushing and shoving or thrashing and fighting to get a look at the arrival of more fuel for the furnace.

"I'll go ahead to speak with the warden," Lillehorne told Matthew as they continued along the tunnel. He raised his voice so all could hear the next statement, which was delivered without addressing any particular person. "I trust your keepers will bear in mind that you are here for safe-keeping and *not* for punishment, as you have yet to be officially heard in the crown's court." Lillehorne's gaze returned to Matthew, and it was no comfort to the young man that Lillehorne appeared terrified and ready to flee this monstrous place at the drop of a cinder. "Good luck to you," he said to Matthew, and then with lowered head he strode away at a rapid pace, turned to the right and was gone from the flickering illumination of the torches.

One of Matthew's four guards gave a short, hard laugh. The man with the mean billyclub said, "Gots to be in this damn place for a *reason*, no matter what that fancy cockadoodle crows!" And then, "Move on, baitfish! I ain't gots all day to be nursin' ya!"

A dozen more hobbling steps and Matthew was guided to the right by the prod of a billyclub, thankfully not the one primed with stickers. A massive, ugly slab of a door with, perversely, the faces of two smiling cherubs carved upon it was opened for him and he shuffled into a cold chamber with pale yellow walls and a floor that looked as if all the stains of London had been gathered in one place. A beak-nosed man in a topcoat, a brown cravat and wearing a wig that was more or less the same color as the walls sat at a desk with a ledger, a double-wicked candle, a supply of quills and an inkpot before him. A small pair of spectacles was balanced on the beak.

"You are Matthew Corbett, so sayeth Mr. Lillehorne?" the man asked without looking up, quill poised over stained paper. "Two 't's, both?"

"Correct." Obviously Lillehorne had passed this way on his errand to see the warden.

"Age?"

"Twenty-four."

"Place of birth?"

"The Massachusetts colony."

That earned only a brief rise of the arched eyebrows. "You are consigned here for holding purposes until your trial date, so sayeth Mr. Lillehorne?"

"Yes." God, it was cold in here! A grimy, wet cold; the cold of the grave.

The man scribbled, and scribbled, and scribbled some more. His writing, what Matthew could see of it, was illegible. "Calculate these figures," the man said abruptly. "Twenty-one plus ten minus four."

"Twenty-seven," Matthew answered almost at once.

"Sound of mind and memory, it appears." The man made a mark next to the scrawl that was the new prisoner's name.

"I try my best."

A billyclub bumped the base of Matthew's spine hard enough to bring from him a gasp of pain.

"You were not being asked a question," said the bewigged master of admittance, with no emotion whatsoever in his voice. "Refrain from speaking unless an answer is required. This prisoner is assigned to…" He paused while he checked some bit of information or another. "Cairo. Mr. Lillehorne has vowed to pay your entrance fee, as well as one month's worth of lodging, food and water."

"An *entrance* fee? You're joking!" Matthew dared to say, and this time the billyclub meant business. Matthew's knees nearly buckled and he had a few seconds in which he feared he couldn't regain his breath.

"Fees are required for all processes." A quick scan was made of Matthew's person. "No value to be had from your clothing. Your shoes, such as they are, have a value in their leather. Remember that if you desire anything extra. You gentlemen are dismissed," he said to the two courthouse guards. And to the others, "Take him away."

Three ordinary words. Combined in this situation, horrific.

In nearly a shocked state of mind Matthew was removed from the admissions area, was taken along a corridor past other various offices and to a narrow iron door that only one human body could pass through at a time. This seemed to Matthew to be the boundary between worlds. The noise of the prison, the slow animalish rumble, was more pronounced here, and absolutely terrifying. As one guard put a billyclub at the back of Matthew's head, the other unlocked the iron door from a ring of ancient-looking keys. Matthew noted there were only four keys on the ring, which likely meant that they were skeleton keys or that the locks in here were not much varied one from the other. He knew from his reading that the first incarnation of this prison had been built in the year 1188, and perhaps the structure had been altered over the centuries but the atmosphere of dread, violence and horror remained constant.

The iron door was pulled open. The hinges shrieked like a chorus of banshees. Through the opening came an incredibly vile odor of dampness, rot, unwashed bodies and something else even more debilitating in its heavy, putrid essence. Matthew thought it might very well be the smell of despair.

"Go through," he was told, and the rest of that sentence could have been *And welcome to Hell.* At his first step he was shoved through, then followed by the guards. More walls of mortared stone stood on either side of the cramped corridor, these walls wet, dripping and blotched with clumps of black and green fungus. Dim gray light entered from a single barred window at least twelve feet above the floor. At the far end of the corridor was a doorway formed of an iron grating, the entrance to a cage, and beyond it Matthew could make out figures watching his progress as he drew nearer. A few weak candles burned in the dankness over there, and voices of all manner whispered and grunted and shouted, laughed with mad merriment or evil intent, rasped like sawblades and gurgled with disease.

"More fuel for the furnace!" someone hollered over there. The cry was taken up by another voice, and another and another, and echoed hollowly along the walled corridor as a macabre greeting to the fresh meat that approached the cage. Only his chains rattled in response.

"*Stop!* Don't move until I say so," the guard with the wicked billyclub hissed in Matthew's ear. Bodies in rags pressed against the grating. Grime-blackened faces stared at Matthew and the guards with watery eyes.

"Give 'em a knock, Baudrey!" said the other man.

The guard referred to slammed his club against the door with furious force and gave an unintelligible yell that yet had the promise of bloodshed in it. The prisoners scattered back like frightened mice. Matthew saw that the metal had been scarred and actually bent inward at several places, indicating that billyclubs found this a suitable knocking place.

"Stay back, ya dogs!" Baudrey shouted. He slid a key into the door's lock, turned it and pulled the door open. No prisoner dared to rush him, though there seemed to be dozens all jammed up together within ten feet of the grate. *"Ira Richards!"* he hollered, ever louder. "Get yer ass up here!"

"Yes sir, yes sir, yes sir," came a weak-lunged voice, and following it was a bent-backed, thin figure that seemed more crab than human being. This individual held a punched-tin lantern with a candle stub burning in it. His flesh appeared the same dingy gray color as his clothes, and he wore no shoes; his hair was shaved to the scalp and his scalp mottled with the red bites of vermin.

"New prisoner," said Baudrey. "Name of Matty Cubitt. He's to go in Cairo."

"Yes sir, yes sir, yes sir."

"Well don't stand there breathin' on me, ya stinkin' mongrel! Take him on!"

Matthew, who felt delirious from the sights, sounds, smells and reality of this nightmare, said, "My name is—"

Baudrey clutched Matthew's throat with a hairy hand and put the billyclub up to the prisoner's lips, threatening to slash flesh at the least provocation. "Yer name," he growled, his sunken eyes devoid of life, "is Sir Shitface, Lord Lay Me, Lady Cockplay or anything I damn say it is. Don't matter to me what ya done or what ya *ain't* done…in here yer allllllll the same fuckin' garbage. *Garbage!*" he shouted at the mass of prisoners, and the crablike Richards scrabbled back as if desperately searching for his hidey-hole. Baudrey pushed Matthew forward, into the guts of Newgate. "Good day to ya, baitfish," he said, and then he slammed the mesh door shut, relocked it, and he and the other guard walked away. The second man slapped Baudrey on the shoulder and gave a noise one might present as appreciation to the most noble champion of law and order.

"This way, Matty," said the crabman, and motioned with his lantern.

"It's Matthew," the prisoner answered, but no one seemed to be listening. Most of the others had begun to drift away from what was perhaps an eating-chamber for there were a number of chairs and long wooden tables in it, but not a speck of food. Unclean hay was scattered about on a floor of damp stones. A few of the prisoners converged around Matthew, plucking at his clothes, his hair and his beard; they spooked Matthew because they were grinning and whispering to him as an ardent suitor might whisper to an object of affection.

"Don't mind them, they're only half here," said Richards. "Come on, get you settled."

Matthew shuffled along after him, and the others let him pass. Within a few seconds it was apparent to the new arrival that Newgate was indeed built in the fashion of a medieval castle, for there was a mazelike corridor that snaked through the guts of the place and archways leading a few steps down into chambers where lived the denizens of these depths. Filthy hay was strewn across the floors. Some of the prisoners lay upon straw-filled bedding of indescribable condition on wooden bedframes, some lay on mattresses on the floor, but most clung to dirty blankets as their only meager succor. Only men were present, the female prisoners being housed elsewhere, and Matthew saw a range of ages from boys of maybe fourteen or fifteen to men past eighty. Everywhere was filth. The deeper Matthew ventured into the prison the worse the conditions seemed to become, as if those furthest away from the outside world had lost the understanding of what it meant to be a civilized human being.

In the corridor, which seemed to have been constructed by a mad architect intent on destroying the prisoners' sense of direction, stone staircases ascended into darkness and descended into deeper darkness. Matthew could barely make out another iron grate of a door at the top of one of the stairs, and the glint of eyes peering through as he passed. This was a huge place with many levels, all of them bad.

By the light of a few candles and the occasional obviously highly-prized lantern, Matthew was presented with a strange array of sights as he followed Ira Richards through the corridor and had time for a look down into the chambers: two men fighting, both of them already bloody and in tatters, as a circle of onlookers savagely urged them on; in the same chamber a group of men sitting together in the hay, several smoking clay pipes, and seemingly calmly holding a discussion as if at the finest teahouse in London; a madman with no legs trying to haul himself around on a little wooden-wheeled cart and hollering the Lord's Prayer at the top of his lungs; a pair of naked men engaged in sexual intercourse while other prisoners idly looked on and what appeared to be a gray, open-mouthed corpse lay sprawled in the hay not two yards distant; another totally nude and nearly skeletal man standing on a wooden box and giving what sounded like a rousing political speech, though no one gave him a scab of attention; an old man huddled up and sobbing in a corner, a young man with a terribly-scarred face absorbed in straddling another prisoner and striking him repeatedly to the bloody, crumpled mouth in the leisurely occupation of fearsome violence; a frail long-haired youngster of perhaps sixteen wearing a pink petticoat and flouncing around the chamber to the shouts and catcalls of his fellows; and other sights that made Matthew feel he had entered not only a different world but a universe of different worlds mashed together, all of them overlapping but none quite conjunctive, and most of them perverse, tragic or simply wicked. Eyes caught sight of Matthew as he passed; some gazes quickly dropped away while others held, with ominous implications.

"Here's your place," said Richards. They had come to the corridor's end. Six steps down, the chamber was the same as the ones they'd passed, just as densely populated and equally dirty if not the worst of the lot. "Cairo, they calls it. Myself, I'm in Cartagena. You'll hear a bell ring for your meal. Four strikes of the bell. Got to warn you, though...sometimes they run out of food by the time they call this section up. And don't try to sneak into another section, everybody knows who belongs where. Them guards'll beat you blind, they catch you at the tables without bein' belled. The inmates'll do you worse."

Matthew had no comment for this. By the looks of the half-starved population, it was not surprising news. "I see some in chains and some without," he said. "You're not wearing chains. Why am I?"

"I paid the chain removal fee," Richards explained. "Pay it every month, God bless my lovin' sister. Oh...another thing...don't try to take nobody's blanket unless they're dead. Same with the beddin'. Even then, you'll have to fight for it. Well...I brought you here, my duty's done."

With that pronouncement, the crabman turned away, took his lantern along the corridor and scrabbled off at his painful-looking gait.

Matthew descended the steps and thought crazily *in for a penny, in for a pound.* What he thought might happen did not; he was not rushed upon by the other inmates seeking to tear him to pieces. In fact a few looked at him and then looked away again, a few more seemed to be talking about his arrival behind hands that shielded their mouths, and no one stirred themselves from their blankets, their plots of hay or their mattresses. Over in the far corner a card game was going on, with five or six players and a dozen or more onlookers, and that likely had much to do with the pallid reception. But Matthew was in this case glad of pallidity. He wished to make no impression, just to be left alone. He needed time to think, to get his senses in order…and now the next problem was, where to find a resting place among all these bodies.

As he crossed the chamber in search of a space of hay long enough for himself, he noted that not only did some wear chains and others not, but not all wore shoes. A few prisoners were completely nude. Again, a wide range of ages was represented and a wide range of states of health, it appeared, though to call anyone in this chill and fetid clime healthy was stretching the bounds of sanity. A few thin and wasted figures looked to be on the edge of receiving their otherworldly rewards; if they were to receive punishments in the afterlife, Matthew thought that even God would have lost His equilibrium.

"Move on!" said a voice as raggedy as the man who owned it, speaking from his threadbare blanket on the floor. Matthew did so, and in his journey across the chamber discovered something he recalled hearing from that unfortunate but wicked individual he'd uncovered in Fount Royal: a channel in the floor moving raw sewage along from a pipe that ran down the far wall to a hole in the opposite wall, and needless to say no one had encamped around that. Neither did Matthew. In his next faltering step he accidentally trod upon one of the prisoners who appeared to be near death. The poor gent let out a harsh rattle of pain but no one paid any attention and the noise of the players at the card game didn't falter for an instant.

"Over here, young man!" An emaciated, white-bearded prisoner with dirty fingernails three inches long was motioning to him from his own mattress. "Over here, there's a place for you beside me!"

By the various low lights Matthew saw that indeed there was, though it was right up against a fungus-streaked wall. Today Matthew realized he was the most beggardly of the lot, and though the prisoner looked less than trustworthy he couldn't turn this down. He started toward the man, his chains as heavy as London's sins.

Someone stood up in his path. This man was short, had been probably stocky before he was starved thin, had a shaved head and also was in chains.

"Don't go over there," the man cautioned. "Old Victory bites."

"Um...Old Victory?"

"Was a musketeer at the Battle of Dunbar, to hear him tell it. As I say, don't go over there. He'll be on you like the plague. Take a chunk out of you, even if you ain't a Scotsman."

"Thank you." Matthew saw that Old Victory had already decided the new prisoner was not worth chewing on, because he'd settled back down on his mattress and was busy at intently counting on all eight of his fingers. "I'm new here," Matthew said, dazedly. "I don't know what's what."

"Takes some gettin' used to. Got to be careful while you do. You're wearin' your chains by choice?"

"No money for the fee."

"Ha! I wouldn't pay it if I had it. A few others in here still wearin' 'em, it ain't so bad after awhile." He looked Matthew up and down before he spoke again. "Name's Winn Wyler. Bargeman by trade."

"Matthew Corbett. I am—was—a..." It seemed ridiculous to talk about problem-solving in a place like this. Death was the only solution to the problems here, and Matthew figured that when one of these prisoners died he was rewarded with a moldy winding sheet, a muddy hole, and a wish of good riddance. "I was a magistrate's clerk in the New York colony," he said.

"Damn, you're a long way from there! Took a hell of a fall, you must've!"

"I fear I haven't landed yet."

"Well spoken." And no sooner had those words left Wyler's lips that he coughed once, then again, a third time more violently, a fourth time and a fifth more violently still, and after the sixth he wiped dark threads of blood from his mouth with a corrupted sleeve and drew in air with a bubbling sound. "Beg pardon," he croaked. "Get my wind back…shitty thing…dyin' in here."

"I'm sorry to hear that."

"Why? You ain't done nothin' to cause it. Hey, Gimlet! Move your ass a little ways and let Matthew Corbett have a space! Danley, you too! Hell, you're takin' up enough room for a fat man's pride! Come on, the both of you show some…some…" He looked at Matthew for help, because he couldn't find the word.

"Fellowship," Matthew offered.

"Yep, that's it. I knew you was a smart one, bein' a law clerk. Go on and move, the both of you! We're fellowshippin' today!"

The man Wyler had referred to as Danley was completely nude, as thin as a whistle and dark with scabs, but there were worse in here. And worse to come; when Matthew inquired about the proximity of water he was pointed toward an open barrel with an attached cup and chain, but there was so much scum on the water's surface and such an evil odor rising from it that he lost his thirst.

"That's all right," said Wyler knowingly. "We was all like that. You'll drink when you get thirsty enough. And waitin' won't help, they don't change the water out but ever' month."

Matthew settled himself in the hay. He realized he was elbow-to-elbow with a naked man covered with scabs and about six feet away from a stream of slowly moving human refuse. Danley turned on his side and slept, but Wyler and Gimlet—a pale small man with bright green eyes that still held the spark of intelligence—wanted to talk. Wyler was in for his debts, being hurt in a fall and unable to work his trade; he had been here for four months. Gimlet proudly announced himself as a professional thief and said he had been here for nearly a year. Wyler helpfully explained that the chambers in this part of Newgate were called Cartagena, Budapest, Helsinki and Cairo, the last being the worst and furthest from the eating room. There were some in here, Matthew was told, been in Newgate ten, twelve, fifteen years. Like Old Victory over there. Likely to die here, Wyler said. Look at us poor sufferin' lot, he said. We're all likely to—

He was interrupted by a figure standing over Matthew.

"Your shoes," said the man, in a low and menacing voice. "Give 'em here."

Matthew looked up into a fearsome face. The man had a wide chin bearded over with gray-shot black, a low slab of a forehead, narrow eyes under heavy black brows, and half a nose. The other half had been lost to either sword, dagger or razor, and exposed as if in a scientific display was the nasal passage and the brown, hardened tissues. Though thin, this man had the broad shoulders and large hands of a brawler, and neither did he bear the burden of chains. Matthew saw that he held cards in one of those hands; the man had run out of money in his game, and he was looking for replenishment.

"Shoes," the man said. "You want me to take 'em off for ya? Want me to break yer fuckin' legs while I'm at it?"

"Jerrigan," said Wyler, "have a heart. This fella just—"

"You want to give me yours, then?" A taut silence told the story. "Thought not. So shut yer damn hole."

Matthew saw that the card players were all watching, and so was everyone else who wasn't sick or dying. He understood; this was a test of the mettle of the new fuel for the furnace.

"I'd like to help you," Matthew said, "but I'm afraid I—"

He didn't finish. The fist that came down and hit him across the jaw like a flying anvil knocked him senseless.

The next thing he knew he was struggling to a sitting position with blood in his mouth and what felt like two or three loose teeth, a roaring in his head, a watery redness to his vision, and no shoes on his feet.

"Bad luck, that," said Wyler, with a shrug. "Turk Jerrigan used to hire himself out as a pair a' fists, 'fore he murdered his mother. You don't want to get on his bad side."

Matthew spat crimson for the second time today. His jaw felt as if it was hanging off his face. He shook his head to try to clear it, heard hard laughter and saw Jerrigan and a few of the others looking at him and grinning with absolutely no humor. Then they went back to their game. Matthew realized he had just been marked as a weakling unable to defend himself, and open to whoever else in this cattle corral decided they wanted something from him...and he didn't have much left to offer, that being the central problem.

"Enjoy the day while you can," said Wyler, as if reading Matthew's thoughts.

Matthew could hardly speak, his jaw was so sore. "I don't think there's much enjoyment to be had in here."

"You'll see," Wyler said, with an expression of prison wisdom. "Night comes mighty early in here."

That was just what disturbed Matthew the most. The new fuel, held in chains, weak to this world of predators…nowhere to hide, nowhere to run to, every man for himself.

And night, indeed, was coming.

Twelve

Sleep was impossible. He'd known it would be. In his room at the Curryford Inn on the edge of the little town of Hobb's Square, Hudson Greathouse sat in a chair by a rain-streaked window. The time was near half-past one, the candle was a stub, the rain was still falling but…a good thing…his bottle of stout ale still had about two cups' worth in it, and he was determined not to waste a drop.

He poured himself a fresh drink. Did the rain thrash a bit harder against the glass, or was it his imagination? He wondered if Berry, in the next room along the corridor, was finding it easy to sleep. He doubted it; she was as much on edge as himself. They were still over a hundred miles from London, the road to that city—such as it was—had become a quagmire in this miserable weather, and to cap the pleasantries this afternoon the rear right wheel of their coach had snapped off its axle and he and Berry had had to walk nearly a mile to this inn. Their trunks had been of necessity left with the coach, and the coachman left to negotiate a solution to the problem, which meant leaving the second driver—armed with a sword and a blunderbuss—to guard the goods while the first man trekked into the hamlet of Hobb's Square to find a new wheel or have one made. Hudson and Berry had been told they might get back on the road within a few days, depending on the talents of the local wheelwright. In the meantime—tomorrow, which was today—a wagon would be secured to deliver their trunks to the inn, so at least they could have a change of clothes.

Thinking about it, Hudson wanted to dash his ale bottle against the wall, cry havoc and let slip the dogs of war. There was no telling when they'd reach London, and just last night when they'd been eating their dinner at a tavern in the village of Chomfrey, Berry had expressed her feeling that Matthew was in terrible danger, and that she feared beyond fear that when they found him it would be too late.

"We either find him or not," Hudson had said, pausing in his delectation of a kidney pie. "What do you mean, 'too late'? As in, he'll be hanged for murder by the time we get there? No, they'll put him in some gaol for awhile. He'll have to be tried by the crown's court. Anyway, there are so many to be hanged before Matthew gets the noose, it'll be summer before—"

"You're not helping," she'd said, and she pushed her bowl of parsnip soup aside.

"Sorry. What I mean to say is, he's a big boy. You know he can take care of himself. We'll find him and we'll clear all this up, don't worry. And if you don't want that soup, pass it over here."

"It's the gaol part I'm most worried about. What if they...what if they put him somewhere dreadful? I'd imagine that all gaols there are dreadful...but I'm sure some are worse than others."

Hudson had taken a drink of his mulled wine, listened to the wood popping in the hearth for a few seconds while he formulated his reply, and then said, "You heard what Moncroff told us. Matthew's gotten himself sent to London so he can find Gardner Lillehorne. God help London, but Lillehorne can surely help Matthew." He flashed her a quick smile but she was too disturbed to return it. "Anyway, it'll serve him well that Lillehorne knows Matthew's history."

"You think *that* will serve him well?"

"Lillehorne may be a...excuse the word...*shit*, but he won't let Matthew flounder. If he's got any kind of pull at all there by now, he'll speak a good word."

Berry had been quiet for awhile, also staring into the crackling flames. Then she'd returned her calm gaze to Hudson but he immediately saw that it was a thin disguise, that she was holding herself together with pins and needles just as he was.

"What I fear," she told him, "is that without me...someday he's going to run out of luck. I just hope it doesn't happen before we find him."

Now, in his room at the Curryford with rain striking harder at the window and the chances of their reaching London anytime soon diminishing by the wet and muddy hour, Hudson knocked back his last cup of ale and considered Berry's statement about luck.

Though Lillehorne might hold a grudge for past grievances, imaginary or not, surely he would be a helping hand to Matthew. Lillehorne was a bumbling blowhard, but he wasn't *evil.* Yet Lillehorne had not been in his position long enough to have much clout, politically speaking, so that was anyone's guess. Where might they put a man accused of murder on the high seas? A holding cell, of course. Better that than...

No, they wouldn't put him in Newgate. Perish that thought, stab it and kill it. There were other gaols, none of them gentle, but surely not Newgate. Lillehorne wouldn't let that happen.

Hudson understood what Berry had meant about finding Matthew when it was too late.

The gaolhouses of London could kill a man in a very short time. Not necessarily a physical death—there was that danger too—but a death of the spirit and soul. He had known several who'd gone into that system on minor offenses and ended up so changed they were from then on worthless to the outside world.

That couldn't happen to Matthew. He was too strong to be broken that easily.

Wasn't he?

Hudson suddenly wanted to scream. He found the ale bottle in his hand and his arm cocked back to smash the bottle against the wall...but he took a long breath and quietly set the bottle down upon the table again, because it wouldn't do to disturb Berry on the other side of that wall.

There was nothing to be done but wait.

And hope, as Berry did, that Matthew continued to be a very lucky young man.

⁂

Because he could not sleep for all the coughing, muttering and moaning that came up from the denizens of this dark realm… because he did not *wish* to sleep, since this was his first night in Newgate and he had been marked as a weakling, Matthew knew when they were coming.

He did not hear them so much as feel their presence. It had occurred to him that at night prisoners from other chambers would be on the prowl, and the only reason they needed for violence was their own history, their own torments and unnamable sins that gnawed at them and found release only in the fist or the stranglehold or the rape. They were coming, and he felt them gathering in the dark around him as the stormclouds had gathered around the *Wanderer.*

He sat up in the hay. His chains rattled; it was a common sound, many chains rattled as someone moved. His eyes were not used to this darkness, but he reasoned that theirs were. He heard harsh breathing, very close to him. Not the bubbly breathing of Wyler, not Gimlet's breath nor Danley's shallow sips of air. This breathing was from lungs heated by passion…either the passion to kill, or the passion to dominate in the worst possible way.

How many of them? Three? Four? Yes, that many. He had no idea if Jerrigan was part of the group, for he realized that his parade through the different chambers today had likely caused all manner of predators to sniff his scent. Whoever they were, they were moving nearer…and now someone was stepped on in the close confines, and this prisoner gave a ragged howl of pain that sounded like a wild dog…and Matthew started to stand up to defend himself as best he could but the chains prevented quick movement, and—

Then they were upon him.

An arm locked around his throat. He was pulled up by several hands. His cry was a strangled bleat, his thrashing of no consequence. The offended prisoner was still howling and now the place exploded with noise, shouts and curses in a mélange of rough voices. Matthew tried to get his legs around anything to stop his progress as he was dragged across the hay and across other bodies but the chains around his ankles would not allow it. A fist drove into his midsection and burst the breath out of him. A hand clamped around his mouth and another gripped his hair. He was lifted off his feet like a gunnysack, and one of them said in what was nearly an inhuman grunt of triumph, "We gots 'im, we gots 'im!"

Still Matthew thrashed, and he would not give up. A hand slapped him across the face. Another hand gripped his still-sore jaw like a blacksmith's vise. "Easy, be easy," a voice curled into his right ear. At the same time a fist punched him in the back and another set of hands began to pull his trousers off. It seemed to Matthew in that moment a ridiculous thing, that some of these creatures wished to kill and some wished to rape. Either way, it would not go well for him.

He tried to fight. It was going to be a losing battle. He was aware that several of the other prisoners had used their tinderboxes to flame their precious tapers and were holding lights toward the scene of Matthew's impending ruin. He got an arm loose and, chains or not, threw an elbow that struck a bearded jaw and brought a hiss of pain. This action earned him a meeting with the wall, as he was flung against it so hard his bones were nearly shattered. In the candlelight the chamber was a world of moving shadows. A hand grasped Matthew by the hair again and a mouth with cracked lips pressed against his ear. "Easy, easy," it whispered, and someone laughed like a storm of stones.

His trousers were down around his hips. An arm snaked around his belly. A fist belted him across the back of the neck. His senses were going, everything was a blur and a roar. He was pressed down into the hay on his knees, a painful position to his spine because of the chains. A weight got on his back, increasing the pain. This man was thrown off by another, who took his place. Matthew tried desperately to rise up but it was hopeless, and the man astride him laughed and began to cuff him across the shoulders and back of the head, seemingly just for the fun of it.

Quite suddenly, all noise ceased.

There was an intake of breath, the sound from many lungs.

The weight left Matthew. A hand in his hair released its hold.

The silence lingered.

With great effort Matthew got himself turned around, his own breath rasping and sweat on his face. His assailants stood in a circle with him at the center, none of them moving.

The candlelight caught gold and made it gleam.

A new arrival had descended the stairs and entered the chamber.

This figure wore a black cloak, a black hood and a pair of sleek black leather gloves. Where its face should be was a golden mask. The features were serene. There was a small golden beard carved into the material which was certainly not real gold, Matthew realized even in his distress, but some painted material. It resembled the depiction of a Roman god come to earth, the eyeholes taking in this sorry world as the human kind had shaped it.

The figure also held a saber that shone with reflected light. It was aimed in the direction of the four men who'd attacked Matthew.

The prisoners in the chamber had moved away from this figure as surely as night retreats from day. They had given him all their space and were crowded together like rats. Candles trembled in the hands that held them.

When the figure advanced a single step, the villainous quartet around Matthew retreated. Matthew looked at them and recognized only one: the scar-faced young man who'd been so absorbed in dealing out violence the day before. Now his face was contorted not just by the terrible scarring, but by dread of the nightwalking figure that somehow had gotten past all the doors and locks into Newgate Prison.

A phantom, Matthew thought. But no…he realized he was looking at Albion.

The figure stood motionless for a few seconds. Then, with slow and regal purpose, it pointed the saber's tip at Matthew Corbett.

With this motion, the four men scrabbled as far away from their would-be victim as Newgate's walls would permit.

Albion's gloved left hand rose up, gripped the air, became a fist, and pressed against the center of its chest.

The message was clear.

That one is mine.

Albion held the position for a few seconds more. The golden mask of an ancient god seemed to be regarding Matthew, the head slightly cocked at an angle. Then the figure, still holding the saber out at full length, began to back away. It ascended the steps with a swordsman's sure-footed grace. Under the archway it hesitated. The masked face scanned the stunned assembly, as if daring anyone to follow. No one moved. Albion stepped back further, out of range of the candlelight. The last glimpse of it had been a faint shadow sliding across a wall. Then gone.

For a long time it seemed that no one in Cairo could breathe.

"Blimey!" said someone, breaking the silence.

Two of the most daring, or foolhardy, prisoners entered the corridor with a lantern in the wake of Albion's exit but they certainly did not rush. The four assailants had backed against the wall. Matthew got painfully to his feet and pulled his trousers up where they ought to be. When he caught the eye of the scarred young man this prisoner averted his gaze, his vicious impulses quelled at least for the moment.

"Blimey!" the same fellow repeated.

"Y'know who that was!" a bug-eyed prisoner said, speaking to all. "I mean to say, *what* it was! Albion, come right into Newgate like a bleedin' ghost! God knock my eyeballs out if I ain't seen what I seed!"

Matthew was still jangled by these incidents and his brain was fogged, but even so he reasoned that copies of the *Pin* got in here on a regular basis, if one could afford the fees. He staggered and caught himself by grasping a bit of hairlike fungus hanging from the wall. His reserves of strength were almost gone.

"Albion, standin' right here in Newgate!" The bug-eyes found Matthew. "I know what he was sayin' to you, too! Come to tell you that when you get out of here, he's gonna kill you like he done them others got out their cages!" This brought a rumble of assent.

"You're wrong!" Winn Wyler spoke up. "Albion was givin' a warnin' not to do him no harm!" This opinion also brought an assenting rumble. "Think you oughta take that to heart!" he said to the four assailants, at least one of whom belonged to the mob in Helsinki and appeared very uncertain about whether he wanted to return there by the same corridor Albion had disappeared into.

"He was sayin' he's gonna kill the fella, if that one ever gets out!" came the adamant response.

"I saw it as a warnin' to every man here!" said Wyler. "Why the Devil would Albion slip into Newgate to say he was gonna kill somebody on the outside? He don't know even know if the boy's ever gonna get out!"

"He knows, all right!" said a gray-bearded wretch who held a candle. "Albion ain't human...he knows ever'thin'! Gonna slice that fella's throat or run 'im through, soon as Newgate spits him clear!"

There was agreement to this by others and it was met by forceful denials by those who saw the incident as Wyler had. As Matthew clung to both his consciousness and his sanity, he thought the chamber was going to soon erupt into an epic shouting match between the tribes of differing opinion. All Matthew was concerned with for the moment was that he was alive and relatively unharmed, and the four nasty villains had begun to slink away from him as if seeking to hide their faces in the darkest corner.

The men who'd gone into the winding corridor returned, along with five others from the nearest chamber. "Ain't nobody there," said the man who held the lantern. "They heard the noise over in 'Sinki...but they ain't seen nobody pass through."

"Albion's a fuckin' spirit!" someone else in the chamber said. "You ain't gonna catch that one!"

"He may be a spirit," replied a man who had taken a moment to pack his pipe and light it from a candle's flame, "but his sword's real enough. Killed how many, Simms?"

"Six so far," croaked the prisoner who Matthew figured was able to procure the *Pin* from the outside, and from him it was passed around to the others. "Seven, when this poor soul gets out."

"That ain't what Albion was *meanin'*!" Wyler insisted, with a measure of annoyance. He looked for someone in the throng and found him pressed up against a wall trying to pretend to be just another formless shadow. "Jerrigan! You got some sense! What d'*you* say?"

The half-nosed mother-murderer said nothing. Others were looking to him expectantly. Matthew figured the man—whatever he otherwise might be—held some clout among this tribe. It was a moment before Jerrigan responded at all, and when he did he came toward Matthew with his head lowered, as if in deep thought.

He stopped before Matthew and held out the pair of shoes that were amongst his winnings from the card game. "Take 'em, they're yours," he said. "I'm clean with you." And then to Wyler and the rest of the room: "I dunno what Albion was sayin' exactly, but I know I don't want no part of it. I ain't gettin' a blade 'cross my neck in the middle of the night, nossir!" His fear-struck eyes returned to

Matthew, who reached out and retrieved his shoes. "We're clean, ain't we?" Jerrigan asked in the manner of a small child needing reassurance. "Say we're clean."

"We're clean," Matthew answered, in a croak that was even more froggish than Simms's.

"*Clean*, we are!" Jerrigan hollered it toward the corridor, just in case the golden-masked phantom had not heard distinctly. "Turk Jerrigan's mindin' his own bloody business, ain't causin' nobody no trouble!"

"Good to hear," Matthew said, his ears ringing in addition to all his other pains.

To complete his absolutions, Jerrigan clapped Matthew on the shoulder as if they were as close as bread torn from the same loaf. Matthew thought for an instant that Jerrigan was going to hug him, with one eye on the corridor, but then the brawler turned toward the four offenders. "You lot!" he snarled. "Shame on all your heads, and 'specially yours, Jonah Falkner! You with a wife and three children out there!"

"Two wives and five children," Jonah Falkner corrected, contritely.

"Ahhhhh, the Devil with all of ya!" Jerrigan waved a disgusted hand at the group, which was the cue for the scar-faced young man and another thin brute to make their way across the chamber, up the steps and out, while Falkner and the fourth offender settled down on their bedding.

"Let me help ya," said Old Victory, appearing suddenly beside Matthew and perversely licking his lips, but Matthew had the sense and strength enough to decline. With shoes in hand he made his unsteady path back to his own piece of hay. A couple of the others went to pains to help him along, and they too cast fearful glances at the corridor.

But if Albion still lurked there, he did not reappear.

Sleep for this night was impossible. Matthew put his shoes on as if he were actually going somewhere, but at least they were a link to the outside world. The talking back and forth continued on with no sense of time, as time was meaningless here anyway except for the burning down of the candles.

"I still say Albion's markin' him!" said the bug-eyed prisoner, whose name Matthew had not caught.

"Markin' him for protection from the likes of in here!" Wyler fired back. He turned his attention to Matthew, who with bruised throat, sore jaw and rattled bones felt as if he might pass out at any minute, yet the vision of Albion was still sharp in his mind. Wyler kept his voice low when he asked, "What'd you do to stir Albion up?"

"I have no idea."

"The whole prison'll know about this by first light. Maybe it'll help us get some damned food." Their section had been skipped for the evening gruel, as the pots had gone empty. Wyler's face lightened. "We might be what they call celebatories."

"Celebrities," Matthew corrected. His gaze kept sliding toward the corridor, for in the dim light of the few candles the prisoners feared to blow out he continued to imagine he saw furtive movement there.

"Yeah, that. Well…to tell you the truth I don't know if you've got a friend or an enemy in Albion, but ride the horse while it's saddled."

Matthew nodded. The entire episode was beginning to seem more and more like a dream within a nightmare. What indeed had he done to stir Albion up? And for that matter, how had he become of interest to Albion, since he'd only been in London a few days and all that time in gaol? And the central question: who was Albion and what the hell was he *about*? Not to mention the fact that getting in and out of Newgate Prison was no easy trick, even for a phantom.

"Lord, what a thought I just had!" said Wyler, his excitement further heightened. "We might make mention in the *Pin* for this!" Then he lay down on his mattress and stared up at the cracked stones far above his head, as the voices quietened to muttering. Two of the candles reached their end and hissed out. Wyler had a coughing fit, spat up blood and looked at the streamers of it on his hand, then he licked the blood away as if unwilling to give any part of himself up to the crushing confines of Newgate.

Matthew lay on his side in the hay. He realized that if he thought too much about what had happened since he'd left New York for that damned Sword of Damocles ball in Charles Town he might lose what was left of his diminished sanity. The Herrald Agency… Berry…Hudson…all his friends in New York…everything he'd gone through and survived, to wind up here in a sorry bedding of stinking hay with a shrunken belly and a golden-masked maniac pointing a saber at him and making some kind of demonstration of either friendship or enmity. It boggled the mind, which was already double-boggled.

For a terrible moment he thought he might be reduced to tears, and where would that put him here, among this den of criminals?

Six months in this place? How could he stand another *day*?

He heard sobbing. At first he thought it was himself, and so alarmed was he about this breakdown of willpower that he brought his knees up higher so he could press both hands to his mouth.

But it was not him, he realized in another moment. It was some other inmate across the chamber, someone who likely had a family outside these walls and who for one unfortunate reason or another had been sentenced to this perdition for more years than were left in his life.

Still, Matthew kept his hands pressed hard to his mouth, just in case.

THIRTEEN

"MATTHEW *Corbett! Get yer ass up here!*"

The brassy holler had come from the guard Baudrey, who stood under the archway with his leather tricorn tilted rakishly on his head and the glass-spiked billyclub resting against one shoulder. Behind him stood a second guard, a lean whip of a man Matthew hadn't seen in his three days of confinement in Newgate.

"That one calls, you'd best move quick," Wyler advised, and so Matthew hauled himself up in the chains that seemed ever heavier, or perhaps it was just because his diet consisted of one bowl of brown gruel and a piece of cornbread per day. An added bit of nutrition, however, were the scores of weevils in the cornbread; Wyler said he thought those were better than the bread, and Matthew had to agree with him. Matthew had tried the water, had thrown it all up, tried it again from sheer thirst, and now had no telling what swimming in his internals.

"Hurry it up there, baitfish! You're agin' me!"

Matthew went up the steps to where the two men waited. He was aware of being watched; it had been rare in the last two days, since the incident with Albion, for him not to be watched, or spoken about in whispers by the other prisoners. No one knew quite what to make of Albion's visit, and by now word had circulated throughout Newgate though neither Baudrey nor any of the other guards had mentioned it to Matthew; it appeared that the officials had taken the route of willful ignorance.

"Move on!" Baudrey gave Matthew a shove, which was not unexpected. Matthew shuffled along the circuitous corridor, passing the archway into Budapest. They came to a staircase leading up to a door of grated iron. "Halt," said Baudrey, and Matthew obeyed.

A ring of keys made a metallic, almost musical noise, though music of the rudest sense. "The things they have me do 'round here," Baudrey complained, as he slid a key into the cufflock. The cuffs fell away. "I ain't bendin' for no piece a' garbage like this 'un," he said, and he gave the keys to the other guard. "You do the honors."

The second man muttered his own complaint, but nevertheless he bent to unlock Matthew's ankle shackles. Then the chains were off and the second guard put them over his shoulder while Matthew stood rubbing his raw wrists.

"Your fee's been paid," Baudrey said. "Mind you don't do somethin' that warrants 'em on again."

"Paid?" Matthew felt as if his brain was becoming as useless in here as a brick of soap. "Who paid it?"

"Up them stairs." Baudrey pushed Matthew's shoulder with the wicked billyclub. He took the keys from the other guard, followed Matthew to the top and unlocked the grated door. "In with you," he said, but this time he didn't give the shove. He aimed an evil eye at Matthew, whose gait was still that of a shackled man, and then he closed the door and locked it between Matthew and himself. "The things they have me do," he repeated, and then he shook his head, turned round, and he and his companion descended the stairs again.

"Mr. Corbett." It was a quiet voice, the name spoken with respect.

Matthew turned to his left. In a corridor similar to the one on the lower level stood a man with a high mane of curly dark brown hair that may or may not have been a wig, it was difficult to tell. He wore a wine-red dressing gown imprinted with a pattern of small gold paisleys. "My name is Daniel Defoe," he said. "May I have the pleasure of your company?"

"Well…"

"I promise you no harm. My quarters are just along the corridor. Shall we?"

Matthew took Defoe's measure. He was a tall man, but slight, possibly in his early to mid forties. He had a long narrow face, a nose equally long and narrow, and intelligent dark brown eyes that were examining Matthew with the same interest. He was clean-shaven and appeared to be in relatively good health for this place that so easily destroyed the health.

"You'll pardon me," Matthew said, "if I ask what this is about?"

Defoe offered the merest hint of a smile, which seemed awkward on a face constructed for only the most serious of expressions. "The human condition," he said. A couple of other prisoners, both of them very well-dressed and clean compared to the rabble below, were peering from open doors made of wood instead of bars or grated iron. One of them removed from his mouth the pipe he was smoking and called out, "Is he the one, Daniel?"

"Yes, he's the one. Please, Mr. Corbett…come along, we can have some privacy." He motioned to his left.

Matthew's curiosity was inflamed. He had always thought such would be his undoing but for the moment it had to be satisfied. He followed Defoe to an open door just past the others, was motioned in, and found himself in a room that—if not quite the equal to New York's Dock House Inn—was certainly a royal palace compared to Cairo. The man had a writing desk with a leather chair, a second leather chair for visitors, a small round table beside the chair, and an actual bed with real bedding and pillows. On the floor was not dirty hay but a dark red rug. Atop a dresser was a burning candle clock, a waterbowl and a handmirror. A small shelf held a dozen books. To top this veritable paradise was a window allowing in gray morning light and overlooking the courtyard his coach had entered that first day. Through it he could see the slowly moving banners of black coalsmoke that somehow reminded him of the tentacles of Professor Fell's octopus symbol, but it was a window an imprisoned king would kill for. It mattered not that the stone walls of Defoe's private cell were damp and streaked with fungus and the cell itself was quite chilly; one could survive here in relative comfort.

Matthew was further surprised when Defoe produced a key from his clothing and locked the door. “Privacy assured,” the man said. “Please sit down. Ah, I expect you'd like a cup of clean water? I say *clean*, but let's remember where we are.”

Matthew sat down. My God, he'd nearly forgotten what a comfortable chair felt like! It was almost too much for him, he nearly had to stand up again to get his equilibrium.

Defoe poured water from a bottle into a wooden cup and offered it to his guest. “I wish it were a nice claret, but that must wait for another time.” He took the other chair at the writing desk. “We have ninety minutes, by the candle clock. I asked for two hours, was offered one, and I had to negotiate further, with some success. Now,” he said, as his eyes took even more of an intensity that Matthew took as a true need for knowledge, “tell me about yourself.”

Matthew drained the cup. The water, obviously from a well beyond the prison walls, was not quite clear but not at all scummy nor did it smell like it had been strained through a dead horse, as did the liquid in Cairo's communal barrel. “Ahhhh, that's good!”

“More, then?”

“In a moment. I never realized plain water could make one tipsy.” He put the cup aside and cast his gaze again around the fabulous quarters. “I'm assuming you paid my chain removal fee?”

“I did. I inquired as to whether you wore chains and I was told you did. I have a little money to spare. I believe it was for a good cause.”

“My most grateful appreciation, sir. But…tell me…what is all this? I mean…this is—”

“Unexpected?” Defoe's brows went up. “Of course. You know by now that the part of Newgate not run by prisoners is commanded by the most venal of officials. Those inmates who can afford to buy a little space, a little privacy, a little…shall we say…*civility* in here, are allowed—*encouraged*—to do so. Now, I am far from being rich but I have wealthy friends. Unfortunately not wealthy enough to pay the debt of my sentence for sedition against the crown, but I am able to be comfortable here, as much as possible.”

“What's your occupation?”

"Writer. Traveller. *Thinker.* Philosopher upon the balance of good and evil in this world. Such does not allow me to bask in the glory of gold, but I am satisfied with my position. Now...*you.* I wish to know your history, why you are here, and consequently why Albion chose to visit you in Newgate Prison, something that I believe has never happened before."

"Oh," said Matthew, with a frown. "That."

"Of course, *that.* Oh, how Lord Puffery would love to get hold of this tidbit!"

"Lord Puffery," Matthew repeated. "By name Samuel Luther, printer?"

"I've never met him nor do I know anyone who has." Defoe placed the tips of his long fingers together. "It wouldn't surprise me for this item to appear in the next *Pin.* I'm sure someone from the prison has already sold it to Lord Puffery and it will be embellished beyond all belief. Though I have to say, Albion's appearance in this formidable pile of stones needs no embellishment to be utterly fantastic. He was there for only a moment, I understand? He pointed his sword at you and made a motion of threat?"

"Some say threat. Some say he was offering protection from... you know...the others."

"His method so far," said Defoe, "is to murder ex-prisoners released from gaol. Six so far. All men of low repute, but delivered from their sentences by able and cunning lawyers." Again, he gave just the slightest hint of a smile. "Do you have an able and cunning lawyer, Matthew?"

"Absolutely not. The only friend I have in London is a man who despised me in New York."

"New York? We have time and there's a story here. Tell it."

Where to begin? Matthew asked himself. The beginning, of course.

As Matthew told his story, starting with his position as clerk to Magistrate Isaac Woodward, God rest his soul, the light that came through the window moved. Constant stayed the coalsmoke banners, spitting fiery bits down upon the already-seething city. The noise of London was a low hum, punctuated by the sound of horse hooves and carriage wheels beyond Newgate's portcullis. Matthew left nothing out of his tale of the Queen of Bedlam, nor did he refrain from telling Defoe about Mrs. Sutch's sausages in the recitation of his search for Tyranthus Slaughter. With words he painted a picture of Pendulum Island and the lair of Professor Fell, and then he dredged up the sorry story of the trip to Charles Town that was supposed to be so easy a task and ended with the loss of his memory, the murder of Quinn Tate and his falling into the clutches of Count Dahlgren. A summary of what had happened aboard the *Wanderer*, a truthful admission that he really had committed an execution, the rather bitter recounting of his experience with Judge William Atherton Archer, and he had come to the present moment.

The light had dimmed. Clouds had thickened above the coalsmoke and beyond the bars the rain was coming down again in sheets. The noise of it for the time being muffled London's heavy heartbeat.

"May I have another cup of water?" Matthew asked, for Daniel Defoe seemed to be transfixed; the man's mouth was partway open, and he looked to be as dazed as Matthew had been upon being thrown into the gaolhouse at Plymouth.

"Oh...yes, of course. Better still, help yourself." He watched as Matthew poured water from the bottle. "You've been a very busy young man," he said. "How old are you?"

"Twenty-four, but lately I've felt forty-two."

"Forty-two is nearly my age," said the writer. "I am just past it. Appreciate your youth and vigor. Your tale...the story of your life... is amazing, Matthew. Of course I've heard of the Herrald Agency, though I've never had need of their services. And Professor Fell...I also have heard that name, but I thought him a myth, something to scare the children with when they misbehave."

"He's the most real myth I've ever met. Interesting...Archer also considers Fell a myth. I'd think that in the course of his career he might have been charged to give trial to someone in Fell's circle."

"Judges are first and foremost people. Sometimes they don't wish to see the truth, particularly if they can't do anything to change it. I just hope my own situation changes for the better. I had the misfortune of being brought before Judge Salathiel Lovell, who is cut from even sterner and more unreasonable cloth than Archer. Well...here we are, islands to ourselves, and shipwrecked by circumstances. But tell me now...do you have any idea why Albion might have considered you of some importance?"

"None. The greater question is...how did he get into Newgate? And...might he still be here, either as a guard or an official of the prison? Perhaps someone here with a bent for the law that's a bit warped, and who didn't think those six men should have been released under any conditions. The problem with that line of thought, though," said Matthew, "is that all the six were not confined to Newgate. In fact, I don't know if any of them were, but I do know one had been recently released from St. Peter's Place."

"Hm," said Defoe, with a slight nod. "You're not in a position to do much problem-solving, are you? But I can tell the steed is champing at the bit."

"My nature, though sometimes regrettable. What I'd like to know is, was there any connection among the six men, other than their being prisoners and released by either craft or graft? Did they have the same attorney? Did the same judge pass sentence on them? Albion has gone to a great deal of trouble to get himself dressed up in that gold-painted mask, and he's not shy about attracting attention, either. So...what's his point, and what his story?"

"A tale of woe and madness, I'm sure. Unless Lord Puffery has hired a murderer and nightstalker to provide grist for the mill. Readers are eating that up."

"Possibly a tale of woe," Matthew agreed, as he watched the rain coming down beyond the bars. "Of madness, possibly not. It seems to me there's a cogent plan behind this...and for some reason I have been entered into it. I don't think Lord Puffery cares much about *me*." He turned his full attention again upon his host. "You say you're a writer? And you're sentenced here for sedition?"

"I wrote a political pamphlet that was not appreciated by the crown," said Defoe. "I meant to stir up a stewpot of discussion, but instead I stirred up a firestorm that quite nearly roasted me. But I will see my way out of this difficulty, in time." The gathering of the lines upon his face as he spoke belied the confidence of his words. "Better to be imprisoned in Newgate than imprisoned in ignorance," he mused. "Some gaols are of the soul, and they can be the most cruel."

"I agree. Unfortunately life itself can have a very cruel soul."

"Ah!" Defoe's face brightened. His smile was broader. "I like that, Matthew! The sound of it: cruel soul. *Cruel soul*," he repeated.

"I'll find a place to slip that in somewhere...sometime or another." His smile faded. "You know, I'm not the only man of letters here. How quickly one's star can rise and fall...but that's the human condition, isn't it? There are some great intellects here, locked away in the curse of disuse. Just offhand...there's Edmund Crispin, Thomas Love Peacock, Peter Greenaway, William Knowles, Thomas Tryon, Theodore Sturgeon, John Collier, Charles Godfrey Leland, Ronald Firbank, Max Erlich...all locked away here, all bypassed in the rush toward the future. As I will someday be...and you...and all who live and breathe and fight now to be heard...to be *known*. But I think...if a man can be known for a little while...if he can be recognized for having given to his earthly kin something that provided joy, or thought, or comfort when it was needed...then his life was worthwhile." He looked at Matthew with sad eyes. "Don't you think?"

"Yes," said Matthew. "I do think."

"A true champion you are," Defoe answered, and just that quickly the sadness left him like a banished blight. He took measure of the candle clock and saw that time was growing short. "I have enjoyed our conversation. Be sure I will continue to pay your chain removal fee. I wish I had more funds to spare. As I say, my friends are keeping me from the dungeon."

"I understand. Thank you very much for what you've done. I wish I could repay you in some way."

"But you already have! Being able to talk like this, and my hearing your story...it's very inspirational, though I'm surprised you've not been killed at the hands of some extremely formidable adversaries."

"I suppose I've been lucky," Matthew answered. "So far, that is."

Defoe rose to his feet. Matthew knew it was time to return to the lower realm. "The guards will be at the door soon," the writer said. "I'll walk back with you."

At the grated door, as they waited, Matthew decided to ask about a word he'd been chewing on since it had been spoken. "You mentioned a dungeon. I saw a couple of staircases going down. Who's sentenced there?"

"Prisoners who have attacked the guards, or who are raving insane and murderous."

"As opposed to being sane and murderous?"

"Point well taken," Defoe said, "but that's how it is. Also a prisoner sentenced to be hanged is sent to a dungeon cell for his last two weeks, is kept in solitary and is put on a diet of bread and water."

"A kind send-off, I'm sure," said Matthew with dripping sarcasm. "But tell me this, if you know...is every cell down there occupied?"

"I don't know. Why do you ask?"

"I'm wondering...if Albion is not a guard or an official here, and most likely not a phantom able to walk through solid walls, then he is a man who has found another entrance into Newgate. I would imagine there's quite a network of passages under a city with such ancient beginnings."

"Oh yes. In fact many live down there. Mostly beggars."

"Albion may be a beggar by day and an avenger by night. Or, at least, he may be passing himself off as a beggar. I just wonder if one of the empty cells in the dungeon doesn't have a few loose stones... enough to be moved to allow a body to crawl through."

"Even if that were true, how would Albion know? And how would he know if the particular cell would be empty? It seems to me he could well have crawled into an encounter with a screaming lunatic who might even be too much for his sword to handle."

"A good question and an even better observation," said Matthew. "That would indicate, again, that Albion has some knowledge of what goes on in Newgate, therefore a connection here."

Defoe asked, "You do know the meaning of the word 'Albion', don't you?"

"No, I don't."

"'Albion' is the ancient name of England. It was referred to as such in Greek writings dating back to the sixth century Before Christ. It also refers to the elemental force—the strength of a giant—that is fabled to be England's protection again harm. Whoever Albion might be, he has a sense of both the classical and certainly the dramatic. Ah, there's a light! Someone's coming up. I can tell by his walk...it's Parmenter, not Massengill or Baudrey. Those two are to be avoided if at all possible. Good afternoon!" said Defoe cheerfully, speaking to the guard who was wearily climbing the stairs.

"Good if yer a flippin' frog," Parmenter grunted as he followed the yellow circle of his lantern. "Stand back." When the prisoners obeyed, he went about unlocking the door.

"Thank you for coming to see me," Defoe told Matthew. "You've given me some things to think about." He offered his hand and Matthew shook it. "I hope everything works out for you."

"And I you, sir."

"Come on through," said Parmenter with a scowl as he opened the door. "Yer jawin' time is done."

On the walk back to Matthew's section, as they moved through the twisting corridor, Matthew asked, "Do you know if all the cells in the dungeon are occupied?"

"Why? You wantin' to curl up in one of 'em?"

"No, Mr. Defoe was just telling me that prisoners due to be hanged are put there. Also those who might be considered to be…um…problems. I was simply curious."

"Do tell."

They went on a little further, Matthew leading and the guard a few paces behind, before the problem-solver tried again. "So are all the cells down there taken?"

"A few are empty. I could work it out so's you can see for yourself, spend a couple a' nice nights down there in the dark all by your lonesome."

"I'm content to use my imagination. But one more thing: is there a locked door one must pass through to reach the cells?"

"Under an archway, across a little bridge over the shit pond and then you come to a locked gate. Y'sure you don't wanna see it? Sweet smell down there to drift off to."

"I'm sure," Matthew said. He was considering the facts as he knew them to be, and he came up with another question. "How long have you been working here?"

"A lifetime, seems like. This place gets to a fella. Been here eight years next month, and don't know whether to be proud a'that or not."

Matthew was grateful that at least Parmenter was somewhat civil; he could imagine the response if he'd posed questions like these to Baudrey. "In your eight years, has anyone ever escaped?"

"Two I can recall. And one a'them was nabbed less'n an hour later. Two ain't a whole lot compared to how many been through here, so…hey, wait a bleedin' minute!" He gave Matthew a half-hearted cuff to the back of the head. "You ain't got the right to be askin' me such!"

"My apologies, I forgot my place," Matthew said. They passed by one of the descending staircases. "One more, please: did either of those two escape from the dungeon?"

"Hold your tongue, Corbett," came the curt reply. "I ain't answerin' nothin' else."

"Very well. That's unfortunate, because I was going to trade information with you. I was going to ask for that question to be answered in return for telling you what I saw when I looked into Albion's face, and what I've told no one else."

A body was sprawled on its back in the corridor ahead. Parmenter stopped to shine his light downward on the thin, wasted form. He gave the man a quick kick to the ribs and the prisoner moaned and turned over on his side. "Up with you, Eddings!" said Parmenter. "I come back this way and you're still here, you'll be stretched for the lash!" He stepped over the body and continued on, and Matthew did the same. Parmenter said, "Albion don't have no face. He wears a mask. Anyway, the warden's told us we're not to talk about that."

"Pity." Matthew had the feeling that Parmenter's shell was not so hard that it couldn't be breached at some meeting of joints and angles. "I'm bursting to share this with someone. It's the kind of item I'm sure the *Pin*'s readership would find intriguing."

"You ain't got nothin'. And I don't know what that fancy word means."

"It means that it's likely Lord Puffery would pay for it. Worth a guinea, I'd say."

Parmenter didn't reply.

They were nearing the archway into Cairo. Matthew calculated a couple more turns of the corridor before they got there. Water dripped from the cracked ceiling and ran down along the stones of the walls to make dirty puddles at their feet.

Suddenly a hand reached out and grabbed Matthew by the back of the collar. Parmenter was stronger than he looked—or Matthew just that much weaker from lack of food—because the young man was stopped in his tracks. Parmenter shoved Matthew over toward the right side of the corridor. "Listen here." Parmenter lifted his lantern so it shone fully into Matthew's face. "I don't like your ways and your ear-bustin' words."

Matthew's shoulder ached where it had met the wall, but it was better than being struck by the guard's billyclub, which remained hooked to a leather belt around Parmenter's ample waist. "Sorry," Matthew said. "Let's forget this discussion. This *talk*," he amended. "All right?"

Parmenter ignored the request. "I got a question, then." He cast his voice low, though they were currently alone in the corridor. "What'd you do to stir Albion up? He ain't never set a ghostly boot in here before. So what'd you do on the outside to bring him in?"

"Nothing I can think of."

"You kill somebody? He don't care for killers."

"Is that what the six victims did? They each killed someone?"

"Naw. Well...two of 'em did. Of the other four, two were roughers, one a cracksman and the other a dog buffer."

Matthew nodded. Parmenter was describing two murderers, two common ruffians for hire, a housebreaker and a thief who stole dogs, killed them and sold the skins to furriers. He decided to press his luck, for he might not get another favorable spin of the numbers wheel. "Did one of those escaped prisoners get out of Newgate through a dungeon cell?"

Parmenter looked to right and left. Then into Matthew's face again. "You first. What do you have I can sell to the *Pin*?"

Quickly, Matthew conjured something up. "Mark this: his eyes were ablaze behind that mask. They were like two windows into Hell. Shuddered my soul to look there, but I had to. Not only that, but I heard him speak. Not with the ears, mind you, but in here." He tapped his skull. "I heard him say he's got three more men on his murder list. One's got the letter 'A' in his first name. I heard Albion say he's sharpening his sword, and he's going to strike soon. Maybe tomorrow night, if his plan goes well. But he'll be out there stalking. That's what I heard him say."

"Go on!" Parmenter's mouth crimped. "You ain't heard nothin' of the sort!"

"I did. Do you know why Albion came here to speak to me? Because...he and I are connected by murder. Yes, that's right. The man I killed was on his murder list. He told me that, too, and he came here to *thank* me."

"Go on!" This time it was spoken in a whisper. Parmenter's beady eyes had widened, as much as they could. The guard's hand left Matthew's collar. "Who was it you knocked off?"

"A Prussian by the name of Dahlgren. Why he was on Albion's list, I don't know, but there you have it. Now tell me the *Pin* wouldn't buy that, seeing as how it's coming directly from my mouth."

"Christ's bloody nails!" said Parmenter. "If I was to see that in the *Pin*, I'd snatch it up in a second!"

"The information is yours. Just don't give it away for free to anyone here...especially not to Baudrey."

"Oh, I can't stand that swaggerin' Tom Turdbag!" Parmenter hissed. "He's killed a baboon and stole its face! And I happen to know he's on the White Velvet, too. Disappears for days at a time, don't remember nothin' about where he's been or what he's done."

"The White Velvet?" Matthew asked. "What's that?"

"Cheap gin that knocks a man senseless. Just stay away from that pi'sen is my advice...if you ever get out of here, I mean."

"Very well. Now...about the dungeon cell and the escape?"

"If I tell...you won't cause me to sit on thorns, will you?"

"It will be as if you never told. It's only to feed my curiosity." Matthew plowed ahead when Parmenter hesitated. "Have some mercy on me. I need something to think on!"

One more look to right and left, and then Parmenter gave it up. "Yep, one of 'em slipped the cage through a dungeon cell. Happened a year or so after I got here."

"Which cell?"

"Ohhhhhh, no! This is as far as the horse wanders. Get on with yourself." Parmenter motioned with the lantern.

Matthew started walking again. It was such a relief to be out of those chains, but he found himself still wanting to hobble with the same constricted gait. His legs had gotten used to the shackles. He could see how a man could become inured to the darkness and despair in this place, and give up hope of ever walking in the sun again. A hope all Londoners probably shared right now, with all these days of dreary downpour.

He could sense Parmenter counting his shillings from sale of that item to the *Pin*. It would probably make Lord Puffery squeal like a little girl. Facts be damned, Puffery wanted puffed-up fantasies, the better to feed his hungry audience; Lord Puffery probably gave thanks for the murderous presence of Albion at every mealtime.

And so too, did Matthew give thanks for Albion. He realized, as he came to the entrance archway to Cairo, that Albion's appearance in Newgate and the figure's puzzling display—a vow of either life protection or death promise—was keeping his mind from becoming a sloshy bowl of pudding. It would be easy here to lose all sense of purpose, all interest in anything but removing itchy lice from the beard, all curiosity save the question of how long a sick man like Wyler had left to live, all dignity, all empathy, all everything.

But now to keep his head square and steady Matthew had Albion, plus the dungeon cell from which one bird had flown out of Newgate. He still might have—God forbid—six months to fester in here, but at least he'd been presented with a problem to solve, and that to him was like a little gift of life.

Parmenter left him. He went down the steps into the chamber, where nothing ever changed very much, except for the removal of bodies.

One thing particularly bothered him. Though Matthew did not believe in omens, it seemed in retrospect he'd made a very poor choice. Why...*why*...in his fictional tale of "hearing" Albion speak had he told Parmenter that one of the next murder victims had an "A" in his first name?

Had he become so dumbfounded in here that he'd forgotten how to spell his own?

Fourteen

"MATTHEW *Corbett! Get yer ass up here!*"

Baudrey was calling him again from the entrance archway. The man had a tremendous bellow but a miniscule range of expression.

Matthew stirred himself to get up from his little bedding of hay. "Popular fella, you are," said Wyler, from his own resting place. "You ain't doin' somethin' you wouldn't tell your grandkids, are ya?"

"No."

"What's he wantin' with you, then?"

"I have no idea." Matthew wondered if Defoe wished to see him again; their visit yesterday had been a bright spot in this dismal picture. At least up there with Defoe he could get a cup of clean water and a look at the outside world.

"Watch y'self," Wyler cautioned. And added: "Whatever it is you're doin'."

"Do I have to come down there, fishbait?" Baudrey hollered. "You wouldn't like that, I'm warnin' ya!"

Matthew made his way across Cairo's tortured landscape. A card game was in progress, and the other prisoners were in the process—as they always were—of finding something to occupy their time and minds or otherwise dying a little more. A couple of sad candle stubs attempted illumination. Baudrey stood in the glow of the lantern he held, and truth to tell he did have a face that resembled a baboon's. Matthew climbed the stairs, suffered a brief cuff to the back of his head for being tardy, and then was pushed along the corridor.

"Where are we going?" Matthew asked when they were a few yards along the passageway.

"You'll find out."

He didn't like the sound of that. In fact he didn't like this at all. He had learned a sense of time in here, according to the rhythms of waking up, eating and sleeping. The citizens of Cairo had been herded into the eating-room about two hours ago, by his estimation, for a supper of black bread and thin yellow soup that Parmenter had told him was pea soup, and Matthew thought it wise to ask no further questions. But if supper had been two hours ago, then it was likely seven or eight o'clock on the outside—maybe later—so what was this evening excursion about?

Last night he'd entertained the thought of slipping down into the dungeon just for a gander, but as the candles were as precious as food and water he realized there was no way to get hold of a light. There would be the locked gate to get through to reach the cells, thus his exploration of the darkened dungeon was stymied. His theory that Albion had gotten into Newgate the same way one of the escaped prisoners had gotten out would have to remain a theory. But if the theory was true, and say part of the wall had been cracked and the stones loosened by time and the movement of the earth under the city itself, then why hadn't the warden repaired the wall in that particular cell? If a couple of stones could be moved and a body could crawl either from or into London's underworld, why had the work been left undone? Surely the warden and the guards had gone over the cell the prisoner had escaped from and found the route he'd taken…or had they? And if that was indeed the way Albion had gotten in and out, how had he known about it?

One possibility, Matthew had realized: Albion was the escaped prisoner, therefore he knew about the cell and he knew the inner workings of Newgate.

But...another question...how had Albion gotten through at least one lock to reach Cairo? It did seem, at first consideration, the movements of a ghost. And what was so important about an imprisoned, bearded and filthy young man from New York that Albion would even care to make some sort of contact?

Matthew had no idea, but he relished the questions; now, though, the questions became more immediate, as he didn't like being pushed ahead of Baudrey along this dank and dripping corridor. "I'd like to know where I'm being taken," he dared to say, because they'd passed the steps leading up to where Daniel Defoe and the others were kept.

"A little trip," came the reply.

"A *trip*? To where?"

"To the bleedin' infirmary if ya don't keep your trap shut. Keep movin'."

They stepped over and around several bodies, but otherwise the journey to the outermost iron door was uneventful. Baudrey unlocked it and pushed Matthew through. On the other side were two hard-faced men in dark cloaks and tricorn hats that glistened with moisture. Both of the men carried lanterns.

"You're bein' moved," Baudrey said. "From here to Houndsditch prison, over in Whitechapel."

"*Moved?* Not that I'm unappreciative, but why?"

"I ain't no man of the courts. Papers come across from the Old Bailey, signed by Assistant Master Lillehorne and Judge Archer. You're out of Newgate, but don't think they'll treat you lightly at Houndsditch. Fishbait here, fishbait there. Want him shackled?" Baudrey asked the two men, who were obviously guards sent by the court or the constable's office.

"He's a pip of a squeak," the larger of the men rumbled. "Won't give us no pains."

"He's yours, then," said Baudrey, and as a last measure of low regard he flicked Matthew's ear with a thumb and forefinger.

With a guard on either side of him, Matthew was taken out of Newgate by the same route he'd entered. In the courtyard a black coach with barred windows awaited him. The dim light of evening was blurred even further by a low-lying yellow fog that smelled of chalkdust and wet stone. Torches burned along the walls, their glow weirdly diffused through the vapors. The air was chill yet clammy at the same time, a disagreeable condition to the lungs. Matthew was pushed into the coach and the two guards sat facing him. Because he was such a pip of a squeak and the guards evidently thought so mightily of themselves the doorbolts were not thrown. Then the coachman started them off, they passed under the open portcullis, and Matthew's last impression of Newgate was a sound of imprisoned humanity that might have been a moan from the tortured walls of the prison itself.

"Settle in," said the guard who was the slighter of the two. He had a narrow face that appeared to have been crushed inward at birth, the eyes, nose and mouth all much too close together. "We got a few miles to travel."

Which spoke volumes of the size of London, Matthew thought. He couldn't imagine the length of the town of New York ever being a few miles of travel. But then again, who could foretell the future? Surely the Romans—and whatever ancient tribe had preceded the Romans in planting their territorial stones in the earth of what would become London—would never have believed such a city would grow from Caesar's ambitions. So too, might Peter Minuit—and Matthew Corbett—never believe the future size and shape of New York in a hundred years. A city, Matthew realized, was itself a living thing; it either grew or died, and there was not much in between.

The horses clopped on. Through the bars Matthew made out the shapes of people moving about the streets in their cloaks of fog, heard shouts and laughter and rough music. Smears of fire indicated torches burning here and there, and oil lamps along the streets showed more civilized sparks of light.

"So you're the one," said the larger man.

"Pardon?" Matthew asked, turning his attention away from the window.

"You're the one says he seen Albion. That right?"

"It wasn't just me. The whole of the chamber saw him."

"That's the damnedest lie I ever heard spouted." It was spoken with the curled lip of the born bully. "Ain't no such bastard as that. Made up by the *Pin*, he is, to get a fool's pennies. Oh, that tale a' Albion gettin' into Newgate has made the rounds of the Old

Bailey, you can be sure." He leaned toward Matthew with a dangerous grin. "But I say it's a damned lie and you're a damned liar. What say you, Petey?"

Petey said, "Damned lie, damned liar," and it was spoken by a man who knew what was good for him.

Matthew brought up a bemused smile and aimed it at the bully. It seemed to him that neither of these two were going to do anything hurtful, seeing as how he had been rescued from Newgate by the "Assistant Master" constable himself. He would forever be grateful to Gardner Lillehorne for pulling whatever strings the man had to pull for that to happen, and he vowed he would find a way to repay him. It remained to be seen what Houndsditch was like, but surely it wasn't as bad as what he was so gladly leaving.

"Wanted to get your name in the *Pin*, is what I'm thinkin'," said the heavy-set guard. "Pack of lies, all of it."

Matthew remained silent. There was nothing more to say to these two. Neither did he care to listen to their foolish jabbering. He looked out the window again, at the moving shapes and the blurs of flame in the fog, and allowed himself the luxury of thinking what he would do when this was settled and he returned to New York. Approach Berry and try to make amends, if that was possible? Try to tell her what he'd been thinking that day he was so callously cruel to her? He wished he could bring her back to him but there was the problem of Professor Fell, who certainly would never forget the fact that Matthew had blown up his gunpowder supply and basically destroyed his home island. So...bring Berry back to him, with Professor Fell certainly set on revenge?

No. He could not.

The coach rolled on, the ride getting rougher over rougher streets. The blocks of buildings seemed to grow tighter together, and the streets more narrow. Darkness ruled in this part of London, though it was interrupted by the occasional glow from the windows of what must be taverns. The fog had thickened and the tavern signage was impossible to make out. The denizens of this area must be rougher as well, for a stone thwacked against the coach's side and following it was a shouted snarl of curses, indicating no love for the law. In the distance could be heard a man's ragged hollering, the words indistinct but the tone one of pure rage, the words rising and falling on volcanic tides. From another direction came the high thin scream of a woman that abruptly ended. Out in the fog, very close to the coach, a man laughed quietly and Matthew saw the flare of a flame as a pipe was lighted. It occurred to him that Houndsditch might not be so bad as Newgate, but the Whitechapel area itself was no walk of saints.

He'd no sooner thought that than two hands gripped the bars of the window next to Matthew. A bedraggled young girl with sharp features and one eye blackened and swollen shut cried out into the coach, "Shillin' for a blow! Shillin' apiece, all a' ya!" She tried to create a smile but the clay of her battered face would not cooperate, and all she could present was a desperate, gap-toothed grimace. "Free for a sip of the velvet!" she cried out again, as if her life depended upon it.

"Off with you!" said the larger guard, and he leaned over to slam his hand against her fingers, breaking her grip on the bars and causing her to fall away. She let loose a string of oaths that would have made the inmates of Newgate blanch bloodless, and then the coach had gone on deeper into what Matthew began to suspect was a London tarpit the likes never seen in the New World.

"Holy Hell, Johnny," said Petey with an expression of dismay. "I could'a spared a shillin'!" Then, dejected, he slunk down in his seat.

In a few minutes, Johnny peered out one of the windows to get his bearings. Though all Matthew could see were vague shapes in the yellow fog, the guard must've spied a landmark of sorts—a tavern sign, a familiar window or some such—because he said with satisfaction, "We're near the gate. Won't be long now."

About ten seconds after he said that, something bumped against the side of the coach. Then against the top. There came a muffled cry. The horses seemed to lose stride and the entire coach shuddered.

"What the damned hell…!" Johnny said.

The coach rolled on a few more feet and then stopped.

The brake came down with a hard *thud.*

"Nelson!" Johnny slammed a fist against the coach's ceiling. "What're you stoppin'—"

For, he was going to say, but it was forever left unsaid.

The door on the left swung open. A swordblade entered first, gleaming in the lantern light. Its tip pricked Johnny's brick of a chin.

"*Sit easy,*" came a low whisper.

Johnny may have soiled his breeches. Or Petey may have. One of them certainly did, for Matthew smelled it. He, himself, was shocked but he was able to keep his already-filthy trousers at least clean of that.

The figure behind the saber wore a dark cloak and hood. Within the hood was the golden mask with the ornamental beard. The color of the eyes were impossible to make out. A black glove held the sword, which shifted smoothly to the tip of Petey's narrow nose.

Albion whispered, "*You*. Give him your cloak and hat."

"What?" Petey blinked, his eyes watery.

The saber twitched. Blood spooled from the sliced nostril. Petey cried out but did not move.

"*Cloak and hat*," Albion whispered.

The items were rapidly removed and set in Matthew's lap.

"*Your money*," came the next demand.

The two guards gave it up, putting two small leather drawstring pouches on the seat beside Matthew as if they had become as noxious as what freighted an unfortunate pair of breeches.

The golden mask angled toward Matthew. "*Take them*," said the swordsman, and the order was delivered so fiercely that Matthew's arms gathered up everything as if they were on poppet strings to Albion's control.

Then, a command also directed to Matthew: "*Out*."

Here Matthew was suddenly frozen, for terror hit him hard. Did this creature mean to roust him from the coach and murder him in the street?

"*Now*," said Albion.

Matthew found his voice. "If you mean to kill me, you'll have to do it here." He was preparing a kick to the center of Albion's chest, and if he could get in another one before that saber kissed him it would be a miracle...but worth the chance.

"*Fool*," came Albion's raspy whisper. "I'm *helping* you. Out!"

"I don't care to be helped by you."

Albion might have laughed behind that mask. Or groaned...it was difficult to tell.

"Mr. Corbett," said the voice, "you are also going to help *me*. Out, or..." He paused, thinking. Then: "Out, or I kill the thin one." The saber went to Petey's throat.

"I understood you only killed criminals who had managed to escape justice."

"True until now." The sword's point pressed into Petey's flesh. The guard had gone deathly pale, and he trembled and moaned but otherwise was paralyzed with fear. "Your decision," said Albion.

Matthew nearly said *Go ahead and kill him*, but he wasn't far enough gone for that. He was desperately thinking what he should do when he stepped out of the coach. Throw these items in Albion's masked face? Then run for it? But what did the creature mean by saying *you are also going to help me*?

"*Please,*" Petey croaked.

Matthew moved toward the door. Albion lowered the sword and stepped back. When Matthew's shoes had crunched down on the street's cinders, Albion plunged the saber forward into the coach...not to pierce Petey, but to pick up one of the lanterns by its nailhook. He withdrew it, said to the two guards, "Stay," as if they were nothing more than dogs, and then shut the coach's door with his free hand. He turned toward Matthew. "Put on the cloak and hat," he ordered, still speaking in a whisper. "Take the money. Take the lantern." He offered it on the saber. Matthew donned the cloak and tricorn. He pushed the pouches into a pocket in the cloak. When he took the lantern, he found Albion's golden mask pressed forward into his own face.

"Midnight," said the voice, up close where it could not possibly carry into the coach. "Tavern of the Three Sisters. Flint Alley. Hear me?"

Matthew was fully and completely poleaxed. But he heard himself say, "Yes."

A black-gloved hand went into Albion's cloak and emerged with an ivory-handled dagger in a cowhide sheath. "Guard yourself," said Albion. "Dangerous here."

Matthew took the weapon, as he could not disagree.

Then, abruptly, Albion turned away and strode quickly off along the street, and within a few seconds the fog had swallowed him whole.

Matthew swayed on his feet. The world seemed to spin around him. He realized it wouldn't be too much longer before one of the guards found the courage to look out the window and see that Albion had left the scene, and what then? He had no idea where Flint Alley was, or where he stood in this vast city. Time was moving, and so he must make a decision. In truth it flitted across his mind to return to the coach and deliver himself to Houndsditch, for surely with Lillehorne's influence he could soon get out of this predicament.

You are also going to help me.

Spoken by a golden-masked avenger, most likely the prisoner who'd escaped Newgate.

Spoken to what purpose, and what meaning?

His curiosity was roused to a feverish pitch. How could he go forth to Houndsditch and vegetate there for many days—if not weeks—with this problem to be solved?

He did not remember starting off but suddenly he was walking in the direction Albion had gone, with the sheathed dagger beneath his cloak. In another moment a figure came staggering out of the fog. The man was holding his left shoulder and his face was bloodied. Nelson had obviously been thrown from his perch atop the coach when Albion had climbed up to rein the horses in. The coachman glanced only quickly at Matthew and then averted his eyes, for this was indeed a dangerous place. He staggered on past in search of his charge.

Matthew kept going for awhile, his mind still mostly stunned. He stopped in a darkened doorway to check by lantern light the contents of the money pouches and discovered enough money to buy a good meal and a bottle or two of ale, if he could find such. He heard fiddle music adrift in the fog and the sound of male and female laughter. Then, a free man wearing a warm cloak and with money in his pocket, a lantern to light his way and a dagger close at hand, Matthew set off to follow the noise of humanity to its source.

Fifteen

MATTHEW sat at a corner table in the Horse Head Tavern on a street called Gower's Walk, with his back to a wall of brown bricks. Before him was a wooden platter of boiled pig's feet, some kind of mushy greens, a mashup of figs and apples sour enough to curdle the tongue, and corncakes baked to break the teeth. The ale in his tankard was bitter and smelled of long age in a musty cellar.

He ate and drank and thought himself for the moment a king in a delectable dream, for food and drink that would have seemed indigestible at the beginning of Matthew's ordeal now equalled any delight put before him at Sally Almond's in New York. He hadn't realized how starved he was, and so down the hatch went everything, the sour with the bitter and the mush with the tooth-crackers.

This was not the first tavern he'd entered on his exploration of Whitechapel, but at the Goat's Breath a fight had broken out before he'd taken a chair, and finding the chair he was about to take smashed across the shoulders of one gin-raged blowzabella by another, and men throwing their coins down and clearing the floor for this violent entertainment to continue, Matthew eased himself away from the maddened crowd and back into the foggy street.

Therefore he used caution in studying the tavern signs before committing himself to life-threatening error. The Scarlet Hag, the Leper's Kiss, the Four Wild Dogs, the Broken Cherry...heavens, no. And as he walked along these narrow, dirty lanes in the weak circle of his lanternlight, with an occasional other lamp or torch sliding past him in the gloom, he was aware that many other figures were on the move with him, all going somewhere or another, some calling out with voices impossible to decipher as if they were speaking haughtily not to anyone on earth but rather to gods unknown, in the manner of daring lightning to strike. Most, however, moved in ominous silence, either singly, doubly or in packs of three, four or more. Matthew kept his lantern uplifted and his other hand on the dagger's hilt, and he stopped every so often to press his back against a rough wall and make certain he was not about to be jumped from behind.

He had had at least one close call of which he knew. Several times he'd passed bodies sprawled on the ground, one with a head so bashed it was impossible for that broken cup to hold a drop of life. But in one instance Matthew had been called—"Gentle sir! Gentle sir, I beg you!"—from a doorway next to an alley, and found by the lanternlight a not unattractive young girl in dirty rags huddled there holding a baby. The infant was not moving. Matthew had thought its pallor a shade too blue. The girl had asked for coin to feed her child, and asked in so poignant and tearful a way that Matthew almost did not sense a slow uncoiling of something from the alley to his left. He did not wait to see what it was, because the sensation of evil that emanated from it was too horrible to contemplate, and so he quickly retreated as the girl called out with practised sorrow *Gentle sir, gentle sir, please help us.*

He did not turn his back on that alley until he had put a little distance between it and himself. The last he heard from the girl was a seething release of breath that had all the damnation of the world in it.

Then Matthew had gone on, thinking that anyplace where there was a market for dead infants was a place he did not be needing to wander, yet here he was. His appointment was at the Tavern of the Three Sisters at midnight, and he could not be late for that.

Now, as Matthew finished his meal at the Horse Head, he considered the subject of Albion. Surely there was some connection between the person who wore that mask and the historic meaning of the name. What Defoe had said: *It also refers to the elemental force—the strength of a giant—that is fabled to be England's protection again harm.*

Judging from what he'd seen so far, Matthew thought that the elemental force of the fabled Albion had given up the cause and left the country.

But...was it possible that a human being had taken up the sword?

What...one man was going to puncture this evil bladder and release all the devil's piss? Then London would be a shining example of order and purity, and so bring England back to some golden condition it had never really known?

It was madness.

What had been his impressions of Albion? It was worth summing up. The figure had been slim of build and not quite as tall as Matthew. Male, of course, though age was hard to tell because the whisper had been an effective disguise for the voice. A swordsman, for sure, and not just using the saber as a prop. And, obviously, Albion had to know that Matthew was being transferred to Houndsditch, what time he had left Newgate and what the route would likely be. Matthew recalled that Johnny had said they were near the gate. Albion had been most certainly lurking there, hidden by darkness and fog, awaiting the coach's arrival. Then he'd taken a leap, climbed up the coach's side, thrown the driver off and brought the coach to a sudden halt.

But *why*?

The serving-girl, a dark-haired wench with bruised eyes, came over to ask if he required anything else. He had noted her misshapen nose, obviously broken by more than one fist, and her downcast countenance. It seemed to him this was a city of beasts bound to battle each other because the larger circumstances of their poverty and plight could not be fought by human hands.

He checked the candle clock on the bar and saw that it was burning down toward ten. "Tell me," he said to the girl, "do you know the Tavern of the Three Sisters in Flint Alley?"

"Heard of it."

She needed prompting to continue. "Well, is it near?"

She had to ask the barkeep, who replied, "South toward the river. Maybe…oh…half a mile, I'd reckon. But sir…if you're thinkin' of goin' down in there I'd take another think. Awful mean down that way. Wilders left and right, ain't nobody safe."

"Cut yer throat for a sniff a' snuff," one of the patrons added, and the drunken blonde doxy astride his lap slurred out, "Ain't got no fuckin' morals down there."

"I was afraid of that," Matthew said resignedly. "Thank you, all." He asked for another tankard of ale and gave the serving-girl his best effort at a smile, but if she knew what a smile was she had forgotten, for she turned away with the same lifeworn expression she might have had if he'd spat in her face.

A choice lay before him, and here in the warmth of the tavern with a few candles flickering and a low fire burning red in a small hearth, he had the luxury of time and space to consider it. If he ventured forth to reach the Tavern of the Three Sisters at midnight he would undoubtedly learn who Albion was and what in the blazes this was all about. Of course, before he reached there he might suffer a little thing called murder, which would cancel the rest of his evening.

The other half of his choice involved throwing all this to the wind and finding his way back to Houndsditch, where he would humbly turn himself in. He would ask to speak to Gardner Lillehorne on the morrow to both thank him for getting him out of Newgate and explaining that this Albion business was none of his doing, and all he intended to do was be nice, quiet and timid until he could go before Archer in an official court function and state his case.

He drank and considered. Either way, sooner or later he would have to brave the streets of Whitechapel. It appeared from the number of people staggering into the Horse Head that this area was only beginning to come to life as the candle burned toward midnight. He might have one more tankard of ale for courage, but his money would be gone and so would his senses; best to face the rest of this night with a clear head.

He gave it another hour, nursing his ale and watching the denizens of Whitechapel come and go. A dice game was begun, the barkeep's billyclub slammed the drinkers' deck to stop several arguments before they became violent, a few garishly-made up dollies sauntered in and out, various mutterings and whispers indicated nefarious plots being planned by shadowy figures that stayed their distance from the light, and then it was time for Matthew to turn his attention to the task at hand.

He had decided. He would go to the Tavern of the Three Sisters, find out what all this was about, and then he would report himself to Houndsditch. The life of an escaped criminal was not for him.

"Would you direct me southward?" Matthew asked the barkeep, who gave him directions as far as the Oak And Eight tavern on Pinchin Street. "Thank you," he replied, and he left the barkeep and the serving-girl an extra coin. Then he took his lantern outside, pulled his cloak tighter because the night had gotten colder, situated his tricorn a little more westward, and began striding south.

He had been correct about this area coming more to life as the night moved on, for now though the fog had lifted and the chill wind had picked up figures were walking on the street in numbers that would have been New York at midday. There seemed to be four taverns on every block, and all of them doing a brisk business. A body came flying out the door of one of them as Matthew approached, and this was followed by a heavy-set black-bearded brute in a leather apron coming out to dump a bucket of foul unmentionables upon the man's head, much to the amusement of the throng who seemed to materialize from the air in search of such tragic comedies.

The street curved to the left and downward, sinking toward the Thames. Matthew walked at a brisk pace, his head on a swivel. A rider on a horse came galloping past with two more in pursuit, what appeared to be a chase with violent ramifications. Matthew smelled the ashes of burned buildings and had to sidestep many times to keep his shoes out of a nasty mire. From somewhere or another a woman was screaming and then the screaming became a high-pitched, nearly hysterical laugh. Up ahead, out in the gloom, there came a pistol shot.

The first thing Matthew was going to do would be to ask the man behind the golden mask why in the world he'd had to make this trek into such badlands. Then again, one did not ask too many impertinent questions of a phantom who had already murdered six men and had a saber eager for new blood.

He walked through an area where the painted wagtails marched back and forth like soldiers of a determined army, flagging down coaches by dropping part of their garments to reveal their gifts or actually trying to seize the horses' bits. But it was apparent that the coaches would not be here if they weren't bringing customers, and so the wanton troops did not have to wage their campaigns too ardently. In this area the wooden houses seemed to all be crooked and leaned one upon the other, as if their roofs might slide off at any minute like the top layers of rotten cakes. In the light of pink lamps Matthew was nearly lifted off his feet in the arms of fervent females and carried into one or another of the houses while their pimps, armed with stout clubs and hatchets, looked on approvingly and called out prices and practices for male consideration, though Matthew noted a few genteel-looking ladies emerging from some of those coaches. He got out of there with his clothes and his skin still on, but he thought he would be forever haunted by the sight of little girls aged eight and ten, all dressed up and decorated like gaudy candies, who hung back in the doorways while the big bawds launched themselves like fireships.

In another few minutes he was treated to the sight of a mob of men shouting around a sunken pit, and glancing in he wished he had not, for in the windblown torchlight a chained bear was fighting two snarling dogs, and the bear itself had scarred holes where its eyes had been removed. He put his head down and hurried past.

When he got back to New York, he decided, he would kiss every plank of the wharf and by God he would find Lord Cornbury and kiss that horsey face too, for on that day everything would be beautiful.

A cry to his left pierced his reverie.

Matthew dared to look in that direction. He was passing an alley. A thrust of the lantern revealed three men beating a slight figure—a young boy, it looked to be—that had tried to crawl into a mound of crates. One of the men's eyes flashed scarlet as he looked toward the offending lamp, and Matthew saw that his face was marked with streaks of red and black warpaint. One of the others had the boy's legs and was dragging him out, and just in that second Matthew had a quick look at the young face and saw that both eyes were already blackened. Then the three fell upon the boy and began to pound away with their fists like workmen intent on any task that called for full concentration.

Matthew went on.

It was not his business.

He had somewhere to be.

This was a city where you were on your own, and God help you.

He wasn't strong enough to take on three fierce ruffians.

Shit.

He stopped.

The boy cried out again, a high bleat of pain. Matthew could hear the sound of blows connecting.

Why? he asked the fates. And though there was no answer from them, his own reply was *Because you are here, and you are not yet so far a citizen of London as to keep walking.*

He returned to the alley. The boy was fighting wildly but only gaining a little time. All three of the men—young men, they appeared to be—wore the warpaint on their faces. One of them sported a headband complete with a spiky patch of feathers. That individual fell down across the boy's back, planted a knee on the spine, and began to pull the boy's head upward by the chin as if to break the neck.

"That will do," said Matthew.

Instantly the three figures froze. The boy continued to fight, clawing to get to the dubious safety of the crates.

"Away with you!" growled the man who'd looked into Matthew's light. "You don't want none of this!"

"I don't like what I'm seeing. Three against one, and a young boy too. You should be ashamed."

"Fuckface," came the gruff voice of the one with the Indian headband, "you move on or we'll cut your balls off and feed 'em to you." He let go of the boy's chin. His hand moved toward his fringed deerskin jacket and returned with the shine of a knife.

Matthew had seen, to his right, a jumble of flame-blackened boards. He drew out one that bore a couple of twisted iron nails toward the end that would meet flesh. He was frightened of this confrontation, for sure, and later—if possible—he might think himself stupid for having stuck a sharp nose in, but after all the misery and corruption he had seen in this city he could not be a part of it.

"Let him up," he said.

"Carve him a grin, Black Wolf," said the feathered gent, who remained with his knee pressed down on the boy's struggling form.

The one who Matthew had first seen pulled a knife as long as Matthew's forearm. The second one also brought out a blade.

Matthew stood his ground. "*Black Wolf?*" He nearly laughed, but he was too tight inside. "Do you apes fancy yourselves real Indians?" He readied himself to throw the lantern into a warpainted face and follow that with a nailboard blow; then, his hand would go to his own dagger, which unfortunately was of a pitiful size in this circumstance.

Black Wolf slinked forward, the league-long knife making little circles in the air.

One more step, Matthew thought, and then the lantern would fly. *Come on, you—*

A monstrous stormwave hit him from behind, coupled with a bellow of voices, and for an instant he was back on the *Wanderer* fighting the whole of the roiling Atlantic. He tried to twist around to use the board, but a club struck him on the shoulder and the makeshift weapon dropped away. He had a fleeting second to recognize that in the blur of faces he was seeing, all of them had blackened eyes. Then a fist caught him on the jaw, another one hit him high on the chest and took his breath, he was thrown to the ground and was aware of his attackers attacking those who had been about to attack him. Blades gleamed, fists flew, cries of rage and pain spewed out, bodies tumbled, the boy had gotten up and was fighting like a fiend, and Matthew struggled for air and tried to get to his feet.

He had made it to his knees when flesh smacked flesh in the riotous melee and a body fell upon him, and in the confusion he saw a boot coming but he could not get his head out of its path.

And so, ingloriously but completely...to sleep.

Three

Enemies Old and New

Sixteen

"LET me make sure I have heard you correctly. You just said Matthew Corbett has been sentenced to *Newgate Prison*?"

"Not sentenced," Gardner Lillehorne answered, with but a slight quaver in his voice. "Sent there for containment."

Berry Grigsby did not wait for Hudson to speak again. She had been silent during Lillehorne's recitation of Matthew's appearance before the judge and his subsequent banishment to Newgate, but now she found her face burning and her tongue wanting to burst through her clenched teeth. Even she knew the horrors of that prison, and this was more than she could bear. "How *could* you do it?" she asked, with a flame in her voice that nearly set fire to Lillehorne's pale blue suit. "You stood there and let this so-called judge send Matthew into that hellpit? Oh my Christ! How long has he been there?"

"A few days, only," came the weak response. Lillehorne had his desk between himself, Hudson Greathouse and the red-faced girl, and he gripped both hands to the desk's edge as if he might have to heft it up and use it as a shield against feminine fury. "But…

listen…I tried my best to help him. I swear I did. It's just…well, he antagonized Judge Archer. It was a horrible scene."

"As horrible as a few days—and nights—in Newgate? I doubt that very much!" Berry had come to the end of her patience. She was weary to her bones but ready to fight to their marrow. The travellers had finally arrived in London this morning, about an hour ago, had found rooms at the Soames Inn just off Fleet Street, and had come directly to the office of the assistant to the head constable as soon as they could get directions and hail a carriage. Berry's coppery-red hair was a wild tangle of multiple birds-nests, her eyes were hot coals in a florid face, and her mouth was ready to bite off the head of a blue-suited snake coiled up behind a desk with a stupid simpering half-grin on his face.

"He must be let out at once!" Berry said, her voice rising to dangerous heights. "I swear to holy God and Mother Mary I'll spend the rest of my days seeing *you* in that damned hole if you don't get him—"

"*Out?*" said Lillehorne, with admirable calm in the face of this heated whirlwind. "I was about to tell you. He is already out."

Those four words brought for a few seconds a sudden silence to this storm, but it was only the pause before a bigger blow.

"Christ's blood!" Hudson thundered, himself on the edge of going berserk. "Why didn't you say so in the first place?"

It was a moment—a precious moment, in which the assistant to the high constable evaluated his past life and determined he would like to live at least several more hours—before Lillehorne spoke again. His voice broke when he began, so he had to start over. "There is a problem," he said. "I was just about to walk over to the court of sessions, it's only across the courtyard." He stood up; even his bones were trembling in the presence of the man and the woman who had come from New York to find Corbett and burst past his clerk into this office like human hurricanes, and surely in the next few minutes he would have to hang on to his skin. "Would you accompany me?"

"What's the problem, then?" Hudson fired at him.

"Please. Just go with me, and all will be explained." Which, Lillehorne thought, might be one of the biggest lies ever to leave his crimped lips.

Hudson and Berry left the office with Lillehorne, they descended a staircase to the courtyard and strode along one of its precise geometric paths under a low gray sky. They entered the massive courthouse and presently found themselves standing before the young straw-haired clerk named Steven, in an office with filing cabinets, bookshelves and on the white walls portraits of famous dead men.

"I know, I know," said the young man as soon as he saw Lillehorne. He lifted a hand to remove his square-lensed spectacles. His eyes appeared dazed and beneath them were purple hollows. "How this has happened…I have no idea."

"What's happened?" Hudson nearly shouted. And then, restraining himself, he said, "I'm Hudson Greathouse and this is Berry Grigsby. We've come all the way from New York to find Matthew Corbett, and now we're told he was sent to Newgate Prison. When was the trial?"

"There was no trial, sir," said a voice from the doorway, and there appeared a slim but decidedly solid-looking man with blonde hair tied in a queue by a black ribbon, his apparel a dark blue suit with gleaming silver buttons, a gray waistcoat and white stockings. His aristocratic face was unsmiling. "I was on my way here when the power of your voice almost blew me back to my office. You might lower your volume so as not to blast the pigeons off the roof."

"Judge William Atherton Archer," said Lillehorne to his two New York acquaintances, and then he retreated a step as if wishing to merge into the wall behind him before this war truly began.

"Oh, so *you're* the one!" Hudson brought up a wolfish grin that in its history had caused many men to count their moments. "The *judge*," and he let that word drool out, "who sent my friend to Newgate. As I asked this clerk, when was the trial?"

Archer approached Hudson. When he got within the range of which any other man would stop, he kept coming two steps nearer, until he was looking up at the larger figure as a bulldog might stare up the nostrils of a bull. "And as I have already said, there was no trial. *Sir*," he added, his expression impassive. "Do they still understand English in the colonies?"

"Yes, and they understand stupidity too, of which London judges need to be educated."

Lillehorne gave a noise that sounded as if a great pain had issued deep in his bowels.

The clerk seemed to rouse himself and think it best to intercede. "Judge Archer, these two are asking about—"

"I know why they're here!" The words were snapped at the clerk, but the intense dark blue eyes were still fully focused on Greathouse. "I heard the introductions. My ears are still ringing. Yes, I sent Corbett to Newgate. Without trial. That will come later, when he's found." A fly buzzed between himself and the other man's face. Archer quickly brushed it away. "Look what you've let in here, Lillehorne!" It was said with the burning eyes still fixed upon Hudson's fiery orbs. "A little flitting nuisance to add even more joy to my day!"

Near tears, Berry spoke up. "All we want to do is find Matthew!"

"Then you share my desire. Mr. Jessley, tell the tale."

The clerk lowered his head. He took a deep breath. The fly circled his head and landed on his right cheek. He brushed it away with nerveless fingers and began. "Late yesterday afternoon…I received a messenger from the constable's office. It was nearly time to close up and go home…all the judges had already gone, and I was on my own. The messenger brought a document. Judge Archer has already seen it."

"A document on official parchment, bearing the official seal. It's in my office right now," Archer added. "Go on, Mr. Jessley."

"The document," said Steven, "requested an immediate transfer of the prisoner Matthew Corbett from Newgate Prison to Houndsditch prison, in Whitechapel. The way it was—is—worded…left no doubt that immediate meant just as it said. And…the devil of it…was that not only was it scribed on official parchment with the proper seal, but it bore three signatures: those of Master Constable Patterson, Assistant to the master Lillehorne, and—"

"My own," the judge said tartly. "A forgery, of course, but very well forged."

"Very well forged," Steven agreed. "As was Sir Patterson's and Mr. Lillehorne's. I know I should have waited until morning, to ask you about it," he said, addressing Archer, "but—"

The young man's countenance was distraught, his blue eyes without their spectacles watery-looking and fixed on the judge. The fly came in toward his face again, and suddenly his hand streaked out and snatched the thing in midair seemingly without even looking at it. "I thought I'd been given a direct order," he said, and all in the room heard a small crunch as the clerk's fingers ended the life of a London pest. As if in a trance, he wiped a small smear across the front of his starched white shirt. "I'm sorry, sir. I have made a grave error."

Archer released a long breath that he must have been holding for several seconds. He moved past Hudson and Berry, and he walked around the clerk's desk and laid a hand on the young man's shoulder. "Steady up," he said quietly. "An error was made, yes, but with that document in hand, how would you know the order was not genuine?"

"All right, we've gotten that part," said Hudson. "So Matthew is currently in Houndsditch prison, is that correct?"

"Lillehorne?" Archer prompted. Some of the acid had returned. "Since these are *your* people, you should do the honors."

Lillehorne wore a pained expression, as if that disturbance in his bowels had risen to his throat. "We have had…a problem here recently. The last several months, as I understand it, though it predates my presence. So…I…have to tell you…that—"

"That a maniac who calls himself Albion," Archer interrupted, "waylaid the prison coach last night, assaulted the driver and one of the two guards Mr. Jessley had assigned to take Corbett to Houndsditch, rousted your man out and disappeared with him. This after garbled and insane reports came out of Newgate saying that Albion had materialized *inside* the prison and made a threatening gesture toward Corbett."

Neither Hudson nor Berry could speak. Hudson thought he heard a little whuff of air that might have been from either one of them trying to find words, but no words were produced.

"So…no, Corbett is not in Houndsditch," Archer went on. He gave the clerk a pat on the shoulder, and Steven nodded a thank you for the gift of stability and put his spectacles back on. Hudson found himself staring, dumbly, at the little smear of fly guts on the young man's shirt. "It is unknown where Corbett currently is," said Archer, as he came back around the desk. "Or…and I have to say this…whether he is dead or alive. Since his first appearance in May

Albion has murdered six men by the sword. I have myself interviewed one of the guards this morning. Albion's sword was put to work on the other's nose and neck, and I'd say both those men got off very lightly. Though…a mystery…Albion demanded that a cloak, a tricorn, a lantern and two money purses be handed over to Corbett, and the guard swears Albion spoke kindly to him, offering him *help*, which indicates…I don't know what."

"*Albion?*" Hudson finally asked. "What kind of name is that?"

"The made up identity of a murderer who goes around in a hooded cape wearing a golden mask. I am told he strikes usually around midnight or in the early hours. No one has seen his face."

"Damn," said Hudson. He was aware then that Berry had grasped hold of his arm and he was the only thing holding her up. He put his arm around her, the better to keep her from falling. "About faces, then." He spoke to the clerk. "Who was the messenger yesterday? Someone you know?"

Steven shook his head. "This is particularly where I failed. I didn't recognize the man, but he told me he was new to the department. He was very convincing. He knew the proper names and the positions, when I inquired who he was working with."

"A description, please?"

"What, you think it might be someone *you* know?" Archer asked. "And you just recently arrived? Mr. Jessley has already given myself and Patterson a description, and it's no messenger we've ever seen."

"Let me say," Lillehorne ventured timidly, "that Mr. Greathouse is, like Matthew Corbett, an associate of the Herrald Agency."

"Oh my Lord!" came the reply. "Yes, we certainly need more hands stirring this bowl of confusion, so by all means stir away!"

When it had appeared the judge was giving his consent to continue, Steven said, "A young man, he was." He pressed a hand against his left temple, as if that might further sharpen his recollection. "Maybe twenty or so. Around my age. Of medium-height and slender build. Well-dressed. Neat in appearance. Brown hair, pulled back in a queue. Brown eyes…I suppose. Maybe they were more gray than brown. He seemed intelligent and capable, but otherwise simply a common messenger." Steven shrugged, ending the labor of memory.

"Scars?" Hudson asked. "A cleft in the chin? Anything irregular at all?"

"No, sir."

"Eureka!" said Hudson, with a false smile that became a grimace. "I suppose that narrows it down to several ten thousands!"

"The City of London is not paying any associate of the Herrald Agency for assistance in this sorry matter, sir," Archer advised, sending forth another fiery glare. "Both and I and Sir Patterson have Mr. Jessley's testimony consigned to paper, and that didn't cost us a bent shilling."

"I'd like to see this document," said Lillehorne. And then, as if fearful he'd pressed too hard, "At your convenience, I mean."

"Of course. Your name is well-forged on it, too. It's a first-class job. I'm going to have it framed to keep with my other remembrances...that is, until it's brought before the court as evidence and someone pays the price for this crime." Archer's gaze travelled to the clerk. "You're all right now, young man?"

"Yes, sir. I didn't sleep too soundly last night. I think I must've had a premonition that something was wrong."

"See that you get some rest tonight. Drink yourself into a stupor if you have to, but be sharp tomorrow. Good day to you, sir, and to you, miss. Lillehorne, if you want to take a gander at the parchment come with me."

"Just a moment!" Hudson protested. "Is that *all*?"

"All what?"

"All to be said and done? With Matthew out there, maybe in the clutches of a murderer?"

"What would you have us do?"

"*Search* for him!"

"Hmmm," said the judge, with a finger tapping his chin, "I'm sure our army of constables will get on it right away, as soon as the hundred and ninety-four other murders, assaults, abductions and various other violences committed in the last two days have been remedied. By the way," he said to Lillehorne, "how goes the investigation into Madam Candoleri's kidnapping? I was too preoccupied this morning to ask."

"The same as before. Not a word demanding ransom."

"That makes no sense! Why would anyone kidnap her unless they wanted money?"

"Perhaps," said Lillehorne, "they desired a private opera performance?"

Hudson jumped at this. "What, you've got a missing opera singer on your hands?"

"If she was on our hands, she wouldn't be missing," Archer said coldly. "Teachers of logic must sorely be lacking in the colonies."

"We make up for that," Berry was able to answer, "by teaching good manners."

"That and six pence will buy you a cup of sour cream. Now go about your business and leave us to ours. Can you find your own way to the street?"

"We'll go by the coal chute," said Hudson, "since we're being shovelled out."

"Then slide on and be gone," Archer said, and Lillehorne followed him from the office with a last quick helpless glance at Hudson that said *I have done all I can.*

"Is he always such a prick?" Hudson asked the clerk after the sound of their shoes on the corridor's floor had clacked away.

"He's a very able man. A little prickly, yes, but he has the necessary temper for this job."

"I'll take your word for that. Is there nothing more you can recall about the messenger?"

"Nothing more than what I've already related." The young man's eyes behind the square-lensed spectacles went to Berry. "I… presume you have a…special interest in Mr. Corbett?"

"Yes," she said firmly. "I do."

"And come such a long way. Indeed it must be special."

"She loves him, that's the interest," Hudson blurted out. "And he loves her too, but he's too stupid to tell her."

"Oh," said Steven, and he seemed for a moment to be examining his own hands. When he looked up at her, his face had softened. "I regret what has happened. Judge Archer does too, but he…he has his own way of expressing things. If it's any help to you, Mr. Corbett seemed to me an extremely capable man. I mean, I only saw him in this office for a few minutes, but in that short time he seemed very sturdy. I would think he is a…I suppose the word would be *survivor.*"

"Yes, he is that," said Berry. "But even so, I can't bear to think of him out there at the mercy of some creature of the night."

"Well," the lad said, "it's daylight now, so he's in no danger from Albion."

"I wish we knew that for certain," Hudson said. He motioned toward the office's oval window. "And you call that *daylight*? I'd forgotten what London gloom was like."

"One gets used to the gray. If there's anything else?" Steven pulled a sheet of paper toward himself and picked up a quill.

"Nothing else," Hudson said. "Good day."

"And to you, sir, and miss."

On the way out, they were halfway down the central staircase when Hudson said, "This is a damned strange barrel of pickles."

"An understatement," Berry answered. "Lord, I'm tired...but I couldn't sleep unless I was knocked unconscious."

"We both need to eat something. Get a cup of tea or coffee somewhere. Figure out what to do next." He shook his head as they descended the stairs. "All that about Albion...the messenger and the forged order...what has Matthew gotten himself into *now*?"

"Something I pray to God he can get himself out of." She stopped suddenly, a few risers from the bottom, and Hudson paused two steps further down. Her cheeks appeared a bit flushed. "He... *loves* me, you say?"

"I do say."

"He has a very peculiar way of showing love."

"Perhaps so. It's something we need to talk about, but first let's go find a meal."

"All right," she said, with a faint smile that held hope, and she followed him toward the courthouse's set of finely-painted white doors while he tried to figure out how to keep her mind off the fact that the man she loved—and who certainly loved her—might be by this time long dead.

"I think he's comin' 'round."

The voice—not quite a voice, but the mere echo of a voice—made Matthew realize he was returning to life, though it did flit through his aching brain that the voice was feminine, and might belong to an angel, thus he was dead and by God's grace gone far from London, unless the Devil was tricking him for past misdeeds and bad wishes, and when he opened his eyes they would be greeted by—

"Yep, he's turned color. Comin' 'round, he is. Hey, wake up!"

A hand grasped his arm and jostled him, none too gently.

"Give him a pinch, see if that don't do it." That was a male voice.

And another male voice: "Pinch his pecker, that oughta make 'im jump."

Instinctively, Matthew's hand went south to protect his privacy. He discovered it was already stolen. He was as naked down there as the man in the moon.

His eyes opened. Bleary light shut them again. His head felt as heavy as an anvil, his neck a fragile stalk of wheat.

"Almost there," said the girl, for indeed the voice was girlish. "Come on, fella, try it again."

"Lemme pee in his face," said one of the men. "That always works."

"A moment," Matthew was able to say, though it was the weakest whisper. "A moment," he said, louder. "Hold your water, please."

They laughed. Two men and a girl, laughing.

Of all the indignities he had lately suffered, being laughed at was the one that galled Matthew the most. It flamed his temper, and by that heat and power he climbed out of the darkness to which he recalled being consigned by an unfriendly boot. He opened his eyes. Swimming into focus came three faces, daubed yellow by lamplight. The rest of the chamber, wherever he was, remained dark.

"There you are," said the girl, and in her blurred face he saw the offering of an honest, toothy smile.

"Where is...*there*?" Matthew managed to ask. He found he was covered over by a thin blanket and lying on a mattress that was lumpy with straw.

"Our cellar," said one of the men. "'Bout two blocks from where we put you under."

"Yeah, Roger's quite sorry for that," said the other male, a higher and more nasally voice than the first. "But it was your head got in the way, so he can't be too contrite."

"My head. Yes." Matthew brought a hand out from the blanket and felt the side of his jaw. Every hair of his beard registered pain. He was swollen up pretty good, so there was no use in examining himself any further. But—strangely enough—he felt *clean* and a bit raw, as if his skin and scalp had been rather violently scrubbed. Also...was that a soapy scent he was smelling? "Have I been given a bath?" he asked the three still-indistinct faces.

"And it was a messy job, too," said the girl. "Turnin' a half-dead body back and forth to get at all that nastiness. Time it was done I filled up a bucket we can use for hard core, plug some of the holes 'round here."

Time, Matthew thought.

Midnight at the Three Sisters! Flint Alley! Half of him shouted to leap up, the other half was his own sea anchor.

He did try to get up at least on his elbows, which was itself a difficult task. "What time is it?" he asked one of the faces.

"Here now, do I look like a fuckin' clock?" The first of the men had spoken.

"Go soft on him, Kevin," said the girl. "He still ain't all to earth yet. Well...I'm thinkin' it's likely past eleven."

"Got to get to the Three Sisters. Flint Alley. Have to be there by midnight."

"By *midnight*?" She gave a small chuckle. "You got some time, then. More'n twelve hours, and Flint Alley's just a few minutes' walk."

"Twelve hours?" It dawned on him. "You mean...it's past eleven in the *morning*."

"Right-o."

"Oh," said Matthew. He sank back down again into the lumps. His appointment, directed by Albion, was lost. "*Damn*," he said quietly.

"The Three Sisters ain't goin' nowhere," Kevin told him. "Neither are you, by the looks of you."

Matthew could apply no comment to this. It occurred to him that not only had the boot knocked him out for so long, but his weakness and lack of decent sleep had combined with the blow to keep him insensate.

"You must've been mighty thirsty for tavern brew," said the girl. "That explains why you started twitchin' and turnin' somethin' awful 'round about midnight. I know, 'cause I was sittin' in here with you and saw it." She turned her head to speak to one of the others. "Rory oughta know he's come up."

"I'll fetch him," said the second male, and there was the noise of boots clumping away across a stone floor.

"Lots 'a questions to ask you," the girl said to Matthew. "Figure to wait on Rory for that."

"By all means," Matthew muttered, still cursing himself for missing the meeting and, furthermore, for missing a chance to clear up some of this mystery. "Let's wait on Rory. In the meantime..." He had to pause a few seconds, because to his swollen jaw speaking all these words was like chewing on cannonballs. "You say...Flint Alley's a few minutes away? I realize I'm in a cellar...but...who are you people?"

The girl's face came out of the dimmer dark, was fully illuminated by the light of an oil lamp sitting on a crate beside Matthew's head, and she looked down upon him like an angel from above.

"We're your new fam'ly," she said, "if it pleases you to be so."

Matthew's vision had almost completely cleared. He saw she was first of all maybe sixteen or seventeen, was slightly-built and had curly brown hair cropped short like a boy's. In a heart-shaped face with untended, wild dark eyebrows her brown eyes caught the light and showed glints that could only be described as golden. Except her right eye was bruised and puffed, there was a purple knot on her scraped chin, her right cheek bore the bruise of a couple of knuckles and a small cut lay across the bridge of her pug nose.

This, Matthew realized, was the person he'd thought was a young boy suffering an attack by three bullies. Her statement, given earnestly, made not a whit of sense to him, but then again very little did these days. "What's your name?" he asked.

"Pie Puddin," she said, and her good and wounded eyes searched his face with intense interest. "What's yours?"

"Matthew Corbett."

"'lo, Matthew," she said, and her bruised face smiled again.

"Hello...Pie," he answered.

"Has our brave but foolish and *very* lucky warrior come to his senses?" The voice echoed in the cellar, as its owner had not yet reached Matthew's side. Matthew heard the clump of a number of boots again, the girl named Pie moved away, and a man stood next to him. "Roger, look what'cha done," the man said, speaking to someone out of Matthew's field of vision.

"Pity," returned yet another voice. "'Course it was just a graze. The next kick got that buster square in the chops. Sorry, mate," he said to Matthew. "No hard feelin's?"

"My choppers are still there. Didn't bite my tongue through. Little hard to talk, but…no hard feelings."

"Just what we want to hear." The new arrival knelt down beside Matthew, uncorked a bottle and offered it. "Gift to you," he said. "Best rum we could get on a moment's notice."

Matthew took the bottle and had no hesitation in drinking. In fact, he wouldn't mind getting extremely drunk. The rum burned his mouth and throat and sizzled in his stomach but he thought he'd never tasted finer.

"His name's Matthew Corbett," said Pie Puddin.

"Rory Keen," the new man told him. "I'm what y'might call lord of the manor."

Matthew took another long swallow. "Lord of what manor?"

"All you see here below, and above. Three blocks to the south, three to the west, four to the east, two to the north. Workin' presently on increasin' our territorial holdin's, in a manner a' speakin'." His ruddy face grinned, showing three silver teeth in the upper front and two in the lower. His deep-set, fierce pale blue eyes were frightening in their fervor. "You're in the land of the Black-Eyed Broodies, and welcome to such a gallant soul. Wadin' in there and savin' our Pie—though she didn't need no savin'—was quite the show a' balls. I like balls, though not in the way some do."

Another girl in the group who had entered the cellar laughed, and ended the laugh with a most unmaidenly snort.

"Now," said Rory Keen, who had hair the color of flames and so thick, wild and wiry it appeared that trying to use a comb on it might've reduced the instrument to char. "Drink up plenty, friend Matthew, and we've got plenty a' questions to ask you, and we hope you answer 'em all right as rain, 'cause we would sorely hate to think kindly of you one minute, then the next send you to your grave with a second mouth in that throat a' yours."

And, so saying, he placed a wicked-looking knife upon the crate next to Matthew's head, and Matthew noted with some distress that its hooked blade already wore a proud crust of some enemy's dried blood.

Seventeen

PERHAPS it was the potent rum. Perhaps it was the fact that Matthew was coldly enraged at himself for missing his midnight meeting. What it most likely was, was the fact that a few seconds after Rory Keen had spoken and the knife set down upon the crate, a whirlwind of memories whipped through Matthew's mind, of all the things he had done and seen, all the tight scrapes he'd gotten out of, all the people he'd loved who had died, all the pain of having to keep Berry at a distance and the continual fear of that greatest shark in the sea of sharks, Professor Fell.

Therefore with all these in mind, and with Rory Keen staring holes through him and an instrument of violent death about twelve inches from his head, Matthew looked into the ruddy face of the master of the Black-Eyed Broodies and said with tightly-controlled fury, "Don't you dare threaten me."

Rory Keen had been wearing a mocking half-smile. Matthew saw it melt away as if the man's face had become a mask of hot wax.

"I don't care who you are. Who any of you are," Matthew went on, just as strongly. "I was on my way to the Tavern of the Three

Sisters, I saw someone who I thought needed help and I tried to do so. I got a kick in the jaw for it, and for it also thrown into a cellar on a dirty mattress and now threatened with death if I don't answer questions 'right as rain'. Take your knife, stick it up your ass and back away from me, because I'm having none of it."

The silence of doom stretched out. Keen's face was blank, absolutely unreadable.

"You forgot somethin', Matthew," said Pie.

"What?" he snapped.

"You got a nice bath out of it," she said softly.

Still Keen did not move nor did he register a speck of emotion. No one else spoke.

After what seemed a crawl of eternity, Keen's hand came out and retrieved the knife. He drew it towards himself and it went into the folds of his brown coat. Matthew had gotten a glimpse of a tattoo—a stylized eye within a black circle—on Keen's hand between the thumb and forefinger. Keen regarded Matthew as one might study a dead fish. "My apologies," he said. "But, y'know, we have business interests. We have competition in those interests. Got to be careful these days, who you trust. Dog-eat-dog world out there, am I right?" He waited for Matthew to agree, but Matthew remained quiet.

"Alrighty, then," Keen went on, "I'll give it to you that you've been struck hard, your brain rattled, and a few swallows of rum gone to your head. I'll give it to you that you got a league-long cock. I'll give it to you that you was wearin' clothes look like they come outta some prison or workhouse, and you was just as dirty, so you got some kind of rough history. I see that scar on your forehead; you didn't get that by bein' sliced on no children's playground. I'll give you all these things," he said, "but I'll not give you another chance to live if you ever speak to me that way again." His face during this discourse had never shown the slightest hint of any emotion. "Are we clear on that?"

Matthew wanted to lead with his chin and say, decisively, *no.* But he realized this short rope had a bitter end, and therefore he said, "Yes."

Still Keen's face remained unchanged. Then, slowly, the smile crept back. "You wantin' somethin' to eat?" he asked. "Bet you do. Paulie, go get 'im some food. Beef stew do for you? Comes out of the Drunk Crow Tavern 'cross the way. Mostly horse meat, but it's tasty. That do you?"

Matthew nodded.

"Good. Paulie, bring 'im another bottle. Bring me one too. Go on with you." There was the sound of someone walking away across the stones, then going up creaky wooden stairs. "I'll leave you for now," Keen said to Matthew. "Pie'll stay with you, keep the rats away. That suit you, Pie?"

"Suits me," she answered.

"Fine, then." Keen stood up. "We'll have us a good talk later, Matthew." And then he turned away and, with a group of the others Matthew could not see, left the cellar.

It was a long time before Pie spoke. Then she said, quietly, "Rory killed his first man when he was twelve years old."

"Do tell."

"I'm tellin'. He split the man's head open with an axe. It was just after his pa beat his ma to death right in front of him, and that axe was a few minutes late. His pa was gin-mooned, Rory says it was kill or be killed."

Matthew considered this, and then he replied, "We all carry a bloody axe of one sort or another. I just don't like being threatened for no reason."

"Rory's got a reason." Pie knelt down on the floor so he could see her face, and she could see his better. "One of our own got hisself killed 'bout two weeks ago. Murdered in Crescent Alley one street north from the Three Sisters. Fact is, he'd just been drinkin' there. So when you said that's where you was headed, and you a stranger and all…it's put him on edge."

Matthew had a sudden start. The Black-Eyed Broodies. So-called, he presumed, because of the black eye makeup they used when they were on the prowl; that was what he'd seen on the faces of the other gangmembers as well as on Pie's face. But his sudden start was because he'd recalled a conversation in his cell at St. Peter's Place, when he'd been interrupted in reading to Broken Nose and White Hair from a recent issue of the *Pin*.

The headline had been *Albion Attacks Again*, *Murder Done In Crescent Alley*.

Matthew remembered that the victim's name had been Benjamin Greer, recently released from St. Peter's, and White Hair had said *Benny…damn, he was a good feller. Ran with them*

Black-Eyed Broodies over in Whitechapel, and maybe he did some things that weren't so upstandin', but...hell...he had a good heart.

Matthew decided it would not be in his interest to reveal that he knew the name of the Black-Eyed Broodie who'd been done in by Albion's sword. Now was not the time to go any further along that crooked and dangerous road, though the burning questions fairly flared from his mouth.

"Were you 'bout to say somethin'?" Pie asked, because evidently he had started to speak before he'd caught himself.

"No."

"Seems like you were."

"I was going to ask," he dodged, "about the situation last night. You in that alley with those painted play-Indians beating you. What was that about?"

Pie, who not only had the cropped hair of a boy but wore a boy's clothes and boots, busied herself by bringing from a small horsehair bag a clay pipe, which she began to fill with coarse-looking tobacco. "I was set on by the Mohocks. They do fancy themselves Indians. Try to copy the Mohawks, from the colonies. They all give 'emselves Indian names. Sometimes they come at you with tomahawks and spears. Fire Wind's the big chief."

"You've got to be joking."

"Am not." She started her own fire with her tinderbox, and her wind pulled the flame into the pipe's bowl. She puffed a cloud of blue smoke that drifted between her and Matthew. "See, we're at war. Not just with the Mohocks, but with the others too."

"The others?"

"For sure. We're surrounded by 'em. To the north the Mohocks and the Amazon Nation, to the east the Plug Uglies, to the west the Bitter Roots and the Luciferians, to the south the Savage Circle and the Cobra Cult."

"Hm," said Matthew. "Are the Killer Clowns in there somewhere?"

"Huh? Oh, no!" She gave a little laugh that spewed smoke. "That would be damn silly. But the ones I told you, that ain't all of 'em. Them are just the ones right around here."

As Pie smoked her pipe, Matthew saw that same tattoo of a stylized eye within a black circle on her hand between the thumb and forefinger that he'd noted on Keen's hand. "I'm guessing," he said, "your tattoo is your—how shall I put it?—gang symbol?"

"Fam'ly mark," she corrected. "The Black-Eyed Broodies, they're my fam'ly. Could be yours too, if you're wantin' such…after what you did for me and all. Wouldn't be a hard pull to get you in." She gave him a sidelong long as she puffed her pipe. "You got a fam'ly?"

"Not really. I was raised in an orphanage."

"Me the same!" she said from her smoke cloud. "There's where they gimme my name. Found me in a basket laid at the front door. Note pinned to my swaddlin' said 'Take care of my puddin' and pie, 'cause I cannot.' Leastwise that's what the nuns told me. So that was my name, but they put it backwards: Pie Puddin."

"A nice name," Matthew offered.

"I wouldn't change it, not even if I knew my real name. If my ma gimme a real one, I mean. I always thought…my ma must'a been a lady 'cause of the way she wrote that note. 'I cannot', she said. Don't that sound like the way a lady would speak?"

"It does." Matthew was listening with one ear. He was taking the measure of how he felt and if he could stand up. It had occurred to him that though he'd missed the appointment last night, he might get to the Three Sisters tonight and possibly…well, he would find out when he got there. Then following rapidly on the heels of that realization was the thought that one could go nowhere without clothing.

"Answerin' your first question," Pie was saying, "I was out doin' my job. We was poachin' on Mohock territory. My job is findin' out where they're gatherin' and where their headquarters might be. I go out front, and the others are always close behind."

"They weren't close enough last night."

"I don't mind gettin' banged up a little. I heal fast. Anyway, we do the same to them, or any other bleedin' gang tries to poach. I'm a scout. What they call a promised rider."

"Providence rider," Matthew corrected. "Yes, I'm familiar with that."

Pie smoked her pipe and watched him while he took another swig from the rum bottle. "Real unusual, somebody buttin' in like you did," she said, and the silky tone of her voice told him what he'd suspected: that she was not down here to guard him against rats but to get answers from a question mark that had resisted

Rory Keen. Possibly some signal had passed between them for her to take prominence in this particular rat-hunt. Matthew understood that everything she'd been telling him had been to soften him up. "Your clothes and you all filthy," she went on, "and you too handsome to have a beard, if you don't mind me sayin'. So you been somewhere you couldn't get hold of soap or a razor. What gaol was that?"

Now the territory was getting swampy. Matthew said with a pained expression, "I appreciate talking to you, Pie, but my head's still ringing like ten church bells. Do you mind if we talk later?"

Her mouth on the pipe's bit. Puff...puff...puff.

"Ain't no shame to have been behind bars," she said. "Most of 'em been. What'd you do to get y'self hooked?"

He was saved, mercifully, by the sound of a door opening and boots descending the creaky stairs. It was a good thing, because he'd had not an iota of an idea what to say. She would want to know—acting as Keen's ear—how he got out of Newgate and why he was in Whitechapel on his way to that particular tavern, and what would he say that she couldn't see through?

"Here's your food comin'!" the girl said. "Paulie, come sit with him awhile, lemme go up and do my business." She stood up over Matthew as Paulie, a skinny boy about seventeen with shaggy brown hair, brought their guest a clay pot of stew and a fresh rum bottle. "I'll be back directly," Pie said. She started off and then abruptly stopped and turned toward Matthew again.

"That's a fine dagger you had in that cloak. Expensive ivory grip, real fine. Got the cutler's mark on it. Where'd you get that from?"

"It was a gift," he had to say.

"Who from?"

"A friend."

"Matthew," she said with a tight smile in her voice, "you're makin' all this sound so mysterious. Rory ain't right about you, is he? That you're either workin' for the Mohocks or—worse yet—the law? See, Rory thinks that after I cleaned all that stink off you, you still smell like the Old Bailey. Is he right about that, Matthew?"

She was doing her job, he thought. After all, she was a providence rider. He said, "I need to eat and get some rest. But I'll tell you this and tell you truly: I am wanted by the law for murder. I am not working for the law and certainly not for the Mohocks or any other band of rowdy idiots. Can we leave it at that?"

An answer was a moment in coming. It arrived with the pungent odor of Virginia's finest.

"For now," she said, with a harder edge, and she went off to do her business, part of which Matthew figured would be to report to Keen everything he'd said.

"You really murder somebody?" Paulie asked, all big eyes and misplaced admiration.

"I really did." And there it was: the truth. He had killed a man in cold blood and with forethought. Did it matter that Dahlgren would be trying to kill him and toss his body over the side all the rest of the way to Plymouth? He likely could have protected himself, by stating his case to the others. Maybe they would've put Dahlgren in chains, down in the hold. That damn Dahlgren, he thought...why the hell hadn't that bastard stayed in Prussia where he belonged?

He looked into Paulie's grinning face and then quickly away. After the eating would come the drinking. He could forget about the Three Sisters tonight. Even if he felt up to the stagger between here and there, the bawds and headknockers of Whitechapel had never seen a nude man parade into a tavern and sit there waiting to be contacted by a maniac wearing a golden mask. He had traded one prison for another; the Black-Eyed Broodies were not going to give him clothes and let him leave here until he gave Keen an explanation that made sense, and mentioning Albion and the murder of Benjamin Greer to Keen would not be so keen. Not for awhile, at least.

Sitting crosslegged with the blanket more or less covering him, he started in on the stew with a wooden spoon Paulie had brought. The food and drink was far better in this prison than in any other he'd recently visited. Paulie sat down on a crate and watched. "Rum?" Matthew asked, and offered him the second bottle. The boy took it with an eager hand, uncorked it and put down a swig.

Matthew waited until a few more swallows had gone down Paulie's pipe, and then he said casually between bites of the peppery stew, "Pie told me one of the Broodies was murdered a couple of weeks ago."

"Yep."

It was necessary to wait for a swig or two more to go down. "Wasn't there something about that in the *Pin* just lately? Do you know that news sheet?"

"Every'body does. Yeah, they done some writin' 'bout Ben. How he got murdered in Crescent Alley." Paulie drank again, and then said in a hushed tone, "Albion done it. Will was there when it happened."

"Will?"

"Will Satterwaite. He was down here awhile ago."

"Albion didn't try to harm Will?"

"Went for Ben. Stepped out of a doorway and got him clean 'cross the neck." The boy made a motion with a finger across his own throat. "Will said it happened so fast it was over and done 'fore he could pull his blade. Then Albion run off and he was gone."

Matthew recalled something else in the *Pin*'s story. "No one claimed Ben's body? Not even the Broodies?"

"Naw, 'cause Mousie took care of the buryin'."

"Mousie?" Matthew's brows lifted.

"Humphrey Mousekeller," said Paulie, and he drank once more from the bottle and ran the back of a hand across his mouth. "Our lawyer," he added.

Matthew pondered this new information and found it most intriguing. "The Broodies are able to pay a lawyer for his services?"

"We don't pay. Somebody does, but I don't know who."

"What else does he do for you?"

"Things." Paulie shrugged. "He's just there when he's needed, I s'pose."

"I see," Matthew answered, but in truth he was as blind as the proverbial bat. He would have to feel his way toward answers in this puzzling cavern. Of what need did a street gang have for a lawyer? And—most interestingly—who was paying the legal fees? Certainly not Rory Keen. That one didn't seem the type to spend two pence on anything to do with the law, and the service of even a cheap London attorney likely was not cheap. No, it definitely wasn't him.

Matthew decided not to press the issue, for he doubted that Paulie could supply him with any deeper knowledge. He continued to eat and drink, but now he only sipped infrequently at the rum. Sooner or later Keen would be back down here wanting to know Matthew's full story, and this time he would not leave it to Pie to glean bits and pieces of information. But Matthew had his own questions too, and an intriguing theory based on what Paulie had just told him.

The Black-Eyed Broodies might have a silent benefactor who had used Humphrey Mousekeller to spring Ben Greer from gaol… and in so doing, had brought the wrath of Albion down upon the unfortunate victim. Will Satterwaite had been in no danger. Albion was making a statement, scrawled in blood.

"Know what a pawn is?" Matthew asked the boy.

"A *paw*?"

"No," said Matthew. "A pawn. A chess piece of the lowest rank. Usually fated to die on behalf of a greater purpose."

"What're you talkin' about?" The young man frowned, completely lost.

"I'm talking," Matthew said quietly, "about *Ben*."

Eighteen

FOR the next two days Matthew was treated well. Though he was never offered clothing and he knew better than to ask for any, the blanket kept him warm against the cellar's chill. Relatively warm tavern meals and jugs of fresh-tasting water were regularly brought to him, he was afforded the oil lamp, a chamberpot and a modicum of privacy. When he asked for something to read, he was promptly brought two small volumes: a dictionary that appeared to have never before been touched and a grimy dog-eared pamphlet entitled *The Adventures Of Peter Gunner, Or How The Ladies Learned To Shoot*. On several occasions he was left alone and took the opportunity to wander around the cellar, finding it to be a large space holding two dozen crates and a half-dozen barrels, four brick columns supporting the floor above, and here and there a skittering of rats. At the top of the wooden stairs the door was always locked.

As he was left alone much of the time and he neither wanted to learn new words or investigate Peter Gunner's adventures, his curiosity turned toward the crates and barrels. All were unmarked.

With an effort that demanded more than an hour and some skin off his fingers he was able to subvert the nails and pry the top off one of the crates. He uncovered several rows of small blue bottles packed in wood shavings. The crate held thirty bottles. Thirty times two dozen...a lot of small blue bottles in this subterranean chamber. The barrels were heavy, but a liquid sloshed within when Matthew moved one. He returned the top to the crate and decided it was best to leave these unknowns alone.

Over this period of time Matthew learned from his various keepers some of their names—Paulie McGrath, Tom Lancey, Lucy Samms, Billy Hayes and John Bellsen—and what the Black-Eyed Broodies were about. Paulie was the best source of information, though Lucy also had an unguarded tongue. At the moment the Broodies were a collection of twenty-six outcasts from London society who had come together simply to survive. The twenty males and six females ranged from the ages of fifteen to twenty-seven, Keen's age. They all had criminal histories, mostly theft and acts of violence before they'd joined the Broodies. Paulie's loose lips revealed that Tom Lancey was a good forger, Will Satterwaite a very able cracksman, and both Jane Howard and Ginger Teale such practised pickpockets they could, as he put it, "steal the cock off Sad Dick and turn him Mary."

The main occupation of the Broodies, it seemed from what Paulie told, was keeping order in their territory. It wouldn't do, he said, for a tavern to burn up overnight or a shop to lose all its windows, or the owner of that tavern or shop to take a tumble and break something they needed to walk around on. Thus, money was paid to the Broodies to keep those foul things from happening. The Broodies could walk freely from their territory into enemy territory by day, just as could all the other gangs freely move, but with nightfall came the rule that payment was due by pain and blood if a rival gang member was caught poaching. And, according to Paulie, the scouts were always out watching the streets and those scudders knew who was who.

But, also according to the talkative boy, the Broodies did perform services for their territory other than demanding tribute. They settled disputes among tavern owners and other business keeps without need of court, and somehow—at least this was what

Matthew garnered from the revelations—the Broodies were able to maintain the constant flow of commerce in the area, such as making sure a shipment of spoiled wine from a merchant in Clerkenwell was repaid by the burning down of the merchant's house. Thus the Broodies sent the message to all merchants dealing with their territory in Whitechapel that respect given was respect earned, and as Paulie put it, "vicey versey."

What seemed to be the particular bone of contention between the Broodies and the Mohocks was the pink-light area of bordellos Matthew had passed through; for awhile the Broodies had claimed it, as well as a percentage of the take for protection services, and then with the death of the last Broodie leader in combat the Mohocks had taken it over. Now the Broodies wanted it back, and they were scouting to learn the Mohocks' strength and find their head-quarters, which like that of the Broodies was frequently moved to avoid such detection.

On this third day of his confinement—morning it was, because Jane Howard had brought him a bowl of oatmeal and a small pot of tea, as she'd previously done at the same time the morning before—the door at the top of the stairs was unlocked and Pie Puddin walked into the glow of Matthew's lamp.

"Time for you to get acquainted with my friend," she said, and she held up an open razor, which appeared to be no friend of Matthew's.

"I'll say hello at a distance," he answered, but his calm flippancy was a lie. He was calculating the geometries of throwing his blanket over her head, somehow evading and gaining control of that blade, and—

"Go on with you!" said the girl. "How am I to shave you at a distance?" She lifted into the light the shaving-bowl in her other hand.

"Oh. Well...thank you, but—"

"Hush. I'm gettin' them whiskers off that face, and that's the fact of it." She knelt beside Matthew and got her position comfortable. She set the shaving-bowl down and drew the lamp nearer. Matthew saw a cake of soap in the bowl's water. Pie closed the razor, put it into a pocket of her brown leather waistcoat, and drew from another pocket a pair of scissors. "First we gotta trim the hedges."

"Really, it's not—"

"There's a handsome face under that scruffle," she said. "Let's get some light on it." She began the task of trimming. "Lordy, you been long without a shave!"

"Yes, a long time."

"Not that I'm sayin' some don't look fine and gallant with a beard. Roger's got one, and Will too, but I expect you to clean up better'n they would."

"I hope I don't disa—*ouch*!"

"Tough ol' hairs don't want to give up the ghost," she said, as she continued to cut. "Y'know, Jane's got an eye for you. She's the one asked me to do this. Also wanted me to ask if you was taken."

Matthew didn't know how to respond to this. Jane was probably about Pie's age, sixteen, as thin as a beggar's cloak and with limp brown hair that had been weeks without a wash, but she did have very beautiful, luminous green eyes.

"She can clean up real good, too," Pie told him as if reading his thoughts. "And she ain't been so rough used as to be muffin-dead. She got out of the crib 'fore it killed her."

"I'm glad of that. She seems very kind. I have to say, I *am* taken."

"By who?" The scissors chattered away.

"Pie," he said, "you have the damnedest way of trying to get information from me. Did Rory put you up to this?"

"Little a' him, greater part a' Jane. So who's took you?"

"A girl in New York."

The scissors stopped. She peered into his eyes. "You're from the colonies?"

"I am. Came over here and was put directly into gaol at Plymouth. To answer the question you're about to ask, the murder I committed was aboard the ship."

"Ahhhhhh." She nodded and began trimming again as if this information involved nothing more serious than a tricorn lost at sea. "Who'd you off?"

"A very wicked man. A Prussian, who certainly would've tried to kill me if I hadn't…*offed* him," he said.

"You got an interestin' story. There, that's the best trimmin' can do." She brushed all the hair off the blanket, put the scissors away and began to rub the soap between her hands to make lather. "Where'd you get such a scar?"

"I had a fight with a bear."

"Oh, don't be throwin' me Adam's rib! Really...where'd you get it?"

"Honestly. I fought a bear in the wild. It nearly killed me, but I'm still here."

She looked at him with new appreciation. "Ain't many can say that. *If* it's true. How 'bout all them other small marks you got? Little scar here, little scar there. Them's from the cubs?"

"No," said Matthew with a small laugh. "They're from...other circumstances."

"Circumstances can kill you," she said, and then she began applying the lather to her subject's face. "I never killed nobody. Good thing I heal fast, though, 'cause I've took some hard circumstances." Matthew had already noted that her injuries were mostly gone away, the cut across the bridge of her nose scabbed over, the bruises faded, the chin scrapes and knot disappeared and the swollen and discolored right eye nearly back to normal except for a small smear of purple. "Got to go scoutin' again soon, though. Take my lumps like always, I reckon. Worth it in the long run, to get rid'a them Mohocks." She brought the razor out and opened it. "Where to start?" she asked, studying the angles of the face that was being revealed. "Maybe I'll just cut your nose off and call it a day." She laughed at the widening of Matthew's eyes. "I'm throwin' you Eve's apple! Let's start on that chin."

As the shaving progressed, Matthew could not suppress his curiosity a moment more, and though he knew this condition of his would likely be the end of him, he had to follow its lead.

"Tell me," he said as Pie worked on his right cheek, "what's in all those crates and barrels. Sure are a lot of them."

"Oh yeah," she answered, without an iota of hesitation. "That's the White Velvet. Bottles in the crates, gin in the barrels."

Matthew recalled what Parmenter had told him in Newgate: *Cheap gin that knocks a man senseless. Just stay away from that pi'sen is my advice.*

"What's it doing down here?" Matthew asked, aware than any one question could be one too many. She was very deft with the razor; perhaps too much so.

"We dole it out ever' so often. Fill up the bottles, sell 'em to certain taverns. They pay good money for it, 'cause the stuff's special."

"Special? How?"

Pie stopped shaving him. She drew the razor away from his face and looked deeply into his eyes. "Listen here, and listen good," she said firmly. "Don't you never take a drink a' White Velvet. Know why they call it that? 'Cause they say it's like sippin' white velvet...goes down clean and easy. But you take a gander at them crates. Thirty bottles apiece in 'em. You drink one bottle a' White Velvet, your goose is fuckin' good and cooked. One bottle, and you'd sell your granny for another...and if she was dead, you'd dig up her carcass and try to sell that. Believe you me, that shit is *devilish*."

"Oh," said Matthew. He was remembering something. Gardner Lillehorne in the conference room at St. Peter's Place, saying *Bring a new influx of cheap and mind-robbing gin to the equation, and you have the makings of Dante's Inferno upon English earth.*

"Stick with rum," Pie advised as she went back to her task. "We had a Broodie drank White Velvet in secret, back...oh...it was last year. Wasn't a secret too long. Pert soon he looked like a walkin' skeleton and all he gave a damn about was gettin' another sip." She stopped the razorwork, the better to concentrate on the telling. "We tried to give him the hemp cure...y'know, tie him to a bed for as many hours as it took, but he was too strong for us. Him weighin' maybe ninety pounds. Jumped out a third-floor window. Hell of it was he landed right on a lady gettin' out of a carriage. Busted his leg but he was still a runner, crazed as he was. Horse reared up, caught him underneath, bashed his head in. You can bet we hightailed it."

"If the stuff's so bad, why do you sell it?" Matthew asked.

She gave him a look she must've reserved until she'd met the dumbest man in the world. "*Money*, dear heart. Them that wants will find a way to gets. Anyway, we ain't the only ones sellin' it. We just cover our own—"

"There's the gentleman!"

The door had opened, letting in a shaft of light. The voice belonged to Rory Keen, who entered the cellar followed by three other Broodies. He carried a lantern and by its light wore a merry smile. "How goes the shavin', Pie?"

"Little more to do."

"Step aside," he told her.

"Huh?"

"Aside," he said. His smile was aimed at Matthew, who felt a sudden chill and not only to his newly-exposed face. "*Step*," said Keen.

Pie obeyed. Keen put his lantern down on the crate beside the oil lamp. He sat on the floor next to Matthew, took the razor from Pie's hand, washed it off in the bowl of water, ran a cautious thumb along the edge and gave a low whistle of admiration at the razor's sharpness. Then he said, "Let's finish up your throat. Lift your chin up. Little more. There you go!" The razor went to work, even more deftly than Pie had handled it.

"Ever'thin' all right?" Pie asked, also evidently feeling a chill. Her smile and bright demeanor were gone.

"Fine. Just dandy. Peachy," said Keen. "Look how pretty Matthew's gettin' to be. Like his mug now, Jane?"

Jane, standing among the others, did not answer.

"Jane went out a little while ago," said Keen as he continued to work the razor across Matthew's throat. "Know why? 'Cause she knew the latest *Pin* was on the street today. Got herself a copy, brung it back here to read. She's a right good reader. 'Course, she saw that first story soon as she got her hands on it. Read us that top part, Jane."

In her small, reedy voice, she read what must have been set in bold type: "*Monster Of Plymouth Compatriot Of Albion.*"

"Oh, careful!" said Keen. "You jumped a bit, Matthew. Don't want to do that with this razor slidin' back and forth and forth and back. Pie, you can read...pick up that book a' words there and find 'compatriot'. I am real curious as to what that means. Jane, go ahead and read us the next line. Chin up, Matthew, I don't want to do you no damage."

"*Villain Loose in Whitechapel*," she read. "You want me to keep goin'?"

"Go."

"*Officials report*," Jane continued, "*that the so-called Monster of Plymouth, by name Matthew Corbett of the New York colony in the Americas, lately has escaped Newgate Prison with the help of that golden-masked fiend of the night we know as Albion. Corbett, who murdered at sea an important Prussian dignitary on his way to England for a meeting with the crown, is also accused of the murders of three women and five children in Plymouth."*

"*Nice*," said Keen. "Lemme get this little patch right under your lip. Go on, Jane, you're gettin' to the good part."

"*The Monster of Plymouth*," she went on, in a voice that seemed to fade in and out or perhaps that was just Matthew's hearing under the pressure that squeezed his brain, "*cut the heads off his victims, painted them in bright colors and planted them atop fenceposts to be, in his satanic mind, admired by all. He escaped custody of the law with help from Albion, who waylaid the prison coach in which Corbett was riding and afforded the Monster with clothing, money, lantern, two daggers, a pistol, and a garotte made of human hair.*"

"Almost done here," Keen announced. "You're gonna be all shiny. Jane, read that next amazin' part."

"*Reports to this news sheet say Albion visited the Monster in Newgate, walking through walls as only the phantom can do, and in that noble prison vowed to loose Corbett upon London, the better that they become brothers in murder and terror.*"

"That is awful fine writin'." Keen lowered the razor. He smiled into Matthew's face, but his eyes were dark and deadly holes. "Now tell me this: what're we gonna do with you?"

"If you'll—" Matthew began...*listen to me*, he was going to say, but the hand at his throat and the razor under his right eye said that his words had become of no value.

"I could *cut* you," Keen whispered, up close to Matthew's face. "I could carve you into a hundred fuckin' pieces, put you in a bag and then in the river, and...looky here...I done killed me a monster and brother to that fuckin' Albion. You find that word, Pie?" She nodded. "Read it!" he commanded.

She did, rather haltingly: "*Compatriot...of the same country... holdin' the same politics...allied in beliefs.*"

"Allied in beliefs," Keen repeated. The razor had begun to sting Matthew's flesh. "Ain't that a kick in the fuckin' head?"

Though most of his attention was of necessity riveted to the ominous razor, something had begun to work in Matthew's mind. It was like the humming of industrious wasps around a nest, coupled with a sudden burst of light in absolute dark.

"Jane," he said, his throat tight, "would you…please re-read the sentence that ends with the words 'human hair'?"

"Huh?" she asked.

"What, you're so high on y'self you want to hear it again?" Keen's breath smelled like the kind of acid that could burn a man to his bones. "Go on then, Jane. Consider it a last request."

She read: "*He escaped custody of the law with help from Albion, who waylaid the prison coach in which Corbett was riding and afforded the Monster with clothing, money, a lantern, two daggers, a pistol, and a garotte made of human hair.*"

"That suit you?" Keen asked.

"A moment," said Matthew. "If I may speak without fear of being sliced?"

"You think you can talk your way out of this? You workin' on Albion's side, and that bastard puttin' the snuff to Benny? What're you doin' here? Wantin' to murder *me* next?"

"I am not working on Albion's side. Who Albion is and what he wants, I have no idea."

"You *lie*," came the next heated response.

"I think," Matthew said carefully, "we can all agree that Lord Puffery's pen—and *Pin*—turns saplings into orchards. He seizes on a small statement of truth and expands that into a tome of fiction. I would have you consider: someone brought this story to Lord Puffery, who has greatly embellished it. Did Albion enter into Newgate? True. Did Albion waylay the prison coach? True. Did Albion give me those items? Both true and false, and here is a mystery."

"What the hell are you goin' on about?"

"The guards witnessed Albion giving me possession of clothing, money and the lantern. But they did *not* see him give me a dagger. When the dagger was mentioned to Lord Puffery, it became two daggers, a pistol and a garotte, as per sapling into orchard. Only Albion knew about the dagger…therefore—"

"Therefore I think I'll start my cuttin' on them flappin' lips."

"Therefore," Matthew pressed on, "the person who submitted that story to Lord Puffery is Albion himself."

Was there ever a deeper silence? The candle in Keen's lantern hissed, and that was all.

Then: "Why the *fuck* would Albion have told all that to Lord Puffery?" Keen's razor had not moved a hair, neither had its dangerous pressure lessened.

"I don't know. All I do know is that when Albion pulled me out of that coach he told me to be at the Tavern of the Three Sisters at midnight. He spoke in a low whisper. I would imagine when he spoke to Lord Puffery he used his regular voice, and he stood unmasked."

"You mean…Lord Puffery got a look at who Albion really is?"

"Yes, but unless Lord Puffery is actually sponsoring Albion's endeavors, he had no idea to whom he was speaking."

Still the razor did not budge. "You really murder all them women and children?"

"I killed a dirty Prussian killer aboard a ship from Charles Town. He was as much a dignitary as I am the king of Siam. Again—"

"You're sayin' some of what's in the *Pin* is *made up*?" It was a shocked question not from Jane Howard, but from Tom Lancey, who obviously had put much stock in the publication. He sounded stricken. "What about Lady Everlust and her two-headed child?"

"Oh Jesus," Keen muttered. The razor left Matthew's face but the hand remained clenched to the problem-solver's throat. "Why should I believe you ain't workin' with Albion?"

"I don't know what Albion's trying to accomplish. I understand he's—would you remove your hand, please, it's very uncomfortable." After a few seconds, Keen did. Matthew continued. "I understand he's murdered six men, Benjamin Greer included. All of them have been criminals charged yet released from prison by legal machinations."

"By *what*?"

"Able and cunning lawyers," Matthew amended. "I would imagine that bribery had a hand in it as well. I think Albion holds a grudge not only against those six men but against the entire English legal system…or rather, what he considers the corruption of such."

"You're in water over my head," said Keen.

"Deep water indeed. Almost over mine as well. I have many questions, but one foremost is: what does Albion want with *me*? When he got me out of that coach—and I can tell you I feared for my life at that moment—he said he was not only helping me but that I was going to help *him*."

"What? To murder the rest of the Broodies?"

"No, certainly not that. But I wonder...I understand that Ben Greer was killed after he'd been drinking at the Three Sisters? And then Albion wanted to meet me there...presumably, in an unmasked condition, just entering as any patron would." Matthew's brow furrowed. "What is it about the Three Sisters that might draw Albion's attention?"

"Don't know. But I do know that place is our best customer."

"Customer? For what?"

"The White Velvet. Over in them barrels. We bottle it and sell it around to the taverns. The Three Sisters would buy ever' drop, if they could." Now it was Keen's turn to frown. "Hm. I'm thinkin' maybe I shouldn't have told you that. The Mohocks would sure like to get their claws on what we got down here." He looked to one side. "Pie? You believe him?"

She hesitated.

Matthew felt very cold indeed, and very much alone.

Then Pie said, "I do believe him. Look at him, Rory! He may be scarred up and hard on the outside, but he's got soft innards. He ain't killed no women and children."

"He's got a handsome face," said Jane. "For a monster, I mean."

"He ain't no monster," Keen decided. "He's just a man got hisself in a right sticky Londontown mess. A smart man, though, and one I could put to good use."

"Pardon?" Matthew asked.

"One way to show us you're on the level," said Keen, his eyes fiery again. "You join the Broodies. Take the oath and get the mark, you'll be bound for life. Means you ain't gonna wander far from our sight, either."

"Well...I appreciate the offer, but what I need to do is get some clothes and be on my way to find Lord Puffery. He knows who Albion is, though he likely doesn't know he knows."

"You talk like you're blowin' smoke rings. Kinda entertainin', to hear you." The razor came up and rested against Matthew's jugular vein. "I wouldn't kill you here. Too bloody. But there's places it can be done, easy. Two ways you're endin' this day: either in pieces in a burlap bag in the river, or proud to be a Black-Eyed Broodie. Which is it gonna be, Mr. Corbett?"

He didn't have to hesitate very long. The razor meant business, and as he needed the full use of his legs to locate Lord Puffery, he didn't have much of a choice.

With a smile so tight it could have been its own Roper's Window, Matthew said, "I would be proud to be proud."

"Good. Then you'll be with us tonight, when we raid the Mohocks and kill that fuckin' Fire Wind."

Nineteen

"Satisfied?"

"Another moment, please," said Matthew. He had seen the welcome sun appear from the clouds for perhaps forty seconds, shining a yellow glare upon the streets of Whitechapel. Then the clouds had closed up again, their gray bellies pregnant with more rain, and the cold wind grew colder still.

"Nothin' much to see out here," Rory Keen told him, standing at his elbow.

And that was true, if one was looking for beauty. Matthew was looking for the substance of the neighborhood, and indeed it was not a lovely sight. Standing on the front steps of the dilapidated and abandoned warehouse the Broodies called home, and dressed in a ghastly purple suit that had been procured for him from a local tailor's shop, Matthew had been given time to take stock of where he was in the scheme of things.

It was, first and foremost, a pleasure to not have a razor threatening his life; secondly a pleasure to be wearing clothes and sturdy boots, and thirdly to be out from the confines of that damp cellar into the air, though the air be equally as damp. To the west amid the awesome crush of buildings stood the larger constructs of London, the stately and grandiose towers of the government meant to endure into eternity. To the east new parts of the metropolis were being born, a landscape of hundreds of wooden frames rising amid a sprawling tent city set up to house workmen and their families, and from where he stood Matthew could see all that and the sparkle of small fires on muddy hillsides. Horses, mules and oxen were pulling wagons loaded with bricks and timbers along paths yet to be made into streets. He couldn't see much to the south, for all the buildings in the way, but he figured the warehouses were sardine-packed side-by-side down there amid the river wharves.

Somewhere, he was sure, there were elegant gated neighborhoods where the lords and ladies dallied on the plush luxury of their estates, where the snow-white wigs were always of the current fashion, where the carriages were kept spotlessly clean by the loyal servants and the horses in the barns were fed the finest oats and pranced beneath the smoothest of leather saddles.

Wherever that was, it was a world away from Whitechapel.

Here the very sky was filthy with the crisscrossed black banners flowing from dozens of industrial smokestacks, and the ebony effluvium came down and settled as dirty dew upon the squat and crooked buildings so that no roof nor window nor brick nor chink between bricks could ever be anything but the color of midnight. If there was a wig-wearer passing by, he was staggering drunk and likely moony, and his wig looked as if someone had burned it as tinderbox cotton. The wagons that trundled along the streets, which were mud covered with cinders, all appeared to have been recently wrecked and bound back together with ropes and pieces of other wrecked wagons either smaller or larger than the original, for none seemed to be of the correct proportions. Even the horse teams were mismatched, as one big and slow-hoofing beast that had been trampled by the world was yoked to a smaller animal straining at the bit, or as Paulie would say, "vicey-versey". Every wagon, and there were many in the progression of local commerce, moved as if on its way to the driver's funeral.

Matthew saw clearly that the territory of the Black-Eyed Broodies was simply the black eye of London. He had the impression that the industries here—mostly tanneries and slaughterhouses, from the odor of scorched blood and rotten guts wafting in the wind—were vital to the city's progress yet a blight on the senses of those same elite lords and ladies who lived a world apart, thus it had been necessary to further the distance. The buildings were most made of rough stones and bricks but there remained a few wooden ones like the warehouse upon which steps Matthew stood; the old timbers and roofs of these structures had taken quite a beating, and seemed to be either slowly caving in or bending toward the earth in defeat. The sun had for its scant appearance found glass beneath the grime and gave a falsely merry glint off the many windows, though most were only large enough to allow a single face at a time to peer out from the dark interiors.

To be such a hellish pit, the area of course offered a paradise to the determined drinker. Nearly directly across the street was the Drunk Crow Tavern. Three doors to its right was the Sip A' Courage, and across the way and further to the east stood the Long-Legged Liza. A goodly number of pedestrians were on the move, all of them—men, women and children of varied ages—looking as if they'd just awakened from long alcoholic binges or particularly frightening nightmares.

"Had your fill?" Keen asked.

Matthew realized he was not adding to the beauty of the scene. The hideous suit he wore was a shade of purple that boasted an undertone of green in the nubby cloth, plus a bright green piping at lapels and cuffs. He refused to wear the purple-and-green-checked waistcoat that had been presented to him with this getup; it was bad enough that his shiny stockings were a pale lavender hue. But the cream-colored shirt was bearable even with its unfortunate froth of vomitous green ruffles down the front, and the brown boots didn't squeeze his feet too painfully. It was the best Keen said they could get anywhere near his size from the unsold merchandise at a tailor's shop the next street over, so—as Keen had put it—"take it or go jaybird, up to you."

"Had my fill," Matthew replied to Keen's query. It was time to do whatever he had to do to get this Broodie business over and done, though the prospect of raiding the Mohocks and killing anyone tonight was a plan he wished to object to once the formalities were finished.

Keen followed him back into the building. All the windows were boarded up. There was a large central chamber and a warren of rooms around it, these being the rooms the various Broodies inhabited. Pigeons by the plenty roosted up in the rafters. Some of the holes in the roof were large enough to drop a wagon through and under those holes the planks of the floor were stained black by sooty rain. Various rusted chains and pulleys hung from the ceiling, indicating that heavy weights were once hoisted here for whatever purpose.

All twenty-five of the other Black-Eyes were waiting for Keen and Matthew. Each one held a candle. True to their name, they had put circles of black greasepaint around their eyes and they stood in a circle. They appeared more raccoons than rowdies, but far be it from Matthew to say anything. He wondered if he was going to have to eat bugs or something, or have to recite an infantile creed that would have him laughing before he finished it; beware a blade to the throat if that happened, he thought.

"Stand in the center," Keen told him. Matthew obeyed as Pie applied the black grease to Keen's eyes. Then Keen lit a candle of his own from Pie's flame and regarded Matthew with his ebonied orbs. "We won't be hard on you," he said. "Ordinarily to start with I'd put you up against two men and let 'em beat the tar out of you, but as I need ever'body in good health tonight that'll have to wait for later."

"Makes sense," said Matthew.

"Shut up and don't try to be cute," Keen told him. "This is damned serious, whether you think so or not. The Black-Eyed Broodies been a fam'ly for near twenty years, been takin' care of each other and guardin' the streets since I come in when I was ten years old. Came in when Spencer Luttrum was the head man, and a finer more honest gent there never was. I was there when a Cobra Cult bastard stabbed him in the heart, and I was there when we run that fella down and skinned him alive. I seen 'em come in hungry and tattered and we fed and clothed 'em, gave 'em a reason to keep on livin'. I seen 'em so mad at the world they could fight their own shadows, and sometimes their own shadows were what killed 'em. I seen 'em rise to greatness from the dirt of the streets and I seen 'em fall back to that dirt bloody and dyin', but they didn't die as nobody's dogs. They lived and died as Black-Eyed Broodies, part of a tradition. So what I'm sayin' is, we got a lot of *history* here, and anybody don't take history with a serious mind has got a lot of woe in his future. Who wants to be first?"

First? Matthew tensed; he didn't like the sound of that.

"I'll choose," said Keen. "We'll go 'round the circle, startin' with Tom."

Tom Lancey stepped toward Matthew, hawked up a spit and delivered it squarely into Matthew's face.

"Let it run," Keen instructed as Matthew lifted a hand to wipe away the offending spittle. "Touch it and we start over again. Paulie, you're next. Keep it movin'."

To bear a spit in the face from twenty-six mouths was not how Matthew had figured this was going to go, but at least he was not going to be thrashed. As the members of the Broodies stepped forward to perform this solemn duty, Keen intoned a speech that Matthew suspected had been repeated time and time again through the years.

"We give of ourselves," Keen said tonelessly, "and in givin' we receive new blood and new strength. So doth the Black-Eyed Broodies live on. Long may the Broodies live, long may we take refuge in each other, protect each other and what we have, and subject our enemies to 'orrible deaths."

Jane Howard had been about to spit in Matthew's face. She paused, and with the others in unison repeated the last sentence of Keen's speech. Then she spat a good greasy one in Matthew's left eye and stepped back for John Bellsen to take his turn.

"State your name," said Keen to Matthew, who wisely waited until the spittle splashed his forehead before he opened his mouth. "Log it in your hearts, scribe it on your souls," Keen intoned to the others. Then, again to Matthew, "State your reason for joinin' the Broodies," and before Matthew could reply—and what he was going to say he didn't know—Keen answered for him: "To uphold the laws of this fam'ly and give honor to your brothers and sisters, and damn you to a mongrel's death and eternity in the shittiest hole of Hell if you don't."

Kevin Tyndale gave Matthew a full blast that he must've been saving in a phlegm-pouch at the back of his mouth since midmorning, for it was heavy with bits of oatmeal. Next up, Angie Lusk equalled the force of that spit and more, and the mucous that flew out of that small mouth streaked across Matthew's face like the strike of a whip. The following spit, delivered by Billy Hayes, sealed Matthew's right eye and effectively blinded him for he dared not lift a finger to clear his vision. Besides, he didn't care to see any more strings of spit flying into his face, anyway.

But the wet initiation continued. The next spitter—Will Satterwaite, it would have been from the continuation of the circle—took a diabolically long time hawking up clumps of goo, and when all of it hit Matthew's face it was at very close range and with such power that Matthew actually staggered back before Keen's hand caught and steadied him.

The mess drooled down Matthew's forehead, cheeks and chin. His eyes were glued shut. It went on for so long Matthew suspected Keen had gone out into the street to recruit the beggars with the foulest breath and saliva he could haul in; surely the end of the circle was near, or was it in this case a horrible example of the circle being unbroken and the treatment would continue until Keen decided it was done?

Matthew took it, with his hands down by his sides. At last—long last!—there came a fierce spit into the morass of Matthew's face that was followed by...nothing.

"You are now the lowest of the low of the highest of the high," came Keen's voice.

"Repeat this: I solemnly swear..." He paused. "Well, go on, we ain't waitin' all day!"

Matthew, his eyes still shut and the rivulets still dripping, said, "I solemnly swear..."

"To be faithful and true to the Black-Eyed Broodies..."

Matthew repeated the same.

"...and hold my brothers and sisters..."

The same, again.

"...in the highest regard and respect, show no mercy to their enemies, and do no harm to nobody who is and ever was a Broodie."

Matthew repeated it.

"And if I don't," Keen went on, "I take it plain that I am worse than dogshit and give my brothers and sisters leave to remove me from this earth without complaint. I swear this a hundred times a hundred."

"I swear this a hundred times a hundred," Matthew said, with tight lips because some of the mess was getting in.

"That finishes the oath. Here, stand still." A cloth that smelled of musty dampness was wiped over Matthew's face several times, unsticking his eyelids. He opened his eyes to find Keen offering him an uncorked bottle of rum. "Take a swig." Matthew did, and then Keen took a drink and passed it around to the others, who still remained in the circle. Keen sloshed the liquor in his mouth and Matthew had the fright that now came a group spritzing, but then Keen swallowed it down and the fright passed.

"We'll whip your ass later," Keen vowed. "But you ain't a full Broodie quite yet. Pie, come on and do the honors."

Matthew realized she had stepped out of the circle. Now she returned carrying a silver tray on which rested a small blue bowl and a couple of strange-looking sticks. She said, "Over here," to him, and he walked out of the center of the circle to where a table had been set up, two chairs pulled close together, and two oil lamps atop the table. "Sit down," she told him. He took one chair and she the other. He saw black ink in the blue bowl and realized the sticks were tattoo instruments: one was called a rake, being a length of wood like a Chinese chopstick with a small piece of bone with little needle teeth attached to its end, and the other a more blunt piece of wood called a striking-stick. A multitude of nail holes pocked the tabletop.

He knew he was about to get his, as Pie had put it, "fam'ly mark".

As the main part of this ceremony seemed to be done, the circle of Broodies broke up. Some drifted off and others came nearer the table to watch. The rum bottle was still being passed around, and then someone put it on the table within reach of Matthew's left hand. A few small pieces of sponge were also on the silver tray.

"Pie's our artist," Keen said, pulling up another chair to sit and watch.

"Not near as good as Ben was. He had the touch." She wet one of the pieces of sponge with rum and cleaned the area of Matthew's right hand between the thumb and forefinger. "It don't hurt too bad," she explained. "Just takes a little time."

"Oh, make it hurt *bad*," Keen said, with a crooked smile. "And draw it out it 'til he screams."

"He's playin' your fiddle." Pie darted Keen a disapproving scowl. "Gent needs to be *relaxed*, Rory!"

"I'm relaxed," Matthew said, though the rake's needle teeth, as tiny as they were, did appear fearsome.

Will Satterwaite suddenly leaned over him and with a mallet drove a nail into the tabletop. "Thumb against that," he said.

Matthew saw the method in this; it was to stretch his hand so the area to be tattooed was smoothed out. He placed his thumb against the nail, Will took a measurement by eye and then drove in a second nail. Matthew stretched his hand and placed his index finger on the other side of this nail. It was a bit uncomfortable, the nails being spaced widely enough so that Matthew imagined the tendons between thumb and forefinger were in danger of tearing, but he could stand it; he just hoped he didn't have to hold this position very long. He took the bottle of rum with his left hand and had a good deep drink.

"Ready?" Pie had already dipped the bone needles in the ink bowl, just a touch at the tips.

He nodded, noting that Jane Howard was standing nearby watching him with hungry, black-ringed eyes. He thought she needed a good stomach-filling meal of chicken and biscuits more than anything else.

"Here we go," Pie said. She placed the needles in position and used the striker to make contact between sharp bone and stretched skin. The pain compared to what Matthew had endured lately and in other situations was miniscule, more of an irritating itch like the biting of a battalion of bedbugs. He considered that Pie might not be the best at this craft but she was indeed very smooth and fast, the noise of the striker against the rake being rapid bursts of *ta-ta-too, ta-ta-too, ta-ta-too*, from which the procedure had received its name.

"May I ask a question?" Matthew had directed this to Keen.

"You can *ask*, but you might not get an answer."

"Fair enough. What crime did Ben Greer commit that sent him to St. Peter's Place?"

"Easy question. A snatch and rough-up."

"Translate, please?"

"Stealin' somethin' and knockin' the fella 'round a bit. To leave him a lesson, so to speak."

"What was stolen?"

"A calf's-skin carry-all. You know, one of them things the lawyers are always totin', to make 'emselves look important."

"Really?" Matthew frowned. "Of what use was that to the Broodies?"

Keen shrugged. "It was what was inside the case was wanted. My orders were to send a strongarm or two over to High Holborn Street on a certain day and a certain time and nail a fella as he was leavin' a buildin'. Take the carry-all, boot the gent a bit to leave him bloody, and get gone. Ben nabbed the goods, but the gent called out for help and there happened to be a pair a' constables comin' out of a bakery right up the way. They caught Ben and gave him a conkin'."

Matthew took all this in as he watched Pie's process of dipping the tips of the bone needles into the ink and then *ta-ta-too*ing again with a rapid beat of the striker. Tiny dots of blood appeared, which Pie blotted with a bit of sponge. "I'm not getting something," he said. "What do you mean, your *orders*?"

"Just that. Word come down from above."

"From above? From *whom*, above?"

Keen grinned, his silver teeth glinting in the light. The black circles around his eyes gave him a savagely sinister appearance. "You're just *full* 'a questions, ain't you?"

"Help me become empty of them."

"Somehow I doubt that would ever happen." Keen was silent for awhile, watching Pie work with the rake and striker, and Matthew let him deliberate. Then Keen said, "Way it's been since Mick Abernathy struck the deal. He was head of the Broodies a'fore Neville Morse, who was just a'fore me. Mohocks killed Neville and Georgie Cole last April, jumped 'em comin' out of the Brave Cavalier on Cannon Street. Cut 'em to pieces, and Georgie swelled up with Neville's kid. Anyway, the deal was struck and it holds. We do things, we get paid. Simple business."

"Things? Like what?"

"Such as I've told you. Little errands here and there. And we move the White Velvet for 'em."

"Them? Who?"

"Lordy, Matthew! Some things you need to let be."

Matthew decided the wind from this direction was in danger of dying, so it was time to tack. "The White Velvet," he said, watching the tattoo on his hand take shape. "Where does it come from?"

"From a wagon," Keen answered, and followed that with a harsh laugh.

"Driven by…?"

Keen's smile went away. He leaned forward and sniffed the air. "Smell that, Pie? That stink? I told you before, Matthew reeks of the Old Bailey."

"I'm just curious," Matthew said. "Really. If I'm to be a Black-Eyed Broodie, shouldn't I—"

"No, you shouldn't. Not your first fuckin' *hour.*" Keen sat very still for a moment. His eyes were dead, and suddenly he reached up with both hands and smeared the black rings as if trying to wipe them away. "I got things to do," he said, and he abruptly got up from his chair and left the area. A few of the Broodies remained, watching Pie work, but most had gone off to their various interests. Jane Howard was one who'd stayed, and Matthew noted that she was slowly coming closer and closer.

"How's that feelin'?" Pie asked.

"Stinging a bit. Otherwise, fine."

"Little details to be done right in this here area. Ben was lots better at this than me, and faster too."

"I have time."

She nodded, and then she said quietly, "You shouldn't ask about the Velvet. It bothers him, us sellin' it to the taverns and knowin' what it did to Josh."

"Josh?"

"Yeah, Joshua Oakley. He's the one I told you went crazy, jumped out the third-floor window."

"I see." He was aware that Jane Howard was right at his shoulder. She needed a bath, in the worst way.

"Bothers him," Pie went on, "'cause he wonders how many others gone out of their minds on it. He's told me so, number of times. Wonders how many women drank the Velvet and threw their infants in the fire thinkin' they was throwin' in a log on a freezin' cold night, or how many men drinkin' it and gone crazy thinkin' they was fightin' back in a war, and wound up killin' ever' soul in the house. Those things have happened, mark it."

"Sounds like more of a drug than a drink. I know it makes money, but why keep selling it if it weighs so heavily on him? I think if I were in his position, I'd—"

"You ain't," she interrupted, with perhaps a sharper blow of the striker than was necessary. "And you don't know the kind of people got us in this deal to sell it for 'em. Harder cases could not be found by lookin' under ever' rock in London. Anyway, like I said...and Rory knows it, too...if we weren't movin' the Velvet somebody else would be, and it ain't like we're the only ones sellin' it. So just let it be, Matthew." She gave another little severe strike. "Let it be."

It seemed to Matthew that the spindly Jane was now nearly about to sit upon his lap. To forestall this from happening, he looked at her with a smile and said, "Jane, would you do me a favor?"

"*Anythin'*," she answered, gushily.

He had to figure out quickly what that favor might be. "Would you...oh...find that copy of the *Pin* and bring it to me?"

"Sure will!" she said, and she rushed off.

"You wantin' to read about y'self again?" Pie asked.

"No. Just wantin' to—I mean, *wanting* to—get myself some breathing room. Besides, if you don't care to answer any further questions about the White Velvet, or who's really in charge around here..." He paused, leaving the gate open.

"I do *not*," she answered, slamming the gate shut and tossing away the key.

"Then," he continued, "I might as well read about Lady Everlust's two-headed child." As he waited for Jane to return with the news sheet, he was vaguely bothered by something he had himself said just a moment before, concerning the Velvet: *Sounds like more of a drug than a drink.*

That stirred up dirty water from a swampy place inside him, but he didn't quite know what it was. Something he ought to remember, he thought, and he wondered if indeed his memory was in places still faulty.

Jane returned with the sheet, which was so wrinkled and crinkled and smeared and smudged that every hand in the house must have been on it sometime today. Except for twice reading through the story with his name in it and verifying his suspicions that only Albion would have known about the dagger, he'd wanted nothing to do with the paper. Now, though, it would be a nice barrier between himself and Jane while Pie finished up the tattoo.

"Want me to read it to you?" Jane asked, her eyes bright in the bony face.

"No, thank you. I imagine you have something else you should be doing?"

"Naw, not a thing."

Matthew reached for the rum bottle and took a swig before he accepted the *Pin*. "Well," he said, "if you'll just sit quietly somewhere, I'd like to read."

"I'll stand right here, close by, in case you're needin' anythin' else."

Pie gave a soft little chuckle. Matthew mentally closed both of the women out and regarded the renowned rag. The article about himself, the fearsome Monster of Plymouth, and Albion had indeed pushed the continuing tribulations of Lady Everlust further down the page. Lady Everlust shared column height with an article about a certain Lord Haymake of Rochester who had hanged himself after making love to five wenches in one night, the hanging commencing because apparently the seventy-year-old letch could not raise his falstaff for the sixth—as the Pin put it—'moist valley of Paradise'.

"Have mercy!" Matthew muttered to himself, but a line at the end of the article read *Next Issue: A Wench Comes Into Fortune* and Matthew was horrified to realize he was rather interested in which wench it was.

Then there came a few paragraphs about the kidnapped Italian opera singer, Madam Alicia Candoleri, headlined *Opera Star Still Missing* and, below that, the question *Murder Claims The Songbird?*

"Done here in a few," Pie said. "Devil's in the details."

Matthew nodded. The stylized eye in the ebony circle on his hand was taking shape. His other two eyes went to the next story down nearly at the bottom of the page.

Coalblack Amazes Audiences, read the boldtype headline. Below that, *African Strongman In Almsworth Circus.*

The first line caught Matthew's attention, with a jolt.

The amazing, massive African strongman known as Coalblack, who cannot speak due to loss of tongue, is currently in his third week of nightly showings at Almsworth Circus in Dove's Wing Alley, Bishopsgate.

The second line caused Matthew to nearly bolt upright from his chair.

As the reader recalls, the huge African with the strangely-scarred face who has become our famous Coalblack was found last June clinging to a bit of wreckage from a ship at sea, and brought to England by Captain James Troy of the Faithful Marianne.

"You jumped!" said Pie, who had stopped striking and raking. "What's the matter?"

Matthew was speechless. Was this an article about the Ga tribesman Zed, he of the tattooed face and tongueless condition, who had been an aide to Ashton McCaggers in New York, later such a great help in the dangerous situation on Pendulum Island, and when last seen had been aboard Captain Jerrell Falco's ship *Nightflyer* about to be sailed back to his homeland?

...clinging to a bit of wreckage from a ship at sea...

"*No*," Matthew heard himself whisper.

Was it possible one of Professor Fell's pirates had come across the *Nightflyer*, and recognizing it by its name as a vessel and captain cursed to destruction by Fell, given chase? Then, before the *Nightflyer* could fly into the night, cannonfire put an end to the ship? If this was indeed Zed, rescued from being adrift at sea, then what had happened to Falco? Death by drowning? Or captured by Fell's pirates?

"No, *what*?" Pie prompted, the instruments no longer *ta-ta-too*ing.

"No," he said, with an effort steadying the whirligig of his mind, "I'm just reading this...this utter *trash*. That's all."

"Alrighty. Hold firm now, just a bit more to be done."

He read the article over again.

Zed. Could it really be?

"Um...where is Almsworth Circus from here?" He was trying very hard to sound somewhat disinterested. "That would be...on Dove's Wing Alley, Bishopsgate."

"A far piece. Why?"

"I thought I might go sometime. I've always enjoyed them."

"Best go durin' the day, dearie," she said as she tapped out the last of the work, and though it wasn't as clean as what Ben Greer might have done, it was still a decent piece.

"The show doesn't start until after dark." He looked further into the article. "Says here it starts at eight o'clock."

"Good luck, then."

"What do I need that for?"

"Wellllllll," she said, drawing the word out, "you're marked as a Broodie now. Know how many gang territories you'd have to cross to get to Dove's Wing Alley off Bishopsgate? You ain't got that many fingers and toes to count on. Odds are you'd cross a few without gettin' rousted, but if you was to get rousted by a gang we don't have a peace treaty with...well, you wouldn't be comin' back home from your circus."

"Oh," Matthew said grimly, still staring at the *Pin*'s article. "I see."

"Not worth it, my sayso." Pie began to clean the ink and blood off the bone needles.

Home? he thought. This was certainly not his home. He didn't know if he'd ever see New York again, but he had to find out if this was Zed, and if so what had happened to the *Nightflyer* and Captain Falco.

First, though, there was the task of talking Keen out of attacking the Mohocks tonight. He thought he could at least make a good case, it being that discovering Albion's identity took precedence for the moment over an attack on make-believe Indians who had gained control of the brothel district. That would keep. He hoped Keen would agree, particularly when he made the suggestion that Keen accompany him tomorrow to hunt out the Fleet Street lair of Lord Puffery.

And that was well worth it, he thought.

His sayso.

Twenty

It was early afternoon of the following day. Hudson Greathouse leaned closer to Berry and said quietly, "Just continue to eat. Look to neither right nor left, but I want you to know we've picked up a tail."

She restrained herself from swivelling around in her chair to scan the tavern's occupants. "Where is he?"

"Far left corner, sitting with his back to a wall. Late forties, dark hair with gray on the sides, grizzled-beard, tough-looking but well-dressed for this area."

"Aren't you describing yourself?"

"He's a striking-looking devil, at that. I make two of him in size, though." The movement of a smile across Hudson's face was very rapid. He solemnly went on. "Man came in a few minutes ago and situated himself where he could watch us. Every once in awhile his eyes come over this way."

"You're sure he's following us?"

"He was standing at the bar with a second man in the Scarlet Hag. Then I caught a glimpse of him on the street, behind us. He was dawdling in a doorway across from the Leper's Kiss. Now here. He's not as good a tail as he believes himself to be."

"What about the second man?"

"He left the Hag before we did. I haven't seen him since."

Berry continued eating her meal of beef-and-kidney pie; there was not much beef, if it really was beef, but there was a plenitude of kidney. They were sitting at a table in the Four Wild Dogs, and Berry did not wish to think that these ingredients were of a canine nature. Hudson had before him a platter of calf brains and cornbread soaked in brown gravy, which he ate with his usual gusto, no matter the less-than-sociable and definitely dingy surroundings.

It seemed that the Whitechapel area was as full of taverns as a porcupine was full of quills, and the majority of them just as painfully nasty. It had been soon after their meeting with Gardner Lillehorne that Hudson had knocked on Berry's door at the Soames Inn and told her he was done waiting for inept London constables to search Whitechapel for Matthew; he was going to the office of the Herrald Agency on Threadneedle Street the next morning to ask help in finding the boy.

At the office Hudson had met an old friend, Sheller Scott, with whom he'd shared many battles against the infamous Molly Redhand. Hudson had explained the situation and learned that at present the agency's other four problem-solvers were at work outside London and Sheller himself was due in Maidstone on the case of a missing child. Sheller had said he hoped to be back within the week, but he couldn't say exactly when.

Thus Hudson had presented Berry with the reality that if Matthew was to be found, he was going to have to comb through Whitechapel. Berry had followed this with a suggestion: that he find for her paper, ink and quill and allow her time to sketch a rendition of Matthew's face so that the tavern keeps, serving-girls and patrons might have a more exact description. And, also, she'd stated that she would not be remaining at the inn while he was out in Whitechapel, and she would be going with him. He had agreed with the drawing part but argued strenuously against her presence in Whitechapel, as he knew that to be a particularly rough area of London and he didn't want to be responsible for her safety.

Strenuous argument or not, her determination had won the day and so it was settled over Hudson's objections.

Hudson had procured the necessary items, and then came the question of how to depict Matthew. Bearded or clean shaven? They hadn't asked Lillehorne, but Hudson figured Matthew had had no need of shaving aboard the *Wanderer* and would not have been afforded a razor or shaved by anyone else at either St. Peter's Place or in Newgate. So bearded it would be. To err on the side of caution Berry had made a second drawing of a clean shaven Matthew, and so the job was done.

For the past two days they had departed the inn in the cold and drizzly mornings and taken a coach to Whitechapel. The coachman had been given strict instructions and the promise of extra money to meet them at a certain time where they'd been put out, which somewhat limited their range of movements for the day. Hudson had no intention of their being cast adrift in Whitechapel as night came on, and in this foul November weather night came on early. The nearest they'd gotten so far to discovering Matthew's whereabouts was when a serving-girl yesterday afternoon at the Giddy Pig recognized the name from a story about the Monster of Plymouth in *Lord Puffery's Pin*, and she would have shown them the news sheet if it hadn't been stolen ten minutes after she'd paid a good solid coin for it.

The serving-girl, up until then lethargic, had become quite excited. "Killed eight women and a dozen children, the monster did, and now Albion's pulled him out of a prison coach and loosed him on Whitechapel to kill more. Ha! Like we don't have murderin' enough goin' on 'round here! And that's the monster's face, is it? Can't be! He looks too much a human. You the law? Smells so."

"Your smeller is correct," Hudson had decided to say. After the girl moved on, he had nearly gnashed his teeth. Hudson said, "One of those damned guards has sold his tale to some liar's news sheet! We'll see if we can't find a copy somewhere. Damn all publishers of rotten fiction!" He caught himself, for it was certain that Berry's grandfather had on occasion published in the *Earwig* fiction that foully masqueraded as news. "Apologies to present company and her absent grandfather," he amended, and she had returned to him a snort, a bemused half-smile and the raise of a coppery-red eyebrow.

During the course of yesterday's route, they had several more times come upon readers of this *Pin* who recognized the name but knew not the face. Finally, in the Goat's Breath, the barkeep had supplied an already tattered copy of the rag, and after reading the article of concern Hudson with reddened face had torn the thing to pieces, marched to a latrine hole behind the tavern and dumped the shreds in with the shits. "Not suitable for your eyes," he'd told Berry, taking upon himself the role of gallant protector.

As all people did, they had to eat sometime and somewhere, and since there did seem to be a menu of some variety at the Four Wild Dogs and many of the other patrons were having food with their various poisons it was agreed to pause here and replenish.

"What are you thinking?" Berry prompted to Hudson's silence.

"The two men," he said, "were standing at the bar when we asked the keep and the serving-girls about Matthew. I saw both men glance at the drawings, but one—the gent who's sitting over there—regarded the pictures a few seconds longer than the other. I meant to ask him if he'd seen the face, but before I could he pulled his companion aside and they had a little conversation of a guarded nature. A minute or so later, the second man left. At first I thought they were setting us up for a robbery, but between here and there they had plenty of opportunities to strike. Therefore…" He hesitated to sop up a little brains-and-gravy with a chunk of cornbread. "They may have some knowledge that I would like to get."

"And how will that be done?"

"We'll see," he told her, and attended to his meal and cup of red wine.

Now Berry found herself on edge. Did every new patron who entered the tavern cast a shady and lingering gaze upon them, or was it her imagination? Her interest in her food was gone. Though she had known London and had lived in Marylebone for eight weeks as a teacher, before an unfortunate incident with a goat and a lantern had burned the school down, this part of the city was utterly alien to her. She had entertained the thought yesterday of going to visit her father and mother in Coventry but that was nearly a week's coach trip from the city and likely a full week due to the weather and the roads. Neither one of them could help her find Matthew, and so she could not spare the time for them even though she loved them dearly. Possibly—hopefully—when this ordeal was over and Matthew was safely by her side she could suggest that they all go to Coventry for a few days, if for nothing but to get this vile city grime and smell off them; until then, Coventry must wait.

"Hm," Hudson said, a small noise of importance. "The two men who just came in," he said with a goodly mouthful of brains, "are going back to see our friend in the corner." He swallowed his food and followed it down with a drink of wine. "One of them is the man who left the Hag. Seems we're being ganged-up on." He wiped his mouth with a brown cloth napkin. "I expect all three of them will follow us when we leave here. Did you ever imagine that today you'd be leading a parade?"

He amazed her. She asked, "Aren't you in the least *afraid*?"

A tight smile rewarded her question. "Now there's an interesting word for you," he said, as he crumbled the last of the cornbread between his fingers. "I am *cautious*. I am *aware*. I am cognizant of my abilities and shortcomings. Am I afraid of those three men over there? Who now are all staring at us quite openly, by the way. Afraid? Not for myself, because I know I can give as well as I can take. But...I'm afraid a little bit that when whatever is going to happen begins, I won't be able to protect you. Which is *why*, Miss Adamant, I wished you to stay behind."

"I couldn't stay behind. You know that."

"Yes, I do know." He gave a sigh and patted her hand in the most fatherly way. "Let's pay for our slop and get out into the wild again, shall we?"

On the street, a light rain was falling from the drear sky and a cold wind sneaked around the edges of the buildings. Hudson was hatless and gave not a care about the wet, but Berry drew up over her head the hood of her violet cloak. Within an inner pocket of the cloak were the two drawings of Matthew, rolled up with leather cords and protected as much as possible from the weather. "Walk in front of me," Hudson told her, and motioned in a direction that would take them westward. In a little over two hours they were due back at their first stop of the day, The Bat And The Cat, at the crossing of Whitechapel Road and Plumber's Street. It was Hudson's opinion that if Matthew remained in this vicinity he had to be eating and drinking somewhere, therefore the taverns were the targets of investigation. Ahead through the rain Berry could see another tavern sign that proclaimed itself to be The Seat Of Judgement, and assumed this would be their next destination.

She hadn't gone very far when a figure lurched out of an alley to her left and clutched at her with skinny claws. The suddenness of the attack scared a scream out of her. At once Hudson was between her and the assailant and had thrown the man up against the bricks.

"Please sir...please sir," said the man, who had a gray beard matted with straw and a mass of tangled gray hair. His flesh was so filthy it too was gray. He wore the thinnest of rags, his face was swollen and malformed both by the violence of blows and the ravages of disease, his lips being corrupted with sores, and from him issued the foul odor of wet grave-rot. "Please, sir," he rasped. "Please...have mercy. A few pence, please...beggin' you, sir...and lady...beggin' you."

"Away with you!" Hudson said, though he still gripped hold of the beggar's shirt.

"Please...sir...got to have a sip...just a sip to get me back on my feet. Just a sip, sir, and that'll do me right."

"I think you've had a sip too many, old man!"

"The velvet'll get me back," he said, one eye bright with what was likely madness and the other as dark as a river stone. "God praise the sweet velvet, sir, one drink'll bring me back from all this."

Hudson released him. "I think you should go find a *man* of God instead of a bottle."

"Please, sir...please...just enough for a sip."

"Here." Berry was opening her purse. "Take—"

A small riding-crop whipped out and struck the beggar across the face. It had come from behind Hudson and Berry, and as Hudson whirled toward the new threat he damned himself for losing his concentration due to this Godforsaken beggar.

The three men were standing there, all of them in dark coats and tricorns. The man who had wielded the whip was the one who'd been sitting in the corner at the Four Wild Dogs; at a distance he may have resembled Hudson, but at close quarters the man had a broader face, thinner eyebrows and a hooked nose that looked like it could impale someone with a dangerous sneeze.

"Get away from here, shit rags," said the man in a voice as cold as the wind. He lifted the riding-crop for a second blow.

The beggar scrabbled back into the alley, his good eye full of fear. Hudson could see an empty crate in there and a threadbare blanket on the ground. Suddenly the beggar seemed to come to whatever senses he had left, for out of striking distance of the crop he straightened himself up, smoothed his pitiful shirt with his frail hands, and said to Hudson in a tone of whispery dignity, "I'll have you know...sir...that I *am* a man of God." The eye blinked. "*Was*," he said. Then, "Will be, again. Annie can tell you. She died but I raised her from the dead. She'll tell you true, my Annie will." Then his ravaged face broke and what was underneath was the horror of a soul destroyed. He sat down on the blanket and rocked himself with his bony knees up to his chin, and he sobbed as he whispered, "A sip...a sip...God save me...a sip..."

"Don't," said the man with the riding-crop as Berry's hand emerged from her purse with several coins in it. "Throwin' your money away, miss. Hundreds of 'em like that around here. Better off left to die rather than live tortured." The man's smoke-colored eyes were emotionless, the hook-nosed face impassive. His gaze shifted to regard Hudson. "Wouldn't you agree?"

"Who am I agreeing with?"

"Name's Frost. This is Mr. Carr and Mr. Willow. You've been asking about a young man by the name of Matthew Corbett."

"That's right. And you've been following us a ways."

"Also right. We know someone who might be able to help you."

"Really?" Hudson's thick brows went up. "Three good Samaritans in Whitechapel? I doubt that very much. Who are you and what's your angle?"

"Come with us. Two streets over, the Gordian Knot. You'll find out."

"I don't think so. I have a fighting chance in the street. My friend and I don't care to be knocked over the head, robbed and dumped down a chute into the river today."

Frost laughed, but it was just a chilly sound; his eyes and face were uninvolved. "We ain't..." He stopped and tried that again. "We're *not*," he said, "violent men."

"Every man, woman and child in Whitechapel is violent. It's called *survival.* Tell me another one."

"As you please. There is a woman in the Gordian Knot waiting to speak to you on the matter of Matthew Corbett." Frost was trying very hard, Hudson thought, to sound as if he came from anywhere in London but these few hundred acres of mean despair. "She can be of great help to you."

"What's her name? Bertha Billyclub?"

"I'm not at *liberty,*" Frost said, pronouncing the word with care, "to reveal her name. Come along and you'll find out."

"No, thank you."

Frost shrugged. His face was a blank, as were the expressions of the two others. "Suit yourself. It would be a bit ridiculous to let this opportunity go slidin' by, but that's your choice, inn'it?"

"'Tis," Hudson replied, his own face equally unreadable.

"Good day to you, then. Good day, miss." Frost offered a tip of his damp tricorn to Berry. "Let's be off, friends," he said to the others. They crossed the street between a passing haywagon and a team pulling a load of what appeared at first to be a mound of pallid dead bodies but was revealed with lessening distance as broken pieces of statuary, old saints pulled from some collapsed church or dislocated graveyard, arms reaching to the gray vault of Heaven and the faces washed serene and smooth by the water of time.

"Are you *insane*?" Berry asked, with a bite to it.

"Not the last time I looked."

"Aren't you at all interested in what this woman has to say?"

"I am," he admitted. "But I'm not walking into any damned tavern with three men at my back. Not violent! *Really*...did you see the scarred knuckles on Frost's hands? Knocked plenty of teeth down throats, you can be sure." He pushed a lock of rainwet hair away from his forehead. "We don't know what we'll be going into. Damn it!" A hand came out and slapped the bricks. "I don't suppose it would do a bit of good to ask you to go back to the Bat And Cat, wait for the coach, and if I'm not at the inn by...say...eight o'clock you'll have a message sent to Lille—"

"Not a bit of good," she interrupted.

"All right. I'll save my breath, I may need it later." Hudson peered into the alley. The old beggar had crawled into his crate. He was shivering, wrapped up in his nearly-useless blanket. Hudson reached into a pocket of his breeches and flipped a few coins to the ground beside the crate. As the old man sprang upon them with a cry that would have made the angels weep Hudson turned away, his face drawn tight. "Save your coins," he told Berry. "God willing, you can buy me a very strong mug of ale back on Fleet Street. Let's go."

Misters Frost, Carr and Willow were waiting for them under the sign of the Gordian Knot, which Hudson had known they would be.

"Changed your mind," said Frost, he of the frozen expression.

"You gentlemen enter first," Hudson told him. "I want none of you at our backs."

"Very well. Our route will be this: once inside the doorway, we'll cross the tavern floor to the bar. To the right of the bar there's a staircase going up. We'll be ascending."

"After you, then."

The Gordian Knot was no different from any of the other taverns they'd entered; a change of name, but the same planked floor, the same candled lamps, the same round tables scarred with use and the same woozy patrons, the same long bar and the same beleaguered keep, the same weary serving-girls, the same the same. "Stay close to me," Hudson said quietly to Berry as they crossed the floor behind the three men. For the first time he noted that Frost wore a pair of spurs on his expensive-looking boots. The trio went up the narrow staircase, Frost first and then Willow and Carr. Hudson ascended with his hand reached back behind him to grip Berry's.

They emerged from the staircase into a circular room much finer than the rest of the tavern below. Lanterns of blue and green stained glass hung from hooks on the exposed oak beams, giving the upper portion of the room an underwater cast, while regular lanterns with burning white candles were set on several large round tables. The planks of the floor were covered with what appeared to be a very fine dark green Persian rug.

"Here they are, ma'am," said Frost to someone else in the room.

Hudson and Berry saw a figure sitting in a high-backed leather chair, over in a corner at one of the tables.

The woman spoke in a voice that, like Frost's, made an attempt to disguise its common birthing. "Bring them closer, if you please."

"We're close enough," said Hudson. "We've been told you have information about Matthew Corbett?"

"Firstly, welcome to my tavern," said the woman. "Do sit down, the both of you. We have a fine selection of mulled wines here." The candlelight caught a smile on the woman's mouth, exposing small peglike teeth beneath a knuckle of a nose and a pair of eyes that Hudson could only describe as froggish.

"We'll stand," he answered.

"You're *afraid*," she said.

"Cautious."

"A big, strong man like yourself ought to be able to take care of business, if necessary. Look at you! You're an ox!"

"I grew up to be big and strong by being cautious," he said. He was very aware of where the three men stood in the room and if any bootstep tread upon the risers. He kept hold of Berry's hand. "We're leaving in ten seconds if you don't offer us something."

"I've already offered you wine. Oh...the other thing, you mean. Matthew Corbett. Well...that young man *does* get into scrapes, doesn't he? He makes for an entertaining story in the *Pin*. And now he's associated himself with that dreadful Albion! You *have* seen that, haven't you?"

"Your time's up."

"If you won't be sociable, I fear we have nothing more to communicate. I don't like rudeness, Mr. Greathouse. Either you and Miss Grigsby come sit down, or I agree...time is indeed up."

"I know you," Berry suddenly said. "Don't I?"

"We've never met. Come, come...sit." She shrugged her broad shoulders. "Or leave, if you like. The way out is open."

Hudson didn't like the smell of this. As far as he knew, he'd never met this woman before, and yet...something about her was familiar. He had a decision to make. "Do *they* have to be here?" He motioned with a lift of his chin toward the three misters.

"Certainly not. If they offend you, they shall be gone."

"They offend me."

"Be gone," she said, speaking directly to Frost. Hudson pulled Berry aside as the men passed them and descended the stairs without another word or glance at them. "*Now*," said the woman, "can we talk like civilized people?"

"To the brass tacks," Hudson replied. "We're looking for Matthew and we've been told you have information. You seem to know us from somewhere. And no, we don't want any wine, thank you. Do you have information, or not?"

"Oh, I do." The woman pushed back from the table and stood up. She approached them across the fine Persian rug. She was of formidable build, a thickly-set woman not fat but crudely powerful, though she moved with a practiced grace. The froggish brown eyes in the work-seamed face were fixed upon Hudson, the mouth crooked with a peg-toothed smile. She wore a dark blue gown with bright pink ruffles down the front and along the sleeves. On her big, workman-like hands were pink lace gloves with the thick sausages of her fingers exposed. Hudson took measure of the deep lines in her face and the cottony cloud of her hair done up with golden pins, and he decided she must be sixty years old at the youngest but there was the attitude about her of the strutting Whitechapel brawler thirty years her junior. He knew her from somewhere…surely he did, and now she was close upon him and she was about to speak.

"My information to you," she said, still smiling, "is that you are now the property of my employer, Professor Fell."

Her name burst upon both the brains of Hudson and Berry at the same time. She was just as Matthew had described her.

"Ah," said Hudson. "Mother Deare." A muscle jumped in his jaw. "Matthew wondered if you'd survived the earthquake."

"You can see I did. So too did my friend Augustus Pons. And so too did the professor, who I'm sure would like to see the both of you."

"He's somewhere near?"

"Somewhere," she allowed.

"I suppose our wandering around Whitechapel asking about Matthew brought us to the attention of your…shall we describe them as your *people*?"

"Yes, my people." Her smile broadened. The froggish eyes seemed to bulge a bit more. "I like that, Hudson. May I call you by name?" She didn't wait for his approval. "Hudson, I like being civilized…being *intelligent*."

"I imagine you've come a long way in both areas."

"Oh, yes. I was born a quarter-mile from here in the most dreadful hovel. Now I have a very fine house in the central city, I own several taverns, and I do like to make the rounds."

"Whitechapel's in your blood, I suppose."

"Well expressed," she said, with a little bow of her head. When she looked into his eyes again her gaze was all iron and no nonsense. "Let me tell you what's going to happen. You are both going to walk down those stairs to where my *people* are waiting. You can be sure all three have pistols in their hands by now. None of the patrons down there will give a flying flip. In fact, they will have likely already cleared out at the first sight of the weapons. Then, being on your best behavior, you will sit at a table of your choice and enjoy a cup of that fine mulled wine as we wait for a coach that has already been summoned."

"And the coach will take us where?"

"To my home. You'll be treated well there this evening. My *people* will continue to search for Matthew. If he's found—as I expect he shall be—all the better. In any case I'm sure the professor would like to get hold of you sooner than later."

Hudson said, "Nice plan, but you forgot one thing."

"Oh? Please enlighten me."

With a short drawback of his right fist he hit her as hard as he could on the forehead just above the left eye. She staggered back but made no sound, and he expected her to fall like a chopped tree as he said, "This ox can—" *punch*, he was about to continue, which would have made no sense to anyone but himself. But he held the word in amazement, for not only did Mother Deare not topple from a blow that would have sent a regular-sized man into dreamland, but she shook her head and touched the reddened place of impact on her forehead as if she'd only been bothered by a mosquito.

"Oh my," she croaked. "That smarted a bit." Then, her eyes fierce, she thundered:

"Frost!"

Immediately boots clunked on the stairs. Hudson picked up a chair and threw it, catching Frost in the chest as the man came up. Frost fell backward, the pistol in his hand went off with a loud *crack* and burst of white smoke, the lead ball went up somewhere amid the colored lanterns, Frost collided with the other two men behind him and they fell down the stairs in a tangle.

And then, as Berry cried out a warning, Mother Deare was upon Hudson.

Sixtyish or not, the woman still carried the brutality of her birthplace. The lantern she'd picked up from the nearest table was smashed into the left side of Hudson's head, pieces of glass slicing into his cheek and jaw and putting him on the path to being a bloody mess. He swung at her and missed as she dodged aside, and then she kicked for his balls. Before the kick could connect Hudson grabbed her booted foot and heaved upward, crashing her to the floor with a violence that likely puffed dust from every fiber of the Gordian Knot. Blood burned and blinded his left eye. As he retreated from Mother Deare and tried to clear his vision with the back of a hand, the woman squirmed toward him like a serpent, took hold of both his ankles and with sheer brute strength upended him. The back of his head bashed a table and he fell, stunned and very near to having his neck broken.

As Mother Deare was standing up from the floor, Berry grabbed hold of the woman's white hair with one hand and with the other fist struck her full in the nose. There was the sound of fabric or some kind of fastener tearing, and the blow separated Mother Deare's head from her hair.

Berry stood dumbly looking at the golden-pinned wig in her hand.

Mother Deare got fully to her feet. Both her nostrils were bleeding. The bulbous eyes leaked tears of pain. She was completely bald, her scalp a tortured battlefield of thick and ghastly dark red and brown burn scars, the tightening of seared flesh being the cause of her eyeballs to bulge from their sockets.

The sight of that blood-smeared face beneath such a horror petrified Berry. Mother Deare approached her with a blank expression, reached out to grasp the wig and headbutted Berry into instant unconsciousness. As Berry fell like a bag of laundry, Mother Deare pressed the wig back upon her head and, though it was on backwards, turned her attention to the dazed and bloody man—formerly an ox, now more of a poor lamb—who was struggling to his knees.

Frost, Willow and Carr had made it up the stairs, though Hudson would've been pleased to see that Carr was holding a broken wrist. The men approached their victim. Mother Deare said, "*Wait*," and they halted in their tracks.

She removed from her bodice a pink lace handkerchief, which she used to blot her bloody nose. Hudson was attempting to stand. She put a hand atop his head and exerted force to keep him where he was.

“Look what happens,” she said to him, “when people forget their manners.”

Then she grasped his hair and drove a cruel knee into his face, and his last thought as he was crushed under a red wave of pain was that this mother was a bitch.

Twenty-One

"I SUPPOSE this is the place," said Keen.

"It would appear so," Matthew answered. On the signboard of the shop before them was the designation *1229 Fleet Street* and below that, *Sm. Luther, Printer.* It simply looked to be, in spite of Lord Puffery's probable wealth, a perfectly ordinary printshop and actually the door and windowsills were in need of painting.

Light rain was falling, forming puddles on the walks and in the street. Keen said, "Never thought I'd have any need to go into such a shop. I'm feelin' kinda funny about it."

"How so?"

"I don't know…meetin' Lord Puffery face-to-face. He's like… you know…somebody *important*."

"He'll be just a man. A man with quite an imagination and very few scruples, but he pulls on his breeches the same as any other. And…he holds the key to Albion's identity. Come on, buy you an ale when we're done."

"What, with *my* money?"

"*My* money, that you took from my cloak and still have not returned."

"You didn't have enough money on you to buy a rotten apple! Ahhhh, damn it all!" Keen said, bridling at a sore spot. He looked around uncomfortably at the traffic of pedestrians, wagons, coaches and carriages. He was dressed in a mud-colored suit with gray patches at elbows and knees. The cravat he'd wrapped around his neck was dark with grime. His shirt had been white at one time in the distant past but currently was a sick shade of yellow. He had done himself up like this at Matthew's urging, to present a gentlemanly front to the printers' shop they would be visiting.

But Keen knew he was out of place here in this central part of the city, where even in the rain the gentlemen and their ladies strode about showing off the height of fashion. He had noted the passage of roofed carriages and teams of exactly-matched horses that cost fabulous amounts of money, and within the plush interiors beautiful women with high-topped hairdos and their handsome escorts who appeared to have been born in a world where everyone had a bathtub and used them quite frequently. He knew that he could not—should not—go with Matthew to visit Lord Puffery looking as he usually did, and he readily admitted to himself that this would be offensive to the Fleet Street toffs and their toffettes, so it was this suit last worn by a dead man and purchased from an undertaker that had to do.

"All right," said Keen, his steely grip on courage returning. "Let's get to it."

About twenty-four hours ago, after Matthew had taken the Black-Eyed Broodie oath and been tattooed, he had sought out Keen in the Whitechapel warehouse and presented his premise: that it was more important to learn on the morrow who Albion might be than it was to attack the Mohocks that night. After all, was Keen absolutely certain he knew where the Mohocks were headquartered?

Two buildin's, Keen had said. We figure we know which one Fire Wind lives in. We get him, that's a good night's work.

Matthew had pointed out that the Mohocks were going to have lookouts up on the rooftops all night, just as the Broodies did, so it was imperative that if an attack be made it was to the correct building and not a chancy affair. Any attack on the Mohocks was sure to cause Mohock deaths, of course, but Keen should bear in mind that some of the Broodies would not be returning from this jaunt, so was he prepared to go in helter-skelter?

The alternative: postpone this attack until it was certain without a doubt in which building Fire Wind lived, and how best to wage the battle without throwing Broodie lives away. Tomorrow, Matthew had said, put on a suit and go with me to find Lord Puffery.

Keen had delayed his response until after nightfall. Then he'd sent Pie to Matthew with a one-word message: *Agreed.*

A matter of concern had developed in the morning. "What do you mean, we hire a coach?" Keen had asked. "I've never ridden in a fuckin' coach in my life! Anyway, the treasury don't have coin to throw away! And you don't know these people lookin' over my shoulder about the money...they want to know where every penny of every shillin' is spent!"

Matthew had decided to let the matter rest of who *these people* might be, but he'd answered, "First of all, is the address of 1229 Fleet Street within walking distance?"

"I don't know exactly where that lies, but I figure I could get there in a few hours."

"I don't want to look like a drowned rat when I speak to the man and neither do I want you to appear the same. Travelling by coach makes the most sense. If you have a problem with the accounting, pay with the money you took from me. And I don't want to get there and have to walk back, either."

Of the return trip by coach, Keen didn't argue because he knew, as Pie had pointed out, how many gangs were out there just hungering to catch a Broodie in their territory after dark.

"There wasn't enough money left in them little bags of yours to pay for a drayhorse, much less a coach! Put my neck on the choppin' block, spendin' this kind of loot," Keen had fretted. "How am I gonna square it with the old woman?"

"Old woman?"

"Yeah...the old fancy-dressed woman who comes to collect. Her and her three hard cases. They come by once a month to check the book and get their cut."

"The *book*? You keep a financial ledger?"

"Have to. Well...Tom keeps it, he's got the head for numbers."

Matthew was bursting with questions, but he thought it wise not to push Keen just yet. There would be time for that in the coach ride to Fleet Street, and indeed he had starting throwing them when they were settled—one gentleman in a mud-colored and patched suit and the other in a purple and green-piped horror—and on their way.

"This ledger book you keep," Matthew had begun as the team clopped along westward in the direction of the central city. "You scribe a record of the money paid to you by the local merchants for protection?"

Keen had given him the evil eye.

"I'm a Broodie now," Matthew had reminded him. "You see?" He held up his tattooed hand, which today was a bit swollen. "Aren't I to be trusted yet?"

"The oath and the tat don't mean but half of it 'til I see you in action, which you talked y'self out of last night."

"Fighting war-painted idiots is not how I plan to leave this earth."

Keen gave a fierce grin. "*Rowdy idiots*, don't you mean? Ain't that how you put it to Pie? Meanin' the Mohocks, the Broodies and all the others fightin' for territory?"

"Yes," Matthew said. "It's my opinion the Broodies are being used for purposes far beyond a battle for territory. The Mohocks may be as well, and every other gang." He let that simmer for a bit before he stirred the pot again. "You may be in charge of the Broodies," he said, "just as Fire Wind—Lord, I can barely speak that with a straight face—is in charge of the Mohocks. But you likely both have something in common: someone else is in charge of *you*. Just look at your ledger book, at the restrictions put upon you, and think about the old woman and the hard cases. What does she call herself?"

"The *boss*," he answered, a bit grimly. He had sunken down in his seat.

"You know what I'm saying is true. These people take a monthly cut of what you get, correct? And they expect you to, as you put it, run 'errands' on their behalf? Putting you at risk with the law, but not them."

"Mousie sprang Ben from the coop. They paid for it and worked an angle," Keen said. "Mousie's our—"

"Lawyer, yes. Paulie told me. He's another individual I'd like to have a talk with. I wonder how many of those other five men Albion murdered were represented at court by Mousie."

"Huh?"

"I wonder if Mousie—or some lawyer paid by the same individuals who are running this show—worked angles for those other five men, got them 'sprung' and in so doing put them at the point of Albion's sword. That's what I'd like to know."

"You'd like to know a whole hell of a lot you probably shouldn't *ought* to know. What do you do for a livin', anyway? Educated fella like y'self, a high talker and all...what's your game?"

"I was a law clerk at one time. Lately, in New York, I've been what is called a 'problem-solver'."

"Law clerk," Keen repeated. He nodded. "*That's* the smell of the Old Bailey I've been gettin'. The other thing...solvin' what kind of problems?"

Matthew felt that a moment was upon him. He steadied his gaze upon Rory Keen and said, "I have one very large problem I'm trying to solve, other than the current one involving Albion. Do you know the name of Professor Fell?"

Keen was silent. He studied the Broodie tattoo upon his own hand. "Used to be," he said in a guarded voice, "the name would put terror in me, and the others too. You never knew what that bastard was up to, and where his people might show up. 'Course we keep low to the ground, we never did fly 'round his belfry. But of late, word's gotten out...he ain't what he used to be."

"Go on," Matthew prompted.

"Word is he's been fucked in a couple a' deals. Ain't been able to get a grip on the colonies like he was intendin'. Somethin' about runnin' gunpowder to the Spanish...that was fucked too. Word is he's left London, holed up somewhere to lick his wounds. Still dangerous, for sure, but...see, here's the rub of it."

Matthew waited, as the strident noise of London's streets buffeted the coach and rain tapped upon the top.

"Some of his people have...like...gone over to his competition," Keen continued. "Left him, 'cause they think he's had too many teeth knocked out. Think he's gotten weak. That's what I hear, at least."

"His *competition*? Who would that be?"

"New blood," said Keen. "A younger gent. Already done some murders that's made talk. Killed a judge a couple of months ago, is what I heard. Man by the name of Fallonsby. Beat him to death and strung the body up from a flagpole outside the house. Offed the wife, the daughter, the butler, the maid and the family dog too. It was in the *Pin* for awhile, but I think Lord Puffery dropped it 'cause even he got scared."

"Do you know this new man's name?"

"Nobody does. Oh, he left his mark carved into Fallonsby's forehead…leastwise that's what the *Pin* thought it to be. A Devil's Cross. One carved upside-down," he explained.

"Hm," said Matthew, looking out the window at the passing carnival. He heard the deep tone of a tolling bell from a nearby church, and he wondered if it was for someone's funeral.

"What I'm gettin' at," Keen offered, "is that when the cat goes soddy, the rat gets cheese. Fell's been the big cat 'round here for a long time. Now the rat's eatin' cheese, and gettin' mighty…" He hesitated, searching his brain for an apt description. "*Mighty*," he finished.

Due partly—mostly?—to myself, Matthew thought. Exit the black-hearted villain, enter the blacker-hearted? He had one more subject to broach with Keen.

"Where does the White Velvet come from?" he asked.

Keen stared squarely at him. The eyes were, again, dead.

"*No*," said Keen, and that had been the end of that.

Now, as Matthew and Keen entered the printshop of one *Sm. Luther*, a little bell tinkled merrily above the door. The place smelled of bitter ink. Barrels and crates stood about, along with stacks of various qualities of paper. Behind a long counter, standing beside his press in the light of several oil lamps and the dim illumination from a nearby window, was a slim white-haired man occupied in the arrangement of rows of wood-carved letters in their print trays. He wore an ink-stained leather apron over his clothing and he was smoking a stubby black pipe. At the music of the bell he looked toward his visitors with gray eyes behind thick-lensed spectacles, the seams of his face deepened by the presence of ink that likely had collected there, dot by dash, over a period of many years and now had become part of the man.

"Help you?" he asked, his fingers still poised over the trays of letters, which by necessity he had to arrange in the mirror image of what the finished product would be.

"We hope so," said Matthew. "Samuel Luther?"

"The same."

"Am I speaking to Lord Puffery?"

The man had not offered a smile. He offered none now. "You are not."

"Oh...pardon. But this *is* the shop where the *Pin* is printed?"

"It is."

"Then I assume you're in contact with Lord Puffery?" Matthew had noted a closed door beyond the press area, which was guarded by a waist-high wooden gate at the far end of the counter.

"Lord Puffery," said Luther, "is indisposed. If you have a story to sell, I would be the man to see." He motioned toward a desk to his left where there were two chairs, a stack of cheap paper and writing tools atop the blotter.

"But you would need to ask Lord Puffery if the story I wish to sell would be worth his money? Correct?"

"Correct."

"All right, then. Before we begin, please tell Lord Puffery that Matthew Corbett, the Monster of Plymouth, has arrived from his chamber of horrors in Whitechapel. Tell the kind sir he wishes to sell an account of the decapitation murders of umpteen women and double-umpteen children."

Luther did not move. The gray eyes, greatly magnified by the corrective lenses, blinked. He reached for a rag to wipe his hands. "I'll relay the message," he replied, with steadfast calm, and then he went to the door, rapped on it and stuck his head in. "Matthew Corbett's here," he said to the person within. "The Monster of Plymouth. Got a story to sell, he says."

An exchange was made that neither Matthew nor Keen could hear. It went on for perhaps thirty seconds.

Luther pulled his head back out. "Come on," he told the two.

They went to the gate, which Matthew reached down to unlatch and open. They crossed the print area. Luther stepped aside for them to enter the domain of Lord Puffery.

It was a nice office, but no rich man's haven. In fact, no man's haven at all.

The middle-aged, rather plump gray-haired woman behind the desk was sitting in a brown leather chair that had known better times. So too had the desk, for all its nicks and scratches. Behind her were a few books on shelves. An oil lamp burned on the desk. She had been scribing in a record book, as it was still open before her and the quill returned to its rest next to the inkjar. Facing the desk was a chair and another one stood the corner. The floor was of rough planks, the walls the same except upon them were various framed copies of earlier *Pin*s and a couple of advertising broadsheets indicating the other work that Luther did.

"Leave us," she told Luther.

"But ma'am—"

"Leave us and close the door," she said. Her accent was neither highbrow nor low; she was an educated woman and certainly very wealthy but no mistress of an ostentatious castle, for her clothing was plain and unadorned by frills. Her bearing, as well, gave Matthew the impression of directness and simplicity, which surely were not qualities of the London gentry.

Luther withdrew and the door was closed.

The woman's right hand came up. Perhaps it was accustomed to holding a quill, but for the moment it held a very serious-looking pistol aimed in a direction of damage.

TWENTY-TWO

WHICH one of you is Corbett?" Before an answer could be made, the woman's sharp gaze found him. "*You.* Cleaner than the other and a look of inquisitive nature, but the brutal scar of past misdeeds upon your head." Her eyes narrowed. "Are you colorblind?"

"No, madam. I haven't had a chance to find a proper tailor. This is my friend Rory Keen. Would you mind moving that pistol to one side? I didn't come all the way from Whitechapel to have my hair parted by a ball."

"Are you here to take revenge?"

"I am here to feed my nature. Which, you must know, is not an appetite for the murder of countless women and children in Plymouth."

"But you've murdered at least *one* woman and child?" The pistol's barrel had not moved the length of a flea.

"Sorry. Not one."

"The next issue of the *Pin* will have the authorities uncovering more of your murders from beneath the dirt of a rose garden in Exeter. What do you have to say to that?"

"I say...before I leave here I'll give you the address to which you might send my share of the take. That would be the colonial branch of the Herrald Agency, Number Seven Stone Street in the town of New York."

Now the pistol did waver, the length of a hand. *"What?"*

"Indeed," Matthew answered with a genuine smile of pleasure at upsetting this particular applecart. His smile had no longevity, though, because of the truth of his next revelation. "I did kill a man aboard a ship from New York. A past associate of Professor Fell...and I see from your face that you know the name. This particular man wished to use me to return to the good graces of the professor. Things developed as they did." His eyes had darkened. *"Praeteritum est praeteritum."*

"Hold on just one damned high-wigged minute!" said Keen, in what was nearly a bleat. "I'm seein' that Lord Puffery is a *woman*? And I'm *hearin'* that you killed one of Fell's people? Holy Hell, Matthew! What have you dragged me into?"

"Real life," came the answer. "A far cry from the fiction of the *Pin*. Please put that gun down," he said to the lady of the house. "And now that the introductions have been made on this side, may I ask your true name?"

The woman's calm had not diminished. The gun did drop a few inches, but wasn't completely harmless at that angle. "Firstly," she said, addressing Keen, "if you go out into the world and shout from the highest rooftops that Lord Puffery is indeed a woman, you'll find yourself laughed at from here to Land's End. Quite simply, no one will believe you. Who but a crude and crass vulgarian of the *male* breed would smear upon good stationery such nuggets of scandal and malice?" Her cool, pale green eyes in the full-cheeked and matronly face turned upon Matthew. "Secondly, I know of the Herrald Agency and I do know the name of the individual you've mentioned, and for that reason both myself and my pistol request that you leave this office, never to return."

"Has the kitchen suddenly become too hot?" Matthew asked. "Odd, for one who has flamed up so many tinderboxes and touched off so many fires."

"Get out." She cocked the pistol. "I won't tell you again."

Matthew knew she meant business, but he dared the moment. With an effort, he kept his voice light as he said, "I'm not going anywhere, Lady Puffery, until you tell me who Albion is."

"What? Are you *mad*? How should I know?"

"He's been to this office and sold a story to you through Mr. Luther. Do you keep records of the names of persons who sell you these tales?"

"Yes."

"Very well, then. What is the name you have for the person who sold you the tale of my being released by Albion from that prison coach? There's a detail in the story that only Albion would know... one I'm sure you have exaggerated in your smearing of good stationery. A single dagger became two...your invention, correct?"

"The more is always the better," she said.

"As I suspected. Really, madam...please uncock the pistol and put it away."

At that moment a knock sounded on the door. Luther's tremulous voice asked, "Are you all right, Mrs. Rutledge?"

"A moment," she replied, because she hadn't yet decided.

"It's the truth," Matthew prompted. "Albion was here. You have his name in your book." *Book of lies*, he almost said, but he didn't wish to help her pull the trigger.

He waited.

"Yes, Samuel," the woman answered at last. "I'm all right."

"Do you...need me to—"

"I need you to bring me the payment book, at once."

"Yes, ma'am," he said, and moved away.

Mrs. Rutledge carefully uncocked the pistol. She put it down upon the desktop, but within easy reach. "Matthew Corbett," she said, as if fully seeing him for the first time. "You've killed an associate of Professor Fell? I'd say you're the one who's touched off a fire."

"He's not the first of them I've had to...shall we say...condemn with rough justice."

"Oh sweet Jesus!" For all his swaggering toughness, Keen was melting. He took a staggered step and got himself in the chair before the woman's desk. "Killed *more'n* one? Matthew, you're a harder case than I thought...but you ain't toyin' with tykes, gonna take their jacks and waddle on home." He gave Matthew a suffering look. "Even weaker'n they were, them mashers play for keeps!"

"Believe me, I know."

"I'd want to stay far, far away from 'em. Hell, just knowin' you puts me in the same bloody soup!"

"Esther Rutledge," Lady Puffery said.

Keen ceased his quailing.

"My name," she said, speaking to Matthew. She tilted her chin up. "You do understand that I am running a business here, and a business sometimes runs on—"

"Lies?"

"The low road," she continued, with no change of her solemn expression. "Ah, here's our book." Luther had knocked at the door again. "Come in," she instructed.

Luther entered with a book bound between covers of a suitable flammatory red. The pages, Matthew saw as Luther passed the volume to Mrs. Rutledge, were marked off in lines and columns, with dates at the top. From the looks of it, there was no lack of items for the *Pin* to pursue. It occurred to Matthew, as the woman put the book in front of her and her finger found the proper line, that the *Pin* was misnamed; instead of puncturing gaudily-colored soap bubbles, it created them, only in this instance soap was not the material that came to mind.

"Here," said Lady Puffery, tapping the line. "The story about Albion attacking the coach and the two guards. We paid a crown and two shillings for it. To—"

Matthew leaned forward to see.

"Joshua Oakley is the name," she announced. Her gaze came up. "He's Albion?"

"Josh Oakley?" Keen looked as if he might be strangling, and sounded worse. "That's a nutter's nightmare! Josh Oakley ain't Albion! Hell, Josh is long dead!"

"You know this individual?" Lady Puffery asked, again with steady calm.

"I knew *a* Josh Oakley! Can't be the same one! He's bones and worms by now!"

"That's the name in the book."

"And the name I was given," said Luther, who had put a distance between himself and the Monster of Plymouth. "I remember the young man quite well."

Matthew felt as if his head was swimming. Who was Joshua Oakley? Oh yes! He recalled the name. The member of the Broodies who had been so crazed by the White Velvet that he'd leaped from a third-floor window and been brained by a horse in the street below.

"Im-fuckin'-*possible*!" Keen was on his feet, craning to look at the name. "At least that can't be the Josh Oakley I knew!"

"I daresay," retorted Lady Puffery, "that there are several Joshua Oakleys in London and the environs."

"Wait, wait," said Matthew in an attempt to steady the chaos in his own brain. "Mr. Luther, can you describe this man?"

"I can. He was young, well-dressed, of slender build, and had light-colored hair."

"Not much to go on. Anything that stood out about him?"

Luther shrugged. "He seemed quite ordinary. A gentleman, he was. Soft-spoken. Oh…he wore spectacles with square lenses."

That touched a chord with Matthew. The description of the spectacles with square lenses. Of course that was not out of the ordinary, but who had he seen lately who wore such a pair?

"I'm sorry," Luther said. "That's all I have. He attested that he was a cousin to one of the guards involved, and so had been given the tale first-hand. I paid the young man his coin, thanked him for coming in, and he left." Luther's head seemed to shrink a bit into his shoulders. "Please understand, we are…um…how shall I put this…?"

"We are not sticklers here for absolute truth," Lady Puffery chimed in. "We did send a messenger boy to the constable's office to verify the fact that this event occurred, with a letter requesting the verification on behalf of the citizens of London, but the boy was rudely thrown out. That was an answer of sorts. Thus I took the raw material of what we'd been given and worked it into—"

"Dough?" Matthew interrupted.

The woman pushed the book aside and leaned back in her chair. She regarded Matthew with hooded eyes, and for the first time he noted the lines of pain in her face. They seemed to have risen to the surface of the skin all at once. "How little you must know of the baser instincts of human beings," she said. "Either that, or you delude yourself."

"I do understand the baser instincts, madam, but I don't wish to enrich myself by stroking them."

"I'll have you know," said Luther, who had decided to play a shining Lancelot in spite of the presence of these two dingy ruffians, "that Mrs. Rutledge does not enrich herself on earnings from the *Pin*! Quite the contrary! After business expenses and costs of living are met, every shilling goes to feed the poor and aid the hospitals! You being from Whitechapel, you should know there's a hospital on Cable Street that serves the poor and can't survive without financial help! There's another one within a few blocks of here! And others a'plenty, I can tell you! Without the money from the *Pin*, they'd likely—"

"*Samuel*," the woman said quietly. "Cease and desist. It's not as if we keep all those institutions afloat just by ourselves."

"Well, it's almost so!"

"Hush," she told him, but gently.

Matthew nodded, having been given a new view in this light of illumination. "Pardon me. I understand you have altruistic motives, but…I am very curious as to how a woman of your obviously clean character has chosen to play in the grime of the streets."

She didn't answer for a moment. Her gaze seemed to be fixed on a faraway distance.

Then she took a long breath and said, "There could be no cleaner character than my husband. A printer by trade. An honest man. Honest to a fault. Crushed by creditors, and squeezed by costs. Like any business it is a demanding competition for customers. Zachary died early…too early. After his passing I at first wanted to sell, but Samuel insisted I try my hand at the reins of this ungainly horse. We couldn't keep up with the other printshops, who were well-established and dropping their prices to drive competitors out of business. We were at the bitter end of our rope. One night, it came to me: why wait for business? Why not *produce* it? I thought…what is it that the common man of London would pay five pence a sheet for? I was thinking of volume sales even then. But what *was* it, that would find itself in demand by the masses?"

She lapsed into silent memory, and Matthew allowed her to linger there.

"I decided," she continued after her repose, "that what every man and woman wishes is to feel equal to, if not superior than, the most notable lords and ladies of the moment. Thus I began a news sheet relying on stories of the absurd habits and peccadillos of those individuals, their spending sprees, their spats in public and in private—if I could get the information—and anything else that would make them appear more...well...*common.* We almost instantly began selling out, and so we soon went to a twice-weekly schedule. Of course at that rate, even though London is a vast cocoon of tawdry moths dreaming they are butterflies, news of the wealthy and infamous began to be more difficult to procure. Oh, we had our share of threats and broken windows. A fire was started here once, but Samuel lives upstairs and he was able to douse the flames before any real damage was done."

She offered Matthew a wistful smile. "It was not my intention to become a factory of exaggerations and—often—outright lies, but our readers demand more and more. Whatever I might concoct sends thousands of copies of the *Pin* sailing off into eager hands. Perhaps I'm doing my part at helping people learn to read. At least...I tell myself that. We have outlasted a score of competitors. The names of Lord Puffery and the *Pin* carry considerable weight. Would I do this again, in the same way?" It took her only a few seconds to answer her own question.

"Yes. I think of my Zachary laboring as he did. I think of the creditors hounding us, day and night. I think of how it was when the rent was due and our daughter and her family were offering money they did not have to keep us out of the house of poverty. Then I write a stirring or sordid tale that may or may not be based upon fact, and I sit back in this chair, Mr. Corbett, and in the vile but sometimes accurate expression of the street, I say to all those who live in their ivory castles, hide behind their false masks of civility and bare their fangs at Lord Puffery's *Pin* and the citizens who read it...*fuck you.*"

There was a stretch of silence before Luther nervously cleared his throat. "And to add that the poor and the hospitals are *very* generously aided."

"Zachary died in a public hospital," the woman said. "The wealthy here take everything, even down to the proper equipment and doctors for themselves. The hospitals particularly are in need." She waved away any more talk of what the *Pin* was doing for the public. Her gaze had sharpened again, and Matthew could tell that something else was on her mind. "Samuel," she said, "fetch the document."

"Yes ma'am." He was gone at her command.

"We received an interesting document in an envelope sometime last night or early this morning. Slipped under the door," she explained. "I wish you to see it."

"Coalblack," said Matthew, as it came to him to bring this up.

"Pardon?"

"The African strongman at the Almsworth Circus. Do you know anything more about him?"

"That he was found drifting at sea, that he is huge, has a tattooed face, cannot speak as his tongue has been cut out, and that he draws quite an audience every night. I myself haven't seen him. Why?"

"I think I might know him."

"Lord Steppin' Lightly!" said Keen. "Do you know the flippin' *queen*?"

"I've had occasion to meet one."

Luther returned with a piece of paper that had been folded several times. "Give it to Mr. Corbett," she instructed. Matthew took the paper and opened it. Scribed upon it in a neat, small and concise handwriting were six lines.

He read aloud: "A gauntlet thrown,/ and D.own I.t fell..." He had to comment on the punctuation marks before he went on: "Interesting use of periods behind the 'D' and the 'I'."

"Very interesting," said Lady Puffery.

He continued. "Seek Clotho, Lachesis, Atropos/ at the midnight bell./ Come test your fate and dare to ask/ what lies beneath the gilded mask." He scanned the lines once more before he looked up. "Gilded mask? Albion?"

"Albion, or someone posing as such. Along with it in the envelope was a guinea coin."

"He wishes you to print this?"

"What else? We're setting it up for the next issue."

Again Matthew studied the lines. A bit of his interest and reading of Greek mythology surfaced. "The three names. Sisters, I think." He frowned, going through the overfilled filing cabinets of his mind. "Let's see...Clotho...I believe...was one of the mythological sisters of Fate. Of course...Albion spells that out. 'Test your fate', he says. Yes, I recall. Clotho spun the thread of life, Lachesis drew the lots and determined how long a person would live, and

Atropos...ah, yes. Atropos chose how someone would die by cutting the thread of life with her shears."

"This is all moon talk to me!" Keen huffed.

"Moon talk or not," said Matthew. "This is a challenge directed to someone. 'A gauntlet thrown', he says. Thrown to *whom*?"

"Obviously," said Lady Puffery, "he expects it to be read in the *Pin* by that someone."

Matthew directed his attention to that word.

That single word.

Right there, upon the paper.

The word 'fell'.

Whenever and wherever he saw that word, however it was used, he couldn't help but feel a little twinge of unease as if someone, somewhere, had just stepped upon his grave.

"The three sisters," he said, mostly to himself. "That must be the Tavern of the Three Sisters. The same place Albion wished to meet me, by the way. Albion is making a challenge to this person to meet him there. But...how will the person know he's meeting Albion unless he already knows who Albion is? And he's not giving a specific date or time...just saying, after midnight. Unless the date and time are hidden in code? A request: may I copy this down on a piece of paper and keep it?" She gave him paper and a quill. When he was done he returned the original to Lady Puffery and folded the copy into his pocket, having digested as much of its innards as he could currently manage.

She refolded the original. Then she picked up the pistol, opened a side drawer of her desk, put it in and closed the drawer.

"You do realize," she told him, "that the Monster of Plymouth must live on awhile longer."

"I'm sure he must be compelled to kill again, and many more times, and each more brutal and shocking than the one before?"

"Of course." There was a devilish spark in her eye. "Your public demands it."

"How will the story end?"

"If you're not captured and hanged by the neck at Newgate Prison before you can get yourself out of this fine box of thorns, the Monster of Plymouth will likely be hunted through the winter, and in the spring—depending on what else rears its head—you will be shot by a little boy who has come to the defense of his younger sister while their mother and father lie bleeding and nearly dead. Mortally wounded but yet as strong as Satan, you will climb to the rooftops to attempt your escape, and in trying to evade the constables by climbing into a chimney you will fall into an industrial furnace and your body be burned to atoms."

Matthew nodded. "I like that. Can I purchase a subscription?"

"Hm!" she said. "Subscriptions! Now there's an idea!"

"Moony!" said Keen. "A thousand times moony!"

"We'll be on our way, then," Matthew said. "Thank you for your time and good luck in your endeavors. Thank you also for showing me that letter and allowing me to copy it. I find that a very interesting thing to ponder."

"To ponder is one thing," she said. "To supply an answer is altogether another." She stood up from her chair. "I sincerely hope the reign of the Monster of Plymouth ends in that fiery furnace. In the meantime, good luck to Matthew Corbett."

Fuel for the furnace, Matthew thought. It was going to get him one way or another. He said goodbye to Esther Rutledge and Samuel Luther, and he and Keen left the office. He had more questions than before. The rain had lessened to a nasty, irritating drizzle, the air smelled of wet horses and their manure, and now Keen was thankful for the coach and its driver awaiting them at the curbside.

"That was a damned strange visit," said Keen as they walked to the coach. "Lord Puffery a woman! Who would've believed it?"

"No one, and no one will if you tell it, either."

"I won't tell it. But another thing...stranger still than hearin' Josh's name...that thing about Cable Street."

They reached the coach. The driver tipped his water-logged tricorn at them, for this was just a day's work.

"The hospital there?" Matthew asked as Keen opened the door. "What was strange about that?"

"Bugger it all, but Josh went crazy on that Velvet, and we tried to tie him down to give him the cure."

"Yes, Pie told me."

"Did she tell you that when Josh jumped out the window of a three-story buildin', he came down on Cable Street?"

"No, she didn't."

"Right there's where he landed." Keen had paused halfway into the coach to relate this. "Ain't that strange…hearin' Josh's name like that, and hearin' the name of the same street where he died?"

"Yes." Matthew had so many questions in his mind his brain felt as swollen as the coachman's hat. He let Keen get into the coach, and then he said, "Rory, I'm not going back with you." He held up a hand before the other man could speak, because the words were near bursting from Keen's mouth and his eyes had flared like dangerous torches. "Listen to me, please. I have things to do that I can't do in Whitechapel. I've got to find my acquaintance who's the assistant to the head constable and—"

"God A'mighty!" Keen said. "There's that stink of the Old Bailey again!"

Matthew rolled on: "And let him know what's been—"

Suddenly he stopped, for with mention of the Old Bailey the memory of a well-dressed, soft-spoken young man with light-colored hair and wearing a pair of square-lensed spectacles came to him.

Steven, the clerk.

"What's wrong with you?" Keen snapped at him. "Somebody pee in your porridge?"

"Maybe so."

"Huh?"

"Just thinking. Trying to figure something out that doesn't make any sense."

"Good for you. So you're leavin' me to fend for myself with the old woman, are you? Damn it, Matthew! I thought you'd help me set her straight about why we hired the coach! Let her know about Albion and all. She'll skewer my ass for this, if you ain't there to back me up."

"You're smart, you can come up with something."

"Like hell I can! Mother Deare can smell a lie six leagues from the Sabbath!"

That name nearly put him on the cinderblack paving stones.

"Who?" His voice sounded like that of a stranger choking on a bitter lemon.

"The boss. Calls herself Mother Deare. Mother to a snake in swaddlin', if she ever was, scares the shittles out'a me but I can't show it in front a' nobody."

Now Matthew's voice was truly lost. He heard the sounds of London rising around him as if it were a gigantic creature gathering itself in mad power and evil fury to crush him into dust.

"Where to, gentlemen?" asked the sodden coachman. The horses snorted and wanted to start pulling.

"I won't stand in your way if you want to leave," Keen said. "But after *you* stand with me and square it with the old woman. I could get in terrible trouble, spendin' this kind of coin. I swear it, Matthew. Oath or not, you can take a powder."

"Mother Deare," Matthew rasped.

"That's right." Keen blinked. "Oh Jesus, don't tell me you know *her*!"

Matthew looked up into the drizzle for a few seconds. Up against the dark, slowly-moving clouds a parliament of ravens crossed the sky.

With an effort he focused his attention upon Keen again. "You get the White Velvet from her, is that correct?"

It was obvious that this was the moment to come clean on that subject. "Yes," he answered, with a sour twist to his mouth.

"Then you should know that you and the Broodies are in the employ of Professor Fell."

"*What?* No, Matthew, you're wrong. Mother Deare's her own company."

Matthew lifted his tattooed hand to urge the coachman's patience. "She works for Fell, and I can swear to that. You work for her. See how that circles? I imagine the Broodies is not the only gang Fell's using to get the Velvet on the streets."

"All right then, whatever you say. But she'll be along anytime now to collect her due and go over the book. I'm thinkin' that if you offed one of Fell's people, you ain't too well appreciated by Mother Deare? That is, if you're on the level."

"I am. Mother Deare would know me on sight."

"Please…listen…I ain't as good a thinker as you. Hell, none of the Broodies are!"

"You sell yourself short."

"No…hear me out. Just come back with me and help me cook up a story that she'll buy, and it'll have to be a good one. Then you can leave and go see your good friend the flippin' Pope, for all I care.

If the old woman shows up a'fore you leave, we'll cover for you. I swear it."

What was the right thing to do? Matthew asked himself. He was in, as Esther Rutledge had said, a fine box of thorns, and it seemed he'd put Rory in one as well. Getting them both out was going to take some very careful maneuvering. Should he do it, or should he go on his way?

Matthew said to the coachman, "Back to Whitechapel, same place we hailed you." He got in and closed the door. He settled himself on the cracked leather seat and stared balefully at his companion. The thought *more drug than drink* was prominent in his mind.

The name of the lately-deceased Dr. Jonathan Gentry, he of the sawn-off head and delicacy to an octopus, had also come to mind.

As had the book of poisons, drugs and concoctions Gentry had created in support of Fell's efforts, one of which was called the "Juice of Absence", and had rendered its creator insensate while his head was being cut off in Fell's dining hall on Pendulum Island.

He recalled part of Gentry's description of the juice: *it removes one...takes him away...eases the mind and deadens the nerves...causes one to leave this realm of unhappy discord, and enter another more pleasant...*

"I want you to tell me everything you know about the White Velvet," Matthew said. "I mean *everything*. Hold nothing back, do you understand?"

"It's a fuckin' liquor, is all! A potent gin, to be sure, and I regret it took Josh away, but...it's just a drink."

Matthew shook his head. "It's much more than that. It's a drug."

"Yeah...well...I suppose any liquor's kind of a drug, ain't it?"

"Not like this one. It has something different in it. Some additive...some ingredient that makes a person nearly insane for the want of it." Matthew remembered the desperate girl grabbing the bars of the prison coach's window that night. She had wanted to bargain her body for "a sip of the velvet". And Pie talking about Joshua Oakley: *Pert soon he looked like a walkin' skeleton and all he gave a damn about was gettin' another sip.*

"What d'you make of it?" Keen asked, uncomfortably.

"I make of it," said Matthew, "that Professor Fell has a new enterprise, and it is centered on drugging an entire nation."

Four

The Things We Do for Love

Twenty-Three

Matthew stood in the Broodie cellar, looking at the crates of blue bottles and the casks of what he was certain was Professor Fell's latest plot upon the world.

"But you can't be...like...bettin' your life on it, can you?" Keen asked, standing beside him with Pie on Matthew's other flank. All of them held lanterns, uplifted to throw light upon the holdings. "I mean...about it all bein' drugged. You can't say for—what would be the right way to put it, Pie?"

"One hundred percent," she supplied.

"Let me ask both of you one question," Matthew said. "Would you want to drink a whole bottle of it?"

Neither answered.

"Well, why not?" Matthew prompted. "If it's only gin, perhaps with a high alcohol content, why wouldn't you want to?"

"I wouldn't care to throw up my guts," said Keen.

"You know that's not all. You told me in the coach that you've never tasted a drop of it. You told me you've seen what it can do to more people than Joshua Oakley, and Pie's told me the same. There's a reason you forbid any of the Broodies to drink it."

"That don't come from me, it comes from Mother Deare. She don't want to cut into the profits."

"She doesn't want her sellers to become addicted wretches and spoil the play," Matthew said. He looked from Keen's face to Pie's and back again and saw they were both struggling with the morals they thought they'd abandoned many years ago. "It's one thing to release upon the city—and I daresay the whole of England—a liquor of low cost and high volatility. It's quite enough to be knowingly selling a drug meant to turn its users into mindless maniacs who would do anything to get more of it."

"We don't *know* that!" Keen's face had reddened. His eyes were shiny, and he looked like a smoldering torch about to burst into flame.

"Yeah," Pie added. "And anyway, it's like I told you...if we wasn't sellin' it, somebody else would be." She turned her lantern upon the accuser. "It's about the money, Matthew! See, you don't understand it! You *can't*! You ain't a part of Whitechapel, you don't know what a person has to do to survive here! All right, maybe there *is* some drug in the Velvet that keeps 'em cravin' it, but we ain't the keepers of every poor fool out there! I wouldn't touch the shit, neither would Rory nor anybody else got any sense in their head, but plenty do and they pay good coin for it and that's all the matter!"

"Wrong," Matthew said firmly. "Rory, you told me you wanted to stay far away from Professor Fell. Well here you are in his waistcoat pocket! All the Broodies are, and have been since Mother Deare came to Mick Abernathy to strike the deal. That was four years ago, you say?"

"Near four."

"I would imagine the Velvet's gotten more and more highly dosed as time's gone on. It probably started off with just a light touch from Jonathan Gentry's book of potions."

"This doctor you're tellin' me about," said Keen. "Fell's chemist, he was?"

"In a way, yes."

"So...why would Fell want to spread a drugged gin 'cross the city? And the whole *country*, if you're right about this. Why not just make a cheap, strong gin and let it go at that? He'd have plenty a'customers."

"That's not enough for him. He wants to make sure his brand is the one drinkers crave...that they feel they can't live without.

And I believe there's another, darker reason." Matthew let his light move across the six barrels, which probably held more than enough to fill the bottles in the crates. "He knows it's not just the beggars and prostitutes who are going to become addicted. He knows the Velvet is going to find its way to the higher positions, to the businessmen, the attorneys, the constables and the judges. A blind need makes for blind corruption. The Velvet becomes a kind of currency he can use to buy those who might otherwise resist the influence. This moment, I'll wager there are politicians, officers of the law and maybe a judge or two who are getting a private supply. They're hiding their weakness, and Fell is preying on it. That's his way, believe me. Right now he's got some powerful people in his pocket who've been snagged by the Velvet, and those people are the ones he's really after but he's had to hide that by...shall we say...drowning the market in it."

"But he don't drown the market," Keen persisted. "Look at them barrels. They been sittin' here for quite a while even though the taverns are wantin' more!"

"He's building demand so the price will go up. Also maybe conducting a little social experiment to see what the addicts do when they find they can't—"

"Rory?" The door at the top of the stairs had opened. Tom Lancey had come in. "They're here," he said quietly.

"You mean, *she's* here?"

"Not her. Frost and Willow. They're wantin' to speak to ever'body all at the same time."

"They're wantin' the ledger book?"

"Didn't ask for it. Just say they got some questions."

"Be there directly," Keen said, and Lancey left and closed the door. Keen's light came up into Matthew's face. "Peculiar. She's always with 'em, and there's always three. *Questions.* Shit, I don't like the sound a'that. Must not be wantin' to go over the book, though, 'cause she's the one with the numbers nose." He lowered the lantern. "All right, we're in for it. Listen good, Matthew: they're not likely to come down here 'cause all the business is writ up, but if I was you I'd still dowse my light and find me a place behind them casks to bellydown awhile. Got it?"

"Got it." He was already looking for a place.

"Come on," Keen said to Pie, and they went up the stairs, out of the cellar and shut the door securely at their backs.

The two men were waiting in the central chamber, standing next to the table where Matthew had received his Broodie tattoo. Night had fallen outside; no light showed through chinks in the window's boards. The other Broodies had assembled at Frost's command. The two men both held lanterns and so did several of the others. Raindrops glistened on the men's coats and tricorns. By the yellow glow Keen saw that Frost looked a little worn and weary, and Frost was pressing a gloved hand to the center of his chest and breathing raggedly.

"You take a tumble?" Keen asked, as he put his lantern down on the table.

"Never you mind." Frost took a moment to hawk and spit on the floor. Keen quickly noted that the spit had a red shine to it. "Everybody here?"

"Looks so. Carr not with you? Or Mother Deare?"

"Not an accountin' visit. We're lookin' for—" Frost had to stop, because his breathing did sound impaired. "Tell 'em, Willow."

The other man, lean and long-chinned with a blonde goatee and deep-set dark eyes that regarded the Broodies with more than a smudge of arrogance, said, "Mother Deare's sent us out lookin' for a young man. Mark's name is Matthew Corbett. Last seen wanderin' in Whitechapel, as we hear it. We're makin' the rounds. Gent's in his young twenties, stands about six, wiry build, black hair, gray eyes. Handsome, Mother says he is. Might have a beard. Seen him?"

Keen was about to say *no* when Jane spoke up.

"What does she want with him?"

Keen darted a savage glance at her but he had to quickly lower his head; he did not have that much freedom of the mask.

"Does it matter?" Willow asked. "Seen him, or not?"

No one spoke. Keen felt Pie's arm pressing against his side. He knew she was likely thinking the same thing he was, that anyone who now wanted to step into being leader of the Broodies had a golden opportunity to chop off the head of a fella named Rory Keen. That would probably include Will Satterwaite, Jesse Lott and John Bellsen.

Keen put his mask of toughness back on and looked into Willow's face. "We ain't seen such a person."

A guinea coin hit the table, drawn from Frost's pocket. "For whoever sights him," Frost said, still speaking with an effort.

"You don't sound too good," Keen remarked. "Lung trouble?"

"Chair trouble," came the answer. Frost reached out, retrieved the coin and put it back into his pocket. "We got places to go. You see this mark, you—tell 'em, Willow."

"You see this mark, you bust 'im up so he can't walk. Then go tell the keep at the Lion's Den and give him your name. He'll get the word to us."

Keen nodded. "Sure will."

Frost's gaze wandered toward Jane once more. Keen felt his heartbeat quicken. Did the bastard sense it? Did he have an inkling that Jane knew something she wasn't spilling? For a few seconds Keen wondered how he might kill Frost and Willow, if it came to that.

"Accountin' visit next week," Frost said. "Have your numbers ready." He took in a hitching breath, pressed his hand to his chest once more as if to help his lungs perform, and then he and Willow left through the narrow door that to the passersby also looked boarded-over.

"That gent's got a serious problem," said Keen after they'd gone.

"It's *us* got the serious problem!" Will said. "What're we doin', lyin' to those men? Hell, Rory! What's the jig here?"

"The jig is that Matthew is a Black-Eyed Broodie, and though he ain't proved hisself in combat yet he still bears the sign and by God that makes him my brother. Yours too. Long as I'm wearin' the crown here, ain't no Broodie turnin' another Broodie over to no-fuckin'-body."

"What're they wantin' him for?" Paulie asked. "Seems like they're real bent on findin' him. How come?"

"If he's done an offense against Mother Deare," Jesse Lott added, "then we're all in for some heavy shit."

That caused a few of the others to bubble up and spew their mouths off, but Keen held up both hands for quiet and got it. "Ever'body just calm down, now. Believe me when I tell you, I got all this under control."

"Don't seem it!" said Will, his eyes narrowing. "That fella down there, when he ought to be in the gaolhouse but Albion turned him loose, and Albion killin' Ben right in front of me, and now them men comin' here and—"

"*And and and!*" Keen snapped. "Shut up your *andin'*! Hell's bells!" He cast a fiery look upon the group, pausing for a particular throw of flame at Jane Howard for opening her yap, and then he said, "Will, you, John and Billy go collect somethin' from somebody. Hit up the Piper's Folly and the Brass Bell."

"We done that last week."

"Do it *again*! Tell 'em they ain't paid enough, I need a new Sabbath suit. Jesse, you take Micah and Paulie and go to…I don't care…*somewhere.* That old bastard at the Golden Slipper's in need of a shakeup. Go lean on him." Keen clapped his hands together with a noise like a pistol shot. "I ain't just jawin'! *Move!* The rest of you…go get drunk or fetch your supper or bag a whore or I don't care what the hell you do. Pie, come with me."

He decided to turn a deaf ear to the muttering, but in truth he knew he was out on a mighty thin limb. He and Pie returned to the cellar with their lanterns.

"It's us, Matthew!" Keen said into the dark. "They're gone."

Matthew raised himself up from the floor behind the barrels, and not a moment too soon because a couple of rats had been scurrying around him and getting braver. "She wasn't with them?"

"Naw. Two of her men, Frost and Willow. They described you good. Nobody quailed. But she's lookin' for you, and those two are gonna turn Whitechapel upside down. I'd figure she's got others on the hunt too. *Damn it*," he said quietly. "Maybe you were right, back on Fleet Street. Go on about your business and hope you don't get killed doin' it. I sent some men out to press extra coin, I figure we can cook the ledger that way. Mother Deare knows how much we take in ever' month. Maybe we can scare up enough to cover that fuckin' coach."

"Thank you," Matthew said, for he knew what it would mean if Mother Deare's people learned the Broodies were harboring him and had lied to their faces. "Sorry I've gotten you into this."

"Matthew?" Pie asked, coming closer and shining her light on him. "If those men took you…would they kill you right off?"

"I doubt it. I think they would take me to Professor Fell, wherever he is. Then…well, the professor is a bit angry at me for destroying his island in the Bahamas."

"Oh Jesus! I don't want to hear it!" Keen would have put both hands to his ears if he hadn't been holding the lamp. "Christ, you're a rounder!"

"I knew that," Pie said with a gamin-like smile, "when he walked in that alley to save my skin."

"I believe we done paid that debt. Matthew, in the mornin' you're off. We can't have you here with them bloodhounds sniffin' your trail, it's way too risky and there's some here I think would like to turn you over. We don't have much to give you, but you can keep the suit and the boots."

"Thanks again." The purple horror was due for a burning, but for now that and the boots were very much appreciated. "Let me ask…do you know the time?"

"Ten or so, I reckon. Why?"

"At midnight," said Matthew, "I plan on being at the Tavern of the Three Sisters."

"What? With them neckbreakers out there huntin' you? I thought you had some *sense*!"

"Unfortunately, sometimes my sense and my curiosity go to war. Often my curiosity wins. I'm thinking that Albion might have been haunting the Three Sisters since that night he told me to meet him there. This near to midnight, and so close to the Sisters…I have to go."

Keen was about to protest again, but he sighed and simply said, "It's *your* funeral." He added, "Just be a good ol' oak and if them fellas get you, keep clammed about ever knowin' any of us." Keen's light fell upon the barrels. "*Oak*," he repeated, his eyes hazed over, and both Matthew and Pie knew who he was thinking about. "You're right," he said after a space of time. "The Velvet killed Josh, no doubt about that. It's killed a whole hell of a lot of other people, too. Either put 'em in their graves or made 'em into the livin' dead. What I hear the Velvet does…it's a bad thing, all right." He moved his light to take in both Pie and Matthew.

"You know what I think about sometimes?" he asked, in a faraway voice that sounded as if it were coming from a different man. "It comes on me awful sudden, and I can't shake it. You remember, Pie…when Josh went crazy and jumped out that window…you remember…he landed smack on a woman gettin' out of a carriage down on Cable Street. I recall hearin' her give a cry. Just real quick, and then she went down. She was dressed like a lady. I can still see her, all splayed out like a broke doll on the stones. Even when that horse bashed Josh's head in…I was lookin' at that lady, and wonderin' what she was doin' all dressed up gettin' out of a fancy carriage on Cable Street. And wherever she'd come from and whatever she was there to do…she sure hadn't gone to bed the night before thinkin' that a skeleton-weight piece of Whitechapel insanity was gonna fall from the sky and strike her down."

"Did she live?" Matthew asked.

"I don't know. We cleared out fast. We was using that place as a hideout, next to the hospital we was told about today. That's why I thought it was so strange…today, hearin' Josh's name and seein' it writ down, and hearin' about the Cable Street hospital, and all of it come back to me in a flood." His light moved amid the casks. "Seems like, when you think about it, it was the Velvet struck that woman down. 'Cause that's what Josh was at the end…ravin', and sittin' in his shit, and pleadin' for a drink, wantin' to fight and goin' mad with rage…then huddlin' up in a corner and sobbin'. All he was at the end was what the Velvet made him…ate up with poison, and wantin' to find some dream it give him that it took away." He turned the light upon Matthew. "If there's a drug in it, tastin' so sweet and then poisonin' people in that way…it ain't fair, is it?"

"No," Matthew said. "It isn't."

"What's to be done about that?"

"Are you asking me what *I* would do?"

"Maybe I am."

"If it were up to me," said Matthew, "I'd get an axe and I'd go to work down here. Let the rats dream."

There was a long silence. Then Keen said, feebly, "I can't do that. If I was to, there'd be no place I could hide, and they'd kill every Broodie who draws a breath."

Matthew gave no reply, but it seemed to him that London could be a city of prisons. The Broodies and the other gangs were imprisoned by the powers that controlled them, and doubly imprisoned to their territories. Whitechapel was a prison as much as Newgate, and likely the lords and ladies of the city were imprisoned in their silk-lined boxes of strict behavior and family heritage as much as the town's rowdies were constrained in their freedom of movement. One could be blinded by the bars, which might be made of gold as well as iron. And there was Professor Fell, himself a prisoner to his way of life, imprisoned by his rage after the beating death of his precious and much-loved twelve-year-old son Templeton, set upon a road of conduct that was of course his choice and his sin, and so twisted now as to be desirous of imprisoning thousands of other humans in cages of both greed and affliction. There was a pity in that, if Matthew stepped back and considered it with a mind unfreighted by emotion, for before the murder of Templeton the professor by his own admission had been a stellar member of society and a champion of science. Clotho, Lachesis, and Atropos were tireless workers, and those three sisters viewed the world of Man with eyes as cold as gravestones.

"I have to go," said Matthew, impressing upon himself the importance of visiting the appointed tavern at the appointed time.

"'Course you do," Keen answered. He ran a hand through his flame-colored hair and made a sound like he needed to spit out something foul. "Damn it all, I can't let you walk into the Sisters by yourself! Hell, even with the proper pointin's you might miss it and wind up on Drybone Lane, and that's even worse than Flint Alley! You start wanderin' 'round out there, you'll soon be poachin' on the Cobra Cult and with that Broodie sign on your hand they'll cut your eyeballs out."

That was a beautiful thing to ponder, but Matthew said, "I believe I can find the place on my own."

"You likely can, but do you really *want* to? What'll you do and where will you go if he don't show up? Better question…what'll you do and where will you go if he *does*?"

"I'll figure all that out when the time comes."

"By the time you figure it all out," Keen said, "you might be *dead*."

Matthew couldn't disagree. The logic of his going alone into such a hellhole was definitely faulty. Actually, the logic of his leaving this warehouse alone in the dark wasn't too solid either.

Pie said, "Rory's right. It's a mighty low dive to have a high-soundin' title. You got to be real careful in that place."

"Second that. They're our best customer for the Velvet, so you can imagine what it'll be like in there. And 'round midnight the thieves are gonna be stalkin' about." Keen paused to let that nice picture work in Matthew's mind. "You come an awful long way from New York to die in Flint Alley. Hell, you ain't goin' alone. That settles it."

"I'll go too," Pie said.

"No you won't! The more ain't the merrier when we're talkin' about Flint Alley at midnight. You just stick here. I mean it, Pie," he said to her defiant thrust of the chin. "You don't have to prove nothin' to nobody, but if I see you where we're goin' I will be mighty unhappy. Do you hear me?"

She resisted until he asked her again, more sharply, and then she responded with the briefest and most petulant nod.

"We'll fetch your cloak, your tricorn and that fancy dagger you came in with, and you can take a lantern too," said Keen. "We can eat and drink for free in the Sisters if we want to, since they're always beggin' more Velvet."

Suddenly Pie approached Matthew. She got up on her tiptoes to give him a kiss on the cheek. In the lamplight her brown eyes with their flecks of gold were shining, but they were sad.

"That lady of yours in New York is a lucky one," she said, and gave him the best smile she could offer. It didn't stick very long. "I'd be with you if I was let by that horse's ass over there. But watch them close shaves, Matthew," she advised, with a serious face. "Sooner or later you get cut."

He knew that was true. The trick was surviving the blade. Was it worth going there and hoping that Albion in his real identity also would choose this night to maintain watch at the Three Sisters? Yes, it was. His curiosity...his burning desire to wrap up all loose ends... the power that pushed him to often throw caution to the winds and dare those Sister Fates at the cost of life and limb...his need to think of himself as *good*, in this world of increasing evil...

The bars of his own prison?

Perhaps.

It was time to get ready.

Twenty-Four

THE rain had stopped and the wind had died. Following the black ribbon of the winding Thames came the damp yellow fog that began to slowly and silently spread itself block by block, street by street, and mile by mile across the great metropolis.

This night, approaching the strike of twelve, the fog held trickery. It transformed the moving coaches and carriages into misshapen creatures of demented dreams, their eyes ablaze with red centers of flame, their drivers dark blots in the gloom laying lash upon snorting fog-smeared behemoths. The buildings became of grotesque shape and size as if seen through rippled and dirty glass, and distances seemed elongated as if the fog had corrupted the very nature of space and time itself. Footsteps echoed here and there, with no one walking. A blurred face faintly touched by candlelight might appear at a broken window where murder was most recent, and no one living there anymore. A riderless horse might burst from the fog and then be swallowed up again in an instant, and a black dog might trot along at the heels for a spell before it wheeled and was swept away like a whirl of dead leaves. Voices or the memory of voices might issue from this room with a blood-stained floor, or this alley where the bones were found so gently wrapped, or from the chinks in this wall that held the beggar when he died standing up.

Fog set free the ghosts of London, Matthew thought as he followed Rory Keen through the labyrinth of hauntings. He could feel the spirits in the air, and he was not much one to dwell on such things...but still and all, they were here. Was the gnarled woman real who reached her thin arms toward him, and said in a ragged whisper, "My boy"? Was the fat man in a long coat and feathered tricorn real, who called, "Come here, come here" and gave a laugh as if he knew the central secret at the soul of the world? Was the little auburn-haired girl in the stained green dress real, who simply stood and stared at him with a lamb's-gut condom in her hand as if to an offering of the god of Whitechapel?

They must have been real. When Keen said harshly to all of them, "*Away!*" they were gone when Matthew looked back. So, yes...they must have been.

"Not much further," Keen told him. Even at this short distance, his voice seemed to come not from in front of Matthew but behind him, another directional trick of the fog. The lanterns they both carried cast weak beams that penetrated only a few yards into the miasma; all around them were walls of slowly undulating mist.

Matthew pulled his cloak a bit tighter. The weight of the dagger in its sheath at his side, beneath the cloak, was a small comfort; in truth he didn't want to have to stab anyone with it, and so doubly feared the furtive movements he imagined he caught in the doorways and alleys they passed. Keen had put on a brown cloak and skullcap; beneath his cloak he also carried a dagger, and Matthew noted that he always kept his lantern in his left hand so the right was free to quickly draw the blade.

High-pitched laughter floated in and away. There came the distant sound of a woman's voice, singing a song that must have been bawdy for the raucous hollering that accompanied it, and then both those noises of the night also faded out. An infant cried somewhere nearby, really startlingly close...then abrupt silence. More spirits wandering the void, Matthew thought. In spite of his rational nature, the hairs prickled at the back of his neck.

For the fourth time he was sure he heard the sound of bootsteps behind them, crunching the damp cinders on the walk. For the fourth time he stopped to shine his light in that direction, but once again there was nothing. No...wait...was that the faint glow of a lantern approaching? Or some ghostly orb growing in size and strength as it bore down upon them?

Keen had stopped just after Matthew had, and he too was directing his light the way they'd come. The noise of spectral gibbering came floating through the fog; it became a giggling that seemed to be emanating from all points at once, and Matthew now could make out a strange three-headed shape shambling toward him. It was coming fast and would be upon him before he could draw the dagger for his senses and his hand had become afflicted by the noxious spells of Whitechapel.

Then two drunken men with an equally soused female between them came out of the fog, the woman giggling and chattering and grasping onto the shoulders of both men. One of the gents, on the edge of a stumble, stopped abruptly at the sight of Matthew and nearly caused the other members of his tipsy caravan to go crashing to the paving stones. A lantern was lifted. By Matthew's light he could see that the woman's garish makeup was so smeared it appeared she had a second face on the side of her head and could have hidden at least three birds in the tangles of her hair, yet the two men were clean-shaven, wore expensive-looking cloaks and leather tricorns.

Matthew had the impression that the gentry had come here to wallow.

"*Sir*," slurred one of the men, and instantly the other gave a hard guffaw as if a deballed bull had been given this salutation. "*Sir*," it came again, and a laugh the same, "may I ask if you...hold a moment...Wilfred, stop her from squirming. Sir, may I ask if you have any Velvet?"

The question so disarmed Matthew that he couldn't answer.

"We have money," the man said. "Our last bottle...gone to piss, I fear. We have *money*," he repeated, as if reciting a magic charm.

"We were told we could find some Velvet here," said the second man, also slurring. "Somewhere. We're out."

"Pay him some money, sweetie," the woman told him. She was hanging onto both men to keep from falling. "Bet he's got a bottle hid."

"I have no bottle," Matthew said.

"How about you?" The first man was asking Keen. "Lord God," he said to the others when Keen didn't reply, "these two are dumb as stumps."

"Stumps as dumb!" the woman cackled.

"You won't find any for sale around here." Keen's face was devoid of expression. "There's none. Go home where you belong."

The three seemed to waver back and forth as if this information had been a shock wave.

"*Jimmy*," the woman whispered to the first man, and she busied herself fussing with the upraised collar of his cloak, "I told you...I told you...I *want* some Velvet. It's all fun and games to you, dearie... all fuckin' fun and games, but...Carrie needs her Velvet. Now...you said we was gonna—"

"Shut up," he growled, and when he pushed her face away he got her greasepaint all over his fingers. His mouth above the lantern had twisted. "There's *got* to be Velvet here somewhere! Stupid fucks...got to be, in all of Whitechapel!"

"Good luck to you, sirs...and madam," said Keen.

"These two don't know nothin'!" the woman squalled. "They're just common trash! Come on, let's...oh...oh...*shit*!" A puddle of urine began to widen around her scuffed shoes. "Find me some Velvet, Jimmy," she said, in a falsely-giddy voice. "Willie, find me some Velvet." She sounded like a child begging for a sweet, but underneath the plea there was a touch of terror.

"We'll bathe in it before morning," the gallant Jimmy answered, thrusting his chest out like the prow of a battle frigate. Then the three-headed monster staggered away, past Matthew and Keen, and were taken by the fog.

"They'll be bathin' in their own blood a'fore mornin'," Keen opined. "Come on, it's 'round the corner."

Unnerved by this encounter, Matthew again glanced back the way they'd travelled. Once more...was that the glint of another lamp? Well, of course it was. Midnight in Whitechapel was the midday of New York; they'd already seen a score of people with lanterns on the streets—and certainly not all of them citizens of the spectral realm—so what of it?

"Buck up," Keen told him, mistaking Matthew's hesitation for a loss of resolve. "But you know, you can still jump out a'fore the wagon catches fire, if you like."

"No, I can't. Lead on."

Keen took him to the next corner, where they made a quick turn to the left and went down a flight of stairs under a stone archway. The walls squeezed in to a width of about three feet. "Watch your step," Keen cautioned, because there was a man lying on his side underfoot. A second man was sitting on the ground with his back to the wall. His eyes were closed, he was snoring and appeared to have thrown up all over the front of his cloak.

About twenty feet on there was a slab of a door with the simple sign above it that said *3 Sisters*. The place looked like it had no windows. Keen asked, "Ready?" Matthew nodded and Keen pulled the door open.

Pipesmoke, the fumes of alcohol and the smell of unwashed humans rolled out. Matthew followed Keen inside and the door closed at his back. A few of the patrons glanced their way, but immediately dismissed them. It was not a large place. It was dimly-lit by lanterns on some of the tables. A portion of the cracked walls were painted, oddly, a pale robin's-egg blue which helped the lighting though the painter had given up about a third of the way through and left the rest mud-colored with fist-sized chunks of plaster missing down to the timbers. There stood the customary bar with a bald-headed, gray-bearded keep behind it. Two weary-looking serving-girls were tending to the wants of the customers. The room was nearly full, eight of the ten tables taken. Matthew quickly noted that the prime tables in a place like this—those in the corners with the protection of the wall at one's back—were already occupied. A scan of the room through the blue pall of smoke showed him several figures sitting alone. Two of them wore cloaks with hoods and their faces were in shadow; their ungloved hands were busy emptying mugs of ale into the unseen mouths. The noise of conversation here was a quiet mutter, though suddenly someone might cackle madly or a fist might pound a table to drive an opinion home.

"Rory! Rory!" the barkeep called him, waving him over. Matthew followed Keen to the bar, where the keep leaned forward with glinting eyes and a sparkle of sweat on his florid cheeks. "When we gettin' a batch?" he asked, keeping his voice low.

"Soon."

"When's *soon*? I could'a sold a dozen casks' worth in the time I've had nothin' to sell!"

"I've had no orders to move anythin'."

"They're gettin' restless! I don't start sellin' 'em Velvet real quick, they're gonna be tearin' this place down."

"They look tame for the moment," said Keen.

"Says you. You ain't in here hour after hour. Well, *shit*," he said, in exasperation. "But I'm first on your list, ain't I?"

"You are."

"Hell…I don't like this way a' doing business." The barkeep, perhaps realizing he was walking on unsteady ground, righted himself. "What'll you two have?"

"Ale and ale," Keen answered, ordering for both of them. "The nutbrown. And don't be waterin' it. We'll find a place to sit."

"Pardon," Matthew said to the keep. "Do you know what time it is?"

"Near midnight, I'm guessin'. Who is *this*?" he asked Keen. "Fella in the Sisters with the manners of a duke? I'm like to swoon away!"

"Come on." Keen took hold of Matthew's elbow and guided him to the nearest vacant table, which was toward the center of the room and in an unguarded position but that couldn't be helped. They had just seated themselves and Matthew had removed his tricorn when an argument broke out two tables over among four patrons engaged in a dice game. Foul curses were thrown, a knife flashed, there was a flurry of motion and the man with the blade was restrained by another gent from attacking his accuser; then when the voices had quietened and the tempers cooled all the men sat down again and the game went on as before.

The serving-girl brought their ales and she gave a laugh and swatted at the hand when Keen pinched her bottom. Matthew gazed around. The two silent and faceless hooded figures continued to drink. He saw no one he even remotely recognized. There were some faces in here that, once seen, could never be forgotten in terms of grotesquely-shaped noses, bulging foreheads and lizardy eyes.

"Drink up," said Keen. "If he shows, he shows. If not..." A shrug ended the comment.

"I won't know him, but he'll know me. I hope." He realized not having a beard might make a difference in recognition, but still...the whole thing was quite the frail fishing-line thrown upon stormy waters.

He brought from his pocket the paper with the six lines scribed by Albion and studied it again. What continued to grasp his attention was the line *and D.own I.t fell.* Why the periods behind those letters? Was this a message from Albion to Professor Fell? A challenge of some kind, the gauntlet being thrown down?

He took a drink of his ale. One of the hooded figures suddenly began raving, half-shouting and half-weeping, calling out the name of Angela. None of the other patrons paid him a straw of attention, and even Matthew's was fleeting. That definitely was not his man.

But who *was* his man? It intrigued him that the name Joshua Oakley had been left at the *Pin* by a young man who fit the description of Steven, the clerk at the Old Bailey. Of course that could be a common description, but for the moment Matthew let his imagination run wild.

He had thought that Albion might be the prisoner who'd escaped Newgate and knew about the underground passage in and out of that particular dungeon cell. Who else would know about it? A clerk at the Old Bailey? Who might have access to keys that would allow him to unlock both the cell and the gate out of the dungeon into the upper reaches of the prison? A clerk at the Old Bailey?

That made no sense.

And why go to the extreme trouble of getting *into* Newgate in the first place? For the simple reason of making an appearance in Cairo, and performing the theatrics of a gesture?

And yet...there it had been in the payment book at the *Pin*. The name Joshua Oakley, and then from Mr. Luther the description of the young man with the square-lensed spectacles that made him think of Steven the clerk.

How did it all work together? If, indeed, it did work together, for at the moment it seemed—

The door opened.

Matthew thought it must be just touching midnight.

A heavy-set man with a blonde bawd on his arm sauntered in and they went directly to the bar.

"That made you come to life," said Keen, who had finished more than half of his ale. "Doin' some thinkin', I perceive."

"Yes." Matthew folded the paper and put it away.

"I wouldn't be you for all the tea in China," Keen said.

"Why is that?"

"Your head must be awful heavy, all them brains in it. Can't figure how your neck holds up."

"It holds."

"Yeah, but I'll bet that when the sun shines on your face you start wonderin' how it is that a fuckin' orb in the heavens can be so hot and not explode. I'll bet when the wind blows a sweet breath up your nose you wonder where it came from and what makes it blow. And when a girl kisses you, you're thinkin' of how the lips work to make that kind'a pucker. Am I right?"

Matthew was silent.

"*Knew it.*" Keen gave a silver-toothed grin. "See, I'm smart in my own way. Hell no, I wouldn't be you. Too much thinkin'...it kills life. That's a curse, much as any man ever was cursed."

"I've never thought of it that way."

"'Course not. Likely it's the *only* thing you don't give much thought to: thinkin' itself, and that bein' a chain around you. What do you *enjoy* doin', besides workin' the brain?"

"Chess."

"Oh, hell! That sure don't count! What else?"

"I enjoy..." Matthew stopped and scowled. He had reached into a well and found it dry. "This is kind of pointless."

"Pointless *is* the point! Ain't you ever wanted to do somethin' just for the fun of it?"

"What, like robbing someone or raiding a rival gang's hideout with the intent to kill?"

Keen laughed out loud, which was not the reaction Matthew had expected. "No, not that," he said when the laugh had gone.

He took another drink of his ale and turned the mug between his hands. His voice was very quiet when he spoke again. "Do you know that I killed—had to kill—my pa?"

Matthew decided to let Pie keep that secret.

"I did. Long story, that is. He was a hard drinker. But he was a right good fella, when he was in his senses...and this was long a'fore the Velvet got loose. I don't even know if he was my real pa or not... my ma was kind of a cat. But he was the one who stayed on. One time when I was ten or so...he took me to what used to be a stone quarry. Ain't far from here. They hit water and it filled up, but the sides were high cliffs. He said to me, 'Rory, today I'm gonna teach you how to fly'. And know what he did? He stripped himself naked right on that cliff, and the sun shinin' down...it was hot July, I think...yeah, hot July. He stripped himself naked and he said for me to do the same, and I asked him, 'Why, pa', and he said, 'Son, you got to let the feathers breathe.' So I took 'em off, and there we stood in our splendor on what seemed like the bleedin' edge of the world.

"Then he says to me, 'Fly, Rory. Don't think about nothin', just fly.' I looked at that water way down there, and just a little rugged path to climb back up on, and God only knew what kind of monsters were down in those deeps and I said, 'I can't, Pa. I'm afraid'. And he reached out and took my hand...and I never held a hand so strong as that one was, a'fore or since. He said, 'Don't think about the fear...think about the flyin'.' I said...I remember I said...'But Pa, we'll fall,' and he gave me a big-toothed grin in that rough-seamed face, and he said, 'Son...to fall, first you got to fly.'"

Rory continued to turn the mug between his hands. He was staring at the scarred and stained table with eyes that had seen much misery, but Matthew was certain he was at that moment looking down from a cliff upon a shining surface of water with eyes yet full of trust and wonder.

"'Let's go,' pa said," Rory went on. "He said, 'Don't think...just go'. We went, both of us together. I was never so scared in my life, way up in that air, just him and me...but then I went into the cool water and it closed over my head but my pa...he didn't turn my hand loose. Not for a second. And when we come back up, spittin' and laughin', the first thing I said is, 'I want to go again'. 'Cause it *was* like flyin', just for a few seconds. You could spread your arms out and just feel like you was hangin' there in midair, and in those few seconds nothin' on earth could chain you down."

He looked quickly at Matthew and then away again. "Never told this to nobody, but…I still dream about that. It's a funny thing, though…in my dream I'm holdin' onto my pa's hand and we jump off the cliff…we jump and we sail in that bright summer air…and we never, ever come down." He finished off his ale. "Yeah," he said, the small voice of a lost child. "Yeah. Had to kill him."

Matthew was about to say *I'm sorry* when the door opened again.

In came a slender figure of medium height, wearing a black cloak with a hood over the head. On the hands were black leather gloves. Matthew's heart jumped. He had the quick glimpse of a face within the hood—no golden mask tonight—as a pair of eyes scanned the room.

This was the man. He knew it.

He pushed his chair back, stood up and dared to lift a hand in greeting.

Albion—for it had to be Albion—took a step toward Matthew, yet Matthew was still unable to fully see the face within the hood.

And suddenly the cloaked figure was pushed aside as two more men entered the Three Sisters like battering-rams, both wearing fog-damp cloaks and tricorns and carrying lanterns. In their fast appraisal of the room Matthew saw them freeze their gazes upon both himself and Keen. He heard Rory gasp, "Jesus! They've found us!"

The two men—Frost and Willow, Matthew presumed—strode across the planks toward them, after the one in the lead gave the cloaked figure another shove to clear the way. Albion—if it truly was—turned aside and approached the bar.

"Gentlemanly of you to stand for us," said the lead man. His pallor was waxen and his breathing labored. He pressed a hand to his chest. "Figured you was holdin' out, Rory. Shame on you! That girl…had to know somethin'. Christ, I can't talk. Willow?"

"Waited outside the warehouse," said Willow. "Long wait, but you come out."

"Figured to see where you was headed. Damn fog," Frost rasped. "Lost you. Went from tavern to tavern. And here you are!"

Matthew looked past the two men. Albion was speaking to the barkeep, the hood still up.

"Mother Deare," said Frost to Matthew. "Wants you."

Now was not the time for panic. Matthew judged what the effect of throwing the table over might be.

Willow must've caught the thought or perhaps the two toughs were used to dealing with desperate men, because the snout of a pistol suddenly appeared in his right hand amid the folds of his cloak.

"*No,*" he said, which pretty much covered all the angles.

"Double that," said Frost, as the barrel of his own pistol made its ugly self known. "We got a ways to walk."

"You been bad boys," Willow said. "Mother's gonna spank you."

"Up." Frost's pistol made the motion to Keen. "And *out*, easy as you please."

As they were herded toward the door Matthew looked over at Albion, but if the cloaked figure really was the golden-masked avenger he simply seemed to be ordering an ale from the keep. He had not yet lowered his hood; Matthew couldn't even see the man's hair color.

On an impulse, as they reached the door, Matthew called out, "Steven!"

The keep and several of the patrons looked up. The cloaked figure did not turn from his position at the bar.

"Go on," Frost commanded, sounding terribly out-of-breath.

When they were in Flint Alley and walking toward the steps, avoiding the two men sprawled on the ground, Frost gave three deep coughs followed by a ghastly wheeze. He placed the barrel of his gun against the back of Keen's head. "Damn it!" he croaked. "Tell 'em, Willow!"

"This is how it is," said the second gunman. "Mother wants you alive, Corbett. You make a move we don't like and ol' Rory gets it in the brainpan. Keen, you try to run and you get it in the brainpan. Either way, you get it. Got it?"

"Seems to me I'll get it in the fuckin' brainpan either here or there, so what's the difference?"

"The difference is that—Christ, I can't breathe. The fucker and that chair. Should'a kicked his head in." He gasped for air, a painful sound. "Tell 'im the difference, Willow."

"You can live to see tomorrow if you play nice," said Willow. "Would you rather lose your life or your left hand? You're gonna lose one or the other for sure. Your choice."

Matthew knew they had thrown Rory a bone of hope, but he also knew Mother Deare and the nature of Fell's people. What Willow wasn't saying is that they would *start* with the left hand. Likely use a redhot iron to sear the stump, make him live that much longer. Sometime around six in the morning they would be getting to the footless legs.

They climbed the steps out of Flint Alley.

"To the right," Frost told them. They walked into the wafting wall of fog.

"Just go easy," Willow cautioned.

Was there any other way? Matthew had a brief impulse to just run for it, but Frost's bullet would surely go into Keen's skull as soon as he tried, and he figured Willow wouldn't shoot to kill but wherever the ball went into his own body, it would be an agonizing night. Still, Mother Deare was not going to be gentle, even after venting her rage and cutting Rory to pieces. However one looked at this picture, it was not pretty.

A few paces onward and Frost had to stop for a coughing fit. He lowered his gun from Keen's head and doubled over but instantly Willow's pistol took its place. Frost coughed violently for perhaps eight seconds, spat red on the stones and then coughed some more. "Ahhhhh, *shit*!" Frost said when he could get hold of his voice again. "That bastard...fouled my chest, Willow."

"I think you need a doctor," said Keen. It was the wrong thing to say because suddenly Frost was up in his face with a savage, twisted expression that could only signify impending carnage. By the lanternlight, Matthew could see that Frost's lips were flecked with blood. Two pistols pressed against Rory's head.

"Ought to kill you right here and now, you low traitorous...tell him!" Frost wheezed.

"You low traitorous sonofabitch!" said Willow, ably conveying the sentiment with his own twisted mouth.

"*Move*," Frost commanded.

Matthew and Rory moved on, at the point of the pistols.

And here Matthew wished that from any of the fog-shrouded doorways would lurch a beggar, a prostitute or some other creature of the night, and in so doing might afford a chance to disrupt this caravan of the doomed. Matthew thought he could get hold of

Frost's gun-hand, if Rory could take care of Willow. But as they walked on no such thing happened, and even when a pair of drunks stumbled past from the opposite direction they went by as peacefully as doves.

Frost had to stop to cough and wheeze again, and Matthew thought that now was the time but the gun against the back of Rory's head turned his resolve into a fleeting idea of misguided heroics. They continued on when Frost's fit had passed. Matthew began to wonder how he might talk Mother Deare down from her pinnacle of revenge, but though he might survive the night in one broken form or another he was sure his friend's every step led nearer the grave.

The light of an approaching lantern glinted through the fog ahead. A figure was coming closer.

"Keep goin'!" Frost said, his voice nearly gone.

Matthew heard the sound of drunken laughter and a slurred voice. The man approaching them staggered from side to side. He was talking and laughing to himself, and now he was almost upon them and Matthew thought if he grabbed the man and threw him into Frost, what would be the outcome?

He suddenly realized the figure wore a hooded cloak.

"Pardon, pardon, pardon," the man said, the voice muffled as he stumbled toward Frost, and Frost let out a curse and lifted the lantern and there in the hood was the golden mask of Albion, who without further hesitation smashed Frost in the face with his lantern and was already drawing his saber from beneath the ebony cloak.

Many things happened in a rapid succession and a blur of motion.

Frost gave a cry, his face bloodied, and fell backward. Matthew swung for Willow's head but missed because the man had already moved. Willow's pistol was coming up to fire at Albion. Rory backpedalled, fearful of the saber and what he thought was a mad killer. Willow's gun went off with a *crack* and a billow of smoke, but the hand holding it was already half-cleaved from the wrist by Albion's blade and the ball ricocheted off the paving. Albion followed the first cut with a slash across Willow's eyes and as the man's head tilted up the next swordswing caught him squarely across the throat. He spun past Rory like a bloody pinwheel.

Another shot rang out and more smoke puffed. Matthew heard Albion give a grunt and a gloved hand went to his left side low on the body. Frost was on the ground, his back to a wall and blood in his eyes but his pistol's eye had targeted well enough. Matthew kicked the gun from Frost's hand though by now it was merely a club; then he was shoved aside by the surprising strength of Albion, who brought his saber down upon Frost's head like the judgment of God. The blade crushed Frost's tricorn through his skull into his brain, and gray matter streamed over the man's ears as if a bowl of moldy oatmeal had been poured on his head.

Albion pulled at the saber to free it, but the blade had gone deep and the avenger's strength appeared to be quickly ebbing. Voices shouted through the fog. The sound of one shot going off may have been a drunken accident; two shots was a bloodletting. Albion let go of the sword. The golden mask turned toward Matthew and hesitated only a second. Then Albion staggered, still holding his wound, and ran away into the fog from whence he had come.

The voices were getting closer. Matthew saw that Willow's lantern had been shattered but Frost's was lying intact and still lit. He picked up the survivor, put his foot against Frost's mushy skull and yanked the saber free. Then he said to Rory, "Come on!" He had to give Rory's arm a jerk to bring him back to the moment. "Follow me!" he said, and took off running in the direction Albion had gone. He didn't look back to see if Rory was coming or not; time was of the essence.

He began to see the scrawls of blood on the ground. A half-block ahead, the blood showed that Albion had crossed the street. Matthew followed and picked the trail up a few yards onward.

Not much further, the blood trail turned into the doorway of a money-lender's shop.

There, on the ground with his back against the door and his knees pulled up toward his chest, was Albion. He was breathing raggedly, but breathing. The mask had gone crooked in the confines of the hood.

"He's hurt bad," said Rory from right behind Matthew, which made Matthew nearly jump out of his skin.

"Hold this." Matthew gave him the bloody saber, and never was a sword more reluctantly received.

No 3

Matthew knelt down. He saw that the eyes in the slits of the mask were closed. The wound was bleeding profusely through the gloved fingers.

He reached out, under the man's chin, found the bottom edge of the mask—shiny gold-colored fabric, the 'beard' a tooled piece of gold-painted leather—and lifted it.

Before him was the face of Albion.

Before him was the face of Judge William Atherton Archer.

"You know him?" Rory asked, for Matthew had given a startled jerk.

"Yes," Matthew managed to reply, though still stunned. All that blood...the ball had hit something vital. "We've got to get him to a doctor," Matthew said. "Somewhere." He looked up at Rory. "*Where?*"

"I don't know, I can't—wait...wait. The Cable Street hospital. It ain't too far...couple a'blocks."

Archer's eyes fluttered and opened. The bloodshot orbs stared up at Matthew, who slipped the mask off the man's head and put it away in his cloak.

"We're going to take you to the hospital on Cable Street," Matthew said. "Can you hear me?"

Archer tried to speak but could not. He nodded. A little trickle of blood ran from a corner of his mouth.

"Let's get him on his feet," Matthew said. And as Rory helped him pull the wounded Albion up, Matthew hoped they could get this man to the hospital before the life departed from him, because then forever would depart the mystery of why a respected and upright justice of the Old Bailey would transform himself into a masked and nearly maniacal killer.

They set off into the fog, as the ghosts of London silently kept their watch.

Twenty-Five

The tall, distinguished-looking but very weary surgeon on duty came along the hallway into the small lantern-lit room where Matthew and Rory sat on a bench next to the high-topped desk of the admissions nurse. He had just removed his blood-smeared green apron outside the operating chamber. He wore white stockings, brown breeches and a yellowed shirt that used to be white. His sleeves were rolled up. His hands had been freshly scrubbed of blood yet some traces of it always stubbornly remained beneath his fingernails as a reminder of his work.

He ignored the hollow-eyed woman whose husband had been brought in with a knife wound to the right shoulder, for the man was out of danger, and likewise he ignored the two ragged wretches who had carried a third in after their companion had gone into a Velvet-charged rage and attacked a brick wall, shattering the bones of both his fists; that man, too, would survive and the leather straps on his bed would keep him secure after the knockout recipe of laudanum, belladonna and whiskey wore off.

The surgeon strode directly across planks stained with the blood of countless victims of Whitechapel violence. He and the other three doctors who volunteered their services here had seen everything from axes still sticking in the heads of living people to faces obliterated by malicious vials of flesh-burning acid. But never—*never*—had he expected to see what he had first seen two hours ago, when the nurses wheeled the body of a gunshot victim back to the operating chamber and called him from his treatment of the knife wound.

"Gentlemen," he said, stopping before Matthew and Rory. These were the two Mrs. Darrimore had said brought the body in. "I'm Dr. Robert Hardy. You are?"

They introduced themselves. Matthew noted that Rory called himself "Mister Rory Keen".

"Fine. Now tell me why in the name of God William Atherton Archer is lying gutshot and near to death in this hospital."

It had been a gruelling and desperate journey from where they'd found Albion to the entrance of the Cable Street Publick Hospital; gruelling because Albion's legs had given out soon after they'd begun and they'd had to carry a dead weight, and desperate because it was certain he would soon be simply dead if they didn't hurry. Matthew had told Rory to ditch the saber and so the saber had been ditched, in a sewage ditch that ran along the street. When they'd gotten the wounded man into the hospital, Matthew saw that his face was slack and pallid from loss of blood. The nurses had quickly set Archer upon a small wheeled carriage, torn his shirt away to expose the wound, and rushed him back to the operating chamber; they had been silently efficient except to ask the question of how many times the victim had been shot in case they'd missed a second and third wounds, and the question posed to Matthew and Rory asking if either one of them had been the shooter. Matthew figured that there had to be a weapon or two behind that nurses' desk, and the sturdy women here would know how to use such since violence here was obviously a daily—and particularly nightly—matter.

"*Speak*," said Dr. Hardy.

Matthew did. "Sir, how is it you know Judge Archer?"

"He has a history here. Judge Archer has been influential in aiding this hospital. Now that I've answered you, return the request: how did he come to be shot? And what in God's name is he doing in Whitechapel at this time of night?"

Matthew could feel Albion's mask in the pocket of his cloak, which lay across his lap. He realized that anything he said now could lead to dire consequences, and without the proper answers from Archer the wisest course was to say, "You'll have to ask the judge when he awakens."

"*If* he awakens," the doctor replied. "Shall I send for a constable to shake the information out of you?"

Rory laughed. "That ain't gonna happen, doc! You'd find the flippin' Queen in Whitechapel 'fore you'd find a constable, and you know it."

Hardy cast a withering glare at Rory, and then his eagle eyes found the tattoos on both their bloody hands. "You're Black-Eyed Broodies, I see. That's highly ironic."

"Why is that?" Matthew asked.

"It was one of yours who caused the death of Judge Archer's wife, as you must already know."

All of Matthew's senses immediately went on the alert. "His *wife*?" He caught himself and asked in a steadier voice, "No, I didn't know that. How did it come about?"

Hardy stared at him in silence for a few seconds. Then he said, "You're not a Broodie. You've got the mark, yes, but..." His eyes narrowed. "You say your name is *Matthew Corbett*?"

"Yes."

"I've heard that name mentioned recently...somewhere."

The Monster of Plymouth strikes again, Matthew thought uneasily. He figured at least one of the nurses and possibly a physician or two here were readers of the *Pin*. Even so, he had no choice but to forge ahead. "Sir, I'd like to hear what happened to Judge Archer's wife."

"Why? What's that to *you*?"

"Doc," Rory said with a bit of heat in his face and voice, "we brung the gent in, didn't we? We could'a left him on the street to bleed to death. We been sittin' here for the like a' two hours, waitin' to hear what state he's in. Don't that count for nothin'?"

"It makes me wonder *why* all the more."

"You say a Broodie killed his missus? That right?"

"I didn't say *killed*," Hardy corrected. "I said, *caused her death*."

"Ain't that the same?"

Hardy turned his attention to Matthew again. "His wife—Helen by name—was a great asset to this hospital. She volunteered her time and services at every opportunity, and ours was not the only institution she favored. One day she arrived in her carriage to perform her volunteer work and she was struck down in the street by a falling body."

Matthew's mouth had gone dry. He thought he felt the flesh of his face tighten.

"Don't you know this?" Hardy probed. "How long have you been running with these children who think themselves so grown-up?"

"*Josh Oakley*," Rory said, in what was nearly a stunned exhalation of breath.

"That was his name," Hardy went on. "We found it out from a tavern keep. The tattoo on his hand further identified him as one of your odious tribe. We also learned from others in the neighborhood that he was addicted to and likely made insane by the White Velvet, which is not only the scourge of Whitechapel but a damned blight upon this entire city."

"Go on," said Matthew. "About Helen Archer. She didn't die in the street?"

"Thank God, no. I say that, but…it might have been better if she *had* died there. No…she was brought into the hospital with a broken neck, a broken back, and severe internal injuries. We considered transferring her to a better-equipped facility but she was in tremendous pain and begged not to be moved, and…in truth…no other facility could have done any better for her." Hardy's eyes were cold. "Does it give you some measure of *pride*, hearing this?"

"No pride," Matthew answered. "Sorrow for one and all."

"A little late for that, young man. Helen lingered here for nearly two weeks. In time the pain-killing concoctions we prepared for her lost their power and so we had to keep her sleeping. Mercifully—*for one and all*," he said with dripping sarcasm, "she passed away in her sleep. Now Judge Archer shows up here, after midnight, with a gunshot wound that may yet kill *him*? What's the game?"

"I'm not sure," Matthew said, partly to himself. "But whatever it is, it's deadly."

"I believe you two should leave," said the doctor. "This room is hard enough to keep clean as it is."

"We don't have to sit here and be fuckin' *insulted*." Rory rose indignantly to his feet. "Come on, Matthew, let's scrape this shit off our shoes." He took two steps toward the door and then stopped when he realized his brother Broodie was still sitting. "Come on, we're not wanted here!"

"You go ahead."

"*What?* You're gonna stay here and take this?"

"Yes," said Matthew.

"I want you *out*," Hardy told him.

Matthew looked the doctor in the face. "You'll have to throw me out. I intend to stay here in case Judge Archer wakes up."

"He won't. Not for many hours, if indeed he wakes up at all."

"Then for many hours I'll be right here."

"*Why?*" Hardy asked. "All right, so you brought him in! You can give yourself a pat on the back and an extra slug of rum…or Velvet, if you're stupid enough." He took a few seconds to examine Matthew from head to foot. "You're not a Broodie. You're play-acting as one. Who and what are you, really?"

Matthew said, "I'm the person who's going to be sitting right here until Judge Archer wakes up. I can tell you that he'll want to see me."

"And why might that be? To thank you? You expect a reward?"

"In a manner of speaking," said Matthew, for answers would certainly be a rich reward.

Hardy turned on his heel and stalked away.

"My ass has gone t' sleep," Rory said. "I can't take no more a' that flippin' bench."

"You should go home," Matthew advised, if one considered *home* to be a room in a dirty warehouse full of the vilest corruption ever to be poured upon the desperate souls of London.

"Yeah, I'll do that." But Rory didn't move any nearer the door. He looked around, saw that the hollow-eyed woman was dozing and the two wretches were sitting on a similar bench, talking with their heads close together as if planning where to nab their next nip. Sleeping ass or not, Rory eased himself down again beside Matthew.

"Can you figure that?" he asked quietly. "Josh came down on a judge's *wife*? And that judge turned out to be Albion? How come you don't want to tell the doc?"

"I want to hear what Archer has to say first."

"Brain me with a cod! A judge is a fuckin' *killer*? And I carted him in, knowin' he was the one cut Ben's throat! Not to mention he got hisself into Newgate just to see *you*? And then..." Rory shook his head; it was all too much for him to comprehend. "What do you make of it?"

"I make of it...a puzzle. Many pieces are missing. I think only Archer can supply them."

"If he dies you'll never get 'em."

"I know. One thing we can both be very thankful for: he took care of our predicament tonight, so in effect he saved our lives."

"My life saved by a flippin' judge. Who would've ever thunk such a thing?" Then Rory's shoulders sagged and he lowered his face, and he was silent for a time but Matthew knew what must be going around and around in his overburdened mind. It had to do with Oakley, Helen Archer, the bountiful and corrosive supply of Velvet in the Broodies' hideout, and the far-from-motherly hand of Mother Deare. "She won't stop lookin' for you," he said. "You know. *Her*."

"Yes."

"It'll get back to her 'bout Frost and Willow by first light. Then she'll send out more of her hounds." He looked up into Matthew's eyes. "You mean the Broodies are really workin' for Professor Fell? And we been doin' it for years?"

"Ever since the deal was struck with Mick Abernathy."

"Years," said Rory. "Do you think Albion killed Ben 'cause of what happened to his wife? I mean...him bein' a judge and all, and knowin' people...he could've found out some of the Broodies hang 'round the Sisters, and likely went in there as a regular fella and maybe saw the marks on Ben and Will's hands?"

"Perhaps, but that doesn't explain why he killed the other five. They weren't Broodies, were they?"

"No."

"I think it has to do with something else. Possibly the death of his wife is part of it, but I believe it's far from being the whole story. We'll just have to wait and hope he awakens."

"That White Velvet," said Rory. "It's done an awful lot of damage, ain't it?"

"It has."

"How can I just put an *axe* to it, Matthew?" Rory's face was lined with pain. "If I did that, they'd kill every one of us. And right now...I'm not sure Will, or John or somebody who wants to take my place would stand by and let me do it."

"Likely not," Matthew agreed. It was clear Rory had little choice in the matter, unless he was to throw off his ties to the Broodies and simply walk away. But where would he go? And the Velvet would continue to be sold to the taverns, no matter his involvement or not. The demand, and the power that had cultivated it, was just too great.

They lapsed into silence. For the next hour they watched a tragic parade of people being helped, carried or in some cases dragged into the hospital. A screaming woman with a face covered in blood was brought in by two other females. A well-dressed gent staggered in with what appeared to be a multitude of knife wounds all down his left arm, blood dripping from the fingertips to add their pattern to the floorboards. Three young men carried in a fourth whose head had been bashed in and looked to have already slipped the bonds of life. A thin and ragged woman entered leading a silent, heavy-set man by the hand, but as soon as a doctor came out to speak to them the man became suddenly enraged and attacked the physician with both hands to the throat, whereupon one of the nurses used a club to subdue the offender with a single quick blow to the skull.

From Dr. Hardy there was no word, though he did reappear from time to time to speak with other patients and accompany them to the back. He cast not even a glance in the direction of Matthew and Rory, and Matthew surmised there was no change in Archer's condition.

At last, as it must have been near daylight, Rory stood up and stretched so hard his bones popped. "I can't do no good here," he said. "I'd best get back to the others, they'll be wonderin' what's happened."

"I'll need to stay," Matthew said.

"Figured. Listen...it's almost light, so...if you want to go your own way, that's fine. If not, can you find you way back to the warehouse?"

Matthew nodded.

"Ain't too far. Like I say, you want to get on with what you need to do, that's your business, but if you need a place to roost you can always come back. You're one of us."

"Even without proving myself in combat?"

"I reckon we just had us combat enough. Don't fret on that. If you hang with the Broodies you'll have plenty of chances for fightin'."

"You're not worried about Mother Deare knocking at your door to find out what happened to her men?"

"Naw. Frost and Willow ain't gonna be doin' no more talkin'. Yeah, she'll send more men, but she ain't gonna know what happened out there, and I'm in the clear. So...anyhow...decide whatever you please."

"Thank you," Matthew said.

"Welcome." He started to move away and then hesitated, for there was something else he needed to convey. "Matthew," he said, "that doc was right. You got the mark, but you don't belong here. You're flyin' in higher air than me. Ought to fly on 'fore Whitechapel gives you a fall."

Matthew nodded at this but he could neither add nor subtract from what Rory had expressed, as it equalled the truth.

"All right, then," Rory said, and he turned away from Matthew, walked across the blood-stained boards and out of the Cable Street hospital.

Murky daylight was beginning to show through the room's windows. Beyond the dimpled glass in their unpainted frames, carts and wagons were trundling along the street through the dwindling tentacles of fog. Matthew wondered if the sun would ever shine again upon London. He placed his hand upon Albion's mask in the pocket of his cloak. He longed to inspect it more closely, to see how it was sewn, but here was not the place. He caught one of the square-bodied, husky nurses staring at him; he hadn't given anyone but Dr. Hardy his name, and he sincerely hoped that on one of the woman's many excursions to the patients' ward Hardy hadn't mentioned his name to her, and her a reader of the *Pin*, and now that the nightly dramas of life-and-death here had quietened she wasn't putting a face to the Monster of Plymouth.

He couldn't help it if she was. He smiled at her and she quickly looked away, but leaned toward another nurse to speak softly in her ear. Well, he wasn't leaving and that was that. Bring on all the constables you please, he mentally told her. Albion is lying back there, so bring on the devil if you please but I'm sticking.

He situated his back against the wall and closed his eyes. For all the questions that whirled in his mind, he was asleep within a minute and slept in a dreamless void.

He was awakened seemingly only seconds after his eyes had closed. Someone had grasped his shoulder and given him a shake. He looked up into the face of not Dr. Hardy but another man, this one older than Hardy with white hair tied back in a queue and wearing spectacles. "Corbett?" he asked.

"Yes." Matthew realized the light through the windows had strengthened, though it could barely be called strong, and the faces of the people in the hospital's waiting-room were all different. "What is it?"

"Judge Archer has awakened and is asking for you."

At once Matthew was on his feet, though still a bit groggy. He took his cloak and tricorn and followed the man out of the room, along a hallway and through a door into the patients' ward, which was a long chamber crowded with beds. Not a single bed was empty. Mercifully most of the patients were sleeping, but some were raving as they fought against the leather straps that constrained them. One—a woman—was sobbing and shrieking, while a little boy stood next to the bed holding her hand. The smells of sickness and infirmity overpowered the bittersweet odor of the soap used to clean the linens and scrub the floors. Nurses moved back and forth to give aid, but all in all it was a hellish scene.

"We have him in a private area," the man—another doctor, Matthew presumed—said as he led the way through the ward. He stopped briefly to confer with a nurse and check something off with his pencil on a sheet of paper, and then he continued on through a door and into a short corridor with two rooms on either side. The doctor motioned toward the nearest room on the right. "Your name was the first he spoke. I can only give you a few minutes."

"I understand."

"Oh," the man said before he retreated, "Dr. Hardy has told me he's sent a messenger to the Old Bailey to give them word."

"I see." Matthew still felt dazed. "Can you tell me what time it is?"

The doctor referred to a very fine-looking silver pocketwatch. "Sixteen minutes before nine. I'll send a nurse to inform you when you should leave. Judge Archer is still in a precarious condition."

"All right." Matthew entered the room, the doctor withdrew, and there upon a bed of snow-white linen with the topsheet pulled up to his chin was the Hanging Judge himself, his pallor gray, his breathing all but imperceptible, his eyes closed.

Matthew waited a few seconds but the eyes did not open. He said, "I am here, sir."

The eyelids came up with sluggish strength, as obviously the drugs in Archer's system were highly potent. They drifted down again before, seemingly by sheer force of will, he corrected the descent.

"*Mr. Corbett*," he whispered, in a frail voice no one on earth would have recognized as belonging to the fiery and combative William Atherton Archer. "*Closer*," he urged.

Matthew stepped nearer the bedside. Archer simply stared at him, as if trying to gather enough strength to speak again. To the judge's silent struggle, Matthew said, "I thank you for saving the lives of myself and my friend."

"Fool," whispered the judge.

"Sir?"

"Not you. That…fool…who kept coughing. Might have lost me…in the fog…otherwise."

"Ah. I presume you saw them take us from the Three Sisters and you got around in front of them in the fog?"

"'Course. Didn't…hop…like a cricket, did I?"

"I'd be surprised if you couldn't. Albion can walk through walls like a phantom, so hopping like a cricket would be a minor effort." Matthew was aware that time was passing fast and the judge's strength might collapse at any second. "I have Albion's mask," he said. "Can you tell me what all this is about?"

"Professor Fell," Archer answered, still in a tenuous rasp. "The White Velvet. Murder…and despair. The…*corruption*…of…everything I hold dear."

"I thought you believed Fell to be only a—"

"*Don't interrupt*," came the reply, with surprising force. Then: "Who were…those men…Albion sent to their graves?"

"Fell's men, working with a woman who calls herself Mother Deare. She—"

"Yes, yes. I know that…odious name. You see? My plan…my plan has *worked*."

"Your plan, sir? What would that be?"

"My plan," said the judge, "to…lure Fell out from hiding…by using *you* as bait."

"*What?*"

"All this…to lure Fell…or his people…to show themselves. To let him know you…a…formidable foe…who has bested him…are in London…and your only friend…is Albion, the…killer of his underlings."

Matthew had the sudden memory of the vicious guard named Baudrey at Newgate, calling him *baitfish*. It seemed that he had been the sardine on a much more important hook than Baudrey had ever dreamed.

"I knew…sooner or later…they would find you. But I had hoped…Matthew…that I would be at your side…when they showed themselves. I fear my…plan…has not quite…succeeded as I intended."

"That's all right, Father," said someone at Matthew's back. "God willing, it shall yet succeed."

Matthew was startled, but he already knew who he would see when he looked behind.

The story in the *Pin*…the name of Joshua Oakley…the person who knew the comings and goings at Newgate as well as did Judge Archer, and the one also who had lost a loved one to the tragic insanity of the White Velvet.

"Greetings, Steven," Matthew said to the young man with the straw-colored hair and the square-lensed spectacles.

"And to you, sir," Steven replied, with a quick and respectful bow of the head.

TWENTY-SIX

"IT is time," said Matthew, "for answers."

"Agreed," Steven said.

"The whole story. Leave nothing out."

"*The whole story*," Steven repeated with an air of bitter sarcasm. He spent a moment to stir a spoonful of sugar into his cup of coffee. "The story of at least two lives, if not two hundred thousand."

Matthew had decided to take his coffee strong and unadorned. He took a drink of it and imagined feeling renewed vigor race through his veins, a sensation he sorely needed.

They were sitting in a small coffee shop called the Rising Sun, one street to the south and a block to the west of the Cable Street Publick Hospital. It was the nearest place they could find that guaranteed a modicum of privacy. The brown brick walls were cracked and the place wasn't very clean, but the coffee smelled good and the tables were more or less level, so this establishment suited the purpose.

Barely thirty minutes had passed since Matthew had been called to Judge Archer's bedside. Steven had gone to his father and hugged him, they'd spoken quietly for a short time, and then it was clear the judge's strength was again ebbing because he couldn't raise even a whisper. A nurse came to tell them it was time to leave, and so after Matthew had washed the blood off his hands in a horse trough they'd taken their discussion to this house of the Rising Sun.

"I should tell you," said Steven, "that two people from New York are here looking for you. Their names are Hudson Greathouse and Berry Grigsby. They're—" Matthew's gasp gave him pause, and then he went on. "They're staying at the Soames Inn off Fleet Street. Very near the printer who produces the *Pin*, by the way."

"I visited the *Pin* yesterday." Matthew had to down nearly half his cup, for he'd been shaken to the core by the news Steven had just delivered. It figured that Hudson had likely gone to Charles Town in search of him and located someone who could help—possibly Magnus Muldoon—and therefore had been put on the track to Rotbottom. Much of that remained a painful blur, but it stood to reason that Hudson had followed the trail to the departure of the *Wanderer*, because he was after all a very able problem-solver himself though in his case muscle won over mentality. Matthew thought how much he could use the Great One's help now; going to the Soames Inn and finding him was nearly a scream in his ears, and yet…

Berry was with him.

Damn it! he thought angrily. And here he'd been thinking he had no other skin to worry about in London but his own! Why the hell had she come? Why the devil hadn't she stayed in New York, where she…

Then he realized that she was here, searching for him with Hudson, in spite of those terrible things he'd said to her. She was here because she had put those soul-crushing things aside. Her feelings for him were stronger than the pain he'd dished out to her. There was much to be said for that, and again he was shaken by the thought of someone with that much devotion. She must believe in me very much, he thought. She must love me with a conviction that overcomes the lies of a moment, and by now Hudson has made her understand that they *were* lies.

Still…she shouldn't be here. He couldn't go to Hudson for help. Couldn't even let the man know where he was. No, this was now a deadly battle with three sides: Matthew Corbett, Professor Fell, and Albion.

"You can begin," Matthew said, "whenever you like. But please start at the beginning."

"You're aware of the beginning," Steven answered. Though younger than Matthew, the eyes behind the spectacles held the darkness of experience gained only through suffering. "It begins with Professor Fell." This was spoken in a guarded tone that would carry no further than to Matthew. "His crimes and his ambition. His desire to destroy everything my father has spent his life to preserve and protect. Fell might not consider this, but my father certainly has: if Fell is not stopped, he will destroy the very fabric of England itself. Right now it strains and rips. You see it, with the spread of the White Velvet. And you've seen it before, I'm sure, in your other encounters with him."

"I have. But please tell me this: *why* was I was sent to Newgate?"

"For your protection."

"My *protection*? Ha! Excuse me while I laugh again."

"Consider," Steven said calmly, "that as the general clerk for all the justices, I was the first to see Mr. Lillehorne's plea to Judge Greenwood to hear your case. In that plea was mentioned your connection with the Herrald Agency in New York, and your past experiences with Fell by way of explaining the unfortunate incident at sea. Never—*ever*—have we had access to anyone who has gotten as close to the professor as you have. I immediately took the document to my father and he deliberated over it. Very quickly he saw how you could be—excuse the term—*used*. He approached Judge Greenwood with the intent of meeting you and hearing what Lillehorne had to say, and as Judge Greenwood is a younger man and my father has a few years seniority there was no argument."

"A question," Matthew said. "Is it known at the Old Bailey that you're the judge's son?"

"It is not. I am hidden from view under a false family name and a false history. He thought it best that when he petitioned for my employment—as his eyes and ears, so to speak—our relationship should not be known. My father has always been a private man, and the justices by nature are not social animals. Also...we know that two of them are in the employ of the professor. There was a third, but someone murdered him back in September."

"Not your father?"

"No. My father concluded long ago that he should not visit violence upon a justice or an attorney, no matter how tainted the robes and the purse. To expose the corruption of those offices would have to be done by legal means. Judge Fallonsby's throat was cut and he was hanged from a flagpole. His entire family was—"

"Murdered as well," Matthew recalled hearing from Rory. "I know this story. Fallonsby was found with an inverted Cross cut into his forehead?"

"That's correct. He was for several years instrumental in dismissing criminal cases that Fell wished to be dismissed. My father has no firm proof of that, of course...the trail leads into a dense thicket of lawyers and a politician or two. But he and I both have been keeping records of the proceedings, and we've seen the connections between Fallonsby, Fell's legal machine and the goings-on on the streets."

"Do you know if Fell had Fallonsby killed, and why?"

"We believe," said Steven, "that Fell had nothing to do with that. Fallonsby was an important part of his apparatus. Whoever murdered Fallonsby is a new player on the scene, and obviously extremely vicious...also obviously somewhat anti-Christian."

"Ah." Matthew nodded. "The soddy cat and the throat-cutting rat."

"Pardon?"

"This new player seems to be wanting to attract Fell's attention as much as Albion is...or *was*. Now, about Newgate. *Why*?"

Steven couldn't hide a small, wicked smile. He took a drink of coffee to urge it away. "My father," he said, looking into Matthew's eyes, "was quite taken with you from the beginning. He told me how he paused at the door before he entered the courtroom...he was reticent, and my father is hardly *ever* reticent. He said he didn't know how he was going to handle you, and what he would find if he pushed you. He said...if you weren't tough enough to fight back against what he was going to throw at you, you would be no use to us. He was afraid, really...that this chance to lure Fell from his hiding-place might be an illusion. But...you passed with flying colors, obviously."

"My flag was almost lowered to half-mast in Newgate. Why the hell did he put me in there?"

"Again, to test your toughness. To see what you were made of, he told me. But he knew he had to act quickly, because there's a pattern to the attacks on new inmates there. If it's going to happen, it will be the first night and a two-hour period roughly between one and three o'clock."

"Oh, there's a formula to this?"

"Records of attacks clearly show the pattern. That is, of those who survive. We're not barbarians here, Matthew. We do keep such records and the guards are told to make their rounds in that period of time, especially if there's—as they call it there—more fuel for the furnace."

"Yes," Matthew said. "I nearly got my ass burned."

"Unfortunately," Steven continued, "the guards won't do very much without being bribed. My father knew that the only way to protect you in Newgate was to enter on the first night and basically scare the hell out of everyone there, at the same time giving a gesture that he hoped would convey a measure of protection."

"That worked smoothly enough, but how did he manage it?"

"Well," said the clerk, with a slight shrug, "since I'm a bit more slim than my father, it was my role that night. You were placed into Newgate for another reason: that reason being, a cell in the dungeon has a hole in the wall at ground level that leads to an underground passage. It's not a rare thing, there are passages everywhere under the city. A man dislodged the stones and escaped through that hole several years ago. Money has continually been afforded to Newgate to seal up the hole, and the money has continually been used in the purchase of bad wine, bad women and off-key songs for the officials who should be in charge of the prisons. My father knows this. He also knows the layout of Newgate very well and can draw a suitable map. While you were travelling by coach, I was walking across the Birdcage to Newgate with orders signed by Judge Archer to have you placed in Cairo, which is the nearest chamber to the dungeon."

"Nice," said Matthew. "You had a skeleton key, I'm presuming?"

"Years ago, my father attended a ceremony of appreciation in which he was given a key that fits all locks in Newgate Prison. He keeps it in a frame in his office. Very proud of that, really. There were two locks to defeat: the cell door itself, which is kept locked even though the cell is unused, and the gate that separates the dungeon from the rest of the prison. I left my lantern at the top of the steps. Had to feel my way along the wall. I heard all the commotion, put on the mask, and it seems I reached you at a critical moment."

"Not an inch too soon."

"I performed my little show, I backed up—nearly fell on my ass climbing the steps—and I got out the same way I came in. The departing of the phantom," said Steven, "leaving *you*, sir, with the respect you so honestly deserve."

"Hm. Then I'm supposing you and your father worked out the arrangements for me to be sent to Houndsditch? And of course you knew the route that was always taken."

"Yes, always. The coach drivers are creatures of habit. That is the shortest route, and therefore the least taxing to man and beast. But my father was waiting very near the gate, so it would be impossible to miss you. I arranged your release from Newgate with some—I will admit—artful forgery, since I do have access to all the signatures and wax seals."

Matthew pondered that for a few seconds. He looked out through the front window and watched wagons and pedestrians going by in the dim gray light. Wind whipped cloaks and caused people to grab hold of their hats. "Great effort was expended for this," he said, returning his gaze to Archer's son. "What's the ultimate purpose? Luring Professor Fell out of hiding, yes...but what then?"

Steven sipped his coffee and took his time formulating the reply.

"Albion was born," he said at length, "on Cable Street, in front of the hospital. When my mother was struck down by a member of the Black-Eyed Broodies who had been made insane by the White Velvet, my father...became a different man. Oh, he'd always been high-minded, perhaps rigidly so, but he realized—as he told to me—that the entire civilization of England was being threatened by this one man who considered himself an Emperor of crime beyond the reach of the law. Fell hides behind so many layers of underlings, attorneys, judges and politicians...and now even deeper, because of the influence of the Velvet. My father believes there's some drug in it that hastens the process of addiction."

"I believe the same," said Matthew.

"This singular drug," Steven progressed, "is responsible for a tremendous rise in the rate of crime, stemming not only from Fell's hand but from the despair of the streets. Fell has unleashed a demonic force upon England...a corrupting brew of need, greed and violence that reaches the highest levels of our entire country. When my mother lay dying in hideous pain in that hospital, my father came to the conclusion that Fell must be challenged...he must be brought into the open, and possibly by responding to this challenge he will make some mistake that will open him to the judgment of the law, which at the present time is too overburdened to attempt to seek him out."

"A plan, but still a vague one. Your father decided to begin this challenge by murdering criminals who'd escaped the courts?"

"All individuals who'd been freed by the machinations of Fell's attorneys acting upon compliant judges, two of whom are themselves addicted to the Velvet."

"I doubt," said Matthew, "that some of these men he's murdered even knew who they were working for."

"That may be, but the deaths were statements made to Fell... that, indeed, someone knew he was behind their crimes and their subsequent releases from gaol. It was...*is*...my father's belief that a dramatic figure was needed to present this challenge. He was always very athletic and an excellent swordsman...at one time in his youth he was a fencing instructor. He's also taught me very ably."

"So he caught on the idea of wearing a mask to appear an avenging phantom?"

"Yes. He also knew that if he created a character dramatic enough, the *Pin* would fix upon it. In fact, it was the *Pin* that supplied the name of 'Albion'."

"The mythical protector of England," said Matthew. "It suits the costume and also the purpose."

"It does. I bought the gold-colored fabric from a merchant in Oxford. My father's elder brother lives in Colchester and is a saddler, and from him we got the tooled piece of leather to create the beard. The leather was painted, a bit of stitching was done, holes for the eyes were cut out and a leather strap was attached to hold the mask in place...and there you have a golden-masked hope for the future of England."

Matthew said grimly, "Your father has been playing a dangerous game."

"Is there any other, when a creature like Professor Fell is involved?" Steven let that sentence hang for a few seconds. Then he said, "My father says there is a freedom of the mask, but it is also a wearying responsibility. And…you know…he has come to consider his true mask the one he wears every day…and in particular, the mask he was wearing when he first spoke to you in his courtroom at the Old Bailey."

Matthew thought that now was the time to produce the paper with the verse he'd copied at the *Pin*, and so he brought it out and spread it upon the tabletop. "Explain this to me."

Steven knew it by heart so he had no need of study, but he did express surprise. "Interesting that you have this! Well, I suppose your visit to the *Pin* was worth your while. You may have already known who it was that gave the name of 'Joshua Oakley'?"

"The description Mr. Luther supplied rang a bell, but I wasn't sure in which direction the tower stood. Now, about the verse?"

"A direct challenge to Professor Fell to come to the Tavern of the Three Sisters after midnight, to be delivered in the next issue of the *Pin* a few days hence."

"The date is not indicated?"

"My father and I have taken to haunting the Sisters as regulars, complete with tattered clothes and dirtied faces. That, we'd learned, was a center of the Velvet being poured upon Whitechapel, and a source of revenue for the Black-Eyed Broodies. We'd been to the Sisters often enough to recognize the other regulars from strangers, and we thought it would be quite apparent when someone came in who didn't belong. We planned to hold vigils there every night for one week after that challenge sees print."

"It's a nice verse," said Matthew, "but rather a lame challenge, isn't it?"

"No, it's rather a very powerful challenge."

"How is that?"

"It conveys to Professor Fell," Steven said, "the fact that Albion has learned his first and middle names. You see the initials 'D' and 'I' in the second line? The full name is Danton Idris Fell, and that information was gleaned from sources mined very carefully by—shall we say—friends of Judge Archer. And if he walked into the Sisters one night at the tolling of the bell, we would immediately know him."

"Why would that be?"

"Professor Fell is a mulatto," said Steven. "He is fastidious in his dress and his demeanor. In a tavern like the Sisters he would be instantly recognizable...by us, at least."

A mulatto, Matthew thought. That complemented what he'd already suspected, since Fell was the son of the governor of Pendulum Island, in the Bahamas, and that his own son was tormented and beaten to death on a London street partly due to the color of his skin.

"My father has been counting on Fell's curiosity driving him to the Sisters." Steven finished off his coffee with a final sip. "Fell has to be wondering who Albion could possibly be, and he would be somewhat nettled at the idea that his underlings are being executed by this person. He would likely wonder how much is known about him, and surely he would rather this irritating golden-masked individual be put to death...after a period of severe interrogation, of course. So...when he enters the Sisters Fell will find at least two ragged wretches drinking their ales and muttering their complaints, and they will quickly leave while the professor waits for a meeting that will not happen. But when he exits...Albion will strike him down on the steps in the narrow confines of Flint Alley, where the movement of defense by his bodyguards will be severely constricted."

Matthew said, "Of course this plan is sweetened by the fact that Danton Idris Fell or someone of his circle reads in the *Pin* that Matthew Corbett has allied himself with Albion, and by a midnight meeting at the Sisters Fell might brush aside the latter and get hold of the former, whom he *really* wants?"

"As I say...you are the bait in this."

"*Was* the bait," came the quick reply. "If you recall, your father is currently lying gutshot in the hospital, which actually is to the good for both of you. Does your father wish for you and he to follow your mother so recklessly? That plan was suicide! It hinged on too many 'ifs'."

"It was our best chance of getting at him."

"It was *no* chance!" said Matthew. "All right, maybe he might have showed up at the Sisters. But getting through the men he'd have around him...close enough to drive a sword into him, and his men likely to have pistols? No. It was a desperate plan that would end with both of you dead...if you were lucky." Matthew shook his head, amazed at the foolish audacity of what he'd just heard. "Your father...he's a pillar of the law, yet he's let himself become a murderer! And your plan wasn't to deliver Fell to the law, but to kill him on the Flint Alley steps! Don't you see the irony in this? Your father has let Fell corrupt him as much as the Velvet corrupts the drinker!"

Steven said, "I understand what you're saying. I understand it clearly. But as I say...Albion was born that day on Cable Street. My father—and I—loved her very much. She was not perfect, but she was very near an angel. To think of the misery that Fell has caused, and will continue to cause...to think of all the suffering, and the deaths, the despair, the betrayals, the darkness that is already descending on this country. It's not just for the love of my mother that we've done these things...it's that we love our country, and we don't wish to see it destroyed from within. If someone—someone—does not act, it *shall* be destroyed." He looked across the table with tortured eyes. "The things we do for love," he said, "are sometimes themselves crimes...but if no one dares to do *anything*...then all is lost. Don't you see?"

"I see your point and I wish it were an answer, but no two men, however well-intentioned, can save people from themselves...or save a country," Matthew said. "Fell and others like him always aim for the easiest target, which would be the baser instincts of human beings. Against that there is no defense."

"I'd say an able defense would be a swordblade across the throat."

"There will always be another to take his place. That's why your father is better serving England as a real-life Judge Archer than as a mythological Albion."

Steven stared into his empty cup. He looked out upon the street scene, and Matthew could tell by the slump of his shoulders that his battle had come to an end.

"Your father should go to the constables' office with what he knows," Matthew offered. "He should give any information he has to the proper authorities."

"*Proper authorities*," Steven repeated, with obvious gall. "Don't you understand that we don't know who to trust? Not even the new man, Lillehorne. And upwards from the constables' office, the bribery is rampant. Any information about Fell would likely be burned in a fireplace grate and the man who brought it to the *proper authorities* murdered or made to appear killed in an accident. It wouldn't be the first." Steven balled up his fist and Matthew thought he was going to strike the table with it, but then all the fight seemed to go out of Steven and the fist came down to quietly bump the tabletop.

"Luring Fell to Flint Alley and killing him on those steps…that was the only way we could see that might work," he said. "Now…I can't do it alone."

"And don't *try*," Matthew said. "Your father needs a son, not another gravestone."

"I pray he doesn't soon become one."

"They greatly respect him and your mother there. They're going to do everything possible."

"I know." Still looking out the filmy window upon the gray day, the young man drew a long breath and let it out as a sigh of resignation. "I'm going back to the hospital and stay with him. What will *you* do?"

"Walk," said Matthew. "Where to, I'm not certain."

"I'd say we were sorry we got you into this, but you were already well into it long before you came to England."

"That's what made me valuable to you as bait, isn't it?"

"Of course. When you return to the colonies, I'd keep a watchful eye out. If two men can't save a country, neither can two men save a collection of small countries bound together by commerce and circumstance. I'd suspect the White Velvet will likely be showing up in New York soon."

"You may be right."

"I *am* right." Steven gave Matthew a thin, cold smile. "When you sit at a table amid the wreckage of what *was* and ponder what *will be*, raise a cup of the Velvet and remember this conversation, for we had here a chance to change the future."

"Speaking of which," Matthew said, "you told your father that his plan might yet succeed. Why did you say that, knowing it's come to its conclusion?"

"He needs something to cling to. Without that, he might give up and pass away. I love my father as I loved my mother, sir. I'm sure you would do the same, in my place."

Matthew didn't respond, but he knew that was the truth.

"Good day to you," said Steven. He put down coins for their coffees and stood up.

Matthew watched him leave the shop, pull his dove-gray cloak tighter around himself to brave the biting wind, and walk past the front window in the direction of Cable Street.

Then Matthew sat alone for a time, just thinking. Finally he returned to a pocket the paper with the challenge to Professor Fell upon it. He stood up, put on his cloak with the mask of Albion within, donned his tricorn, and walked out to find the future.

Twenty-Seven

Matthew found himself nearing the Black-Eyed Broodies' warehouse.

The wind was truly vicious, the sky layered with clouds that looked as thick as armor plate. He'd walked in circles for awhile after leaving the Rising Sun, on this day when the sun had hidden itself. He was in need of sleep. He thought if he could grab an hour or two of it, he would have a clearer vision of where to go and what to do. Two hours of sleep, and then he might be on his way to the central city to find Gardner Lillehorne. He sorely wished Hudson had come to London without Berry; what was to be done about that?

The street was quiet but for the constant rumble of wagons of various size. Matthew started up the steps to the door that appeared to be boarded-over and nailed shut, the windows the same.

Then he saw the bloodstains beneath his boots, and quite suddenly the cold pierced him like an iced blade.

He pushed through the artfully-disguised door…

…and entered a slaughterhouse.

The first body he saw was Paulie's. The boy was lying crumpled in a heap, the face covered with blood. His heart pounding, Matthew knelt beside the body to search for signs of life. There were none. The throat had been cut, the face misshapen by blows. Both eyes had been gouged out. On his forehead there was another wound that had crusted over, indicating it had been some hours since this murder had taken place. The forehead wound was an inverted Cross.

Matthew stood up. He staggered back a step, for on one wall was another splatter of blood and lying at the bottom of it was a figure he had to get closer to identify. He thought it was Will Satterwaite, but he couldn't be sure. Again, the throat had been slashed and the forehead marked. And, again, the eyes were missing.

The place smelled of gore and the heat of violence beyond description. Matthew came to a third body; this one, a young man, he couldn't identify and it did not bear the forehead mark. The man had been slashed across the stomach with a blade, and from the gruesome trail he'd left it appeared he'd crawled some distance before expiring. His throat was also cut open.

Matthew intended to shout *hello?* into the silent darkness but his voice would not come. He leaned against a wall and stared at a bloody handprint and smear of gore. His gorge rose and he choked it down.

"Hello?" he called. There was no answer. Above him the pigeons cooed in the rafters. "Hello?" he tried again, louder. Then he knew he had to go deeper into the place; as much as he feared it, he had to go.

In the dim shafts of light that pierced the warehouse, Matthew stumbled on. A half-dozen steps further, and he nearly fell over the body of a woman. He turned her over with trembling hands. It was Jane Howard, her eyeless bloodmask of a face frozen in a rictus of terror, a blade wound near her heart, her throat slashed and the Devil's Cross carved into her forehead.

"Rory!" he shouted into the gloom. No answer. "Pie!" he shouted.

Silence, still.

He went on, and began to count the corpses. Whoever had done this had made sure no one would survive. The bodies had been stabbed multiple times and there was evidence of cudgels at work, battering the faces into unrecognizable lumps of putty. All their throats had been cut, and to sign the job a sharp blade had carved the mark.

"Rory!" Matthew shouted once more.

He stepped over what he thought had been John Bellsen, and then Lucy Samms and Tom Lancey, lying so close together their blood had become a small lake. The first flies had arrived in spite of the cold, and soon this warehouse would be swarming with them as they came through the cracks on the coppery scent of murder.

Matthew was very suddenly overwhelmed. He thought he had steeled himself, but after counting twenty bodies his knees sagged and he grabbed at a bloody wall for support. It was denied him and down he went. He threw up his guts, retched and retched and threw up again, and then there was nothing more to expel. His mind reeled; it seemed that every Black-Eyed Broodie had been killed in a savage attack, the throats cut to ensure death and that damned mark cut into their foreheads as an exclamation mark of Satanic triumph.

Matthew forced himself up and onward. "Pie!" he croaked. With the next step his boots stirred a bloodpond, and flies arose to whip him in the face. A slender body lay at his feet. He saw a mass of short-cut curly hair. The face was averted, the body lying as if nearly broken in half. He bent down to turn her over.

"Don't do that," someone said.

Matthew froze, his heart a crash in his chest, his entire body trembling and tears of surprising rage upon his cheeks.

"Don't," Rory repeated. His voice was hollow and otherworldly. "Come closer to me. Watch where you step."

Matthew obeyed, as if locked in a nightmare beyond human endurance. He saw a meager glow in a far corner. Rory was sitting on the floor, and when he shifted himself the small light of a single candle was exposed; the candle looked to be stuck with wax to a floorboard at his side.

"Closer," said the eerie, strengthless voice.

Matthew nearly tripped over yet another body. That would make number twenty-two. He bent over, feeling again as if he might throw up.

A bottle came rolling across the boards. It stopped a few feet short of the dead man at Matthew's feet.

"Drink," Rory said; it was a command.

Matthew picked up the bottle. It was not the small blue bottle of the Velvet, as he'd thought it might be; it was a large brown bottle of rum, corked, with maybe three swallows left in it. He pulled the cork out with his teeth, drank almost all the rest of it, and pushed the cork back in. The horror of the moment would not be dulled by any rum, no matter how potent. He stood where he was, wavering on his feet.

"A massacre," said Rory. "Ain't that the right word for this?"

"Yes," Matthew said.

"They're all dead."

"*Jesus*," Matthew answered.

"Hm. Yeah. Any a' that left?"

Matthew took him the bottle. Rory reached up, grasped the bottle, uncorked it and finished it off. When he was done he set the bottle quietly down beside him, as if in respect to the sleepers.

"*All* of them?" Matthew asked. He thought he'd heard movement and soft cries, but he realized it was only the pigeons.

"Three extra dead men," said Rory, whose own face in the candlelight was pale and ghostly. "They were vicious bastards. Finished off their own wounded, I reckon if they figured they was gonna die anyway."

"The Mohocks did this?"

"No," Rory said listlessly; the absolute evil of this wholesale slaughter had drained him of emotion just as he'd drained the rum. He sat upon the floor like a shattered shell. "Not the Mohocks. The men they left behind...they ain't war-painted. And the way they done it...no, not the Mohocks."

"Who, then?"

"I've been sittin' right here...I don't know how long...tryin' to figure that out. *Who?* But I know the *why*, Matthew. That's clear enough."

"Tell me."

"The cellar's been cleaned out. They took ever'thing. Likely brought two wagons...one full a' killers, the other empty to haul the Velvet in. Took it all...except for one thing."

"What?"

"I'd take you down there and show you, but...I can't move from here, Matthew. Been sittin' here...for hours, maybe? Right here, and I don't really care to move. You could go see for y'self, but I won't put that on you." Rory looked up at Matthew. Sweat sparkled on his face and his eyes were hollow holes. "They left one blue bottle, right in the middle of the room. One blue bottle. Know what they filled it full of?"

Matthew dared not guess. He thought of the bodies he'd seen, and in particular the eyeless faces of Paulie and Jane.

"Yeah," said Rory. "Left it there, I reckon for a constable to find…or whoever would come in here lookin'. Would that be what an educated fella like y'self might called a 'statement'?"

"A declaration of war is what I would call it," Matthew managed to answer. "War against Professor Fell."

Rory nodded. "That cheese-eatin' rat…he's swelled up to be the size of a monster now, and…I'll tell you…I'll tell you…" His voice cracked. He shivered, his silver teeth clenched together, and he had to fight back from the precipice. "I ain't never seen such a sight. These men…they took delight in this, Matthew. They took delight in killing ever' one of my fam'ly…not just once, but two or three times over. Took delight in it." He nodded again, a little too vigorously, and he reached for the empty bottle and uncorked it and drank rum that was no longer there. For a moment Matthew thought that a cry might burst from Rory's strained face that would level the warehouse's blood-smeared walls.

But instead Rory peered up into Matthew's face, the bottle softly settled back down to the boards, and the terribly-crushed voice rasped, "They're all gone…all of 'em…and I'm a man without a country."

Matthew heard Rory make a sound of muffled pain, as if his back had broken and he was by the sheerest force of will holding the scream at bay. He began to crawl across the floor, away from Matthew, and when Matthew reached down to grasp his shoulder he said, "Don't touch me," in what was nearly the snarl of a wounded animal. Matthew let him be.

Rory crawled away a distance where the light from the single taper made him only a mass without detail, and there he lay on his left side with his knees pulled up to his chest. The next noise he made was a soft whine that went on and on; it was an unbearable sound of torment to Matthew, and so he walked away as far as he could without again entering the death area.

How long was it before Rory was silent? Two minutes? Three? Matthew waited, the smell of blood up his nose and the memory of those dead, brutally mutilated faces at the dark edges of his mind.

"Figure whoever it was," Rory's husky voice reached out, "must've stormed the place…so fast there wasn't no time to put up much of a fight. Must've been a lot of 'em. A wagonful, I'm thinkin'. Likely had a ramp with 'em, put that down on the cellar stairs and rolled the barrels up after the killin' was done. Rolled the barrels up a ramp into another wagon, carried the bottles out, and they was gone. Left three a' their wounded behind with cut throats so there wouldn't never be no talkin'. You with me?"

"Yes," Matthew said listlessly.

"Seen that mark on their heads?"

"Yes."

"Devil's Cross. Like what was given that judge. Fallonsby, his name was. You recall I told you?"

"I do."

"Likely came in…two or three o'clock, I reckon. Caught most of the Broodies in their beds. Happened while I was with you at the hospital. Can you beat that, Matthew?"

"Beat what?"

"You and me. We're the last of the Black-Eyed Broodies. Won't never be no more. Just you and me, and we're the last." Rory lapsed into silence again.

Matthew waited; it was all he could do.

"No, they wasn't Mohocks," Rory suddenly said, as if this question had just been asked. "This was done by those who enjoy it too much, Matthew. This was done by dark things looked like men, but they wasn't. Must've been fast…must've come in like the wind… just carved ever'body up. We're the last, Matthew. Last ones alive."

"Surely someone *heard* this," Matthew said. "The noise of fighting…the screams. Surely."

"Not much screamin' can be done with a cut throat. Yeah… maybe they heard somethin' of it at the Drunk Crow or one of them other taverns…but nobody wants trouble so they just kept on drinkin'. Just put their heads down, and when they was drunk enough they all staggered on home and the taverns closed up and nobody knew ever'body here was dead 'fore I walked in this mornin'.

Maybe somebody saw that blood on the steps, or they looked in here and saw Paulie lyin' dead. Then they turned tail and beat it for home, 'cause they don't want to get 'emselves killed. I would'a done the same. Maybe you would've too."

"Maybe," said Matthew.

Rory did not speak again for a long time. Gusts of wind whipped across the roof and made shrill banshee sounds, the rising and falling of ghostly voices. Pigeons fluttered and fought up in the broken rafters and made the rusted chains and pulleys creak. This was now truly a haunted house, Matthew thought. He would not wish to be here when the next fog rose and drifted through the cracks; in fact he wished to never again set foot across that bloody threshold.

Rory asked in a voice that was weakening once more, "Who's gonna bury 'em, Matthew? Don't you think they oughta get proper graves?"

"Yes, I do."

"Whoever did it...they knew the Velvet was here. Oh yeah... they come ready to take it. Left one bottle in the cellar. One single bottle. Know what's in it, Matthew?"

"Listen to me," Matthew said forcefully. "We've got to get out of here. There's no use in staying a minute longer."

"Caught most of 'em in their beds. But they got three. If I'd been here...if I'd been here maybe—"

"Stop that. If you'd been here, I'd be the only Black-Eyed Broodie left. Have you got any money?"

"Money? I got a little bit."

"Enough for a coach to the central city?"

"No, not that much. Our treasury box...had nine pounds and some shillin's in it, but that was took. They knew where to find that, too. How'd they know, Matthew? Who told 'em?"

Matthew couldn't answer. He'd thought of searching through the pockets of the corpses. It was a passing thought because it made him shudder and there was no way he could do that. Anyway, he doubted that any of the dead would have more than a few pence. "We'll walk, then."

"I don't have nowhere to go."

Matthew had made a hard-edged decision; he needed Hudson's help in the worst way, and it was unfortunate that Berry was with him but the time had come when that would have to be somehow managed. For his part, he would wish to send her in a coach to the next ship leaving Plymouth for New York.

"We're going to the Soames Inn off Fleet Street," Matthew said.

"What for?"

"For help. Just trust me."

"Ain't nobody can fix this." Rory made no move to stand up. Matthew thought he'd been in a state of shock for the several hours he was sitting in here with the bottle of rum at hand. Likely he'd already gotten drunk and slept, awakened to this nightmare, slept again and awakened again. "Somebody's gotta bury 'em," Rory said. "You help me do that, Matthew?"

Matthew knew the man was talking out of his head, and in that moment he pitied him and wished to put a hand of support upon his shoulder; he knew also that Rory's rough character would never accept such a touch. "We have to go now," Matthew told him.

"Bury 'em first. They was my brothers 'n sisters. Yours too. Mousie buried Ben for us in the potter's field...we oughta do the same."

Matthew stared down at the floor. It killed his heart that these souls had been born into violence and tragedy and been destroyed by it. The image of Pie Puddin, bright-eyed and saucy, trimming his beard and shaving him was a sharp blade of pain. The others... what chance had they ever had, really? And knowing that, the tentacles of Professor Fell had emerged to manipulate them just as the lawyer Mousekeller and the deliveries of White Velvet to the addicted masses were manipulated.

The sorrow he felt was very suddenly replaced by anger. Rory Keen was alive, and Matthew intended him to stay that way.

"Stand up," Matthew directed.

"Go on with y'self. You ain't earned the right to give me orders."

"Yes I have," Matthew said. A whirlwind of past encounters went through his mind: Jack One Eye, the killer hawks, Mister Slaughter, Sirki the murderous giant, and the treacherous dangers of the Carolina swamp. "Oh *yes*," he repeated. "Stand up or I'll drag you up. We're leaving here together."

Rory's voice was slurred when he taunted, "Come on and drag me—"

Matthew was on him before he'd finished. He leaned over, took hold of Rory's shirt with both hands and got him halfway up before Rory bellowed with pent-up rage and drove his fist into Matthew's stomach. It was a hard punch, delivered well, but Matthew realized his test of combat had been presented; he let go his grip with his right hand, balled it into a fist and struck Rory on the point of the chin. When Rory's head snapped back, he followed the blow with a left to the jaw. His next right-handed strike missed, as Rory ducked beneath it and came up wildly swinging...and at the same time, screaming.

A fist grazed his left cheek. The next blow connected only with air because Matthew had dodged aside, and the strike after that likewise came up empty. Rory was flailing like a madman, as if he were fighting the very atmosphere of Whitechapel itself. Matthew backpedalled and let Rory come after him, and then abruptly Matthew changed direction, saw his opening and threw his weight into a punch to Rory's chest that stole his breath and stunned him. The next blow he wished he didn't have to deliver, but the leader of the Broodies was crazed and only a strong fist would stop him.

Matthew dodged another pair of wild swings. He steadied himself and struck Rory once more directly on the point of the chin, again not holding anything back. Rory made a gasping sound and fell backward. Matthew charged in with two more punches...one, two in quick succession to the right and left sides of the jaw.

Rory collapsed.

Before the back of Rory's skull could hit the planks, Matthew caught him and got his hand between fire-colored hair and rain-blackened wood. Rory's body twisted and struggled involuntarily, but for all intents and purposes he was out.

Matthew eased him down, and then he walked away as Rory curled up on the floor and began to sob. The crying became a wail of torment, and in it was all the agony of a life twisted by hideous circumstances that a young boy could not prevent. Matthew realized that Rory and so many others like him had never had much of a chance to fly, but all of their lives had been the falling.

Matthew waited silently. He rubbed the knuckles of his fists. Rory Keen possessed as much of a hard jaw as a hard head.

In time the tortured noise subsided.

There was just the sounds then of Rory's harsh breathing, and the pigeons playing above.

Rory blew his nose and snuffled, and then he said, "I'm sorry," which might have been the only time in his life he'd uttered that statement.

"You have the right idea but the wrong opponent. I suggest we leave *now*. Mother Deare will be sending more men out to find Frost and Willow, if they haven't been found already. It's a matter of time before someone comes here."

"Yeah. Yeah, we ought to get out." With an effort, Rory stood up. He staggered on his feet but then righted himself. He wiped his face with his shirt and looked through the gloom at Matthew. "The Soames Inn?"

"Yes."

"Take us awhile to get to Fleet Street. Any reason for that particular place?"

"A friend of mine is staying there. I think he can help our situation."

"Okay." Rory still seemed unsure of which leg to move to get him started. "Albion," he said. "Did he die?"

"No."

"That's good. Been an awful lot of dyin' today." He put a hand to his forehead. Matthew could see that it trembled. "Matthew," Rory said, "will you help me get through?"

Matthew knew what he was meaning. Help him get through the bodies of his family, the blood and carnage that lay between him and the way out.

"I will," Matthew promised.

Twenty-Eight

The bewigged and rather priggish clerk at the Soames Inn reported that the errand boy he'd sent upstairs had received no answer to knocks on the doors of either Mr. Hudson Greathouse or Miss Beryl Grigsby. He could not say where they had gone or when they would return.

"May we wait for them?" Matthew asked, in his most gentlemanly tone.

The clerk looked Matthew and Rory over and obviously did not like what he saw. These two ragamuffins would surely befoul the overstuffed blue cushions of the chairs in the parlor, and this one in the horrendous purple suit spoke like a gentleman but his eyes bore the dark gaze of a born ruffian.

Matthew read the man's thoughts. "I can assure you that Mr. Greathouse will reward you with an extra pound if you allow us to wait, and I can also assure you he'll tear your little paradise to pieces if you don't."

Thus it was that the clerk's initial startlement at the Great One's size and brusque manner convinced him to comply, and Matthew and Rory found themselves seated on the blue cushions in an oak-panelled room where a civilized fire burned in the brown stone hearth and an ornate grandfather clock ticked away the minutes. They were glad to be off their feet, for the walk from Whitechapel in the bitter wind that shifted directions like the thrusts of a demonic swordsman had taken them several hours and worn them to the nubs.

Matthew noted a recent copy of the London *Gazette* atop an ivory-inlaid table. When he picked it up, underneath the newspaper like a little toad beneath an eagle's wing was the latest issue of the *Pin*, with that abominable bold headline *Monster Of Plymouth Compatriot Of Albion.*

He started to fling it into the fire, but the line *Coalblack Amazes Audiences* snagged his eye and stayed his hand.

He read the article again. *African strongman...cannot speak due to loss of tongue...strangely-scarred face...found last June clinging to a bit of wreckage from a ship at sea...*

Was it Zed, or some other? If it was indeed Zed, had Captain Falco's ship been destroyed by vengeful cannonfire from one of Fell's roving pirates, and Zed cast upon the waves?

"Thinkin'," Rory suddenly said, as he stared into the crackling fire.

This required a response. Matthew pulled his attention away from Coalblack. "Yes?"

"You say whoever killed my people and took the Velvet was declarin' war on Professor Fell?"

If there had been anyone else in the parlor overhearing this, they likely would now have gotten up and retired to their Bible closet, but Matthew and Rory were the only ones and Rory's query had been cast low.

"The same individual who murdered Judge Fallonsby," said Matthew. "He—or God forbid, *she*—has decided the time has come to make a move. I suspect that Fallonsby was one of the justices in Fell's employ, so that was a blatant strike against the professor. And I wouldn't doubt that this person has a chemist available to examine the Velvet's ingredients in hopes of copying the recipe."

"Tangled bag a' snakes, huh?"

"All knotted up," Matthew said.

"All right, so this new sonofabitch wants war with Fell. But—sayin' it's a he—how'd he know we had Velvet in that cellar? I mean, sure we ain't the only ones been holdin' cellars full of Velvet, but how'd he know?"

"Someone's talk slipped out here or there. Some slip of the tongue made in a tavern, and a careful ear listening. Could be someone associated with the Sisters. Then one or more of the Broodies was identified and followed, the warehouse staked out over a period of days—or weeks—and notes taken as to the unloading of barrels and crates from a wagon in front of that warehouse late at night."

"The last shipment we got was over a month ago," said Rory. "Came in 'bout four in the mornin'."

"It was likely being watched. I suspect this new individual wasn't ready, for whatever reason, to undertake a raid at that point. Maybe he didn't have enough men. Who knows?"

"*Damn*," Rory said, frowning into the fire. "I just...I just can't think about it, Matthew. It hurts my head and my heart at the same time. God bless 'em all, but I failed 'em."

"Don't go down that road. I don't think what happened could have been avoided. Of course you very well could have perished with them, and therefore have no current pain of head and heart, but you're not the cause of it. It's Fell...Mother Deare...the White Velvet...and now this new...*creature*," Matthew said. The hideous images of the Devil's Cross and the gouged-out eyes came to him, and he had to brush them away by reading once more about the famous Coalblack.

The grandfather clock ticked away but could work no magic on the movement of time. It crawled. From where he was sitting Matthew had a direct view to the clerk's desk and the red-carpeted staircase leading up to the rooms. He watched several people come and go, but none of them were Hudson or Berry. An hour passed, and then another.

"You sure they're gonna come back here?" Rory asked.

"They're on the register, so why wouldn't they?" Matthew figured they were out looking for him. He hoped they stayed far away from Whitechapel.

"How much longer you gonna give 'em? Light's fadin' out there."

From what Matthew could see through a slice of window, late afternoon's light was the same gloomy gray as midday's. The grandfather clock chose that moment to chime five times.

"Another hour," Matthew said.

"And if they don't come, then what?"

Then what, indeed, Matthew thought. Surely they wouldn't be allowed to remain in here all night, no matter the promise of reward or threat of breakage. "We'll figure something out," Matthew answered, but he was presenting a lame horse.

In precisely thirty minutes the bewigged clerk came into the parlor. He squared his thin shoulders and took on an expression of severity. He said, "Sirs, I shall inform you that at six o'clock the management of the Soames Inn closes the parlor to all persons who are not guests or not accompanied by guests. I regret your friends have not returned, but at six o'clock you shall have to leave."

"What if we don't choose t' leave?" Rory thrust his chin out in haughty defiance.

"In that case, sir, we have the benefit of common ownership of the gymnasium across the street, which includes a very popular prize-fighting club. At all hours of the day what they call the 'ring' is in constant use, and a group of men who appreciate the sport are always seeking new targets of practice."

"Oh," said Rory.

"It's our management's policy," the clerk said, thawing a little. "For the safety and security of the guests, really."

"I see," said Matthew. "All right then, we'll leave at six."

"My appreciation," the clerk replied, with a stiff-backed bow. He was starting to retreat when Matthew, already trying to figure out where he and Rory might go, had a sudden idea.

"Pardon," Matthew said before the clerk could withdraw. He checked the article about Coalblack in the *Pin* once more. "How far a walk would it be to Dove's Wing Alley at Bishopsgate?"

"That distance would be in the approximation of three miles. May I ask if you're interested in the Almsworth Circus?"

"Yes, exactly so."

"I've attended it myself. Very entertaining, but quite a walk from here. May I send an errand boy to hire a coach for the gentlemen?" This was said with only a hint of sarcasm.

"No, thank you, but I'd appreciate walking directions."

"I shall write them down for you." The clerk bowed again and went on his way.

Matthew stood up. "Rory, exactly how much money do you have?"

He checked his pockets and came up with three shillings and six pence.

"That ought to be enough to get us into the Almsworth Circus."

"What?" Rory got out of his chair and winced at the pain in his feet from their earlier walk here, which had been nearly double that distance. "You want to go to the flippin' *circus*?"

"I do. The show begins at eight. If we leave now, we can make the opening."

"*You* say. My dogs are barkin'!"

"Well, we won't walk as fast as we did coming here."

"Why the bloody hell are you wantin' to go to the circus, pray tell?"

"I might know someone who's involved there," said Matthew. "I have to see him to make sure."

"Do you know the flippin' man in the moon, as well? Jesus, I ain't never met a gent with so many acquaintances in high and low places!"

"I *must* see this one," Matthew replied, and added, "If nothing more than to ease my curiosity." *Ease his fears* was more correct, for he dreaded the thought that the brave Captain Falco had been destroyed in retribution for the destruction of Pendulum Island.

"Hell's bells," said Rory. His voice was strong, but his eyes were still dark-hollowed and every so often his body gave an involuntary tremble or outright jerk. Matthew had caught him staring into space with a half-open mouth and a frozen countenance as if he'd just stepped into the warehouse again and found the first of the dead upon the floor. "Ain't quite the day for a circus show," Rory went on.

"It's just the day for it. I have to see this man and we have to go *somewhere*."

"Uh huh. And with these marks on our hands, if any of the dozen or so gangs between here and there find us poachin' at night, we're dead men. If we get there in one piece, we still got to get back!"

"If this man is who I think it might be, then I believe my story to the owners of the circus might improve his value, and from them it's possible to earn a coach ride back here." Matthew was sure the owners would appreciate learning that Zed was a member of the fighting Ga tribe and something of his history...but then what? Leave Zed in the circus, when he knew the man so ardently wished to get home to his tribal land? Just turn a back on him, and leave him here in this seething cesspool? But that bridge had to be crossed later, and first things first: was this African strongman Zed, or not?

"Lord have mercy," said Rory, and then he was silent.

Matthew got the written directions from the clerk. He left instructions with the man to inform Hudson Greathouse that he had gone to the Almsworth Circus and it would be good to be met there with a coach if Hudson could manage it; if not, he would return to the inn later that night. They left the Soames Inn, setting off to the east. They were heading back toward Whitechapel, as the Bishopsgate area lay just to the northwest of it. Chill winds gusted through the streets, plucking at hats and cloaks and tugging the hems of ladies' gowns. Matthew kept one hand on his tricorn and the other grasping the collar of his cloak as the garment billowed around him. Streetside torches flared in the wintry currents, and lanterns appeared in the hands of passersby. The central section of the city was jammed with traffic, pedestrians rushing about and carriages, coaches and wagons clogging the ways. Rory kept pace with Matthew but Matthew was aware of his friend's discomfort and so eased his stride. The larger buildings loomed on all sides, lanternlight yellowing many of the windows. In the hurry and crush of the well-to-do, beggars of all ages and descriptions hobbled back and forth, some of them children, some of them young and bedraggled women holding infants. Some people walked upon the streetsides as if the devil snapped at their bottoms and whole groups of others meandered as if measuring the length of cow pastures on a hazy midsummer morn, and therefore the collisions were numerous and constant. Matthew hoped New York never became as this, for he was sure the pastoral beauty of the town would be destroyed.

Matthew and Rory crossed a multitude of streets and braved a multitude of wild drivers. They witnessed a man and woman run down by an ornate carriage less than twenty feet from them as they went across Lombard Street; the carriage might have continued on had not a wheel broken off and gone rolling past the two circus-bound travellers. Matthew was glad to see the two lucky victims of this near-murder helped to their feet, and all was good except for the fact that they'd unluckily tumbled into a sewage ditch.

At last the directions Matthew had several times stopped to consult indicated that Dove's Wing Alley was within three blocks, just past the Spittle Yard. For some time Rory had been keeping his head on a swivel, but though they walked along some streetsides that looked like gangs had already done their ravaging and left ruins in their wake the only distress they experienced came from the nasty curses thrown at them from a number of young women and young men who approached them with lascivious offers, all ignored.

Finally, after seeing plastered on several walls broadsheets advertising the Almsworth Circus—*Jugglers! Dancers! Acrobats! The Mighty Coalblack! You Shall Be Amazed!*—they heard a commotion of drumming, gonging and shouting ahead. At the sign of Dove's Wing Alley under a guttering, windblown torch, a rotund fellow with green greasepaint on his face had a contraption of drumheads, cymbals and gongs strapped to his body, and he was hammering his sticks at these as if beating his mother-in-law. "Come one, come all!" he shouted every few seconds into the night, and he bowed his head slightly at Matthew and Rory as they passed and gave an extra oomph to a drumhit.

As at Flint Alley, a set of stairs led down into a crevasse, but this one was festooned with ropes upon which were hooked multicolored lanterns. At the bottom of the steps, there was a small courtyard where a clown with white-painted face and wearing a belled jester's cap stood before a doorway covered by a red curtain. He was making such foolish, tongue-wagging and goggle-eyed expressions as a clown might make at the dozen or so patrons who'd gathered, at the same time taking coins into a pewter bowl and giving out tickets. Beside him a petite dark-haired girl in an extremely revealing black outfit with white stripes was walking on her hands, while her twin, identical except for wearing a white outfit with black stripes, was performing perfect flips over and over again, both girls receiving the applause of the gathering.

The clown announced to Rory an entrance fee of one shilling apiece, a sum that made Rory visibly bristle, but the coins came out and went into the bowl. Tickets in hand, Matthew and Rory went through the red curtain into a small lamplit theater with four rows of bench seats that already held another half-dozen patrons.

Matthew wished to sit on the front row. As more of the night's customers came in, he removed his tricorn, took off his cloak and folded it, and then took his place beside Rory.

"A *shillin'* for this?" Rory fumed. "It ain't nothin' but rank robbery!"

"We're out of the wind and we're sitting," Matthew reminded him. "Be glad of that."

"A fool *circus*! What good are these things?"

Within thirty minutes, after the crimson-costumed master of ceremonies had emerged to welcome the audience and tell a few ribald jokes, the drummerman had taken the stage and played not only the drums at a thunderous rhythm but also the mouth harp at the same time in a stirring show of talent, a fire-eater had swallowed a torch or two and puffed out twenty rings of smoke, a man wearing a huge blue bowtie had engaged three small dogs in jumping through a number of hoops—and one of them aflame—Matthew heard Rory give an excited intake of breath as the two petite twin acrobats jumped back and forth with effortless ease from swings suspended above the audience.

When this display of the defiance of gravity was ended, Rory perhaps clapped the loudest in the audience, and when he looked at his companion with a silver-toothed grin and said, "Have you ever *seen* such a sight?" then they both knew of what good circuses were.

The clown came out upon the stage and performed a number of pratfalls, a show of juggling with flowerpots and bricks, and some other tricks that involved colored handkerchiefs and a few sprays of water at the audience from a false rose in his lapel. Matthew was gratified to hear Rory laugh. The horror of the morning would never be forgotten but for the moment it was held at bay, which in itself was a miracle of mercy.

A woman with long red tresses and wearing a violet gown came out to sing, accompanied by a stout little man playing a fiddle. The song began as a soft, slow recitation of a maiden's love for a young farmer. Very suddenly the bottom dropped out of it. The fiddler began to saw like mad and the songstress belted out rhymes using words like "cock-a-doodle" and "ruptured duck", which likely accounted for the fact that in looking around Matthew had seen no children in the audience, but the grownups hollered along at the chorus like delighted ten-year-olds.

Then after that whoopsedaisie the master of ceremonies came back to the stage and in the yellow lanternlight looked out upon his listeners with a solemn face. He said in his leathery voice, "Ladies and gentlemen, please be aware that our next act hails from a savage land. A land of lions, tigers, fierce bears and venom-dripping reptiles! A land where one might step into a pit of quicksand and be pulled down to his doom from the face of the earth..."

Oh, Matthew thought, *I've already been there*, but he remained silent. His heart was hammering and he felt sweat at his temples.

"...a land of pitiless horrors, where death lurks under every tree of thorns!" The master paused, sweeping his eyes back and forth across the theater. "Yes!" he boomed. "Such a land shapes a man! He either perishes there or he becomes a mighty force to break the bonds of destiny! But...*is* he a man? Or is he a beast? I shall let you decide the answer, fair audience." As he was speaking, the clown and the drummer wheeled out an object about seven feet tall and five wide and covered over with brown canvas. They left it at center-stage and withdrew, returning with a long piece of iron bar carried between them with obvious effort. "I give you, for your amazement and speculation," said the master, as he motioned toward the covered object with a flourish, "*the Mighty Coalblack!*"

The clown and the drummer whipped the canvas away. There was a catch of breath among the onlookers. Underneath the canvas was an iron-barred prison cell on wooden wheels. At the bottom of the cell was a layer of hay, and crouched upon the hay was a large figure covered over with an ebon cloak.

The master of ceremonies clapped his hands twice. The shrouded figure stirred. It began to rise from the hay, and as it stood to its full height of well over six feet the black cloak fell off. The man exposed beneath was equally as black. His immensely-broad and muscular back was turned toward the audience. He was wearing only a lion's skin around his waist, the mane and flattened head curved up over his right shoulder in Herculean fashion and secured in the front.

Was it Zed? Matthew asked himself. It had to be! This man was huge, just as Zed was! Yes! It had to be!

Coalblack growled, a guttural and terribly menacing sound. A few women in the audience gave little noises of fear and clung closer to their thin and pallid men.

Then Coalblack whirled around, gave a resounding but mutilated shout that made even Rory jump a few inches off the bench, and attacked the bars of his prison. His knotty hands gripped the iron and began to force the bars apart. Two women shrieked and a man cried out as if he'd just wet his breeches. Matthew saw the corded muscles move in the mighty arms, saw the chest swelling with tremendous power, saw the bars beginning to bend under Coalblack's relentless force, saw the tribal tattoos that scarred the fearsome, black-bearded face…

…and saw also, that it was not Zed.

This African was a Ga, yes. Perhaps his tongue had been removed by the same tribe of slavers that had captured Zed, and perhaps the slave ship carrying him to London, or Amsterdam, or New York, or Charles Town had been attacked by pirates and destroyed, with this man the sole survivor…

…but Zed, he was not. His face was broader, his features different. His bald head was as round as a cannonball.

No, not Zed.

Coalblack had already burst a sweat. His teeth were clenched, a pale slash in the ebony face. He worked the bars apart with steady pressure and then, showing a display of stagecraft that even the most primitive elder of the Ga tribe would have admired, he thrust himself between the bent bars and out of the cage with a roar made more horrible by the loss of tongue.

Matthew thought that the audience was going to have a fit, and indeed some ran for the exit. But as Coalblack stood there fiercely flexing his awesome muscles for the crowd, with sweat gleaming on his face and his eyes tracking back and forth as if searching for the next lion to kill, the fiddler emerged from the lefthand side of the stage playing a spritely tune and Coalblack, whose grimace became a grin, began to dance.

It was like watching a bear try the minuet, but the sight calmed the crowd. What might have elicited laughter at any other time instead brought forth a sense of wonder, that such a massive creature could move so gracefully. To the crowd's absolute silence, as the fiddle played, Coalblack flexed various parts of his body from shoulders down to calves. The master of ceremonies invited a man and woman at random up to test the validity of the iron bar. The man stepped up, but the woman declined. He almost fell on his face when he tried to lift the bar, much to the laughter of the audience. Then he returned to his seat and Coalblack stepped forward to the task. The Ga picked up the iron rod as if it were a length of hollow painted wood and proceeded to bend it ten different ways from the Sabbath.

Matthew felt satisfied. He'd had to see for himself. Now he was fairly sure Zed and Captain Falco had escaped Professor Fell, and even now Zed might be with his tribe, and Falco returning to New York to be with his wife Saffron and his son Isaac. That would be a very good thing. And now, watching Coalblack upon the stage and hearing the audience applaud the African's feats of strength, he thought that Coalblack had found a place to belong as well, for though he obviously was many leagues from home he smiled warmly as he accepted the acclaim, and when he lifted the acrobat twins, one in each hand, and they did handstands upon his shoulders he treated them as carefully and respectfully as if they were living pieces of art.

So...that was also a very good thing.

When Coalblack's act had ended, he joined the other performers in bowing to the crowd. He looked, really, to be a contented man. As the drummer, the fiddler and the singer put up a caterwaul to bid the audience goodnight and the master of ceremonies blew exaggerated kisses to the crowd, Matthew and Rory made their way out into the courtyard.

"Not bad, Matthew," said Rory as they started up the steps. "For a circus, I—"

"Pardon me, please."

Matthew looked around, for a hand had grasped at his cloak.

A young man—handsome, with a clean-cut face, high cheekbones and blonde hair beneath a rakishly-tilted dark green tricorn—was smiling at him. "Is your name Matthew Corbett?"

Instantly Matthew sensed danger. The cool gray eyes under thick blonde brows stared at him impassively, awaiting an answer.

"You have the wrong man," Matthew said.

"Oh, pardon," came the reply. "I thought you were he, because I have a message from Hudson Greathouse."

Something was very, very wrong. "Sorry," Matthew said. His guts were tight and roiling. He continued up the stairs under the merry multicolored lamps.

The young man climbed up beside him, with a brief glance and smile at Rory. "You bear quite a resemblance," he offered. "I saw you in there, with your tricorn off. Not many people carry such a scar on their foreheads. It *does* mark you."

"You are incorrect."

"Really? Oh...well...I thought I heard your friend there speak your name just as I reached you. Was I also incorrect about that?"

Matthew turned his head toward the man to tell him, quite brusquely, to be off; in so doing, he saw the quick motion that was given to two other cloaked and hulking men waiting at the top of the steps, and he knew he and Rory were done.

"Mr. *Corbett*," said the young man, who placed a firm grip upon Matthew's shoulder. "Let's go right up here to the coach we have waiting, shall we?"

"Hold on!" Fear jumped into Rory. He looked for a way out. Other people were coming up the stairs, pushing him forward. He couldn't retreat, and he saw the two men waiting and recognized them not by name or by having seen them before, but as the killers he knew them to be. Then he was at the top of the stairs and the huskier of the two came over and put his arm around Rory's shoulders as if they were the longest-lost of friends.

"A fine show, wasn't it?" the young blonde-haired man in the dark green tricorn said to Matthew as he guided his captive toward the side-lamps of the coach that sat about halfway along the block. "Well," he amended, "it was fine the first time I saw it, two nights ago. Tonight...*eh*!" He shrugged in dismissal. "Please be aware we all have pistols and we all very good shots and we don't mind shooting any of the grinning idiots on this street if you have a mind to yell for help. So be a good boy and don't drag your legs. All right?"

"Where are we going?" Matthew dared ask, but he already knew.

"*You* are going," said the calmly-smiling young man, "to get a terrible spanking. Come along now, Mother's waiting."

FIVE

THE BEAUTIFUL GRAVE

Twenty-Nine

It was a sturdy two-storied house of brown and white bricks with a widow's walk at the pinnacle. A long gravel drive that curved up from the main street through a gate that had to be unlocked by the young blonde man in the dark green tricorn before the coach could pass through. Afterward, he walked back and relocked it.

The house had many windows, all of them aimed toward the central city. Lanterns shone through the glass. The appearance of the house indicated that a party might be in progress.

But Matthew and Rory found themselves the center of attention at this gathering. They had been delivered to the house in absolute silence, no one even volunteering a name. They were herded through a pair of oak doors and through spacious rooms carpeted with bright Persian rugs and adorned with leather-upholstered furniture. They were taken through another door toward the rear of the house and down a staircase. In a lantern-lit cellar with a gray stone floor they were ordered to undress, and one of the men took their clothes away.

"A bit drafty down here, don't you think?" Matthew asked the men as he stood in his nakedness, but he received no reply. Two of the men left the room. Another man, this one wearing a brown skullcap and smoking a small clay pipe, came in to stand with the blonde-haired gent, but they did no talking. They held their pistols down at their sides. Everyone remained that way for fifteen minutes or so, no one saying a word but all eyes focused on the prisoners.

Matthew might pretend to be oblivious to whatever was in store, but in fact he was scared to death. He thought the men had removed their clothing to make them feel even more defenseless and to watch their bodies involuntarily tremble. Matthew stared at the floor and tried to figure a way out of this, but he was fully and terribly aware that there was no way out.

Rory said to the two men, "You could at least give a sufferin' bastard a coat, couldn't ya?" His face was hard and his eyes defiant, but the shivering of his skin betrayed him. "What the fuck is this all about?" he demanded, but received only the ominous silence.

In another few minutes the other two reappeared, some words were quietly spoken, and Matthew and Rory were pushed out of this current room through a short corridor into another chamber. Oil lamps were fixed to the walls and smoked ever so slightly. In the room were four high-backed chairs with armrests, all about six feet apart. Matthew saw that the chairs had been either built or altered for a special purpose, for they had runners that had been fitted into the grooves of concrete blocks cemented to the floor. The chairs could not be overturned or otherwise moved when someone was sitting in them. He noted several nailheads nearly flush to the backs of the chairs, about where the head would rest. Around the chairs and on the concrete blocks were so many bloodstains it appeared that more than a single quartet of poor wretches had been skinned here.

Presently, Matthew and Rory were pushed upon two chairs side-by-side. Both of them were already wet with fear-sweat. The young blonde-haired man kept his pistol aimed at Matthew's head and another man did likewise to Rory as leather cuffs locked wrists to armrests and ankles to chairlegs. A leather strap drawn tightly across the chest completed the securement.

"You got the wrong men," said Rory. His voice trembled. "Swear to God you do."

Everyone left but the blonde-haired man in the dark green tricorn. The last one of them out closed a door that looked to be three inches thick. No sounds would be escaping this room. Matthew figured that even if any noise got out of this torture chamber and then out of the house, the main street was still too far away for anyone to hear a peep.

Torture chamber, Matthew thought. That's exactly what this was. This was a place where, obviously, up to four unfortunates could be tortured at a time. He wondered how that number had been decided upon. A roll of the dice? Was 'four' Mother Deare's lucky number? He was sweating and shivering, hot and cold at the same time. The blonde-haired man had put his pistol away beneath his cloak, and he was leaning against a wall next to the door, dozing with his eyes closed.

"How'd you find me?" Matthew asked.

The eyes did not open, nor was there any further response.

"You were haunting the circus?" Matthew probed. "Mother Deare put you on guard there? How did she figure I might show up?"

There was absolutely no reaction.

"These fuckers are *deef*," Rory said, with a nervous cackle. "Fuckin' dumb, too."

"But obviously they can read. Someone can, at least." Matthew had an idea how this capture had been devised. "So Mother Deare's a devotee of the *Pin*? Is that right?"

The blonde-haired man dozed on.

"Fuck you, blondie!" Rory called out. "You look like you et a bowl a' man-nuts for your supper!"

Even this drew no reaction. Rory swore softly and lowered his head. "Shit, Matthew!" he muttered. "We're in for it."

"They're not going to kill us. If they wanted to, we'd be dead already." Matthew didn't like hearing that from his own throat. The bloodstains around the chairs made the statement that in some cases death might be preferable to the long, slow...well, whatever technique was to be used, and Matthew chose to shut his mind to any further imaginations.

An hour might have passed, during which the blonde-haired man stirred himself and left the room for fifteen minutes or so. In his absence Matthew and Rory struggled to either loosen their bonds or test the stability of the chairs; in both cases, the security was beyond assault. When the man returned he was smiling thinly, for surely he knew what had been tried here and what had failed.

The door opened again. Matthew's body jerked; he had the thought *this is it*. Two of the men he'd previously seen brought in a small round table and a stool and put them between Matthew and Rory. Then another man, previously unseen, entered.

"Hello, fellows," he said, and he gave them the grandest smile with a mouthful of large white teeth. He was dressed in a light gray suit with a pale blue waistcoat and carrying a black leather bag, which he placed upon the table. "My name is Dr. Noddy. May I ask yours?"

"You already know them. She told you," said Matthew.

"Quite true. Just trying to be friendly." He drew from the black bag a piece of green cloth. He spread that out on the table-top. "Matthew Corbett and Rory Keen," he said. "Strapping young men, you both are." His hand went into the black bag again, and he began to neatly and precisely lay out on the cloth an assortment of instruments that caused the hairs to ripple on the back of Matthew's and Rory's necks.

Shining in the lamplight was first a small pair of pliers, then joined by a thin silver rod with a fishhook on the end, then joined by several pairs of forceps, then joined by a collection of ivory-handled tools with various spear or spade-shaped ends, then joined by another thin silver rod with what looked to be a coarse-toothed file on the end, then joined by a silver tool holding a little square mirror, and finally completed by two assemblages of metal rods adorned with leather straps and hooks.

"My beauties." The man beamed at his captive audience. "I'm a dentist," he said.

Matthew felt sweat crawling down his face. Noddy was perhaps in his late fifties or early sixties, a rotund man with chubby cheeks and a reddish complexion. He was bald but for curly waves of white hair on the sides of his head, and he wore a neatly-trimmed white goatee and round-lensed spectacles that slightly magnified his brown eyes. He had a plentitude of laugh lines in his face, indicating a merry disposition. He was certainly a man who seemed pleased by his position. Matthew uneasily noted that his hands were not large in keeping with the rest of his body, but rather sinewy. Just right, he thought grimly, for working with the teeth.

"Tell her I'm ready," Noddy said to the young blonde-haired man, who immediately left the room and closed the door behind him. Then Noddy, grinning widely, returned his attention to the two men in the chairs. "Beastly weather we've been having lately, don't you think?"

Suddenly neither Matthew nor Rory wanted to open their mouths.

"Oh come, come!" said Noddy. He adjusted his spectacles, which had slipped slightly down his knob of a nose. "I'll tell you in all candor," he said as he sat down upon the stool and got himself comfortable with a few wiggles of his buttocks, "that *everyone* talks. No matter how stout and sturdy a fellow thinks himself to be, or how sealed his secrets...everyone talks." His thick white eyebrows jumped as he spoke, as if to accentuate the sentences. "It is just, as they say, a matter of time. And loss of blood. Oh, dear me! You'd think someone with *her* wealth would have servants clean this chamber once in a while, wouldn't you?"

What was the proper response? There was none. Matthew remained silent. Rory lost control and wrenched at his cuffs for a few useless seconds. Noddy watched as if observing the difficulties of a trapped dog.

Then the door opened again. The mistress of the house had arrived.

Mother Deare—her real name Miriam—wore a crimson-colored gown with black ruffles down the front. Her rough workwoman hands were stuffed into black lace gloves. The cottony cloud of her hair was done up with the golden pins Matthew recalled. She was the same as he remembered—a solid, powerful body, a smug expression of superiority, a flophouse madam trying to be the belle of the ball—but there were three glaring differences. Both of her froggish eyes were blackened and swollen, as was her snout. Recently she'd received a good knock.

"Our Matthew," she said, but the voice was cold and flat and the mouth crimped around the small peg-teeth. Her eyes shifted in their hoods of flesh toward Rory. "And you." She made a clucking sound of disapproval. Her gaze returned to Matthew. "Enjoyed the circus, did you?"

"I did." Matthew was trying very hard to keep the terror out of his voice. It was an effort even Coalblack could not have matched. "And I didn't expect you to have that place staked out."

"I have people watching for you in many places. It's going to take some time to call them all in. We have the docks covered, and the roads leading out. My men are going through every coach and wagon, on the pretext of constables searching for the Monster of Plymouth who might be trying to escape the justice he so severely deserves."

"Good idea. You don't want that sonofabitch getting loose."

"Exactly. I happen to be quite a fan of the *Pin*. I read there about Coalblack—who I went to see last week, and particularly I enjoyed the clown—and I thought…hmmm…he greatly reminds me of the tongueless African giant—your scar-faced friend—we had caged on Pendulum Island. I wondered…not knowing what became of that ebony gent…if you might be interested in seeing someone very like him. After all, I'm sure they're rare. Well." She shrugged.

"Since we had the roads and the docks under watch and searchers roaming through Whitechapel, I thought…send a man or three out to Dove's Wing Alley for the next few nights, just to have a looksee. See?"

Matthew remained silent.

"I admire a man who is being hunted by the law of London and the law of Professor Fell, and who chooses to hide in public view by attending a circus," said Mother Deare, with a faint smirk. "But we all have to get our minds off our troubles in some fashion, eh?"

Matthew said nothing. His gaze kept slipping toward the hideous-looking instruments on the table.

"Yes," said Mother Deare, "you are right to fear those, darling Matthew. What a mess you left of Pendulum Island! My God, that beautiful castle and nearly a third of the island…gone into the sea. Do you have *any* idea what that has cost the professor?"

"I do," Matthew decided to say. "He's gone somewhere to lick his wounds and in the meantime there's a new player in town. He signs his work with a Devil's Cross, and early this morning he—"

"Raided the Black-Eyed Broodies, killed all of them and stole the Velvet. Yes, I was there this afternoon." The eyes went to Rory. "I should say, killed all of them but *one*. Where were you when that was going on?"

"He was with me," said Matthew.

"Oh? And did either of you have anything to do with the murders of Frost and Willow very near the Tavern of the Three Sisters?"

Matthew again remained silent, and Rory looked at the floor.

"Of *course* you did! Or...rather...you were mixed up in it, weren't you? Because Frost and Willow were killed with a sword. That dagger you had in your cloak is very nice, but it didn't do the job on them, did it?"

Matthew's mouth was dry. All the liquid in his body was sweating out. He knew exactly where Mother Deare was headed. *The cloak.*

"Julian," she said, "bring those items in, please."

The young blonde-haired man had been waiting just outside the open door. He came in, carrying in one hand the folded paper upon which the verse of challenge was written, and in the other hand the mask of Albion.

Mother Deare took them. She fanned herself with the paper. Her expression had not changed one iota from when she'd first entered the room. "This verse...it's a ridiculous dramatic," she said. "Of no consequence to anyone."

"Danton might think differently," said Matthew.

The fanning stopped. Then began once more.

"Oh, forgive me, gentlemen," Matthew said to the four men in the room. "Now that you know Professor Fell's full name is Danton Idris and he's a mulatto, Mother Deare will have to kill you."

"Shall I step out?" Dr. Noddy asked nervously. A little sweat had begun to sparkle on his forehead.

"Certainly not," Mother Deare replied, still fanning away. "We're beyond such secrets now, and as I say it's of no consequence." She smiled froggishly at the dentist. "Though do mind what your lips spill, Theodore. He wouldn't care for that to become common knowledge."

"You may rely on my discretion, as always."

Suddenly Rory blurted out, "What are you gonna do to us?"

Matthew winced. That question was not one he wished to have answered anytime soon.

Mother Deare ignored him. "I see," she said to Matthew, "by the mark on your hand that you've become a Broodie. How charming! A young gentleman from New York come to London to be transformed into street trash! What a lovely proposition!"

"Did you think the Broodies were street trash when you enlisted them on the professor's behalf to move all that White Velvet to the streets?"

"I think I should step out," said Noddy.

"Stay where you are!" she said sharply. Then, in a falsely-gentle voice, "Matthew, this is all business. Every bit of it. There is neither *good* nor *bad* in business. There is simply profit or loss. Do you understand that?"

"I understand there's a drug in the Velvet designed to hasten the process of addiction."

Noddy said, "I really should—"

"Hush," she told him. "You've heard worse, just put a cork in it." She regarded Matthew for a moment in silence, and he couldn't be sure but he thought he saw a measure of respect in those swollen eyes. "*Business*," she repeated. "There are other brands of gin out there, Matthew. Many others. Why not create one that has... shall we say...an extra added ingredient, so that this product might truly shine? And people love it, Matthew! They can't get enough of it! They work their fingers to the bone and break their backs in their low, menial and dirty jobs and have little to show for it. The suffering and despair out there is truly shameful! So we give our fine customers a little escape...for very little money, really. What's wrong with that?"

Matthew said, "Everything. The Velvet causes more suffering and despair, and the profits go to pay for Fell's other *business* activities."

"I'm listening, but I still don't hear anything wrong with it. We have created a product and a demand. We control the market in that particular potion, and therefore we—"

"You might not control the market very much longer," Matthew interrupted. "This new player will likely take a sample of the Velvet to a chemist in his employ and seek to duplicate the formula."

"Action will be taken, I assure you."

"It's Professor Fell you should be assuring. That warehouse was really *your* responsibility, wasn't it? When he finds out about the theft—if he doesn't already know—he may invite you to dinner and put your head on the roasted pig."

One of the other men made the mistake of giving a chortle. He rapidly disguised it by clearing his throat, but Mother Deare's eyes shot flames at him and the man actually ducked his head and retreated a few paces.

When she returned her attention to Matthew, she was all licorice-sweetness and dirty light. She held up the mask of Albion. "Who is he?"

Matthew had known they were coming to this. God, the cuffs were tight! So too was the strap around his chest.

"*Albion*. Who is he? And where is he? You see the dried blood on this?" She turned the mask between her thick fingers to show him. "Is it his, or that of my men?"

Matthew figured that both Frost's and Willow's pistols had been stolen by the time Mother Deare's men reached the scene, therefore she couldn't know that Albion had been shot.

"Rory, do you have anything to say?"

To his credit Rory was bravely silent, but he also was looking at the dental instruments with a blanched and sweating face.

Mother Deare said, "Matthew, *listen* to me. I'm going to ask you those questions once more, and then Dr. Noddy will go to work. There will be no stopping him when he begins. He enjoys his craft. Now: who is Albion?"

Matthew swallowed hard. He heard Rory do the same.

"Where is he?" She paused a few seconds, staring holes through him, and then she sighed. "All right. Noddy, work on Matthew first."

At that pronouncement, two of the men rushed forward. One squeezed Matthew's nostrils shut with an iron hand and the other pressed his fingers hard into Matthew's throat. He was unable to keep his mouth closed. Before Matthew could clench his teeth, Noddy had thrust one of the constructions of metal rods into his mouth. Matthew tried to thrash but was held tight; he thought the corners of his lips were going to be torn. Sharp prongs of metal pressed into the soft tissues. The solid framework kept his mouth from closing. The men took the ends of smaller leather straps that hung from the device and hooked them to the nailheads sunken into the back of the chair, which made his head immobile.

When it was done, Matthew's mouth was stretched wide open and he had no chance to oppose what was coming. The assembly even had a flat metal piece that kept his tongue depressed.

The men stepped back, giving Dr. Noddy plenty of room.

"Let's have a look," the dentist said, with a smile. "Julian, will you bring a lantern over here, please?" It was done. Noddy used the tool with the little mirror fixed to it. "The fine little invention that is currently affording me a view into your mouth—and plenty of space to work, I might add—was created by a Dr. Northcutt a few years ago in order to forestall the effects of lockjaw," he said. "It has also been used in the beneficent care and feeding of patients in Bedlam." Matthew felt the little mirror bump against a tooth. "People," Noddy said, "just don't take care of their teeth as they should. A pity, really. There's a great future in dentistry, I firmly believe that. Oh! There's a small cavity back at the gumline, lower left. Just begun, it looks. Otherwise…a nice set." He withdrew the mirror and stared into Matthew's widened eyes.

Noddy's smile had taken on a sinister twist. "*Pain* is the problem," he said. "Why people fear the dental profession. The mouth… the teeth…the gums…so sensitive to injury. I was telling Mother Deare once…I think some men have more feeling in their gums than they do in their balls. I mean, really…you cut a man's balls off and he's going to scream, certainly, but the pain fades. You start pulling his teeth one by one and then exploring the empty sockets with the probes…as I told you, young man, *everyone* talks."

"Pay close attention to this procedure, Rory," Mother Deare directed. "If you have anything you wish to say, I would advise you to be forthcoming."

Rory didn't answer.

The rush of blood sounded like a raging river in Matthew's ears. His face was hot but the rest of him shivered involuntarily, as much as it could against the pressure of the cuffs. Tears of anger bloomed in his eyes and ran down his cheeks. There was nothing to be done, and no one was coming to save him.

Noddy picked up the pliers. He positioned the little mirror where he could see what he was doing, as Julian held the lantern close. The pliers went into Matthew's mouth and bumped against front teeth as it moved toward the back. Matthew felt them seize a tooth on the lower left of his jaw.

He heard himself moan.

"Steady," said the dentist. "We'll have that out in a jiff."

Thirty

NODDY'S arm moved with unsuspected power.

Matthew heard the tooth crunch. Heard it being pulled from its root, and then the pressure and pain ripped through his jaw and still the crunching noise went on as Noddy's wrist twisted the pliers back and forth.

"Stubborn," Noddy remarked.

Panic hit Matthew yet he could not fight. He could not move, he could not close his mouth. The only thing he could do was grip the armrests harder with his fingers. His tongue fought the restraint, but it was no contest. The pain felt like the side of his face was about to explode. Then with a final twist of his hand Noddy withdrew the pliers with the bloody tooth clamped in it. Blood streamed into Matthew's mouth; he had no choice but to swallow it down.

"A fine specimen," Noddy said, holding the tooth up for all to see. Suddenly he frowned and looked closer at it. "Oh me," he said. "Oh me, oh my! A thousand pardons, Matthew. I've extracted the wrong one. It's the tooth behind this one I meant to get. Well, let's remedy that." He dropped the tooth upon the green cloth and with no further hesitation pushed the pliers again into his victim's mouth.

Where can I go? Matthew asked himself as he heard the tooth crack under pressure. *Where can I go to escape this? At the Trot, playing chess? Working with Hudson in the office? Walking along the Broad Way, with Berry beside me? Yes...that. A brisk autumn afternoon...the hills turned gold and purple...*

"Another stubborn beast," said Noddy. "Deeply rooted."

...our conversation light, the sun sparkling on the windows, nothing to worry about, nothing at all, others stopping to converse, her hand stealing into mine, and no Professor Fell in the world...

"Ah!" The tooth came out, with a last furious twist of the dentist's wrist. More blood flooded Matthew's mouth. The pain pulsed with his heartbeat. He coughed and gagged, fearing he was going to choke on his own life fluid.

"Swallow," Noddy urged. "Little swallows, a bit at a time. Yes, this is the tooth I wanted. See the little spot right there? In time, that could've caused you real trouble."

...holding Berry's hand, walking along the Broad Way, talking about nothing in particular but knowing we are approaching the future...a fine future...one free of terror and violence...yes, a fine future...

"Before we go on," Noddy said to Mother Deare, "might I have my reward a bit early? It does so relax me in times of tension."

Through a blurred red haze Matthew saw the woman give a motion to one of the men, who left the room. Noddy spent a moment wiping the pliers off with the green cloth.

"Now that we have openings," he said when he was done, "we can explore them a bit more deeply." He began to pick up one after another of the ivory-handled probes, trying to decide which one to use from his bounty of beauties.

"Anything to say, Rory?" Mother Deare asked.

Matthew tried to shout out *No* but it sounded like something mangled by a tongueless Ga.

Rory remained silent.

"Your time is coming, young sir," she said to him. "We're not going to kill Matthew, because Professor Fell will want to speak with him. You, on the other hand, are garbage and have no value.

Therefore when your time comes we have no restraint in what may be done to *you*, and afterward we are going to kill you. If you cooperate, we can end your life with a quick ball to the brain. If not, you will endure the fires of Hell before you go to the Devil. Are you hearing me?"

Rory said nothing.

"You always were an idiot," she sneered. "Ah, here's your solace, Theodore!"

The man had returned with a small blue bottle, which he gave to the dentist's outstretched hand. Noddy uncorked the Velvet and took a long drink. Afterward he closed his eyes and held the bottle against his heart. "A noble vintage," he said.

"Yes. Last Tuesday."

"I might wish to ask what chemical is in this that makes it so very...soothing, would be the word. But I—"

"But you have work to do," said Mother Deare.

"Exxxxx*zactly*," Noddy replied, with joyful enthusiasm. He took another long drink of poisoned courage, corked the bottle and put it aside. "All right now...let's see...I think this one will be of use."

Matthew was unable to see which probe the man chose. The sweat burned his eyes and dripped from his chin. He smelled his own fear, a bitter animalish scent. The liquid flowing down his throat caused him to start choking and gagging again.

"We'll have none of that!" Noddy scolded. "This is one of my best suits! If you mar it in any way you shall pay the piper!"

Mother Deare replied, "I'll buy you ten fucking suits! Work him."

The probe clattered against Matthew's front teeth.

...the Broad Way in autumn...a slight mist over the hills...sailboats on the river...and Berry, walking at my—

A black whirlwind took him. It was a jolt of agony that at the same time coursed up his skull and down his neck to his shoulder. The chair creaked as his body convulsed against the cuffs, and in so doing he nearly dislocated both arms. He heard the dying echo of a strangled scream.

"I believe that touched bone," said Noddy. "A little more to the right this time."

Again the horrendous, burning pain tore through his jaw, skull and shoulder. It caused his body to jerk and shake so hard the chair came close to breaking apart at its joints. The scream echoed again, to his fevered brain a distant and alien sound. He had the sensation of rapidly rising and then falling into a pit that seemed to have no bottom.

"...coming around, I do believe," he heard Noddy say spritely. "Yes, he's awake. Open your eyes, Matthew. Let me ask your opinion."

Matthew's eyes opened. Sweat seared them shut again. When he tried once more the world was a place of glaring light and distended shadows. What appeared to be a shining piece of metal shaped like a miniature spade was presented before his face.

"Shall we try this one?" Noddy asked. "It's useful for digging abscesses out of the gums."

"I'll talk," Matthew heard Rory say, his voice choked.

Matthew tried to shake his head back and forth. It was impossible. He tried to scream *No*.

What issued from him was a garble that might have been the Ga language, or Prussian, or any dead tongue yet unknown to man.

"Who is Albion?" Mother Deare's voice was itself a bludgeon.

Matthew heard himself sob. His mouth was a firepit, his entire face in flames.

"You'll stop torturin' him if I tell you?"

"Tell."

"His name is...I'm sorry Matthew, I swear to God I am. His name is Archer. He's a judge."

"*Archer?* William Atherton Archer?"

Rory was silent. In Matthew's fever-dream he imagined that his friend had nodded *yes*.

There was a long moment of stillness. Matthew heard the bottle of Velvet being uncorked once more by the giddy dentist.

Mother Deare said quietly, "I don't know how you came up with that name. I suspect Matthew in his current tribulations with the law heard the name and perhaps mentioned it to you. But if you expect me to believe that an English *justice* masks himself as Albion and goes around killing the professor's errand boys, you will next expect me to jump into the chocolate sauce of the Thames and dive for a cherry. Fuck you, your dead mum, your fuckin' dead Broodies, and every inch of fuckin' skin I'm gonna flay off your shit-sack body."

In her barely-controlled fury, the foul-mouthed street brawler had made an appearance. "Theo, this time stop playin' and *hurt* him."

The probe slid into Matthew's mouth. It searched for one of the raw and bleeding holes.

"It's God's truth!" Rory shouted. "Albion's the judge! I'm swearin' to—"

With a very slight thrust of the spade-tipped probe, the pain that ignited Matthew's nerves had no precedence. His body fought the cuffs and strap. Sweat flew from his face. The bones of his jaw were being melted by Satanic fire. He let loose a mangled scream that echoed back to his ears a dozen times from the cold stone walls. He had the sensation that an iron spike had been driven deep into his jawbone and now it was being twisted to crack the hard tissue and dig out the marrow. His frantic mental efforts to reach the Broad Way in autumn, with Berry at his side, failed. There was no escape.

Voices faded in and out. Matthew's eyes opened, again to a world of distortions.

"...tellin' you true," Rory was saying. He sounded as if he were near weeping. "It's that judge, Archer. Go to the Cable Street hospital and see for y'self."

"This wound he received was life-threatening?" Mother Deare asked, her fiction of proper composure returned.

"Yeah. Ball put him in a bad way."

"Hm," she said, and then was silent.

The cork was pulled on the bottle of White Velvet once more. Noddy noisily drank, smacked his lips and returned the cork.

Mother Deare said, "Julian, you and Harrison go to the Cable Street hospital. Find out who was brought in last midnight with a pistol wound. He should be a man aged about forty-two or so, blonde hair, the look of an aristocrat. Definitely not the rabble they usually treat. He would have been brought in by two young men. Ask what name they have on their records."

"We didn't give 'em a name," Rory said. "We told the nurses we didn't know."

"Your tale begins to sound interesting, Rory, but if you're lying to stall your own fate you can be sure you'll pay for it in the worst way I can devise. And, little man, I can devise the *worst*."

"It's all true, just like I said."

"We shall see. I know Archer by sight, so I'll go along for the ride. Noddy, take that thing out of Matthew's mouth. Then go upstairs. There's another bottle of your delight in the kitchen cupboard, but be aware I may need you to continue."

"Yes, and thank you most kindly!"

"We should be back within an hour." Mother Deare and her men left the room. Before Noddy complied with the woman's orders he put a spear-tipped probe up one of Matthew's nostrils as an act of caution. Then he removed the small straps and hooks from the nailheads and with a deft movement born of practice he withdrew the wicked device from his victim's mouth.

"Procedure finished for the time being, at least," said Noddy. "We might have to do some more exploratory work later. And you would be my next patient, I believe." He gave a little bow toward Rory, then he began to return his instruments to the leather bag. "Keep the teeth cleaned, gentlemen! People are far too lax in this regard! If you don't scrub them in your mouth, you'll wind up scrubbing them in their glass. That's what I tell all my patients." He picked up the bag and the blue bottle, which was nearly empty. Noddy's eyes behind the spectacles were shiny. "'Til later," he said with a jolly inflection. Then he left them alone, closing the door at his back.

In the silence that followed, Rory said, "I had to do it."

Matthew spat blood upon the floor, adding to the coloration.

"I couldn't let 'em keep doin' that, could I? I mean...what's that judge to *me*?"

Matthew thought he must've lost three pounds, for all the sweating he'd done. His jaw and the entire side of his face still throbbed with pain, the muscles of his neck and shoulders felt as if they'd been stretched nearly to the point of tearing loose from the bones, and he was sick to his stomach. Blood from his mouth glistened in streaks down his chest. The memory of the more excruciating pain was close enough to make him tremble all over again.

"I couldn't!" Rory went on. "You're a Broodie! How could I let 'em do that and keep my mouth shut?"

"A Broodie," Matthew said. His voice was almost unrecognizable even to himself. The left side of his face was puffing up. He kept his tongue away from the two holes where the teeth had been. He felt so weak and worn-out he could be folded up and fit inside a very small box, or they could wring him out and pour him into a little blue bottle.

"No sense to go on like that," Rory said. "Ain't human."

Matthew spat more blood and took a deep breath. He released it and said, "Agreed."

"You *do*?"

"They weren't going to stop until they got what they wanted." His speech was becoming more and more muffled, as if he were trying to speak through a mouthful of feathers. "God help Judge Archer, though."

"You think they'll kill him on the spot?"

"No, but they'll take him out of the hospital. Fell will want him." Matthew leaned his head back, oblivious to the nails. He shivered involuntarily. A bloody tide rose from his gullet. When he was done, he was a total mess and all he wanted to do was escape into the false comfort of sleep. He had the strength of a ripped-up rag. Even so, he realized that Rory's minutes were numbered. When Mother Deare returned, Rory was doomed.

Matthew began looking around for any hope of freedom. He tried to move the chair. It was impossible. The little round table was of no help. The oil lamps smoked on the walls, a continent away. He tried to wrench the cuffs loose. When it was apparent they were not going to yield a fraction of a fraction of an inch he put his tenuous strength to the ankle cuffs. Again, there was no movement.

Rory began to quietly laugh.

"What's wrong with you?" Matthew's damaged mouth was as hard to work as a rusted pump. "What's *funny*?"

"You. Fightin' the chair and them cuffs. In the shape you're in, still fightin'. That's right commendable, Matthew, but it's stupid."

"Why?"

"The flippin' cow's got us cooked. You know it, pure 'n simple. Well...I reckon I'm the one to be cooked. But you best save your strength. No use in fightin' what can't be beat."

"There *has* to be a way out of this!"

"I 'magine that's been said before in here. Or *thought*, at least. All the blood on this floor...lot a' poor buggers been here and gone."

He drew a long breath, and there was some satisfaction in it when he let it go. "I got enough tooth problems, I don't need no more 'fore I kick off the skin."

Matthew's tongue wanted so badly to investigate the holes. The taste of blood in his mouth was sickening. He thought he was going to throw up again, but by force of will he kept everything down and himself steady.

"That was a bad 'un," said Rory. "Lost two teeth and went through all that, for *what*? You don't owe that damn judge nothin'. Hell, look at the tight he's got you in! I should'a spoke up soon as they put that flippin' cage in your gabber!"

"I owe him the chance to get away," Matthew answered. He realized that very soon he wasn't going to be able to talk at all; his very own case of lockjaw was creeping up on him from the strained muscles. "I don't know what I was thinking...maybe that by the time..." Damn, it was hard to speak! "By the time they got what they wanted...he'd have been moved out of Whitechapel...to another hospital." And maybe that had been done today, he thought. Maybe Steven had arranged for his father to be moved. Maybe taken him out and placed him in a private hospital. Yes! There was a possibility of that, for sure. It was something to hope for.

"Reckon so," said Rory. "Still and all, he got you into this mess. Now, concernin' me...I'm thinkin' I got my own self into it. Or maybe takin' charge of the Broodies did it. Or that deal Mick Abernathy did with the old bitch that I had not a thing to do with." He was quiet for awhile, and then he said, "Don't matter, really. Way of the world. Sometimes you stray from the right path, sometimes the right path strays from you. Don't matter much now. Matthew, I got to pee somethin' fierce. Do you mind?"

"Go ahead." Matthew was thinking furiously. This was a deadly game of chess he thought he'd lost before his first move had even been made. "What we have to do," he said with increasing effort, "is...make you valuable."

"Me? My guts and bones might be worth somethin' to a grave robber. That's 'bout all I got."

Matthew could only come up with one solution, and it was flimsy but worth a try. "I'll pay her," he said.

"*What?*"

"Pay her," Matthew repeated. "*Money.* That's...all they hold of value."

"You got a stash hidden somewhere on you?"

"Bargain with her. Pay her...from the Herrald Agency. I'll work it out."

Rory didn't answer. Matthew's head was swimming. He closed his eyes and jerked them back open again when he realized he'd faded out for a time. How long, he didn't know.

"You awake?" Rory asked.

"Yes."

"You went out for awhile. Figured you needed it."

"How long?" Now the muscles of Matthew's jaws were so stiff every word was an effort.

"Maybe ten, fifteen minutes."

"I'll pay her," Matthew said, as if to validate the idea. "Like...a ransom. She'll value that."

"Maybe she will," said Rory, but his voice was listless and already seemed far away. "Y' know," he went on, "I ain't never been more'n ten miles out of Whitechapel my whole life. Hardly that. You travel much?"

"Wish I didn't."

"I'd like to have travelled. Seen somethin' of the world. You stay in one place so long, you think that *is* the world. Then you forget how much is out there. It's mighty big, ain't it?"

"Big," Matthew agreed.

"A sea voyage," Rory said. "That's what I wish I'd done."

"What I wish...I *hadn't* done."

"Sailin' on a ship. Yessir. Nothin' 'round you but the wide blue ocean, and the wind in your hair, and them sails spread wide over your head. That's sure what I wish I'd seen. I can hardly 'magine lookin' out and seein' nothin' but water. Bet that scares some men to the core. Me...I would'a liked it, I think."

"Pay a ransom," Matthew said. "Valuable, that way."

"What's New York like?" Rory asked.

"Home."

"Reckon so. That would be good, to have a place you think of as home. Me, I just been passin' through. Travellin', I guess...from nowhere to nowhere. Wish I'd taken me a sea voyage."

"You will," Matthew said.

"They're gonna kill me when she gets back," Rory replied, with a calm that told Matthew he had already dispatched much of his spirit to the other world. "Ain't no way to make me so valuable they won't kill me. It was a good thought, though, and I thank you for it."

"We'll get out of this," said Matthew.

"We will...but in different ways. One thing I'd like to ask you, Matthew...Broodie to Broodie. Hearin' me?"

"Yes."

"If you can...find out who was in charge of killin' 'em all. Make whoever did that pay for it, Matthew. I mean it. Make 'em pay."

"We'll find out together."

"No," said Rory. "No, we won't." He was silent for a time, and then he laughed again.

"What?" Matthew asked.

"Funny. A real rib-breaker. That *you* should be the last of the Black-Eyed Broodies, and carry the torch on. Find out who gave that order, Matthew. Find out what kind of monster could do a thing like that."

"We both will."

"As stubborn as your flippin' teeth," Rory said, with a snort. "Listen...I'm not much on the Bible and all that, but I figure prayin' might be a good idea right about now. Would you just hear me?"

"Yes," Matthew said.

"All right. Well...this is to God I'm speakin'. I'm sorry for the bad things I done. Bet you hear that a whole hell of a lot from people 'bout to die. Hope you don't turn a deef ear to me. Sorry I stole that horse from that man give me a job. His boy liked that horse, give it the name of Sandy for its color, and there I sold it to a fella run the gluepot house. Well, maybe he figured the horse was for better things and put it in the races or somethin'. Sorry I whipped Joe Connor in front of that girl he was tryin' to show off to. Sorry I stole the coin from Mary Kellam and lit out in the night when I told her I was comin' back for supper. Sorry for...all of it. Sorry in an awful big way for what happened to Josh, and me knowin' what the Velvet was doin' to people. Now, if I'm goin' to Hell, that's why I ought to go. 'Cause I knew the Velvet was different...bad different... and I closed my eyes to it. So if you say I need to go to Hell, I can understand that, and I won't fuss about it. But...listen...I sure hope them others don't have to go to Hell. I was the one leadin' 'em about. They just followed what I said to do. So...don't blame them and send 'em to Hell for what *I* done."

Rory was quiet. Matthew didn't even try to speak.

"One more thing I'd like to ask," Rory continued, his voice now very small. "Watch over Matthew. Watch over him, hear? He's a right good fella, and he's got some important things to do. Watch over him so he can find the sonofabitch gave that order to kill our fam'ly, and he can cut that bastard's black heart out and feed it to the crows. I guess that's all I have to say."

Rory said no more.

Matthew faded in and out. He was rehearsing what he would say when that door opened. A ransom for Rory's life. Money drawn from the Herrald Agency. A certain amount per month to keep Rory alive. He could work it out. Mother Deare would accept it, because it was all business. It was profit for her. It made sense. His tongue gingerly felt the holes at the back of his mouth. Mother Deare could be reasoned with, she wasn't stupid. No, far from stupid. A profit was a profit, no matter how—

The door opened.

Mother Deare entered the room, with Julian and another man behind her.

"Listen to me!" Matthew said, but his voice was a garbled mess through the swollen mouth. "I can—"

Mother Deare lifted the pistol she was holding at her side and fired into the center of Rory Keen's forehead.

The *crack* of the shot was deafening. Blue smoke roiled through the room.

Julian put a leather bag over the dead man's head and drew it tight with drawstrings around the neck. He knotted the drawstrings twice.

Matthew was no longer in the room. His body was, yes, but his mind had reached out for Berry, there on the Broad Way under the cool breeze and soft sun of autumn.

"We have *Albion*," Mother Deare told him, but he hardly heard her. "A young man, two nurses and a doctor tried to stop us. We left them regretting their actions." She handed the still-smoking pistol to Julian. The other man had begun to remove the body strap and cuffs from Rory's body.

The young man, Matthew thought with a start. *Steven?* Had they killed Archer's son? He couldn't speak. To his numbed amazement, he realized he was weeping.

"There, there," Mother Deare said, with a touch of motherly sweetness. "You're going to be taken upstairs. Clean you up, get you some nice clothes. A cup of warm tea. Something harder to drink, if you'd like that. Noddy says you shouldn't try to chew anything for awhile. We're going to be preparing for a trip of ten days. Stopping at inns along the way, so you're going to be on your best behavior. If you're a good boy, you'll be treated as such. Which means not trying to cause us any trouble, as we would not like to have to dispatch anyone who has no stake in this. You see, we're reasonable people."

"Archer," Matthew managed to croak. "You're going to kill him?"

"Certainly not. The professor will want to entertain both you and the noble justice. As I say, you have value. This one's value," she said, with an uptilt of her chin toward the body, "lies in being cut into chunks and fed to my dogs. They do so like to chew on bones. Now don't give me such a look, Matthew. I'll tell you that you have something to greatly look forward to."

"What...might *that* be?"

"Hudson Greathouse and Beryl Grigsby are already on their way to visit the professor. They will reach him before we do. So you see, you have a grand reunion to look forward to."

Matthew closed his eyes. What sharper blade than this could ever pierce a heart?

All, it appeared, was lost.

"Let's get you out of here," said Mother Deare. "Bring you back to proper civilization. Shall we?"

Julian began to free Matthew from the chair. There was no use striking out, which was Matthew's first instinct. He could do no good here. He would have to wait, bide his time, come up with some sort of plan and hope for...

...a miracle?

"Thank you," he told Julian when he'd gotten to his feet and staggered, and the young blonde man in the dark green tricorn had steadied him. They led him out of the chamber across the blood-stained floor. Though the leather drawstring bag covered Rory's face, Matthew was very sure that the eyes of the Black-Eyed Broodie—perhaps the eyes of all of them, now spirits in the London firmament—were fixed steadily upon him, the last of their family.

Thirty-One

On the fourth evening, Julian Devane knocked at the door of Matthew's windowless but otherwise spacious room. Devane informed him to dress for dinner, that he was not to dine in the room alone tonight but that Mother Deare wished him to attend the evening meal with her promptly at eight o'clock.

How could Matthew refuse such an invitation? Since emerging from the torture chamber, he'd been living a life of luxury. Mostly of the solitary variety, but luxury nonetheless. His room might have been copied from the royal bedchamber of a Persian prince with all the excesses of carved wood and eye-dazzling patterns of carpet and curtains. He was presented with three meals a day, none of them feasts but all of them delicious and quite filling. An occasional knock at the door summoned him to find a bowl of apples or pears offered by one of the black servants, who locked the door again when the offering was accepted.

Twice the knock had brought a wicker basket holding such items as philosophical pamphlets, folios of works by the Cavalier poets, and dramatic pieces by authors like Thomas Middleton, John

Fletcher and Francis Beaumont, whose *Love Lies A-Bleeding* in particular caught Matthew's interest. He was afforded a dark blue silk robe, and three new suits—two black and one gray and all of a very fine quality—appeared in his room the first afternoon, when they let him out for Dr. Noddy to gently apply cotton saturated with pain-killing and disinfectant medicine to the sockets where his molars had been.

He was given a silver pocketwatch to keep the time. On the back of it was the engraving *To My Precious Phillip From Your Devoted Caroline.* He had to wonder if precious Phillip had gone toothless to the grave and coughed this out of a pocket on the way.

Dinner at eight with Mother Deare? He hadn't seen her since she'd ushered him from the cellar after shooting Rory in the head. The cup of tea that had been given to him by, again, one of the black servants must have been laced with something, because he'd passed out in the little tearoom next to the kitchen and awakened here, with precious and likely-departed Phillip's pocketwatch on his pillow and the time reading eleven forty-two. Of the next morning, he'd found, because a knock at the door brought him a copy of the *Gazette* and not only a bowl of shredded wheat with sugar and cream but a little cup of chocolate pudding. It was only when he spooned to the bottom that he discovered the cherry.

As eight o'clock approached, Matthew used the washbasin to scrub himself. He dressed in one of the black suits—in mourning, he told himself—with a lightly-starched white shirt, a white cravat, a black waistcoat, white stockings and a new pair of black boots that fit him very well but would need considerable breaking-in. He was unable to shave, for here as in any other gaolhouse he'd recently occupied, no razor nor any implement with a sharp edge was allowed within the circumference of his eye. He had considered the possibility of using the glass in the pocketwatch and the little metal hands as weapons, for what they'd be worth, but to what end? No, better to keep track of time and withhold all thought of demanding payment in full for the cold-blooded murder of Rory Keen.

He combed his hair, brushed his teeth, and dabbed a bit of the medicine Noddy had left with him into the healing sockets. At precisely seven fifty-five the knock came at the door, and Matthew was ready.

He was taken by the vigorous Devane and the cadaverous-looking Harrison along a corridor and down a wide staircase to the lower level, which was decorated much like his own miniature Persian palace. He thought that for a bawd from Whitechapel, the old lady had done pretty well for herself.

But his attempt at keeping a light spirit was in fact a heavy burden. He knew there was no point in pretending he wasn't facing his own grisly execution at the hand of Professor Fell. How that might come about he dreaded to think. As for Hudson and Berry in the grasp of the professor...what was to be done about that? Nothing he could engineer, and though he could worry himself sick and white-haired over it, he was currently powerless. He had to trust that both of them would still be alive when he reached them. Therefore he chose to live moment-by-moment, as long as the moments lasted, and if he was given a soft bed and fruit bowls, poems and plays and discourses on philosophy, new suits and shirts that still smelled fresh of the tailor's art, a washbasin with a steady supply of clean water and a dead man's timepiece, then by God he was going to embrace it all. It was a prison, yes, and the thirteen steps were waiting for him further down the road...but right now this was a far cry from Newgate.

He smelled the fragrantly-gamey aroma of roast venison.

"Matthew!" said Mother Deare with a peg-toothed smile in the glow of many candles. She was seated at the dining table in a room that was more comfortable and sensible than Matthew would have imagined. It did indeed resemble the dining room of an upper-class matron who kept her fortune in boxes in the closets and doled the money out to worthy charities, favorite nieces and nephews and occasionally the horse race betting parlor. There seemed to be enough dark oak in the room to build a fifty-gun warship. The polished table gleamed, as did the elaborate silver service, in the light afforded by two eight-taper candelabras. Beyond the table a door led to the kitchen. A pair of heavy dark purple curtains were drawn across a picture window that gave a view, Matthew presumed, upon the rear of the estate. As Matthew took the place next to Mother Deare that the woman indicated, Devane left the room but Harrison stood guard beside the doorway they'd just come through.

Mother Deare said, "You look very fit tonight. Catching up on your rest, I would think."

"Absolutely, and thank you for your compliment." Matthew was determined to be his charming best at this dinner, but he had to draw the line at returning the pleasantry. Mother Deare was done up in pale pancake makeup and blue eyeshadow that made her even more repulsive-looking than ever, though her recent injuries of bruised nose and darkened eyes had subsided. She was wearing a voluminous pink gown with a thicket of red ruffles around the collar and down the front, and on her manly hands were red lace gloves.

Matthew noted that Mother Deare's place was set with silverware, including a very substantial blade for the meat, but he had not a baby-sized spoon.

"I'm glad you could join me," she said. "Now let me ask you a question, and answer it truthfully. Do you need a guard standing in here during our dinner? I mean to ask, are you going to be inclined to want to cause a scene?"

"I need no guard." He glanced quickly in Harrison's direction. "I have no desire to want to escape or cause anyone harm. I want to see that Berry and Hudson are safe and well-treated."

"Spoken like the gentleman I know you to be. Harrison, you may leave us."

"Yes, mum," he said, and he slinked away.

Mother Deare picked up a little silver bell on the table and rang it. Two black servants in spotless black suits, white shirts, white cravats and white gloves entered. One of the men was nearly the size of Hudson Greathouse and looked ill-at-ease in his formal getup. So Matthew realized he was going to be guarded after all, as this man would be stationed only steps away in the kitchen.

"Let's begin," she told them, and they retreated at her command.

The larger servant returned with a silver setting for Matthew. He put down the same knife that was set before Mother Deare. Did he linger just a few seconds, looming over Matthew like a threatening storm cloud? Perhaps. But then he left, Matthew put his napkin in his lap, another servant emerged to pour them glasses of red wine, and the first course of what Mother Deare announced was pigeon soup with a side saucer of pigeon blood to add flavor as one desired.

"I intend," said Mother Deare as they drank the wine and ate the rather delicious soup, "to give you a lesson in economics. I feel I should explain why Rory is no longer with us."

"A lead ball to the brain makes one permanently late for dinner," Matthew said, and he studied the saucer of blood for a few seconds before he decided his soup was fine as it was.

"It's plain and simple *economics*, Matthew. We're leaving in the morning at first light for a ten-day trip. Rory had outlived his usefulness. Feeding him on the journey would have been a wasteful expense."

"I see," said Matthew. Her frugal attitude made him wonder if the pigeon meat in this soup didn't come from the birds in the rafters at the Broodies' warehouse. Something struggled up and screamed inside him at the idea of Rory dying because this wealthy criminal and possible madwoman did not wish to buy him a few crackers for his supper, but he swallowed the scream down with a drink of wine.

"I hope you do. We're going to be in close quarters for the next ten days, so I would regret any action toward you if you decided you had an issue over Mr. Keen's departure."

Matthew nodded. His mind was elsewhere, on a pressing matter. "May I ask where Judge Archer is?"

"He is at another location, and has been receiving medical treatment to ready him for the ardors of our journey. He'll be travelling in a separate coach."

"He hasn't lost any teeth, has he?"

Her smile was crooked and utterly hideous. "Certainly not. I want him healthy to present to the professor. By the way, that verse has been printed in the latest issue of the *Pin*. And Lord Puffery declares that Albion and the Monster of Plymouth continue to haunt the East End."

"Well, that just goes to show you shouldn't believe everything you read." There was another matter on Matthew's mind that called for careful phrasing. "I hope no one else was injured when Judge Archer was removed from the hospital?"

"The doctor who tried to intervene had to be turned away with a broken arm. I personally knocked the hell out of one of the nurses."

What about the young man? Matthew wondered. Had it been Steven, or not? He feared fishing in dangerous waters, lest the woman's sails be turned toward nabbing Archer's son.

"And," she went on, with a spoonful of blood-laced pigeon soup at her thick lips, "we did have to give a lesson in manners to a young man who interfered. We might have damaged him a little, but then again he was already in the hospital."

"He was also a doctor?" Matthew dared venture.

"No, he was in the waiting area. Why do you ask?"

Matthew shrugged and took another drink of the wine. Did Mother Deare even know that Steven was Archer's son, if indeed this had been the young man? Archer may have done a good job in keeping Steven's identity a guarded secret, even from Mother Deare's informants. "There's been an awful lot of violence lately," he said. "I don't like the idea of innocent bystanders being harmed."

"When an innocent bystander interferes in my business, he is no longer a bystander," she replied. "We didn't do serious harm to anyone, so calm yourself."

The second course of pickled meats and smoked cod's roe arrived, along with a platter of sliced black bread. Fresh glasses of wine were poured.

"I saw the carnage in that warehouse," Matthew said. "Also the fact that the Velvet was taken. Do you know who was responsible?"

"A new individual on the scene."

"Yes, and he signs his brutal work with a Devil's Cross. Do you know his name?"

"I do not."

"Really?" Matthew looked at her over the rim of his glass. "Has your network of information failed?"

"This new individual has so far defied identification," she said. "But you can be sure we'll find him, given time."

"It seems he knows more about the professor's operation than Fell knows about him. Could it be that the professor's slipping? Losing control over the empire, so to speak?"

Mother Deare busied herself spreading cod roe on a slice of bread. "If the professor is in any way disengaged lately, you may be proud of yourself in causing such a temporary condition. The loss of his home on Pendulum Island struck him deeply, and the destruction of the goods there dealt him a setback in our agreement with the Spaniards."

"Forgive me if I feel no empathy," Matthew said. "So I assume that as soon as we reach him—wherever he is—he's going to kill me?"

She added a piece of pickled meat to the concoction she was creating. "I wouldn't know his intentions in that regard. I can say he's *extremely* angry at you. How that anger will resolve itself, I have no idea."

Matthew figured that Dr. Noddy's treatment would seem a delight compared to what Fell could devise. He stared into the flames of the tapers on the candelabra nearest him and thought *Moment-to-moment, and each in its own space.*

"Which leads me," said Mother Deare, who licked cod roe from her lips, "to a question I'd like to ask *you*. What do you know of the man the professor is seeking, by name Brazio Valeriani?"

Matthew put aside his own slice of bread. He recalled the eerie voice of Professor Fell emanating from the false mechanical figure in the dining hall at Pendulum Island: *I am searching for a man. His name is Brazio Valeriani. He was last seen one year ago in Florence, and has since vanished. I seek this man. That for the present is all you need to know.*

Matthew recalled also the price Fell was putting on finding his quarry: *I shall pay five thousand pounds to the person who locates Brazio Valeriani. I shall pay ten thousand pounds to the person who brings him to me. Force may be necessary. You are my eyes and my hands. Seek and ye shall find.*

Matthew said with an attitude of careful indifference, "I know he's Italian."

"*Very* intelligent of you." The peg teeth flashed. "Of course you have no idea *why* the professor seeks this man, do you?"

"I'm not sure I really care."

Mother Deare's hideous smile widened and a sudden glint of wildness jumped into her bulbous eyes. "You *should*," she said. "The entire *world* should care. Do you have any idea what the professor's speciality of research was?"

"I recall he told me he was interested in...how did he put it... the specialized life form."

"Biologics was his study," she offered. "The study of life forms in all their intricacy and variety. He was—and is—particularly fascinated by marine life."

"Yes, I remember him saying that too," said Matthew. "As he put it, he had an interest in 'the creature from another world'. That would explains the octopus with a taste for human heads." For some reason he wished to stay away from the cod roe, and in general his appetite was dwindling.

"I'll tell you, dearie, he's a very smart man. He's talked to me about these things before and I wound up with so bad a brain ache I had to stay abed for two days. His mind is far beyond me."

"And far beyond mine, I'm sure."

"I wouldn't jump to that conclusion so readily. As a matter of fact, he informed me that he enjoyed your company…the short time there was of it, that is. He enjoyed your discussion."

"He did the discussing. I just listened." Matthew knew Mother Deare was referring to Fell's recitation of the murder of his twelve-year-old son and his subsequent entry into the criminal world, beginning with a vow to execute not only the boys who had beaten Templeton to death but their entire families. The success of this venture and his newfound imagination for crime—and deep-seated yearning for power that had been repressed until this incident unleashed it, Matthew suspected—had attracted a fledgling gang of toughs and the professor's kingdom had grown from there.

"So," Matthew said, "exactly why does the professor want to find Brazio Valeriani? I'm assuming it has something to do with marine life? Does he possess a talking dolphin?"

She gave a quiet little laugh. "Valeriani possesses information the professor needs. It has not to do with marine life, but…in a way it does involve the deeps. Certainly it involves the professor's interest in life forms." She angled her head as if contemplating how much further to go. Then the froggish eyes blinked and Matthew knew she'd come to the end of that particular road. "No, I'd best let him tell you, if he chooses."

"You say the world will be affected by this…whatever it is?"

"I would say the world will never be the same."

"Charming," said Matthew, for he had the feeling that in speaking of this thing the entire room had seemed to become more shadowed.

The main course was served. The venison was still sizzling on its huge brown platter. There was a plate of boiled and sliced potatoes and carrots and a bowl of steamed apples.

The servants carved the venison, prepared the plates, refilled the wine glasses and then left the room again.

In spite of his memory of Fell's pet octopus taking Jonathan Gentry's head for its morning meal, Matthew found his appetite regained by the sight of this feast and launched into his food.

Mother Deare watched him eat for a moment, her eyelids at half-mast, and then she said,

"You've heard the professor's story. Would you care to hear mine?"

Matthew realized it was more of a declaration than a question. He dreaded anything this creature was bent on relating to him, but he wondered if there might be something in the tale to stave off Fell's wrath. "Of course," he replied, with a polite but quick smile.

She drank a bit from her refreshed glass. She peered into its depths, as if some recollection lay there.

"I was born to a bordello madam," she said. "Over in Whitechapel, not three blocks from the Broodies' warehouse. The house isn't there anymore. It burned down quite a long time ago. When I turned six years old my mother set me to work…not with the bawds, but gathering up the sheets and helping the regular laundress. My mother—Dorothea—was a cunning and very able businesswoman, but she was not well-educated. She simply acted on her instincts. Dorothea Darling, she called herself, and that's what the others called her. One of the ladies' mothers had been a school teacher. She became my teacher. She taught me to read, taught me proper English, taught me…many things."

She swirled the red wine around and around in her glass. "Heady times, Matthew," she said, her eyes somewhat glazed by the mist of memory. "My mother believed in showing the customers a good evening…the place was dressed up for a party every night. Some nights we even had musicians in the parlor. Of course we were under the thumb of the local gang and my mother had to pay protection, but that was the game. Sometimes she was required to pay more than money…but that also was the game. I can see the house now, just as it was. Two floors…white curtains at the windows…rooms of different colors…strawberry red, midnight blue, deep green and sunny yellow. And she kept it clean, too. Well…I mean to say *I* kept it clean, sweepin' and moppin' and such after the washin' was done. A place to be proud of, really. My mum didn't use two-pence whores and none of 'em were under sixteen. If one of 'em got preggers, she didn't get thrown out. Usually gave the baby up to the church, but none of 'em was ever strangled and buried in the backyard like they did at some of the houses. We had a higher standard."

"Your father was also involved in this business?" Matthew asked.

"Oh, *naw*. My pap..." Mother Deare sipped her wine and gently set the glass aside. "My *father*," she said, in her affected voice of a proper lady, "was unknown to me. My mother never mentioned him, when I was a little child...but...*later*..."

She sat for awhile without speaking. She stared into the candle flames.

"*Later*," she continued, "when my mother began to lose her mind...she did tell me about my father."

Matthew had felt himself tense up. He thought that now a line had been crossed and dangerous ground lay ahead, and it was best that he say no more and simply listen.

"It started in small ways," said Mother Deare. "She became forgetful of details. Miscounted figures. Misspoke names. She developed a very noticeable and alarming facial tic, and her speech began to slur. Then the sores began to appear...first on her body, and then on her face. They would not heal. The ladies began to leave, and those who replaced them were of a poorer class. So too became the customers. My mother took to wearing a veil to hide the sores that only I was allowed to see...and I tell you, Matthew, I wish to this day I had not seen them. The flesh is so...corruptible, isn't it?"

He gave no reply.

"Corruptible," she repeated, and then she went on, quietly. "My mother became known as Dirty Dorothea, for the state of things. Beneath the veil...her face was being eaten away. In her skull, her brain also. Our house was falling to ruin. The gang wanted her out, said she was destroying the business. They said they'd give her one week to pack up and leave...but where were we to go? I was eleven years old, Matthew, and she was thirty-seven. Where were we to go? The poorhouse? The beggars' row? The *church*? Well...there might have been a possibility, but..."

She left that hanging while she drank again. She looked out upon the dinner feast with eyes that told Matthew she was no longer really here at the table, but was a desperate eleven-year-old struggling to survive in a horrid world with an insane mother who may have contracted leprosy.

She said, "On the last night...the house was almost empty. Even the slatterns had deserted us. I think...I recall a couple of them...

drunk and debased, lying in their beds. I recall...how the house looked. The curtains torn and dingy, the paint on the walls cracked and scabbed...falling to pieces. And my veiled mother pacing the floor like an animal, and raging against fate. She stopped very suddenly, was silent, and I knew she was looking at me through the veil, and she said, '*You*'. She lifted a thin arm, with gnarled fingers, and she pointed at me and said again, '*You*'. Then she asked me...if I would like to know who my father was. I did not speak, because I was terrified of her. But...she told me anyway."

Mother Deare's mouth was twisted. Her eyes found Matthew for only a few seconds before her gaze drifted off again.

"She said my father had come to her over three nights. On the first night he appeared as a black cat with silver claws. On the second night, as a toadfrog that sweated blood. On the third night...into the room with the midnight wind...he came as his true self, tall and lean, as handsome as sin, with long black hair and black eyes that held a center of scarlet. A fallen angel, he announced himself to be, and he said he was going to give her a child who would be her joy...and yet...some price must be paid for this, he said, and in his world joy must always lead to misery. My mother said...this demon promised her wealth and beauty with the birth of the child...promised music and light. But...at the whim of Hell this would be taken away, all of it smashed, all of it corrupted...because that was the way of his world. So he said...enjoy it, while you might, for payment must be made for services rendered."

The twisted mouth became still more twisted. "She didn't exactly say those words, Matthew. She didn't speak very well. *Couldn't* speak very well, with her lips as they were. But that's what I understood her to mean. Then she said I had been born from a demon's cock that shot fire, and to fire I must return. So she broke open a bottle of whale oil and rubbed the oil into my scalp...my beautiful red hair the ladies liked to brush when I was little. Rubbed it over my face and neck, let it run down my back and my front. She poured the rest of into a puddle on the floor, and then with a scream she smashed a lantern into the puddle and it burst into flame. I think...I must have been in shock. Would that be the term for it, Matthew? *Shock?* Or maybe...I was thinkin'...my mum was gonna come out of it, any minute. She was gonna wake up, and rush to hug me…and I would let her hug me, even though by that time I couldn't hardly bear to look at her."

Matthew saw her shiver. It was just a quick thing, there and then gone.

"I said, 'Don't, Mum!' 'Cause I saw she was fallin' into a place she couldn't get out of, and how was I to help her? 'Don't, Mum!' I said, but she wasn't listenin' to me no more. Then…she hit me. She was a strong woman, even then. She hit me and I fell down. Next thing I knew…she was grabbin' hold of my ankles, and she was liftin' me up…and then she held me over that fire and she screamed for him to come and take me. She screamed so loud it like to bust my ears…then I kicked out of her hands and I scrabbled 'cross that room. I used the curtains to put out the fire in my hair…but there was so much oil. It was ever'where. The curtains caught, and the floor was on fire. I remember that heat, and how them flames grew so fast. And right there in the smoke and fire I saw my mum start dancin', 'round and 'round in the room, like she was hearin' the music that used to play downstairs. I knew…there wasn't no savin' her, and if I was to live I was gonna have to save myself. That was an awful minute, Matthew, when I saw her dancin' in the flames and I knew I had to leave her there…and all of a sudden she tore her veil off and her face…it was ate up…no nose…ate up nearly to the bone. She reached down with both hands into the fire…and the oil on her hands caught…blue flames, I remember that…and she put the fire to her face like she was tryin' to wash herself with it."

Mother Deare stopped speaking. She stared into space, her mouth partly open. Matthew could hear her harsh breathing.

"Then what happened?" Matthew dared to ask.

A few seconds passed in which Mother Deare did not blink, nor speak, nor otherwise show that she had not herself left the realm of sanity.

At last she picked up her fork, speared a piece of venison and brought it to her mouth. She looked at it as it hung before her lips. "I got out of that room and out of that house," she said.

"It burned down before anyone could think to start a bucket brigade, but by that time no one cared very much about Dirty Dorothea. They were glad to see the house burn to the ground. I was injured a bit. My hair burned away...my scalp...injured. Other burns that healed in time. I was taken to a hospital—not the one on Cable Street, it wasn't there then—and I...well...I *lived*." She offered Matthew a fleeting smile before she put the venison in her mouth. Her pegs worked at destroying the meat.

"Your mother died in the fire?"

She swallowed the food and took a sip of wine before she answered. "Certainly. I heard much later that a local tavern owner found her blackened skull in the ruins. A great story was circulated about her—oh, it would've put the *Pin* to shame!—that she appeared as a ghost to the owner of the Gray Dog Tavern not far from where the house stood, and her ghost said that whoever touched her skull would have good luck in love and money. So the owner of the Gray Dog promptly renamed his tavern the Lucky Skull and put it on display for his patrons to fondle. It was still there, thirty-nine years later, when I bought the Lucky Skull Tavern and renamed it the Gordian Knot, after a story I particularly enjoyed hearing. My first task as the new owner was to take a club, smash that skull to pieces and sweep it out with the trash." She showed Matthew her teeth. "I was never very lucky at love, but *extremely* lucky with money...and, as I do so love money...all is well in the end."

"An unfortunate childhood," Matthew said.

She shrugged. "Most are, in one way or another. I was taken in by the woman who had worked at my mother's house and taught me manners and the proper way of speaking. By that time she was well on her way to becoming a madam herself, which she did very successfully in later years. I grew up in the trade, but after I became involved with the professor—through a series of circumstances that were part coincidence, part hard work and part my willingness to do whatever was necessary to help him succeed—I was moved into another area of the professor's interests, and the business of managing the houses he owned given to a young jayhawk named Nathan Spade. Oh!" She pressed a sausage of a finger against her lower lip. The froggish eyes widened. "You're familiar with that name, aren't you?"

Matthew allowed himself a faint smile. "Nathan Spade" had been his alias and disguise during that nearly-deadly adventure on Pendulum Island in March.

"Nathan Spade is dead," said Mother Deare. She lifted a fork high. "Long live Matthew Corbett." The fork came down with fierce strength and impaled her next choice of meat, her thrust making the entire table tremble.

Matthew had another drink of wine. Wherever they were going on this ten-day trip, it was not going to be an easy journey travelling with Mother Deare and her gang of toughs. And then...at the end of the ten days...the professor would be waiting.

Long live Matthew Corbett indeed, he thought grimly. *Long live Berry Grigsby, long live Hudson Greathouse, and long live Judge William Atherton Archer, otherwise known as Albion.*

They would be gathered together at this mysterious place, in ten days' time, and then it would be seen how much longer they all had to live.

Moment-to-moment, Matthew thought. *Each in its own space.*

He had many things to think about, many mental burdens and fears for Judge Archer and the two who'd come such a long way to find him. Would he ever again hold Berry's hand and stroll along the Broad Way in the cool of an autumn afternoon?

Right now, it wasn't looking too good for that.

Matthew decided he was going to finish everything on his plate and have a second helping. He was going to eat slowly, bite-by-bite, and when the dessert was served he would have his fill of that too. After all, he was a guest in the house of the very lucky Mother Deare.

He held up his empty glass.

"Another bottle," he said.

Thirty-Two

SMELL that?" Mother Deare asked. She inhaled deeply, her nostrils flaring. "The sea."

Matthew smelled the salty aroma of the Atlantic in the chill wind that slipped around the coach's drawn windowshades. He had been drowsing, for this—the tenth day—had been a particularly long haul of travelling, beginning at first light, and night had fallen several hours ago. Usually the coach would pull into an inn at sunset. This meant, he knew, that they would soon reach the lair of Professor Fell.

He closed his eyes again. He was quite sick of the sight of Mother Deare, who never failed to wear her gaudy gowns and variety of lace gloves, which made her froggish appearance and affected manners even more abrasive. He felt a certain empathy for what she'd experienced at the insane hands of Dirty Dorothea, but the reality of Mother Deare's current existence was that she was a cold-blooded killer. He was well aware that if she didn't think Fell would reward her in some way for presenting Matthew to him, he would have gone to the dogs in pieces like Rory Keen.

It had been an arduous and tiring journey, made bearable by the happy discovery that Harrison Copeland carried with him a small chess set and was actually very skilled at the game, having bested Matthew in eight out of nineteen, with four stalemates between them. The half-dozen other men accompanying Mother Deare on this trip, riding in two separate coaches, sometimes watched these games but soon turned away out of disinterest and retired to their sullen corners with bottles of rum or wine. Julian Devane, who sat next to Mother Deare in the coach Matthew occupied, was unfailingly cool and aloof, usually silent, and regarded Matthew as one might watch a cricket crawling across a floor. Matthew had the feeling that Devane would like nothing more than to lift a perfectly-polished boot and crush the cricket into paste.

The sleeping arrangements had been awkward. Some nights he'd stayed in a room with Copeland and Devane, other nights it had been two different men. After the second night, it was determined that Matthew was not going to try to escape. He knew that because he was aware of an easing in the manners of his guards, in that he was allowed to walk outside on the grounds of the inn and no one was right on his tail. He was also allowed to have meals by himself, and no one shook him down to see if he'd swiped a knife. They had obviously come to the conclusion, as he had at the beginning of this caravan, that his priority was in seeing that Berry and Hudson were safe, and one certain way to get their throats slit was to try to slip away or start blabbing about his situation to some innocent bystander.

Some of the innkeepers and tavern owners knew Mother Deare and a few of the other men by name, so it was a certainty that they had travelled this route several times—many times?—before. No one acted as if the slightest thing in the world was wrong. It was simply a business trip, and the inns and taverns were glad to take Mother Deare's money. She kept a record of how much she was spending in a little book bound with calf's-hide, and her habit of constantly licking the tip of her pencil was one of her mannerisms that drove Matthew up the oak-planked wall.

Once they'd gotten out of London, the clouds had thinned and a few rays of sun had touched the earth. By its rise and descent, Matthew ascertained that they were heading northwest in the direction of Wales. It was on the third morning when he was sitting opposite Mother Deare and Devane in the coach, being jostled and jarred by the wheels over a rutted road, that a memory came back to Matthew with a suddenness that caused him to catch his breath.

"What is it?" Mother Deare had asked sharply.

"Nothing," he'd said. "Just this rough road getting to me, I suppose." But what he'd recalled was being in a coach with two men he thought were going to kill him, during the affair of the Queen of Bedlam. Both of them had been working, indirectly, for Professor Fell.

One of them had said: *We don't waste talent, even if it is misguided. Our benefactor keeps a nice village in Wales where people can be educated as to the proper meaning of life.*

So...Wales it was. And the destination was Fell's village, where Matthew was sure the education was applied most severely.

He did smell the sea. It made him think of Rory's desire to make a sea voyage, and the fact that the young man had never before experienced this bracing aroma of windblown brine. It made him think of the promise he'd vowed to Rory to find out who had raided the stronghold of the Black-Eyed Broodies and committed that massacre. It made him also register the fact that at least twice a day for the last two weeks he had either come awake from sleep with the memory of the single pistol shot ringing in his brain, or some loud and errant noise had made him jump because it too reminded him of the pistol's report.

In his meals taken with Mother Deare, hearing her snore in the next room through the wall, sitting across from her in the soft yellow lamplight of this coach...he never forgot who she was, what she had done, and what she was capable of doing.

The coach driver gave out a holler.

"Ah!" said Mother Deare, her eyes upon Matthew. "It's in sight."

"Fell's village," Matthew said.

Her thick lips made an o of surprise and her brows lifted. "You are such a *smart* young man," she said. "I'm sure no one told you. How did you know?"

"My secret," he decided to say, just to nettle her.

"Then you also know what's it called?"

"Purgatory," he answered.

She laughed. "y Beautiful Bedd," she said. "With two 'd's'."

"Surprisingly romantic, but unfortunately misspelled."

"Translated from the Welsh," she told him. "The Beautiful Grave."

That took him aback and silenced him for a few seconds, but then he restored his senses. "His own, I assume?"

"His enemies' and those he wishes to contain. Once there, the lid is closed…yet it is a very pleasant cemetery and surprisingly lively."

"Wonderful," Matthew said, with more than a trace of sarcasm.

He heard the crack of the driver's whip. The horses were being pushed, the coach rocking back and forth. The damned village had to be close, Matthew thought. He leaned over to his left, the seaward side, pulled aside the damp windowshade and peered out.

Little pellets of mist hit him in the face. The odor of the sea—of brine, weed and marine life—was stronger. Of course the professor who was intensely interested in marine creatures would position his beautiful grave on the seacoast. All was dark but a faint glow in the sky perhaps two miles off, though distance was hard to accurately judge. Matthew had brought along the silver pocketwatch once belonging to now-dead Phillip, and in checking it he saw the time was just after eight. The horses must be near exhaustion, yet they were pulling gamely on. Matthew let go of the shade and settled back in his seat, every leather seam of which his aching ass would never forget. He said, "I see he's left the lamps burning for us."

"Not just for us. There's a thriving nightlife. It's run as any small community might be."

"How many people?"

"Oh…at last count…fifty-three, I believe. Add your friends and Judge Archer to that. And you, of course. Fifty-seven."

"I'm to become a permanent resident? And be spared the deadly rod of correction?"

"That's up to the professor," she said. Her flat tone of voice and the dead look in her eyes put quit to any further questions Matthew might throw.

A quick glance at Julian Devane and then away again told Matthew that the silent henchman's cold but slightly bemused expression said a certain cricket was nearly down to its last chirrup.

The coach began to slow. Something popped up above and sizzled away. A signal firework set off by the driver, Matthew suspected.

These nitwits thought of everything. And would that they *were* nitwits, so they'd be easier to deal with. But unfortunately not.

In a few moments the coach had rolled nearly to a stop. Matthew heard the clanking of chains and what might've been the noise of a heavy gate opening. Then the coach picked up speed and they were off again, on a road that curved to the left in the direction of the sea. It wasn't but perhaps fifteen seconds later when the coachman's fist knocked against the top and the vehicle came to a halt. The brake went down with a *thump*.

"We've arrived," said Mother Deare.

"Out," Devane told Matthew, and hooked a thumb toward the door on the left.

Matthew obeyed. He stepped into a scene he never would have expected.

A band had come to greet the coach. There were two fiddle players, an accordionist and a girl striking and jingling a tambourine, all of them well-dressed and looking to be in the prime of health. Their expressions were neither excessively merry nor gloomy, but somewhere in the vicinity of resigned comfort. The tune was lively but dignified. The group of about thirty people who had gathered in what appeared to be a lamplit village square made greetings to the driver and the passengers, as Matthew was the first out. The men doffed their tricorns and the women curtseyed. There were many smiling faces, but Matthew's first impression was that the eyes above the smiles were dulled. A few members of this strange welcoming committee wore blank expressions, as if the slates of their minds had been wiped clean.

So that was it, he thought as Devane gave him a little forward shove. Matthew was very familiar with the situation of losing one's memory by a blow to the head. He figured drugs could do the same, or else work to extinguish the desire for freedom and make this beautiful grave appear a gateway to paradise. He took quick stock of all the people he saw. The eldest in this group was a man likely in his mid-sixties, the youngest was the teenaged girl with the tambourine. No, he had to correct himself. Over there by a well positioned in the middle of the square was a woman cradling an infant in her arms, and a man beside her who must be her mate, holding a little boy of about six years up so he could view the grand arrival.

Then the coach that had been second in the caravan behind them came sweeping into the square, and like automatons the villagers turned their dubious attention, vacant smiles, automatic doffing of tricorns and acts of curtseying toward this new vehicle, which carried four more of Mother Deare's wrecking crew. The band played on.

A tall, lean man wearing a buckskin jacket and a gray skullcap came forward toward Matthew, Mother Deare and Devane. He was not part of the dull-eyed community, Matthew instantly saw. This man's eyes were sharp, his features hard and weathered, and he was carrying an ugly-looking blunderbuss with a short bayonet attached underneath the barrel. He rested the weapon upon one forearm with the snout pointed in the general direction of a New York problem-solver.

"Welcome to Y Beautiful Bedd," he said in a thick brogue, addressing Matthew. Nothing about him was welcoming. Even the statement carried more than a hint of menace. He nodded to Mother Deare and Devane. "Evenin', folks."

"Good evening, Mr. Fenna. We have luggage to be carried to our quarters."

"Yes, 'm. How many arrivin'?"

"Four in the coach that just came in. Another coach with four more right behind. Has Dr. Belyard arrived yet with a patient?"

"No, 'm, not yet."

"He will directly, I'm sure."

"I'll have your bags taken care of. Where's this one goin'?" Fenna nodded toward Matthew.

"The Lionfish guest house. Or is that already taken by the two I sent earlier?"

"No, 'm, it's clear. They were took somewhere else."

"Berry and Hudson?" Matthew looked at the woman. He didn't like that phrase *took somewhere else*. "Where are they?"

"Here, in comfortable surroundings." She gave him a chilly, one-toothed smile. "Julian, will you escort Matthew to the Lionfish guest house, please? I have duties to attend to."

"I want to see my friends," Matthew said. The third coach had just come in. The music had become a touch of madness in this strange environ.

"The guest house," Mother Deare told Devane. Then, to Matthew, "Get yourself settled. If you want anything to eat, go to the tavern on the other side of the square." She hooked a thumb in its direction. "It's open all night. Have a nice dinner, a cup of wine, and relax." She dismissed him and turned to Fenna. "Is he up?"

"Yes, 'm. Workin', as always."

"He'll want to see me at once."

"Yes, 'm," said Fenna. The man threw a menacing look at Matthew that let him know he would like to blow Matthew's brains out with that blunderbuss and hoped he might get the chance. Then Fenna and Mother Deare started across the square, which was paved with neat chalk-white stones. The crowd of greeters was diminishing and the band had ceased their caterwauling.

The pistol that Devane had drawn from beneath his cloak pressed against Matthew's ribs. "Walk on," he said. "Straight ahead and turn right at the next street."

"You know you don't need that."

"I like it in my hand. Walk on."

Matthew obeyed. He then had the opportunity to gather impressions of this tidy little prison, for that's indeed what he realized it must be. He had had his fill of prisons lately, but here he was in perhaps the worst one of all...yet it was clean, people walked about freely, and cheerful lantern light glowed from the windows. No one seemed to mind that a man was being herded along at gunpoint.

There appeared to be four streets radiating from the village square with several narrower streets turning off of those. All of the structures were ground-level only, and most were constructed of the white stone though a few were dappled white-and-gray or white-and-brown. The majority of the buildings had roofs of dark brown slate but there were several with thatched roofs. All local material, of course, Matthew thought. He saw places where the walls had been patched and possibly patched again, and it gave a charming air to the little houses but also left him with the impression that the age of this village had been disguised by patchwork and paint; there was something nearly medieval about their design and about the layout of the village itself, but then again that was only a guess.

Stone chimneys spouted polite whorls of white smoke that rose into a star-filled sky. When a breath of cold wind cast the smoke in all directions Matthew caught a pungent, earthy odor that he'd never smelled before. Peat fires, he reasoned; the village was likely surrounded by marshes and peat bogs.

On the street corners there stood poles holding burning lanterns on hooks, and beneath the lamps were street signs on enamel plates. Matthew noted that he was turning right onto Lionfish Street. He assumed all the streets were named after marine creatures. With Devane at his back, Matthew passed a small building marked with the sign of *Y Beautiful Bedd Publick Hospital.* Only four more cottages stood past that building, two on each side of the street, and then Lionfish curved to the right to presumably lead back toward the square. Lamplight cast a glow upon a wall of rough gray stones about twelve feet high, with a stone parapet at the top. A half-ruined turret indicated that this had perhaps been a fortress back in the mists of history. The gap-toothed nature of the turret stones gave Matthew a particularly bad memory and a phantom jaw ache. A man was up there on the rampart, shouldering a musket as he walked slowly along, his gaze drifting over the rooftops and then out in the direction of the sea. Matthew could see how the wall continued to both right and left. He realized it must be built around the entire village, and the village itself probably encompassed not more than three or four acres.

He did not fail to note a ten-pounder cannon up on the parapet, aimed at the sea through a firing port, and he was pretty certain it was not the only one.

"Here," said Devane, motioning with his pistol to the right.

It was a cottage about the same as many of the others, single-storied, white-and-brown stones with a roof of dark brown slate, a few square windows, a small circular window above the door. No light emanated from within.

"It's unlocked," Devane said.

Matthew went in. He had the impulse to rush the man in the darkness, but it was a stupid impulse and he let it go. "Step back," Devane commanded, the open door behind him. "There'll be a tinderbox in the top drawer of a writing table to your left." He reached over to a lantern that hung from a wallhook beside the door, and this he threw to Matthew who fumbled with the thing, nearly dropped and broke it but then claimed victory over his butter-fingers. "Someone will bring your clothes," Devane said. "That person will also have a pistol. Don't cause any trouble."

"I wouldn't dream of—"

The man retreated and closed the door, leaving Matthew alone and in the dark except for the communal light of the village's lamps that entered softly through the windows.

"*...it*," Matthew finished, for he liked completion.

He drew a flame from the tinderbox and with it lit the lantern he held and two others he found in the room. As the light spread and joined, he walked around to get his bearings. The house had a parlor and a bedroom, both spartanly furnished but certainly more comfortable than the straw-strewn floor of Newgate Prison. The bed had a goosefeather mattress, there was the small writing desk in the parlor and two chairs were situated before a nice-sized fireplace. He had been supplied with a few bricks of peat and fireplace tools. Except for the blackened hearth and some scratches on the writing desk, there was no sign that anyone had ever dwelled in this place before him. He checked the desk's drawers, found them empty, and also checked the dresser in the bedroom. The only thing he discovered was a little cotton lint.

But he did discover that there was no lock on the door, and there was no back door. Of course, he thought; can't have Professor Fell's guests barricading themselves away from their host.

Though he was weary and in need of sleep, he desired to have a look around the village. He stretched, hearing and feeling his backbone pop, and he leaned over to touch his toes several times to get the blood flowing. Then he took one of the lanterns, left the other one burning, pulled his cloak up around his neck and went out to where the cold wind gusted along the streets of Fell's paradise.

The yellow moon was nearly full. A few lights showed in windows, but not very many now as the night had progressed. No one stirred on Lionfish Street and the Publick Hospital was dark. Matthew wondered what the Beautiful Grave's residents had done to get themselves deposited here, and if they were enemies of Fell why the professor just didn't eliminate them. He found a street that aimed toward the wall, and in another moment he could hear the thunderous crash of the sea. He put the lantern down and continued on. Soon he came to a wide gate of heavy iron bars under the parapet that looked out over total ink-black darkness. He gingerly tried the gate, not wanting to make any clanking noise to alert the guards, and found of course that it was locked. No surprise. But what was beyond the gate? Just the sea, which sounded fearsome? Or did the street continue on, and to where? He would have to wait for the sun to find out.

Matthew retraced his steps along the street, retrieved his lamp, and soon found himself entering the village square. The coaches had been moved, likely stored somewhere and the horses taken to a stable. Two men were talking beside the well. Both had muskets fixed with bayonets leaning against their shoulders. They gave Matthew a cursory glance and then returned to their conversation. Matthew knew of course they were guards who likely patrolled the village all night, but it seemed to be no concern to them that he was out and about. Across the square light showed in the windows of the white stone building that must be the village tavern. He saw a wooden sign above the door: a simple black question mark painted on an unlettered scarlet background. The tavern was called the Question Mark? Professor Fell's sense of humor on display, Matthew thought. He decided he had to visit the place.

Within, the tavern was small but well-lit and clean, with seven tables and the usual bar. Two tables were taken. At one sat a trio of men talking quietly. More guards, Matthew saw. Their muskets leaned against the fourth chair. The men were likely either taking a break from their rounds, had just come off duty or were about to go on. The second occupied table held a single man who appeared to have passed out over his brown clay cup, which had spilled and was dripping dark liquid onto the floorplanks. Matthew took a table nearest the bar where he could keep an eye on the others.

"Yes, sir?" said the aproned keep, a slight and balding man with a prodigious nose who had come around the bar to where Matthew sat.

"Can I get some food?"

"The kitchen just closed a few minutes ago, but we do serve drink through the night."

"Oh." Matthew suddenly realized the problem he faced. If Fell was drugging the residents of The Beautiful Grave to keep them docile—and that was certainly how it appeared to Matthew from his first impressions of the gathered throng—the drug could be administered in anything: food, wine, ale, or water. The most innocent-looking broth could be laced with some spirit-sapping potion taken straight from Dr. Jonathan Gentry's book of recipes. Matthew recalled very clearly a statement made to him by the professor on Pendulum Island, after Gentry had been dispatched to the great apothecary in the sky: *I persuaded him some time ago to fill a notebook with his formulas for poisons and other drugs of usefulness, and therefore* he *became useless.*

Of course the formula for the drug that altered the White Velvet from a simple gin to a potent mind-wrecker had come out of that notebook, Matthew reasoned. He thought a weaker variant of it might be at work here in The Beautiful Grave, and how to avoid it if everything could be poisoned with it?

"You're wanting a cup of wine, sir?" the keep asked.

"I have no money."

"Oh…you came in with Mother Deare tonight, didn't you? I didn't get out to the greeting, I was here cleaning up after the evening fare."

Matthew nodded. He thought that even the water used to wash the cups could have a drug in it, and it might linger inside the clay to be activated when liquid was poured. The same with the dishes. A trick of that nature had been used by Fell's compatriots in Philadelphia a few years ago, with deadly results.

"No money is needed here, sir," said the keep. He had very blue and friendly eyes. "Your credit is good."

Matthew saw that the three guards were drinking from wooden tankards. Likely the use of those was specifically by the guards, and they were partaking from a supply of undrugged liquid that was not offered to the regular patrons.

"We have some stout apple ale, if that's your taste," the keep suggested.

"Thank you, but I think I'll just sit here for awhile and rest."

"A cup of water, then?"

"Nothing at all," Matthew decided, and the man nodded assent and returned to his late-night duties.

This was going to be a fine fish kettle, Matthew thought. Unable to trust the food and drink, lest it turn him into an addled idiot. But what of Berry and Hudson? They'd been here long enough to *have* to eat and drink. Were they now reduced to simple-minded obedience? Evidently the drug didn't entirely erase the will to escape, judging from the firearms the guards carried. Or was that a matter of identification more than offense?

He was wondering about this and mulling over how long he might go without food and water when he heard an angry voice raised outside. Into the Question Mark came two individuals, a man and a woman, who definitely were *not* under the spell of the professor's medicine chest.

The woman, perhaps in her mid-thirties, was tall, well-figured and quite beautiful. She had fierce dark eyes and a bounty of glossy black hair that sat high atop her head and also cascaded down around her shoulders. Her beestung lips were bright red. They were spitting rapid-fire words in Italian that Matthew thought would likely redden his ears if he could slow her down enough to decipher them. She wore a dark blue gown with white trim around the collar and a white cloth jacket over her shoulders. Her companion was a smallish man, at least three inches shorter than the woman and delicately-framed. He was dressed in a black suit and waistcoat, had gray hair tied back in a queue with a red ribbon, thin gray brows, a sharp blade of a nose and a look of extreme worry that deepened the lines on his rouged face. As the woman fired her speech at him he took to wringing his hands and looking from side to side as if seeking a way to escape. The three guards had ceased their conversation to nudge each other and grin, and the sleeper at the other table lifted his head a few inches off the wood before his neck weakened and his head thumped back down again.

The woman grabbed at the air as she verbally assaulted her companion, as if pulling forth invisible knives to stab him with. He put a hand over his heart and the other hand to his forehead and staggered under her onslaught as if he might swoon.

Then she caught sight of Matthew watching and her black eyes fixed upon him with a power that he could feel readjust his spine. She pointed a finger at him.

"You!" she shouted, making the earthenware behind the bar tremble on their shelves. "You *might* have some sense! Do you play an instrument?"

"Pardon?"

"*An instrument!*" Her hands became fists and rose up to fight the world. "*Sono circondato da idioti totali!*" she raged. "A musical instrument! Do you play one?"

The Italian she was shrieking wasn't too far removed from the Latin he knew. He did not consider himself a total idiot, as she evidently did. He said, "Piget me nego." *I regret to say I do not.*

She stopped screaming. The silence was as heavy as her accent.

She turned then upon the man, and in his face shouted in English with a force that might have seared the flesh away and sent his gray hair flying off, queue and all.

"*How am I expected to sing Proserpina, Daphne, La Fortuna and La Tragedia with no orchestra?*" Her voice rose to frightening heights. "It is an insult! It is a comedy! It is utter madness, *e un vaiolo su questa intera idea!*"

"Oh my God!" Matthew suddenly said, because he'd realized who she was.

She whirled upon him, her eyes ablaze. "*Si*, you may call for God! Call him down and tell him to bring an orchestra of angels, for that is the only way this damned part will be sung!"

"You," he said. "You are—"

She threw her head back as if to attack him with her pointed chin. "Alicia Candoleri!" she announced with haughty grace, but he already knew.

Before him stood the kidnapped opera star, and it appeared that if indeed a pirate had taken her as his lover, as the *Pin* had speculated, the poor bastard had bitten off more woman than he could chew.

Thirty-Three

MADAM Alicia Candoleri circled Matthew's table like a panther.

When she suddenly stopped next to his chair, she said, "What do you know of me? *Eh?*"

"I know," he answered calmly, "that you make every question sound like a demand."

"You should know I am also a *star*!"

"In Italy, yes. In London and many other cities, I'm sure. Here…you seem to be only a very loud and abrasive woman in search of an orchestra."

"Hear how this one speaks to me!" she fired at her ashen-faced companion, who Matthew thought must be her manager. He recalled the *Pin* had reported that a third member of her travelling party, her makeup girl, had also been taken from the waylaid coach. She snarled at the downtrodden fellow as if she were still addressing Matthew. "*Questo deve avere le palle di ottone per andare con la sue orecchie in ottone!*"

Matthew caught something about brass balls and brass ears. He said, "I'll take that as a compliment. Now…would you like to sit down and ease yourself?"

"Ease myself? *Ease myself?*" The diva's full lips puckered and her ample bosom swelled, and Matthew was tempted to grab hold of the table's edge lest he be blown through the nearest wall by this Mediterranean cyclone. But then the bosom's swell subsided, the lips relaxed from their pucker of passionate rage, the black eyes softened—if just a small bit—and she cocked her head to one side as if to examine him from a different angle. "Who the hell are *you*?"

"Truly spoken like Proserpina," he said, knowing that this was another name for the Queen Of Hades, though he had no idea what opera she was singing.

"*Si*, and I may had better *speak* the part, rather than try to sing it without an orchestra! What is your name?"

"Matthew Corbett. And you are?" He addressed the besieged manager.

"His name is *fango*, for getting me into this! In brighter times he was called Giancarlo Di Petri."

"How do you do?" Matthew said to the man, who looked like a shivering bundle of raw nerves and seemed not to dare answer anything Matthew asked.

"He is *simplicimente eccellente*!" Madam Candoleri replied. She cast a dark glance at the three guards, who resumed their conversation, and then she pulled a chair back from Matthew's table and sat down, her legs splayed out in what Matthew thought was more likely the peasant style than that of an opera star. "Whew!" she said. "What a place is this!"

"I just arrived not quite an hour ago."

"We have been...for the sake of the saints, sit down, Giancarlo!" she instructed, and he promptly sat at another table. "We have been here for eight days," she continued. "Or is it eight *weeks*? *Madre Maria*, I'm going mad!" She narrowed her eyes. "Are you one of them?" She tilted her head in the direction of the guards.

"No. I was brought here much as you were."

"It was a trickery! Giancarlo, Rosabella and I are greeted at the ship by a host we thought was sent from the Earl of—what is the name of the place?" she asked her manager.

"Canterbury," he supplied in a high, thin voice.

"The Earl of Canterbury," she went on, "and then off we go on roads that break the back! And faster and faster the horses run, and

I look into the face of the man who has introduced himself as the Earl's most trusted *ambasciatore* and I say, '*Scusami*, this banging 'round has made me need to...how do you say?...relieve the water.' I say, 'Tell the driver he stop the coach at the next tavern and let me do this, only take a moment,' and he nods and sits there, and then we go fly past the next tavern! And an inn across the way! So I get a little, you know, *upset* at this disrespect, and I demand he stop the coach just immediate! And can you imagine what this man says to me?"

"Shut up?" Matthew ventured.

"*Esattamente!* That is exactly correct! So I say then, stop this coach immediate *now*! I get so...ohhhh, I get so angry thinking of this I would throw something...so red-wild mad I say I am going to jump out of this coach if it does not stop for me to relieve my water...and do you know what this man dares to say to me, Alicia Candoleri?"

"Go ahead and pee?" Matthew asked.

"Correct again! So you know what I did?"

"I can guess."

"You better believe it, *bambino*!" she said, with a crazed grin. "I dropped my skirts like a *donna dei campi* and I let it go all over that man's legs! You should've heard the holler he let out, I'll bet Senetta didn't yell that loudly when he had his balls cut off! So then—*then*—the man is scarlet in the cheeks and cursing like a sailor boy and sudden he pulls a *pistol* out of his travel bag! Puts it right in my face and says if Professor Fell didn't want me he would shoot us all, me first, and that would be fine with him because he says he absolutely positively and supremely *despises* the opera!" She gave a snort that a bull might've envied, and she balled up a fist and looked for a moment as if she were about to spit on the knuckles in the manner of a backroom brawler. "If I ever see that man again, I will turn him inside out and kick him in the kidneys! A whole day spent with him in that racing coach, and then we reached some forsaken inn out in the country with not a light for mile upon mile and there were other men waiting on us. Then I knew...then I *really* knew...I was not being taken to perform for the Earl of Canterby."

"Decidedly not," said Matthew.

"Barkeep!" the lady shouted, startling the man so badly he dropped a rack of wooden tankards he was in the process of putting up on a shelf, making one hell of a racket. "Do we appear to be as the knots on logs? Bring us three cups of red wine! The stronger the better!"

"Um…I'm not sure that's a good idea," Matthew advised.

"And why not? I'm thirsty! The only decent thing I've found here is the red wine!"

Matthew pondered this. If Madam Candoleri was feeling at all sluggish and mind-fogged, she wasn't showing it; in fact, though Di Petri was quiet and nervous, he didn't seem to be drugged either. "When is your performance?" he asked.

"The night after tomorrow, in that little barn they call a *theater* here."

Matthew figured Professor Fell had given orders that Madam Candoleri, her manager and her makeup girl not be presented with drugged food or drink until after the performance. He imagined the effects would interfere with the diva's power of memory and her abilities in general, or perhaps the drug could be modulated to insure varying levels of compliance, or perhaps it just took a few days to show any effect at all. But in eight days Madam Candoleri and the others should be affected in some way, if they were getting even a slight dose. Therefore the barkeep would likely be supplying at least two cups of wine from a more private stock than was commonly given. As for his own cup, Matthew realized he couldn't hold out very long without eating or drinking.

"What is this problem you have with wine?" Madam Candoleri asked as the keep brought the three cups on a wooden tray. To Matthew all the cups looked exactly alike. When the keep offered the tray to him, Matthew reached a bit further to take the cup just to his left, the one that the lady should have taken. The barkeep made no noise or expression that might have been interpreted as a failure to make sure everyone got the right potion, and so Matthew figured they were either all slightly poisoned with a relatively slow-acting formula or there was nothing in the wine but wine.

"No problem," he said, and he waited for the barkeep to move away again before he continued. "Do you know anything about Professor Fell?"

"I do not, except that he must be a criminal with big hands."

"Pardon?"

"I think she means to say, 'with big plans'," Di Petri supplied, after he'd sipped delicately at his *vino.*

"Oh. Yes, I'm sure he does have big plans. You've seen him, then, to discuss this performance?"

"I have not. His request came from his piece of mouth."

"Someone speaking for him," Di Petri translated.

"I see," Matthew said. "But I have to say, you're taking being kidnapped quite well. Why would you want to give a performance for your captor?"

She shrugged. "It is what I *do.* And we will not be here very long, of this I'm certain. Once the dear Earl who made arrangements for this tour pays the ransom, we will return to our...how you say...*programma.*"

"Schedule," said Di Petri.

Matthew took a very tentative taste of the wine. If there was anything in it to addle the brain, he couldn't detect it. But he realized that even without an added drug, Madam Candoleri's brain was fogged. No ransom demand was going to be made on her behalf. For whatever reason, Professor Fell had brought her here to this village of walking sleepers and likely had no intention of letting her go.

"If I may," said Di Petri, asking permission from the diva to speak. She waved a hand to freely release his tongue. "Neither *Signora* Candoleri nor I have seen this professor person, but...it's very odd...on the first day we were here, he sent a man to bring Rosabella to him. She went to his house. She said he was very polite. He gave her a piece of vanilla cake and a cup of tea and they talked for a bit."

Matthew's interest sharpened. "He wished to speak to the madam's makeup girl? About what?"

The diva picked up the story, as she could not bear to be offstage even for a few seconds. "Rosabella said it was...how you say...lunacy. She was in his big house in a room with all his books and his fishy things, and he wanted to know about her life and her growing up. He asked many questions of her that she said made no sense."

"Such as?" Matthew prompted.

"Her family history, as if that really could matter to him. Questions about her mother and her father...particularly about her mother…and she said he was very interested in knowing things about her cousin Brazio."

Matthew had been close to taking another taste of the wine, but this name gave him pause. "Brazio Valeriani?"

"*Si*." The diva's black eyes narrowed with suspicion. "*Un momento!* How do you know this name?"

"I've been aware for some time that the professor's searching for him. I'd guess that Rosabella's mother is Valeriani's aunt?"

"*Si*. What do you mean, the professor's searching for him? Why?"

"He has something Fell wants," said Matthew. "What that is, I don't know."

"My God!" Di Petri suddenly said, without waiting for permission. His eyes had widened. It was obvious he was an intelligent man, because he'd recognized the truth of the matter. "Do you mean…we've been kidnapped simply because this…Professor Fell person is searching for Rosabella's cousin?"

"*Impossibile!*" Madam Candoleri began to flare up again to fiery heights. "Such a thing would be utter madness! We were brought here for my ransom, and only that!"

Matthew decided that now was not the time to press the issue. He noted that the trio of guards had begun to listen in. "Whatever the professor's reasons are," he said, "I'm sure that once the ransom is paid, you'll all be on your way." He felt a twinge of shame at this utter lie, but he'd realized from the quick gleam of fear in the diva's eyes and the slightest quaver in her voice that she used her anger to mask a surprisingly fragile spirit, and she wore this mask as desperately as William Archer had worn his. She simply had to believe that a ransom demand had been made and the money would soon be delivered.

Di Petri, however, caught Matthew's eyes over the rim of his winecup, and a communication was sent: *I understand what you're saying, and she does too.*

Matthew said to the *signora*, "I don't know a lot about the opera, but I look forward to your performance." He stood up.

She wore a frozen expression. "The music may be supplied by two fiddle players, an accordionist, a girl who bangs the tambourine and a twelve-year-old boy who has had four lessons in blowing the trumpet, but otherwise it will be…how you say…spectacular."

"Goodnight," Matthew said to them both. Di Petri attended to his wine and the diva bowed her head the merest fraction of an inch.

Matthew took his lantern, left the Question Mark and stood in the square. The cold wind hissed and whooped around him. The village at this time of night seemed a peaceful place, only a few windows touched by the glow of candles, all the little houses much the same but for small differences in the stonework, no smell or sight of sewage, not a horse fig underfoot. It seemed a world away from the chaotic mess of London, and New York certainly did not lie this untroubled beneath the stars.

Untroubled? Matthew thought. Of course it was an illusion. This entire village was Professor Fell's mask. It presented him as a kindly ruler interested in the well-being of his subjects, who had all done something to either perturb him or draw his curiosity. This neat and clean prison might be Fell's idea of mercy, or his laboratory for further experiments on behalf of his enterprises. As for himself, Matthew was sure his days were numbered; he hoped he would still be alive in four days when Madam Candoleri took the stage. After Fell had wrung all the information he wanted from Archer, Albion was a dead man. And what of Berry and Hudson?

He nearly damned Hudson for bringing Berry into this, but he knew full well that Berry had blasted her way into that sea voyage. And here he was torn…he was distressed at her for being here, but obviously she loved him enough to put the terrible lies he'd spoken to her aside and risk life and limb to cross the Atlantic in search of him. Now, with both their deaths imminent, should he remove his own mask and tell her how much he loved her, and—if there was a minister somewhere in the Beautiful Grave—should he ask for her hand so that they might go together to the eternal?

He was sure that would give Professor Fell and Mother Deare quite the tears of sentimental joy, marching them out after the wedding night to chop their heads off in the square, or poison them with the wedding cake, or however Fell wished it to be done.

Matthew was also sure Fell would want to be looking into his eyes when the moment of murder came, and likely both Berry and Hudson would go first to accentuate the agony.

Damn, he thought.

He felt as powerless to alter the future as he was to reach out and throttle the wind. Nevertheless, on this quiet night in this village of drugged sleepers, it was rushing upon him with breakneck speed.

He gathered his cloak around his throat and walked back to the house on Lionfish Street. Wasn't a lionfish poisonous? He didn't know.

Inside the house, he found that his bag had been delivered containing the new suits and shirts Mother Deare had purchased for him. Atop the dresser in the bedroom, next to a waterbowl, was laid out a small tin of toothpowder, a few toothpicks, a cake of soap, a couple of fresh white washcloths and a straight razor.

Matthew knew Professor Fell was confident he wouldn't use the razor on his own throat before he saw Berry and Hudson and got some answers. But it would be nice to shave and clean up.

He noted also that he'd been brought a corked glass jug of water and a white drinking cup, sitting on the dresser along with the other items.

He would have to thank Professor Fell for the gracious hospitality, and he planned to do so on the morrow, face-to-face, with no masks between them.

Thirty-Four

THE sun was coming up and the sky promised to be a cloudless and most welcome blue. Matthew had been dressed in his gray suit and waistcoat and waiting for at least an hour. The bed was comfortable enough, but the discomfort of his mind had allowed him not quite three hours of sleep, none of it more than a quarter of an hour at a time.

As the light strengthened and moved across the floorplanks, Matthew remained in a chair in the front room. Through a window he could see people occasionally passing by. He wondered how the place was organized. Were there teams of workers? Were they occupied in such tasks as cleaning the streets, making repairs of walls and woodwork, going out in wagons to cut blocks of peat? Of course everything would be supervised by the guards, and if his assumption about the drugs was correct the workers would be easily handled. What did they do for food here? Was there space for gardens? Did the guards go out on hunting trips? There was the sea, if one could get fishing boats out in what sounded like waves crashing against treacherous rocks. Possibly there was a protected harbor nearby, or a beach from which the boats could be launched.

Matthew considered that Y Beautiful Bedd was quite an endeavor. On his cursory examination last night, it appeared the place had possibly been a medieval-era fortress. How had Professor Fell gotten hold of the place? Maybe it had simply been abandoned for many years, Fell had purchased the property—and how much of the surrounding land?—and rebuilt everything. It would certainly be within his power to do so. But the idea of keeping people here as his prisoners...it was, as Madam Candoleri had said, madness. Though with Professor Fell there was always a method, and what might be deemed madness to most was to him simply a means to an end.

Matthew was afraid.

He tasted the fear in his mouth like the most bitter of wines. He had stayed away from the bottle of water. His throat was hot with thirst. As he'd washed his face and shaved, using that same water, he wondered if he'd been contaminated in some way. The fear had gotten down in his chest, coiled around his heart and started crushing it. To be totally in Fell's grip was bad enough, but for Berry and Hudson to also be? And soon Judge Archer would be, if the coach carrying him had not already arrived sometime in the early hours, and him taken to a place without the fanfare of a greeting throng and an off-key band. Did they have a town cryer here who went around announcing the imminent arrival of new residents? And how was the news brought to the Beautiful Grave? By a series of fast horsemen who passed the messages along a certain route, was his guess.

Through the blur of his concentration he saw a figure approaching his door. The knock was delivered. Matthew's heartbeat quickened and he felt sweat on his palms. "Come in," he said thickly.

Julian Devane had been sent for him. The young blonde man wore a tobacco-brown cloak over his suit, and on his head was the dark green tricorn tilted at a rakish angle. This morning he did not offer the threat of a pistol but his face was unsmiling, the gray eyes chilly. "It's time," he said.

Matthew stood up from his chair. "The professor can wait. I want to see my friends."

"Naturally. I'm to take you to them. The girl first."

Matthew had been prepared for a test of wills. He was for a few seconds thrown off balance, but he realized that Fell was in no hurry to drive a spike through his brain.

"After you," said Devane, holding the door open.

Matthew put on his cloak and his own tricorn and left the house, walking into a morning in which the sun shone brightly but the cold wind carried a knife's edge. Devane walked a few paces behind him until they reached the square, and then he came up alongside to guide the direction. In the more revealing daylight Matthew could see the fortress wall of ancient and weathered stones that protected the village. Matthew counted six guards walking up on the parapets with shouldered muskets, but there could have been others out of sight. A large wooden gate could be seen at the end of a road about a hundred yards to the southeast, with what appeared to be a small guardhouse set off to the left. Nothing could be seen beyond the walls.

They passed into the square. Several people spoke good morning to Devane, but he ignored them. A wagon trundled past carrying a load of a dozen or so casks, but these were of a much smaller size than those that had held the White Velvet in the Broodies' hideaway. Was the drugged gin being created here? Such common casks could be made anywhere, but why were they differently-sized from the others? He saw a couple of women and a little boy at work sweeping the stones. Two men, both well-dressed and looking well-fed, stood before a shopfront marked with the sign General Goods. They were engaged in a conversation that might have been about the weather or the state of politics in Parliament, their faces ruddy with the cold but bearing no hint of dismay at being confined against their will within Fell's fortress.

On the other side of the square Devane herded Matthew onto a street that bore the sign of Redfin. Here the small cottages of slate roofs and thatched roofs spouted smoke from their chimneys and in some places there stood neat white picket fences separating one property from another. It appeared an idyllic setting, but there was not a single tree in sight and no birds sang.

A little further, they came upon a middle-aged woman in a blue bonnet and gown dancing in the street as if with an invisible partner. She was doing a slow, graceful movement Matthew knew to be called a minuet. The smile she offered to her ghostly companion was to Matthew nothing less than a horror. Her eyes appeared glazed over. She stopped her movements to bow into the wind.

"Keep walking," said Devane, for Matthew had slowed a step.

The woman began dancing once more. Matthew had noted that she was very thin, and the folds and ruffles of the gown hung off her frame. He wondered if what she'd been given had cursed her mind into believing she was in attendance at a dance that had no end, until she dropped dead from it.

"Here is the house," Devane announced, and motioned toward a thatched-roof cottage that had a frame of pale blue paint around the windows. He gave a tight and unfriendly smile. "I'll wait."

Matthew walked to the door. His heart was again hammering furiously in his chest. He balled up his fist to knock…

…and in the next instant the door came open and a coppery red-haired female of his dearest acquaintance threw herself into his arms. "I saw you coming!" Berry said breathlessly, her mouth up against his ear. "I couldn't wait! They told me someone was coming, and I was to stay here…but I would've been outside to meet you if I'd known…they told me to stay inside, I wasn't to—"

"Shhhhhh," he told her, and he put a finger against her lips and looked at her for the first time in over three months.

She appeared tired, with purplish hollows under her eyes and the dark blue of them also murky, like peering into shallow ponds that had been stirred up by the passage of heavy boots. Otherwise, he thought she was simply and unsurpassably beautiful. Her strong features, her finely-chiselled nose, her freckled cheeks, the wildness of her locks that seemed to have burst free with excitement from the bonds of several small and brightly-colored haircombs, the invigorating lemony scent of her, the warmth of her body and the nearness of her lips…he nearly staggered under the spin of what could only be called dizzying ecstacy. Then she crushed herself into him again, and he held tightly to her and they stood that way for a time, heart-to-heart, as their merged shadows lay behind them almost to the toes of Devane's shiny boots.

"Let's go inside," Matthew said, his voice both weakened and roughened with emotion. Tears had started to burn his eyes. He blinked them away, because they were tell-tales of his fear for Berry's life and he could not—must not—let her see them.

Her abode was not much different from his own, except she'd started a peat fire burning in the hearth. After Berry had closed the door behind them, Matthew just couldn't let go of her hands.

"I still can't believe this!" he said. "That you're here, and I'm here, and…oh my Lord, I'm so glad to see you!"

She hugged him again and he put his arms around her. Once more he felt dizzied with pure and soaring joy, and at the same time terribly frightened for her life.

"I'm sorry for those things I said to you," he told her. "Can you ever forgive me?"

"What things?" Berry asked, with her head resting against his shoulder.

"You know. The things I…well, never mind that, because we should let all that go. Just understand that I only said those things to keep you from harm."

"I do understand," she said. "I know you didn't want me to come here."

"If I'd had my way, neither one of you would've!" He looked into her face again. She was smiling a little wistfully, it seemed to him, and her eyes…they were very murky. He caught sight of a half-drained bottle of clear liquid—water and not the White Velvet, he assumed—on a table next to the entrance to the bedroom. A drinking cup sat beside the bottle.

"Listen," he said, "I'm not going to give up. I'm going to do what I can to get us out of here. You, me, Hudson, and…there's another person I'm going to try to get out too. So I know things look grim right now, and I wish to God you weren't in this situation, but I want you to be strong and brave and—"

"What *are* you talking about?" she asked, and she drew back a little ways.

"The situation!" he repeated. "Being here! I'm going to find a way to get all of us out! Where did they take Hudson?"

"They…" She frowned, and it seemed as if a shadow passed across the freckled, open face and for an awful instant he didn't recognize her. "I suppose he was taken to the house they were so kind to offer."

Matthew didn't reply. *So kind to offer.* He didn't like the sound of that. Her eyes…murky…unfocused…puddles of mud.

"Berry," he said, and he took hold of her shoulders. "Do you know where you are?"

"Of course, silly," she answered, with a lopsided grin that quickly slid off her face. "We're in a beautiful village in Wales. Where do *you* think we are, Ashton?"

His mouth made the word, but he heard it as though muffled through cotton. "*What?*"

"I said, where do *you* think we are?" She gave him a puzzled look, and then she hugged him again and gave him a sisterly kiss on the cheek. She retreated a few steps, leaving Matthew's hands gripping the air. "I cannot *believe* you found us, Ashton! And you came all that way…*why*? They told me last night that someone was coming to see me this morning, but I didn't know who it might be. Then…when I saw you through the window, I…I could hardly keep myself from rushing out. Did you leave New York just after we did? But tell me…really…I know you didn't want me to come here, and…yes…I do recall that you said you thought this trip a wild and dangerous endeavor, but…why did you feel the need to *follow* me?"

He wanted to shake her. Wanted to say *Look at me, and tell me who I am*, but he did not because again he was afraid. He thought he should be very careful now, very careful indeed, for as he looked at her he saw what appeared to be the quick flickering of many emotions across her face, like viewing the tumult of terrible storms at a distance. He glanced again at the bottle of water. Half-drained. How many others had she emptied? And now here stood before him the woman he loved, the woman he had finally realized he needed and wanted to be with, and she was a stumble and a shriek away from Bedlam.

She was seeing Ashton McCaggers when she looked at him, that much was clear. But why? Why *him*? What had the drug triggered in her brain that so clouded and distorted her vision?

He said, "So…" It was a moment before he could steady himself to go on. She was staring at him expectantly, and suddenly she reached out and took his right hand. If she was even able to see the tattoo between his thumb and index finger, she made no mention of it. "So," he repeated, "you haven't found..." God, to speak this meant that she really was afflicted, and this was no bizarre nightmare. He felt near bursting into tears. He had to make himself continue. "You haven't found Matthew?"

"No," she said, and both her voice and her eyes were sad. "Our friend here...he's an educator with a local university, I understand. His name is...Dr. Idris. Yes, that's right. He says he'll help us find Matthew. Hudson spoke to him."

"Hudson told you this?"

"No...another man told me. But he said Hudson had explained everything to Dr. Idris, and the doctor had promised to help us. I haven't met him, but he seems like a very good man to take such an interest."

"I'm sure." Matthew had spoken through clenched teeth. His stomach had lurched; he feared he was going to be sick all over this neat and tidy parlor. "Berry...please...tell me how it was you and Hudson came to this place."

"I had an accident in London," she said, with no hesitation. "I remember...falling. On a set of stairs, I believe. I think I struck my head. I remember travelling in a coach...I remember watching a fly on the wall in a room. I recall eating a bowl of beef broth. But I must've been dazed, quite a bit. My head didn't clear until I'd been here awhile."

"Did Hudson tell you that you'd suffered this accident?"

"No, another man did. The same man I told you about. His name is...oh, that's odd. I can see his face, but I can't think of his name. Well...I'm getting dotty, Ashton. I think I've been so worried about Matthew...I just can't keep all of it in my poor head anymore." She smiled at him, but it was terrible because he saw that her eyes were more dead now than when he'd first arrived. "How it happened...this woman knew Dr. Idris, and said not only could he give us shelter while I...you know...recuperated, but he knew many people and had many connections and he could help us find Matthew, but it might take some time. *Oh!*" she said suddenly, a startled sound that caused Matthew renewed alarm.

"What is it?"

"It's so strange. I thought for a moment you weren't wearing your spectacles."

Matthew had to look down at the floor. He said, "I'm very glad you were so excited to see me."

"I *still* can't believe you're here! That's another strange thing. This man…his name is…Danley? Daniel?…something…asked me who I would go to if Matthew was never found. He asked who I might find comfort in if…you know…Matthew was dead. I told him about you."

"Ah," Matthew said, a small noise.

"And then," she went on, "I began having the strangest dreams about you! It seemed I saw your face in my dreams every night. You came to me…telling me everything was going to be all right…to calm myself and trust in Mr. Daniel and Dr. Idris. I could see you as plain as day, sitting at my bedside, speaking to me. And here you are! Oh, Ashton!" she said, and she rushed herself into his arms again, but as she did a shiver rippled up Matthew's spine. "I'm so grateful to you for being here!"

"I presume," he replied, "that when you told this man about me…he asked you to describe me in detail. Is that correct?"

"I suppose so. Yes, he did. I *think*. Well, I'm sure I did."

"I'm sure," said Matthew.

"We shouldn't have to stay here too much longer. Just for me to get all well again. And while we're here Dr. Idris is going to help us. He knows many people and has many connections and he can help us find Matthew, but it might take some time."

"Yes," Matthew said, "it might." He pressed her close to him, and there were tears in his eyes again because he was going to have to let her go, and when he walked out of this damned bright sunlit cottage in this lovely cemetery he might break down on the street and he could not give Devane the satisfaction of seeing that. And Berry…dear God…what if Berry was lost to him forever?

That was a place he just could not allow himself to go.

"I need to see Hudson," he told her. "I'll come back a little later. All right?"

"Yes. Please. We can have dinner together at the tavern."

Matthew blinked the tears away before he kissed her cheek, and then he looked into her face but chose not to look too deeply, for the Berry he knew and loved was here in body, but in mind and spirit somewhere far distant. "Until later," he said with the best smile he could muster. He squeezed her hand, and then he pulled away from her and started for the door.

He was reaching for the knob when she said, "*Ashton?*"

Her voice quavered. There was something in it of the cliff's edge.

He turned toward her again. "Yes, Berry?"

Her smile flickered on and off. Did she have a slight sheen of perspiration upon her forehead? A wildness came up in her eyes and then quickly receded, for the afflicted mind could not grasp reality.

"I've never known you to call Hudson by his first name," she said. "Only 'Greathouse'."

He thought quickly, though his own mind seemed sluggish. "I'm trying to be less formal than my usual manner," he explained.

"Oh. I'm sure he'll be very pleased to see you."

"I hope." He smiled at her again, she returned the smile like that of a painted doll, and then he got out of the cottage and into the cold wind and brightness of the sun and Julian Devane stepped out of a shadow beside the house and said, "That was a short visit."

Matthew felt an animalish rage leap up within him. He tensed himself to spring at Devane's throat, to tear the eyes from the head, to use his teeth if need be to send the man to his well-deserved reward. The furies of Hell almost came out of him… almost…but Devane said with maddening calm, "Settle yourself, Matthew." He swept an arm along Redfin Street. "Your other New York friend is waiting."

Numbed, Matthew followed the direction of Devane's arm. What else could he do? He felt as much in chains here as he ever had in Newgate; even more so, for all this sunny brightness and blue sky was a hollow shell that seemed to confine everyone he gave a care about.

"Turn here," Devane said.

They turned to the left, onto the way marked with a sign of Conger Street. They were approaching the sea. Matthew saw instantly where they were headed, and had been so dazed by his encounter with Berry that he hadn't noticed above the other roofs the two-storied construction standing about sixty yards away, at what appeared to be the wall's northwestern edge. It was a squat square castle keep of a house, formed of the same stones as the wall and so blending into the larger picture, making Matthew think of a snakeskin camouflaged by the rocks around it. Numerous windows, some made of stained-glass, looked out upon the professor's realm. A balcony circled the upper floor. Upon it stood a dark-garbed figure whose hands gripped the railing. As Matthew and Devane neared, the figure turned away and disappeared through an arched doorway.

An iron gate was open at the bottom of a slight incline up to the house, the gravel pathway ornamented on both sides by small trees, contorted into windblown shapes, that had obviously been transplanted from somewhere else. Devane got in pace beside Matthew and steered him toward a main doorway at the top of a short set of five steps with an ornamental iron railing. He opened the sturdy-looking oak door without hesitation. "Enter," he said, and never had a single word filled Matthew with such dread.

Devane closed the door at Matthew's back. It was quiet in the house but for the ticking of a clock somewhere. There was the chalky smell of old stones and the hint of a sweeter, musky aroma that Matthew thought might be some kind of Oriental incense. He stood in a narrow hallway with walls painted sea green and lined with parchment prints of aquatic creatures in small black frames, all done in a scientific style with the different parts of the organism identified by their Latin nomenclature. Light entered through a window of clear glass at the end of the hallway and filtered in hues of yellow, red, and blue through stained-glass windows on the upper level. A black runner with dark blue swirls in it covered the polished floorboards, and just ahead was a staircase with the same color rug going up the risers. Two lanterns burned on a black lacquered table just within the entrance.

"Take one of those and follow me," said Devane. He picked up a lantern, as did Matthew, and led the way past the staircase to another door off to the right.

"I thought I was going to see Hudson Greathouse," Matthew said, as Devane opened the door and a musty dungeon smell wafted out.

"You are."

"What, he's being kept down *there*?"

"He's being kept," said Devane, his face expressionless, "where he can't hurt himself."

Matthew's throat tightened. "What's been done to him?"

"Come along," Devane said, and started down a set of stone steps so narrow Matthew wondered how they'd gotten Hudson's big-shouldered body down them.

Though he was both seething and terrified inside, Matthew again had no choice but to follow. He thought he could smash Devane in the head with the lantern he held, but what good would that do? None whatsoever. He docilely descended the stairs.

At the bottom, there was a stone-floored circular chamber dimly illuminated by a single lantern burning on a wallhook. The lamps Matthew and Devane carried helped, but to Matthew it seemed that the dark, damp walls absorbed light. Four wooden doors were set equidistantly around the chamber. Each door had a slot through which a tray of food could be delivered, and a small viewport about head-high that could be unbolted, the covering square of wood pivoted out, and an observation made of the prisoner within the cell. Currently all the ports were closed.

Devane approached the first door on their left. Matthew stopped.

"Come on," the man said. "You wanted to see him, didn't you?"

Matthew couldn't get his legs moving. His face felt like a lump of clay. If this was not the worst nightmare of his life he needed no other any more terrible, for he knew Hudson was in that cell and it was not going to be a pleasant sight, and he was completely and totally powerless to help his friend.

Devane unbolted the port and stepped aside. "Have a look," he said.

Matthew moved forward.

All was dark within the windowless cell. He shone his lamp in and angled his head to see.

The walls were covered by some kind of thick, gray padded material. The floor, the same. There was a bare mattress on the floor. There was evidence that the occupant of this cell had been allowed to lie in his own filth. There was a bundle of rags in a corner.

Then when the light touched the bundle of rags it shivered and moved. A voice whimpered, like that of a child facing a brutal lash.

"Hudson," said Matthew. "I've—"

The figure began to try to winnow itself under the mattress. Matthew caught sight of both hands clasped to the face, and as he watched the bare feet and legs work desperately to push the body beneath the mattress either he or the man in that cell gave a heart-wrenching moan that sounded torn from the very throat of a soul damned by all the demons of Hell.

"He's afraid of the light," said Devane. "He's afraid of voices. Afraid of his own name. Afraid of most everything, really."

Matthew spun upon the man. He felt his lips draw back from his teeth in a grotesque rictus. His face was afire. There was nothing in his mind but the desire to kill the bastard who stood so calmly before him.

Devane took a backward step, his eyes heavy-lidded. Before Matthew could leap to the attack, Devane said, "Professor Fell will see you now."

Thirty-Five

"Did you hear what I said?"

Matthew's eyes had been searching the walls, looking for hooks where the keys to these cells might be kept.

"The keys are not down here," said Devane, correctly inferring what Matthew was after. "Shall we go? He's waiting for you."

Matthew gritted his teeth so hard the muscles in his jaw jumped and nearly locked. As his rage settled he reckoned he didn't have enough teeth left to spare in grinding the rest of them into powder. The fire in his face abated, but his head and heart still pounded with the horror of what he'd seen in that cell.

Devane closed the viewport and slid the bolt home. "Better for him to remain in the dark," he said. "After you, please."

Matthew climbed the stairs, with Devane right behind him. In the hallway the man took Matthew's lantern and put them both on the table where they'd been. "Upstairs," came the command. Matthew obeyed as if he truly had no mind nor will of his own.

On the upper level, another corridor led between several closed doors. Again on the walls were hung the framed prints of marine creatures. At the end of the corridor was an open doorway. Matthew could see in that room a large window and beyond it the cloudless blue of the sky. He kept going, step after step, his boots making hardly a noise on the black runner, and then he crossed the threshold into what he knew was the professor's inner sanctum.

It was, as he'd expected, an intellectual's heaven of what must've been at least three hundred books on dark oak shelves. On the floor the black runner had given way to an intricately-woven Persian rug that was swirled with the many colors of the sea in many conditions of light: deep blue, blue-green, pale green, dark gray and light gray, a violet that edged toward ebony. From the ceiling's thick rafters hung a black wrought-iron chandelier holding eight tapers and shaped like an octopus, each tentacle holding a candle. The room's oak walls must have been scrubbed down with some kind of polishing wax, from the way they glistened, and upon them were various framed etchings of sea creatures... yet they were the aquatic beasts of nightmare and fable, for here a tremendous creature with a fifty-foot-long sword at its snout was impaling a longboat as the crewmen jumped for their lives, and there a leviathan of a kraken was enfolding a three-masted ship toward the massive, gaping spear-toothed mouth at its center. A section of one wall held shelves upon which rested a collection of jars of fish, crabs, small squids, mollusks and the like—Rosabella's "fishy things"—preserved in a smoky amber liquid.

A door to the right of the room led out onto the balcony, which was at a height just above the fortress wall. A brass telescope was aimed at the vast expanse of the sea. Sunlight glittered on the ocean's surface, throwing sparks into Matthew's eyes.

And there in the center of the room, his back to the window, sat a man at a writing desk with ornamental diamond shapes carved into the front. Two black leather armchairs for the comfort of visitors were situated before the desk. The man was scribing something with a quill in a ledger book open before him on a green blotter.

He had not looked up as the two others had entered, but continued his writing.

Devane made no sound. Neither did Matthew. A passing flock of seagulls caught Matthew's attention and his gaze followed them out of sight. From here he could see upon the ocean to his left what appeared to be a couple of small fishing boats moving with the swells.

The man still did not lift his face, but his slender left hand made a quick gesture that meant *away*. Devane left the room, closed the door, and Matthew was alone with Professor Fell.

Matthew's host was wearing a black silk robe trimmed with gold down the front and at the cuffs. Though the room needed no more light than that of the sun, a single candle burned in a pewter holder next to his right hand. The scribing went on as if no one else was in the room.

Matthew called up what remained of his courage. He turned his back on the professor, walked to the shelves and began examining this absolutely wonderful collection. In a matter of seconds he took in such titles as John Locke's *An Essay Concerning Human Understanding*, Roger L'Estrange's *Fables*, Ned Ward's *A Trip To New England* and *A Trip To Jamaica*, several astrological almanacs, Cotton Mather's *Wonders Of the Invisible World*, and...

Had he made a sound, or had he imagined doing so? Because the volume his gaze had settled upon, bound in cracked, dark brown leather with faded gold lettering upon the spine might have brought forth from him a small exclamation.

The title was *The Lesser Key Of Solomon*.

He realized it was the third copy of this particular work that he'd seen in connection with Professor Fell. The last one he'd come upon was in Fell's library on Pendulum Island.

He had looked through the volume there, on the island, and found it to be a book that described in great and horrendous detail the demonic royalty of Hell.

Those pages held the Latin script and elaborate woodcuts that depicted hideous combinations of man, beast, and insect as might be created from the seething rage of the underworld to war against the power of Heaven. He recalled some of the names of the demons, which were given titles as befitted such nightmarish nobility: Duke Ashtaroth, Count Murmur, King Zagan, Prince Seere, Marquis Andras, King Belial and on and on through descriptions of the specialties of these infernaradoes, such as the deliverer of madness, the king of liars, the destroyer of cities, the reanimator of the dead and the corruptor of the dignity of men.

He remembered also that within the cracked binding, which itself resembled the snakelike skin of a horned demon, were spells and rituals written out to call these monstrosities from their caverns to do the bidding of men.

The Lesser Key Of Solomon.

A guidebook to summoning demons, with detailed descriptions of their powers.

This…the third copy…

He suddenly heard in his mind the voice of Mother Deare, speaking about Fell's interest in finding Brazio Valeriani.

Valeriani possesses information the professor needs. It has not to do with marine life, but…in a way it does involve the deeps.

Matthew's hand had reached out to take the book, but now he held it just short of the devil's snakeskin.

He thought…*the deeps?*

How much deeper could one descend than to the gates of Hell itself?

"Have you found a book you wish to read?"

The voice, as silken as the robe, was right behind him.

Matthew hesitated. He lowered his hand, took a breath and released it, and then turned to face Professor Fell.

Just as Professor Fell had said at their first meeting on Pendulum Island that Matthew was younger than he'd expected, now Matthew found that Fell was older than he'd thought…or, at least, the wages of the man's life had been paid in the currency of years. Matthew had assumed from the voice behind the automaton's mask that Fell was in his late forties or early fifties, but now it appeared he was closer to sixty, from the hollows of the eyes, the fine lines around them and across the forehead, and from the whiteness of his cropped cap of hair, which was allowed to bloom out in tight curls on either side of his head like the wings of a snowy owl.

The professor was indeed a mulatto, his skin the color of creamed coffee. He was very slender, almost frail in appearance, and stood two inches taller than Matthew, who was himself nearly six feet. But even if Fell's age was in the vicinity of fifty-eight to sixty or so, the man's presence was in no way softened by the approach of those golden years in which a regular man might be assumed to crawl into an easy chair with pipe and slippers and be waited upon by doting grandchildren. No, this man stood a far cry from the scene of loving relatives gathered around the home hearth.

Fell's shoulders might be a fraction stooped and the hands he held clasped before him lined with blue veins, but in his long-jawed and high-cheekboned face, which might be also described as gaunt, there resided the tiger in repose. Or, more fitting to the professor's interest, the slowly circling shark. His thin-lipped smile hung between humor and cruelty and showed the faintest glint of teeth. But it was his eyes in their dark hollows, like luminous orbs in fleshy caverns, that truly communicated to Matthew Corbett the persona of the man who stood before him.

They were the same smoky amber color as the liquid in the specimen jars, yet they were also aflame. They were the eyes of a highly-intelligent and gifted man who had given his life to the pleasure and achievement of academics and found his life changed forever by brutality, and thus in revenging himself upon brutality had become brutal, and been both consumed by its voracious maw and reshaped by its twisted guts. They were the wary, dagger-sharp eyes of a man who had fancied himself passive but who perhaps had always secreted the seeds of violence and the desire for power from youth, and who had suddenly been thrust into a situation where those seeds not only grew into misshapen trees of barbed thorns but entire forests of them. They were the eyes of a supremely civilized man who had released his most primitive reptilian force upon both himself and his world, and perhaps those lines and appearance of age in his faintly-smiling face were the marks of the battlefield his soul had crossed.

Professor Fell was in essence, Matthew thought, a man who had decided that to live he must die, and in dying live. Was the murder of his son Templeton on a London street the only motive for a brilliant academic to find salvation in savagery? Possibly not; possibly the murder had simply hastened the speed of a long-burning fuse, and the man who had lived in the confines of law and order found such existence a prison, his only chance for freedom the taking up of a mask of power that would forever separate him from the world in which loved ones celebrated a life well-lived.

No one loved this man, Matthew thought. They feared and respected him, yes, but never would he know love...and those burning, smoky amber-colored eyes of Professor Fell told Matthew he had cast off the desire for that cloak of honor long ago, and now he wore the black robe of the bad man for it was all he had.

The professor awaited an answer.

Matthew had to steel himself a little further before he could reply. Then he said, "I wouldn't know where to begin."

The gaze moved past Matthew, and Matthew was certain it locked upon *The Lesser Key* before it returned to him.

"Come sit down," said the professor. "Let's have a nice visit." He turned away, went back to the writing-desk, sat down and waited as if about to interview an applicant for the job of groundskeeper.

Matthew removed his tricorn and cloak. He laid the garment over the back of one of the chairs and then eased himself into the seat as one might lower his body onto a bed of spikes. He kept the tricorn in his lap, a most uncertain shield against swordpoint or pistol ball.

"I am *so* glad to see you, Matthew," Fell said silkily. "You look fit enough, though a bit thin. Mother Deare tells me you've been through some hard weather. Newgate Prison...the Black-Eyed Broodies...nice mark on your hand there, by the way...and a little visit by a moony dentist. But you're a survivor, aren't you? Yes, you are. And to be admired for that."

Matthew almost said *thank you*, but he held his tongue.

"I was just about to call for a slice of vanilla cake and a cup of tea. May I offer you the same?"

Matthew decided there was no more use for caution. "Laced with what drug?" he asked.

"Is powdered sugar a drug? The vanilla bean? Flour? Oh, some consider oolong tea to be a drug, of course. Is that your meaning?"

"You know my meaning."

"I know that you'll have to eat and drink *something*, at some time or another, or you will wither away. Why not start here, in my company?"

"I'd rather not."

Fell's smile, which had been soft, now sharpened. More glint of teeth showed. "How do you think dying of thirst and hunger will help your two friends?"

"Is there any help to be had for them?"

"Your third friend is here," Fell said. "He arrived this morning around four o'clock. The good Judge Archer, also known as—excuse my little laugh—*Albion*."

Matthew thought that now was time to throw his own poisoned dart. "Next you'll be telling me you've found Brazio Valeriani and he's been put into the dish closet."

Fell was silent. His smile began to fade.

Matthew followed this jab with, "I presume Rosabella told you where to find him? Madam Candoleri said she was very impressed with this room."

After a silence, the professor said, "You *do* get around, don't you? The problem-solver at work? My providence rider still astride his dead steed? It did you proud to destroy my house and my work on Pendulum Island, didn't it? Destroyed my *heritage*, is what you did."

"I think I just stopped you from destroying many thousands of English men and women with that gunpowder," Matthew answered. "Your house and heritage happened to be in the way."

His face clouded, the professor started to say something but then stopped himself. He nodded, his gaze on a vacant distance. He rose smoothly from his chair, went to one of the walls and tugged a bellpull twice. From the hallway beyond the closed door came the double sound of the bell. Then he returned to his chair, opened a drawer of his desk and drew out several items: a saucer, a knife with a hawkbill-shaped serrated blade, a small white card, a piece of blue cloth and finally a little glass vial containing an inch-depth of what appeared to be blood.

"I want you to witness this," said the professor. He spent a moment using the hooked blade to scrape away wax that gave the vial's stopper an air-tight seal. Then he put the knife aside and from the opened vial poured just a dab of blood onto the saucer.

Matthew knew full well what he was witnessing. Professor Fell was about to create a blood card, his vow of death to whomever received it.

Fell pressed the index finger of his right hand into the blood. The finger then pressed upon the card. Fell wiped his finger clean with the cloth and then held the card up with its bloody print for Matthew's approval. "Like it?" he asked.

"Seen one, seen them all," said Matthew.

"True, but the person to whom this is being sent has never seen one. You know him. His name is Gardner Lillehorne."

Though he felt it like a bellyblow, Matthew made sure he revealed no impact of emotion. "What's he done?"

"Oh...you didn't know? Well, it's a trifling thing, *you* might say. His first task upon arriving in London was to rouse the High Constable to undertake a search of warehouses on the docks. I presume that someone told you a shipment of Cymbeline was stored there, pending sale to Spain, and you passed that information on as soon as you were able. I can guess who squealed the tale. So a similar card will be travelling across the Atlantic to the door of Miss Minx Cutter, and she will be made to pay—as Mr. Lillehorne will—for the seizure of a fortune's worth of *my* gunpowder."

Matthew remembered. Fell was correct. Minx had told him the specialized gunpowder that Fell had created was being hidden in a warehouse and disguised as barrels of tar and nautical supplies. He had informed both Lillehorne and Lord Cornbury when he'd gotten back to New York but thought at that time the message had received only a shrug and a cold shoulder from two personages who wished not to become involved.

"I also gave Lillehorne the names of Frederick Nash and Andrew Halverston," Matthew said, citing other information Minx had given him about a pair of influential and seemingly-upstanding London figures—one in Parliament and the other in the money trade—who were on Fell's payroll. "Are they in Newgate yet?"

Fell laughed quietly, as if he appreciated Matthew's sense of daring in the face of doom. "The first is here, with a new position as mayor of Y Beautiful Bedd in my absence. The second...alas, poor Andrew blew his brains out with a pistol shot when Julian failed to convince him to seek refuge here."

"Oh, you mean to say that Andrew blew his brains out when Devane pulled the trigger for him?"

"It is his pleasure to serve."

"I thought his master was Mother Deare. Where is *she*?"

"Still here, for a time. And...since I am the master—let us say, *guidance*—of Mother Deare, I am also the guidance of Julian Devane. Ah! Here's our repast!" There had been a knock at the door. "Come in."

Speaking of the devil, it was Devane himself who brought in the silver tray bearing two plates of white cake, silverware, two green ceramic cups and a small silver teapot bearing the filigree of—as Matthew saw when the tray came nearer—a dragon with a pair of smooth jade stones as its eyes.

"Right here is fine," Fell said, indicating a place on the writing-desk. "If I need you again, I'll ring."

Devane left the room without a word or a glance at Matthew.

"I said I wanted nothing," Matthew objected, as Fell poured two cups. The teapot was only large enough to hold that much.

"Humor me. You will notice I am pouring both cups from the same pot and you are watching very carefully."

"*No*," said Matthew.

"All right, then. Have a piece of the cake."

"Certainly not."

Fell shrugged and took a sip from his cup. "Back to the card for a moment. It might interest you to know that Mr. Lillehorne is receiving a bloodprint made with *your* blood. It was taken from your mouth on an occasion during which, in Mother Deare's words, you 'went all hazy'. And by the way, we do have a good physician here who can also take care of the teeth…you might want to make an appointment with him, just to make sure Noddy cleaned up after himself."

Matthew watched Fell drink his tea. The professor chose one of the pieces of cake and began to eat it very delicately. "What's in the Velvet?" Matthew asked.

"What you already know. A narcotic from the late Dr. Jonathan Gentry's notebook of fascinating formulas. We have a greenhouse full of useful botanicals here. The dosage is being increased as time moves along. It's as much of an experiment as a business."

"It seems to be you've stirred someone else's interest in the business. Mother Deare told you what happened in that warehouse?"

"She did." Fell's mouth became a grim line. "There is some… let me be a gentleman and call him an *upstart*…who has come upon the territory—*my* territory—with obviously great ambitions. That was not the first cache of White Velvet to be stolen, and not the first of my helpers murdered to get it. Whoever did this also murdered my associate Judge Jackson Fallonsby and his entire family. He is taunting me, just as your Albion did by murdering other members of my...shall we say...circle. But this new man, if I may use that term lightly, leaves an interesting mark on the foreheads of his victims... the mark of a demoniac."

"A demoniac?" Matthew asked, having never heard that term before.

"Someone who either is or believes himself to be possessed by a demon."

"What do you mean, 'is'? Such a thing isn't possible."

The twisted smile on the professor's hollow-cheeked face was frightening. "Oh, Matthew!" he said. "What you saw in London... in that warehouse...and what you've seen elsewhere in your experience...and *you* say such a thing isn't possible? Even your Bible says it is. If you were my son, I would say...*grow up*."

"The closest to a demon on earth I can think of is yourself." Matthew was near mentioning *The Lesser Key*, but for the moment he restrained himself.

"You may find to your educated horror," said the professor, "that as bad as you feel me to be, I am far from the worst."

"Debatable." Matthew's head had begun to ache and his mouth was a dry sandpit. He was thirsty and hungry but he didn't dare take any of the tea or cake. "I want to know more about the Velvet. It's made here?"

"No, we produce the drug here. Or, rather, my very talented new chemist produces it. In the laboratory at the hospital, if you'd care to know...which you *always* do. The gin is purchased as any dealer would, through a middleman in London. We add the narcotic there, and the gin is stored for later delivery. I did *not* come up with that title of White Velvet. I think Lord Puffery did. My appreciation to him."

Matthew felt a bit satisfied that he knew one secret Fell did not. "Your new chemist must be a busy man. I take it that this entire village is a laboratory in which to test Gentry's formulas?"

"Exactly. Also a place for new drugs to be created and tested, and a refuge for those associates whom I deem worthy. You're certain you don't wish any tea or cake?"

"I wish Berry Grigsby and Hudson Greathouse to be returned to normal," Matthew said.

Professor Fell drank down the rest of his tea. He took a small bite of the cake, and then he leaned back in his chair and smiled at the overhanging octopus before he returned his gaze to Matthew and spoke again.

"After Pendulum Island," he said quietly, his face calm but the fire smoldering in the amber eyes, "I spent much time considering how I would deal with you when I found you. And not *if* I found you, but when. I knew...someday, in some way, I would get hold of you again. I considered...drastic things. Drawing and quartering, emasculation and consumption of your own organs, the death of a thousand cuts, death by crushing, strangulation or drowning...or, simply, being tortured nearly to death and then having your head cut off bit by bit starting with pieces of your face. Oh, I spent much time thinking of all the possible ways, Matthew...but one thing I did *not* think of." He paused for a few seconds, smiling.

"I did not think," he continued, "that I would be so fortunate as to get hold of your two friends *before* I got hold of you. That has made all the difference. It has calmed me, as you can see perfectly well."

"I see a monster sitting at a writing-desk," said Matthew, who reached up with both hands to rub his temples. His head felt oddly swollen. "You're going to kill me and I can't stop you. But for God's sake let those two go. Do whatever you want to me, but—"

"I *am* doing what I want to you," the professor interrupted. "Don't you grasp it yet? The volume Gentry left me contains a king's wealth of information on various narcotics and poisons, most of which can be manipulated for different effects. For instance, three seeds of a particular botanical—crushed, put into food or liquid and given on a twice-daily basis—will cause certain death after a period of so many days. But *one* seed of that same botanical, crushed and applied every *other* day, will have an entirely different effect. So it is with many of the formulas in Gentry's book. A poison is not necessarily deadly unless one *wishes* it to be. Which...in the cases of Miss Grigsby and Mr. Greathouse, I do not wish."

Matthew's head had really begun pounding. His tongue had gone numb. In his chest his heart had started beating so madly he feared it might burst asunder.

"You've colored up," Fell said. "I was wondering when it would begin. Listen carefully, now."

"You've pitched a rug out from toomey!" Matthew said, and heard that gobbledygook with his ears, yet in his mind he'd spoken the words *You've given something to me.*

"Hush. *Listen.*" Fell leaned forward in his chair. "Your reward for what you have done to me is to watch your friends be destroyed. Now, now...I wouldn't advise trying to get up. Your brain's sense of speech and sense of reality have been affected, though your hearing has been spared. If you attempt to leave this room you may find yourself climbing over the balcony's railing thinking you're getting on a horse like a good providence rider. *Listen*, I said."

"Zoned see," said Matthew. *Poisoned me.* His mouth weighed three hundred pounds, all gigantic swollen lips and pillow-sized tongue.

"The water in your cottage is extremely potent. But not by drinking. By absorption into the skin, and I know such a gentleman as yourself likes to wash his face in the mornings. Your hands too, I'm sure. It did take longer than I thought. We're still testing this one."

"Shine!" said Matthew, whose mind now lost any idea of what he was trying to say. The room had begun to spin and widened out to huge distances. Three Professor Fells sat in three chairs behind three writing-desks at its center.

"Sit still. Let me continue. Mr. Greathouse has been given what I call an *essential timoris.* The essence of fear. Give him that and while he's slumbering in its embrace have someone recite to him a frightful tale. When he awakens, he lives the nightmare. If he wasn't given the drug daily, he would revive back to normalcy in three or four days." The Fells lifted three index fingers that in Matthew's distorted vision shot up to be iron spears reaching to the limitless ceiling. "As to Miss Grigsby, she's been given an interesting potion using the Jamestown weed that opens her mind to suggestion and has a steadily cumulative effect. She is lost to you forever, because even if the dosage ceased today—which it will not—she would fail to recover without vigorous and steady application of the antidote." His triple grins to Matthew were the keyboards of spinet pianos, and amber-colored spiders squirmed in the eyeholes of his faces. "You are going to watch her decline into imbecility," said the professors. "In the end, she will revert to being an infant in a cradle, and I may let you rock her from time to time."

Matthew tried to rise from the chair. He was no longer sitting in a chair. He was encased in a tarpit, his movements caught by its ebony glue.

"Before you get any worse," the Fells said, "you should eat your cake. The antidote is in it."

With the greatest effort against the sticky tar that now seemed to have gathered from air that was blotched like leprosy, Matthew reached out for the piece of vanilla cake that sat on the middle desk of the three desks before him. His arm went on and on, his hand becoming as small as that of a child's poppet. His fingers, a mile away, spouted spikes. His hand closed around the cake, which came to life like a vicious little animal and tried to bite the spiked digits, as Fell's three faces ballooned larger and combined one into the other to make a swollen, knotty mass. Matthew wasn't sure if he had actually grasped the cake or not, for his fingers were dead. Then he brought the squirming thing to his face and instead of finding his mouth it went into his eyes and nose.

"I wish Dr. Ribbenhoff were here to see *this*," said the talking wart.

Matthew frantically worked to get some of the cake into his mouth, and he thought he'd succeeded...or he *imagined* that he thought he had. He kept pushing the stuff in with his spiky fingers. Swallowing took another effort. Around him all the colors of the room were running together, the sunlight came from a different world where the sun was blindingly red with a pulsing blue halo around it, and the tarpit was dragging him under.

"Close your eyes," said the gnarled and faceless monstrosity that had begun to grow to massive size. It spread out tentacles that cracked in the stained air like bullwhips.

Matthew did. Under his eyelids his eyes stared back at him.

"You will need about half an hour. I'll ring for Julian to take you to a room where you can lie down. I wanted you to understand how useless it is to resist...even a little bit. Nod your head if you understand."

Matthew nodded. He felt his head topple from his neck and swing back and forth on the wires that were holding him together, because at that moment he realized he was a boneless construction not born of flesh but created by Professor Fell, who now had the power to take him apart.

"When you return to your cottage you'll find a fresh and full bottle of water. Drink as much of it as you can. It will be *only* water. I want you in good condition to have dinner here tonight at eight. You and Judge Archer will be my honored guests."

Matthew felt the tentacles around him, gripping his upper body with crushing force while the tarpit trapped his lower body to the waist.

A bell rang.

"You should've had the cake straight away," said the voice beside his left ear. "You see what being stubborn gets you?"

Thirty-Six

So it was, Matthew thought as he lay on the bed in his cottage, that the worst of the worst had come about. All he'd feared for Berry had come true...and even more horrifying, he was too late to do anything about it. Where was Gentry's book of formulas? In Fell's house or in the hospital, under the watch of this new chemist Ribbenhoff? Even if he could get the book, how could he produce the antidote for the drug in Berry's system?

He lay staring at the ceiling. His head still ached and his body was occasionally wracked by a tremor, but at least he didn't see the walls as bulging and cracking with the onslaught of unseen monsters as they'd been in the room at the professor's house. When Devane had guided him back here, Matthew had taken down nearly half of the fresh bottle of water. He wondered if it also had been drugged in some way he didn't yet know. He was absolutely defenseless against any potion Fell chose to experiment on him.

And what of Hudson? In that dark cell, his mind being torn apart by nightmarish terrors...it was the proverbial fate worse than death, particularly for such a man of strength. Add to this recipe of calamities the capture of Judge Archer, and the torments Fell surely had in store for Albion, and…it was hopeless.

Matthew pressed his palms into his eyes. He had to *think*, though his brain was mushy. What was it he could possibly do to dig them all out of the beautiful grave? Before releasing him, Fell had sent word by way of Devane to go to the tavern and get something substantial to eat after his head had cleared, but food was the last thing on Matthew's mind. He dreaded the dinner tonight. What time was it now? He fumbled in his pocket and brought out the watch. Nine minutes after three. He wished to go see Berry again, because she was expecting Ashton McCaggers to go to dinner with her this evening at the tavern, but he couldn't bear to know that she was unable to recognize him, and he thought that in her state of mind the presence of Ashton in her cottage this morning already seemed to her like a dream she'd had last night.

He asked himself once again, what possible weapon did he have to draw upon? Was the situation indeed hopeless, or had he yet to see how the pieces stood upon the chessboard? He could not give up. No. They might all be doomed anyway, but to give up would be an early death he wasn't prepared to endure.

What was it that Professor Fell valued, that Matthew might yet seize hold of?

Matthew's brain continued to work, if thrashing about like a squirrel in a cage could be considered so.

A word came to him. *Information.*

The professor valued information. Particularly concerning one subject.

The whereabouts of Brazio Valeriani.

He sat up. His head spun for a few seconds and then settled itself.

He thought…if he could find out something from Valeriani's cousin Rosabella that Fell did not know…that might be the weapon he needed.

It might be worth going to the tavern. If Madam Candoleri was there, all the better; if not, surely someone could tell him where she was. Or she might be at the theater, wherever that was, rehearsing her program. If he could find Di Petri, that would also serve him well, or he might just stumble upon the makeup girl herself.

In any case, he was doing himself, Berry, Hudson and Judge Archer no good in hiding himself here. He felt able to walk now without staggering like a drunken fool. He stood up to test his legs. They were weak but they held him up. He walked to the wall and back again. Maybe he still couldn't walk a straight line yet, but what mobility he had was all he required.

He put on his cloak and his tricorn and left the house.

At the Question Mark, the barkeep told Matthew he had no idea what cottage the diva occupied, but of course Matthew knew the man was lying. Fell's people were not going to make anything easy for him. The barkeep did tell Matthew that the meeting hall was on Thresher Street just past Redfin and there Madam Candoleri's performance would be given tomorrow night.

Matthew headed off against the wind. Passersby greeted him as if he was already part of the community, their smiles offered below drug-hazed eyes. On the way to Thresher Street he got an idea of some of the communal activities here. He took note of a house with a sign proclaiming it to be Madam Hennischild's School Of Art. Another house was marked Y Beautiful Bedd Basketweavers' Society. And still another, just down from the basketweavers, John Mayes' Stargazers Club. He figured the gardening guild and the bubble-blowers bunch would be somewhere near as well. He passed a shed under which three men were jovially occupied in making the small casks Matthew had earlier seen on the wagon, and he half-expected to see a sign marking the territory of the cooper confederation.

The pair of guards Matthew spotted on patrol with their muskets against their shoulders, however, looked anything but clubby.

He wondered if there had been any instance of someone suddenly coming out of their trance, or having a delayed violent reaction to some potion they'd been given. That might call for a musket ball or two, depending on the circumstances. Matthew shuddered to think that Gentry's book of poisons and formulas, gathered evidently from the botanicals of many countries, might include one that gave a human being an enraged super-strength.

The theater was not hard to find. Though still single-storied, it was a larger structure of weatherworn brown stones that was not a barn, as the madam had so disdained it, but may at one time have been a church, for the belltower atop the roof. Matthew went up two steps to the oaken door and opened it. He stepped into an anteroom where cloaks and hats could be hung.

"Can you not play one single clean *note*?" shouted the thunder before the storm. "*Mi fai cosi pazzo io esplodere!* Giancarlo, make these *idioti* understand the English!"

Matthew entered the main chamber. Light entered through two windows, one on each side of the building, that were probably recent additions. A dozen pews with aisles in the center, on the right and the left faced an upraised platform that appeared to have been newly constructed, for the wood was still green. Steps led up on the right. A colorful and expensive-looking rug had been laid down over the platform's floor. The beautiful but terrifying madam was standing at its center, wearing a voluminous purple gown, her black hair piled high and glittering with golden combs, her hands on her hips and her eyes shooting fire at her poor orchestra.

They sat at the foot of the platform in chairs that had been brought in for the occasion. Music stands had been supplied to hold copies of the score. There were the two fiddle players Matthew had seen in the square and the twelve-year-old boy who'd taken four trumpet lessons, and all of them were clinging to their instruments as if the items might be blown out of their hands. The accordionist and the tambourine girl likely had jumped ship, for they were nowhere to be seen. Matthew did see Di Petri sitting in the front row, along with the person he'd hoped to find: a dark-haired girl who must be the reason Fell had brought them here.

Di Petri was getting up to place himself in harm's way between the lady and her targets of wrath. "Please, Alicia!" he said, holding up his hands in a manner of appeasement. "They're doing their best! Won't you—"

"Their best is *un grande mucchio di merda*!" she shrieked. "How can I sing to such garbage of a noise?"

"Lady," said one of the fiddlers, "I just can't play these notes. There're too many of 'em." He gave an exasperated sigh and got up from his chair. It seemed to Matthew that, even though the men—and likely the boy too—were held in the warm embrace of some happy narcotic, they had all come to the end of their witless smiles. "I can't speak for Noah or Alex, but I believe I'm past done to well-done and near burnt alive. I'm headin' for home."

"Noah can speak for himself," said the second fiddle-player, also getting to his feet. "Right as rain. I'm goin'."

"You cannot walk out on me!" she shot back. "I am one of three females in this entire *world* who sings the opera! Do you know how hard I have worked and what I have done to earn my place among the ball-less men with the child voices?" A quaver of desperation entered. "What am I to do for the *music*?"

The boy had stood up and was following the others to the door. He turned back, trumpet in hand, and he said in the lofty tone of someone much older than he appeared, "Perhaps you can find someone who hums."

Then the three musicians left the theater and did not witness Madam Alicia Candoleri grab at the air as if trying to tear holes in it. Matthew was sure however that the three did hear her scream of outrage; he felt sure Lady Puffery would be reporting in the next *Pin* the sound of a shrieking meteor heard across Wales as it sizzled into the Atlantic.

"*Caro Signore,*" said Di Petri. "Let us all take this one step at the time."

"It is insane crazy madness!" the lady fumed, as she stalked back and forth. "I have not even the dressing room! Am I expected to—" The red mist of her anger must have lifted a bit, for she stopped her pacing and pointed at Matthew. "Do you get a good laugh out of this, mister?"

"Not at all." Matthew removed his tricorn. "I have empathy for everyone involved."

"*In pathy?* What is this he's saying, Giancarlo?"

"He feels sorry for us," said Di Petri, a little too bluntly and incorrectly.

She began looking around, it seemed to Matthew, for something to throw. "*Gloom!*" she shouted, and Matthew thought for an instant she was going to start tearing her own hair out. "*Disperazione! Agonia su di me!*"

Matthew strolled down the left side aisle. He glanced quickly toward Rosabella, who was watching him, and had the impression of a pretty oval-shaped face, large brown eyes and an expression of bewilderment. She was younger than he'd surmised, maybe seventeen at most.

"Pardon me," Matthew said when he reached the platform, "but do you really need an orchestra?"

"Of course I do! Are you mad? What is an opera without the music?"

"Well," he answered quietly, "doesn't the music come from *you*?"

Madam Candoleri gave a strangled sound, indicating she did not follow his line of reasoning. Her hands rose up as claws, her teeth clenched together and Matthew feared that when she threw herself off the platform at him there would be blood.

"Alicia! *Ascoltatelo!*" said Di Petri, moving alongside Matthew. "He has something!"

"He has a brain in his fever!" she shouted, none too sensically.

"No, no, *signora*! Think of this as a challenge! This young man is correct...the music comes from you! Whether you have accompaniment or not is beside the point. You know the score and the *libretto*...what more do you need?"

"Ha!" That single exclamation had almost blasted the dimpled glass out of the windows. "Open your eyes, Giancarlo! *Siamo nel piu profondo di merde!*"

Di Petri drew himself up a bit taller and straighter. It appeared to Matthew that the harried manager realized his time had arrived. Di Petri said calmly, "We are only in the deepest of shit if you allow it to be so."

Madam Candoleri's bosom swelled like the sail of a fifty-gun warship. Her red-lipped mouth began to open to deliver the cataclysmic volley.

"He's right, *signora*," came the soft voice of the makeup girl, who had gotten up from her pew to join them. "No one can defeat you but yourself."

This quietly-delivered truth pinched out the burning fuse. Madam Candoleri looked from Di Petri to Rosabella and then to Di Petri once more. Her warship began to shrink back again to the size of a noble yacht. She released a *whoosh* of a breath and scratched her forehead in dismay like any common human might. "You think I can do this?" she asked.

"I am *certain*," said Di Petri. "And...even if you are off-key once in a little while, who among these wax-eared English will know it?"

"I surely wouldn't," Matthew added.

Madam Candoleri's index finger tapped her chin. "*Si!*" she said after a short period of contemplation. "If I cannot do this thing, no other can do it...for certain no other *woman*!"

"That is the proper attitude, *signora*. We press on into the unchartered territory."

"*Si*, and who can say that before tomorrow night the ransom is not paid?" said the lady. "Very well then, let me start at the beginning once more, without that garbage noise banging my head drums."

"Ear drums," Di Petri corrected.

"May I ask a favor?" Matthew spoke up before he was drowned out. "May I take Rosabella away from you for just a few minutes?"

"*Me?*" the girl asked. "What for?"

"*Si!* For why?" Madam Candoleri looked like she was getting ready to ruffle up again.

"I have some questions to ask you," Matthew said, addressing Rosabella directly. "We can step outside. As I say, it won't take very long."

"Questions? About what? And who *are* you?"

"This is the young man I was telling you about, we met in the tavern last night," said Madam Candoleri. "He was kidnapped, like us."

Matthew decided not to correct the lady, but to let that stand as it was. "I have some of the same questions Professor Fell asked you, about your cousin Brazio."

Rosabella frowned. "Why is it that Brazio is so important? I have not seen him for years!"

"Why Brazio is important to Professor Fell is exactly what I'm trying to find out."

Perhaps emboldened by his success in calming the star, Di Petri said, "Go ahead, Rosabella. There is no harm in speaking to the young man."

"All right," she answered, but still a little uncertainly. It was clear to Matthew that she had not an inkling of what her cousin's value was to the professor, but if Matthew had his way he was going to find out.

Rosabella put on a pale blue hooded cloak over her gown and Matthew donned his tricorn again. They went outside and stood in a splash of sunlight.

"What is it you want to know?" she asked. When she frowned, two small lines came up between her chocolate-brown eyes, even as young as she was. Matthew reasoned that working anywhere near the diva was not a pleasant experience, but he imagined the job paid very well. "I already told the professor everything I remembered about Brazio," she went on. "What more is there?"

"I'm not the professor," Matthew said. "I know nothing about your cousin, except the fact that Fell is searching for him. And very desperately, I might add." He watched a well-dressed man and woman stroll past, arm-in-arm, as if they were walking a high-class London promenade.

Rosabella chewed for a few seconds on her full lower lip. "Is it true...what Giancarlo has told me? That we may have been taken because the professor is after my cousin? He told me not to say a thing about this to Alicia."

"It's true."

"Then...there's not going to be a ransom demand? Is that also true?"

"That I can't say." He thought it best to remain mute on the subject, but he doubted Fell would ever release anyone from the beautiful grave. Once you were brought here, for whatever reason, here is where you would live out your days as subjects of experimentation until you died.

"What is it you wish to know about my cousin?" Rosabella asked, perhaps reading in his eyes the unspoken reply to her last question.

"Just this, and think on it if you will. Professor Fell has a highly-intelligent mentality, though unfortunately of the criminal nature. Look around and see what he's capable of creating. He went to a lot of effort to get you, and I imagine he had contacts in various places to tell him what your sailing schedule would be and who you expected to meet in Portsmouth. Also, he had to have a contact who knew your connection to Brazio. That was a lot of time, effort, and money. Spent for what reason? What is it you can think of—anything at all—that Brazio might offer to the professor?"

"Brazio working with a criminal? Is that what you mean?"

"Not exactly, but possibly. Does Brazio have some talent Fell could use? Forgery? Safe-cracking? Is he a chemist?"

"A *chemist*? I don't know this word."

"Does he make drugs? *Medicamenta?*" He waited for a reply. She shook her head. Of course, he wondered, how might this seemingly-innocent young girl know if a cousin she hadn't seen for years had turned to the criminal life? "Let me ask this: how old is he? Near your age?"

"No, he was...I think...twenty-six or twenty-seven years old when I saw him last. That was more than three years ago."

"So you say he's likely around thirty?"

"*Si*, that."

"What work was he doing the last time you saw him?"

"I don't know. When I saw him it was with the rest of my family. It was in Salerno, at a funeral."

"A funeral? Whose?"

"His father's," she said. "My uncle, Ciro."

"Ah. And had you known your uncle very well?"

"No, not well. He had a house and a laboratory in the hills above Salerno. He was a man of science, but they told me he lost his mind."

Matthew paused. Two things she'd said had caught his attention: *man of science* and *lost his mind.*

"Your face has changed," Rosabella said.

"Pardon?"

"Your face. Something about it changed just then."

"Tell me," Matthew said, probing at a possibility, "what kind of scientist Ciro Valeriani was."

"I don't know, exactly. My mother and father never talked of it. It was only much later I found out he hanged himself in his laboratory."

"*Hanged* himself? Do you have any idea why?"

"What I understood," she said, "was that...well...he had made something. This was all I overheard my parents saying. He had made something that caused him to go mad, and...I know this sounds... as I would say, *pazzo*...but...he tried to destroy it, and it wouldn't let him."

Matthew was standing in the sun, but suddenly he felt very cold. "This thing...was it *alive*?"

"I can't say. That's all I know about it. I asked my mother once, and she said it was not to be mentioned again, that Uncle Ciro was a good man who had broken when Laurena—his wife—had died of a fever, and when he went into dark things he was no longer the brother she knew."

"Dark things?" Again Matthew experienced a chill. "Your mother never explained that?"

"No, never."

"I'm sure the professor would love to get his hands on your mother."

"She wouldn't know where Brazio is. No one does."

"I see," Matthew said. But he was thinking now that Brazio was only a means to an end. Professor Fell wanted to find this creation that Ciro Valeriani had made in his lab. Possibly Brazio had it? Or knew where it was?

He tried to destroy it, and it wouldn't let him.

"So it destroyed him, instead," Matthew said.

"*Perdono?*"

"Sorry, I'm thinking aloud. I suppose you told all this to the professor?"

"I did."

Matthew looked deeply into the girl's eyes. "Do this for me. It's very important. I want you to think hard about both Brazio and his father, and anything you might have overheard about either of them. Can you think of any small detail that you remember now that you did *not* tell the professor?"

"I told him all I know, that the last time I saw Brazio was at Uncle Ciro's funeral in Salerno, and he said to me—" She stopped and blinked as a memory resurfaced. "Wait. I do remember something else! What he said to me at the funeral! I didn't tell that to the professor."

"Yes? Go on."

"He asked how old I was, and I told him thirteen. He said…I think I'm remembering this right…that thirteen was a good age, especially for Amarone."

"Amarone? What does that mean?"

"It's a red wine, very strong."

"Brazio had a particular interest in wine?"

She shrugged. "I just remember he said that."

Matthew couldn't let this go. It seemed he was on the edge of something vital. "Was Brazio living with his father when Ciro hanged himself?"

"No, I believe he had to travel from somewhere."

"Why do you say that?"

"He came two days late. The funeral was delayed until he got there."

"Did you tell that to the professor?"

"Yes," Rosabella said. "He asked if Brazio had been living in Salerno or had travelled there. I told him just the same as I'm saying now. Also that my mother and father had not heard from Brazio for years and they didn't know where he was living."

"He didn't tell your parents or someone else at the funeral?"

"Not my parents. They didn't want to know. My mother...she thought that Laurena had been unfaithful to Uncle Ciro years ago, and that Brazio was not his real son. My mother said she believed the fever was God's way of passing judgment on Laurena, and all that Laurena had done had made Uncle Ciro the way he was. It was a sad thing, but she wanted nothing to do with Brazio."

"But it's possible he told someone else?"

"*Si*," she said. "Possible."

"You told all this to the professor?"

"*Si*."

"Let me guess what happened next," said Matthew. "Professor Fell asked you to write down a list of the people present at Ciro's funeral?"

"Correct. There were five others besides myself and my parents."

"But he doesn't know Brazio mentioned the Amarone?" He waited for her to answer with a shake of the head. "Why do you think your cousin might have mentioned, of all things, a variety of wine?"

"I have no idea," she said, again with a shrug. "Unless...he works in a vineyard somewhere."

Matthew nodded. "Yes. A vineyard somewhere." Of course it could be that Brazio simply liked Amarone and was planning to get drunk on it after the funeral, but...thirteen years a good age for Amarone? Spoken like someone who understood and valued the aging process.

A vineyard worker? Or a vineyard *owner*?

And what part of Italy might the grape that produced the Amarone be grown in?

But this was, as Rosabella had said, more than three years ago. Matthew recalled that on Pendulum Island Fell made the announcement regarding Brazio that *He was last seen one year ago in Florence, and has since vanished.*

Gone home to the vineyard, perhaps? Out in the country, a distance from any city?

Vanished, at least, from the eyes of Professor Fell.

For the present.

"Rosabella," said Matthew, "if the professor calls you back to the house and asks you more questions, it is very important that you *not* mention the Amarone. You, Madam Candoleri and Di Petri are here because the professor wants Brazio. I'm beginning to think he wants Brazio for whatever it is that your Uncle Ciro created in that laboratory, because if it wasn't destroyed then Brazio may know where it is. What happened to the contents of Ciro's house? Did Brazio take anything with him when he left?"

"I was thirteen years old," she said. "I hated the funeral. I just wanted to get back to my dolls that I named and put makeup on. Everything else that was going on…I didn't care. These things the professor has already asked me, and I answered the same."

"I understand."

"I've been with the madam for only a year," she continued. "Tell me the truth. If the professor does not find Brazio, will he never let us go?"

"The truth," said Matthew. "It doesn't matter if the professor finds Brazio or not. He'll never let you—or any of us—go." She staggered back a step, her hand flying up to her mouth, and he reached out and caught her arm to steady her. "That doesn't mean," he said, "that we'll never get out of here. We can't give up. Most of the people here are on some kind of drug to keep them complacent…*opulenti*," he translated in Latin. "You and Di Petri are going to have to be strong for the madam. For the time being, that's all you can do."

There were tears in her eyes. He said, as gently but as firmly as he could, "I wish crying would help. It will not."

He stood with her awhile longer, until her composure returned. She was a young girl, innocent in her ways, yet the year spent in the employ of Madam Candoleri had left its mark on her; she was tougher than she appeared.

"I'm going to be all right," she said.

"We'll find a way," he told her, and even though such a statement sounded hollow at the moment, he hoped he could follow through with it...for the sake, really, of not only Rosabella, Berry, Hudson, Judge Archer, Di Petri and Madam Candoleri but all the poor souls caught here in the beautiful grave, even the basketweavers and stargazers.

He hoped. But damned if he could figure out how.

"Thank you for your time and your answers," he said, and then he turned away.

Six

The Demoniac

Thirty-Seven

THE dining room to which Matthew was shown had wallpaper of dark red. Heavy black velvet curtains covered the room's two windows. Above the dining table, which had legs carved to resemble dolphins leaping from the waves, was not an octopus chandelier but a simple black wrought-iron wagon wheel arrangement that held six tapers. Three more candles burned at the middle of the table around an interesting centerpiece: a blue-and-gold marbled bowl that held not an arrangement of flowers but a tangle of ebony thorns. The sinister centerpiece notwithstanding, all the illumination gave the room a ruddy glow that might have been cheerful on any other occasion.

Clad in a black suit and clean white shirt with a white cravat, Matthew found himself first to the feast. The man who'd escorted him from his cottage back to Fell's battlement was a hawk-nosed gent with a silent disposition, one of the men Matthew had seen during his stay at Mother Deare's but had never spoken to.

The table was set for three, with one chair at the head and two chairs opposite each other. Small white cards—not of the death variety, Matthew was pleased to see—indicated that Matthew Corbett was to sit on the professor's left while William Atherton Archer was on the right. Matthew took his place and waited. His escort left the room through another door. The candles sputtered and fretted, perhaps mirroring Matthew's internals though his external was as calm as a baby's breath. It was hard work, keeping such a disguise in place.

In about another minute there came the sound of footsteps approaching along the same corridor that had brought Matthew to this room.

Entering first was Judge Archer, followed by Julian Devane. Archer's pallidity and the hollowness of his eyes indicated that, though he might be up and about, the severity of his gunshot wound coupled with his entry into the domain of Professor Fell was not a complement to one's sterling health. Still, his expression was resolute, his mouth firm and his chin uplifted with a goodly measure of dignity. His blonde hair was tied back in a queue with a black ribbon and he too wore a black suit, white shirt and white cravat, as formality seemed to be correct for the evening. Matthew wondered if Archer thought, as he did, that it was proper manners to go well-dressed to the grave, beautiful or not.

To his credit, the judge drew up a warm smile that was absolutely a hundred-and-eighty-degree turn from his first glance upon Matthew that day in his courtroom.

"Good evening, young sir," he said. "Whom do I have the pleasure of addressing?"

Matthew was taken aback. Was Archer already made insensible by drugs?

Devane said, "You've been told that your game is up. Do you persist in this?"

"I'm sorry, but I still have no idea what you mean." Archer drew back his chair and sat down, and Matthew noted that he winced just a bit and briefly put a hand to his wounded side. "I've never seen this young man before."

"*Sure.*" Devane gave him a cold smile, and then he exited left the room.

Immediately Archer's index finger went to his lips, and his expression told Matthew to beware any ears that might be listening.

Archer spread his napkin in his lap. "A fine night for a dinner," he said. "Wouldn't you agree, Mister—?"

"Matthew Corbett."

"Ah, Mr. Corbett! Pleased to meet you. I'm William Archer." As he spoke, his gaze was moving back and forth in search of the revealing glint of light through a peephole. "Are you a local resident?"

"No sir, I'm from the colonies. New York, in fact."

"*Really?*" His eyes continued to search, but they snagged for a few seconds on Matthew's Black-Eyed Broodie tattoo. "I understand New York is growing to be quite a town."

"Growing, yes sir, but it'll be some time before it's the equal of London."

"Very few places," he replied with just a hint of bitterness, "are the equal of London. You should wish New York never becomes so." He arranged his silverware this way and that, his fingers nervous though he wore the same disguise of calm that Matthew had manufactured. "I hope," he said, "that the *plan* for New York never becomes as disjointed and chaotic as that of London. Such *plans* can go awry, and yet even if *the result is obtained*, it may not be exactly the result one had envisioned. Then apologies must be offered in a profuse manner, but the fact remains that ofttimes the best intention explodes in one's face. Do you follow, sir?"

"I do."

"You seem a bright young man. Pity we've not met before this moment."

There came the sound of polite applause.

Into the room walked Professor Danton Idris Fell, wearing a silk robe of crimson with gold trim at collar and cuffs.

He smiled and gave a slight bow to his guests. "Pardon the interruption, but I've been enjoying this play and I wished to show my appreciation. You know, I've intended for some time to start a drama troupe here. You two may well be the superlative members."

Archer put on a dumb face. "Sir?" he asked. Then he started to stand to show a feigned respect for his host.

"Please stay seated. Those who have been shot and recently nursed back from near-death have no business getting up and down from the table. Good evening, Matthew. Feeling all better now?"

"Tip top."

"Excellent." Fell took his place at the head of the table. "We'll be having our first course in a few minutes. Oh, here's the wine." A heavy-set, black-haired man who looked as much a kitchen servant as a buzzard could be a hummingbird came in through the opposite door bearing a bottle, which he laboriously began to uncork while standing beside the professor. "A nice full-bodied Cinsault," said the professor. "Free of any additives, on the honor of my house. We'll be having a very fine swordfish tonight so pardon my not offering the white, but my personal taste runs darker."

Matthew nearly broke out in a sweat keeping himself from commenting on that remark. He watched the pair of ham-hands pouring wine into his glass and said, just for the hell of it, "I also prefer the red. Syrah, Pinot Noir, Amarone, Gamay…all those pique my interest."

"I had no idea you were so worldly," came the smooth reply. "An Italian wine included among the French? If one or the other got wind of that, you might be responsible for starting a war. Thank you, Martin," he told the attendant. "Give us a moment or two and then we'll get started." He held up his glass. "May I offer a toast, gentlemen? To your health, to truth, and to the future."

"Hear, hear," said Archer.

Matthew drank with the others. Had there been any reaction to the use of the word *Amarone* other than Fell's observation of its Italian origin? He didn't think so, but he decided not to be rash or stupid. Once a cat was out of its bag, one could not get it back in without being clawed to pieces.

Fell put his glass back down upon the table.

He smiled thinly at Judge Archer. Matthew had the sense that a moment of reckoning had arrived.

Fell said, "I imagine you've heard many interesting cases, sir. Would you entertain us by reciting a few?"

So it went for the next half-hour, as if this dining room sat in a house on a street in high-class London, and the lordly gentlemen here were discussing the stuff of life, business and circumstance much as would be discussed at any exclusive club. A course of squid salad and clam chowder was offered, and Fell insisted they at least try the side dish of boiled green seaweed adorned with small onions. Fell listened attentively as Archer went on about such defendants as Zebulon Whittington the horn merchant who had stabbed his partner to death with a wild boar's tusk, Ann Clark the widow who displayed her hatred of men by murdering eight of them with poisoned mushrooms in her boarding-house, and the notorious and handsome George Parker, the Flower Man, who roamed the well-to-do neighborhoods of London offering young servant girls the aroma of a bouquet that had a nose-cutting knifeblade at its center.

Then the judge stopped speaking, because the main course was served.

The large baked swordfish on a sea-green platter still wore its crusted silver skin. Its head had been removed and replaced with the golden-bearded mask of Albion.

The platter was put down upon the table, and Martin showed he might not be very proficient with a corkscrew but he was the master of an eight-inch blade.

"My, that looks tasty!" said Professor Fell, with a little joyous clasping of his hands before his face.

Martin served swordfish steaks to every plate. Another platter of fried potatoes with onions and leeks was brought out, along with cups of sherry cream and vinegar sauce if one wished to anoint the swordfish. Martin left the room, the professor picked up his knife and fork and began to eat.

A long silence followed. Archer caught Matthew's gaze and his eyes narrowed just a fraction, the meaning Matthew caught being: *Who knows what's next?*

"You two gentlemen," the professor said as he ate, with pauses to sip from the wineglass that Martin had refreshed, "are quite the intelligent ones, aren't you? Or is the word *crafty*? Well, you can't be too crafty or you wouldn't have wound up here."

"Crafty, sir?" asked Archer.

A flash of irritation passed across Fell's face, and then his expression returned to its remote normality. "You might like to know that a compatriot of yours is a resident. The Right Honorable John Mayes has been here for two years. I would have had him killed for his hand in fouling my affairs, but in addition to biologics I also have an interest in astronomy, so here he will reside until he finishes the book he's writing for me on that subject, upon which he is a recognized expert."

Matthew dared to speak up. "I'll wager that book will be a real treasurehouse of knowledge, if he's been given one speck of what I had this morning."

"Indeed. No, he's simply been given something to help him relax and to throw off the chains of the society that bound him. The book is going slowly but surely. Actually, John is quite content here."

"*Content* is an Atlantic's width away from *happy*."

"Oh, not so far. Judge Archer, you're not eating. The fish doesn't appeal to you?"

Archer began to eat, and Matthew hoped he was the only one who noticed the judge's hand tremble but he doubted it. The question was: did the tremble originate from fear, or from suppressed rage in the presence of the man who had not only caused his wife's agonized death but had been such a dark stain on the whole civilization of England? Matthew figured on the latter.

"It seems to me, Danton," said Matthew, "that your affairs have lately been fouling left and right."

Fell laughed like a soft cough. "Unfortunately true enough. William, you allied yourself with a formidable force in Matthew Corbett. He might not look like much, but he has a way about him. You must meet the two people who came from New York to find him, but it should be soon because you can't do much conversing with dishrags."

The urge to take his arm and sweep everything off the table in the direction of Fell's lap gripped Matthew like a fever. He thought if he picked up the wineglass at that moment it might explode in his hand. He stared at the piece of fish on his plate, as the seconds ticked past. Then he swallowed his own rage down and continued eating, but his face felt misshapen by the slow movements of inner pressures.

"Tell me," the professor said to Archer, "just exactly what your masquerade has been *about*? What point was it to execute six of my most underling errand boys? One of them, I might point out, who wore the tattoo of a Whitechapel gang exactly the same as the mark on Matthew's hand...and dear Matthew, as I told you before, you do get around. But tell me, Judge Archer, what did you hope to accomplish by nettling me in these miniscule ways? You seemed to know a lot about me and my influence. Why didn't you lie in wait for Judge

Chamberlin, and cut his throat as he came home from the court? Why didn't you murder the lawyers, Edwin Wickett and Humphrey Mousekeller? Or…better still…why didn't you go dressed as Albion to the halls of Parliament, and use your saber on…well, I'm sure you know at least *three* of the names. I ask the question: why not murder someone whose demise might really cause me an uneasy hour or two?"

Fell smiled at Archer over a piece of fish hanging from his fork. "Because, Judge Archer," he said, "the simple answer is: you are *evil*."

He ate the fish.

Archer sat like a piece of stone.

"Yes, evil," Fell repeated. His smile was gone. "You attacked and murdered six men who had no idea why they were being so brutally dispatched. You attacked men who *did not matter* the least in the larger scheme of things. Of course I had to get them out of gaol, it was a question of honor. But to stalk and murder *small* men, when larger targets were parading around within your sight *every single day*…that is evil, Albion. May I call you that?"

Archer did not answer, nor did he react in any way. He might have been dead with his eyes open and staring but for the slow rise and fall of his breathing.

"*Albion*," Fell said, with a twist of the mouth. "I understand the *Pin* gave you that name, but I'm sure it's one you relished. Do you know the meaning of it, Matthew? I'll tell you anyway. Albion: the great mythical giant and the spiritual protector of the civilization of England. Doesn't that sound lofty and noble? A single man takes it upon himself to attack what he sees as the deep corruption that is rotting our country, and therefore he kills six stupid errand boys? Eight, if you include Mother Deare's pence-a-dozen hired guns. I would laugh about this if I didn't find it absolutely *pathetic*. Is this a problem you have with the blackmailing I'm doing of public figures who put their greed and their idiocy to work and tripped over their own league-long cocks? Does it have to do with the purloining of secret papers that will send a hundred thousand English boys to die in war over a pot of foreign gold? Does it have to do with the White Velvet, which for a short time soothes the agony of souls who live under whips every day of their lives and so must leave their own minds to find a place of peace? Oh, Albion…how you disappoint me! Here I was expecting a great debate, a great verbal and mental contest over the true meaning of good and evil, and there you sit like a fig of filth about to slide into the gutter. Look at Albion, Matthew! See him unmasked, as he really is! *Albion!*" Fell's voice had risen to what was for him a shout. Archer's head turned toward the professor, his eyes dimmed.

Fell asked quietly, "How do you plead?"

Archer didn't answer for a moment. He took a drink of his wine. Then he said, "Guilty, I suppose. Guilty of giving a damn."

"And damned you may well be," came the reply. "You know, I've heard a lot about you. That you are incorruptible, that you are a steadfast man of so-called honor, far beyond my ability to recruit you as a tool. But now I see…you don't even understand the nature of *crime*! How many men have you hanged because you were really hanging *me*? How many men deserved mercy, and you saw in your warped sense of justice a budding Professor Fell, and so you sent them to the rope? I'll wager you can count them on more than two hands! Did you think you were really doing anything to *save* England from itself? What would be your next move, to start sending children to the gallows for cheating in games of marbles, so that the criminal element of England would be destroyed in its infancy?

"*Ha*," the professor said, and he started to take another bite of his fish but then he put the fork down and pushed the plate aside as if he had no more stomach for it. "Crime," he said softly. "You murdered six errand boys, while in Parliament plans are being drawn up to go to war over territory and money for a select few, and in consequence murder sixty-six thousand errand boys. Those in power are the criminals and every day they get away with some form of murder! Yet your eye is turned toward me."

He shook his head, sadly. "I don't even know why I bothered with you, except to put you in your place. Well…yes, I do know. You and Matthew are going to be my guests at the opera program at eight tomorrow night. After the program is ended, Albion Archer, you are going to be worked on. I don't like people knowing my business, and you learned far too much for my comfort. Therefore you are going to be worked on, to get a proper accounting of those who revealed to you my full name and description. Matthew may have spilled that to Mother Deare, but it had to come from you because of that cute little rhyme in the *Pin* that she brought along. We must remedy this breach. After I get the information I want from you, you'll be used as a subject for some experiments. Depending on how those proceed, you'll either live or die."

"Lovely," said Archer, with a tight smile.

"Yes, lovely. Now if I were operating under your conditions, I would let you walk free and kill everyone who was a reader of the *Pin*." Suddenly the professor's face contorted. "You *disgust* me," he said. He took the napkin from his lap, flung it onto the table and stood up. The chair screeched across the floor. Instantly Martin came into the room from the opposite door.

"We are done here," Fell said. "Get out of my house, the both of you. And take your mask with you, Archer. You may wish to wear it to bed tonight to make you dream of being anything but a criminal who thinks himself a hero."

So saying, the professor stalked from the room.

Martin stood where he was, glowering. The message to get out was well-received.

Archer got up from his chair. He reached for the mask and then hesitated. Reached a little further and hesitated again.

Then his hand went all the way, and he took it off the crisped and eviscerated fish.

Thirty-Eight

THE night had gotten colder.

Matthew was walking alongside William Archer, away from the house of Professor Fell. Lanterns glowed on the street signposts and an occasional light showed in a window.

"What street are you on?" Archer asked.

"Lionfish. And you?"

"Bullhead. One over from Thresher."

Matthew nodded. "You're aware that most of the residents of this village are numbed by drugs?"

"From the limited part I've seen, I had that suspicion. I know there are guards here, but how could Fell keep everyone so docile without narcotics?" He was silent for a few paces. "I suppose by being a subject for experimentation I'll get first-hand knowledge of this?"

"Yes," Matthew said.

"Hm. There's a shaving razor in my cottage. I wonder if I shouldn't just—"

"I doubt it will be there when you return." Matthew suddenly stopped, and so did Archer. They faced each other on the street, with the cold wind swirling around them, the near-full moon a bright lamp and the stars burning above. "I imagine you could find a way to remove yourself if you really wanted to," Matthew said. "You might think it wise to do so, to protect your contacts and also to protect Steven. Did they harm him in taking you from the hospital? I understood that a young man tried to come to your aid."

"It wasn't Steven. It was someone else, the husband of one of the nurses I think. I'd told Steven to go home and rest, to come back the next day if he could. Luckily, he took his father's advice."

"I'm glad to hear that. Did Steven tell you that he related to me the whole story of this…I am hesitant to call it a *plan*, so I must call it a desperation."

"He did. I was fading in and out, but I got the gist that he'd told you everything."

Matthew looked up at the moon and the expanse of stars, breathtaking in their splendor, and then returned his attention to the judge. He shook his head. "How could you *ever* think something like this would succeed? Using me as bait to bring Fell to the Three Sisters, where you hoped to kill him on the steps of Flint Alley? You're a learned and intelligent man, and your son also. How could you have concocted such an insanity?"

"It might have worked. Part of it did, at least."

"Instead of bringing Fell to you on your ground, it's brought you to Fell on his. If that's a success, I have lost my bearings on what the word *failure* means." Matthew felt the heat rising in his face. "And how *dare* you use me in that way! Putting me in Newgate…casting me adrift in Whitechapel…all of it. *All of it*," he repeated, holding up the Broodie tattoo in front of Archer's face.

"Yes," said Archer. His eyes had gotten hard and a muscle jumped in his jaw. "I've seen that mark before, on the body of the young man who came crashing down to destroy my Eleanor."

"Perhaps you can be comforted in the fact that the gang to which Joshua Oakley belonged has been reduced to one final member: myself. They're all dead, everyone but their leader murdered at the hand of whoever killed Judge Fallonsby and his family. A demoniac, Fell calls him. Someone trying to muscle his way onto the professor's territory by stealing shipments of the Velvet. The leader of that gang was murdered in front of my eyes by Mother Deare, and he had his rough edges but he was a decent man who deserved much better than what life shoved at him. Now the professor has in hand two of my friends—pardon me...a correction, my *best* friend and the woman I love—in this village of the damned and their minds are so overcome by drugs neither one can recognize me."

Matthew put a hand to his forehead, as a dizziness swept over him. He had a few seconds of sheer panic, in which he feared he'd been poisoned again, but then he realized he was still in control of his faculties and what he was experiencing was the poison of the situation. He said, "I am used to finding a way to solve problems. In the past I've been in complications in which I racked my brain almost to pieces, but I always did devise a solution. This time, I can't find one." He lowered his hand. "If anyone ought to have the right to leave this life by his own effort, it should be myself," he said. "I have caused the worst thing I dreaded in this world to happen, and I'm powerless to change it. The only thing I can do is to hang on for another minute, hour and day, and hope I can conjure an answer that will at least save my friends. So...if you wish to kill yourself you could find a way, but that would *really* show what a misguided attempt this has been." He paused to let that register. Then he said, "Salvage some pride from the ashes, sir. Hang on a bit longer."

"I have only one more day in which to hang."

"I imagine many of the men who were awaiting the rope because of your decision looked at a single remaining day, and they made the best of it. Even the professor believes you to be of sterner stuff than a will toward suicide, or he would never have let you leave the house."

"True," the judge said, in a quiet voice. He gazed around at the little houses for a time, and Matthew could tell that the man's mind—though certainly burdened—had begun to work at the problem. A simpleton could not have played the part of Albion or devised the plan, even as flawed as it was. "This afternoon I walked the length of the wall," Archer said. "I saw the very well-guarded front gate and a back gate over the cliffs. The rocks are treacherous there, but I could see a road that winds down maybe a quarter of a mile to a protected harbor. Two fishing boats and a larger sailing craft were docked there. Do you think it possible to break that gate open and get to one of the boats?"

"I'll have to take a look," Matthew said, but he was already thinking how difficult that would be. Even if there were no guards down at the boats...*locked gate...guards on duty walking the parapet...armed with muskets.* The bars had looked strong enough to defy Coalblack. And on the very slight chance that Archer might somehow get away, Matthew could never abandon Berry and Hudson to save his own skin even if both front and back gates were wide open.

Archer drew a long breath and released it. He stared at the ground for a moment, as if contemplating his place on the surface of the earth. Then he lifted his gaze and said, "Matthew, I will say to you the same thing I said to my Eleanor: I am truly and deeply sorry, and I humbly apologize."

"That will have to do, I suppose." Matthew frowned. "You apologized to your wife for what? The accident?"

"No. For giving her an overdose of laudanum that last night. I couldn't stand to see her in such pain any longer. The doctors said she would linger indefinitely." Archer's own face seemed to have tightened into a mask, but it was one that allowed not an inch of freedom. "Steven doesn't know I sent her off. So you see," he said, "I really *am* a murderer."

Matthew saw not necessarily a murderer standing before him, but a conscience-stricken man of the law who was a prisoner in his own cage of bones.

With that admission, Archer's eyes seemed to have retreated into his head and he had shrunken as if trying to hide himself in a place where there was nowhere to hide. When he spoke again his voice held the rough gravel of pain. "I'll walk on now. Goodnight to you."

"Goodnight," said Matthew, and he stood where he was until Judge Archer had walked to the next street and turned to the left, carrying the mask of Albion at his side.

In his cottage on Lionfish Street, Matthew could not have slept if Spenser's faerie queen had drifted in and blown a shimmering handful of forget-the-world dust up his nostrils. He sat in a chair in the front room and played twiddle-thumbs while in his fevered brain thoughts roamed far and wide and leaped about like wild animals.

Did an hour pass? Did two hours creep by? The candle in his lantern hissed out. Matthew had not the heart to relight it and look at his pocketwatch, for the passage of every minute was a torture. To think of Berry in that house on Redfin Street, her mind devolving into porridge...and Hudson, the Great One, on his belly trying to crawl beneath a mattress to escape his living nightmares...

God, it was too much.

He sat in the dark, with the moonlight through the windows his only companion.

He longed to go to Berry, to hold her and kiss her and tell her that everything would be all right, but it would be the most blatant lie. And when she looked at him, would she see Ashton McCaggers or some other phantom that Fell had ordered inserted into her head?

In the end, she will revert to being an infant in a cradle, and I may let you rock her from time to time.

It was hideous. He would rather have gotten on his knees and let Fell swing the blade that took his head off, rather than to have to watch that slow death.

I will tell you, dear Matthew, that she is lost to you forever, because even if the dosage ceased today—which it will not—she would fail to recover without vigorous and steady application of the antidote.

The antidote. It would be in Gentry's book of potions, and where would the book be? Kept in the Publick Hospital? The building had been dark when Matthew had passed by. If he could break into the hospital...find the notebook...if the notebook was there... if the antidote was there, and clearly marked...if...if...if...

He was no chemist. What if he found Ribbenhoff and forced the man to give him the antidote? *Ribbenhoff.* Another damned Prussian?

Vigorous and steady application, the professor had said.

Meaning what? Once a day for a week? Four times a day for four weeks? Six times a day for six weeks? It was impossible.

Matthew leaned forward and put his head in his hands. He was near weeping. He felt himself coming apart, and he was reasonably sure he wasn't even drugged. No, the professor wanted to keep him clear-minded and open-eyed, so he could witness the utter destruction of the two human beings who meant the most to him in the world.

He needed a drink.

Without further hesitation he got up and put on his cloak and tricorn. He didn't care to take the time to fire his tinderbox and light the lamp. He just left the house and strode along Lionfish toward the square.

The village was silent. All the houses were dark. He saw the movement of lanterns up on the parapets, where the guards were walking back and forth. Surely Fell paid them a goodly sum for such deadening work, or else he paid them in some other currency... perhaps in addition to money, food and drink he gave them the Beautiful Bedd's residents when those were used-up and of no further value to him, to do with what they would. Matthew shook from his mind the images of a group of men throwing themselves upon a wan and stupidly-smiling Rosabella, or a mute and compliant Madam Candoleri, or using their fists and muskets to smash Di Petri into red sauce. He shook those images away because they were frighteningly like what he thought Fell would envision.

Matthew came out of himself when he saw a figure with a lantern crossing his path ahead.

He slowed down, then stopped in the middle of the street.

Who was that? A squat though broad-shouldered and formidable figure, moving with quick purpose. A guard, reporting for duty? No, the moonlight did not reveal a musket. The figure wore a dark cloak and hood. A woman, he thought. Did he recognize the rather mannish walk? And then the wind swept in and fluttered the figure's cloak and hood, and Matthew caught a glimpse of cottony white hair.

Mother Deare. Going somewhere in a hurry.

But not toward the professor's house.

Toward the wall that ran along the sea cliffs.

He stood very still. What time could it possibly be? The moon was sliding down. He judged it to be near three o'clock.

Mother Deare on the move at three o'clock in the morning. Interesting, he thought. And more of a mind-cleanser to tag along after her—just for a looksee, see?—than sitting in that damn tavern feeling the seconds of his, Berry's and Hudson's lives ticking away.

So be it.

He was on the hunt, all senses questing.

He followed her, staying at a respectful distance. He sighted a guard walking toward him and had to duck between two cottages, but the guard turned away and so freed him to continue on.

Matthew didn't have to follow her very far before another interesting thing happened. She met someone waiting for her near the back gate that Archer had mentioned and Matthew had seen the night before. This person—a good-sized man—was also carrying a lantern. They stood together, talking for a moment, and then they went up a set of stairs to the parapet with Mother Deare in the lead.

Matthew positioned himself next to the nearest cottage to be able to watch their progress along the parapet. They were moving to the right. They came to a guard, who they stopped and began talking to. The man who was with Mother Deare called the guard aside and seemed to be talking earnestly with him, and Matthew noted that the man had worked his stance so that the guard's back was turned to the sea.

Then...

...Mother Deare stepped to the edge of the wall, facing the sea, and quickly she lifted her lantern and made a motion with it in the air. It only took a second, after which she lowered the lantern and joined the conversation that her companion was having with the guard.

Matthew's eyes narrowed. Was it his imagination, or had her lantern moved in the shape of an inverted Cross?

She'd been making a signal to someone out there. Whether the signal had been returned or not, he didn't know...but...a signal, just the same.

Meaning what?

Mother Deare and the man were coming down from the parapet on that same set of steps. Matthew had the desire to see who the man was. He could say he had emerged for a walk and just by happenstance had come upon them. Yes, that would hold water.

He started toward them. Should he lift an arm and say hello? He was getting closer. They were going to be crossing his path in—

A hand gripped his mouth, another hand pinned his right arm behind him, and he was dragged on his heels into a darkness beyond the moonlight.

"*Quiet*," whispered a voice into his ear.

Thirty-Nine

Mother Deare and the man walked past. In the glow of the lamps Matthew thought the man might be the hulking Martin, from Fell's house, but he couldn't be sure. The hand continued to seal his mouth and his right arm felt near the breaking point.

A few seconds after the pair had gone by, the hand went away and Matthew's arm was released. Matthew spun around to face his attacker.

"What are you doing out here, you idiot?" asked Julian Devane, still speaking in a hushed tone.

"Walking." Matthew busied himself rubbing the feeling back into his punished shoulder. "Is that forbidden?"

"I think you were following Mother Deare and Martin."

"Really? And why do you think that?"

"Because," he answered, "*I* was following Mother Deare. I saw you start after her."

"I was just walking, that's all." Matthew thought he needed practice on his stalking skills; he'd never realized anyone might be behind him.

"You're a stupid *fop*. Thinking so highly of yourself. I could've brained you a dozen times and you never would've seen the blow coming."

"Thank you for the observation. I'll be on my way now."

"*No*." Devane grasped the front of Matthew's cloak and swung him around so Matthew's back was against a wall and his path of escape blocked. "What did you just see?"

"Pardon?"

"Don't act like an imbecile. You saw something. What was it?"

"I have no idea what—"

"Corbett, *listen* to me." Devane's hand moved to grip the cloak more tightly around Matthew's throat. "I'm going to tell you something, and I think you have enough sense to realize what I'm saying."

"You haven't said anything yet."

"Hear me. I've been in Mother Deare's employ for a little over a year. Over the last three months, she's changed. Become…I don't know…the word I would use is *unhinged*."

"Oh, before that she was *hinged*?"

"It started in small ways, not long after she got back from Pendulum Island," Devane went on. "Losing her concentration, something on her mind interfering with her business…and that's *not* like her. Disappearing for days at a time and not telling anyone where she was going, or where she'd been. Going off alone, without her bodyguards. Again…out of her pattern."

"Mercy me," said Matthew. "I'm sorry to hear such a fine lady is losing her concentration once in a while, and wishes to get rid of her odious bodyguards so she might go shopping for the afternoon on Fleet Street like any ordinary female."

"Stop your feigned stupidity. You work for the Herrald Agency, you're supposed to be so fucking *smart*. I'll ask you again…what did you just see?"

"Two questions to your question: Why are you telling me all this, and why should you care what I think I might have seen?"

"You talk enough to tie a tree in a knot," said Devane. "I'll tell you: Mother Deare may be mixed up in something dangerous."

"I'd say that's an understatement."

"I mean mixed up in something that's dangerous to the professor."

Matthew was about to throw another nugget of wit into Devane's face, but he realized what the man was saying, particularly after seeing Mother Deare give what he perceived as a signal out to sea.

He said, "I saw her lift the lantern in a straight line, draw it down in a straight line and move it from left to right and back again near the bottom of that line."

"Correct. And I'm assuming you know that symbol?"

"Yes," said Matthew.

Devane released Matthew's cloak. He looked in the direction Mother Deare and Martin had gone, looked back at the fortress wall, and then returned his gaze to Matthew. His face was in darkness under the tricorn, and all Matthew could see was the shine of his eyes from a bit of reflected moonlight. "I think she's losing her mind," he said.

"Really? And she hadn't lost her mind many years ago?"

"Maybe she had. Maybe she's just been very apt at hiding it, and now it's come out."

Matthew might not have given a fig whether the woman had lost her mind or not, but for one reason. If that lantern signal of the inverted Cross had anything to do with the monster who'd ordered the murders and mutilations of the Black-Eyed Broodies, he was bound by his honor to give a care. "How do you mean?" he asked.

Devane hesitated, as if deciding whether to go any further with this.

"You've started it," Matthew urged. "Go ahead."

"I have a room in the attic in the house on Seward Street. Mother Deare's house," Devane clarified. "Back in October, she was gone for four nights. Had told her staff she needed no bodyguards, and she left in a hired coach. As I say, off her pattern. But we thought it was her business, we are paid to do as we're told and ask no questions. So...one night I was awakened by a noise on the roof over my head. It was coming from up on the widow's walk, and it sounded like someone was up there dancing."

"Dancing," Matthew repeated.

"Stomping back and forth, actually. I climbed up the ladder to the walk. There I found Mother Deare, dancing around and around and holding a bottle of rum. She was obviously drunk, and her wig had gone crooked."

"Her wig?"

"Yes. Underneath it, her scalp is burn-scarred. I'd never seen it before, but I'd heard tell. Anyway, I neared her and I asked if there was anything I could do for her. She said no, for me to go back down and let her be. But she was grinning and very happy about something. She almost seemed...the way I'd describe it would be *delirious*."

"So you left her there?"

"I did. But just before I started down the ladder she called my name, and she said her father had come back for her."

"Her *father*?" Matthew thought back. He recalled the woman telling him *My father was unknown to me.*

"That's what she said. I went back down and left her alone. Since then, there were two other times she disappeared for several days. The last one was a week or so before she sent me off with Stoddard and Guinnessey to stake out that circus."

Matthew grunted. It was very strange. He recalled that Mother Deare had told him she'd seen the circus that week before his capture.

Had her father taken his daughter to see the show?

Her *father*?

"She told me she had no idea who her father might be," he said. "Except—" He stopped, because the rest of her story had come back to him with stunning force.

Dirty Dorothea...veiled, her face being eated away...in the crumbling wreckage of the cathouse...the madness of the mother, raging against fate...telling her terrified daughter about her real father...

She said my father had come to her over three nights. On the first night he appeared as a black cat with silver claws. On the second night, as a toadfrog that sweated blood. On the third night...into the room with the midnight wind...he came as his true self, tall and lean, as handsome as sin, with long black hair and black eyes that held a center of scarlet. A fallen angel, he announced himself to be...

"Except what?" Devane asked.

"Nothing, just thinking," said Matthew.

"You do a lot of that. Where has it gotten your life?"

"Where has your life gotten *you*?" Matthew shot back.

Devane didn't answer. His hand came up and Matthew thought it was going to seize the collar of his cloak again, but then Devane seemed to think better of it and the hand was lowered.

"At least," said Devane, with a sneer in his voice, "I don't have to watch the mind of anyone I give a damn about turn to pudding."

"Oh? Do you give a damn about anyone, then?"

Again, there was no response. The uneasy silence stretched.

Matthew broke it. "To the point…you saw the same signal that I did. If you suspect that Mother Deare may have any hidden agenda, shouldn't you tell the professor?"

"A hidden agenda? What do you mean?"

"I mean what you already know I mean, but I'm going to spell it out for someone who is more highly intelligent than they wish to appear. You suspect that Mother Deare may have something to do with the man who's been murdering Fell's people and stealing the Velvet. A demoniac, as Fell describes him. She gave the signal in the shape of an inverted Cross out to sea. Why would she do so?"

"Someone's watching on a ship out there."

"Of course. She's not just signalling to the batfish. Martin took care of the guard's attention while she did so, meaning that Martin is also in on this…whatever it is."

"I don't like what you're saying."

"Like it or not," said Matthew, "*something's* going on. How did you come to be following her?"

Devane didn't reply for a moment and Matthew figured he was at his end of sharing confidences. But then Devane shifted his balance a little, as if he'd made a decision which way to lean. He said, "I don't sleep very well, so—"

"I wonder why," Matthew interrupted.

"Do you want me to tell this, or don't you?"

"Right now I'm thinking I am the only one you *can* tell, which is exactly why you're telling me. Go ahead, but for some reason your voice makes my jaw ache."

Devane continued without comment on this observation. "I went to the tavern last night, about this same time," he said. "Mother Deare and Sam Stoddard were sitting in there at a table toward the back, talking. They were alone but for the barkeep. There was an empty chair at their table, so I went to sit with them. Before I could draw the chair out, Mother Deare looked up at me and said they were having a private conversation. Her eyes were strange."

"Aren't they always?"

"They were faraway. Distant. Yet…I don't know…sharp, too. Stoddard's no better than me. He's been with her for about two years, but he's no better. In fact, he's much of a clod."

"Do tell."

"So I sat there, had my cup of wine and wondered why I'd been cast off…which I was, and I couldn't understand it. I watched them talking, but I couldn't hear them. Something about it just wasn't right, especially because of the other things that've happened. They left the tavern and I followed them. They did the exact same thing that she and Martin did tonight," Devane said. "Stoddard took the nearest guard's attention and Mother Deare made that same signal out to sea. The Devil's Cross, they call it. Like what was carved into—"

"Yes, I saw the bodies."

"Right. So tonight I was on my way to the tavern again. I passed her house and saw a light moving inside. I decided to wait and see if she would come out. She did, and then you got between us."

"I see."

"That's not all. A few weeks ago Stoddard and I were on a collection run. Just strong-arming an idiot politician for an extra two hundred pounds. The fool got carried away in a sex game and strangled a young whore to death. Unfortunately for him she was not a nobody, she had a mother and two small children at home."

"Spare me the sordid details of your livelihood," Matthew told him.

"On the way," Devane said, "Stoddard asked me if I was content working for the professor. He made the comment that Fell was losing his grip on events, and that time wasn't going to wait for him to come out from hiding. I remember very clearly…Stoddard said—his opinion only—that the professor was getting weak, and how long did I want to work for a man whose empire might soon crumble away."

"And how did you reply?"

"I told him to watch his tongue, because Mother Deare would cut it out if she heard one word of what he was saying."

"Did he respond to that?"

"He said I might be surprised what Mother Deare would do, and that she might have her own plans that didn't include the professor. Then he didn't say any more, and he didn't bring anything like that up again. I assume he was testing the water and found it cold."

"Agreed," said Matthew. "You haven't told Fell any of this?"

"Jesus, no! For one thing, this is the first time I've been anywhere near him in months, and for me to get in to see him privately would have to go through Mother Deare. There's a hierarchy here, you don't just walk in off the street to see the professor."

"And you think if you made such a request, she would want to know why?"

"Certainly she'd want to know why. She's a smart woman. Cunning, I should say. She'd see right through any lie I told her, and anyway there's no possible reason for me to want to see the professor privately. Any issue I might have is supposed to be taken care of in our own house."

"And I presume you haven't told any of your other compatriots because you don't know whom to trust?"

"Exactly. One word to the wrong person and I'd wind up as dogfood."

Matthew nodded. The moonlight had moved, but still Matthew could not fully see the man's face, only the glint of the eyes. "Don't you think that this is a ridiculous moment, Mr. Devane? You, who brought myself and Rory Keen to Mother Deare at gunpoint, now asking my opinion about what your course of action should be?"

"Who said I'm asking your opinion?"

"You *are* asking it, whether you've stated so or not. But if you don't want it, kindly step aside and let me get to my beautiful bed."

"I don't know why the hell I even stopped you," said Devane, with a hint of anger behind it. "I should've let you blunder on."

"Perhaps you should have. I find myself in a situation that couldn't possibly be any worse."

Devane still didn't step aside.

"My opinion," Matthew said, "is for you to first get me the book of potions and antidotes from wherever it's hidden. Then free Hudson Greathouse from his cell in the professor's dungeon. After that, go to the stable that must be here somewhere, get a horse and ride out, and when you leave this damned place, make sure the gate is left open so whoever can stagger, stumble or crawl can also escape. Get away from here to wherever you can have a new life, and never look back. Your problem is therefore solved, and I won't even charge you a shilling."

"You know I can't do any of that."

"You are free to act on my opinion or not."

"*Free*," said Devane. "Sure I am."

"We have all made our beds, whether they are beautiful or not. And now I'm going back to what passes as four walls of comfort, and I will say good night...or, rather, good morning."

After a brief hesitation Devane stepped out of Matthew's way, and said nothing more as Matthew walked past him and back on the route toward Lionfish Street.

Matthew's head was full to bursting. Mother Deare giving a signal to sea in the shape of a Devil's Cross? Had he *really* seen that? And all that about her father? Then Stoddard's probing of Devane's loyalty?

What to make of it?

Was there a possibility, he wondered as he walked on, that this new figure on the scene—the *upstart*, Fell had called him—had somehow made contact with Mother Deare and convinced her to plot against her master?

If that were so...

...then not only was Mother Deare creating turncoats in her own sphere, but in all likelihood she had told this new man about the White Velvet in the Broodies' hideout, and she was responsible for their murders. Likely also, she was telling this man about the other caches of Velvet stored around the city.

Was it *possible*?

If she'd been holding a low-simmering grudge at Fell's taking away the management of the bordellos and giving it to Nathan Spade...that, and coupled with her own obvious ambitions, insanities, and all this about her father...

Yes, Matthew decided. It was possible.

And...probable, if what Devane had just related was the truth. Matthew guessed that Devane didn't know even half of the story, and if his loyalty remained with Professor Fell he could be in danger of a throat-cutting.

But why the signal? Signalling *what*? And, more importantly, to whom?

It suddenly seemed to him that this silent village might be due for a rude upheaval. Could he find even an hour's mercy of sleep before the sun came up? He didn't know, but instead of being on Lionfish Street he found himself on Redfin, and standing before Berry's cottage.

He thought of her in there sleeping. Did she dream of him? Did she even by now remember his name?

I'll bring you back to me, he vowed. *Somehow, I'll bring you back.*

But not this day.

Matthew returned to Lionfish, a sole figure moving in the village beneath the blaze of stars.

Forty

In his favor, the professor appreciated the finer things of life.

As Matthew approached the theater near eight o'clock with the cadaverous but chess-companionable Harrison Copeland as his escort, he saw that the place had been done up to befit Madam Candoleri's honor. The lamplighters' league must've been in full glow today, for at least a dozen lanterns were festooned on netting that hung along the roof's edge. The two fiddle players and the accordionist were positioned in front of the theater, and though their music was not of operatic quality they were quite accomplished, Matthew thought, at the tavern variety. However, the young trumpeter and the tambourinist had not joined the troupe this evening.

A goodly number of the village's citizens were entering the theater, most of them dressed for a special occasion. Matthew had seen the broadsheets advertising this program up in the Question Mark today, when he'd gone to get something to eat. The special today—and only thing offered—had been crab soup and biscuits. As to the broadsheets, the printmaster who'd created them had done a respectable job with the Italian, listing the program as A Grand Evening With Madam Alicia Candoleri, Performing Arias From The Operas L'Orfeo, La Dafne, Euridice, And L'incoronazione di Poppea, Appearances As Proserpina, Dafne, La Tragedia And La Fortuna, Eight O'Clock, Village Theater.

Matthew had never attended an opera and knew not what to expect. He only knew he was to hear a musicless rendition of selections from four productions, and who could tell how the evening would go? In any case, he was ready for fireworks.

He went inside with Copeland behind him and hung his cloak and tricorn up on hooks in the anteroom with those already hanging there. Within the main chamber, he saw firstly in the glow of many lanterns sitting on small wooden wall sconces that the audience numbered around thirty so far. Then, secondly, he saw standing nearby Professor Fell in an elegant black suit with gold buttons down the front, talking to a heavy-jowled gray-haired man similarly dressed with an elegant gray-haired woman at his side, and between them...

To Matthew's utter shock and jump of the heart there stood Berry, but a Berry that her grandfather would never have recognized and neither would she upon viewing herself in a looking-glass. Her hair was done up in an elaborate construction of coppery curls and sprinkled with blue glitter. Her face was thickly powdered and rouged, which in her right mind she would have considered an abomination. She wore elbow-length white gloves and her costume was a dark blue gown with a froth of white ruffles at the neck.

Before Matthew could speak, the professor saw him and said, "Ah, here's Mr. Corbett! Matthew, I'd like you to meet the mayor of our village, Mr. Frederick Nash, his wife Pamela and their charming daughter Mary Lynn."

Matthew looked down at Nash's offered hand, which he could not bear to touch. Nash's wife was smiling vacantly. Berry stared at Matthew with eyes noticeably bloodshot against the stark white powder. She too, wore a smile that might have been a painted mask.

I'm going mad, Matthew thought. *Either that, or the entire world has gone mad around me.*

"*Matthew?*" spoke a tremulous voice.

All eyes went to Berry, whose white-gloved hand had risen to touch her mouth.

"I *know* you, don't I?" she asked.

"Yes, you met him yesterday," said the professor, taking her arm. His voice was a sinuous snake, coiling about its prey. "The young man is a new arrival."

"Yesterday?" Berry blinked slowly. "What was I doing yesterday?"

"You spent the day with your mother and myself." Nash had forsaken the handshake and put his arm around Pamela. "It was her birthday. We all gathered for the most wonderful celebration."

"Yes, it *was* wonderful," Pamela said, and Matthew realized from the dullness of the woman's eyes and her somewhat labored speech that she too had been given a dose of venom from the snake's nest.

"You remember the cake," Fell said to Berry, his mouth close to her ear. "Vanilla within, with icing of sugared white cream and a very few small red candles on top."

"Oh," Berry said, and her empty smile was one of the most horrifying things Matthew had ever seen. "Yes, I do remember."

The soul-jarring impact of all this made Matthew nearly sick to his stomach. If he'd let himself go he could've vomited all over the elegant clothes and polished shoes. "You forgot a detail, Professor," he said thickly. "Don't you mean it had icing of sugared White Velvet and cream?"

Fell laughed quietly. "Dear boy, you'll have to attend Pamela's birthday celebration *next* year."

"Next year I plan to be in New York." Matthew focused his attention on Berry. "Have you ever been to New York, Miss Grigsby?"

There was a moment in which everyone but Matthew and Fell stood frozen like life-sized paperdolls freshly cut from their patterns.

"I'm sure Mary Lynn has never been to that town," said Fell, who still wore a relaxed smile and still held Berry's arm. He said in her ear, "The young man has had a long journey. Pardon his confusion."

"Of course," Berry answered, and suddenly her eyes were looking through Matthew, for he was no longer there.

"Take Mary Lynn's arm and let's get to our seats," Nash said to his wife. His face had tightened. He cast an uneasy glance at

Matthew though he also still wore his practiced public smile. "Danton, we look forward to the program. There'll be no difficulty, will there?"

"None whatsoever. Enjoy the performance."

As they moved away, Matthew was tempted to call out Berry's name but he thought that if she didn't react—and he didn't think she would—another piece of his hope would go toppling off the cliff.

"She was given a little something extra yesterday after your visit," Fell said. Smiling thinly, he pretended to be brushing crumbs from the front of Matthew's waistcoat. "On her birthday sixteen years ago, Pamela Nash lost her daughter Mary Lynn in a coach accident. She never fully recovered mentally. I thought...why not try a little experiment? It would be a nice birthday present...giving her daughter back to her for one day. Don't you think?"

"I think your pit is deeper than Hell."

"All for science, dear boy. I keep meticulous records, which someday I'm sure will be appreciated by future researchers in the field of human—"

"Corruption?" Matthew asked.

"Manipulation. There will someday be industries—even governments—that will see the value of such. Shall we go to our own seats? Julian has gone to fetch our heroic Albion."

To Matthew's further horror and sense that the world had tilted askew on its axis, Professor Fell put an arm around his shoulders and guided him along the center aisle toward the pew at the front, all the time greeting other members of the community who were all dressed up with nowhere to go.

He had spent the day walking every street of Y Beautiful Bedd and seeing all there was to see. At the rear gate spume was flying up as waves hit the cliffs below. Pressing in closer against the bars, Matthew had seen the road that Archer had mentioned; it wound down amid the rocks to the left, and about a quarter of a mile as the judge had reckoned there was the calm and protected harbor with just the sailing ship moored, as the two fishing boats had likely gone out to sea. Matthew figured the ship was used to sail to the nearest port, which if he was looking out upon the Bristol Channel might be south to Cardiff, but doubtful since in his recollection of reading items from the London *Gazette* in New York that Cardiff was not much of a port nor very highly developed. Likely the ship went north to Swansea, and there loaded up with all the supplies Fell's village required, everything from oats for the horses to printers' ink.

He'd located the stable over on the far northeast of the village, along with a shed in which two coaches and a wagon were kept. There was also a workshop where repairs could be made. Matthew counted six horses in the stalls. Not far from the stable was a chicken coop, a pigpen and a barn holding a few cows. He came upon several men watching another man skin and gut a deer, so obviously hunting was done out in the countryside. The victorious hunter was one of the guards Matthew recalled seeing in the Question Mark that first night.

Back he went to Lionfish Street, and to the door of the Publick Hospital. It was locked and no one about. There were bars over every window. He went around to the rear on a gravel path and saw the arched roof of a greenhouse on the other side of a stone wall about eight feet high. Sharp black iron spearpoints jutted up from the masonry where the stones were mortared together. He followed the wall and found the spearpoints so many in number and spaced so closely that climbing over, even if one could get a good purchase on the stones, would be absolutely impossible. The wall completely enclosed the greenhouse on three sides, which meant that Fell's and Ribbenhoff's garden of delightful botanicals was accessible only through the so-called hospital.

He'd been mulling over the problem when a guard with a musket had come along the path and in no uncertain terms he was told to move on.

At no time today had he seen Mother Deare, Devane or Archer. He presumed the judge had not decided to somehow end his own life during the night with a piece of broken glass or a bedsheet. As for Devane and the story that had been recounted in the early hours, Matthew had mulled that over too, as he'd walked about the beautiful grave. If Mother Deare was indeed plotting something—or rather, working now for the demoniac instead of the simply demonic—there was no way to inform the professor. Devane certainly couldn't, unless he caught Fell here at the opera and made his case, but Matthew surmised that such things just weren't done by the hired help. As soon as Copeland had brought him here, the man had left. The same would be true of Devane when he arrived with Archer, though Matthew did take note of two of the other armed guards standing beside the pew that he, Fell and Archer would be occupying.

A good question to be posed to the professor was—

"Where is Mother Deare?" Matthew asked as Fell sat down. A series of long red velvet cushions had been put down the length of the front row.

"She'll be along soon, I'm sure, though I don't believe Miriam has any interest in the opera." He motioned for Matthew to be seated on his right. Matthew saw the Nashes with their drugged 'daughter' sitting on the front row toward the other side of the theater. Seated on the front row as well was Di Petri, but Rosabella was absent and probably still with her mistress.

Matthew sat down. He took a quick look at the rest of the audience. Maybe forty people were present, including the two guards in the front and two standing at the rear. Archer appeared at the entrance to the anteroom with Devane behind him. Devane spoke to him and motioned him along, and then the judge—looking wan and weary but otherwise still breathing—came down the center aisle while Devane turned away and left.

"Here's our other special guest!" The professor rose to greet Archer. "Good evening, Judge. Come sit right here. This cushion is just the thing for a man who's recovering from a gunshot wound, as the pews do tend to become a bit hard on the hindquarters."

Archer sat on Fell's left. The professor looked back and forth across the audience like a member of royalty surveying his subjects. From the way some of them appeared both so glazed and dazed, Matthew was surprised they weren't drooling.

"Did you have a pleasant remainder of the evening?" Fell asked Archer when he sat down again.

"Pleasant enough, thank you."

"I should have asked you to bring your mask. You could've gotten up on that platform and performed for us. Sort of a masked jester. You would certainly earn some laughter."

Matthew had had enough of Fell's goading of Albion. He said, "Some of these people would laugh if their trousers were ablaze."

"Probably true, at that. Ah, here's someone else I'd like you to meet." Fell stood up again at the approach of a bald-headed, brown-bearded man of about thirty-five or so, wearing a gray suit with a black-and-white checkered waistcoat. "Matthew Corbett, this is Gustav Ribbenhoff."

Matthew didn't stand and Ribbenhoff did not offer his hand. He stood looking down at Matthew as if he'd caught a foul odor. Matthew returned the glare, thinking how much he'd like to knock a dent in that shining bald head and grab the secrets of the drugs and their antidotes as they came spilling from the man's mouth.

"A pleasure," said Ribbenhoff, who had mastered the art of speaking without moving his lips. His eyes, a paler gray than his suit, returned to the face of his benefactor. "All is excitement here, it seems."

"Anticipation would be more the word."

"Ah, ja! I have not attended the opera in quite the few years. Who is this gentleman?" he asked, with a nod toward Archer.

"Your next patient. I trust you'll have something of interest to try?"

"Always."

During this discussion concerning his immediate future, Archer had kept his head lowered. The fire he'd shown Matthew in their first meeting at the Old Bailey was all but extinguished.

Matthew, however, was full of seething flames but he kept himself on a low boil. "What are you a doctor of, Ribbenhoff? The treatment of mange in caged dogs?"

"Very close, sir. I was on the staff of the imperial menagerie of His Majesty King Leopold of Habsburg for several years." Ribbenhoff flashed a fleeting and entirely humorless smile.

"What happened? Were you sacked for having sexual congress with the moose?"

"*Sacked?* What is this meaning, *sacked*?" He looked to Fell for a translation.

Suddenly Archer laughed.

The whole situation must've struck him as absurdly funny, because his laugh was deep, rich and genuine, and it went on like the rumble of stones sliding down a mountainside. Perhaps there was a hint of panic in it, but Matthew reasoned he was the only one to catch that. Archer threw his head back and heartily continued laughing. It might have been the laugh of the damned but Matthew had the sense that it was in some way strengthening him for the tribulations that lay ahead.

"I will seat myself now," said Ribbenhoff, who looked as if he'd been served a plate of fried eggs and sliced turds. He went past Archer and sat a distance away, and Fell also sat back down.

The program would be starting in a few minutes. It appeared that everyone who was coming had arrived. Matthew decided that this was the moment.

He said to the professor, "What does the *Lesser Key of Solomon* have to do with Brazio Valeriani?"

Fell's head turned. He stared blankly at Matthew.

"Or," Matthew said, "I should ask...what does it have to do with Ciro's creation?"

The only change in Fell's face was a slight lift of the eyebrows.

"I don't know what it is," Matthew continued, "but I know there's a connection."

Fell took a few seconds to nod a greeting to someone in the audience before he replied. "You've been speaking to the girl. Bravo for you, your instincts are still sharp."

"Not only that, but I have a proposition," Matthew said. "Bring Berry to herself. Remove Hudson from that cell. Put them safely on a ship bound for New York—and I mean *safely*—and I'll find Brazio Valeriani for you." He paused, but there was no reaction from the professor. He had to go the extra mile. "You've got amateurs searching for him. I can find him. Deep down, you know I can."

Fell's mouth curled just a fraction. "I know nothing of the sort."

"He's in Italy. A big country. Many cities, towns and villages to search through." Matthew brought up a half-smile of feigned confidence. "I know where to *start* looking."

"Where might that be?"

"First...Berry and Hudson go home, in perfect health both physically and mentally. Then—"

Some in the audience began applauding. Madam Candoleri, for want of a dressing room, had simply arrived by way of the front door. She came sweeping down the center aisle, dressed as much like a wedding cake as any woman could be. Rosabella, in more understated finery, was following along behind the madam holding up the ponderous train of her costume. The diva was resplendent in a white gown with so many frills and puffs of white lace that it nearly overwhelmed the eye. She wore white gloves and white boots, and her black hair had been manipulated into an ebony tower adorned with at least a dozen ivory combs carved in the shapes of butterflies.

"*Grazie! Grazie, il mio pubblico bene!*" she called out as she advanced, her smile as brilliant in greeting to this small group as it might have been to the crowd at Rome's finest house of opera. Her face had been powdered and rouged, though not a shade as heavily as Berry's had been, her eyelids darkened with violet and her eyebrows drawn out to make curlicues on the sides of her head. She was ready to do her best, music or not.

There was an anxious moment as Rosabella helped the madam ascend the steps to the platform, the costume almost tripping them both up. The lady positioned herself at the center of the platform, struck a pose that Matthew thought must be suitably operatic, and Rosabella came back down the stairs to take her place beside Di Petri.

Madam Candoleri gave a brief speech thanking them all for coming and saying she would not choose to have been kidnapped for this performance but she was a professional and would act as one, regardless of the fact that there would regrettably be no orchestra. She then proceeded to explain a bit about the first aria she was going to sing, as Proserpina the Queen of Hades from the opera *L'Orfeo.*

As the madam spoke, Fell leaned over a fraction closer to Matthew. He whispered, "Why do you think you know?"

"The agreement first," Matthew whispered back.

"I could extract the information."

"Certainly, but that doesn't get you the man."

Madam Candoleri began to sing. She truly did have both a beautiful and powerful voice, and her art seemed effortless. Even without an orchestra, the music she made was stunning. In fact, Matthew thought that in any other circumstance this would be a magnificent evening, but he kept glancing over at Berry and seeing her painted face and dead smile and everytime he did so he was crushed.

The madam's voice rose to great heights.

Then suddenly a woman cried out, partly a gasp and partly a moan, from the audience. Madam Candoleri's voice faltered and stopped, her eyes wide. Matthew saw, as the others did, that a middle-aged woman in a green gown was thrashing and moaning as a couple of men tried to calm her. She began to foam at the mouth, her head jerking back and forth. One of the guards rushed down the aisle, and the woman was half led and half carried from the theater. Gustav Ribbenhoff hurriedly followed her out.

The professor stood up, as others in the audience were whispering, restless and showing signs of unease that even the potions in their own systems could not fully calm. "My apologies, Madam Candoleri." Fell bowed toward her. "Please continue."

"*Si.* I will, of course." But she looked shaken and confused, her confident demeanor cracked. Matthew realized that the stricken woman in the audience had just awakened from whatever drug was administered to keep her in a world of dreams, and perhaps by now the madam realized why the people of Y Beautiful Bedd were so stupidly happy, and why the faces of this audience—seen from her viewpoint of the platform—were so empty of expression. Matthew thought that after the woman's cry, the diva had looked upon the unfortunate incident and possibly seen herself being carried out at some future time, foaming at the mouth and waking up for just a few minutes in a nightmare that had seemed a pleasant dream.

Madam Candoleri struck her Prosperina pose again, but Matthew thought she still looked lost. Obviously she was trying to pick up where she'd been interrupted, and without music it was made more difficult. She opened her mouth to sing but nothing emerged. Her eyes found Di Petri.

"Giancarlo," she said. "Help me."

He stood up. To Matthew's amazement, Di Petri took a breath and then began to sing what would have been the musical score to the madam's aria. In a strong, clear voice that was nothing like his tone of speaking, Di Petri was offering the madam an accompaniment simply from memory alone.

"*Si!*" she said, nodding gratefully. "*Grazie, questo e quello che mi serviva!*"

But before the diva could continue her aria as the Queen of Hades, there came another sound, this one truly hellish.

Something shrieked past overhead. Its passage shook the glass in the windows. Whatever note Madam Candoleri was about to sing, it stuck in her throat like a fishbone.

From not far away there came the hollow *boom* of an explosion.

At once Professor Fell got to his feet. One of the remaining guards was already going out the door onto the street. There came a second shrieking noise overhead, and a second explosion off to the left somewhere. Matthew saw a leap of fire through the window that faced in that direction.

Fell's calm dissolved in an instant. "Out!" he shouted. "Everyone, get—"

The third blast hit to the right of the theater. The window on that side blew in, sending deadly pieces of glass flying into the chamber. The entire building trembled, dust puffing from between the stones.

Matthew was on his feet. Dust swirled past his face. Some of the lanterns had fallen over, cutting the light to a murk. For a few seconds there reigned an eerie quiet…then came the sound of sobbing, followed by the wails of several people severely injured. To the left through the cracked window, at least one cottage could be seen on fire. Another shriek passed overhead, and another explosion that was likely nearer the square. He saw figures staggering toward the door.

He was dazed not by drugs but by the violence of the moment. He realized that Professor Fell's beautiful grave was under attack, and he pushed past a stunned William Archer in search of Berry.

Forty-One

AMID the moving shadows in the theater, Matthew found Nash, his wife and Berry in the center aisle, heading toward the door. He reached out and grasped Berry's arm, and she turned her powdered face to look upon him with an expression that was a ghastly mixture of bewilderment, fear and dulled sensibilities.

"Berry!" he said. "It's *me*! Matthew! Please try to—"

"Unhand her!" Nash, who had blood running in rivulets down his right cheek from a glass cut at his hairline, pushed Matthew away. His wife began to wail, from terror or pain or the awakening from her soporific drug that the calamity had hastened.

Matthew took hold of Berry's arm again and now it was she who cried out, a sound that tore at Matthew's heart. She jerked away from him and clung to Nash, her father by way of whatever foul potion that damned Ribbenhoff had fed her.

"Please!" he tried once more, as another shriek ripped through the air and a blast perhaps fifty yards away made the floorboards tremble. But she was moving away with the Nashes, and the man was now pressing a handkerchief to the wound at his hairline, and

Pamela was weeping and trembling, and Matthew thought that the gates of Hell had surely opened and were going to swallow them all.

Should he forcibly take her from Nash's side? He didn't know what he should do. Without the antidote and time, she was lost to him. But neither could he simply stand here and watch her go falling away. Still…he feared that if he did take her by force, some mechanism in her brain might employ itself like a coach brake thrust into the earth at too high a speed, and cause an abrupt and total wreckage of the whole.

For the first time in his life, he *wanted* to find Professor Fell, but the man had already gone.

Several wounded and bloody people had collapsed upon the pews on the right side of the theater. Still another shriek and blast told him that in all likelihood bombard mortars were throwing their explosive shells into the village. But from where? Land or sea?

And then he realized why Mother Deare must have been giving a signal out to sea.

She'd been showing a light at the top of the parapet so the mortar gunners on the bomb vessel that was out there somewhere could calculate the range and trajectory.

From where he stood, it appeared that Mother Deare's betrayal of Professor Fell was not just about the stealing of the White Velvet, but the destruction of Fell's empire and possibly the professor's execution.

She said her father had come back for her, Devane had related.

Her *father*? The same demoniac that had killed Fallonsby and engineered the slaughter of the Broodies? It was impossible! If Mother Deare was sixty years old, the man would have to be at least near eighty, and eighty-year-old men did not usually take up lives of violent crime and demonstrate a passion for all things Satanic.

He had to get out of here before a mortar shell came screaming through the roof, which was precisely what the first shells had likely been aimed to do, thereby wiping out Fell and most of the citizens.

"Matthew!"

He turned to find Di Petri standing before him, blood spattered over the front of his suit jacket and a nasty-looking, gory slash across the bridge of his nose. "Please!" he said, his voice ragged. "Help us with Alicia!"

Matthew saw that Madam Candoleri had collapsed upon the platform, where bits of glass glinted in the firelight that issued through the broken window. Rosabella knelt at the lady's side, trying to revive her. Blood could be seen on the upper shoulder of the elaborate white gown.

He followed Di Petri up the steps to the platform. Outside, two more mortar shells came whistling in, one exploding close enough to make the building shake and the rafters groan, and the other hitting more distantly. As Matthew bent down to offer aid, he thought that the bomb vessel had at least a pair of mortars aboard, and the vessel itself likely stolen from a Naval wharf.

Rosabella spoke to Di Petri in Italian. The madam's face was unmarked, her only wound appearing to be a gashed shoulder. Most of the butterflies had flown out of her hair and the construction had fallen into a mass of tangles. She was starting to come around. Matthew thought she'd probably passed out not just from her injury but from the shock of the moment.

"Matthew! Do you know what's happening?"

Archer was standing at the foot of the steps. His suit was dusty but otherwise he was unharmed. Matthew said, "Fell's competitor has decided to make his move."

"His competitor? *Who?*"

Matthew recalled two things Lillehorne had told him, at St. Peter's Place. *There are worse than Professor Fell out there.* And: *Time moves on.*

So time had moved on, and whoever this was that Mother Deare considered her father had decided he wanted all the vanilla cake.

"I don't know his name, but—" Matthew had a sudden jolt. There were two items in Y Beautiful Bedd that he could not let get away from him: Gentry's book of potions and Gustav Ribbenhoff, who knew how to apply the drugs.

The book must be somewhere in the hospital, probably locked away and hopefully in a fireproof strongbox. If Mother Deare had told her 'father' about that, and how much power it held, to create both poisons and mind-altering drugs, then…

…that could be the entire motive for this attack, for even Mother Deare likely didn't have the key to get to the book, if indeed it was locked away.

Madam Candoleri had come awake and was chattering in Italian, her voice rising and falling in the manner of someone who was still riding the horse of confusion.

"Let's get her to the street," Matthew said. He had no time to aid the others lying wounded in here, and he could only hope that the building wasn't demolished by a direct hit.

Outside, the street was empty of people but the shouting of several voices could be heard. Down the way two cottages had been reduced to rubble and the thatched roof of a third was ablaze. Smoke and stone dust hazed the night and had turned the full moon a dirty yellow. Several other thatched roofs were burning on different streets. Under her own uncertain power Madam Candoleri was guided by Di Petri and Rosabella a distance away from the theater, and then with a cry of "*Mi arrendo!*" she fell again upon the ground.

The shriek of another incoming mortar shell announced itself. A red streak across the sky made an arc into the center of Fell's village, followed by an explosion of smoke and debris into the air. Now could be heard the basso booming of cannonfire. New flames leaped up along the parapet as the gunners applied matches to touch holes and the weapons shot their ten pounds of red-hot iron ball at the offending bomb vessel, which might be situated beyond range of the cannons and be sighted only by the flash and streak of the ascending shells.

"Almighty Christ!" said Archer, who had ducked his head as the last explosion bloomed. "Are we in a *war*?"

"Yes," Matthew answered, "a war between two evils. I've got to get to the hospital. Will you help me?"

"I will."

Matthew was gratified to see that some of Albion's strength had returned to Judge Archer. They left Madam Candoleri with Di Petri and Rosabella and headed for Lionfish Street. Cannons were still firing from the parapets, their smoke blowing back from the cliffs to add to the miasma, but Matthew noted that the shellfire had ceased. Perhaps the cannonballs had hit their target and silenced the mortars.

Matthew and Archer saw that a number of houses had been crushed as if by the boot of a rampaging giant. The flames from burning thatched roofs were shooting higher. From the smoke that clung closer to the ground came the bloodied figure of a man with his clothes in rags about him, having been torn off by a blast. In his arms he carried a crumpled and bloody mass that might have once been a child, and Matthew hoped it wasn't what was left of the young trumpeter.

A war indeed, he thought. As always, it was those caught between the powers who suffered the most.

The man walked past in silence, heading to a destination that only he could fathom.

Matthew and Archer were crossing the square, where other buildings lay in ruins and fires burned, when another explosion belched flame and debris over toward the entrance gate. A guard with a musket rushed past, running toward the scene of the blast, and another followed a few seconds later. It occurred to Matthew that the mortar fire had simply been the beginning of this onslaught, and now a gunpowder bomb had blown the gate open for the second attack to commence.

"Hurry!" he told Archer. He broke into a run, and the judge followed as fast as he could under the constraint of a still-nagging wound.

They passed a group of three men and a woman huddled together against a cottage wall, in the manner of frightened children trying to take refuge from a particularly violent thunderstorm. Before he made the turn onto Lionfish Street Matthew heard the distinct high cracks of musketfire, and looking back both he and Archer saw that a pair of Fell's guards had discharged their weapons into two of the huddled group, gunsmoke still swirling about the bodies, and were in the process of stabbing the others to death with their bayonets.

It was clear that Mother Deare had converted more than Martin and Stoddard to the rebellion. Not all the guards in Fell's village considered him their master any longer, and thus Matthew realized he and Archer must beware everyone with a weapon.

They reached the hospital, Archer showing no ill effects from their haste other than being out of breath. The cannons had stopped firing. More musket shots could be heard from the direction of the front gate. At least a few of the guards were still loyal to the professor, but it appeared at the moment a losing proposition with so many enemies striking at once.

Matthew saw through a window a light moving within the hospital. The light spread: a second lantern had been lit, and then a third.

He went to the door and found it locked. With the strength of desperation he slammed a kick against the door, just below the handle. It did not give. A second effort cracked the door, but the lock still held.

"Hold up!" said Archer. "Together, on three!"

They knocked the door halfway off its hinges with a combined effort. Matthew rushed ahead into the hospital, following the glow of the lamps toward the rear of the building.

A lantern suddenly came flying out of a doorway at him and past his right shoulder, shattering against the wall. Burning oil dripped down the plaster and made a flaming puddle on the floor. Gustav Ribbenhoff emerged from the doorway holding in his left hand a small book of probably forty pages or so, bound in red leather. His right hand gripped a saber.

"You Prussians and your damned swords," Matthew said, backing away from the blade as Ribbenhoff advanced.

"I am going to pass and go out of here," the chemist said. "There is no need for bloodshed." He caught sight of Archer blocking his way. "*You!* Step aside!"

"That's Gentry's book of potions?" Matthew demanded, but he got no answer. "Where are you taking it?"

"I have orders to put it in the professor's hands should I feel it necessary. Now, it is necessary. Get out of my way, please."

"I think someone else is coming to get it."

"My thought exactly. It is worth gold and jewels to whoever can concoct these formulas. I know most of them by memory now, but the book itself must go to the professor."

Matthew made a snap judgment. He had to make a choice between the two warring evils, with Berry at the center of the decision, and at the moment it was all he could think to do.

He said, "All right. Some of the guards have turned against him, and it'll be a dangerous trip between here and there. Do you have any other weapons?"

"*Nein*. This one came from my house."

"We'll go with you."

"*What?* Why should you of all people help *me*?"

"Don't waste time. Let's go."

Still wary, Ribbenhoff kept the sword at the ready as he passed Matthew and Archer. They started for the open doorway, but before they reached it a black coach pulled by four horses halted in front of the hospital.

Matthew's heart was hammering. "Is there a back way out of here?" he asked Ribbenhoff, but just that quickly two men burst from within the coach and were already drawing swords as they hurled themselves into the hospital.

For a few seconds Matthew was paralyzed. One of the men held a lantern and was the pipe-smoker in the brown skullcap who Matthew had seen in Mother Deare's torture chamber, the other one unknown to him. Then from the coach and into the hospital came two more figures, moving at a more stately pace. One was squat and thick-bodied and also carried a lamp. The other was an anatomical freak, a slender man nearly six and a half feet tall. He had to duck his head several inches to clear the doorframe.

"How wonderful that all of you are present!" said Mother Deare after she'd taken stock of the scene. She clung to one of the man's pale hands with her workwoman's paw, clad in a pink lace glove. She looked giddy with delight, dressed for the occasion of betrayal in a pink gown with lavender frills and a dark purple cloak and hood. Her grin, if not that of a demoniac, was at least half-insane. She was speaking directly to Matthew, her eyes bulging, when she said, "I want you to meet my father, Cardinal Black."

Before he gave a slight bow, the man showed a glint of teeth that looked sharpened into points.

Then Matthew realized the true depth of the madness of Miriam Deare.

Her father, yes.

Her father, if one believed the demented tale Dirty Dorothea had told a terrified child in a decaying whorehouse.

The man who was called Cardinal Black was the exact image of the figure Mother Deare had described to Matthew. It was open to conjecture whether that entire tale was true or not, or if Mother Deare had manufactured a memory.

Cardinal Black was clad in an ebony suit and glossy cloak that had settled around his body like a pair of ravens' wings. *On the third night…into the room with the midnight wind,* Mother Deare had said, *he came as his true self, tall and lean, as handsome as sin, with long black hair and black eyes that held a center of scarlet.* So too was Cardinal

Black, who appeared to be fifty years short of eighty. The abnormalities of his birth had made overlarge his hands with their long slender fingers and sharpened nails. On his fingers he wore a multitude of silver rings formed into skulls and satanic faces. His own face, framed by a long mane of sleek black hair, had been stretched to what seemed a disturbing dimension. The pallid flesh looked drawn drum-tight against the jutting cheekbones and the point of the chin, and perhaps the flame of the lantern Mother Deare held did throw a scarlet cinder into the center of the eyes, which seemed to hold within their depths all the darkest secrets of the night.

"Mr. Corbett," he said in a quiet, well-bred voice. "I've heard much about you."

Matthew was unable to find his own voice for a few seconds. Then he said, "Should I be pleased?"

"I'm sure you've heard the saying: any kind of attention is better than none." The eyes shifted toward Archer. "And I understand that *here*," said Cardinal Black, "we have the famous Albion, otherwise known as the upstanding Justice William Atherton Archer. I have made acquaintance with one of your breed, Judge Fallonsby."

"He was not of *my* breed," Archer answered.

"Men are all the same breed, sir. They have inherited the sin of Adam. What simply separates one from another is the price they place upon their souls." The eyes found the red leather-bound book in Ribbenhoff's hand. "That is the volume?" he asked Mother Deare.

"Yes, Father."

"I will have that," said Cardinal Black. He gave the flick of an index finger adorned with a silver skull whose eyeholes held the coils of a snake. The man Matthew had recognized from Mother Deare's cellar stepped forward. The sword had pierced Ribbenhoff's guts before the chemist could act to defend himself. Ribbenhoff cried out and staggered backward, dropping the book and his own blade as his knees buckled. A swing of the sword slashed across his throat as he was on his way to the floor, and the lifeblood spurted from a severed artery.

Matthew and Archer had retreated several paces from this display of ferocious murder. Cardinal Black drew a small hooked knife from his cloak. Matthew made out enigmatic lettering and figures etched into the steel. The man bent his long body over to place a hand atop the bald pate of Ribbenhoff's shuddering shape, and with the blade he carved the Devil's Cross on the dying man's forehead.

"I commend your soul to the Master," he said. Then he wiped the blade clean on the front of Ribbenhoff's coat and retrieved the red book of Gentry's potions. He straightened up and put the hooked knife away. "That business is concluded," he said, with a faint smile toward Matthew and Archer.

"I'll get the other book," Mother Deare said. "Martin will have cornered the professor by now. I want the honor of finishing him and taking my time in doing so."

"Certainly. And these two?"

"Kill them, of course."

"Commend them in my image," Cardinal Black said to the swordsmen. Then, to Mother Deare, "I will meet you at the tower." As he turned to leave, Mother Deare clutched one of his hands, drew it to her face, and kissed his rings. They both went out together, Cardinal Black got into the coach with the book of formulas in his possession, and Mother Deare turned to the left on her way to—

Get the other book? Matthew thought. *What* other book?

The coach driver snapped his whip. With a snort from a couple of the horses the vehicle moved on as the two swordsmen advanced upon their victims.

The Lesser Key of Solomon, Matthew realized. It had to be that. With its spells and incantations...of course that would be a fitting gift from insane daughter to demoniac father.

The man Matthew had recognized lifted his lamp, the better to aim his first strike.

Archer picked up Ribbenhoff's sword and put himself between Matthew and the two killers. "Give me space," he said.

It was Albion speaking.

The swordsmen came forward, one on either side of Archer.

He parried the first blow and then an instant later had knocked aside the second. The lamplight glinted off the deadly lengths of steel as the swords crashed together, swung and feinted. Matthew stepped back but was desperately looking for something to use as a weapon, for even though Archer was highly accomplished with the blade the two men were pressing in and at any instant an edge might find the judge's flesh. Still Archer held them off, his confidence with the weapon causing the pair to restrain their enthusiasm at this work, but suddenly a sword got through Archer's guard and a line of blood appeared across the judge's right cheek. He feinted, dodged nimbly aside to avoid another thrust, and drew blood at the shoulder of the man from Mother Deare's cellar. The second man pulled back a distance, calculating the possible angles of attack.

Matthew shrugged out of his coat. He coiled it around and around and whipped at the face of the wounded man as the next thrust was made. The man was struck between the eyes and retreated, and in retaliation he flung his lantern at Matthew, who narrowly missed catching it in the teeth.

Archer lunged forward and his sword, a blur of steel, entered the man's chest just below the heart. The man's free hand clasped the blade, trapping it, and struck a blow that cleaved into Archer's left shoulder at the base of the neck. Then Archer had jerked the sword out of the body, the mortally-wounded man toppled like a dead tree and his weapon went with him, and though bleeding profusely from a terrible cut William Archer—Albion, in full rage against the evil of the world that no man could fully contain—attacked the remaining killer.

Matthew picked up the second sword. In desperation and perhaps knowledge that he had also sustained a mortal wound, Archer was throwing all caution to the wind and battling like a man truly possessed. At once Matthew, recalling his own lessons in the deadly art, attacked the swordsman from the weaker side, being the left since the man was right-handed. He got a deep slash in on the meat of the man's forearm that showed a gleam of bone before the blood filled it up.

Suddenly the man had had enough. He got his back to a wall, dropped his sword and lifted both hands.

"*Mercy!*" he cried out.

Archer, his chest heaving and the blood running like a stream from the wound at the base of his neck, said, "*No.*" He drove his sword into and through the unprotected throat.

When the blade was withdrawn the man gave a terrible gasp and gurgle and, his eyes shining like coins offered to Charon, slid down the wall to a sitting position and did not move again.

"I commend your soul," Archer said hoarsely, "to wherever the hell it's going." Then he looked at Matthew, his face—but for the red line across his cheek—white as opposed to the dark blood that flowed from him. He dropped his sword, took a step forward, and sank to his knees.

Matthew knelt down beside him. There was too much blood. The wound was too deep, and at a vital conjunction of nerves and arteries. Even if a doctor had been there on the scene, Matthew knew full well that Archer would soon be gone.

Archer lifted his hands before him and stared at them. They had begun to tremble. He balled them into fists and let them fall to his sides.

"I'm sorry," said Matthew.

"As am I." He reached out to grasp Matthew's arm, but somewhere along the way he seemed to forget what he intended to do and his hand dropped once more. He blinked slowly and heavily. He said, "Have I been evil, Matthew?"

"You've been human," was the reply.

"Ah…that. Whoever and…whatever that *thing* was…he is correct. All men have inherited the sin of Adam. Our challenge, I suppose is…how much we compound it or seek to heal it…with our purposes." He brought up the ghost of a smile that nearly wrecked Matthew's heart. "I do so love England," said Albion. "What is to become of my country?"

"I expect it will survive the White Velvet *and* Professor Fell," said Matthew. "It will even survive *Lord Puffery's Pin*."

"That one…I'm not so sure of. Will you help me lie down?"

"Yes."

Matthew folded up his coat to serve as a pillow and gave aid in getting the judge in the position he'd wanted.

Archer breathed harshly a few times, and then he whispered, "Thank you. If you are able…tell Steven—"

And with that unfinished request, Albion left the world that had so terribly crushed both his Eleanor and himself.

Matthew stood up. He had no further time to lose.

With bloodied sword in hand he left the hospital and ran toward the house on Conger Street, aware of any movement in the dust and smoke that still drifted over the beautiful grave.

Forty-Two

THE iron gate had been left wide open. So too was the door to Fell's house. Lamplight glowed from the upper windows. A broken lantern lay on the floor just inside the entrance, and the glass crunched beneath Matthew's boots. With his sword held in the ready before him, he started cautiously up the steps towards the professor's study.

He could hear more gunshots outside, but in the distance. On his way here he'd witnessed one guard shooting another, and he hoped it had been a score against Cardinal Black's men. He had no idea what the situation was out there.

All was quiet in the house but the sound of the ticking clock. Had he gotten here before Mother Deare? He'd run as fast as he could the most direct way possible, and he was yet breathing hard. The quiet was ominous. He winced as a riser beneath the black runner betrayed him with a soft squeal that sounded to him as loud as a scream.

At the top of the stairs Matthew saw that the door at the end of the hallway was open into Fell's study, and the room was illuminated by two or three tapers. From this position he could see neither Fell's desk nor the professor. His attention then went to the body that lay sprawled on the floor in the doorway, and from the condition of the back of the black-haired head a bullet had passed through on its way to the opposite wall.

Martin had cornered Professor Fell? Indeed.

Matthew had difficulty getting past the bulky corpse and nearly slipped in the blood. His right elbow banged against the wall. He got through the doorway and there stood Professor Fell in the glow of a double-tapered candelabra that sat atop his desk. The single-shot pistol that had delivered death to Martin lay next to it. The professor's hollow-eyed face was blanched. His hand had been reaching for a book from the wall shelves.

Fell's gaze ticked to Matthew's right.

If Matthew had not instantly recognized that as a signal, the crashing of the door against his right side might have broken his ribs. As it was, his shoulder was nearly dislocated from its socket when he threw up his sword arm to deflect the blow.

He staggered across the room, his arm buzzing with pain, as Mother Deare came out from behind the door. Her pegteeth were tightly clenched, the muscles in her jaws twitching, and her bulbous-eyed face was contorted into a soundless shriek. Without hesitation she threw herself at him. Her ivory-handled dagger—the blade, Matthew realized, given to him by Albion—was upraised for a killing strike.

He tried to get his sword in between them but his arm was too heavy. She knocked the feeble attempt aside with her own free arm, and the knife came down at Matthew's throat. He caught the wrist and hammered at her ribs with the hilt of his sword as they careened about the room. A pink-gloved fist struck Matthew in the jaw and shot crimson stars through his brain. He desperately hung onto the woman's wrist as they battled back and forth. Suddenly she head-butted him with the vicious strength of the back alley brawler and he was knocked to the floor, his lights nearly extinguished.

She lumbered toward him, a mistress of monstrous power.

In his haze he realized he was dead if he didn't act fast. He swung the sword at her ankles but she leaped over it to slam a boot down upon his forearm. His fingers spasmed and opened. As Mother Deare leaned over to pick up the sword he brought his hips up off the floor and kicked her in the face with his right foot. She went flailing away from him and crashed into the bookshelves, as Professor Fell cringed back toward the shelves that held his jars of preserved marine specimens.

Matthew got to his feet. His right arm was bruised, throbbing with pain, and useless. Mother Deare pushed herself away from the bookshelves. Her mouth was bleeding and the cottony cloud of her wig was dangling halfway off her head. Matthew could see the horrible patchwork of dark red and brown scar tissue on her scalp, and even in this fight for his life he felt a twinge of pity for a little girl that he thought had never had a chance. But now in the revelation of her insanity her father had come for her, and in obeying him she had put herself even beyond Fell's brand of wickedness.

Part of the wig was hanging in her face. She tore it away from its fastenings and threw it on the floor. It landed between them like the hide of a skinned little dog. She wiped the blood from her mouth and advanced upon Matthew with the dagger making small circles in the air.

Matthew saw that Fell was reaching for a jar amid the specimen shelves. To keep Mother Deare's attention he did the only thing that came to mind; he stabbed the wig with his sword and lifted it off the floor.

Mother Deare stopped, her bulging eyes large and her warped mouth gone crooked.

Matthew put the wig at the end of his sword to the burning tapers on Fell's desk, and the hair instantly began to crisp and burn.

She screamed, a big-knuckled hand flying to her throat as if to squeeze the scream off before it escaped...but too late.

Perhaps it came from a childhood place, and a memory of her own hair crisping away. Perhaps it came from the memory of the burn, or the memory of her own deranged mother, or the fact that without her wig the crude Whitechapel brawler stood fully revealed to the world, and the shame of what she really was came suddenly up like a beast to eat her alive.

Who could say? But it was the most terrible scream Matthew had ever heard.

"Miriam," said Professor Fell, and when her head turned toward him he flung into her eyes the liquid from the specimen jar he'd just opened.

Whether it was alcohol, or brine, or some mixture of the two was unknown to Matthew, but the solution carried with it a twisted white squid that for a few seconds plastered itself to Mother Deare's forehead. Her scream changed from outrage to a higher pitch of pain. Her free hand went to her eyes, but she held onto the knife and suddenly became a frenzied whirlwind, spinning this way and that, the blade slashing wildly in all directions. Blinded or not, she propelled herself toward Professor Fell. He was nimble enough to dodge the first swings of the dagger but then her hand found and caught the shoulder of his coat. With an animalish roar she lifted the knife to plunge it into his chest.

Before Matthew could move, a figure rushed past him. In the blur of motion he saw a pistol's barrel being pressed against the side of the madwoman's head, and the sharp *crack* of the shot was followed by Mother Deare's brain matter spraying across the specimen shelves.

The knife at its zenith was halted by a hand that gripped the wrist. Mother Deare's knees buckled, her squat body began to fall, and Julian Devane let her go.

She crashed to the floor. Incredibly, even brain shot, she pulled her knees up beneath her and tried to rise again. Both Professor Fell and Devane drew back through the blue smoke curling across the room, and Matthew saw in their faces the stark expressions of fear, that the woman's lifeforce was powerful enough to keep her moving with deadly purpose even with a bloody hole in her scarred skull.

She almost got up to a full standing position. Her bloodshot eyes appeared to be near bursting from her face. From her mouth came the mangled words that sounded like the voice of a child crying out as she tumbled into a bottomless pit.

Then she went down again in front of Fell and Devane, her chin smacked against the floor, she shuddered a few times and at last lay still.

No one moved.

Matthew realized he was trembling, and he fully expected Mother Deare to draw in a breath and begin to rise again, a brain-dead phoenix energized by the strength of her ambition and the strange love she had for Cardinal Black.

But...she was gone.

Fell staggered. He put a hand against the nearest wall to steady himself. He gazed around the study and said listlessly, "Look at this terrible mess."

"You can drop that sword," Devane said to Matthew.

Matthew was still stunned. He looked at the sword and at the burning wig impaled upon it.

"I suggest," said Devane, "that you drop the sword *now*."

Matthew heard him as if at a distance. It came to him that Devane's pistol was another single-shot weapon and could not be reloaded fast enough to defend against the blade. Devane had a purple knot on his forehead above the right eye, a mottling of bruises across his left cheekbone and a show of blood from a split lower lip, indicating he'd endured his own travails elsewhere in the village.

Could the man be taken?

Matthew decided he was in no shape for any further combat. And what would the point of that be?

He dropped the sword.

"Ribbenhoff is dead. Not by my hand," he said. "The man Mother Deare was working with…he calls himself Cardinal Black. He came to the hospital…"

"The *hospital*?" Fell's sense of urgency had returned.

"He took Gentry's book," Matthew went on, and he had to lower himself into one of the chairs before he lost his own equilibrium. "That's what all this was about. Somehow Cardinal Black convinced Mother Deare to help him break in here and get the book. She's been telling him where the Velvet was stored, too."

"The formulas," said the professor. "With those in hand, and the botanicals he needs…he won't be able to recreate the more exotic drugs, but…" He stared down at the dead woman's body.

"My oldest and most trusted associate. Why did I not *see* this?"

Matthew noted that Devane remained tight-lipped at this question. "Time moves on," Matthew said, recalling that Gardner Lillehorne had spoken this exact phrase to him in discussing the rebirth of the criminal element of London beyond Professor Fell's influence.

The professor grasped Devane's shoulder. "Thank you, Julian. How goes the situation?"

"They've cleared out. We've caught three of the horsemen who blew up the gate and we have two of the turncoats. Otherwise we took many casualties. Among them Copeland, Fenna, Leighton and McGowan."

"We have five tongues to make talk, though."

"Yes sir."

"Start that at once. Strip them and have them tied up in the square. Do we have enough men left to do that and put on watch?"

"Guinnessey had a wagon pulled up to block the way in, if they try coming back. I think we have nine men able to shoulder muskets."

"Not very many."

"Cardinal Black has what he came for," said Matthew, who was fighting against a terrible weariness. "*One* thing, at least."

"Meaning what?" Fell asked sharply.

"Mother Deare came here for two reasons. To kill you and to get a second book. The one you were reaching for when I came in. Had she just gotten here a moment before? I imagine I made some noise trying to get around Martin's body."

"We both heard you on the stairs. She likely thought it might be Julian, the same as I."

Matthew nodded. "The demoniac," he said, "wanted as his second prize the book of descriptions of demons and spells on how to raise them. Tell me, Professor...what does *The Lesser Key of Solomon* have to do with Ciro Valeriani?" When Fell didn't answer, Matthew said, "He created something in his laboratory that Rosabella told me he tried to destroy, but it wouldn't let him. What was it?"

Fell remained in silent contemplation for a bit longer, and then he said, "The girl is incorrect. Ciro Valeriani did not create it in his laboratory. From what I've gleaned, he created it in his *workshop*. It is not an object of science."

"All right, then. What is it?"

"It's an object," said the professor, "of *furniture*."

"What? A chair that tells fortunes? And it ran away from him when he tried to put an axe to it?"

"It is heartening to see that in all this chaos your imagination is unimpaired. This object—which you do not need to hear the particulars about, for I would like to keep you alive for awhile—not only kept him from destroying it, but it killed *him*. Such is its power. What it has to do with *The Lesser Key*, you don't need to know for your own protection."

"Protection from what? A devilish bookworm?"

"No," Fell said. "Protection from *me.* Julian, I'm putting you in charge of cleaning up, since Fenna is no longer with us. After the prisoners are bound, send as many men as you can spare to go through every house room by room. We don't want any of their wounded hiding here." The professor's eyes had become more focused, and his mouth a cruel slash. "As for the prisoners, find a strong sawblade or two. Build a fire in the center of the square. I'll be along in a little while."

"What about him?" Devane jerked a thumb toward Matthew.

"What about you, Matthew? Why did you come here, knowing that Miriam was planning to kill me? Were you intending to *stop* her?"

"That's right."

"And why should that be? I would've thought Albion might have fought you for the pleasure of killing me. Where is that gentleman? Hiding under his bed?"

"He was killed in the hospital by Cardinal Black's men," Matthew answered. "What you don't know is that your White Velvet caused the death of his wife in a freak accident, and for that and your other ventures he saw you as a blight on society."

"*I've* been called that," said Devane, with a measure of twisted pride. "It's an exclusive club. The membership dues are more than most men want to pay."

"Indeed." Fell flashed a quick and insincere smile. "My heart bleeds for Judge Archer. I'll say a kind word over him when we throw his body to the sharks. Now...your reason for wishing to save my life? Listen to this, Julian, it should be interesting."

Matthew said, "You told me Hudson would recover on his own within a few days, if you ceased giving him the drug. He's a strong man both physically and mentally, he'll come out it. But Berry..." He had to stop for a moment, as the memory of her all powdered and painted and made to think of herself as Nash's daughter welled up in him. "But...as you say, Berry's on a path to mental infancy unless she gets the antidote. With Ribbenhoff dead and the book of potions stolen, who but you has the ability to make that antidote and give it to her in the proper amount?"

"Oh," said the professor, with a slight nod. "I see."

"I expect you to give it to her and bring her back, presuming she's not been killed in this onslaught. I still offer the proposition... you put Berry and Hudson safely on a ship bound for New York and I'll find Brazio Valeriani. That's a promise."

Fell seemed to be considering it. Then, very suddenly, he laughed.

Matthew didn't care for the sound. "What's humorous?"

"*You*," Fell answered. "What makes you think I know the formula for the antidote?"

Matthew had the feeling that the floor had given way beneath his feet.

"That was Ribbenhoff's formula, a variation on something Gentry had created. I'm sure he added it to the book, as he liked to keep everything in order...but with him dead and the book gone... the only one who can possibly bring your Berry back to you is this Cardinal Black, and I'm fairly sure he doesn't have access to the proper botanicals."

Matthew had lost his power of speech.

"I admire him, in a way," Fell went on. "A courageous bastard, breaking in here as he did. But that doesn't mean I won't savor cutting him into small pieces. I want to know how he got hold of Miriam's mind and how he took possession of a mortar vessel. That smells to me like someone in the Admiralty is involved."

"To hell with that!" Matthew exploded. "You've got to have a supply of that antidote somewhere! I *know* you do!"

"No, we do not. We have a supply of what is used to keep the general public pacified, and what we spice the Velvet with, but not the more esoteric formulas. As I told you, I never intended to give the girl an antidote."

Matthew got up from his chair. Instantly Devane stepped forward and picked up the sword Matthew had dropped. Matthew was shaking with anger and the realization that without the antidote, the woman he'd decided to share the rest of his life with was doomed.

"*Damn you*," Matthew seethed. "Damn you to hell and back a hundred times."

"Quite so," said the professor. He cast an uneasy gaze upon the dead woman again, as if still expecting her to rise and strike. "Julian, go about your business," he said. "Our valiant Matthew has been reduced to a blubbering shell."

"You don't wish me to take him out?"

"No, let him go where he chooses. Just bind the prisoners, get that search done and prepare the sawblades and the fire. But I shall keep the sword and dagger, thank you."

Devane handed it over. He worked the dagger from the pink-gloved hand, gave it to Fell, and then he cautiously stepped over the body and passed Matthew on his way out.

"*Wait*," Matthew said. The power of his voice stopped Devane short.

"You have something further to add?" Fell asked. He prodded Mother Deare's body with the toe of his boot, just in case.

What Matthew had come up with in the last few seconds had been born of desperation. "Let me go. I'll get the book back."

"Oh, of course you will! The problem-solver on the hunt! Of course!"

"*Hear me*," said Matthew, and again the force of his voice was a strong commandment. "You and I have equal desires to get it back, but either you're in shock or you're pretending that all those formulas at a madman's whim would not wreck what remains of your so-called empire. He'll likely already have a chemist at the ready. He might not have all the necessary botanicals but I'd say he could get them in time...if he's *allowed* to. Now tell me truthfully: how long does Berry have? I mean to say...what's the point of no return for her?"

Fell's face had become grim. He said, "Ribbenhoff told me that beyond thirty to forty days the antidote would be useless."

"How long has it been so far?"

"Six days. A dose was started on her the night they were brought in."

"I am begging you," said Matthew, "to let me *try*."

"We no longer have a chemist here."

"I'll find the book *and* a chemist. If not, I'll die trying."

"A sensible statement. One that may well be etched upon your gravestone."

"You don't have enough men to guard this place and send a group out searching," Matthew said. "You have *me*. I heard Black tell Mother Deare to meet him at 'the tower'. Do you have any idea where that might be?"

"None. We are some twenty miles down the coast from Swansea. The nearest village would be Adderlane, six or seven miles to the northwest, also on the coast."

"All right. That's a place to start." Matthew still read indecision on the professor's face. "I have to go as soon as possible. I expect I can use one of the horses, if they haven't burned down the stable." He had another inducement to offer, as odious as it seemed. "I don't have time to wait for Hudson to recover. Send someone with me. One man is all I need."

"You think highly of yourself."

"Yes, I do. And so does *he*." Matthew lifted his chin toward the third man in the room.

Devane frowned. "*Me?* Are you mad?"

"Here's a chance to make amends for past errors," Matthew told him, and the message between them was clear.

"Meaning what?" Fell asked.

"I believe he means," said Devane, recovering silkily, "that he blames me for the loss of two teeth and a dirty guttersnipe who he considered his 'brother' by that mark on his hand. Is that what you mean, Corbett?"

"Exactly so."

Fell backed away from Mother Deare's body and stepped around it. He approached Matthew and Devane and looked from one to the other, his eyes holding a spark of renewed interest. He said to Matthew, "You would go with Julian out to find the book?"

"Yes."

"Julian? What say you?"

Devane answered, "As always, I am ready to serve."

"Hm." Fell stepped closer to Matthew and stood only a few inches away. "You're correct in that time is of the essence. I don't know the meaning of 'the tower' but perhaps one of our new guests does. We may get some valuable information in the next few hours, so let's don't put you on the road until we hear what's to be said. In the meantime, Julian, go on and do what I've asked."

Devane nodded. He cast a brief glance at Matthew that had a flash of sneer in it, and then he departed.

"I want to get out of this room." The professor was staring down at the remnant of the crisped brown wig on the floor. "Come downstairs with me. I have a bottle of whiskey I'll share."

"I need to find Berry," Matthew said. "I want to make sure she's still *alive* before I go out hunting the book."

"I imagine Nash got them to his house. It's up where Conger Street begins, on the left. He has one with a cellar, and doors that can be locked."

"Thank you."

"You shouldn't miss the festivities in the square," Fell said, "but I'd advise you to try to get some sleep. I can give you something for that, if you'd like."

"I'd rather not get in the habit."

"Of what? Sleeping?" Fell gave him a chilly smile. "You should rest while you can."

"I'll be all right."

"Likely so. I'll tell you this, Matthew: if you bring the book back to me, I will agree to your proposition and I will agree to your terms. By all means go find the girl and make certain she's well." He made not the slightest sign of recognizing the irony in this statement. "If you bring the book to me—and a chemist who can understand the formulas—the first order of business will be creating and administering the antidote. When the girl has recovered, I'll send her and Greathouse safely back to New York. Understood?"

"Yes."

"And the second part," Fell went on, "is that I would then hold you to going to Italy with a team of my men to find Brazio Valeriani. Is that also agreed?"

"It is."

"Then," said the professor, "I believe we are in partnership."

"Don't ask me to shake your hand on it," Matthew said, and with a last look at the dead Mother Deare lying on Fell's floor he turned around, got past the other corpse outside the doorway, and left the house to go find Nash's counterfeit daughter.

Forty-Three

Dawn was a red slash to the east when the two men who'd talked were tied to the mouths of cannons, the barrels elevated over the parapet, and ten-pound cannonballs blasted through the men's bodies out to sea.

The other three deaths had not been so clean, because the execution by cannon was Professor Fell's brand of mercy.

After leaving the professor Matthew had banged on the locked door of Nash's house and been admitted by the bandaged and bloodied man who by candlelight was getting drunk on a bottle of rum in the front room. He'd found Berry asleep and unharmed in a bed beside the sleeping Mrs. Nash. Matthew had caught the man up by the collar and told him that if either he or his wife forgot that Berry Grigsby was under both his and Fell's protection he would kill them without hesitation. As he left the house, he realized that not only was he in partnership with the professor but he was taking on some of the ruthlessness required, because he had meant the threat.

He'd contemplated getting some sleep of his own, but it really would've taken drugs to get him calmed down enough to rest. Anyway, he had such a headache from his fight with Mother Deare that it would be impossible. He would rest when he collapsed and not before.

The festivity in the square was a merry scene, if one enjoyed seeing the limbs of screaming men being sawed off.

By the crimson light of a fire at the center of the square, Matthew had stood to one side and watched the five men be stripped and tied to chairs. A small number of people had gathered. The two fiddle-players, the accordionist and the tambourine girl had been brought out to add the bizarre touch of lively tunes to the proceedings. Austere and solemn in his black suit, Professor Fell had stood speaking to one of his men who held a handsaw. Another man had thought to bring an axe. A brazier and bellows had been set up and a iron put into the coals.

Fell asked no questions of any of the men. He simply gave a command and the arms and legs were sawed off one of the horsemen and one of the turncoat guards, the wounds cauterized with the iron after each limb was severed. In time with the music, the man with the axe chopped the arms and legs into pieces and they were shovelled into a leather bag. Fell announced to his new guests that the pieces would be thrown over the cliffs to attract the sharks, and then the torsos of those unfortunate men with the blood-drained faces and the eyes rolling in their sockets would be tossed over to join the feast. Those who refused to talk would become part of the meal, but if any man offered to at least partially blot this stain on his character he would be given a merciful death.

"Now," Fell said, his arms crossed over his chest, "does anyone have anything at *all* to say?"

The first man who spoke up babbled that he had been a prisoner in the gaolhouse in Cardiff and had been freed with six others in a raid there two weeks ago, he knew nothing but the name of Cardinal Black and all he was doing, sir—kind sir—was taking orders in exchange for food and drink.

"Prepare that man," Fell had said, and the sawblade had instantly gone to work. "I want some real information," he told the remaining two, over the screams and the music. "Give me something of value or follow the others."

It was amazing, what a saw, a cauterizing iron and the image of a torso being torn into by sharks' teeth could do.

As the sun came up, Matthew stood in Berry's cottage. He had no idea how long she would sleep in the bed at Nash's house. He couldn't bear to see her again in there, and it was pointless. He knew what he had to do and that at the very most he had thirty-four days to get it done.

But he lingered in Berry's house awhile. He sat in a chair and watched the sun's rays strengthen, as she might. He had a little time, as the professor had directed that a pair of horses be saddled and supplies be put into the saddlebags, and it would take about twenty minutes for everything to be readied.

One of the horsemen had revealed that Cardinal Black and his men—eighteen in number, subtracting their own casualties—had taken over the village of Adderlane. The harbor wasn't deep enough for the mortar vessel to be kept at wharf, so it was anchored in the bay. There were lookouts all around the town, and they would be expecting retaliation but they were soon to be moving out by coach, horse and ship. When they were moving and where to, the man didn't know. He had also been among the number of prisoners freed from the Cardiff gaol, and admitted that he'd been imprisoned there for the murder of a watchman during a robbery. He said that one gave allegiance to Cardinal Black by having a vein opened in the arm and blood dripped into a sacred jar during a ceremony, you got a burn on the underside of that arm in the shape of an inverted Cross—which had already been shown to all eyes in the man's condition of stark nudity—you repeated some gibberish and thus you belonged not only to him but to the will of the Devil. If you failed to do that, you were gutted on the spot. The man claimed he had no use for things Satanic, but it was said that Cardinal Black had discussions with his own Master in the darkest hours of the night, and it was best to go along to stay alive.

About Cardinal Black's origin and history he had no clue. Why this raid on the fortress village had taken place, the man was not told, but he understood from some of the others that there was something here that Black had spent much money, time and effort to get hold of.

The tower he thought Black had mentioned was a crumbling structure about a half-mile in the forest on this side of Adderlane, a medieval watchtower that was the last thing remaining of what must've been a sprawling castle. The man said he'd never been there, but he'd heard that the 'tower' was where Black went to commune with his Master. The Devil's church, as it were.

The other man, one of the turncoats, said that Martin had approached him over a period of more than a month, had worked into his confidence and told him Miriam Deare was planning an organization of her own, that the professor was old and tired and he'd become too weak to manage the various operations.

"Pardon sir, pardon please, I'm just repeatin' what I was told," the poor terrified wretch had said.

"Go on," Fell had answered, his face showing no reaction to this blasphemy.

The turncoat continued, haltingly, to relate his passage from Fell loyalist to fallen soul. What it came down to was something that Matthew knew the professor could readily understand: the lure of money and power. Those who helped Miriam Deare in what was expressed as a righteous cause in saving the empire Fell had built from breaking down like last century's wagon were to be rewarded with more gold and higher positions of authority.

Matthew thought it was a tried-and-true story, and had made sense to those who'd participated. Thus the two cannons had fired and the two bodies torn apart, their stories ended but a new tale yet to begin.

It was time to get moving. Matthew had told the professor what Fell already knew, that Black had gotten only one of the books he'd desired. By now Black was well aware that since Mother Deare had not, presumably, taken a horse from the stable and met him at the tower he was not getting *The Lesser Key*. Black might find a copy at a bookseller, but it would likely not be in London. The professor had informed Matthew that the book was rare and made more so since Fell had bought up every copy in London at exorbitant prices. There was a possibility Black and his men might attack the Beautiful Grave again tonight or tomorrow night to get hold of it, or he might play a waiting game.

It made sense to Matthew that Cardinal Black would want a book detailing the demons of Hell and the incantations used to raise them, but why was it so important to the professor? On that subject, Fell would give no answer.

Concerning the book of potions, Matthew thought that if a band of Fell's men—as paltry as they were—tried to attack Adderlane they would probably be cut to pieces. Worse than that, even if they succeeded in getting through the defenses Black might well destroy the book before it could be retrieved.

Matthew could not risk that, and the professor had agreed. In this case it was best to send only two men who might slip into Adderlane unseen. Still, two against eighteen?

There was no way around it.

Matthew made one last visit to Berry's bedroom, to look at the rumpled bed where she slept. He sat down and smoothed his hand across her pillow as if smoothing the hair away from her cheek—and he felt something hard beneath the goosefeathers.

Lifting the pillow, he found a slim white box about the size of a sheet of paper. He opened the box and saw that, though the Berry he knew was in dire straits of disappearing, some part of her was fighting to remain.

The box held three worn charcoal pencils and several drawings. He examined the pictures one by one.

They were childlike scrawlings of different scenes. The first was the representation of a sailing ship at sea, people aboard the vessel shown as stick figures and the stick figures of fish leaping up from the water. The second depicted the scene of a town. The buildings and stick figure people were out of proportion, stick figure animals and wagons on the streets, a few black squiggles of what might have been ships in the harbor, everything done as if by an eight-year-old. Matthew didn't think Berry had been trying to draw London, for there was a familiarity to the streets and also the long straight street in the middle.

It was the Broad Way, he realized.

And central in the drawing was a building taller than the rest with a small stick figure standing atop it. Berry had drawn little tears falling from the oval of the face.

Ashton McCaggers? he wondered. Sad because she'd left New York to come find him?

The third drawing made him catch his breath and hold it for a few long seconds.

It showed what might have been a pier with holes where some of the planks were missing. Standing at the end of the pier and facing the viewer were two stick figure people, one with a scribble of long curly hair. Both figures were smiling, and they were holding each others' three-fingered hands. Up in the sky shone a childish rendition of the sun with a few curved lines representing birds.

At the bottom of the drawing, beneath the pier on which the happy couple stood, was laboriously written I LOV YOU.

Matthew stared at it for awhile. His eyes teared up. What was to be said about this, other than what he'd already said to the professor?

I'll find the book and a chemist. If not, I'll die trying.

He carefully returned the drawings to the box, closed it and put it back beneath the pillow, just so. He donned his cloak, his tricorn and a pair of black leather gloves the professor had given him earlier when a present was also made of a pistol, which now resided along with a leather powderflask in a holster at his waist, and the dagger with the ivory handle.

It seemed that, in a way, Albion would still be with him.

Outside it was cold though the sun was bright. It would get colder. An iron plating of gray clouds was approaching from the northwest. December was closing in, the winter yet ahead. On his walk to the stable Matthew considered the life and death of Judge William Atherton Archer. Perhaps sometime soon the *Pin* would cease its tales about Albion, and the golden-masked phantom of the night would fade into folklore. There would always be another darktime creature ripping into the headlines, and the *Pin* would never be wanting for tales of heroes and villains...and sometimes, those who were a little of both.

Perhaps also the more staid and respectable *Gazette* would have already run an article on the disappearance of the famous and rightly-feared Justice Archer, and have reported that the constables of London were searching for him high and low after some mystery of why Sir Archer was forcibly kidnapped from Whitechapel's Cable Street Publick Hospital. And there was a mystery yet unexplained of why Sir Archer was a patient at said hospital, but—according to the young clerk Steven Jessley, who attended to Sir Archer among others at the Old Bailey—there was no trace of him nor any idea where he might have been taken or by whom.

And perhaps the *Gazette*, which probably cast an interested eye in the direction of the *Pin*'s readership, might comment that the editorial staff sincerely hoped Albion would look into this matter, since it seemed that the phantom, like Sir Archer, was the only one who gave a fig about the release of hardened criminals back upon the streets of fair London.

Matthew had seen Di Petri this morning after the cannon blasts, when he'd forced himself to go to the tavern and get something to eat. It had turned out to be a plate of cold beans and two corn cakes washed down with yesterday's coffee, but Matthew put it all down knowing none of it would be drugged since anyone who put a pistol up on the bar and spun it while they were ordering their food obviously had graduated into the professor's elite. Also, Matthew had told the keep that if anything was in his meal to hinder his mind Professor Fell would be loading up a third cannon. That brought him to a whole new level of respect.

Di Petri, his nose bandaged from his injury of last night, had sat at the table with Matthew and had refrained to eat after seeing all the mess being cleaned up in the square but wished to thank Matthew for his help in getting Madam Candoleri out of the theater. She had had a bad night but was resting, her wound being looked after by a man who had some medical knowledge, having related with a drug-loosened tongue that he'd been a student before he failed his courses and then entered the business of procuring cadavers for more earnest medical students in London. In any case, he had some knowledge of stitchery and a limited but adequate grasp of anti-infectant medicines, and he'd been promoted to be the village's general physician.

"Rosabella told me you were asking about her cousin and her uncle," Di Petri said. "Can you tell me what the professor's after?"

"No, I can't," Matthew answered. "Rosabella can tell you about something her uncle created that's attracted Fell's attention, but she doesn't know what it is and he refuses to tell me. She and I did have a nice talk, though."

"Interesting. You say it's something her uncle *created*?"

"Yes."

"I suppose Rosabella told you, then, about her collection?"

"Her collection?" Matthew had put down his cup of absolutely wretched coffee. "Of what?"

"The mirrors," said Di Petri. "She didn't tell you? Every year on her birthday, since she was six years old, her uncle sent her a hand mirror that he'd created. She has two of them with her right now that she uses when she's doing the madam's makeup. I think in some way the mirrors caused her to become interested in the human face, and...being a woman...an interest in the application of theatrical makeup followed."

Matthew paused while that information sank in. Then he asked, "Would you think of a hand mirror as *furniture*?"

"Not really. Why?"

"Just wondering. I wouldn't, either."

Di Petri had appeared puzzled over that question, but he'd brushed it aside to delve into what was to him a more vital subject. "Will the professor ever let us go?" When Matthew was silent, attending to drinking down the bitter brew, Di Petri said, "I don't see how he can. He wouldn't want the law to learn about this place, would he? I think he'd rather have us all killed."

"I don't know," Matthew replied, because he honestly didn't.

"We'll lose our minds here, won't we?" Di Petri asked. "Rosabella told me what you said about the drugs. Of course we've all noticed what most of the others are like. How could we not? Even last night, with all that going on, some of them were wandering around like sleepwalkers. And that woman who screamed in the audience. Alicia said when she looked out there she saw so many empty faces her voice was stolen. I assume we haven't been given anything yet, because of the performance. I would think our food and water would soon begin to be tainted?"

There was no use in denying the truth any longer. "Yes," Matthew said.

"What about *you*? Aren't you in the same boat?"

"I have a task to perform that's going to take me out of here. When I get back I'll—" What? he asked himself. How could he possibly help Di Petri, Madam Candoleri and Rosabella? How could he help anyone escape this place but Berry and Hudson?

"You'll actually come back on your own, without being forced? *Why?*"

"I have a responsibility. That's all I can say."

"*Dio del cielo!*" said Di Petri. "Surely while you're out there you'll help us! Find the law! Find someone who can get us out of here! Won't you please? Not just for myself, but...Alicia is not nearly as strong as she pretends to be. She has had a very unstable life. Yes, of course with drugs making everything happy in our heads, we will all live here as if we would rather be nowhere else. But it's a travesty, Matthew! It's an *evil*! Please...if you can help us, and you won't... then you become part of the evil, don't you?"

Matthew was shaken by this, because there was no way he could avoid the truth of it. Still, all he could think about at the moment was getting that book of formulas back from what he knew would be an extremely dangerous opponent.

"I have to go," he told Di Petri, and stood up from his chair.

"Please, Matthew! *Please!*" Di Petri had called, as Matthew headed for the door. "Don't turn your back on the rest of us!"

With the image of Berry's drawings burned into his brain, Matthew reached the stable. He found his horse, a chestnut steed, already saddled and being held for him by the stablemaster. The saddlebags, containing such items as a tinderbox, ammunition, extra flints for the pistol and pieces of dried and salted fish and beef, were also ready. Julian Devane, wearing a black cloak and with his dark green tricorn tilted at a slight angle upon his blonde-haired head, was standing beside his own roan horse. He wore a sword in a sheath at his side. Devane nimbly swung himself up into the saddle, spurs glinting at the heels of his boots. Matthew mounted his horse, set his boots in the stirrups, and without a word the two riders set off toward the front gate.

On the way, Matthew glanced toward Fell's house and saw the figure of the professor standing upon his balcony watching them depart. Matthew thought of Hudson in the dungeon cell, but at least he'd been assured that no more of the 'fear drug' would be applied, and in a few days time Hudson would be getting a lantern down there, and a cot and chair. They passed on, and neither Matthew nor Devane looked back again.

A wagon had been situated in front of the entrance, the oaken gate itself having been destroyed by last night's gunpowder bomb. It was pushed aside to allow the riders to go out, and Matthew followed Devane beyond the walls of the beautiful grave.

In the distance, many miles away, stood a line of blue-hazed mountains. For several hundred yards around Fell's village the land was an unsightly morass of dark gray bogs streaked with brown and yellow, patches of knee-high grass likely hiding quicksand pits, and a few scraggly wind-sculpted trees reaching up as if for mercy from the brutal earth. The road that stretched from southeast to northwest was no more than a hardly-recognizable track across the ground. Ahead, in the direction the two riders must travel, the track curved into forest.

They had gone only a short distance when Devane reined his horse in and turned the animal to block Matthew's progress.

The purple knot above Devane's right eye had receded somewhat but the mottling of bruises had merged together to form a dark patch across his left cheekbone. His mouth curled when he said, "You're well aware that this is a suicide mission, are you not?"

"I'm aware it's a *mission*," Matthew replied. "I don't consider it suicidal."

"Then you're a bigger idiot than I suspected. And here you've dragged me into it!" He reached into his cloak with a black-gloved hand and brought out a pistol that had four short barrels, two atop two, and double triggers. "Should I kill you now or later, and tell the professor this was a fool's errand?"

"It should be later," Matthew said calmly. "The guards up on the parapets could likely hear the shot from this distance."

Devane urged his horse forward until he was side-by-side with Matthew. The sun faded; the ironwork of clouds had arrived.

"Hear me well, Corbett," Devane said. "I don't like you, I don't like this damned circumstance you've gotten me into, and if I somehow survive it I will make you pay. But I will do this to the best of my ability, because I've given my word and I abide by that rule. I have killed many and most of those deaths I enjoyed dealing out. If I have to kill you, I will...and you have my word on that. Understand?"

"Without question," said Matthew.

"I am the bad man," Devane said. "Just so you know."

Again without question, Matthew thought, but he remained silent.

Then Devane put his gun away and wheeled his horse toward the northwest. Matthew gave his mount a flick of the reins and followed behind, his resolve ready for both saving the woman he loved and meting out justice to the killer behind the deaths of his brother and sister Broodies, as he'd vowed to a lost friend.

They went on along the road, the good and the bad across the ugly landscape.